A SCENT OF LAV

Elizabeth Elg
Sweet Promis
chain Summer,
Wedding, *On*
Willow Pool.
the Second Wo … usband on
board a submar … ship. A keen gardener,
she has two daughters, five grandsons and a great granddaughter, and lives in a village in the Vale of York.

By the same author

Whistle in the Dark
The House in Abercromby Square
The Manchester Affair
Shadow of Dark Water
Mistress of Luke's Folly
The Rose Hedge
All the Sweet Promises
Whisper on the Wind
I'll Bring You Buttercups
Daisychain Summer
Where Bluebells Chime
Windflower Wedding
One Summer at Deer's Leap
The Willow Pool

Writing as Kate Kirby:

Footsteps of a Stuart
Echo of a Stuart
Scapegoat for a Stuart

ELIZABETH ELGIN

A Scent of Lavender

HarperCollins*Publishers*

This novel is entirely a work of fiction. The names, characters and incidents portrayed in it are the work of the author's imagination. Any resemblance to actual persons, living or dead, events or localities is entirely coincidental.

HarperCollins*Publishers*
77–85 Fulham Palace Road,
Hammersmith, London W6 8JB

www.harpercollins.co.uk

This paperback edition 2004
1

First published by HarperCollins*Publishers* 2003

A catalogue record for this book is available from the British Library

ISBN 978 0 00 783382 5

Typeset in Sabon by Palimpsest Book Production Limited, Polmont, Stirlingshire

Printed and bound in Great Britain by Clays Ltd, St Ives plc

For my mother
Katie Wardley
and for
my first great-grandchild
Katie Hall

ONE

Backs to the Wall

1940

The month of June, and the world so impossibly beautiful that it hurt. Her world, that was; the little part of it that made her ache inside just to think she might lose it, now that losing Ladybower could happen. And losing Nun Ainsty, too, and everything that was dear and precious and familiar and safe.

Lorna flung her hat on the sofa then angrily tossed her prim white gloves to join it. Angrily, because she wasn't getting her priorities right; because today her husband had gone to war and William going away into danger was surely more important than being invaded, even though invasion was a real possibility. Soon, some said. The tides were right. Stood to reason, didn't it, that nothing would stop Hitler now.

'What a time to be leaving you. God knows when I'll get leave, the way things are.' They had stood on the platform, waiting for doors to be slammed shut the length of the train, when couples would snatch one last kiss, whisper one last goodbye. 'You'll be all right, Lorna?'

'Yes. You're not to worry about me.'

Dammit, she wasn't the only woman to see her husband go to war. Other wives managed, and so would she!

'At least you'll be all right for money – won't go hungry waiting for the Army allowance to come through. You're sure you can manage the bills?'

'Yes, dear.' William was talking pounds, shillings and pence again. 'I do know how to write a cheque.' She smiled to soften the rebuke.

'And if you need help, there's Gilbert and Nance, don't forget. You've only got to ask, Nance said.'

'Yes.' Ask? Nance Ellery would be there in her WVS uniform, asked or not; self-appointed chatelaine of the village. And since the village had no resident vicar, Nance Ellery had taken to running the church, too, with a zeal fit to frighten St Philippa off her plinth. 'You mustn't worry about me, William. Take care of yourself. I'll be fine.' She wasn't as helpless as he thought; she really wasn't. All she wanted was the chance to prove it. 'And I think it's time . . .' Doors were banging at the far end of the train.

'Yes. Best be getting aboard.' He reached for her, holding her close, patting her back, kissing her. 'And I don't want to be waved off. Too upsetting for you. Just give me a brave smile. No tears, eh?'

So they kissed once more and she waited until he was settled in the window seat of the first-class compartment, then held up a hand, wiggling her fingers in a gesture of goodbye. Then smiling tremulously she walked off, head high; was still smiling as she handed in her platform ticket.

And she *would* manage, she thought fiercely as she drove home. Grandpa had indulged her, then William had taken over. She had been a cosseted, obedient granddaughter and now, in the second year of her marriage was a cosseted, obedient wife. Nothing had changed. Not even her name. She walked down the aisle Lorna Hatherwood and had walked up it still Lorna Hatherwood. But when you marry a distant cousin, there's a fair chance that you both share the same great-great-grandparents. And their name.

She drew in her breath then let it out slowly in an effort to sort out her muddled thoughts, find a reason for her dry-eyed lack of concern. And she *should* be concerned. Her husband had gone to war; she should be distressed and dismayed, and she was not, because William would be all right. William was always all right; he spent a great deal of time arranging his life so that absolutely nothing could or would dare to go wrong, even to joining the Army Reserve in 1938, when it was peace for our time, and Hitler had no more territorial demands in Europe. It was as if William knew a war would come and had set about arranging things to his best advantage.

He was an accountant, he had stressed, and it was a waste of a good brain to wait until war happened and he was forced to volunteer. And he was right, she supposed, because her husband would have made a poor job of being a foot soldier; would not have liked it one bit. So even before war was declared, William was a second lieutenant in the Royal Army Pay Corps of the Territorial Army, all set to become a barracks stanchion and to survive the fighting – if war happened, that was – whilst those less astute would stand a fair chance of being sent into danger. Or worse. And she did not blame him for doing such a thing, Lorna thought as she stuck out an arm and turned sharp right into the lane that led to Nun Ainsty. In his own mind he was doing his bit for King and Country, available for call-up long before his age group which, at thirty-two, probably wouldn't have happened for many months. The fact that he had manoeuvred himself into a relatively safe job in the Pay Corps was up to him and his conscience, Lorna shrugged. As long as he was wearing a uniform she supposed it was all right. As always, William had got what he wanted and she would not weep for her loneliness. She would manage, she had vowed at the station, and discover for the first time in her twenty-three years what it was like to live her life without a man to protect her and smooth her way. Grandpa had gone to heaven and William had gone, nine months after war broke out, to the Pay Corps Somewhere in Wiltshire and from this minute on, Lorna Hatherwood had no one to look after her and no one to please but herself!

She fished in her pocket for her car keys and threw them to

join the hat and gloves on the sofa, then gazed at the framed photograph of her husband in his uniform.

'I'm not really as flippant as I'm trying to make out, William. I *will* miss you and I *will* worry about you even though you'll be quite safe in Wiltshire for a time,' she whispered. 'But I need to find out what being my own woman is like, and not having to do what is expected of me, dear. I really do.'

Come to think of it, though, he didn't have a lot of say in the matter. William was a long way away, and all alone. But then, if you thought about it, so was she.

She looked at the clock. Too early for lunch and anyway, she wasn't hungry. Maybe a tin of soup, later on, and a chunk of bread. Right now, though, she was restless; she needed to come to terms with things, like William being a soldier for the duration and she being alone, rattling around in Ladybower like a pea in a tin can. Now, she must work out a timetable, eat three times a day as she had promised she would. Pity she couldn't join something. She had thought, fleetingly, of asking Nance Ellery if the Women's Voluntary Service needed anyone, but the thought of being bossed about by Nance put her off the idea. She would, of course, have to care for the garden now; seriously care for it and grow more vegetables as the government constantly reminded everyone. Digging for Victory, they called it.

'So, Lorna – and this is the first and last time you'll talk to yourself! – you'll get smartly upstairs,' she whispered to the frizzy-haired woman in the mirror, 'change into something cooler, then go for a long walk and sort yourself out!'

And oh my word, she thought as she took the stairs two at a time, wasn't life going to be one big barrel of laughs? She was tetchy already and William only three hours gone.

She made a *moue* of her mouth. She always screwed up her lips when in danger of tears, and tears would not do! There was a war on, the Germans were little more than twenty miles away across the Channel and hundreds and hundreds of our soldiers had died, not a month ago, on the beaches at Dunkirk.

So behave yourself, woman! Stop feeling sorry for yourself. Straighten your shoulders and get on with it like half the women in the country are having to do!

She took off her costume and best blouse, peeled off her stockings, slithered a flowered cotton frock over her head, then pushed her bare feet into scuffed brown sandals, tying back the thick mass of hair that William said she must never cut short. It wasn't very ladylike, she supposed, to go out stockingless and gloveless but wasn't she, from this day on, pleasing no one but herself?

Defiantly, she made for the front door.

The village of Nun Ainsty lay at the end of a long straight lane, the only way into it and out of it. At the top of the lane and across the busy main road was Meltonby, which had a general store and a school which Ainsty children – had there been any – would have attended. Meltonby also had a post office with a bus stop outside it and a regular bus service to York.

Lorna stopped at the lane end. Its real name was Priory Lane, but to Ainsty folk it was 'the lane', which they walked up to the main road or walked down to the scatter of houses that was Nun Ainsty. Not big enough to be called a village. A hamlet, really, a backwater, and she loved it.

She paused, watching the busy road, then looked down at her shoes as a truck of soldiers whistled at her as they sped past. She felt her cheeks redden. Men still dismayed her – apart from Grandpa God-rest-him, and William. Those two she felt at ease with but strange men, or men en masse like the whistling soldiers, she found difficult to cope with. All to do with her sheltered life, she supposed; because Ladybower and Ainsty had been the centre of her life ever since she could remember. She recalled when William, a tall, almost grown-up young man, had patted her head and given her a chocolate bar. She had blushed furiously and run into the garden. She would have choked on that chocolate had she known that little more than ten years on she would marry him.

But William had gone to war and she was trying to clear her head, get things in order in her mind. She turned her back on the main road and started off towards the village, face to the sun, and when she reached the pillar box, she would know she had walked a mile exactly. Thereafter, still trying to clear her head, she would walk around the Green, passing each house, maybe even stopping to tell anyone who might ask that yes, thank you, William had got away on time this morning and she was waiting to hear he was safely there, and what his new address was. She reached the pillar box and was about to turn left to walk the Green clockwise, when an unmistakable voice called,

'Lorna, my dear! A minute!'

'Nance. Hullo. What can I do for you?' Nance Ellery always wanted something doing and Lorna had grown used to asking what it was.

'A word. A word to the wise, you might say. I'm going to Meltonby.' She nodded to the parcel in the basket of her cycle. 'Half an hour, say . . . ?'

'Fine. Anything of importance, or just a chat?'

'Tell you later.' She never wasted time or words. 'William got away all right, did he?' she called over her shoulder as she pedalled off.

A word to the wise? Lorna frowned. A word of warning was it to be to a young wife newly deserted, about the dangers of being alone and fair game for serving men away from their wives and missing the comforts of home. And bed.

She turned right at the pillar box instead and walked the few yards to her home, because Nance Ellery was going to have her say and fill her head with doubts and innuendoes so that clearing it would be well nigh impossible.

She decided against soup for lunch and ate a chunk of

bread instead. Then she took a hairbrush from the dresser drawer and pulled it through her thick, corkscrew curls, wincing as she did it, wishing her fair, frizzy hair was straight and sleek and black.

She glanced up to see Mrs Ellery leaning her cycle against the gate. She had been to the post office and back, and found time to change into her WVS uniform all in the space of half an hour. And because she was wearing her plum and green, Lorna knew that the word to the wise must also have a ring of officialdom about it because anything to do with the war or the church, anything remotely authoritative, warranted the wearing of the uniform.

'My dear.' Nance was a big woman and puffed a little, on occasions. 'Can we sit down? The garden, maybe? We won't be overheard?'

'The garden it is. And there'll be no one listening.' The garden of Ladybower House was overlooked by Dickon's Wood, and completely shut off. 'But whatever is the matter? It seems urgent.'

'It is, in a way. The thing is, Lorna, how many bedrooms have you got?'

'Five. You know we have.'

'Yes! But how many available? You've cleared the attics, haven't you?'

'Of course. As soon as the government said we had to.' And the directive had made sense, Lorna supposed. Any room built into the roof space of any house was to be emptied immediately, because of the risk of fire bombs. Nasty things, fire bombs. They pierced roofs then burned fiercely and it wouldn't have been a lot of use having to clear a way through years of clutter to get to the thing and put it out with sand. 'We threw a lot of rubbish away, but what was left is stowed away in the small bedroom.'

'Which virtually means you have two bedrooms only?'

'I suppose so, but why do you ask?' Nance was putting words into her mouth; that she had only one spare bedroom.

'I mean, are you billeting again? Are you looking for places for evacuees?' Lorna felt uneasy.

'Not at the moment, though the way things are with the war, I soon will be, nothing is more certain!'

When war broke out, children had been evacuated from towns which would almost certainly be bombed. A straggle of children had walked around Nun Ainsty, labels on coats, possessions in brown paper bags. It had been Nance Ellery's job to help the Billeting Officer find homes for them, Lorna recalled. She and William had been landed with four, and William had hated it. William and Lorna had no children of their own, nor were any planned in the near future, and William took exception to other people's being thrust upon his peace and privacy. That they had quickly returned to Leeds and Manchester had been a relief, and her otherwise patriotic husband said he would set the dogs on the next Billeting Officer who showed her face at Ladybower's door – if they'd had dogs, that was!

'So it's children again?' Lorna was clearly worried.

'Not just yet, and if you're clever you can fill that spare room with an adult who'll be no trouble, and company for you now that William's away. A female, of course.'

'W-what kind of a female?'

'A female for Glebe Farm. A land girl.'

'A woman at Glebe Farm?' Kate Wintersgill wouldn't take kindly to that! 'Are you sure they need a land girl? Can't Bob and Rowley manage?'

'Seems not. They want more help. And it would be better for the woman to live elsewhere, and Kate knows it. Well you would, I mean, with a son with only one thing on his mind, if what I hear is to be believed!'

'His mind? Rowley? *What* on his mind?'

'You know full well what I mean! Young Rowley isn't to be trusted when it comes to women. There's no way I could stand by and see one exposed to *him*! And his mother knows it!'

'But a land girl would be working there during the day, Nance . . .'

'Then let's hope she carries a pitch fork around with her, that's all I can say. Anyway, Kate has agreed to a female worker, but not to sleep in. I'm asking you to take her, Lorna. Can you do it? It's either her, or yelling kids.'

'We-e-ll – I'm not sure. If William were here, you see . . .'

'If William were here he'd say yes, you know he would. And there'll be a billeting allowance of fourteen shillings a week and she'll bring her own rations with her from the hostel.'

'Hostel? The one at Meltonby? Then why can't she stay there, like all the other land girls round these parts?'

'Because the hostel is full to bursting. Now, are you going to take her or not? And before you answer, remember that this is a tiny place at the end of a lane, and if Hitler did decide to invade, he'll probably never even find it! But there's a real war going on at the top of that lane, and it's fast catching up with us!'

'I know it is, Nance. William went to join it, this morning.'

'Sorry, my dear. You'll be feeling cut up. Shouldn't have sprung this on you so soon after, but it's got to be today.'

'Why has it?'

'Because I've got to find her a billet and I thought about you – so will you take her?'

'But when will she be coming? The bed isn't made up. And will she keep decent hours – not come in late, or be noisy?'

And take over the bathroom and want to have her boyfriends in? Or would she be common, or swear? Taking another woman into your house, Lorna frowned, wasn't something to be decided in half an hour!

'She can make up her own bed, and I'm sure she'll respect your home. If I were you, m'dear, I'd lay down house rules the minute she arrives. That way, you'll both know where you stand.'

'Arrives? You've decided then, Nance? Do I have a choice?'

'Entirely up to you, but she'll be the lesser of two evils. The way things are going with the war, the air raids are going to start, mark my words, then they'll be closing city schools and evacuating the children again. And you know William doesn't like other people's children.'

'William isn't here to object!'

'No. But if he knew . . .'

'I know! He'd tell me to take the woman in.'

'That's settled, then! Mind if I use your phone – tell the warden at the hostel that Miss Nightingale can come?'

'Be my guest. You know where it is.'

She knew when she was beaten, and even as she heard Nance Ellery ask for the Meltonby number, Lorna found herself wondering if her new lodger's name would be Florence. Just to think of it made her want to giggle hysterically.

The land girl was not in the least bit Florence Nightingal-ish. She was, in spite of the pale blue shirt and overalls she wore, strikingly beautiful.

'Is this Ladybower House, and are you Mrs Hathaway?'

'Hather*wood*.' Lorna held out a hand. 'And your name isn't Florence – is it?'

'Nah! Though a lot of people call me Flo! Actually, me Nan wanted me to be called Ariadne. "They'll never shorten that to Flo," she said. But me Mam hit the roof and said I'd have trouble for the rest of me life with a name like Ariadne and said it was to be Agnes, after me auntie. So if you don't mind it's either Ness or Flo.'

'Will Ness do?' Lorna smiled.

'Smashin'. Now, mind if I leave these cases? There's a couple more I'll have to go back for. You'd be surprised how much kit they give you.'

'It's a long way. Surely you didn't walk?'

'Nah! They gave me a bike. It's at your front gate. Won't be long.'

'I'll be making tea at three-thirty, Ness. That should give you enough time, there and back.'

Ness Nightingale. Lorna stood at the gate and watched her go. Hair black as the night, eyes dark and mischievous, and the loveliest smile you ever did see. Maybe it would turn out all right. Maybe she and Miss Nightingale – Ness – would be able to get along fine, given time of course, and a bit of give and take. After all, there *was* a war on and, if Nance Ellery was to be believed, it wouldn't be long before everyone, civilians included, would know about it. Granted, Nun Ainsty was a tucked-away little place, but the war was only at the top of the lane, the whistling soldiers were proof of it! So best she count her blessings, take in the land girl, dig like mad in the garden for Victory and write every day to William, Somewhere in Wiltshire. That, and keeping cheerful as the government wanted everyone to do in times such as these, would be sufficient to be going on with.

'Right, then! Airing cupboard!'

There was the spare room bed to be made up and towels put out, and the wardrobe and drawers checked for dust and clean lining paper laid in them. She would do all she could to make her lodger comfortable, even though she wasn't at all sure she wanted another woman in her house so soon after William had gone.

But she couldn't be sure of anything just now. Strange, that only this morning William had sat at the kitchen table, eating his breakfast in the most normal way, yet now they were miles apart, and she had a lodger.

'Oh, damn Hitler and damn the war!'

Lorna heaved the mattress over, letting it fall with a thud and a bounce, feeling better for doing something physical. Then she gave all her attention to Ness Nightingale and her black, shining hair and thought how very unfair life could be at times.

* * *

'Would you like to see the village?' Lorna asked when supper had been eaten. 'I could show you who lives where. It won't take long, and it's such a lovely night and – and . . .'

And she felt so restless, truth known, and almost certainly the cause of it was the woman who had taken over her spare room, eaten supper in her kitchen and was now saying that yes of course she would like to see the village and would it be all right for them to walk as far as Glebe Farm – just so she would know how long it would take her to get there in the morning?

'I'm to start at seven. Better not be late on my first day, had I?'

'You won't be late, Miss Nightingale. It's only a cock's stride away. I'll show you. Leave the dishes. I'll do them later.'

'*We'll* do them later. And could you call me Ness? Miss Nightingale's a bit formal, innit? You *do* want me here? It wasn't my fault the hostel was full.'

'Miss – Ness – I *do* want you here. It's just that this morning I had a husband at home, and tonight I've got a land girl, and it'll take me a little time to get things sorted in my head. And I think you had better call me Lorna – if it's all right with you?' she whispered uneasily.

'Mm. Better'n Mrs Hatherwood – especially as you're younger than me.'

'Am I?' Lorna was unused to such directness. 'I – I'm twenty-three.'

'I'm twenty-five – just. And I promise to try not to be too much of a nuisance. And you mightn't have to put up with me for too long. I'm sure they'll take me into the hostel as soon as there's a place.'

'Would you prefer that – being with a crowd of girls?'

'Nah. Being here's going to be better than that old hostel. Me bedroom's lovely and it's smashin' being able to look out and see nothin' but trees.'

'That's Dickon's Wood.'

'Oh, ar. And who's Dickon when he's at home?'

'Tell you later. This village has quite a history, you know.'

'An' it's got a funny name, an' all – funny-peculiar, I mean.'

'Nun Ainsty? We mostly call it Ainsty. But I'll tell you how it got its name as we do our tour of inspection. It won't take long, that's for sure. There are only ten houses – eleven if you count the manor. But the manor's been empty for years and years. So, if you're ready . . . ?'

They walked around the village, past Dickon's Wood and the White Hart public house and the Saddlery. And Throstle Cottage.

'Throstle?' Ness wrinkled her nose.

'It's the old name for a song thrush. There are a lot of them in the wood. They'll probably wake you early with their singing.'

'Don't think I've ever seen a thrush – not even in the park. Sparrows, mostly, and pigeons down at the Pierhead.'

'Pierhead? I thought you were from Liverpool.'

'S'right. Good old Liverpewl. I love it to bits, but I couldn't wait to get out of the dump. There's a big munitions factory being built outside Liverpewl and people reckon there'll be work for thousands, when it's done. But I decided on the Land Army. Always wondered what life was like in the country.'

'And you'll soon know. You'll be living in the country for the duration.'

'I know. Scares me a bit. I didn't know there was so much space, so much sky, till I seen this place. Sky everywhere, isn't there?'

'Everywhere, as you say. But often there are bombers in it – ours, of course. There are quite a few bomber stations around here. Sometimes the planes fly very low, but you'll get used to it. But over there – look! You can see Glebe Farm, with the ruins behind it.'

'Ruins of what? Cromwell at it around here, was he?'

'Actually it was Henry the Eighth who was responsible for the priory. Fell out with the Pope, and turned against the Church; said it was getting too rich and above itself. It was he who turned the nuns out of the priory, sent his hangers-on to take off the roof. Then they looted everything of value and left the place to decay. Pity, really, because it was run by a nursing order. They took in lepers. It was the only building here, apart from the chapel and the three almshouses. It had to be well away from habitation.'

'Lepers? Aren't they the poor sods who had to ring a bell and shout "Unclean" so people would know to get out of their way?'

'The same. They made their way to the priory to die, I suppose. If you look beyond the ruins to your right, you can see the back of the manor.'

'Pity,' Ness sighed, 'about the ruins and the manor all empty. And a pity about them poor lepers, an' all.'

'Suppose it is. See the little church over there?' Lorna pointed to the small, stone chapel, surrounded by green grass. It had no stained glass windows, no belltower. 'St Philippa's. Only tiny. The nuns built it as a chapel for the lepers to pray in. Henry's wreckers left it alone, thank goodness. The lepers were buried around it when they died. And people who died of the plague or cholera were brought here for burial from other parts, too, because it was so out of the way. No gravestones for them, but at least they'll never be disturbed. Did you know, Ness, that even now, no one is keen to disturb a cholera grave? They say it lives on, in the soil, though I very much doubt it.'

'There was a cholera epidemic in Liverpool about a hundred years ago. I think a lot of the dead were thrown into an old wooden ship, then it was towed down the Mersey and out to sea, and blown up. Reckon them poor people would've rather been here.'

'Well, if you're interested, we have a service at St Philippa's every other week.'

'And you aren't worried about catching anything?' Ness frowned.

'Not at all. It's a dear little chapel. Are you C of E?'

'Me Mam is. I'm nuthin', though I suppose if I had to stand up and be counted, I'm Church of England. In Liverpewl we're called Protties – well, that's what the Cathlicks call us. A lot of them around Liverpewl. Came over from Ireland, because of the famine. Suppose it's what makes Liverpewl what it is – the people, I mean. I'll miss the people, but it'll be smashing, bein' in the country, hearing birds singing.'

'It'll make a change. Walk past quickly! There's Nance Ellery in her garden and I don't want to see her, if you don't mind. She's all right, but she likes to boss people around so don't say you haven't been warned. Beech Tree House, her place is called, because of the three beeches in front of it.' Lorna slowed her step once more. 'And next to Beech Tree is Larkspur Cottage, where the district nurse lives. Then right at the end, near the lane, are the almshouses – they survived the wreckers and vandals too. Pillar box to your right, and that's about it. You've toured Nun Ainsty, Ness, in fifteen minutes flat, walking slowly!'

'And it's beautiful. All trees and flowers and – and –'

'Sky?' Lorna grinned.

'Yes, and birds. But you never told me about Dickon – him the wood was called after.'

'We-e-ll, Dickon was an ostler. Looked after Sir Francis Ainsty's horses in York. Sir Francis had a daughter Ursula, who became a nun.'

'At the priory here?'

'Yes, though reluctantly. Ursula, an only child and heiress, couldn't get a husband. She was considered ugly, you see. And since no man wanted an unmarried daughter on his hands in those days, Francis Ainsty sent Ursula to the nuns, paid them a good sum of money to take her, and made his nephew his heir.'

'The miserable old devil! Surely Ursula wasn't that ugly? I mean, wouldn't her father's money have made her just a little bit attractive?'

'Seems not. Anyway, legend has it that no one offered for her, so her fate was sealed, as they say.'

'Was she a hunchback, or somethin'?'

'No. Far worse than that in the eyes of the people of Tudor England. Ursula had a harelip and a cleft palate too, I think, because she was supposed not to be able to speak properly.'

'But things like that don't matter these days. There's an operation for it, isn't there?'

'Yes. As you say, it can be fixed nowadays. But four hundred years ago, people were very superstitious, and anyone born with a harelip was avoided like the plague, because they thought that if a hare ran across the path of a pregnant woman, it caused her baby to have a hare's lip. Witchcraft.'

'What a load of old rubbish!'

'Ah, but was it, Ness? In those days, people believed in witches and a hare – a black cat, too – were thought to be familiars of a witch.'

'Sorry, you've lost me.'

'A familiar was another form a witch could take when she was up to no good, so a pregnant woman, startled by a hare, paid the price for it.'

'Or her poor little baby did! But what about Dickon?'

'Dickon was ordered by Sir Francis to deliver Ursula to the convent, the two of them riding horses. Ursula wept all the way there and Dickon was so upset that he proposed to her – or so the story goes.'

'But she wouldn't have him, him bein' a peasant, sort of, and her bein' high born?'

'Wrong! Ursula accepted. Dickon had always been fond of his master's daughter and protective towards her and couldn't bear to see her locked away. And he wasn't marrying her for her money because she'd been disinherited. You've got to admire Dickon.' Lorna pushed open the back garden gate. 'I feel like a cup of tea. Will you put the kettle on, Ness, and I'll see if there's been a call for me.'

'From your husband? Lucky you've got a phone in the house.' Few people had their own telephone. There had not been one in Ness's Liverpool home. Very middle class, telephones were. She set the kettle to boil and had laid a tray by the time Lorna returned.

'No joy. Mrs Benson from the telephone exchange at Meltonby said she hadn't had any trunk calls from down south all day. Says her switchboard has gone over all peculiar since Dunkirk. Anyway, I wasn't really expecting a call. More chance of a letter tomorrow, or the next day.'

'Sorry, Lorna. Must be rotten when your feller goes off to the Army.'

'Rotten. But I haven't really taken it in. It feels like I'm in a daze, kind of. I – I haven't cried, Ness. Not one tear.'

'No, but you will when it hits you, queen. But if you don't feel like tellin' me about Dickon and Ursula, it's all right.'

'Oh, but I do. Having someone to talk to helps a lot, believe me. Where were we?'

'We'd got to the bit where Dickon asked Ursula to marry him, even though she didn't have a penny to her name.'

'And Ursula accepted him, but I suppose they couldn't just gallop off into oblivion. After all, Sir Francis would expect his servant back in York – plus two horses – so they decided Ursula should wait until the next saint's day to run away. Sir Francis always gave his servants time off to go to church on saints' days, so that was when it would be. Dickon would come and wait for Ursula who would slip away when no one was looking.'

'And he'd wait for her in the wood – bet I'm right!'

'Yes, but it wasn't as easy as they'd hoped. Three saints' days came and went, but getting out of the priory wasn't as easy as Ursula had expected. In the end, she became desperate and tried to climb out of the window of her cell. But she fell and hurt herself badly. It didn't stop her, though, from dragging herself to the wood. She died in Dickon's arms.'

'Gawd. And what did Dickon do then?'

'No one seems to know. He just faded out of the picture, so to speak.'

'So why is it called Dickon's Wood?'

'We-e-ll – and I tell you this tongue in cheek, Ness – Ursula is supposed to haunt the wood, waiting for Dickon to come for her!'

'Ooooh! You haven't seen her?'

'To be honest, no one has seen her.'

'But there must be some truth in it, or why did they call this village Nun Ainsty after her? Like keeping her name alive, innit?'

'I rather think the people who came here all those years ago kept her name alive to make sure not too many more joined them. It wasn't long after Ursula died that the nuns were turned out of the priory, and once the king had taken all he wanted, a blind eye was turned to the looting that went on. With the roof gone, the building started to decay. All that was any use was a pile of stones and quite a lot of land.'

'And the people who came here weren't afraid of germs an' things the lepers had left behind?'

'Seems not. Would you be, when there was priory land for the grabbing and stone to build your house with? Of course, the building material soon ran out. The manor took the lion's share, and then Glebe Farm was built. Very soon, all that was left was what you see now – archways and columns and some of the cloisters.'

'But weren't people worried, pulling down a holy place? Didn't they fear punishment from God?'

'Why should they? Henry had made himself head of the English church. If the king could help himself, then surely so could anyone else.'

'You reckon?' Ness was clearly impressed. 'You live nearest to the wood. Can you say, hand on heart, that the nun has never been seen there?'

'You mean the nun's *ghost*? Well all I can say, hand on heart, is that if she has I haven't heard about it. Mind, Grandpa told me people said they'd seen her ages ago, on the odd occasion, though maybe they'd had a drop too much at the White Hart. But I wouldn't lose too much sleep over Dickon and Ursula, if I were you.'

'But haven't you thought,' Ness was reluctant to let the matter drop, 'that every house in this village is built with stone from the priory, so who's to say that every house isn't haunted by Ursula? Or Dickon?'

'Because they *aren't*. It's all a lot of nonsense. I'm sorry I told you now. You aren't going to keep on and on about it, Ness?'

'N-no. But I've got to admit I'd like to know more about those two, 'cause there's no smoke without fire, don't they say? And had you thought, maybe it's only certain people the nun appears to. I mean, I don't suppose everybody can see ghosts.'

'No one in this village can, that's for sure. Anyhow, I think I'll go and settle down. I want to write to William so there'll be a letter ready to post as soon as I have an address.'

'And I still have unpacking to do,' said Ness reluctantly. 'By the way, thanks for takin' me in. This is a lovely house and I don't mind it bein' so near to Dickon's Wood.'

She said it teasingly and with a smile, so that Lorna smiled back, silently vowing to say not one more word on the subject; wishing she had left Ursula Ainsty where she rightly belonged. Very firmly in the past!

Ness closed her eyes and breathed deeply on air so clean and fresh you wouldn't believe it. Around her, all was green. Every front garden was flower-filled and roses climbed the creamy stones of age-old houses. This was an unbelievable place; so tucked away – smug, almost, in its seclusion at the end of a lane. People back home would be amazed to see so much space belonging to so few people. But one thing was certain. It wouldn't take long to get to know the entire village. She had already passed the almshouses and Larkspur Cottage where the nurse lived and now, to her left, was Beech Tree House where someone called Nance lived; someone, Ness suspected, who could be a bit of a martinet, given half a chance.

She stood a while outside the tiny chapel, wondering about the sleeping dead around it and how the lepers had fared when there were no nuns to care for them. Probably they were doing a bit of haunting, an' all, ringing their pathetic bells still.

Then she stopped her dawdling and daydreaming. There was a war on and Agnes Nightingale from Liverpool was about to become a part of it, a land girl for the duration of hostilities. At seven on the dot she was supposed to join her war, and it was almost that now.

She began to run, turning the corner to see the farmhouse ahead of her, and to her right the stark ruins, already throwing long, strange shadows in the early morning sun. A dog barked and she hoped it was friendly.

'Hey! You!'

'You talkin' to me?' she demanded of the young man who was closing a field gate behind him. 'Me name's Miss Nightingale!'

'And mine's Rowland Wintersgill and you're late. Milking's over. Still, suppose you can muck out. Better go to the cow shed – make yourself known to my father.'

'Yes *sir*! And can you tell me, if you don't mind, if there are any more at home like you, 'cause if there are I'm not stopping!'

Head high, she followed his pointing finger, then carefully crossed the yard, avoiding pats of dung.

The cow shed smelled warmly of cows and milk. She supposed she would get used to it. And sweeping it.

'Hullo, there. Our land girl, is it?' A man, leaning on a brush, smiled and held out a hand. 'I'm Bob Wintersgill. I'll take you to meet Kate. Have you had breakfast, by the way?'

'I – well, yes. Before I came.' A piece of bread and a smear of jam because she had been unwilling to eat Lorna's rations.

'Well, we usually eat after we've got the cows milked. You'll be welcome to a bite.'

'Sure you can spare it – rationing, I mean . . . ?'

'I think it'll run to a bacon sandwich and a mug of tea. Farmers don't do too badly for food.'

'Then I wouldn't mind a cup of tea – if you're brewin'.' She returned the smile. 'And to meet the lady of the house. I'm sorry I was late. Seven o'clock I was told to be here.'

'That'll be fine, till you get used to things, and oh – a rule of the house! You wash your hands after you've been in the cow shed. In the pump trough. Towel on the door; soap beside the pump. Very particular, Kate is.'

She would like Farmer Wintersgill, Ness thought as she lathered and rinsed; hoped she would like his wife, too. Yet she knew without a second thought that she would never like their son. And that was a pity, really, because she was going to have to work with him for years and years, maybe. For the duration of hostilities, she supposed. And how long that duration was going to last was anybody's guess. Especially since Dunkirk, and the mess we were in now!

'I'm sorry,' Ness said when she had eaten a bacon sandwich and swallowed a mug of strong, sweet tea, 'if I'm not goin' to be very good at farming at first. Being in the country is new to me and I know I've got a lot to learn and that I'll make mistakes. But I hope you'll be patient with me.'

'And the answer to that, lass, is that the woman who never made mistakes never did any work! You'll learn, and I hope you'll come to like it here,' Kate Wintersgill said softly. 'And don't you take any nonsense from that son of mine. Just give back as good as you get! Now, want some toast? Another cup?'

'Ooh, no thanks. That butty was lovely.'

'Ah. Home-cured bacon, you see. Anyway, Rowley's working in the top field, so can you help my man with the mucking out? It's a messy job, but it's got to be done. Have you got gum boots with you? If not, there's plenty in the outhouse by the back door. There'll be a pair to fit you. Off you go then, lass!'

Ness sighed. She had laid out her working clothes so carefully last night: dungarees and a pale blue shirt over a chair to avoid creasing, yet now here she was, folding her trouser-legs around her calves, shoving her feet into gum boots a size too small. And what she would look like when she had helped clean the cow shed was best not thought about. Thank heaven soap wasn't rationed and that there was a wash house at the hostel if ever she needed it! She wondered, as she began to sweep, what the girls in the salon would say if they could see her now. Trying not to breathe too deeply, she shut Liverpool and everything connected with it from her mind.

'You'll get used to it,' said her new employer, who cheerfully hosed water up walls and splashed it over the concrete floor.

'Ar.' She forced a smile then thought about the bacon sandwich and wanted to be sick. 'Reckon I will, at that!'

Lorna received William's first letter, which was very short.

Arrived safely, three hours late. This far, Army life doesn't appear too bad. This brief note is to send you my address.
I miss you. Take care of yourself.

Lorna smiled tremulously, then taking the already-written letter, she added a postscript.

Thanks for yours. I miss you, too. Take care and write again as soon as you can.

Then she sealed the envelope and made for the pillar box. There was only one collection in Ainsty; at noon, when the red GPO van delivered parcels and envelopes too bulky for the postman, then emptied the pillar box outside the front gate of Ladybower House.

Soon her letter would be on its way to William, and she wondered why she had not mentioned that hardly had he been gone when Nance Ellery arrived with a land girl. But she knew she had not mentioned Ness because having got rid of troublesome evacuees, William would not be at all pleased to be told that his home had once again been invaded. And without his permission, too!

'Hullo! Are you Mrs Hatherwood – does Agnes Nightingale live here?'

A young woman dressed in a short cotton frock stood at the gate. 'I'm the warden of the hostel at Meltonby. I've brought you Agnes's rations and a week's billeting allowance. Think it's best we do it on a weekly basis – not knowing how long she'll be with you, I mean . . .'

'Just as you wish. Ness – er – Agnes seems no trouble at

all. Got herself up and off to work this morning without awakening me. I felt quite guilty.'

'Then don't, Mrs Hatherwood. You aren't expected to wait on her, you know. And I'll give her a bed at the hostel just as soon as I can.'

'B-but I thought she was with me permanently.' Hadn't Nance said it would be either the land girl or children?

'Only if you want her to be. I must say we're full at the hostel, though, and it would help if she could stay permanently with you. Be nearer her work, too.'

'Well – I've got a spare room and I don't think Agnes will be any trouble.' Not as much trouble as children. 'Shall we give it a try for a month? See how things go?'

'Very well. Next week I'll leave you a ration card for four weeks when I bring the billeting allowance.' She smiled, holding out her hand. 'And thanks a lot.'

Lorna thought afterwards that she would have to tell William about Ness and that she had practically offered to have her in the spare room on a permanent basis. And then she reminded herself there was a war on and no one, not even William, had the right to expect that an Englishman's home was his castle, because it wasn't; not any longer. And she liked Ness. She was cheerful and appreciative and would be company for her, especially through a long, dark winter. Did she really have a choice when the war was going so badly for us, with Hitler's armies waiting to invade. And France and Belgium and Holland and Norway and Denmark occupied. And as if we weren't deep enough in trouble, Italy ganging up with Hitler and declaring war on Britain in the biggest back-stab since the Battle of Bosworth!

So she would tell William about Ness; she would have to. But she would not apologize for taking her in. Being stuck at the end of a lane in the back of beyond would not guarantee Ainsty's safety if Hitler chose to invade or sent his bombers to fly over it!

'Sorry, William.' She picked up his photograph. 'I love you

dearly and I wish you hadn't gone to war, but even in Nun Ainsty things must change.'

Every village, town and city was at war and it was up to her to make the best of it, like every other woman. And she would try, she really would, to take care of Ladybower so that when it was all over and William came safely home, they could carry on as before – have the child she wanted so much.

Gently she replaced the photograph then stood to gaze out of the window at a garden glorious with June flowers. The grass so green, the roses so thick and scented, and behind it Dickon's Wood to shade it in summer and shelter it in winter from the cold north-easterly winds.

Dear Ladybower, in which she had grown up. She loved it passionately and could find it within her to hate anyone who would take it from her or bomb it or set it ablaze in the name of war. So she would care for it and fight to keep it until the war was over. And Ness, who had left her home to do her bit for the war effort, would be made welcome at Ladybower for as long as it took, and tonight, when she wrote again to her husband, she would tell him all about her and how lucky they were to have her and remind him, ever so gently, how much better Ness would be than the evacuees he'd been glad to see the back of.

But then, William had never really liked children – not other people's. She hoped he would like his own – when they had them, that was. When the war was over. In a million years . . .

And she wasn't weeping! She damn well wasn't!

TWO

''S only me!' Ness kicked off her shoes at the back door, then sniffed appreciatively. 'Sumthin' smells good!'

'Stew. The warden brought your rations today. Gave me a piece of shin beef; enough for both of us for two days. Vegetables nearly done. Do you want to change?'

'Not 'alf. Can't you smell me?' Ness couldn't get the cow shed stink out of her nostrils. 'Bet everybody in the village got a whiff of me on the way home.'

'You aren't too bad – honest. Probably your shoes. How was it today?'

'Tell you when I've got out of these overalls. And I've got messages to give to Goff and Martha at the almshouses, but it'll wait till after supper. Won't be long!'

And she was gone, taking the stairs two at a time before Lorna could tell her what she had read in the morning paper; something so frightening that it had to be shared.

'Look – before we eat,' she whispered when Ness appeared wearing a cotton frock and smelling of Vinolia soap. 'This morning – in the paper – I haven't been able to get it out of my mind all day.'

'Don't tell me Hitler's askin' for an armistice!'

'Nothing as wonderful as that! Listen – I'll read it. It must have come from the government; the papers wouldn't have dared print it if not. It's headed, WHAT DO I DO and it goes on to say, "If I hear news that Germans are trying to land, or have landed? I remember that this is the moment to act like a soldier",' she said chokily. '"I do not get panicky. I stay put. I say to myself; Our soldiers will deal with them. I do not say I must get out of here."' She lowered the paper, sucking in her breath. 'Anyway, Ness, I wouldn't even *think* of getting out of Ainsty. It's as safe as anywhere – well, isn't it?'

'Reckon this place would take a bit of finding, queen. But is that it?'

'No. There's more. It says I must remember that fighting men must have clear roads. I do *not* go onto the road on a bicycle, in a car or on foot. Whether I am at home or at work, I just stay put. And it ends with, "Cut This Out and Keep It".' She gazed into Ness's eyes, begging comfort. 'It's more serious than I thought. And look at this cartoon!' She laid the newspaper on the table, pointing to it with a forefinger stiff with fear. 'Look at him! It makes you want to weep, doesn't it?'

The cartoon showed a steel-helmeted British soldier, feet apart, rifle in his right hand, left arm extended in defiance at planes flying overhead. And he was saying, 'Very well! Alone!'

'Ar, hey. You're right, Lorna. We're up the creek and no messin'. Suppose we've been trying to kid ourselves everything would be all right, but maybe it isn't goin' to be.'

'Maybe. Ness – when your warden came this morning, she seemed to think that you being at Ladybower was only temporary, but I told her I'd like you and me to give it a try – a month, say – and she said it was OK by her. I hadn't read the paper when I asked if you could be here permanently, but now I really, really want you to stay. I'm not very brave, you see, and if there were the two of us it might not seem so bad.'

'Ar. That's nice you wanting me an' of course I'd like to stay. But hadn't you thought, queen, it's likely to be on the south coast – *if* it happens. It's them poor beggars who'll cop it before you an' me will.'

'William is in the south,' Lorna said dully.

'Ar, but he's with soldiers and they'll have rifles and hand grenades and machine guns.'

'In the Pay Corps?' She ran her tongue round dry lips. 'Mind, William learned to shoot when he was in the Territorials.'

'And he'll be all right, same as you and me will! As for this country being alone, well, I suppose we are. But Hitler's got to cross the channel, hasn't he? And what's it called, eh? The *English* Channel! And we got most of our soldiers back from France, don't forget, and we've got a Navy, an' all! You aren't goin' to tell me our Navy's goin' to let them *Jairmans* set foot on English soil without a fight, now, are you?'

'But Ness, there's something else. Flora Petch – y'know, the district nurse from Larkspur Cottage. Well, she told me she saw men taking down the signpost at the top of the lane; taking the arms down, that was. They told her it was so German parachutists wouldn't know where they had landed if there were no names on signposts. And the men said that railways were doing the same. No more names on stations. Nobody'll know where they are any more!'

'So what? Neither will them parachutists, if they come! Ooh, I hate that Hitler, but let's not let him spoil our supper, eh? It's just what he wants, innit; us running round like headless chickens, so you and me won't oblige, eh? We'll eat our supper and then we'll worry about being invaded.'

'And you'll stay, Ness? You don't mind that I asked the warden if it could be on a permanent basis?'

''Course I don't. And we aren't entirely on our own, y'know. I heard it on the wireless at Glebe Farm that the first convoy of Australian and New Zealand soldiers has arrived to help us out. So bully for them, eh, and good on them coming, just when we need them.'

'You're right. I'd say it was pretty bloody marvellous them coming all that way to fight for a country they none of them ever thought to see. And the word invasion is banned for the rest of the day! Right?'

But for all her sudden defiance, Lorna was afraid and wished desperately that William could be with her. William would have known what to do if parachutists dropped in one of the fields around. But William was a long way away, Somewhere in Wiltshire, so there was nothing for it but to get on with it as best she could; as best she and Ness could, that was. And oh, thank the dear heaven for the land girl from Liverpool!

Ness made for the almshouses to her left, across the Green. Three of them, built more than four hundred years ago for the nuns at the priory and not considered important enough to be destroyed by Tudor vandals. Goff Leaman lived in one of them and Martha Hugwitty in another. Of the occupant of the middle one, Ness knew little, save that he was sometimes there and sometimes he wasn't.

'Mr Leaman?' she asked of the man who stood in the tiny front garden who had already stuck his spade into the ground at her approach, and now regarded her with unashamed curiosity.

'That's me. You'll be the land girl from Glebe?'

'Mm. I've got a message from Mr Wintersgill. He said could you get your body and your shotgun up to the farm tomorrow early. Says he's got cartridges. You're going to be shooting rabbits, aren't you?'

'That's the general idea. And before you start worrying about them fluffy little bunnies, let me tell you they're a dratted nuisance and do a lot of damage. Vermin, that's what. They make a grand stew, for all that. Starting the haymaking, are they?'

'That's right. I did hear Rowley say he'd be up good and early to open up the field, whatever that means.'

'It means, lass, that he'll cut a road round the field so the machinery can get in. Do it by hand, with a scythe, and by the time it's finished, the rest of the field will have the night dew off it and be dry enough for the mower. And you'd better call me Goff. Everyone else does. Short for Godfrey.'

'And I'm Ness,' she smiled. 'Short for Agnes. See you tomorrow, then.'

'You'll not be in the hayfield? Not a place for amateurs, tha' knows.'

'No. I'll be helping in the farmhouse. There'll be the cooking to do for family and helpers, so I think I'll be more use in the kitchen – till I've learned a bit more about things. I'll probably feed the hens, an' all, and collect the eggs and wipe them,' she said knowledgeably, having this afternoon been initiated into the poultry side of the business. She had enjoyed that part of it much more than the cow shed bit.

'Ah, well. See you.'

Goff Leaman watched her go. A bonny lass with a right grand smile and friendly with it, an' all. A town lass, without a doubt, but willing to learn it seemed. Should do all right in Ainsty, if she could stand the quiet of the country.

He squinted up into the sky as a bomber flew over, far too low, in his opinion, for safety. Off bombing tonight, he supposed.

He shrugged, picking up his spade, grateful that having done his bit in the trenches in the Great War, he was a mite too old for this one!

'Miss Hugwitty?' Ness smiled down at the small, elderly woman. 'I'm the new girl from Glebe Farm and Mrs Wintersgill wants to know if you could help in the kitchen, them bein' busy with the hay. Starting tomorrow.'

'Come in, lass. Was wondering when I'd be hearing. Always help Kate at busy times. They're late with hay this year. Usually they like to start about Barnaby.'

'Er –?'

'Barnaby time. St Barnabas' Day – eleventh of June. Mind, we had two weeks of wet weather, recent, so it'll have put things back a bit. Sit you down.' She nodded towards the wooden rocker beside the fireplace. 'And what do they call you, then?'

'Agnes Nightingale, though people call me Ness. And I'm twenty-five and from Liverpool, and I'm not courting.'

Best tell her, sooner than later. Beady-eyed people like Martha Hugwitty always found out in the end.

'Ah. Well, you're a bonny lass, so you soon will be. Courting, I mean. There's not much to choose from in the village with Tuthey's twins away in the Navy – apart from young Rowley at the farm. But there's a few young men across the top road at Meltonby. And York is full of RAF lads; aerodromes all around these parts. You'll not go short of a dancing partner if you're not already spoken for, that is.'

'Like I just said, I'm not going steady and I'm not looking, either. See you tomorrow, then?'

Ness got to her feet. Time she was going. Martha Hugwitty had been told all that was good for her to know about Glebe Farm's land girl. 'And nice meetin' you.'

Martha closed the door, nodding with satisfaction. Interesting, the lass was. Very pretty and twenty-five and not courting. Peculiar, to say the least. Young man been killed, perhaps? Agnes Nightingale, whose eyes held secrets to be probed by someone like herself, possessed of the gift. Likely the lass would have an interesting palm as well, could she but get a look at it. She shrugged, turning on the wireless for the evening news.

The pips that signalled nine o'clock pinged out. The land girl could wait. Until tomorrow.

'There you are!' Ness found Lorna in the garden, pulling weeds. 'Messages delivered.'

'Good. The two of them always help out at the farm. Both glad of the money, I think. But that's enough for one night. I'll come inside now, and wash my hands.'

'That Martha is a bit of a busybody.' Ness followed Lorna into the house. 'Got real beady eyes, like little gimlets.'

'She's all right, once you get to know her. But don't let her tell your fortune.'

'Bit of a fraud, is she?'

'Far from it! A lot of the things she's told people have come true – those who'll admit having been to her, that is. And you are right about her eyes, Ness. They do look into your soul, kind of. It wouldn't surprise me if she were a medium, on the quiet. Oh, drat! That's the phone! Answer it, will you, whilst I dry my hands.'

'Meltonby 223.' Ness spoke slowly and carefully into the receiver.

'Hullo! Lorna?'

'Sorry, no. I'm Ness. Lorna's here now. I think it's your William,' she mouthed, closing the door behind her. And just what the girl needed; cheer her up with a bit of good news and reassurance. But the news it would seem had not been good, and reassurance thin on the ground, judging from the downcast mouth and tear-bright eyes.

'Lorna, girl, what is it? Not bad news?'

'No. As a matter of fact there wasn't a lot of news, good or bad. William spent the entire three minutes telling me off.'

'Why? What have you done to upset him?'

'I didn't tell him about you. He got a shock, he said, when a strange voice answered. I should have told him in my letter and to cut a long story short, he says I mustn't have you here.'

'Well, it's his house, innit? Suppose you'd better tell them at the hostel.' A pity, Ness brooded. She was really getting to like it at Ladybower. 'I'll go as soon as there's a bed for me. And sorry if I got you into trouble – me answering the phone, I mean.'

'No, Ness! It wasn't your fault, and I don't want you to go! I don't care what William says. The evacuees we had to take put him off, you see. He said good riddance to them when they left. But he shouldn't object to a grown-up who's hardly ever in the house.'

'Poor love. He gave you a bad time because of me, when all you wanted to hear was that he was missing you and that he loves you,' Ness soothed.

'Afraid so. Do you know, if anything awful happened to me, he'd have it on his conscience that the last words he said to me were, "See Nance Ellery in the morning and tell her to find somewhere else for the woman to stay. Is that clear?" Then the pips went. He must have known we'd only get three minutes on a long-distance call, and he wasted them.' She blinked hard against tears.

'Never mind, queen. Dry your eyes. I'll make you a cuppa, eh? Don't bother ringing the hostel tonight. Tomorrow will do.'

'No it won't, because I don't want you to leave and what's more, I'll have who I like in this house. It isn't William's, it's mine!' Chin high, she dabbed her eyes. 'Grandpa left it to me. It's *my* name on the deeds, not William's! And I'm sorry, Ness. He isn't usually so rude.'

'Ar well, maybe he's fed up with the war and invasion talk just like the rest of us. Maybe he's worried about you, here on your own.'

'But I'm not on my own. You are here with me and he should be glad! And I *would* like a cup of tea, please, and I'll bet you anything you like that William will phone again before so very much longer, to say he's sorry.'

William had not phoned back. Ness frowned as she stood at the open window, watching shifting shapes in the twilight-dim garden, taking deep breaths of cool evening air. But to give him the benefit of the doubt, calls from south to north weren't all that easy to come by. Sometimes you booked your call then hung around for hours, waiting. Sometimes the call didn't come at all. Because of the war, and the armed forces being given priority over civilians when it came to using trunk lines. And perhaps, she thought, in further mitigation, William was really cheesed off now, him being so awful to Lorna for three minutes when he could have been telling her he loved her.

Yet nothing changed the fact that as long as Lorna's husband wanted neither evacuees nor land girls at Ladybower House, there wasn't a lot Ness Nightingale could do about it – even though Lorna said she must stay.

Sighing she pulled down the blackout blind, drew the rose chintz curtains over its ugliness, then got into bed. Arms behind head she gazed into the darkness. She didn't usually take sides, but tonight her sympathies were with Lorna. How could William wait ages and ages for a trunk call, then waste it giving Lorna down-the-banks and only because she had taken in a land girl.

William's silver-framed photograph came to mind. He wasn't, she was forced to admit, much to write home about. Oh, he looked well in his uniform, but she had noticed an arrogance about his mouth, a down-tilting of the corners of his lips. Mind, perhaps that was the way he wanted to look, all stern and soldierly, but that moustache didn't suit him, made him look years older than surely he was. And there had been something about his eyes, too. She frowned, trying to find a word for them. *Bulbous*, that was it! You noticed them almost as soon as you noticed the walrus moustache.

She had thought, on first seeing the photograph, that he hadn't a lot going for him as far as looks were concerned, but that maybe he had a kind heart to make up for it, and a protective nature – and was good at lovemaking. Not that she would so much as dream of asking Lorna about her private life, but of one thing she was certain. If tonight's phone call was anything to go by, William had a peevish side to his nature, and what had possessed Lorna to marry him only Lorna knew, because it was obvious she wasn't without means. She owned Ladybower House, which must be worth a pretty penny. Five bedrooms and two lavvies, would you believe, and no end of a big garden. And she wouldn't be surprised if Lorna's grandad hadn't left her a few pounds besides!

I mean, she reasoned silently into the darkness, Lorna is quite pretty. Lorna could be better than pretty if she did something about that ridiculous mop of frizz she called hair. Pale blonde it was, and naturally curly, but there was much too much of it. You noticed the mass of hair before you noticed the girl and how blue her eyes were and how beautiful the bones of her face were. Ness's cutting fingers ached to get at that hair, sort it out, shape it properly so it laid soft and close to her head. Lorna's hair needed a short style; one she could comb with her fingers; a style she could wash in rainwater from the tub at the back door – a beauty treatment in itself – and leave to dry naturally without any rubbing or towelling or even, heaven forbid, drying it in front of the fire.

And after she had tamed that tangled mass, Ness thought gleefully, something ought to be done about those eyebrows. There was a beautiful arch to them, but did Lorna have to let them meet at the top of her nose? A little tidying here and there, and they would be a perfect foil for those deep blue eyes. But William, Lorna had said, liked his wife's hair long, and if Lorna was content to drag a wire brush through it and bring tears to her eyes in the process, then it was nothing to do with Ness Nightingale.

'Night night,' she sighed, snuggling into the blankets, wondering if Lorna was asleep, knowing she was not. Worrying, like as not, about that husband of hers, arrogant sod that he was! 'Sleep tight, queen . . .'

Lorna was not asleep. She was, as was to be expected, wide awake and thinking things out. But she was not worrying because as far as she was concerned, there was nothing to worry about. She had taken a land girl into her home, which was the patriotic thing to do, and William had flown off the handle, would you believe; William, who was usually so unflappable and understanding and kind, just as Grandpa had been. One of the good things about her husband had been his similarity to her lovely Grandpa, who had been father, mother and best friend to her for as long as she could remember. But tonight William had been very annoyed. For the first timc in their married life he had shouted at her as if she were a stupid recruit with two left feet and he a drill-sergeant, bawling at the top of his voice at an imbecile.

William had bawled as if he were giving orders, and it wasn't a bit like the William who usually smoothed her path and sheltered her – metaphorically, that was – so that even the wind should not blow on her, and made her smile if anything dismayed or upset her. So there must be an excuse for such strange behaviour. He was lonely and missing his wife and home and the ordered familiarity of his profession. And it couldn't be easy, going from civilian life to the hurly-burly of the Army; taking orders, too, instead of giving them. Because William was only a lieutenant; an officer, certainly, but a junior one, who would be expected to salute his superiors and call them Sir! Poor William.

Her pillows had become quite hot – from her indignation, no doubt – so she plumped and turned them then walked to the window, carefully drawing the curtains, pulling aside the blackout. Then she pushed the window wide and leaned on her elbows, gazing down into the garden, making out the denser dark of the trees that circled it and the rounded shapes that were banks of rose bushes.

In June, total darkness was a long time coming; the extra hour of daylight took care of that. At this time of the year, you could walk round Ainsty at almost eleven at night and not bump into anything or miss your footing on an unseen kerb edge.

Now, the garden below her took on a mysterious, half-hidden quality and the wood behind – Dickon's Wood –

became strange and enchanted and ripe for haunting because surely on nights such as this, on breathless, half-asleep nights, did Ursula come to meet the man who loved her and waited for her. Surely, if the nun's ghost did exist, it would walk tonight. But ghosts glided. Ghosts wraithed and drifted then disappeared into nothing. Ghosts didn't walk like real people – did they?

'Goodnight Ursula and Dickon,' she smiled, covering the window again, turning on the light at her bedside. 'And goodnight William, my dear. Take care of yourself. I know you didn't mean to be angry on the phone. Don't worry. Everything will turn out right . . .'

Of course it would! Ness was staying, and that was the end of it!

Ness closed the gate gently and without sound. She had risen extra early then hurried into the morning, eager to be at Glebe Farm for the first day of haymaking. She sniffed in air still moist with early dew, wanted to hug herself with joy at the beauty of this tiny place, so hidden away from the war. All around, birds sang; everywhere was greenness and flowers and a sky brightening to summer blue as the sun rose to light it.

'Hey! Wait on, lass!' Ness turned to see Martha Hugwitty bearing down on her, and smiled a welcome.

'Morning, Miss Hugwitty. Isn't this goin' to be a lovely day?'

'No, it isn't. It'll be hot and dusty and hard work. And me name's Martha.'

'Hot and dusty in the field, you mean?'

'Oh my word, yes. They'll be stripped down to bare chests in no time at all. Can't make hay in the cool and wet, see. Got to be dry and sunny. I'm glad you're here, Ness. You can take water to the field for the workers – save my old legs. What made you want to leave Liverpool, then?' The question was direct and unexpected.

'We-e-ll – why not? Always fancied living in the country,' Ness hedged. 'People say that women will be called up like the men before so very much longer, so I thought if I volunteered I could go where I wanted.'

'And what are you running away from, lass?'

'*Me*? Runnin'? Nuthin'!' Her indignation was showing; protesting too much shc reminded herself, regaining her composure. 'Why do you think I'm running away? Robbed a bank, have I?'

'Now did I say that? Did I? All I meant was that a young and bonny lass like you shouldn't want to bury herself in a place like this. Isn't natural. There's no picture palaces here, nor dance halls. Wasn't suggesting nothing criminal.'

'Well that's all right then, isn't it? I just fancied a change and like I said, women are goin' to get called up before so very much longer, I'd bct on it!'

'Never! Women aren't built for fighting wars! A woman's place is at home, cooking and having children. Men can't have children so they do the fighting.'

'So what were those women doin' that travelled to York on the train with me, then? In the Air Force, they were, and in uniform. And there are women in the Army and the Navy. There's a lot of Wrens in Liverpewl, it bein' a port. Seen them with my own eyes.'

'Happen so.' It was all Martha could think of to say. The land girl was telling nothing – not this morning, at least. But she would find out sooner rather than later why a good-looking young woman like Ness seemed intent on burying herself in the country. A man behind it, was there, or maybe she really had robbed a bank? 'Mornin', Kate lass,' she called to the farmer's wife who stood at the back gate. 'Nice day for it!'

Nice day! Ness was to ponder. Run off her feet, more like. Hosing the cow shed had been the start of it with no one to help her since Rowley was away early to the hayfield and Farmer Wintersgill getting a bite of breakfast before he joined his son, scythe in hand. And there had been the hens to feed and water, the eggs to collect and wipe and arrange in trays ready for the egg packers who collected twice a week on Mondays and Thursdays. And how many times had she trudged to the field with jugs, water slopping over her shoes. Gallons, the haymakers had downed. Martha had been right! Cutting hay was a hot and dusty job, although it wasn't so much dust as pollen from the long stems of grass, Mrs Wintersgill had explained.

At noon, the workers had taken their places at a long trestle table, set up in the shade of the stackyard, first having cooled heads and bodies at the pump trough in the yard. Rabbit pies, Kate had made, with stewed apples and custard to follow.

'Hungry?' she asked when the men had returned to the field and the table taken down and chairs stacked. 'I put aside enough for you and me and Martha – it's in the oven, on plates. Reckon we should take the weight off our feet for half an hour, eh? Think we've earned it!'

They sat companionably in the stone-flagged kitchen, doors and windows wide open to the day outside, and never had a meal been so well-deserved, Ness thought, nor tasted so good.

'I was telling Ness that she's going to find it boring in the country.' Martha renewed her probing across the kitchen table. 'Wondered what a town girl like herself sees in a place like Nun Ainsty.' The beady eyes sparked a challenge.

'Maybe it's because I like living in haunted places,' Ness avoided the question with a grin. 'And this village *is* haunted, isn't it, Mrs Wintersgill?'

'Now who told you that? Goodness gracious, there's no such things as ghosts. Lorna been pulling your leg, has she?'

'No. She told me about the nun who came to the priory, though – the one whose father didn't want her and sent her to help nurse the sick. Hundreds of years ago, I mean. I'd asked Lorna how the wood at the back of Ladybower got its name and the story just came out.'

'So you believe in ghosts?' Martha's dark eyes prompted.

'I believe some people think they can see them, but I'm not one of them. I feel sorry for Ursula, though. Must have been awful for her. Nice to think that Dickon cared for her – well, if legend is to be believed.'

'It *is*!'

'Load of old nonsense!'

Martha and Kate replied at one and the same time and they all laughed and the subject of the ghostly nun was dropped by mutual consent. It had served, though, to prevent her answering Martha's questions. There *had* been a reason for leaving Liverpool and her Mam and Da and the good job she'd had. But that was nobody's business but her own, and Martha could probe all she liked; it would get her nowhere. What had happened was in the past and to Ness Nightingale's way of thinking, there wasn't a better place than Nun Ainsty to make a fresh start. And to forget what had been.

'Now what do you want me to do, Mrs Wintersgill?' She rose reluctantly to her feet.

'Well, you can call me Kate for a start, like everyone else round this village does. Me and Martha will see to the washing up; I don't suppose you could get the washing in from the line before it gets too dry to iron?'

'I could,' Ness smiled. She liked the drying green from which she could look over towards the hills to her left, mistily grey in a haze of heat. The tops, people called them. And to her right was the back of the manor, where she would try to count all the chimney pots; and could see the stables that were now Jacob Tuthey's joiner's shop; and see, too, the many windows, uncleaned for years, and so she felt sad about the neglect of a once-fine house.

She kicked off her shoes, stuffed her socks in the pockets of her overalls, then walked deliciously barefoot to the long line of washing, curling her toes in the cool of the grass. Overhead, a black-bellied plane droned, flying low. A lot of them had taken off last night. Going bombing, Lorna said, from nearby Dishforth and Linton-on-Ouse. Whitley bombers, all of them, which Ness would come to recognize in time. Plane spotting was getting as popular as train spotting.

Not interested, Ness decided, as the plane dropped out of sight. Of much more importance was a letter from Mam, who should have got her new address by now, sent on a postcard bought in Meltonby post office; a view in colour of Nun Ainsty though only Ladybower's chimneypots had been visible on it. Ness had scribbled her address and *Will write soon* on the back of it, and tonight, tired or not, she would let her mother know she was all right, that she had landed on her feet in a smashing billet – she would not mention William – and that she had spent her day haymaking.

Squinting into the sun, she took down sheets and pillow-slips, towels and working shirts, folding them carefully into the wicker clothes basket. Then reluctantly she pulled on shoes and socks. Tomorrow, she must remember to bring spare socks with her; socks dry and sweet-smelling. Tomorrow, they would mow the second field, Kate had said, after which there would be days of turning the cut grass until it dried out and became winter fodder for milk cows that would spend the cold months in the shelter of the stockyard. And be fed and watered twice a day, and the stockyard cleaned, too.

In summer, Kate said, it was a joy to work a farm; in winter it was dreary, with mud up to the ankles and everything you touched cold and wet. Dark mornings, too, and night coming before five o'clock. Farming, Ness had quickly grasped, had its ups and downs and today was an up day, so she would enjoy it, even though her feet throbbed painfully and her arms ached. Tomorrow she would have to learn to turn hay which would make her arms ache still more – until she got the hang of it. And meantime, she would think of the evening cool at Ladybower and a bath and the cotton dress and sandals she'd had the foresight to bring with her. Tonight, maybe sitting on the bench in the garden, she and Lorna would chat, all the time listening through the open door for the ringing of the phone. Because surely William would phone tonight, to say he was sorry and of course the land girl must stay and that he missed Lorna something awful. And that a letter full of I-love-yous was on its way to her.

Ness dumped the clothes basket on the kitchen table, offering to do the ironing, but Martha said she would see to it, though maybe Ness would take a couple of jugs to the workers, if she would be so kind?

And maybe, Ness thought as she made her way to the hayfield with jugs of ice-cold water from the pump, ironing was too warm an occupation on days such as this; days when the sun beat down from a clear summer sky; days when you could forget that places like Liverpool existed. Almost forget, that was . . .

Two letters had been delivered to Ladybower House; one for Lorna and the other, propped up on the kitchen mantelpiece, for Ness – the one she had been expecting from her mother.

'So did William mention me?' Ness hesitated. 'Did he –'

'Not a word. But today's letter would have been written before he phoned. And he's sure to book a call tonight. It'll be all right, Ness. I want you to stay.'

'Ar, but does your husband?'

'We'll worry about William when I've had his next letter – or another phone call. Now, tell me about the haymaking. How's it going?'

'Like the clappers. Rowley was going to work as long as it was light, he said, so he could get the big field cut. Then tomorrow they'll start on the ten-acre field. And I forgot.

There'll be a rabbit for me tomorrow. Goff shot ten in the big field; half for him, half for the farm. I said I couldn't skin a rabbit, so Martha said she would do it for me. Said she'd ask Goff for a nice young one, then you could roast it.' Ness wrinkled her nose. She had heard of rabbit stew but never roast rabbit. '*Can* you roast them, Lorna?'

'Yes, indeed. Fill the ribcage with thyme and parsley stuffing, then roast them gently on the middle shelf of the oven. Carefully carved, rabbit has a texture like chicken. William says half the chicken you get in restaurants is rabbit.'

'Fancy that, now.' Oh dear, they were back to William again. 'You got any news, Lorna?'

'Yes, I have. Heard it on the one o'clock bulletin, then had it again from Nance. There's going to be recruiting for a Home Army. They're going to call it the Local Defence Volunteers and Mr Churchill wants one in every town and village. Made up of civilians, it'll be, and they'll be trained to shoot and put up tank traps and generally make things awkward for the Germans – if they come. Seems there's no end of things they can do to help out. I think it must be very serious if they're asking older men to fight. Every man who is able-bodied is expected to join.'

'And what about women? Can we join, an' all?'

'Afraid not. Nance says her husband is going to organize the Nun Ainsty men, and they'll team up with the men from Meltonby and do their parades together. Gilbert Ellery will be taking his orders from Nance, I shouldn't wonder. Bet she was real put out it was a men-only affair. But things must be serious, Ness, if the older men have to fight. I mean, Goff was in the last war. He's done his bit for King and Country.'

'What about the farm? Does farming exempt Bob and Rowley Wintersgill from joining?'

'Seems not. All able-bodied men, it said on the news.'

'Then I suppose me Da'll have to join. Mam won't like

that. The letter was from Mam. I'll write to her, tonight. Have I time for a wash before supper?'

'You have. And when we've eaten we'll sit in the garden and leave the back door open so we can hear the phone. Away with you!'

Lorna sighed deeply. The news about the LDV had troubled her, but Ness didn't seem one bit bothered when told about it. Overreacting, she had been; looking for things to worry about when all she needed to hear was that William was sorry for the things he had said on the phone and of course it was all right for Ness to be at Ladybower. That they could be invaded at any time would seem less frightening then. And anyway, she argued sternly, surely Hitler's soldiers, *if* they came, wouldn't be making a beeline for Ainsty; wouldn't be hell bent on destroying the village stone by stone, then pillaging and raping as the Vikings had done around these parts a thousand years ago? She was not their priority target! She was one of many women who had to get on with things as best she could, invasion or not, because her man had gone to war. What was so special about Lorna Hatherwood, then?

She prodded a knife into the potatoes. Two more minutes, then they'd be done and the cabbage, too, to eke out what was left of yesterday's stew, more gravy than meat. A rabbit would be very handy. Two more days' supper taken care of. She wished she could go to York, hunt around, find a fish queue. Fish wasn't rationed; only the petrol to take her to the faraway shops where there was more chance of finding unrationed food. There was the bus, of course, but buses nowadays seemed to arrive and depart at their own times. It was awkward, she sighed, living in so out-of-the-way a place. And then she thought of the invasion – if it happened – and thought that living in Nun Ainsty far outweighed a piece of off-the-ration fish.

'On the table in two minutes!' she called from the bottom of the stairs, then smiled because tonight William would be lucky and be able to phone her, she knew it. Only for three minutes, mind, but you could say a lot of I-love-yous in three minutes. 'Shift yourself or it'll go cold!'

Sitting in the garden, her bare feet on the cool grass, was a sheer delight. The sun was in the west now, and would soon begin its setting, dropping lower in the sky, glowing golden-red. On the twilight air came the scent of roses and honeysuckle, and on the highest oak in Dickon's Wood a blackbird sang sweetly into the stillness.

Ness closed her eyes, hugging herself tightly as if to hold to her this moment of complete peace. Peace? But for how much longer? Was this suddenly-precious country to be occupied by jackbooted soldiers? It couldn't happen to this tiny island that once ruled half the world? Nun Ainsty couldn't be taken, nor her lovely brash Liverpool? Imagine German soldiers billeted here in the manor house, because they would take it, soon as look at it if the fancy took them!

She stirred, wanting to know why all at once she was feeling like this. Had it been today in the so-English hayfield that the love of this island had taken her or had she, when she boarded the train at Lime Street station, uniform in two suitcases, decided that this cockeyed little country was worth fighting for and being a land girl was the best way she knew to do it?

No, she told a red rose silently, the day she boarded the York train she had felt only relief to be getting away to a fresh start, and sadness, of course, to be leaving Mam and the terraced house she had grown up in. And pain. A tearing pain that jabbed deeper if she let herself think of what she had lost and could never find again.

She shook her thoughts into focus and began to read through the letter she was writing.

Dear Mam and Da and Nan,

You'll know by now where I am, but it is ten times

better than the picture on the postcard. You can't see my billet on it but it's a lovely house, with big windows and a beautiful garden with a wood all around it. The lady I live with is called Lorna. Her husband is in the Army, and I think she is pleased to have a bit of company.

Best not go into detail about William's outburst nor the phone call Lorna was waiting for that would put it right, she hoped.

I work at Glebe Farm for Mr Wintersgill. His wife, Kate, is lovely and they have a son Rowland, but I don't see a lot of him.

Best not say over much about young Rowley. A bit sly, Ness thought, and cocky with it. Fancied himself no end.

Today we were haymaking and I was glad I was not in the field with them, but I was on the go all the time, trying to be useful. There's a lot to learn about being in the Land Army, but I don't regret joining so you are not to worry about me. I'm fine, and I'll be given leave, just as if I'd joined the Armed Forces, and be given a rail ticket, too, so you'll be seeing me before long. And Liverpool is easy to get to from York.

A bomber flew over, and another. Best not mention the aerodromes all around Nun Ainsty. Careless talk, that, and you never knew who just might get hold of her letter. There were spies all over the place it said in the newspaper. Ordinary people you'd never suspect.

'Looks as if the lads are flying tonight.' Lorna looked up from her magazine. 'Wonder where they're off to.'

'Dunno.' Ness hoped they would drop one slap bang in

the middle of Berlin, but the bombing of open cities was not allowed, it seemed. Very gentlemanly this war was at times. 'Think William will manage to get through?'

'Yes, fingers crossed. But if he doesn't, there'll be a letter in the morning and everything will be OK. He'll ring, though . . .' Of course he would. Shouting at her wasn't a bit like him and he'd be only too eager to put things right between them. 'Writing home, are you, or to your boyfriend?'

'I told you, didn't I, that I haven't got a boyfriend. Told Martha Hugwitty, an' all, and that I wasn't lookin' either!'

'Then you told the right person! Martha will make it her business to let Nun Ainsty know that the land girl at Glebe isn't courting. And she'll read your palm, if you let her, and find a nice young man for you in it! By the way, what do you think of Rowley Wintersgill?'

'Not a lot. Why?'

'He's got a reputation around these parts for being a bit of a lady's man.'

'That a warning, Lorna?'

'We-e-ll, not exactly. Been a bit spoiled, being an only child. Thinks the world's his oyster.'

'You mean I'm not to encourage him?'

'Something like that,' Lorna said uneasily, though glad, for all that, that she'd put out a warning.

'Well, don't worry. I can look after meself, queen.'

'Good. And I'm disturbing you?'

'No. This letter is just a quickie to let Mam know I'm all right and liking it here.'

'Good – that you like it, I mean. I want you to stay here, Ness.'

'But will I be allowed to?' There was still tonight's phone call or tomorrow's letter, either of which could land her in the hostel.

'I said I wanted you to, didn't I?'

She said it, Ness thought, with a surprising firmness – for

Lorna, that was. Maybe there was more to her than wide blue eyes and a gentle nature.

'Then I want to, an' all.'

The phone rang, and Lorna ran to answer it. Ness turned back to the letter she was writing.

> *Sorry this isn't much of a letter but I'm tired and plan an early night. Will write a longer letter tomorrow. Just to let you know I'm fine and I don't regret leaving Liverpool. It was for the best, Mam. You're not to worry . . .*

All done now. Carefully Ness addressed the envelope to 3, Ruth Street, Liverpool 4, Lancashire. Tomorrow, or the next day, she would write again. Tomorrow, or the next day, she would know how long she would be staying at Ladybower House, because determined though Lorna was, Ness wouldn't take bets on her getting her own way. The cut of William's jib told her that.

'Oh, damn!' Lorna said, back from her phone call. 'It was Nance Ellery, would you believe. I was so sure it would be my trunk call. And Ness – guess what? The Germans have invaded the Channel Islands. It was on the nine o'clock news and we missed it, sitting out here as if it didn't matter!'

'Just like that? Was there any fighting?' Ness whispered.

'Doesn't seem so. It was a peaceful takeover, by all accounts. Nance said it looks as if we're going to need the Local Defence Volunteers now. Oh, she upsets me sometimes. Always the first with bad news! She seems to attract it!'

'Well, we'd have heard it for ourselves, queen, sooner or later. Had you thought them islands are a part of us, sort of. British, and not all that far away, either. I'll bet Churchill's goin' to have sumthin' to say about it! He vowed *Jairmans* would never set foot on British soil, but they have!'

'Technically they have, I suppose. Perhaps that's why William hasn't phoned.'

‘Ar, I wouldn’t worry, Lorna. He’s a long way from there, though it might have affected the telephone lines with calls buzzing all over the place once the high-ups heard about the Channel Islands. I wouldn’t worry too much, girl. It’s getting a bit chilly. Let’s you and me wait inside, eh? If your feller can’t manage to get through, there’s sure to be a letter in the morning.’

‘You’re right. It’s nearly ten. I’ll go round the house and see to the blackouts; you be a dear and make us some cocoa.’ Cocoa thankfully wasn’t rationed.

So they left the enchantment of the garden to the blackbird, a tiny creature that didn’t know there was a war on. Lucky little bird, Ness thought.

THREE

'There you are, then!' Martha Hugwitty met Ness outside Ladybower. 'Another swelterer it's going to be.'

'You could be right. Is Goff coming today?' They fell into slow step.

'There already. Said last night he was going to give a hand opening up ten-acre field. Crafty old devil. Knows he'll get a breakfast out of Kate if he does! They've got home-cured bacon and eggs aplenty at Glebe Farm. And how are you this morning, eh?'

'Fine. Slept like a log. Must be the country air.'

No use telling Martha she had awakened in the night to hear Lorna weeping and lain awake worrying about her, wondering if she should offer comfort; deciding against it.

Was it the phone call that hadn't come or was it that the Germans were so much nearer now? Was Lorna miserable because she was missing William or was it because she knew her husband would win and the land girl be sent packing? Would Lorna give in in the end?

'You're lucky. Woke me up at four this morning, those bombers coming back. Hope they're all safe, for all that. Don't tell me you slept through it!'

'Afraid so.' She had. After lying awake for a long time, she must have dropped off just before. 'Tell me about that wood, Martha. Any truth in it – the nun, I mean?'

'Oh, it's true about Ursula; no doubt about it. But what I s'pose you mean is have I seen her ghost?'

'So there *is* one. She *does* walk?'

'Yes. But very rarely. Lived here all my life you might say, so I know what's what around this village. Mind, I keep my mouth shut. The less you say, the more you hear. And I can tell you there've been women come to my house who have seen her. Admitted it.'

'No men?'

'We-e-ll, men might have seen her, but men don't avail themselves of my services, Ness lass. And I mean services of the occult. I read palms, as Lorna will have told you, and I do the tarot cards, though not often. Too much death and destruction in the cards. I do psychometry, too.'

'That's a big word, Martha!'

'Aye. I'm not as green as I'm cabbage looking, Ness Nightingale. I know a lot of big words, and that particular one means I can pick up messages from things. Now, if you had a young man and you was worried about him, you could give me something he'd handled and I could tell.'

'Tell things about him, you mean?'

'Indeed! Just by holding it in my hands. Or putting it to my forehead where the inner eye is.'

'*Well*!' Psychometry was a new one! 'But did the ladies who came to consult you tell you about Ursula?'

'One or two did, over the years. Probably why they came in the first place. Seeing the nun must be a bit of a shock – well, to the uninitiated, that is. But Ursula don't appear willy-nilly. Only to certain folk. Sometimes it's years and no one sees her and things die down and she's all but forgotten. Then she's back again.'

'In the wood?'

'Always the wood where Dickon waited. Never seen her myself, but then I wouldn't.'

'Why wouldn't you, Martha – with your gifts, I mean?'

''Cause the nun only appears to lovers. *True* lovers. If

they are despairing, like she was, she comes to comfort them – to let them know it'll be all right. Leastways, that's the conclusion I've come to over the years.'

'And you've never been in love, Martha?'

'No. Never felt the need for it. Have you – been in love, I mean?'

'Well I – I . . .' Such directness caught Ness unprepared. 'N-no. I haven't. Not truly in love.' And may her tongue drop out for the lie!

'Then let's hope one day you will be. *Truly* in love, I mean, then you just might meet Ursula.'

'I might at that.'

Ness was glad they had come to the farm and all talk of ghosts and nuns and lovers – and lovers denied! – had to end. She would never, ever, offer her hand to Martha Hugwitty, because those black eyes could see into your soul. And as for her inner eye – well heaven only knew what that could see.

'Morning!' she called to Kate, standing on the doorstep. 'Another lovely day!'

It had been a lovely day, Ness thought as she walked back to Ladybower. Hot and very hard work, but for a few hours the world and the war had been shut out. Not a single bomber had flown overhead, even. She wondered if there had been a letter for Lorna and what was in it. No land girls! *Positively* no land girls. She really, really hoped not.

'Hi there!' She passed a newspaper-wrapped parcel to Lorna. 'One rabbit, skinned!'

'Great! I'll roast it for tomorrow's supper. There's loads of parsley and thyme in the garden. But how did it go at Glebe?'

'They finished the ten-acre field, then everybody mucked in to give the first turn to the field that was cut yesterday. I wasn't very good at it,' she laughed, 'but Mr Wintersgill said I'd be tossing hay like a good 'un by the time it's dry. Given good weather, about ten days, he said. Any news?'

'From William? Yes. He hasn't changed his mind about you, even though he didn't mention you until the last line. *I'm sure you will have found another billet for the land girl before I come home on leave. Ask Nance to help you.* That's the only mention you got, Ness. And as for Nance Ellery helping me find you somewhere to go, it was she who suggested you come here in the first place! I mean, what's it got to do with Nance? If I wanted rid of you, I could see to it myself. I'm not as stupid as William thinks! But I've made up my mind, there's no question of you going. Like I said, this is *my* house.'

'Now see here, Lorna, there's goin' to be trouble for you if I stay. I don't want to be the cause of friction between man and wife.'

'You won't be. I've been thinking about it ever since the letter came, and I've got it fixed. I went to see Flora Petch.'

'The nurse at Larkspur Cottage?'

'That's her. Mind, I had to be careful – couldn't say William was being stupid about you being here. I – I'm afraid I had to tell her that although I loved having you here, I wondered if you could stay at her place when William comes home. She thought I wanted him and me to be alone, so I let her.'

'And?' Ness took in a deep breath.

'And she said fine by her. Any time at all. I said I'd give her your rations and pay her the billeting allowance for the week and she said she'd look forward to having you. So you see, you're doubly wanted.'

'And you're sure . . . ?'

'Ness Nightingale! If you ask me if I'm sure once more I'll thump you! I've got it all straight in my mind now. William needn't have joined up just yet. His age group shouldn't have to register for months, and even then it's anybody's guess when he'd have actually been sent for. He could still be here, but he joined the Territorials even before the war started and risked early call-up so he could get the regiment he wanted. He chose to go, Ness, and I choose to have you here. William can't have it all his own way. There's a war on and, before very much longer, civilians are going to have to be a part of it!'

'A ladies' branch of the LDV?' Ness grinned.

'No. But people like me without encumbrances will have to knuckle down to war work and neither William nor Nance Ellery will be able to do anything about it! So get yourself into something cooler. You've got twenty minutes. It's Woolton pie tonight!'

Woolton pie, Ness thought as she stripped and made for the bathroom, was what was known as a desperate dish, because you were desperately short of rations; of fat to make pastry for a crust and of good red meat to put underneath it. Woolton pie consisted entirely of mixed vegetables, moistened with yesterday's leftover gravy, and atop it a crust made of unrationed suet, courtesy of your kindly butcher!

But tomorrow they would feast on roast rabbit, courtesy of Glebe Farm, delicately stuffed with thyme and parsley from Ladybower's garden. Mind, Ness wasn't altogether sure it was right to kill such nice little creatures, but having been assured they were no better than vermin, caused a lot of damage on the home front, and that they were much in demand as off-the-ration meat, she allowed her scruples to fly out of the wide-open window.

'I was talking to Martha today,' Ness said as they sat companionably in the garden after supper. 'Seeing the wood made me think of it.'

'Talking about the nun? Ursula's got you intrigued.'

'Martha said she knew women who had seen her.'

'I'll grant you that, Ness. There has always been nun talk. It comes and goes, but *I've* never seen Ursula.'

'Neither has Martha, but she said she didn't expect to, bein' as how Ursula only appears to lovers.'

'Yes, I've heard that, too. I've also heard that very few see her – or will admit to it.'

'Why? Did she frighten them or sumthin', because she was so ugly?'

'No, that's just it, you see. Those who saw her – who *allegedly* saw her – weren't a bit afraid, until they realized they'd just walked past a ghost. They must have felt a bit queer when the penny dropped, but by then she had gone – just vanished. But the most amazing thing – if it's true, of course – is that she walks past them looking like a real flesh and blood person.'

'A person in nun's habit?'

'I would presume so. And it's said they can hear her footsteps on the path as if she's – well, real . . .'

'But ghosts don't – *shouldn't* – have footsteps, surely?'

'I'd have thought that myself, Ness. But Ursula Ainsty walks like a real person, it's said, and since you seem so taken up with our ghost, you might as well have the lot! People who are supposed to have seen her say she is absolutely beautiful. It's another reason why they don't realize it's Ursula because people assume she was deformed. But it's just talk. So many different versions that I don't believe any of them.'

'Beautiful?' Ness whispered, turning to gaze at the wood behind them as if she were waiting for the sound of footsteps.

'Well, if you believe in heaven, which I do, you'll accept that all ills are banished, and Ursula would be whole and complete – no harelip or anything . . .'

'Well, I'm not so sure about heaven,' Ness hesitated. 'Think I'd rather believe in the power of love. Dickon loved her, didn't he? Perhaps his love was good – decent. That would be enough for me, if I were in Ursula's shoes.'

'Loving and being loved makes all things right? It's a theory. But I can say, hand on heart, that all I know of the nun is folklore. I haven't seen her, nor have I met anyone who is prepared to say they have. I'm sorry, but until she crosses my path then I'm a disbeliever.'

'But tell me,' Ness urged, 'those women who told Martha they'd seen her – were they women in love?'

'That I don't know. Seems they must have been, but you wouldn't get their names out of Martha for love nor money. Said people would lose faith in her and her powers if she blabbed all over the village.'

'So any of them could have been married, even?'

'They could have, I suppose. Mind, I don't think any of the women in question came from the village – or so Martha said. Perhaps they lived in Meltonby.'

'Ar. Martha admitted to me that she reads palms, though she doesn't like doin' the cards. Martha's got the gift, you know. You were right about her being a medium, even though she doesn't hold seances. Maybe it's her aura that Ursula uses when she wants to do a spot of haunting – zooms in on Martha's vibrations.'

'If what my grandpa told me is true, then Ursula was doing her spot of haunting long before Martha Hugwitty came to the village. So don't get too carried away, Ness. Ghosts are fun. You've got to treat them as fun. Part of the local folklore.'

'Ar. Like you say – fun. Till you see one, that is!'

'When I've seen Ursula you'll be the first one to know, I promise you,' Lorna smiled complacently. 'And what are you looking at me like that for – like I've got a smut on my nose. Have I?'

'As a matter of fact, I was looking at your hair.'

'A mess, I know. I just washed it this afternoon. Hurts like mad to get the brush through it.'

'I know. I've dealt with more frizzy heads of curls than you've had hot dinners, girl. I'm a hairdresser – or was.'

'It follows. Your own hair is so beautiful that it doesn't surprise me. I should have realized.'

'Hmm. Your hair is a lovely colour; ash blonde it would be if you was gettin' it out of a bottle. Women would kill for natural curls like yours, Lorna. But you've got too much hair if you don't mind me saying so – professional opinion, like. It needs shaping and thinning. If ever you want it seeing to, just let me know.'

'Well, I do find it a nuisance. And I agree my hair must look like a bush on top of my head. But William doesn't ever want me to cut it. He likes it long.'

'And you like it long, too?'

'No. I'd like it shorter, but William –'

'Must be obeyed. Even though you have to drag a wire brush through it and do it no end of harm, William knows best, does he? Anyway, whose hair is it?'

'You're right, Ness!' And because William had been dogmatic and dictatorial and had no right to tell her whom she should and should not have in her house, she walked into the hall and gazed into the mirror. Then she turned and smiling said,

'OK, Ness. Let's give it a go! Thin it out a bit.'

'You're sure? Mind, I know what it'll look like when I've finished, but once it's off there'll be nothing you can do about it, till it grows again.'

'I'm sure. And you must let me pay you.'

'I don't want paying. All I want is to get some order into that mass of frizz and for you to throw that dratted brush away – OK?'

'OK! Shall we get on with it, then?' Why was her heart thudding so?

'If you're absolutely sure, I'll nip upstairs for my scissors and get a towel from the bathroom.'

She would enjoy doing Lorna's hair because for one thing it looked quite ridiculous on one so young, and for another, because she was indirectly, she supposed, taking a swipe at William who didn't like land girls!

'Tell me how long it takes to be a hairdresser?' Lorna wasn't really interested, but Ness was trying to part her hair and pin it into sections, which hurt, and talking about anything at all took her mind off the sharp, tugging pains.

'Am I hurting you?'

'A little, but it's all right . . .'

'Well never mind, queen, when I've sorted this lot you'll be able to comb it with your fingers, I guarantee it. You'll wash it and leave it to dry naturally, then you'll run your fingers through it and flick the curls whichever way you want. You'll like it – honest. It took me a long time gettin' to be a good hairdresser, because I *am* good. I was the best cutter in the salon and I had an improver working under me, and two apprentices to teach.'

'What's an improver?'

'It's when you've done two years; when you've been lackey and shampoo girl and sweeper-upper of hair. God! Those first few months, I hated hair! And for the first two years an apprentice doesn't get a penny piece in wages – not where I worked, they didn't. Had to rely on tips from ladies you'd shampooed. And I used to cut kids' hair at home in Ruth Street. Charged sixpence for it. Big money, sixpence was, to an apprentice!'

'But how did you manage for two years without pay?' Lorna heard the first crisp snip and closed her eyes again.

'I managed because Auntie Agnes paid my tram fares into work for two years. She paid my premium, an' all. To get into a good salon there had to be a hefty fifty quid, up front. But Dale's was the best in town and I've got to admit that the tips there were good – thank God!'

'Called after your Auntie Agnes, weren't you?' Another snip, and a shower of fine hair falling to the floor. 'Fond of her?'

'Oh, ar. I was her favourite. She never had kids of her own, so I was the lucky one. She paid my premium without so much as a quibble and I said she would never want for a free hairdo, once I'd learned enough. Oh, it was lovely when I got to be an improver. I could have my own regular customers, then, though I had to do my own shampooing. Fifteen shillings a week I got. Plus tips. I felt real rich and

Auntie Agnes and Mam and Nan got theirs done free. I even cut me Da's hair. I liked cuttin'. Still do.'

'I can see you do.' Lorna gazed, fascinated, at the growing pile of fair hair. 'Will you be long?'

'Just thinin' it first, then I'll shape it; take each strand and cut it between my fingers so it lays just right. A Maria cut, it'll be.'

'I – I see.' Lorna had never heard of a Maria cut. 'And it'll look all right? You're sure?'

'When I've finished with you, Modom, your hair'll look so good you'll wish you'd had a Maria years ago. Now shurrup, will you? You're distractin' me. Just trust me, eh?'

Famous last words. Lorna closed her eyes and counted the snips.

'There now! All done! Took me longer than I thought,' Ness beamed, half an hour later. 'But you can't hurry good cuttin'. Now, you washed it this afternoon, you said, so I'll just rinse it through and show you how to dry it. Hair's got to be treated gentle, not tugged and pulled and dried in front of a hot fire! Now, pop over to the sink and I'll get a jug of rainwater from the tub. And keep your hands off it!'

But too late came the warning. To a cry of,

'You – you've *scalped* me!' Lorna gazed at the pile of hair on the kitchen floor.

'Ar. Enough there to stuff a cushion,' Ness grinned. 'I'll just take the chill off this water then I'll give you a rinse. And I haven't scalped you. All I've done is cut your hair to a length of three inches all over your head, and when it's dry it'll fall into soft little curls – fronds, like. You'll like it, honest. Now lean over the sink, and you're not to look at it till it's dry.'

'I won't.' She *wouldn't*! She had no wish to see herself all bare and shorn. And as for stuffing a cushion – more to the point was what would William say!

*   *   *

Not long after, when Ness had rinsed and patted and dabbed, then gently massaged Lorna's scalp with her fingertips, she said,

'There! You can have a look. And if I say so myself it's –'

'Ness! Oh, I don't believe it! It's marvellous! And so soft, too.'

'Well, then – from now on there'll be no more tearing at it. Just wash it in rainwater two or three times a week, then leave it to dry on its own. You ladies with naturally curly hair don't know how lucky you are. It takes years off you!'

'I know. I look like a little girl!'

'But you like it?'

'Like it? I *love* it!' Lorna sighed. She did. After all the worrying, she really did!

'Then tomorrow night I'll have to go at your eyebrows. They're a lovely shape, but they're like your hair was. Too much of a good thing. They need tidying up underneath and they shouldn't meet at the top of your nose, either.'

'Ness – how come you know so much about things?'

'Because there was a cosmetic department in our salon and the lady in charge taught me a lot. Mind, I did her hair for her for nothing – on the quiet, like. Anyway, a word to the wise, Lorna. She told me that the traveller she orders Dale's beauty products from said there was going to be a shortage of cosmetics before so very much longer. "A quiet word in your ear," he said to her. "You'll not be able to get cosmetics for love nor money before long." So me and her stocked up. I reckon you should go round the shops in York as soon as you can. Keep it under your hat, mind. Get yourself some mascara and –'

'But I don't use mascara!'

'From now on you do – with eyelashes that fair. Get some grey mascara. Black is too stark for your colouring. And you'll need a rose-tinted lipstick and a pot of cold cream and a tin of Nivea. And whilst you're at it, get a box of face powder, too. Rose Rachel shade. Why don't you take a trip into town to celebrate your new hair? I'm tellin' you, queen, there's going to be a shortage on the cosmetics front. And get yourself some eyebrow tweezers, an' all.'

'Whatever is William going to say when he sees me – plucked eyebrows, too.' Lorna took a long look at her hair, flicking curls onto her face, her forehead, loving the freedom of it, and the softness.

'If he's got any sense at all he'll say "Wow!" and let go a wolf whistle.' Yet for all that, Ness knew he wouldn't, especially when he discovered the land girl had had a hand in it! She and William were on a collision course, even before they had met! 'So what say we have a cup of tea to celebrate?'

'Tea? There's sherry in the sideboard. Let's drink to my escape from the frizzies with a *real* drink!'

'Well! Aren't you going to say something, Nance?' They had cycled the length of Priory Lane and waited at the roadside for a break in the traffic. 'You've been giving me looks ever since we left Ainsty!'

'Sorry. Thought it rude to pass comment.'

'So you think I've gone too far?' The haircut no one could quarrel with, Lorna thought apprehensively, but maybe plucked eyebrows and lipstick – even in so delicate a shade as English Rose – was a bit much.

'Too far? It was a bit of a shock at first – you looked so much younger. But since you ask, Lorna, I do like it – the hair, I mean, though I never thought to see you wearing lipstick. You never have before. Whatever made you do it?'

'It was my idea entirely,' she hedged, determined to keep Ness out of it. 'I decided long hair isn't on in wartime; for women who work in factories it can be downright dangerous. That's why they've got to wear snoods. And short hair is more hygienic. They say you can get nits on trains these days. And women in the Armed Forces aren't allowed to wear their hair long, either, so what's so special about me?' she finished breathlessly, making a dash for the other side of the road. 'And why not lipstick?'

'Well, it's all right, I suppose, for special occasions.' Nance remounted her cycle. 'But as regards your hair, you aren't going to join the Armed Forces are you, nor work in a factory? William would never allow you to.'

'If the government said I had to, he couldn't do a lot about it.' Lorna stared stubbornly ahead. 'Things are going to get a lot worse before they get better. Who's to say a married woman won't be asked to work for the war effort – *ordered* to work?'

'Because married women *don't* work!'

'They didn't, but there's a war on now. And there might be an invasion! What would women do then? Just let it happen? Well, *I* wouldn't, Nance. I'd fight at the barricades to stop them getting Ainsty!'

'Wouldn't we all? But Hitler won't be interested in Nun Ainsty. He'd have to find it first! And if his lot came – what would there be for them here? A few houses, a pub, a farm and an empty manor house. The aerodromes, maybe. Probably he'd drop parachutists on the aerodromes around – Gilbert said so, only yesterday. By the way, how are you and the land girl getting on?'

'Oh – Ness!' Lorna was glad the invasion and her new hairdo were not to be discussed further. 'She's a dear. Makes me laugh and she loves it at Ainsty.'

'I thought you'd get on well. Better than being forced to take evacuees, and company for you in these uncertain times. William should be grateful to me. And had you thought that once our Local Defence Volunteers get themselves organized, they'll have to be prepared to turn out at any hour of the day or night if there's an emergency. You'll be lucky. You'll have company, but I shall be alone, Lorna, if Gilbert gets the call!'

'Y-yes, you will. But you'll manage, I'm sure you will.

You're a very capable person,' Lorna soothed. One concentrated glare from Nance Ellery could stop a paratrooper at ten paces!

'I must agree with you there. Between you and me, I've always had to be the capable one. Gilbert doesn't know how lucky he is!'

They had arrived at Meltonby church hall for the monthly meeting of the Women's Institute and a talk entitled *Making Your Rations Go Further – And Then Some!* by a lady sponsored by the Ministry of Food, and Lorna was saved a reply. At least, she thought as they pushed their cycles out of sight behind the outside lavatories, it would seem that Nance would be on her side if ever it came to a showdown with William about her haircut and the wearing of lipstick. All things considered, it might not be a bad thing to have a capable lady on your side.

She wondered, all at once apprehensive, if William would ring tonight, because if he did, Ness would be obliged to answer and it wouldn't help matters at all, especially since William had made no further mention of the land girl, and his last letter had been quite affectionate.

She sent her thoughts winging. *Don't ring tonight – please . . . ?*

'Had a good time?' Ness smiled a welcome.

'Interesting. Got some food leaflets. Learned how to make a shelter cake and before you ask, if the alert sounded and you had to go to the shelter, you could leave it simmering merrily away on the stove.'

'And if there's anything left of your 'ouse when the all clear goes and you creep out of the shelter,' Ness grinned, 'then you'll have a cake in the pan.'

'After you've let it cool – otherwise it seemed to me you might as well eat pudding. But I think there'll be a few shelter cakes made before this war is over. Anyway, what did I miss on the nine o'clock news?'

'You want the good bits first? Well, the RAF boys are stepping up night bombing on Germany and President Roosevelt has laid down five freedoms.'

'Oh, yes? Freedom from bombing, killing and rationing? Very original!'

'Not exactly. Think I can remember what the man on the news said. It was freedom of information and religion and freedom from want and fear and persecution.'

'So what's new? Don't we all want things like that? What else was there?'

'Seems the Luftwaffe bombed Welsh ports last night; didn't say where, but I reckon it was Cardiff and Swansea. All to do with softening us up, if you ask me, because our convoys in the Channel were attacked, an' all.'

'Any more bad news?'

'Yes. There's to be no August bank holiday this year.'

'But there's always been a bank holiday Monday! They can't do that!'

'Well, they have. Cancelled. And before you blow your top, you'd better sit down, 'cause tea is going to be rationed. As from tomorrow.'

'*Tea*? But they've already rationed butter and sugar and bacon and meat!'

'So now it's two ounces of tea each person each week.'

'Four miserable ounces between you and me, Ness? Well, all I can say is that it's a good job I have two packets in the store cupboard! I mean – rationing *tea*.'

Tea was the universal comforter, the bringer-together in afternoons of neighbours and friends. Tea was so – well – *British*!

'I can only tell you what was said on the news. It'll be in the papers in the morning, if you don't believe me.'

'Oh, I believe you, Ness, and rot his socks the Clever Dick who thought of it! Tell you what – shall we have one last cup of un-rationed tea? I'll make it in the silver teapot and we'll use the best cups and saucers.'

'Might as well, queen. Go out with dignity. And it's a good job me Auntie Agnes passed on last year, 'cause drinkin' tea was like a religion to her, God rest her. Rationing tea would have been unthinkable to her.' Go out with dignity all right, Ness pondered. She'd never had tea from a silver pot.

'Put the kettle on there's a dear, and Ness – did anyone phone whilst I was at the WI?'

'No one. Was you expecting one from William?'

'I'm always expecting one from him. What I didn't want was for him to ring and you to answer it.'

'Well, he didn't ring so you're off the hook. You're still jumpy, aren't you, about me bein' here?'

'No. You're staying. But I am jumpy about William, and it isn't just you. He hasn't seen my hair yet!'

'He'll like it. I said so, didn't I?'

'You did. And Nance Ellery likes it, too. She didn't ask me where I'd had it done, thank heaven, so she doesn't know it was you.'

'But why shouldn't she know I cut it?'

'We-e-ll, if William should happen not to like it, then –'

'Oh, I see. It'll be one thing less to lay at the land girl's door, eh? Well, if he makes a fuss, tell him you don't much care for his moustache, but you haven't told him to shave it off! And you *don't* like it, do you?'

'If I'm honest, no. It makes him look older and it's scratchy.'

'When he kisses you?'

'Yes.' Her cheeks reddened. 'But let's get this tea made. Let's forget the awful news and go into the garden. It isn't blackout time just yet. Let's listen to the blackbird and pretend there isn't a war on – just for a little while.'

She was getting good at turning hay, Ness thought. There was a way of holding the long, two-pronged fork so the weight on the end of it was manageable. The only trouble was that her right hand had blisters on it and Kate had been obliged to give her an old leather glove to protect it.

'Your hands will toughen up. When those blisters are gone, Ness, I'll give you some methylated spirits to rub on your palms. Meths will fettle it.'

'Hey! Ness Nightingale!' Rowley was calling from the fieldgate. 'Didn't you say there was someone in the manor this morning?'

'I heard voices when I came to work. Didn't bother to find out who it was. Could have been a couple of tramps, sleeping in one of the outbuildings.' Fork in hand, she crossed to where he stood. 'Why do you ask?'

'Over there.' He pointed in the direction of the back entrance to the manor. 'Two army trucks, and soldiers. What the hell are they up to?'

'Search me, Rowley. Why don't you ask them?'

'I intend to! Glebe Farm rents the manor fields!'

Red-faced, he strode towards the trucks. Curious, Ness followed.

'A moment, please!' Rowley vaulted the gate that divided manor yard from field. 'Can you tell me what you are doing?'

It was almost a command, Ness thought.

'I can.' A soldier in officer's uniform turned slowly, his eyes raking Rowley from head to toe. 'What exactly do you want to know?'

'Well – why you're here, for one thing. This is private property!'

'You own the manor?'

'No. My father owns Glebe Farm and we rent the manor land.' His face grew redder.

'Then our interest is only in the house, not the land.' The officer turned away, speaking to a sergeant. 'Having any trouble with the keys?'

'No, sir. Got in without any bother.'

'Then let's see what's what. Where's the MO?'

'Inside, sir.'

'Right, then.' He turned to Rowley. 'Good day to you,' he said firmly, dismissively.

'Well! What do you make of that, Ness Nightingale? Arrogant sod! Who does he think he is?'

'Who? From where I was standin', I'm almost sure he's a major. And he did say he was only interested in the manor. Don't think you've got anything to worry about.'

'But we *have*! We can do without a load of swaddies next door, making their noise, lifting everything that isn't nailed down. The manor's been empty for years. They're going to get a shock when they take a look inside!'

'Well, it's nuthin' to do with me. I'm away back to the field, though I think you'd better tell your father what's happened.'

The Army, Ness frowned, resuming her rhythmic forking, lifting, turning, interested in the empty manor house. So what might they want it for? What did anybody want with a tucked-away, empty-for-years old house? Rowley had demanded to know, but all he had learned was to be curtly told they had no interest in the fields around. It had upset the young farmer, Ness grinned. Rowley Wintersgill wasn't used to being spoken to like that.

But soldiers in Nun Ainsty! What would Lorna make of it, or Mrs Ellery? Come to think of it, how would the village take to a turmoil in their midst, because with soldiers usually came drill sergeants and trucks and lorries and noise. Guns, too!

Oh, my word! She could hardly wait for five o'clock to come.

'Soldiers!' Lorna gasped. 'Oh, my goodness!'

'That's exactly what Mrs Wintersgill said. "Oh, my goodness. What on earth is going on?" But Rowley was told they weren't interested in the fields. Very curt, that major. Mind, Rowley jumped in with both feet. Silly of him. It's better to ask than demand when you're dealing with the Army.'

'That young man can be very arrogant. Thinks he's God's gift to the opposite sex. Has he – er – ever tried anything on with you, Ness?'

'Lordy, no! Mind, I haven't been sending any signals. He isn't my type. Don't worry. I'd soon slap him down if he came-it with me. But why do you suppose the Army is interested in the manor?'

'Why shouldn't they be? Probably want it for a billet. After all, they've got to find somewhere to put all the soldiers who came back after Dunkirk. How many were at the manor?'

'There was the one Rowley spoke to, with rank up, plus a sergeant and an ATS girl, sitting in the biggest car. She didn't get out. Suppose she was the major's driver. And there was another. I didn't see him. The MO, they called him.'

'Medical Officer. Maybe he was giving the place the once-over – hygiene, sort of. It must be filthy inside, after all that time empty. Maybe he was checking the water supply and the sanitation. It's going to be interesting – seeing if they'll come, that is. The government can take any house it wants, empty or not. They gave quite a few farmers their marching orders, then pulled down the farmhouses when they wanted to build the aerodromes. A shocking waste of good agricultural land, William said at the time. And talking about my husband – there was a letter this morning. He's fed up. He says it looks like the Army doesn't know what to do with him, once they've got him. Says he seems to spend his time doing useless things, or trying to look busy. He hates wasting time. Time is money, he always said. Well, he would I suppose, being an accountant.'

'And no mention of me?' Ness ventured.

'No. I think he assumes that once having told me he didn't want you in the house, I would ask you to go. Once, I might have done; my own fault, I suppose. Grandpa spoiled me, then William took over. They both used to think for me, tell me what to do, and I let them. After all, Grandpa only wanted what was best for me; tried to make it up to me because – well, because of what happened to my mother.'

'Your mother died? Your grandparents brought you up? Where was your father, then? Why didn't he –'

'My father. Never knew him . . .' Her voice trailed away and Ness knew that already too much had been said – or had slipped out.

'If you'd rather not talk about it – I mean – losing your mother must be pretty awful. I'd go berserk if anything happened to Mam.'

'Yes, but you've had your mother for twenty-five years. I can't even remember mine. She died before I was three. I came here to Ladybower, to my grandparents. Grandma died when I was seven. I only vaguely remember her. Of course, Grandpa spoiled me and fussed over me. I was all he had left.'

'And your father?'

'He wasn't around. He'd taken off, I believe, as soon as my mother's morning sickness started. A pity. She loved him very much, even up until the day she took – she committed –' She stopped, eyes downcast.

'Your mother took her own life?' Ness whispered.

'An overdose of aspirin, washed down with gin.'

'Oh, lovey, I'm so sorry. How did we get onto the subject?' Ness whispered.

'My fault. And I'd be glad if you didn't mention it again. I shouldn't have told you. So long ago – water under the bridge.'

'I wouldn't blab, Lorna. You know I wouldn't.'

'Doesn't matter, really, if you do. Nance Ellery knows and they know at Glebe Farm, too. A nine-days' wonder in the village, though I think it hastened my grandmother's death. A long time ago, for all that.'

'Yer right, queen. Now you've got William to look after

you and you've got this lovely house. There's a lot of people far worse off!'

'I know. And I should be grateful, but sometimes I'm not. I've done as I was told all my life, you see. I obeyed Grandpa, then I married William and now I obey him. So it was quite something, me insisting that you stay here.'

'Now, what say I give you a hand with the dishes?' Best change the subject, talk about other things. Lorna was getting pink-cheeked. 'Sorry I can't wash up – my blisters – but I'll dry and put away. Then can we sit in the garden?'

'Fine by me. I've cleaned the house and written to William – nothing better to do. You like the garden, don't you, Ness?'

'Oh, yes. Better than a back yard, if you see what I mean? And make the most of it, eh? You might not have it for much longer – not if you listen to what the government is saying.'

'About growing food, you mean? About flowerbeds and it being wrong, all of a sudden, to have a lawn? Produce food, must I?'

'I don't see why not. Or you could keep hens. Mrs Wintersgill has her hens in arks.'

'Yes. In the little field, behind the cow shed.' Triangular contraptions like a bar of Toblerone in wood and wire netting. 'But you aren't suggesting we have hens on the lawn? And where would I get a hen ark, anyway? I don't think they're available to people like me, now that timber is in such short supply.'

'But wouldn't you like your own hens, Lorna? The man from the egg packers told Mrs Wintersgill that eggs will be the next thing to be rationed. Be nice to have our own – real fresh. But I suppose William wouldn't like hens on his lawn . . .' She said it sneakily, tongue in cheek.

'William? It's my lawn as well, Ness, if push comes to shove. I don't have to ask my husband if I can keep poultry. Come to think of it, I'd get a few hens if it were at all possible.'

'But there aren't any arks nor hen huts nor hen runs any more – well, only for farmers . . .'

'Exactly. Now I've been very good all day – only made one tiny pot of tea, so I think we can spare a spoonful for a cuppa. Have it in the garden, shall we?'

'OK. You take the cushions out and the little table; I'll make the tea,' Ness smiled.

And she continued to smile as she set a tea tray and put the smallest teapot to warm, because having hens would be a lot better than digging up the lawn to grow vegetables. Ness liked hens; loved to see the way they scratched, feathery bottoms wobbling from side to side, and she liked it when they laid an egg and cackled like mad afterwards; knew too that in summer a hen would lay at least four eggs a week, fresh and brown, for breakfast. And, would you believe, it just happened that behind the hay barn at Glebe Farm, she had seen two arks in need of repair and obviously unwanted by the farmer. Been shoved there, she shouldn't wonder, to be chopped up for firewood. Surely Mr Tuthey at the Saddlery could make something of them? A splice of wood here, a few nails there – and the netting wire repaired? Six hens they would be able to keep on scraps and gleanings from the field. Eggs aplenty in the laying season. Ness Nightingale was a quick learner, knew about the laying season and how to feed and water hens, and in the morning she would ask Kate Wintersgill about those thrown-away arks, and could she and Lorna have them, please?

'Won't be a minute,' she called, so concerned with Ladybower's hens that the matter of Lorna's early life, about her poor mother and a father who had left her, slipped into the depths of her mind.

But for all that, thoughts of Lorna's childhood came easily to her that night in bed. The soldiers at the manor, hens and hen arks, were not of such importance when you thought about a small child with both parents gone. Sad, really, even if Lorna had had a good grandfather to bring her up and leave her all his money and possessions. Was nowhere near as good as having a Mam and a Da and a Nan. And Auntie Agnes – until recently, that was. She, Ness, had been lucky in her rearing, lucky all her life, really – until Patrick, that was. Patrick, ever ready to take over her thoughts even now, if she would allow it.

She closed her eyes and hugged herself tightly. She had loved him so very much. He had filled her heart, her life, and then one day it had all ended.

She opened her eyes wide then blinked them against tears that threatened. She *wouldn't* cry! She had wept a lifetime of tears for him, then taken a long look at her life and how best it was to be lived without him. It was why she had joined the Land Army. A new life, a new start far from Ruth Street and memories of a heartache she had thought she was learning to accept.

'Oh, damn, damn, *damn*!' She threw off the bedclothes and pulled back the curtains, pushing the window wider so she could lean over the sill and look out into the near-darkness and the garden below, smell dew-soaked grass and roses and honeysuckle and newly-flowering lavender. And she gazed over to the wood, a darker mass that merged into the sky, where perhaps there was a nun who appeared to star-crossed lovers.

Are you there, you who know about lost love? If I walk in Dickon's Wood will you come to me to let me know you understand?

'Idiot!'

She crept back into bed, leaving the curtains open so the square of window took in the night glow from a darkness that in high summer was never quite complete; from a sky that outlined tree tops and rose bushes and the wooden bench where, only a few hours ago, she and Lorna had sat. And talked, would you believe, about hens!

She burrowed into the pillows, pulling the blanket over her head, trying to shut out what was gone for all time and think instead of the manor, and hens on the back lawn, and Mam and Da and Nan, so far away in Ruth Street, Liverpool 4. And about the invasion, and if it would come. And if she had one iota of sense left in her head, to count her blessings like any other reasonable woman would do, and get on with the rest of her life!

FOUR

There was a strange quiet in the sitting room. It was as if, when the Prime Minister spoke, he was warning them, warning everyone, of what was to come. His voice, low and defiant, had filled the room as he told them, over the wireless, what they already knew, dare they admit it. Britain could resist invasion he said, and, when the time came, could defeat Hitler, too.

'Be the ordeal sharp or long, or both, we shall seek no terms, shall tolerate no parley. We may show mercy, but we, the people of these islands, will ask none.'

Never before, he stressed, had Britain had an army such as it had today. London itself, if German soldiers had to fight for it street by street, could easily devour any hostile forces that might land.

'We would rather see London laid to ruin and ashes than that it should be abjectly enslaved.'

Brave talk. Fighting talk. Talk to make any man straighten his shoulders and vow love and devotion to this bomb-happy, defiant little country, Lorna thought, tears pricking her eyes. Any woman, too. And of the battle raging in the air over the south, Mr Churchill declared that for every one of our own aircraft, we would claim five of the enemy's. Let them come! We would be ready!

'It's as if the government have something up their sleeves,' Ness said when the speech was over, the wireless switched off. 'I mean – he was so confident we'd be all right. Have we got a secret weapon, or something that they aren't telling us about?'

'Wouldn't be a secret if Churchill told us, would it? And I honestly think he was trying to give us a shot in the arm. But talk like that makes you think, doesn't it, Ness?'

'Think that perhaps we really are goin' to be invaded?'

'That Hitler will try – yes. Whether he'll get any troops ashore is another thing. And *where* will he invade? Germany has overrun Holland. An invasion could come on the east coast, and not the south as most people think.'

'Or it needn't come at all.' Ness smiled shakily, trying all at once to be brave.

'So you believe in miracles?'

'I – I, Yes! I do. This is such a daft, cockeyed little country that I believe there'll be a miracle. I *do*!'

'That's putting your head in the sand, Ness. Churchill's as good as warned us it's going to happen.'

'All right, then! But there's no harm *wanting* a miracle, is there? We had one at Dunkirk, didn't we? Thousands and thousands of soldiers taken off the beaches before the Germans could get to them. Those same men are fighting mad now, and wantin' to take a swipe at bluddy Hitler! So why shouldn't we have another miracle?'

'OK. This is the silly season; the season of miracles! And enough invasion talk! Didn't you say we'd go to Glebe and take a look at a couple of poultry arks?'

'Why not? It's still light. And Kate said if they were any use to us we could have them, and the best of British, because, as far as she was concerned, they were only good for burning.'

'So hadn't we better see Jacob Tuthey first, ask him to look them over, see if he thinks they're fit for salvage? No use thinking about hens if we've nowhere to put them.'

'You're right, queen, but it would be a shame if we couldn't have them, especially as I've seen them and taken a fancy to them already. Lovely, they are. Light Sussex pullets, Kate said they were called. She's got fifty or sixty there, not ready to lay yet, but doing nicely. White, with black tail feathers and black-tipped wings. They lay white eggs, Kate said; she chose that breed because they made good table birds when their laying days were over.'

'Ness! I couldn't do that; couldn't eat hens that had been laying eggs for me. At least,' she thought about the miserable meat ration. 'I don't *think* I could.'

'Well you won't have to think of eating them till they get old – three years at least.'

'You seem to know a lot about poultry, Ness Nightingale!'

'That's because looking after hens and collecting eggs is easy learned. Wish I was as good in the cow shed. I can't milk a cow, y'know.'

'You'll learn.'

'That's what Kate says. When Rowley's got a few minutes to spare he can show me how, she said, but milking comes natural to Kate, her being a farmer's daughter and now a farmer's wife.'

'I wouldn't worry, if I were you. Right now we're more concerned with hens, so shall we go to Glebe – see if those arks can be salvaged?'

The hen ark stood in the far corner of Ladybower's lawn. It did not blend into the background as she had hoped it would, Lorna frowned, but perhaps she would get used to it being there and when the hens arrived she would like it a little more, she was sure.

'So what do you think,' she had asked of Jacob Tuthey, four nights ago. 'Could you cobble something out of these two wrecks, or are they past redemption?'

'Cobble? I don't cobble anything, young Lorna! Cobbled jobs aren't for me, but I've got to admit it's going to take a bit of fettling, for all that!'

To fettle, Lorna explained later to Ness, was to repair a thing; to fix it or, at the very outside, make the best of a bad job.

So Jacob had removed the arks one by one on his handcart, pushing and heaving, with Lorna and Ness doing their best to support each one and keep it from falling off when intricate manoeuvres were necessary, like turning a corner or negotiating a gateway.

'I'll see what can be done,' they were told when the two arks had been transported to Jacob's yard. 'Will give it my full attention, to be sure.'

His full attention, Lorna sighed, resulted in one poultry ark in amazingly good order and a large pile of off-cuts of wood which he had sawn into lengths and barrowed back to Kate to be used as kindling.

In short, everyone had been pleased with the outcome, no one more so than herself, Lorna thought, yet now the hens were almost here, now that the poultry run awaited six white and black pullets, she wondered if they had done the right thing. Or, more to the point, she wondered what William would say to the spoiling of the lawn in particular and the entire back garden in general.

But it was too late now. Six little hens would be arriving tomorrow and she had already phoned the feed merchant to order a bag of grower's pellets, a bag of layer's pellets and a bag of layer's mash. She had also agreed a price with Kate for the hens.

Sorry, William. I truly am, but . . .

July more than half over, with high blue skies and warm days to ripen corn, and it was as if Ladybower had always had its own hens on the back lawn. Ness and Lorna, pleased and proud with the rate at which the cosseted pullets grew and matured, waited daily for the cackle that would herald the first egg.

They would only be small eggs at first, but they could

expect larger ones, Kate said, once the pullets got into their stride. And what was more, in their first laying season they wouldn't have a moult as other older hens did. And Ness, who knew all about such matters, had explained to Lorna in detail that in early winter hens had a moult, lost their feathers and went around looking scrawny and dejected. The bright red comb on top of their heads went pink and flat and, worst of all, they stopped laying eggs. But Ladybower's little flock would not suffer so in their first season. She and Lorna would have new-laid eggs all through winter, and for very little trouble, too.

It was as well they had the hens to fuss over, Lorna thought as she spread the morning paper on the kitchen table and set about checking the time at which blackouts must be in place tonight, and read the column which gave details of programmes on the wireless. Only then, reluctantly, she gave her attention to the headlines.

BIGGEST AIR RAIDS OF ALL
RAF SHOOTS DOWN THIRTY-NINE
MORE NAZIS

In smaller print it said that nine of our fighters had been lost. What it really meant was nine young pilots, scarcely out of school, were dead.

The raids had been on the Southeast, the Southwest, and Wales. The south-east, everyone knew, even though the Ministry of Information always withheld place names, was where the fighter stations were; Manston, Tangmere, Biggin Hill. Fighters and fighter stations must be put out of action before the invasion began. Everyone knew it. So now, whilst southern cornfields were ripening, one hundred and sixty-three enemy bombers had been shot down in five days, for the loss of fifty-four of our fighters.

The battle for Britain had begun, it would seem. For as

long as they could last out, hang on to fly yet another sortie, the future of our country was in the hands of young men, most of them not yet old enough to vote. Or to marry without parental consent for that matter, Lorna thought as a choke of tears made a tight ball in her throat.

Yet she was worrying about keeping hens on the lawn; bothered because William – when he found out about them – would be annoyed. Annoyed, too, about her short-cut hair and, if he gave her a closer look, horrified she had plucked her eyebrows! And all that was as nothing when, these past five days, fifty-four mothers and wives and sweethearts would have been told, in words of regret, that their pilot would never come home on leave again. So why, in the name of all that was holy, was she worrying over nothing? Any one of those fifty-four women would be grateful to have Lorna Hatherwood's troubles.

She folded the paper, laying it on the table top so she might not see the face of the young bomber pilot who had deliberately guided his crashing bomber into the sea so it should not hit the streets of houses below him. He had been married just nine months ago, the caption beneath his picture said, so yesterday, too, a young woman called Margaret would have received the small, yellow envelope that would consign her to widowhood, and to grief.

'It's just too awful and there's nothing I can do about it, either,' she whispered to the silent room.

Well, *was* there anything? Was she really, really sure? But you couldn't be sure about anything when you were fighting tears you needed to let fall for fifty-four young men and a broken-hearted widow.

Yet of one thing she was very sure! Her short haircut stayed, Ness stayed, and the six hens, too! And if William didn't like it – we-e-ll, she would worry about it when she had to!

'There's sumthin' going on at the manor.' Ness kicked off her shoes at the back door. 'Everybody thinkin' it was a false alarm, that the Army wasn't interested after all, then there they are! Didn't you see them?'

'No. But I went to Meltonby – ran out of stamps. How many were there?'

'Two lorries and three trucks. Got a good look at them from the stackyard. Kate said she thought they must be a working party, cleaning out, doing repairs and things.'

'And how many soldiers, Ness?'

'Couldn't say. But there was one on the roof and a couple fixing telephone wires. Will you mind them coming?'

'Nothing I can do about it – it's a free country, thank God. I think we should give them a chance before we start moaning about them. After all, William is in the Army and I wouldn't like people to resent his being there, nor think he'd steal anything he could lay his hands on. Rowley shouldn't have said what he did.'

'Rowley Wintersgill's an arrogant little sod. Six months in the Armed Forces would do him the world of good. Most young men his age are already in uniform. I often look at him,' Ness frowned, 'and wonder how Kate and Bob could have spawned such a nasty piece of work. But blow him! Heard any news? Gossip . . . ?'

'No. And I didn't put the wireless on for the one o'clock news. There's such a battle going on, down south. Headlines in the paper that we've lost more than fifty pilots in five days. That lot in London tried to cover it up by saying the Luftwaffe lost more planes than we did. But how long can we hang on, Ness?'

'As long as it takes, I reckon. And why Hitler's hanging back, I don't know – the invasion, I mean.'

'Give it time . . .'

'Yes. But hadn't you thought, Lorna, that time's running out for Hitler, too. Kate said that soon the tides and the weather will be against a landing. Some article she read.'

'Words – articles – are cheap, like talk! But let's forget That Man. We're getting het up, worrying about when we'll be invaded and that's what he wants! Tell me – when is Bob going to start on the corn harvest?'

'Any day now. The wheat first, then the barley. Mr Wintersgill said when they've got the corn into the barn, you an' me can go gleaning. There'll be a lot we can rake up for the hens. Kate said barley makes hens lay better. Maybe it would start ours off!'

'Maybe,' Lorna whispered.

'Now see here, queen, what's to do?' Ness demanded. 'Sumthin's bothering you. Not had a nasty letter from William?'

'No. Nothing in the post this morning. But that's not why I feel so – so *depressed*. It was reading the paper, y'see. All those young men killed, and them hardly a hold on life. And all I can do is read about it in the papers and feel sorry, when all the time I should be doing something useful!'

'But you can't. Married women aren't expected to leave home. And to volunteer for the Armed Forces you'd have to have William's permission, don't forget.'

'I'm not likely to, and I wasn't thinking of making such a grand gesture. I want to stay at Ladybower, yet I know I should be doing more. I'm going to talk to Nance about it, see what she says and – oh, my goodness! The phone!' And as if she already knew that William was at the other end of it, she ran to answer it, closing the door behind her.

'William!' Ness muttered. Lorna could do without a call from *him*! Lately she had been despondent – felt guilty, Ness wouldn't wonder, about taking in a land girl and not telling her husband she was still here. And worrying, an' all, about the hens on the lawn. A call from her William was the last thing the poor girl needed – unless he'd changed his tune a bit and said something nice for a change. Like he loved her and was missing her.

'William, was it,' she asked of a wide-eyed Lorna standing in the doorway. 'Still loves you, does he?'

'He – he never said, but he's coming home; got a seventy-two-hour pass, Ness. Travelling overnight on Thursday.

He'll be here on Friday.' Her face was pale, her eyes filled with disbelief. 'Oh, my goodness!'

'But you're pleased? And it was very thoughtful of him to give notice,' Ness grinned. 'Gives me time to move out – well, that's what we agreed, wasn't it?'

'Y-yes. Said he was being drafted. Very pleased about that. Said he's been floating about like a spare part these past weeks.'

'So where is he goin'?'

'He didn't say. Well, he wouldn't, over the phone. Careless talk, you know. He wants me to meet him at York station; asked if I had enough petrol left and I told him I had. Should be arriving about ten, though I suppose the train will be late.' Trains were always late now. 'Oh, I feel quite peculiar.'

'Of course you do. Excitement, that's what and the shock of it coming out of the blue. More'n eight weeks since you saw him. Bet he'll be glad to get out of his uniform.'

'Yes. Must take a look at his civvies – see if anything needs pressing. And it isn't excitement I feel. It's just – well – *peculiar*.'

But was that the right word? Wouldn't apprehensive or even worried be more appropriate because the feeling, by whichever name, was nothing to do with the land girl who now lived at Ladybower, nor the hens, nor what William would likely call the wanton chopping of her long hair. What she was really apprehensive about, Lorna all at once realized, was *that*!

She thought about their twice-weekly coupling every Tuesday night and Sunday morning; about his scratchy moustache that left her upper lip sore and red afterwards. *That*. Another name for wifely duty. It had been rather nice, she thought, having the bed to herself for two months.

'Of course you feel peculiar,' Ness said, interrupting her thoughts. 'And you're getting yourself into a tizzy over nuthin'. He'll like your hair, queen; bet you anything he does. And he won't mind about the hens being on the lawn

– not if he's patriotic, he won't. And when he's gone, I can creep back and no one's going to be any the wiser – except Flora Petch, that is.'

'Unless someone makes it her business to tell him about you, that is.'

'So will you mind if he does find out, Lorna?'

'No! Of course not!'

She meant it. She wouldn't. And if she thought about it, she had no worries at all. Not real ones. There was nothing so very awful that it couldn't be explained away. William would be so glad to be home again that he wouldn't let anything spoil his three days – would he?

And then she remembered the wife of nine months who would give the rest of her life to see her man again for just five minutes to say, 'Goodbye. I love you. I shall always love you,' and the thought was so awful, so poignant and heart-rending that she burst into tears.

Lorna dropped two pennies into the slot machine and fished out a platform ticket. Then she enquired of a passing porter when and where they expected the Salisbury train, to be told on platform five. In half an hour. If they were lucky!

She was very calm now, though the thought had all at once struck her – and too late to do anything about it – that if William was being drafted, would he not have all his kit with him and how was she to get it, and him, into her Baby Austin? But she would worry about it later. Now there was time to get a cup of tea at the station buffet, to sit and drink it slowly and think about all the news she had to tell him. About the soon-to-arrive soldiers at the manor; about Bob Wintersgill being busy with the corn harvest and about the six pretty white and black pullets in the back garden; tell him that only yesterday they – *she* – had had the very first egg and wouldn't it be wonderful when all six were laying their little heads off to help the war effort! She had decided she would tell him at once about the ark on the back lawn; that way it would lessen the shock – if shock it was to be.

She smiled at the elderly lady who looked too frail to lift so huge a teapot, placed three pennies on the counter, then made for a table near the open door through which she could see platform five.

The tea was weak, but pleasantly warm. She dropped a saccharin tablet into it then took the cup to where a spoon was tied with string to a hook on the counter. Stirring her tea she walked back to the table, looking at her watch, dismayed to find that only five minutes had passed.

Ladybower. She would think of the house, cleaned and extra-polished; of vases filled with flowers from the garden; of the tea tray, set with a starched cloth and the best china cups. She had arisen early this morning, before Ness had clumped downstairs with a case containing everything from her wardrobe and drawers. Best clean the lot out, she had said. 'If we're goin' to be sneaky, best make a job of it – leave no traces!'

Foolish really, Lorna had thought as they drove to the hostel in Meltonby where a bed was available for the weekend, because one of the land girls was away at her brother's wedding. Flora Petch hadn't minded the change in arrangements. Maybe for the best, she had said, since she had a baby due the other side of Meltonby, and babies could start their arriving any time of the day or night!

Doubly foolish, Lorna thought, eyes fixed on the doorway, when you started to deceive, because all weekend she would be watching every word she said, regarding Ness that was, and lies – or maybe *evasions* was a better word – would lead to more evasions, and William would have every cause to be angry when – *if* – he found out.

She sighed deeply, returning the empty cup to the counter, smiled again at the tea lady still heaving her pot, then determined to walk up and down platform five, from one end to the other, for the remaining twenty minutes. She would count the ups and downs. It would give her something to do and prevent her thinking up fresh mental tortures for herself. Yet after ten minutes' concentrated pacing she began to think that perhaps William was not coming; that something had happened to prevent the three days' leave. Something not too serious, that was. And the thought was no sooner a wish when she saw people looking down the line, moving back from the platform edge. The train was arriving; she heard a distant rumbling and the hiss of escaping steam before it clanked and shuddered to a stop.

She saw William before he saw her and was able to take a deep calming breath, observe him dispassionately. He was carrying only a small case and his respirator. He had lost weight. All at once she wondered why she had worried and pushed through the crowd to where he stood.

'William, darling!' She reached on tiptoe to kiss his cheek, because cheek kisses in public were permitted now. Long, lingering goodbye kisses were no longer frowned upon either, though William would never allow such a thing. 'Oh, it's so good to see you!'

'Lorna!' His face had gone very red. He was looking at her in bewilderment and she didn't know why. She was wearing the blue flowered frock he was particularly fond of and her best pearl beads and pearl earrings. She had tried to make herself especially nice for him, yet his look was one of surprise. And then she knew why, as almost involuntarily her hand reached up to her head.

'Lorna! What in heaven's name have you done to yourself?'

'Don't you like my hair?'

'Like it!' Jaws clenched, he strode to the bottom of the footbridge, taking the steps quickly, staring rigidly ahead.

'William! Wait! Please wait?'

He heard her and stopped, then turning to face her, waited for her to speak, to explain.

'William – the car. It's on the right, in the car park.' It

was all she could think of to say as people pushed and milled around them. 'We'd better move. We're getting in the way.'

She picked up his case and hurried toward the steps at the far end of the bridge, across the concourse towards the sign marked Car Park. Unspeaking she made for the little black car, glad to see a familiar object yet all the time not wanting to be enclosed in its smallness with William's right shoulder jammed against hers.

She opened the door, placed the case in the back, then slithered into the driving seat, turning the ignition, grateful she would not have to get out again and crank the engine into life.

'I'm sorry,' she said as they waited for a break in the traffic. 'Are you sure you don't like my hair?'

'A shock,' he said reluctantly, staring ahead. 'I liked it long. You know I did.'

'But it's so easy to manage now. No tugging and pulling. Anyway – I like it!'

'I see. You like looking as if you're fresh out of gymslips, do you, because that's what it does to you! You're a married woman, Lorna!'

'Of course I am, but I do like my hair short. You wouldn't understand, but I feel so – so *free*. And I don't want to grow it. I couldn't bear to cart that great mop around with me ever again. I felt so top heavy! And long hair isn't hygienic – especially when there's a war on!' She was protesting too much, she knew it, yet still she muttered, 'And if I might say so, William, it isn't very kind of you to find fault when I've been so looking forward to seeing you!'

There! Not only had she stood her ground, defended her new image, she had answered back, too!

There were traffic lights ahead. On red. She slowed, and pulled on the brake. Then she took a deep breath, willing the light to stay on red until she got a grip on her feelings, refusing to speak, to say one more word that might get her deeper into trouble. And thank heaven she had decided against lipstick and even the tiniest touch of mascara.

'Sorry!' William, actually apologizing. 'Sorry, old girl. A shock. I mean – well, I'll look like your father when we're out together!'

'Then shave off your moustache!' The traffic ahead was moving. 'You'd look ten years younger if you did,' she smiled, hesitantly. And he smiled back and said that sorry, the moustache was a part of his officer image – gave him dignity, and all that.

'Very well. You may keep it,' she said with mock severity. 'And William, I really am glad to see you.'

Storm in a teacup over, she thought, as relief thudded inside her, and fingers crossed that she would get away as easily with the hens and Ness Nightingale!

They were halfway down Priory Lane and not two minutes from home when Lorna stopped the car, almost without thinking.

'William – are we friends again?'

'Well, of course we are! We'll forget the hair, shall we? Live and let live, eh?'

'Yes, dear, and I'm sure you'll get to like it, but – well – I have something else to tell you!'

Best get it over with; best, if there was going to be an argument to have it here in the lane.

'And what else have we done? Overspent our allowance?'

'Of course I haven't!' She said it more sharply than she intended, because he was talking down to her; talking like he really was her father! 'It's just that we have got – *I* have got – six hens on the back lawn!'

'You have *what*? *Hens*? In heaven's name, *why*?' His face was red again. 'That is a very fine lawn! Whatever made you want to put hens on it? If the grass cutting is too much, why on earth didn't you ask Goff Leaman to do it for you?'

'I'm well able to push a grass cutter, and the reason for

the hens is that it is patriotic to produce food and if I don't, I'm going to get some sly digs from the village. Most people have got rid of their flowerbeds and I thought hens on the grass would be the lesser of two evils.'

'Without asking me?'

'But do I have to ask you!' she rounded angrily. 'You left me in charge when you went away. Can't I be trusted? I thought very long and hard before I put the hen ark there.'

'Ugly things, arks . . .'

'Yes, but tidier than a shed and wire netting and posts all over the place to keep the hens from straying. And next time you come on leave they'll be laying and you'll have lovely fresh eggs for breakfast.'

'You could have bought equally fresh eggs from Kate Wintersgill.'

'All right! But for how much longer? Eggs will be the next thing to be rationed – she said so herself. But if you are determined to put me in the wrong, William, then you have succeeded!'

'No, Lorna. I'm sure you did what you thought best, but I hadn't bargained for hens on the lawn. Sorry if I sounded abrupt.'

'Yes, you *did* sound abrupt and yes, I will accept your apology. And please remember that I'm not a soldier you can shout an order to – or at!' Her voice began to tremble. 'And why are we going on like this? Today should have been wonderful, yet we're having words again! What is wrong, William?'

'Nothing is wrong. It's just that you had your hair cut when you knew I wouldn't like it and you put hens on that beautiful lawn without a lot of thought. But we are *not* arguing, Lorna – at least I am not! You, though, are getting very het up. What else have you done?'

'N-nothing!' Now, really, was the time to tell him about Ness, but she had pushed her luck far enough for one day. 'Nothing else.'

'Oh, but there *is*! I always know when something is wrong. Tell me, is the land girl still in our spare room?'

The question came suddenly, uncannily. It was as if, she thought, panic-stricken, that the words *land girl* were written on her forehead in inch-high letters.

'The land girl is at the hostel in Meltonby, since you ask!' she gasped. Ness *was* there – technically. And why was she lying and please, *please* don't let anyone mention Ness before William's leave was over? Hens and hair she had got away with, but admitting to a land girl at Ladybower, when William had said she must leave, was asking for trouble. 'And if you don't believe me –'

'Of course I believe you and of course I trust you to take good care of Ladybower – and yourself – whilst I'm away. So don't let's quarrel? I've been looking forward to this leave. Can't we pretend I'm a civilian again – just for three days? No more moods, eh?'

'All right. And I'm sorry if –'

'And no more sorries, either.' He pointed ahead. 'Do you realize I can see Ladybower's chimneypots and I want to get home and out of this uniform. So start her up, there's a good girl, and let's be on our way!'

'Yes, dear.' She said it contritely as the Lorna of old would have said it. Her capitulation pleased him and he patted her knee paternally like the William of old had always done.

Sighing, she started the car.

'There are a few things to be washed, Lorna – can you do them? They're in my case – and there are the things I'm wearing now. I'll get out of this uniform and have a bath, if there's any water?'

There was. She had switched on the immersion heater before she left for the station, even though the powers-that-be frowned on such things. Electricity was a munition of war and electrical appliances must only be used of necessity. Higher than average electricity or gas bills would come under scrutiny, everyone knew, and the miscreant warned, though no one, this far, had actually been taken to court for wasting electricity or gas. It would have been plastered all over the daily papers as a warning, had it been so – like the woman who was fined seventy-five pounds for obtaining two pounds of off-the-ration sugar. *Seventy-five* pounds, would you believe? Six months' wages!

'Water, dear? For a bath for a weary soldier?'

'Sorry. I was miles away, thinking about the immersion heater. I'll pop upstairs and switch it off!'

She did just that, checking the bathroom to make sure Ness had not left her toilet bag. And she had not. Then she went into the spare bedroom, glancing around. But Ness had removed every smallest personal thing. Her sheets and pillowslips were already in the laundry basket, Lorna knew, and the blankets folded neatly and covered by the bedspread. It would be all right – just as long as no one mentioned Ness's name during the next seventy-two hours! And why should they?

William put on the white shirt and grey flannel trousers Lorna had laid out on the bed. The bath had revived him after his overnight journey and he regarded his mirror image with not a little smugness. He *had* lost weight! The suspicion of a belly he'd had when he left for Wiltshire was gone. Why, dammit, he could even fasten the belt at his waist a notch tighter!

He walked to the open window, drawing in the scent of the summer afternoon, feeling pleased with himself. Nun Ainsty had not changed. To his left was the pillar box, to his right, Dickon's Wood. And spread out below him was the village Green on which Martha Hugwitty's two geese grazed and nibbled, and the tiny duck pond on which a lonely old duck still swam.

The midday sun was warm, the sky blue and the scent of grass and flowers was good in his nostrils. He was a lucky man, all things considered. A little upset, naturally, that Lorna had been foolish without his presence to guide her, but she was young; younger even than her years. There was nothing worldly about his wife and he knew he could trust her completely – her fidelity, that was – and never have to worry that she would give him cause to doubt her. Lorna had an air of innocence about her for all she was a married woman. He had heard only yesterday about the wife of a fellow officer who had not only gone off the rails but written a Dear John letter asking for a divorce!

He looked in the mirror, smoothing his hair, liking what he saw there; a man in his prime and fitter than ever he had been. He would have an enjoyable weekend, then on Tuesday report to his new posting; a permanent base and in England, thank God! Could have been North Africa or the Far East, but he'd been lucky and got the safe number he had all along intended, and well worth the time spent in the Territorial Reserve. He would survive this war, he knew it.

He fingered his moustache. Had Lorna seriously meant he should shave it off? Would it really make him look younger, complement his flatter stomach and slimmer waistline? He patted the one-notch-tighter belt almost smugly and decided that the moustache stayed. Dignified. Gave him an air of dependability. Clients had trusted his wholesome image. Lorna's grandfather had felt the same way; been glad, in his last years, to give his granddaughter into the keeping of one so steady and reliable. Lorna had said yes the first time he asked her to marry him as if she already knew her acceptance would have her grandfather's blessing.

Yes, William Hatherwood was a fortunate man. He had a compliant wife, a comfortable, well-run home in a picture postcard village. He had also been given a posting to Aldershot, which suited him very nicely. Life wasn't all doom and despair – apart from the invasion, which was never very far from most people's minds. And that being the case, the invasion would be declared taboo for the remainder of the weekend!

'Butter is to be rationed even more on Monday,' Lorna murmured as they sat at the kitchen table having supper. 'And lard and margarine.'

'Oh dear.' William had not noticed a shortage of anything in the Officers' Mess.

'Two ounces of each per person per week . . .'

'Then I suggest you collect yours every two weeks, dear. Two ounces of anything is hardly worth the time and effort weighing and wrapping it.'

'Yes. A good idea . . .' Or it would have been had there not been *two* people living at Ladybower and four ounces of anything seemed rather more collectable. 'Tell me, William, are you near the awful air raids?'

The daylight raids, intended to wipe out the first line of resistance to Hitler's invasion plans, continued with frightening ferocity. For how much longer could Hitler order the Luftwaffe into the air, twice, sometimes three times a day, at such a loss in bombers? And for how much longer could our fighter pilots stay on their feet, let alone take to the air, sortie after sortie? How did you fly Hurricanes and Spitfires when you were almost asleep standing up?

'The raids don't bother us a lot in Wiltshire, nor will they where I am going. Aldershot isn't a target – yet. And I have been thinking, Lorna,' – think about, talk about anything but the damned invasion – 'that I shall take the car with me when I go back – my car, I mean.'

'Why?' Lorna laid down her knife and fork. 'Surely the Army has enough trucks and cars of its own? Why take yours, and how would you get the petrol for it?'

'The same way as you do – with my own petrol coupons. By the way' – he was all at once alert – 'you haven't been using mine, have you?'

'Of course not! Your coupons are where you left them in

your desk drawer, but could you – *would* you – mind giving one of them to me? A one-gallon coupon, I mean . . .'

After all, she had driven to the station and back and even though the petrol ration went twice as far in her small, economical car than it did in William's, she calculated she had used up at least half a coupon in getting to York and back. Petrol coupons were like gold dust and you didn't get anywhere near enough.

'I will, though I didn't think you'd begrudge me a couple of miles.'

'Twenty-five miles, the round trip!' Lorna was surprised that common sense hadn't told her to let the matter drop. 'And you have two months' petrol coupons unused, I know, and more due on the first of next month. Please, William – I'd be so grateful.'

'Very well. I'll put a gallon in the tank for you.' He was surprised she could be so nit-picky. The Lorna he had left behind him wouldn't have made a fuss over a couple of squirts of petrol because, and she had to admit it, that small contraption of hers went for miles on very little fuel. 'And I'll check my own – tyres, oil and water. Quite a lot of the chaps have their cars with them. Handy. If I can wangle the time I'll be able to get home without a leave pass more often – if I've got my own transport.'

'Then you must take yours, William. We'll give it a clean and polish. Shall you drive it back on Monday morning?'

'Think I will. And that was a very civilized meal, dear. I enjoyed it. Think I'll take a turn round the village then pop into the White Hart, treat myself to a glass of decent ale. The further south you go, y'know, the worse the beer is. I've missed getting a northern pint.' He pushed back his chair and the legs grated on the stone tiles of the floor. 'Won't be too long. Reckon I'll have an early night. Didn't get a lot of sleep on the train.'

He left, looking well pleased with himself. Lorna pouted; he was forgetting that when he was a civilian he had always helped with the washing-up after supper. But she mustn't find fault. This was his first leave, however short, and he must be really glad to be home.

But an early night? Just what did that mean? Was she expected to go to bed with him, or was he genuinely tired? Friday wasn't one of their nights. Perhaps he really was tired and in need of sleep.

She smiled, relieved. It was a beautiful summer evening, William had enjoyed his supper and she, Lorna, had got away with her misdemeanours with hardly a protest. And fingers crossed she would get away with –

The White Hart! The thought struck her like a slap. Who might he meet there? Would Mary Ackroyd ask him, innocently enough, what he thought of his wife's lodger and didn't he think the land girl from Liverpool was a very nice lass?

'Mary!' Panic stricken, she sent her thoughts winging to the landlady of the White Hart. 'Whatever you do, don't mention land girls – please?'

'Oh, damn!' she wailed. Not another misunderstanding, another coldness between them? There would be the mother of all rows if he found out about Ness from someone other than herself!

She took a deep breath, folded her arms belligerently and stared out at the hen ark. Then she ran her fingers through her short, soft hair – to give herself courage, that was – and whispered,

'Sorry William, but Ness stays. I don't want to have to remind you that Ladybower is my house; I never have and I never will, if I can help it. But if you bluster and blow and demand, then I shall. I shall tell you, quietly and calmly, that I will have whomever I want to stay here. I'm sorry, dear, but I *will*!'

Then as suddenly as defiance had taken her, it deserted her and flew out of the window and away, taking her brief courage with it.

'*Please*, Mary . . . ?' Talk to William about the harvest and the bombing in the south and the soldiers who could arrive any day at the manor. Talk about ships and shoes and sealing wax but please, I beg you, *don't* talk about Ness?

Lorna slid out of bed and walked on tiptoe out of the bedroom. Last night had been all right. No misunderstandings, no recriminations. William had returned without knowing that Ness still lived at Ladybower, and gone to bed almost at once.

'I won't wake you when I come up,' she promised, and he had slept heavily, arms flung wide, leaving her only the edge of the bed to cling to. She had awakened twice in the night and been surprised to realize that William was there beside her. It had not taken long, she thought guiltily, to get used to having the bed to herself; to go to it master of the house and get up her own mistress! Then she thought shame on herself and ran downstairs, opening curtains as she went, letting in another sunbright day.

She walked barefoot into the garden, curling her toes on the dew-damp grass, loving the way the hens ran to greet her and to stand, heads cocked at the wire, waiting for the food she would throw to them.

I wonder, she thought indulgently, which of you is going to lay an egg today for William – bring home to him what a very good idea hens on the lawn is?

Carefully she filled a can with rainwater from the tub at the back door, then topped up the drinking trough. They were such pretty creatures. Surely William would come, if not to like them, then at least to accept their right to be on his lawn? There was a war on after all, and he might well have come on leave to find it had been dug up wantonly, and potatoes and carrots and cabbages planted for the war effort as the government so often pointed out.

'Another egg today?' she whispered fondly.

* * *

The weekend had gone well. Yesterday morning they made love as they always did on Sundays, and afterwards she had been unable to stop herself pulling the back of her hand across her mouth. She had forgotten how scratchy William's passionate kisses were and lost no time splashing her face with cold water against the redness, then sighed with relief at wifely duty done. And, she had reminded herself firmly, you couldn't get the child you secretly hoped for without duty done. If she were honest, she hoped with every coupling that a baby might happen. She wanted a child; had been amazed to find they did not come automatically when man and wife had relations within the intimacy of their double bed. She had been surprised, too, when William made it plain that children, when another war with Germany threatened, were not a good idea at all. And when that war came, she reluctantly ceased to hope for a child – at least until it was over – and to long, instead, for a mistake to happen in William's calculations so she might find herself pregnant after all.

But there were ways and means of not having babies, she should have known. She had learned that much in her final year at boarding school, when talk after lights out turned, as it often did, to men and the things men did and the things you should not let men do. Men were only entitled to *that* when they married you. It said so in the marriage service, didn't it? *With my body I thee worship*. Stood to sense that that was what it meant – the Church saying it was all right, once the priest had said the words.

Mind, it was the men who wanted *that* before they put a ring on your finger you had to look out for, said the form prefect, whose periods had started ages before anyone else's and who therefore considered herself an authority on such matters.

Ah, yes, Lorna sighed; she had not been a complete innocent on her wedding day and had accepted that doing *that* was part of what was called wifely duty, or conjugal rights; the price a woman paid for the smug gold band on her eager wedding finger.

And now Lorna made sandwiches for William's journey back to Wiltshire; cut them into dainty triangles, then wrapped them in greaseproof paper and a paper serviette. On the draining board stood a vacuum flask, filled with boiling water so the tea she would fill it with would stay hot, longer.

'That's got the stuff loaded.' William, in his uniform once more and eager to be off. 'Best make a start. Due back at 18.00 hours. Don't want a black mark.'

'Going by road will be better.' Lorna filled the flask with tea. 'You never know when a train is going to start, let alone when it will arrive. A good idea, dear, to take your car with you.'

There was a knocking, once, twice, three times on the front door, the calling card of the Meltonby postman. They heard the snap of the letterbox.

'I'll get it.' William hurried into the hall. 'See if there's anything of importance before I leave.'

Of importance to her husband, Lorna thought, were things like the water rates, the council rates, the electricity bill and most important of all, the telephone account, which could run dangerously high when ladies spent so much time chatting to friends. But there were no such missives to excite William's senses; nothing to check for errors or omissions, no telephone account to be queried. Yet for all that, his face was red and angry as he tossed the letter on the kitchen table.

'Miss A Nightingale? And who is she? A land girl, by any chance?'

'Yes. Ness.'

'So why do her letters come to this house? Did she not think to tell her family and friends she no longer lived here?' He looked into his wife's flushed face, saw eyes that would not meet his. 'Or is there some other explanation, Lorna?'

'Ness lives here.' She forced her gaze to his. 'She's in the hostel in Meltonby for the weekend; didn't think it right we shouldn't be alone for your leave.'

She was shaking so much she was sure he must see it, hear the trembling in her voice.

'But you said she'd left. Weeks ago!'

'No I didn't, William. Never. You said she was to go, but I didn't ask her to.'

'So you went behind my back? You let me think she'd gone. Deceit, Lorna, and not at all like you. Well,' he picked up his cap from the table, 'I have no more time to argue with you. I take it you expect Miss A Nightingale to creep back when I have gone?'

'Ness will be back after work tonight.'

'Then you will tell her to go, Lorna; tell her it is my wish and she isn't wanted!'

He put on his cap, picked up the flask and made for the door.

'No!' Lorna moved quickly to stand in front of it. 'I don't want you to leave like this! At least say "Goodbye. Take care of yourself."'

'You seem well able, my dear, to do that. What Lorna wants, Lorna must have. *Why* must you have the land girl in our home?'

'Because Nance asked me to; said the bombing would start again soon, and that she'd be looking for billets for evacuees and mothers with young children. I knew you wouldn't want children again and it seemed better to have Ness in the spare room. And I liked her and was glad of her company. Besides, Nance said there wasn't room for her at the hostel.'

'Very well.' He bent to kiss her cheek. 'I accept that Nance Ellery can be very persuasive and bossy at times and that you are inclined to take the least line of resistance. But the woman must go. Tell her tonight, there's a good girl.'

It was an order, Lorna thought, not a request, and being referred to as a good girl stung her into action.

'William, I'm sorry and I don't want to upset you when

you are leaving, but I won't tell Ness to go. She isn't a bit of trouble – she's mostly at the farm anyway. And it's patriotic to take her in; helps the war effort.'

'I see. I don't know why you had to be lumbered with her in the first place. The minute she wanted to conveniently disappear there just happened to be a bed for her at the hostel, so tell her to go back to it! I mean what I say!'

'But she can't! The hostel bed was only empty for the weekend.'

'Are we to argue over her, then? Is she more important to you than me?'

'That is childish of you, William, and unworthy.' She felt more calm, now, and even more determined. 'And we are not arguing because it takes two to argue and I have nothing more to say.' All at once, her voice was amazingly quiet. 'I don't want us to part like this, though. Please try to understand?'

'You'll do as you wish, I suppose.' He pushed past her and opened the door. 'There is no more to say, if you are determined. I bid you good day.'

And with a banging of the front door and a crunching of wheels on the gravel of the drive, he was gone.

He bid her good day! What a way to say goodbye! He was going back to the war and all she got was a brusque good day!

But he would be back! By the time he got to the top road his temper would have cooled and he would turn the car in the lane and tell her he was sorry and hold her tightly and kiss her. And when he had done that he would use his talking-to-a-little-girl voice and coaxingly ask her to promise to send Ness away.

That was when she knew she did not want him to come back because if he did she was afraid that for the sake of peace and harmony she would promise that Ness would go and she didn't want her to go. Besides, where was she to stay, with all the hostel beds full again?

She was relieved that after half an hour there was neither sight nor sound of William; relieved, too, that in her stubborn trembling defiance she had not needed to fall back on her last line of defence – 'Ladybower is *my* house!'

'Oh, what a mess!'

The shaking began again and she sat down heavily at the kitchen table. The tea in the pot had gone cold, so what the hell! Rationing or not, she needed a cup of strong, hot, sugar-sweet tea!

'Sorry, William,' she said shakily as she filled the kettle. 'Ness stays! No deal!'

At six o'clock the kitchen door opened and a round brown hat sailed across the room and landed on the table.

'What the –?' Startled, Lorna turned, then smiled to see Ness at the open door. 'Now why did you do that?'

'Oh, it's a daft thing us Liverpudlians do sometimes; throw in our hat first to test the water, see if we're welcome!'

'Well, you are!'

'Missed me, have you?'

'More to the point, have *you* missed Ladybower?'

'Ar, norrarf! The hostel's fine, but it's bedlam when thirty women are talking twenty to the dozen. And it's worse once the hot water has all gone and everybody is wantin' to know which sneaky cow's had more'n six inches of water in her bath! But was it smashin', having William home?'

'Smashing.' Lorna reached for the envelope she had placed behind the mantel clock.

'This came for you – this morning.'

'Oooh. And William saw it?'

'He did!'

'And one thing led to another and –'

'And the cat was out of the bag, as they say. He went off in a huff.' Her voice began to tremble again. 'He accused me of being deceitful for not telling you to go.'

'And when he found I hadn't shoved off, he gave you

down-the-banks, eh? So what is going to happen, Lorna?'

'Nothing's going to happen! William said you must go and I told him I wanted you to stay. I really want you to. Say you will?'

'Of course I'll stay, though I don't like bein' the cause of words between man and wife. And you've been weeping, haven't you?'

'On and off – just a little. Angry tears, really. He just slammed out, you see, and I was sure he'd turn round and come back and say he was sorry. But I'm glad he didn't, because there would have been more words, more demands, and I'm not prepared to take orders any longer. And what's more, I stood up for myself – didn't even have to remind him that if push came to shove, Ladybower is my house and I'll have who I want in it – well, within reason, that is!'

'Ar, Lorna girl – you're sure you want me here, that it's worth all the bother? He's going to come on leave again and there'll be another slanging match and – and –'

'More down-the-banks?' Lorna said gravely. 'And you know what? If William had been kinder, if he hadn't practically ordered me to tell you to go, like a Victorian husband, if he'd coaxed and sweet-talked a little and asked me to do it for him because I love him, then I just might have given in and asked Nance to find somewhere else for you.'

'I still think you should, Lorna. It just isn't worth it.'

'Oh, but it is! William must learn that I've got a mind of my own and I'm not prepared to talk about it any more, Ness. I've made up my mind, and that's it! And I will tell you something. After William had gone I felt dreadful and I was longing for something special to happen to put things to rights. Y'know, like when I was little I'd say, "If the next bird I see is a thrush, there'll be jam roly poly for supper."'

'Mm. We all did it, girl. So what happened so special to put the smile back on your face?'

'We've had another egg, Ness! I heard such a cackling and there it was, all warm and new-laid. Something special, see?

So I hard-boiled both eggs and put them in the salad. There's ham left over from William's sandwiches, so what do you say to ham and egg salad and boiled new potatoes for supper?'

'I'd say,' Ness smiled her wide, beautiful smile, 'that this is the best billet I've ever had – and I'm stopping. Well, till Himself's home on leave again, that is.'

'And we'll worry about that,' Lorna said, chin set at defiance, 'when it happens. So where is your kit?'

'At the hostel. I've had the use of a bike these last three days. I'll pedal over after supper; put the big case on the seat, and push it.'

'I've got a better idea. We'll collect your stuff in the car. And before you ask if I can spare the petrol – yes, I can! I wheedled a gallon out of William.'

'You're learning, Lorna Hatherwood! And I'm ravenous. I'll just have a wash, then there's such news to tell you!'

'Potatoes ready in five minutes!'

Lorna let go a breath of relief. It would be all right. Tonight, William would phone to let her know he was safely back and she would tell him to take care and that she loved him.

Yes, of course it would be all right . . .

FIVE

'It was good of you to go to all the trouble. Will you mind doing it again, next leave?'

Lorna sat on the spare-room bed, watching Ness unpack her kit.

'Mind? No. Glad to be back, for all that. And I haven't told you the news.'

They had been so occupied at supper, oh-ing and ah-ing over the amazing home-produced, hard-boiled eggs and trying to sweep the matter of William's heated departure under the mat, that Ness's gossip was still untold.

'Anything new?'

'There is! I was talking to one of the soldiers at the manor yesterday. Said he was in the REME.'

'Electrical bods . . .'

'Oh, ar? Didn't enquire. Anyway, they're getting the place ready for wounded soldiers – a convalescent home, he told me. Makes sense. There were a lot of wounded at Dunkirk.'

'I see. So Rowley Wintersgill can rest easy,' Lorna said tartly. 'I can't imagine men on crutches, maybe men who have lost a limb, rampaging over Glebe Farm land taking anything that isn't nailed down, as he put it.'

'Kate was quite pleased when I told her. At least there won't be drill sergeants yelling orders, nor firearms practice. And talking about firearms, the Local Defence bods have got their uniforms. Bob and Rowley went to Meltonby to collect theirs. But no rifles, as yet, so what they're going to stop them *Jairmans* with, I don't know.'

'Makes sense. The Army blew up our ammunition dumps before they left France. Our lot might be a bit short on rifles. But let's not get back to the invasion.'

'Fine by me. Saw Flora Petch on the way here. The baby arrived at Meltonby early this morning. She said being wakened up in the small hours wouldn't have been a lot of good for me but better luck on the next leave. No more babies expected hereabouts – or none she knows about.'

'Lucky woman. I wouldn't mind a baby, Ness. Oh, I know starting a family in wartime – especially now when things are in such a mess – might not be the wisest thing to do, but if an accident happened, I wouldn't care. Anyway, what else is news?'

'They're getting another worker at the farm. They're still in need of help, and I know I'm not a lot of good to them. I said so, but Kate said to let her be the judge of that; said she wouldn't mind another one like me. But there's no chance of getting a land girl – not till they find another hostel around these parts to put more of them in.

'So Bob got in touch with the Ministry of Labour, oh, ages ago. Had given up all hope of getting more help, then he got a letter on Saturday. Said there's a man available, but it was up to Bob whether or not he took him.'

'Why? Is he fresh out of prison,' Lorna grinned.

'No. Worse. He's a conchie, and men who won't fight are trouble. But Bob said he'd give it a try.'

'Then he must be desperate! How are you going to feel, working with him, Ness? Don't think I'd much like one of those working for me.'

'One of *those*? I don't think he's a Nancy boy, Lorna. He just has conscientious objections to being in the Armed Forces. Maybe he doesn't want to kill. Live and let live, eh? Kate said if there was any trouble he'd have to go, but that he might be a decent young man underneath. And Rowley smirked and said he'd see to it that the conchie would get all the dirty jobs around the place, and see how much he liked being a conchie then!'

'Rowley makes me sick. He should think himself lucky that farming is a reserved occupation and he won't ever have to join up!'

'You don't like him, do you? What's he ever done to you, Lorna?'

'Nothing. He wouldn't dare. But he's got a reputation for womanizing, and I don't like that. Has he ever tried anything on with you, Ness?'

'I told you he hadn't. I can deal with him if ever he gets fresh. So what say we sit in the garden? I missed the garden over the weekend. I think that no matter where I go I'll remember it, and Dickon's Wood and the smell of flowers.'

'Well, now you've got the smell of hens to add to your memories!'

'They don't smell; not if you clean them out regularly. Goff Leaman said that hen droppings make good manure and he'd clean our ark out every week if you'd give him the hen muck. I told him I'd ask you about it.'

'He's welcome, tell him and – oooh! The phone!' She was across the room and down the stairs to snatch up the receiver with a breathless, 'Hullo? William?'

Ness closed the bedroom door, glad for Lorna yet hoping William would say nothing to upset her. Lorna was trying to convince herself she had got the measure of her husband, and that from now on she would stand up to his demands and sulks. But the speed at which she had taken the stairs showed how pathetically eager she was to speak to him.

'Everything all right?' she smiled when a pink-cheeked Lorna opened the door.

'Fine – if you're meaning did he bring up the matter of Ness Nightingale again. He didn't, so I took that as an apology for leaving in a huff like he did. Said he'd had a nice leave, though, and that he was busy getting his kit ready for the move tomorrow. I think he'll be all right now he's got a permanent posting. Said he'd let me have the address as soon as he got there. So do you still want to sit in the garden?'

And Ness said of course she did and was thankful, inside, that things seemed back to normal between Lorna and her man, and the matter of Ness Nightingale shelved, for the time being at least.

But just as Lorna seemed not to like or trust Rowley Wintersgill so she, Ness, had the same sniffy feeling about William. Nothing she could set her mind to exactly; more a feeling of trouble to come!

'We'll see if the hens have gone in to roost,' she said as they went downstairs, 'and if they have we can shut them up for the night.'

The hens, she thought, and the garden and the green-cool of the wood behind it and Ladybower and Nun Ainsty were so amazing to a city dweller like herself. Oh, she loved Liverpool to bits and the people and their sense of humour and the mucky old Mersey, but Nun Ainsty was a special place she would be glad for all time to have lived in and would remember for ever. And she was lucky to have found it when she was so in need of comfort and a new start, away from Liverpool. And from memories of Patrick.

She sat on the wooden bench beside the rose bushes, closed her eyes, took a deep, calming breath then said,

'Them hens *don't* smell, Lorna . . .'

It was all, in that moment of unguarded remembering, she could think of to say.

'Well!' said Lorna, turning off the wireless at the end of the news. 'What does the government think it's doing! Income tax up a shilling to eight and six in the pound – that's more than a third of all you earn! And beer up a penny a pint! They just spring it on us without so much as a thought! Who do they think they are?'

'They're the government,' Ness supplied. 'They've given themselves emergency powers to do exactly as they want! Me Da's goin' to be sick over the penny on beer, though the income tax won't affect him. He doesn't earn enough to have to pay it. Maybe that bloke at the Exchequer thinks he's Robin Hood, taking from the rich to pay for the war. 'Cause it's got to be paid for, y'know. Imagine how much it costs when we lose a battleship or a fighter or a bomber. And think how much it costs to feed and pay all those fighting men.'

'Pay, Ness? How much do you think a soldier gets? Next to nothing! The country calls them up whether they want to go or not, then pays them a pittance for risking life and limb!'

'You, er – seem to know a lot about what soldiers get . . .' Ness was surprised at the ferocity of Lorna's reply.

'Well I do, as a matter of fact. William told me exactly how much a private in the Army gets – after all, it's his job to know. And will I tell you what a woman with two children whose man is in the Army gets? It's thirty-two shillings a week. One pound twelve shillings a week, for God's sake! And maybe her rent accounts for ten shillings a week or maybe her house is mortgaged, which is far worse! And then there's coal and light! How is a woman who didn't want her husband to join up expected to manage?'

'Are you sure, Lorna? It's a bad lookout, if it is . . .'

'Look, I can tell you exactly how the Army arrives at that figure. They call a man up and reckon he's worth seventeen shillings a week; they also give the woman five shillings for the first child and three shillings – *three* shillings! – for the second. And because that isn't enough for her to live on, they take seven shillings out of her husband's Army pay to give to her without even asking! So the poor soldier is left with a few bob a week and his wife has to try to manage on one pound, twelve shillings!'

'Ar, but the announcer gave it out that the Armed Forces are to get a rise – had you forgotten?'

'How could I have? Sixpence a day is such a huge sum!

So the poor private will probably make his pay rise over to his wife when he gets it. I bet she'll be over the moon with an extra three shillings and sixpence, Ness!'

'Hey up, queen! What are you getting so het up about? Life's like that – always has been.'

'I know. And how do you think it makes me feel? Grandpa left Ladybower to me and all his money and stocks and shares and things. It's all invested, but it gives me an income of my own – and I pay tax on a part of it I might add. And I wouldn't complain at all if I could say where my income tax goes and who shall get it – but I can't! The war, like you say, has got to be paid for!'

'So where would you have your tax go, if you could?'

'I'd give it to a young woman in Meltonby. She's got two children and was drawing her Army allowance at the post office when I was in buying stamps. The post office sells other things as well you know, and the other day they'd got sweeties to sell – rationed out to an ounce for each child. "Would you like a few dolly mixtures," Mrs Benson asked the lady, but she said, "No thanks. Sweeties cost too much." That woman probably thought that when everything was taken care of out of the one pound twelve shillings she'd just drawn, she hadn't enough to pay sixpence for dolly mixtures. After all, sixpence buys two small loaves of bread!'

'Ar. Poor kids. But I suppose you bought the sweeties for them?'

'Of course I didn't! How could I, without hurting her pride? Because when push comes to shove, pride is about all that woman has left!'

'Well, for a lady who's pretty well-heeled, you can do a very good imitation of a Bolshevik, might I say? And how did we get onto this subject?'

'We got onto it because of a pesky sixpence a day rise for a man who is fighting for King and Country! And I'll bet you anything you like he'd rather be at home with his wife and two little girls! And they aren't called Bolsheviks now. They're called Communists, and Joseph Stalin has just confirmed his pact of non-aggression with Hitler, did you know? And what an unholy alliance it is! Communists and Facists the best of friends and each not trusting the other farther than either could spit!'

'Now see here, Mrs Hatherwood, you've got yourself into a real state! What's to do, then? Time of the month, is it?'

'I – I suppose it might be, but the dolly mixture thing happened last week and I keep remembering it and wanting to do something for that poor young woman.'

'Well, you can't, and that's all there is to it. Mind, you could offer her charity, but I can't see that going down very well, can you – her pride, an' all that?'

'You're right. Charity is a cold thing. But when I last saw Mrs Benson, she did mention that her postman is expecting his call-up any time now and she's going to split his round into two. She's got a man – elderly, he is – to do Meltonby and said if I knew of anyone who'd care to take on Nun Ainsty, she'd be glad to hear from them. The pay isn't all that good – not for the few houses I'd be delivering to – but there's the morning paper round as well. Easy enough to push a paper through the letterbox with the mail. I'm thinking of –'

'*You'd* be deliverin' to? You're not thinkin' of bein' a lady postie and paperboy? Flamin' Norah! What would Himself say!'

'He'd say, as would most patriotic men, that I was doing the right thing by the war effort. I mean – young men have got to join up, so someone has to take on their jobs. Why shouldn't I help out? I've thought for a long time I ought to be doing more to help the war effort.'

'All right. You fancy bein' a postie – so how's that going to help the soldier's wife who can't afford to buy her kids a few sweeties?'

'I don't know, yet. I have a feeling her mother lives in Meltonby, too, so she might be willing to look after the little ones for a few hours a day – and let her daughter earn a little to help out.'

'You've got it all worked out, haven't you? You're goin' to do part-time work and if I'm not mistaken you're goin' to offer that woman a cleaning job? My, but there's a devious side to you, Lorna Hatherwood! I wonder what William's goin' to say when he hears about it?'

'Look – I haven't exactly taken the postlady's job, and I don't even know the name of the woman with two children, so it isn't all worked out – yet.'

'No, but it will be! And how much will you pay her, then?'

'I – I thought a shilling an hour – it's the going rate. If I paid her two shillings a day for two hours' work – five days a week that would be –'

'Ten bob. Would be like she'd won the Sweepstake, wouldn't it? Mind, when you find out who she is, she mightn't want your charity.'

'It wouldn't be charity! And if she didn't want to come, I'd still take on the job at the post office – if it's still on offer, that is. I'm determined to do something other than be a housewife. And a pretty comfortably-off housewife at that! D'you know, Ness, if I wasn't a married woman, I might just be seriously thinking about volunteering for nursing or even the Armed Forces. They do say that women who volunteer for the Army can do all sorts of things – like working on a gun site or being a despatch rider or –'

'Lorna! What's got into you? Had a rush of blood to the 'ead, have you? Why all this patriotism, all of a sudden?'

'It isn't sudden patriotism. And I don't know what on earth has got into me, truth known.'

But she did know. She had defied William and got away with it and it was giddy making! And now she was thinking of doing part-time war work – and asking a woman whose name she didn't even know to help clean Ladybower, five days a week. Heady stuff without a doubt!

'No more do I, but a mug of hot cocoa might help – it's getting cold out here all of a sudden. And then we'll see to the blackouts and you an' me can have another chat about your war work, eh? And I'm not going to try to talk you out of it, Lorna. As a matter of fact I'm proud of you, girl. Only sleep on it tonight? See how you feel in the morning – then have a word at the post office if you still want to do it.'

And she would still want to be a lady postie, Ness sighed as she bolted down the flap of the hen ark. And she'd still be willing to push morning papers through doors for little more money than she was prepared to pay her daily help!'

Mind, it was still all up in the air – a wait-and-see situation that well might come to nothing and no harm would be done. Though if she became Ainsty's postie – and paperboy – and the soldier's wife was willing to help out five mornings a week, then Lorna could be heading for trouble, because William wasn't going to like it. Not even in the name of patriotism!

September, loveliest of months. Now the harvest was in and Ness still nursing her scratched and sore arms. Ears of barley, as she too-late discovered, bore needles that played havoc with unprotected flesh. Another year, she smiled ruefully, she would know to cover up!

Now, weary fighter pilots found it difficult to believe that the fury hurled against their stations was now directed at London. An amazing daylight raid on the capital had sent the War Cabinet into angry retaliation. Berlin, hitherto unbombed, received its first heavy raid. At night-time. Open cities, it seemed, were no longer to be immune to bombing.

Now, at Nun Ainsty, the leaves on the trees in Dickon's Wood were darkening as autumn neared. In Ladybower's garden, six hens were in full lay. Not what you could call large eggs, yet, but white and perfect and in the opinion of Lorna and Ness, very beautiful.

Minnie Holmes, soldier's wife and mother of two, had

gladly accepted Lorna's offer of housework. She particularly liked ironing, especially if the wireless was playing *Music While You Work;* liked polishing so you could see your face in things; liked Mrs Hatherwood who was a very kind lady. Minnie particularly liked Fridays when she received the ten-shilling note that made all the difference.

For Lorna's part, delivering letters to Nun Ainsty's few houses presented no problem. She had been given the use of a red GPO bicycle on which she pedalled to Meltonby post office each morning to collect letters, small parcels and newspapers. Going to work was doubly enjoyable because she had never worked before. No one in Ainsty thought it strange that she had taken it into her head to do her bit for the war effort. Nance Ellery thought it admirable, though she was of the opinion that the Women's Voluntary Service would have been more appropriate, the plum and green uniform would have complemented Lorna's fairness and been far smarter than the trousers, old gardening coat and GPO armband in which she set out for Meltonby every morning except Sundays. For this Lorna was paid fifteen shillings a week which she promptly returned to Mrs Benson's counter in exchange for a savings certificate – further to help the war effort.

With past experiences in mind, she had written at once to William, telling him of her need to do something useful and that she had given two hours' work each day to Mrs Holmes, who was grateful for the extra money, as William, with his knowledge of Army pay, would appreciate.

. . . Nance approves of my job, though I think she was disappointed I didn't join the WVS. I like to tell myself that perhaps my very small contribution to the war effort will bring you home just that little earlier. Please write and tell me you are proud of me?

And amazingly, William replied that though there was absolutely no need for her to work, he was coming to accept that this was everybody's war. There were even ATS girls at Aldershot and two women officers who ate in the mess, and were no trouble at all.

'Thank heaven for that!' Lorna breathed, determined that from now on she would make sure her husband was told of anything she did which might be considered out of the ordinary.

'William seems to be settling in nicely at Aldershot,' she said to Ness. 'In his last letter he said it had been rumoured there could be promotions all round and it was fingers crossed that I could soon be addressing my letters to Captain Hatherwood! But whether or not it happens, at least he seems more – well – amenable.'

'Good.' And not before time, Ness thought, returning her concentration to the letter she was writing to her parents, hoping Liverpool would not soon be bombed like London, without mercy. Blitzkrieg, the Germans called it. More than a thousand civilians killed and London hospitals hardly able to cope with the wounded. And a new word *blitz* added to everyday language. Ness was sorry for London, especially for those who lived in the East End, and hoped with all her heart that the city on the banks of the Mersey would be spared such savagery.

Deliberately she turned her thoughts to Ainsty, where the only bombers to fly overhead were our own. When would the soldiers come? There was still activity at the manor. Surely it was ready now? The windows had been cleaned inside and out and she wouldn't be surprised, she had remarked to Kate, if the place hadn't been given a thorough going over as well, after all the years of dust and neglect.

'They do things wondrous slow,' Kate sighed, for Glebe Farm had still not received the man promised by the Ministry of Labour, though he was expected any day now.

'And when he does get himself here,' Kate said meaningfully, 'he will not be referred to as *the conchie*, but treated as normal – even though he might have ideas some folk don't approve of. He'll be treated decent!' She paused to glance across the table at her son. 'Until he gives us cause to think otherwise of him.'

'And if that happens he'll be on his way, be sure of it,' Bob Wintersgill had firmly wrapped the matter up, 'and that lot at the Labour can find me some proper help!'

And the British – who now accepted how much so many owed to the few who had kept the invasion at bay this far – thought uneasily of what seemed to have been postponed until next spring; thought too of the second winter of the war which would bring the blackout with it and cold houses because coal was rationed and gas and electricity not to be used except when necessary.

It was at the height of the blitzkrieg on London that two things happened at Ladybower. William wrote to say he was coming on leave on September 7th and, to Ness's shock and horror, it was announced on the wireless that Liverpool had been bombed.

'Lorna!' Her face paled, her eyes were wide with fear. 'What about Ruth Street? What about Mam and Da, and Nan? God! What'll I do?'

'You'll get on the phone at once. Liverpool isn't all that far away. Maybe trunks will have a line. Tell Mrs B it's urgent, ask her to do her best.'

'But we aren't on the phone!' Did Lorna think phones were everyday pieces of equipment? In little houses like Ruth Street? 'There's a phone at the pub at the top of the street, but that's all . . .'

'Right! Do you know the number? No? Then we'll ask for enquiries. They'll tell us. And you'll be going home, won't you – we'll have to get in touch with the forewoman at the hostel.'

'Home? Y-yes, I suppose so – if I'm allowed.'

'Of course you'll be allowed, especially if – well, if your folks need you there. It's called compassionate leave, Ness, and anyway, you're due a week off, aren't you?'

'Yes. Kate said only the other day it might be a good thing if I took what leave was due to me soon. Before they started lifting potatoes and things. But ring the exchange, Lorna? See if we can get the pub. It's called the Sefton Arms – the landlord's name is Rigby.'

'Mrs B? Look, Liverpool has been bombed,' Lorna whispered when the exchange answered. 'It was on the wireless and Ness is worried sick. Can you get us the number of Rigby, Sefton Arms public house, in Ruth Street, Liverpool? Will it take long?'

'No. I'll ring you back. And tell Ness I'm sorry, will you . . . ?'

'Well, that's got Mrs Benson on our side. And Ness, Liverpool is a big city; it's unlikely the bombs have been anywhere near your home. More likely the docks . . .'

'Ar. The docks. But you'd have thought Mam would have rung me here, wouldn't you? There's a phone box at the end of the street. If they'd been able, they'd surely have got in touch to let me know they were all right.'

'Ness! No news is good news don't forget and maybe there's a good reason why they haven't been in touch. There'll be a lot of people phoning in and out of Liverpool since it was given out about the bombing. Maybe their trunk lines are extra busy at the moment. There's all sorts of reasons for them not phoning. And put the kettle on? A cup of tea, eh?'

'Yes. Of course,' Ness whispered as if tea would put everything to rights. 'And it'll be all right, won't it?'

'Of course it will.' Lorna ran her tongue round suddenly dry lips. 'We'll be through to the pub in no time, just you see and –'

'But you said the trunk lines would be busy, didn't you? Mam hadn't rung me, you said, because there was probably a waiting list for long-distance calls . . .'

'Yes – we-e-ll – that was only one reason! There are dozens of others. Maybe your folks have gone to relations.'

‘Without ringing me first?’

‘Probably. Do they have relations locally? Are they perhaps on the phone?’

‘There’s Uncle Perce and Aunt Tizzy. Perce is Da’s brother. They live over the water . . .’

‘Where’s that?’

‘Other side of the river. People call it living over the water. They might’ve gone there, but Uncle Perce isn’t on the phone, either. Lorna – what’ll we do?’

‘Like I said – kettle! Then, as soon as we’ve got a number we’ll put in a call. It’ll be all right, you’ll see. And I’m sure you’ll be allowed leave. We’ll get in touch with the hostel after you’ve phoned your folks.’

Long before the kettle boiled the phone rang and Lorna ran into the hall to lift the receiver with a shaking hand.

‘Yes? Mrs B?’

‘Hullo, dear. I have that number and I’ve booked a trunk call – is that all right?’

‘Bless you, of course it’s all right!’

‘Then if you’ve got a pencil and paper handy you’d better write it down, then fingers crossed it won’t take too long to get through.’

Lorna wrote, then whispered,

‘Thanks, Mrs B. We were just going to have a cup of tea.’

‘Then have one for me, will you? This switchboard’s going mad tonight. Thank heaven the post office is closed, that’s all I can say! Cheerio, now. Can’t stop!’

‘That’s the number of the pub.’ Lorna laid the scrap of paper on the table. ‘And Mrs Benson has booked the call already. She says the switchboard is busy tonight; maybe it’s the same all over. It’ll be all right, love. Try not to worry too much?’

‘No. I won’t. Bless you for being here, queen. I seem to have gone to pieces. Stupid, aren’t I?’

‘Of course you aren’t! And there’s the kettle. Sit down,

Ness. Close your eyes and breathe in and out. I always deep breathe when I'm worried – and there you are! Phone! Go on then and answer it! It'll be for you!'

Lorna smiled and stirred the tea in the pot. It was going to be all right. The call had come through quickly which only went to prove it was!

'But why?' Ness's agitated voice came clearly from the hall. 'But didn't they say any more than that? Shall we try again, then?'

There was a pause, then Ness stood in the doorway, her face ashen, eyes brimming with tears.

'Mrs Benson got a trunk line, but the Liverpool exchange said they couldn't raise the pub; said the number was dead. Mrs B says she'll keep trying, though. Oh, Lorna, what's to do at Ruth Street? Has Mam been bombed?' She sat at the table, head on hands, shoulders shaking.

'Listen. Just because one phone number isn't available, doesn't mean your folks aren't all right. Maybe there has been a bomb a long way off – one bomb can burst a water main and everybody for streets around has no water. And if the telephone cables have been damaged, even a mile away, it could –'

'Listen! I'm goin' home! Tonight! *Now!* And I don't care what anybody says!'

'No, Ness. By the time we can get you to York, the last train to Liverpool will probably have gone!'

'I can try, can't I? Maybe get as far as Manchester – pick up an overnight train?'

'And what good is hanging about on a Manchester platform in the small hours going to do you? Drink your tea, why don't you, then I'll run you over to the hostel and we'll tell them that Glebe Farm said it was all right for you to have time off. We'll be on our way good and early in the morning. You'll be in Liverpool by midday – bet you anything you like! And before you say what about my petrol, I can spare it – honest.'

'But what about the letters and papers?'

'The round won't take five minutes! The GPO van from York delivers letters at the post office by six in the morning. The papers come early, too. I can have the lot done by seven if I shift myself.' She laid an arm round the drooping shoulders. 'I promise it's going to be all right. Tomorrow at this time, you'll be with your folks and wondering what you were worrying about.'

'But what if the call comes while we're out, Lorna?'

'We'll ask Mrs B if there's been one when we get back, then try again.' They could not, Lorna considered, spend all evening waiting for a call that might not come.

'You're a good sort.' Ness lifted her cup in salute, a small uncertain smile tilting the corners of her mouth. 'There's more to you than a pretty face, isn't there?'

And Lorna smiled, and lifted her own cup and said,

'Come to think of it, I can be quite a bossy boots when I set my mind to it! And Ness – it *will* be all right. I promise!'

It was half past two when the train reached Lime Street station more than an hour late, yet Ness was never so relieved to see the place. Unswept, littered and crowded as most stations were these days, it was still good to hear the familiar Liverpool accent, know that just across the road she could get a tram that would take her to Ruth Street.

The ticket collector clipped her green travel warrant without saying a word or raising his head. Probably worried sick, just as she was, Ness thought.

The breeze that blew in from the Mersey brought with it not the usual river smell but a stink that was acrid and strange; the smell of bombing, was it? Of dust and debris and burning – and of death?

She cleared her mind of such thoughts. The tram was coming; green and brassy with a get-out-of-my-way air about it. Aggressive, sort of. The conductor clanged the bell, the driver swung his handle and they sailed past the soot-stained, sand-bagged bulk of St George's Hall. Home soon.

Nothing changed, Ness thought. All right – so Liverpool had been bombed, but this brash and bawdy place was benevolent, too, and looked after its own as surely no other city on earth did. She was back, and soon she would know why there had been no answer to last night's call; why her mother had not walked down the street to the telephone kiosk.

It struck her, all at once, that there might be no one at home, that Mam and Da and Nan might have upped sticks and gone over the water to Perce and Tizzy's. On the other hand, they might all be lying unrescued beneath a pile of rubble.

She swallowed hard, recalling newspaper pictures of London's blitz and men tearing at rubble with bare hands to rescue people entombed – oh, God! What a world!

She jumped off the tram, calling her thanks to the conductor, running towards Ruth Street and the Sefton Arms. And it had not been reduced to rubble. It stood there the same as ever. No broken windows, no damaged roofs. Lorna had been right. The docks had been the target. Ruth Street's name had not been on any of those German bombs – not this time, at least.

'Mam!' she called. Her mother was there, putting out a milk bottle. 'Oh, Mam, you're all right!'

They ran towards each other, arms wide, and hugged and kissed and did a little jig on the pavement.

'Well, it's our Ness and don't you look well, girl? Why didn't you think to tell us you were coming?'

'Oh, it's a long story. It'll keep. Put the kettle on, eh?'

Tomorrow at this time you'll be wondering what you were worrying about, Lorna had said, and oh, my word, there was more to Lorna Hatherwood these days than met the eye. That haircut had done her the world of good!

* * *

'Funny, innit, the way things work out,' Ness said that night as they sat round the kitchen fire. 'Yesterday they gave it out on the wireless that Liverpool had been bombed and today – here I am, and you're all fine.'

'You weren't worried, girl?'

'Mam, I was worried sick! And what's to do with the Sefton Arms? We put a call in and the exchange told us that the line was dead – well, what would you have thought? And then I wondered why you hadn't gone to the phone box to ring me. I tell you, if there'd been an overnight train, I'd have been on it! Were the phone lines damaged, or something?'

'Nah!' Nan put down her knitting. 'That landlord should pay his phone bill a bit more reg'lar. Always gettin' cut off, he is!'

'Your nan's right. More off than on, that phone at the Sefton Arms. Not to be relied on, Ness.'

'But if there are any more raids, Mam, could you let me know you're all right – nip down to the phone box? Oh, I know you might have to hang around a bit, but you just might get through straight away. Lorna would take a message if I was at work. Will you do that?'

'Well of course I will – and did! Said to your Da that I'd give you a ring, just in case you'd heard we'd been bombed and were worried. No use, for all that. The coin box was jammed full of money. Couldn't get any more in. I told the girl on the exchange that someone ought to shift themselves and empty it before some scallywag made off with the lot. Get the phone mended, too! And she said it was shortage of manpower, and she would do what she could. I tell you, this war has become the excuse for any old thing that goes wrong! "There's a war on," people say, as if it pardons everything!'

'Ar,' Nan nodded, taking up her needles again. 'And if your Da's goin' to the Sefton, he can queue at the chippy on the way back. My treat.' She nodded to where her son-in-law snored gently, newspaper over his face. 'Give him a shove, Ness, there's a good girl.'

So Ness told her father they had decided on fish and chips for supper and to remember to get them salted and vinegared before they were wrapped up, because it was never the same if you put salt and vinegar on when you got them home.

There wasn't a chippy in Nun Ainsty, Ness had to admit, nor in Meltonby, either. Those two beautiful, hidden away, safe little villages didn't know what they were missing, she sighed. But then, you couldn't have everything, could you?

Relaxed now, she gazed into the fire, wondering what Lorna was doing. She would be all alone in Ladybower – until William came home on leave tomorrow, that was. And wouldn't Himself be pleased to find the land girl had gone on leave? And why on earth had a lovely lady like Lorna married the likes of him? Why hadn't she looked around a bit, tested the water a time or two instead of jumping in at the deep end, head first.

'Hope your Da gets himself home from the chippy before the siren goes,' Nan said, wriggling in her chair.

'There won't be a siren tonight. Not when I'm home,' Ness sighed. 'Oh, it's absolutely beautiful at Nun Ainsty but it's so good to be home, bombing or not. Didn't think I could miss Liverpool so.'

Her Mam's kitchen with its black-leaded iron fire grate, and Da, having his forty winks with the Liverpool Echo over his face, and her gran, always knitting. And vinegar-soaked, well-salted fish and chips, wrapped in newspaper!

It wasn't until her father had left for the Sefton Arms, and Nan had gone to sleep that Ness was asked,

'Are you all right, girl? I mean – is it getting any better? Oh, I know you joined the Land Army to help put it behind you and I can understand that, but was it worth giving up a good job for? I often think about what happened, y'know, and I sometimes feel you should have stayed and faced it out.'

'No, Mam. I did the right thing. And I like it where I am. Ladybower is a beautiful house; very old with big rooms and a wide staircase. And Lorna is a love and Kate at the farm, too. And you said yourself I was looking well – in spite of the fact I'd been awake all night, worrying.'

'So you're getting over – *things*?'

'Getting over Patrick? Yes. And Mam, sooner or later they're going to call up women of my age. From twenty-one to twenty-five, it'll be. Hairdressing is classed as a luxury trade now, so there'd have been no way I could have stayed at Dale's much longer. And talking about my trade, your grey bits are showing. What say I give you and Nan a hairdo before I go back? And Da's hair is in need of my scissors, an' all!'

'Well, I told him he looked like Shirley Temple with his hair so long, but he said he'd wait till you came home. You've spoiled him for going to a barber, you know. Says no one can cut his hair like our Ness.'

'Spoiled him 'cause I don't charge like the barber does!' Ness laughed, relieved Mam had had her little say and that it wouldn't be mentioned again – not this leave, anyway.

But getting over Patrick? There were some days she was shocked to find she had not thought about him at all, but there were other days when the hurt of it was still with her, keen as on the day it happened. Get over him? She would have to.

She lay wide-eyed in bed that night listening, she told herself, for the wailing of the siren, though really it was the strangeness of the little room that kept her awake. The bed she had once thought comfortable made her back ache, and though the room was very dark she knew that the walls pressed in on her and that if she drew back the blackout curtains and squinted into the night, there would be no outlines of rose bushes, nor of the wood behind them; no starbright sky that was wide and stretched for ever; no precious village built from the stones of a priory where lepers once came, in hope.

Outside her, in the shifting darkness, would be streets and rows of rooftops and rubbish-strewn jiggers because there was a war on and street sweepers in short supply. And outside, too, the city waited for an alert – her city, the place she was born in and grew up in and worked in. Liverpool was every bit as precious, in a roundabout way, as Nun Ainsty. Both equal in her affections. It was just that it suited her to live at Ladybower now, and work at Glebe Farm and be a land girl for the duration of hostilities, because that was what she had signed up for. And how long a duration lasted no one knew.

She closed her eyes and pretended she was in her bedroom at Ladybower with Lorna next door and the hens, secured for the night, on the lawn. William would be home tomorrow. *Gawd* . . . !

'Thanks for the card, by the way.'

'Thought you'd like it. View of the Liver Buildings with the birds on top. Sailors coming home, up river, can see them and know they've made a safe landfall.'

'The Liver Birds. Fat and funny. Wonder what they're supposed to be?'

'Dunno. They've been there all my life and all Mam's life, an' all. People say that if ever they're taken down – or are destroyed in the bombing – then Liverpool is at risk. And you're saying it wrong. If you came from my part of the country, you'd call them the Liver *Bayds*. And when I left they were still there. There were no more raids, but at least I went home – saw they were all right.'

'So you didn't have to run to the shelter?'

'No. And anyway, they've got their own, at home. Our house is old; built solid, for all that. When I was growing up, I always wanted Mam and Da to move out; get one of the little sunshine semis that were all the rage. I wanted a bathroom, see, and a garden at the back. Well, when you haven't a bathroom and only a yard that opens onto a jigger,

– er – alley, then of course you want a sunshine semi. But I was glad Mam didn't say yes. Them little new houses don't come with coal cellars, like Ruth Street's got. You should see it now! Mam said that since coal was rationed she could keep all we were likely to get in the yard, and she set to and cleaned that cellar and whitewashed the walls. Uncle Perce works in a timber yard, and he got Da some hefty props, cheap, to support the ceiling, and Mam put old lino down and old rugs and bought a kitchen table in Paddy's Market for two shillings – a big one. And Da shortened the legs so it was nearer to the floor and said that if the bombing got really bad, then they could all creep under it for extra protection. It's the best little shelter in Liverpool. I reckon they'll be safe enough, down there, even if Hitler decides to blitz Liverpool like he's doin' to London. But how did it go for you – and William?'

'Just fine. We went to church last Sunday – it being a national day of prayer, of course. William was in his uniform and the Local Defence Volunteers were all there, in theirs. I didn't do a lot of praying, Ness. I just knelt there and thought – about that tiny chapel and the hundreds of people who must have prayed there, over the years, for England.'

'Ar. By the way, I knew it'd be all right to send you a card; that it wouldn't drop on the doormat and get William upset like that letter did.' Best get off the matter of religion. 'I figured that you bein' the postie, you'd be able to slip it in your pocket! Was William bothered about your war work, by the way?'

'No, he wasn't. Never said a word. And when Nance Ellery asked him if he was proud of me doing my bit, he said that yes, he was! I – I think he had things on his mind, things he hadn't been able to leave behind him. I suppose he was preoccupied with that promotion he wants. Anyway, my week passed all right; quite enjoyable, in fact.'

Enjoyable, was it, Ness shuddered inwardly, when it

should have been wonderful and full of love and kisses and early nights and – and –

'Bags of passion, eh, Lorna?'

She bit on her tongue. She shouldn't have said that. What went on between a man and his wife who haven't shared a bed for weeks wasn't open to skitting, and she was glad she had the grace to blush at her clumsiness. Or at least until Lorna said, quite off-handedly,

'Oh, yes. Nothing's changed in that department. The usual twice a week!'

'Beg pardon?'

'William and me, I'm talking about. We always do – er – make love twice a week; always did, right from the start,' she smiled.

'But twice, Lorna? Never once, or three times? I mean – has it got to be *twice*?' She was missing something. She had to be!

'We-e-ll, William and I were very frank with each other before we got married. It was good of him to consider my feelings, though I knew what went on in the privacy of the bedroom. You learn a lot, you know, at boarding school.'

'Didn't know you'd been away to school,' Ness floundered, amazed at such directness.

'When I was thirteen. Maybe Grandpa thought it was best – that I needed a woman's hand. Gran had gone, you see, and I suppose he felt a bit awkward with a girl growing into puberty. And it wasn't exactly boarding. I wasn't all that far away; came home every weekend. Thought I'd told you. I was there for three years. Quite fun, really.'

'So you and William talked about – *feelings*?'

'Of course. He bought a book on the subject of – you know – and I put a brown paper cover over the jacket, just in case Grandpa picked it up. One of the things it said was that the average British man and wife made love twice a week – so that's what we decided on. Tuesday nights and Sunday mornings.'

'And that's it?' Ness had no answer to such directness, such ill-informed directness. Twice a week, come rain or shine, was it? 'And always in bed, of course.'

'Well, of course! Where else would you do it?'

Where else? Oh, Lorna, girl! Everywhere else you can think of! In bed – all right – but how about in a field in summer; how about on a hillside with not a soul for miles and only the clouds to see you? How about on a winter evening with a log fire blazing and the two of you on the hearthrug? It's good in the firelight, Lorna . . .

'Where else indeed?'

'Oh, I'm sorry!' Now Lorna's cheeks pinked. 'Here's me going on about things private and you not knowing! Sorry, love. Didn't mean to embarrass you. And it's quite nice, really – especially when every time you do it there's a chance of a baby.'

'So you still want children?'

'Of course. It's William who – who pointed out it wouldn't be very sensible, in view of the world situation.'

'Yes. Sensible, I suppose.' Flamin' Norah! How had they got onto the subject? And how could Lorna be so blind, think that what she and William shared was passion – or even love? And why, oh *why* was she sitting here, saying nothing when she longed to cry, 'Wrong, Lorna! Loving and being loved can be so different!'

'Anyway, now that you're unpacked and you and I are back to normal, shall we take a turn round the garden? The hens will have forgotten who you are, Ness. And I didn't tell you, William said the eggs were delicious boiled for breakfast though he won't admit, yet, they were a good idea. I think he still secretly winces to see them scratching on his lawn. Now – blackout is nine, tonight. Shall we see to the windows, then have a stroll outside before it gets dark? And something else I forgot! Glebe Farm's conchie came yesterday, late. And I shouldn't have called him that! He's probably a brave young man, sticking up for what he believes in. He's probably had to take a lot of flack, not wanting to fight. I haven't seen him yet. Goff Leaman told me – Goff's been giving them a hand whilst you've been away. Anyway, you do the upstairs blackout and I'll see to down here. And oh, it's so good to have you back, Ness!'

Which was a very peculiar thing to think when your husband has just gone back to his regiment and you should be aching all over, missing him, wanting him.

'Good to be back, queen.' All things considered, she really meant it.

'Good to have you back. Lorna said she'd had a card from you and that your folks hadn't been hit.'

'Great to be back, Kate, and yes – reckon I panicked more'n I should have.' Ness waited in the kitchen for early drinkings. 'But it was good seeing Mam and Da and Gran. I feel a bit better about things, now I've seen the air-raid shelter Da's rigged up for them.'

'I read in the paper this morning that London's copped it again. Eighteen nights without a break; two thousand killed and heaven only knows how many injured,' Kate murmured. 'Said they were starting evacuating mothers and children – again. But save my legs will you, Ness? Nip along to the dairy and get me a jug of milk? And whilst you're there, tell them I've made a brew and ask them if they want it in the shippon.'

Ness crossed the yard. Ahead of her the cow shed and the steady chuck-chuck of the milking machine. New-fangled contraption, Kate called it, though her husband and son had been set on buying it. Save hours of hand-milking, Rowley had argued, and he was right, Ness had to admit. And fingers crossed that machine would never break down because where would Ness Nightingale be, then? Stuck with her head against a cow's flank, trying to squeeze milk out of the dratted animal!

'Mornin',' she called from the dairy. 'Just come for milk and do you want your drinking here or in the kitchen?'

'Good morning to you, too.' The voice was unfamiliar and Ness turned in her tracks.

'Ooh! You – you're the –'

'The new farm hand. Michael Hardie – Mick.' He held out a hand. 'And you must be Ness.'

He was slim and dark, though his eyes were blue. He had a lovely smile, too. Look smashing in uniform, Ness thought. Pity he was a – a . . .

'Ness Nightingale – that's me.' She took the hand he offered. 'An' – an' I hope you'll like it at Glebe.'

'I already do. And they want drinkings in here. I was on my way to tell you. No sugar for me.'

He smiled again and Ness was struck by the way he looked straight into her eyes when he spoke, as if being a conchie came naturally to him and no way was he going to hang his head for it.

'Right, then. Three teas it is.'

'They want it in the shippon,' Ness said to Kate, 'and the – and Michael doesn't have sugar in his, he said.'

'So you met him? I know about his tea, and we call him Mick,' Kate smiled. 'He seems a decent lad, though Rowley and he have hardly exchanged a dozen civil words since he came.'

'Ar, well,' Ness tilted the teapot, 'that won't bother him a lot – Mick, I mean. I got the impression that people could take him or leave him. Pity, though, that him and Rowley can't get on with each other. This war might last a long time.'

'Oh, it's our Rowley. He's been giving Mick all the dirty jobs and it's grieving him that it doesn't seem to be having any effect. A nice-looking young man, don't you think? Tall, and handsome with it.'

'Nice enough,' Ness smiled, placing mugs on a tin tray, 'but I don't fancy him.'

And with that she whisked out of the kitchen, having

had her say and put Kate right – if Kate was matchmaking, that was.

'Got a bit of news for you, from Ladybower,' she confided on her return. 'Lorna's William told her, actually. Said there was a strong rumour in Army circles that Hitler has put off the invasion till next spring.'

'And how do they know what that Hitler's thinking, then? Rang up Mr Churchill, did he?'

''Course not! But it seems the tides aren't favourable any longer; not until next April, or May. And it could be a fact, because William said that a message had been picked up from Moscow and it said the RAF had bombed the German invasion fleet and destroyed a lot of it.'

'Now how do they know that? How can our lot tell what's being said in Moscow?'

'Haven't a clue. Seems we have operators listening all the time; just scanning the airwaves and writing it all down.'

'And do you believe it, Ness?'

'I'd like to – about Hitler's invasion barges bein' bombed and the invasion put off for six months. An' I'd like to think that when winter comes, there won't be so much bombing of London.'

'Ah, it's a bad do, there. I'm glad that Ainsty doesn't seem worth an air raid. And it isn't just the East End that's getting bombed. The posh bits are getting it, too – and Buckingham Palace has had another hit. Where's it all going to end, will you tell me?'

'Dunno, Kate. What I do know is that it must be awful to creep out of a shelter when the all clear goes and find your 'ouse is a pile of rubble.'

It was a terrible thought. There were times when she wished she knew how to pray, because sure as eggs was eggs, it was going to be Liverpool's turn to suffer, just as London was suffering now. Stood to reason. Liverpool was a port. Before very much longer it could be backs-to-the-wall time in Liverpool, too.

So count your blessings she reminded herself sternly, silently, that you live and work in a backwater called Nun Ainsty, and can sleep easy in your bed at night and not in an Anderson shelter or in the Underground in London.

'Ar, well – I'll be off to the shippon to give a hand,' she sighed, wondering as she crossed the familiar yard, how our lot could listen in to Moscow, and decided it was William, trying to sound important. It was at that moment that she looked up and saw ambulances at the back of the manor. Four of them.

'Kate!' She ran back to the kitchen. 'Come and look – over there! They've come, then, at last!'

SIX

Country people always said that St Simon and St Jude's day – at the end of October – marked the end of the fine weather. After the twenty-eighth, people said winter was near at hand, yet this first day of October was mild and bright with a sun rising golden above the far hedgerows.

The morning was still light because the clocks had not been put back an hour, but kept instead on summer time to give an extra hour of daylight to the benefit of all. And if this proved successful, the government said, then in spring clocks would be put forward an hour – as indeed they always had been – to give *two* extra hours of daylight. Which meant, Lorna calculated, that when summer came again it would be light until almost eleven. Quite sensible, really.

The sun threw a long shadow from the early morning sky, making cycle and rider look high and lean. It was going to be a beautiful day. Leaves were now a darker green, their summer tenderness long gone. Soon, they would yellow and wither and fall, yet the leafless trees would seem every bit as beautiful; bare branches and twigs laying like black lace on a winter sky of soft grey.

Yet on this sweet morning, summer still lingered. Elderberries, once the sweet-smelling flowers of July hedges, now hung in clusters of deep purple berries. This year they would be left ungathered; this year no one had sugar to spare for elderberry wine.

She stopped at the top of Priory Lane, balancing the cycle with the toe of her shoe, waiting for passing traffic, then crossed the road for Meltonby and the post office which would have been open – though not to the general public – since six, when the GPO van from York sorting office delivered letters, packets and parcels, which Mrs Benson would sort into three piles; Nun Ainsty's delivery, Meltonby's delivery and the remainder returned to the van driver (who by that time would have finished his mug of tea) for delivery to outlying farms and cottages.

At this time, usually, the night man – an ex-soldier from the Great War who looked after the switchboard from 8 p.m. to 6 a.m. – was also ready for his mug of tea before leaving for home and bed. By this time, too, the bundle of morning papers would have been left on the front step by the conductor of the early-morning bus, which arrived in Meltonby at six-thirty and departed for York, and all villages between, at six forty-five.

It was a cosy scene which Lorna enjoyed. She was a worker, now, and depended upon by the people of Ainsty for their morning papers, letters, and packets small enough to push through letterboxes. It gave her a feeling, if not of pride, then certainly of usefulness. It meant, too, that Mrs Benson, the night attendant and the driver of the post office van had become her friends. And friends were more important than ever in wartime.

She sorted her pile of letters on the long narrow table, starting with Ladybower House, then Mary at the White Hart, then the Saddlery, which always had more mail than anyone else – except now, of course, the manor.

The mail for the manor which since two weeks past was a military hospital, was kept to one side and secured with a rubber band. Eight assorted newspapers were folded and placed beside it. Since the twenty patients arrived, plus orderlies and a medical officer, the bundle was quite large and the order for newspapers grew larger each day.

She called goodbye, placed letters and packets in the front basket of her cycle and newspapers in the back basket, waved to the driver and conductor of the red bus, and pedalled off.

This morning, Lorna felt especially pleased because Pearl Tuthey at the Saddlery had been worrying about the lack of letters from her son Luke, away at sea. 'I just don't know what that ship of his can be up to, and that's a fact.'

Well now, Lorna smiled, Pearl would be more than pleased by five letters all at once from the younger of her twins on HMS *Illustrious*, and the worried look gone from her face. This morning, Lorna decided, she would bang extra hard on the brass knocker at the Saddlery to bring Pearl hurrying to pick up the post.

No doubt about it, she liked being Nun Ainsty's postlady; liked everything about her life except, she thought all at once serious, it would be nice to get more than one letter a week from William and just sometimes get a phone call from him, no matter how troublesome it was these days to get through. Just the occasional call, Lorna sighed, would be rather nice, though her husband had more to worry about than ringing up his wife. His army duties for one thing; his promotion not yet through for another. And he did write to her, actually, every day – something like a diary. Pity he saved it all to arrive each Saturday. Seven letters, if only to say *Terribly busy, darling. Take care, Love you, love you . . .* would have been much, much nicer than one chunk. But there was a war on and she was lucky; especially lucky when she thought, as she often did, about London and the terrible bombing in the south.

An Army truck with a red cross on its side passed her, hooting cheekily, and she raised a hand in greeting. They rarely saw soldiers from the manor. Most of them, she had found, were learning to come to terms with lost limbs, and how to walk again or make do with one arm when you'd always had two. Terrible, to lose a limb, she frowned, stopping outside the White Hart. No letters for Mary this morning. She pushed the morning paper through the letterbox, bringing the knocker down once.

She thought as she propped her cycle against the gatepost at the back of the manor, she could bet a shilling that the kitchen door would be opened by a cook with three stripes on the sleeve of his overall and that he would smile broadly and say,

'Here she is, the love of my life! And how are you today, sweetheart?' and to which she always replied,

'I'm very well indeed, sergeant!' returning his saucy grin with a wink. Only this morning she would have lost her shilling because the door was opened by a soldier wearing a white coat.

'Morning,' he smiled. 'You must be the sergeant's gorgeous postlady!'

'The love of his life, actually.' She tried hard to return the smile because she was a little taken aback – if aback it was – to be confronted with a tall, slim man with fair hair and a smile that would charm Martha Hugwitty's geese off the Green. When you'd expected a small, balding sergeant, that was! 'Er – letters and papers,' she said chokily, furious that her cheeks were blazing, annoyed he made no move to take them from her.

'Ewan MacMillan,' he said, offering his hand.

'Lorna Hatherwood,' she whispered, 'postlady and paperboy of this village. Er – how do you do?'

To which he smiled again and said it was nice to meet her and looked forward to seeing her again sometime. And since there was no answer to that she turned and ran, grabbing her cycle as if it were a long lost friend, pedalling furiously up the lane to Glebe Farm.

'*Well!*' was all she could think of to say.

* * *

It wasn't until she and Ness were eating supper that she gave an airing to the matter of the man in the white coat.

'I met Ewan MacMillan today. Looked like one of the doctors at the manor. Said he looked forward to seeing me again – and of course he will,' she said, eyes on plate. 'Well, I do take their mail, don't I?'

'Good-looking, was he? Scottish?'

'I – well, yes. I suppose he was, and he did have a Scottish accent. Why do you ask?'

'Oh, nuthin'. Only I was talking to him the other day – just in passing. He's a doctor. Was wounded at Dunkirk. Said he's doing light duties whilst he gets himself pulled together – his words, not mine. Walks with a slight limp.'

'Hadn't noticed . . .'

'So what was there about him that's making you blush, Mrs Hatherwood?'

'Nothing! Nothing at all! I – I suppose I was surprised to see him in the kitchen.'

'They call it the cookhouse.'

'All right. I was expecting the sergeant. Usually have a bit of a joke with him. And I suppose he *was* good-looking – if you like your men fair and blue-eyed.'

'Whilst you, of course, like them gingery with a moustache?'

'Of course! I'm a married woman, don't forget.'

Indeed, being a married woman entitled her to think that a man was handsome and had a lovely smile, because thinking didn't matter one bit when she was wearing William's ring.

'And being a married woman makes you immune to handsome men, Lorna?'

'Of course it does. I mean – I think Clark Gable is gorgeous. I can even wonder what it would be like to be kissed by him without a twinge of conscience.'

'Kissing Clark Gable would be a bit like kissing William.'

'Mm. Scratchy,' Lorna grinned, 'and please can we get off

the subject of men? I've got one of my own. You can have the handsome doctor, if you like.'

'Thanks a lot, queen.' Ness pulled down the corners of her mouth, deciding to let the matter drop, because if Lorna thought for one moment that being married made her immune to attractive men then she had better think again! The wedding ring she wore wasn't a magic charm. 'Cut me a slice of bread to mop up this gravy, will you?' she said instead. 'It's too good to waste!'

And Lorna, cheeks back to normal, was glad to oblige, asking,

'How's the new man at the farm?'

'Mick? He's fine. Never talks about it, though – him bein' a conchie, I mean.'

'Well, he wouldn't. He'll have done all the talking necessary. You know, he would have to face a tribunal to get out of the call-up. They give them a pretty tough time, I believe, ask them all sorts of questions. Aren't too particular what they say, either. I should imagine they think all conchies – conscientious objectors – are yellow. William says they ought to be horsewhipped.'

'Oh, ar? Surprised he says that. I mean – well, he's in a pretty safe job, isn't he?'

'William volunteered for the Pay Corps because he's an accountant and firing guns and jumping out of planes is a waste of his knowledge. I – I suppose there's sense in what he says.'

'Oh, absolutely.' Cold, calculating sense, Ness thought. 'And Mick Hardie's just as much entitled to his beliefs as your William is.'

'Which brings us back to square one again. So let's talk about you and why you never get letters from young men.'

'Because I don't write letters to young men.'

'But why, Ness? You're really attractive. Even in your overalls with muck up to the elbows. So why haven't you got a man of your own?'

'Because I was too busy getting on in me job. Career-minded, you might say I was.'

'Then why did you leave it to be a land girl? There isn't compulsory registration for women.'

'Not yet, there isn't.' Ness pushed back her chair, taking her plate to the sink. 'But there will be, and when the time comes I'll be glad I'm where I am instead of having to go into the Women's Forces or work on munitions. I wouldn't like to be sent on munitions. There's a great big factory out in the country from Liverpool. They say it could take over from Woolwich Arsenal, if that place ever got bombed. Wouldn't want to work there. And anyway, I can still do a bit of hair-dressing if I'm of a mind to – keep my hand in. Must say that you could do with a trim, Lorna – just the ends tapered. Get a towel for your shoulders and I'll do it now. And get my scissors, will you – top left-hand drawer of my dressing table?'

The only way, Ness sighed as she cleared the table and put dishes to soak, to stop Lorna talking about men and that every girl of twenty-one and over should be married or at least spoken for. And no way, Ness thought, was she ready to explain why she was twenty-five and still without a man of her own. Not even to Lorna.

Potato picking, Ness very quickly decided, was one of the worst jobs a land girl could be called upon to do. Worse, even, than hosing down the cow shed or barrowing manure. Potato picking caked your hands with cold earth, and damn near broke your back. Up and down, filling buckets; emptying buckets into a sack and your boots so clogged with earth that it felt as if they had lead soles.

At least she was not expected to manhandle the sacks. That was Rowley's job. He could lift one, then swing it onto the cart as if it weighed a pound instead of a hundredweight. Rowley's arms were muscled and tough. Mick's were not. Ness felt sorry for Mick because he hadn't got the knack, yet, of doing things the easy way.

She remembered when she first came to Glebe Farm and how heavy a forkful of hay seemed, until she had learned just how to hold it and how to toss it. There had been blisters, too. She wondered if Mick had blisters and knew that even if he had, he wouldn't complain. Not complaining, taking curtly-thrown orders, doing more than his fair share of dirty jobs was part and parcel of being a conchie and learning to stick to your principles, no matter who thought you had a yellow streak. For that, she gave him credit, even admired him.

'Hurry up, there!' Rowley yelled. 'I'm stood here waiting for sacks!'

'Then shift yourself, why don't you, and help us fill them!' Mick said quietly, stopping to straighten his back, looking directly into his tormentor's eyes.

'Because I'm the boss and you're the hired hand! And one word from me and you're out on your ear, and into the Army where you belong!'

'Now see here, you two!' Ness clumped over to the cart. 'Just stop it, will you. There's your mother coming with drinkings. Do you want her to hear you?'

'Don't much care if she does! And watch it! Don't forget we can do without you, too, Ness Nightingale!'

'Can you, now? Y'know, times like this make me wonder if you were born with it, or if you had to work very hard to acquire it,' she smiled.

'Acquire what?'

'The ability to be such a nasty little swine, Rowley dear.' She turned to greet Kate, still smiling. 'You're a sight for sore eyes. I'm frozen right through.'

'Poor lass. Taters isn't a nice job. But I've brought something to keep you going till dinner.' She took jug and mugs from her basket and a plate covered with a cloth. 'Dripping toast. Come on, then. Get it eaten afore it gets cold! You an' all, Mick! You look fair nithered.'

'Fair nithered means very cold,' Ness laughed. 'He'll learn the language, won't he, Kate?'

'If he stops long enough!' Rowley scowled.

'Oh, I'll be stopping,' Mick said softly, wrapping his hands round his mug. 'I'm getting to like it here.'

He smiled at Kate as he said it and she blushed with pleasure and said she was glad about that, because he was shaping up very well.

But Rowley said nothing. He was clever like that, Ness thought; careful of what he said in front of his parents, sly little sod that he was.

'Cheers, Kate.' She lifted her mug. 'Bless you!'

'I've put the basket and cups and things on the cart, Rowley,' Ness said when they had finished. 'Take them back will you, with the next load of potatoes?'

'Try *please*?'

'OK. Please, Rowley. That suit you?'

'I suppose so. And whilst we're about it, don't put me down in front of the conchie again – is that understood?'

'Perfectly. Next time I'll do it when there's no one around!'

'You know your trouble, Ness Nightingale? You fancy him and he isn't taking a blind bit of notice of you!'

'No, Rowley. I think he's a decent feller who's got principles and is man enough to stick up for them. And whilst we're on the subject I don't fancy you, either, so next time you smack my behind when I'm bending down, I'll land you a fourpenny one! Just keep your hot little hands to yourself – understood? And if you don't mind, there's work to be done so why don't you stop watching me and Mick fill sacks and pick up a bucket and do a bit of scratching yourself!'

'I heard most of that,' Mick said quietly when Ness joined him and began picking. 'Watch yourself, Ness. Don't get into trouble for me – OK? I appreciate you sticking up for me, but don't put yourself in the wrong with Rowley. I don't much care for him and I wouldn't trust him either – not with women.'

'Thanks, but I knew about him when I first came to Glebe

Farm. Kate didn't want a land girl to live in – that's why I'm with Lorna. She's got spare bedrooms, but not for female workers. Are you comfortable there, by the way?'

'No complaints. I've got a nice warm room – it's directly above the kitchen. I spend a lot of time there. Not right to intrude on the family.'

'And what do you do, all alone above the kitchen?' Ness grinned.

'I write home – read. Mostly I sleep. Farming's hard work. It's going to take a bit of getting used to.'

'Mm. I'm only just learning my way around after six months. Are you married, Mick? Got a girl?' She was amazed at her directness, amazed she could care.

'No to both. Fresh out of university. I registered at twenty-one with the rest of my age group and the powers that be let me finish my course first. Architect,' he supplied. 'Think there'll be a lot of call for blokes like me when this lot is over – the rate they're knocking things down, I mean. What about you, Ness? Married? Engaged?'

'No, to both.' She held up a ringless left hand. 'And I'm not lookin', either. And as for Rowley – I can take care of myself if he gets a bit heavy-handed. Thanks all the same, Mick. Don't get yourself in deeper than you are. He's got it in for you.'

'I know. And I can take care of myself, too. But thanks again, Ness – and I do believe we've got help,' he smiled at the approach of a scowling Rowley carrying a bucket.

He winked slowly, mischievously, and Ness winked back and grinned, and said not one more word.

Saturday, and last night a gale had blown fiercely, rattling windows, hurling itself against doors, stripping the last of the leaves from trees.

'Kept you awake, did it?' Ness asked. 'Well, at least there'd be no bombers out last night – ours nor theirs. Not in conditions like that.'

This afternoon they were very conscious of bombers. Not only of raids on London but, two days ago, a viciously concentrated attack on Coventry. It had left the city looking, one newspaper reported, like towns in the last war after prolonged shelling had lain them to rubble and waste. Even the beautiful old cathedral had been destroyed. The destruction and killing had been awful to come to terms with; the wanton razing of something so old had only added to the disgust of people everywhere; stiffened their need to fight back.

'Don't let's talk about bombing,' Lorna said softly. This morning her Saturday letter had arrived and she had left it unopened beside her armchair to be read and read again, later. 'Look – if you haven't got anything special to do this afternoon, how about we forage for wood? There's bound to have been a lot blown down. We could saw it into logs – eke out the coal ration.'

'OK by me. Think we'll meet Ursula?'

'Of course we won't! Martha told you, didn't she? Only lovers see her – or so I've been led to believe. Star-crossed lovers, like she and Dickon were.'

'She comes to give them a bit of hope, you mean?'

'Yes. Oh, *no*! Ursula is a myth, Ness. Nobody ever admits to actually seeing her, not even Martha. As far as I'm concerned, no one ever has! So how about putting your afternoon off to good use? The wood should be dry enough for burning in a few weeks; we can have a fire in the sitting room at Christmas then.'

'Christmas. Doesn't seem right, having Christmas when there's a war on – well, only for the kids. I bet there'll be a lot of bombed-out youngsters worrying how Santa's going to find them this year.'

'Oh, I think not even Hitler will stop Santa getting around, though there'll be precious few presents in the shops. Awful, isn't it, toys being classed a luxury like perfume and make-up and jewellery. Hard on children.'

'Hard on everybody, but let's get on with it. Like you say, at least we'll have a fire in the parlour at Christmas.'

They came on him without warning. He was leaning against a tree, sketchpad in hand.

'Cor! Thought you was the nun, hidin' behind a tree!' Ness gasped.

'Sorry I startled you, ladies. Am I not supposed to be here? Is the wood private?'

'No. If everyone has their own, I suppose it belongs to the manor.' Lorna was the first to gain her composure. 'We're here to scavenge branches.'

'And I'm sketching trees. Beautiful, aren't they, when they are leafless. Especially beeches.'

'An' here's me thinking you was a doctor,' Ness smiled, eyeing the pad. 'That's real good! You could do that for a living.'

'I once thought I would, but medicine won. My father is a doctor, my mother was once a nurse, so there was a bit of bias. I still draw and paint. Find it relaxing. But let me help you? Be glad to, if you wouldn't mind.'

And Lorna said she wouldn't mind at all and the more the merrier, and smiled at Ewan MacMillan without blushing. Which made her so pleased with herself that when the pile of wood was stacked to await sawing she said, 'That was very kind of you, Doctor,' and almost decided to ask him to share a pot of tea.

'No trouble. But could you call me Ewan? I already know your names are Ness and Lorna. I'd like very much if I could use them.'

And Lorna said that was fine, but not in public if he didn't mind, Nun Ainsty being such a small village and prone to gossip and undue speculation. And the young doctor said he was from a small Scottish village himself and understood perfectly.

It was then she almost changed her mind again. After all,

what was wrong in giving a cup of tea to a wounded soldier? With Ness as chaperone who could point the finger? Why, not even Nance Ellery!

Yet still she erred on the side of caution, because she remembered that her husband's letter lay unread, still, and had the grace to feel shame she should have left it unopened for so long.

She dismissed tea and wounded soldiers from her mind completely and thought instead of the letter with the Aldershot postmark.

Yet Ewan MacMillan, she was to find, was not to be so easily dismissed. The following Monday morning the kitchen door at the manor was opened not by the sergeant-cook but by the young man she had almost invited into her house.

'Oh! Good morning, Doctor! We meet again!' She laid letters and newspapers on the large, well-scrubbed kitchen table.

'And this time not by accident. Y'see, I've thought about it a lot since Saturday in the wood, and made up my mind to ask you about it – about the nun Ness mentioned. She seemed quite startled, for a moment.'

'Oh dear,' Lorna sighed. 'Sadly I told Ness about Ursula – the nun – and now she half believes it. And it's only fairy tales, truly it is!'

'So tell me a fairy tale? Sounds intriguing – especially when you deny it so vigorously.'

'I protest too much, you mean? Look – sorry, but I haven't finished the round yet. Could we leave it for the time being?'

'Of course. How long will you be?'

'We-e-ll, there's Throstle Cottage and the Saddlery and the pub . . .'

'Then I'll walk with you, if you don't mind?'

'No! I'll be quicker alone. But if you are determined to know, I'll pop back to the manor, tell you then. But don't get excited. Like I said, it *is* a fairy story – OK?'

'I'll be waiting.'

'Outside, if you don't mind.' She wasn't telling anything with the sergeant listening, nice as he was, because Ursula's story was open to ridicule by someone as down to earth as an Army cook.

'Outside it is. Ten minutes?'

'So?' Ewan MacMillan smiled on Lorna's reluctant return. 'Tell!'

'There's nothing to tell. Nothing concrete, anyway. Ursula Ainsty was a nun at the priory, and I don't know how the story has grown around her. Nonsense, as far as I'm concerned,' she said as offhandedly as she was able.

'Even though this village seems to have been named after her?'

'Oh – you know what villages are? Ursula's hauntings are just a bit of fun. Not to be taken seriously. My grandpa said it was the strong ale at the White Hart that caused her to materialize.'

'I'd still like to know, Lorna. Please?'

So, leaning on the fence that separated the manor yard from Glebe Farm paddock, she told him about the priory and the nuns and lepers and St Philippa's chapel; about Ursula and Dickon and the alleged visitations, none of which had ever been substantiated.

'Like I said,' she finished breathlessly, 'not to be taken too seriously. And only then if you are a star-crossed lover and pining unto death,' she laughed.

'Yet when she appears she's beautiful, with no trace of any deformities?'

'People say that's the way it is. But people would say anything, wouldn't they? They would want her to be beautiful. After all, it seems – *seems* – she had a pretty hard time just because of her lip and cleft palate – either of which mean little, these days. A witch's doing, people would have thought, four hundred years ago. I'm surprised the Prioress even took her in. Her father must have paid handsomely to get her off his hands, poor girl.'

'There you are, being sorry for her, and she only a myth!'

'I'd be sorry for her if it were true, but it isn't. And if you don't mind, Doctor – er – Ewan, I really must go. It's been nice talking to you again. Take care.'

'And you. And I, too, must fly. Three new patients expected any time, one of them with eye injuries – blind. That's three we've got.'

'How awful. I mean – a limb is bad enough, but not to be able to see again . . .'

'Like you say – rotten.'

'Yes. I nearly said I hope to be able to bring letters for your blind soldiers, but they won't be able to read them, will they? Nor to write back. But I'll see you around, I suppose, in my travels. And don't repeat the story about Ursula Ainsty, will you?'

'If you say so,' he smiled, raising a hand as she closed the gate behind her, standing to watch her go.

Not true about the nun? He shrugged. He'd never thought it was. He had put two and two together after Ness's surprised cry in the woods; nun, Nun Ainsty, a ruined priory. He hadn't cared if the wood was full of rampaging nuns. All he had wanted was to talk to Lorna again which was pretty damn stupid, considering he'd known all along she was married. Her wedding ring was the first thing about her he had noticed, after her incredibly blue eyes that was.

So tough, Lieutenant MacMillan. She's spoken for. Some lucky so-and-so got there first. Probably a fighter pilot with a chest full of gongs or a dashing marine. Wouldn't look twice at a limping medic with back and buttocks covered in scars from shrapnel wounds. Not very glamorous, getting wounded in your backside.

So count your blessings, Ewan old son. At least now you can sit down without a cushion under your hindquarters and sleep on your back again. You've got two of everything, as well, unlike most of the blokes in the wards and the new arrival who might never see again.

Yet somehow not even soul searching nor blessings counting helped a lot when you'd been smitten right from the start with so-blue eyes and a delightful blush. Not even when you told yourself you'd been one-hundred-and-one per cent lucky to get off those beaches with your life!

'Tough!' he said out loud, then made for the kitchen door.

'Tea, Doctor?' the sergeant-cook asked. 'Just made a brew.'

Tea. Civilized tea, in thick Army mugs. Down to earth with a bump.

SEVEN

The logs they had cut after the November gales were piled in a basket beside the hearth. A fire in the sitting room was a luxury; most families saved their coal ration for the kitchen if they were lucky enough to have a cosy kitchen with a fireplace, and closed parlours and sitting rooms until warm weather came again. But at Ladybower, Ness and Lorna sat snugly either side of the hearth, flames mellowing the old white walls and lighting brass and copper, polished lovingly by Minnie, making them remember if only for a little while, the way it had once been. Years and years ago, it seemed, in another world called peace.

'Shall we listen to dance music, or talk?' Lorna snuggled into a big saggy chair.

'Talk. Reckon since it's New Year's Eve we should think of all the good things; look back, sort of. Then say goodbye to 1940 and have our wishes ready for when the clock strikes.' Say goodbye, Ness thought achingly, accept that nothing could be quite the same again.

'We're supposed to make resolutions, Ness.'

'Yes, but who keeps them? Let's make it a wish, instead, and no telling if we want them to come true.'

'There isn't a lot I want, except what everyone wants. For the war to suddenly stop; for it all to have been a bad dream.'

'Well, it isn't goin' to stop, queen. Not just yet, anyway.

And it isn't a bad dream. For some, it's a nightmare.'

'The bombing? We haven't a clue how lucky we are, here. How much more can people take? It makes me feel guilty. Here's you and me, Ness, toasting our toes, yet there are people in shelters and huddled in the Underground and living in Rest Centres because they haven't got homes any more. I felt really badly done to when William wrote to say he wasn't getting a seventy-two-hour pass over Christmas after all, but it was fair, I realize, for men with families to be given the leave.'

'It solved a problem for me,' Ness was bound to admit. 'At least I didn't have to move out. And OK' – she held up a hand – 'I know it's best for me to move out, I just didn't want to. I mean, who wants to play gooseberry?'

'Well, he had a good Christmas and he's still got his weekend pass in hand. It was strange, for all that, for Boxing Day to be cancelled. Imagine – everyone told sorry, no bank holiday this year. There's a war on, so get yourselves back to work pretty damn quick! How can *They* just cancel Boxing Day?'

'Because *They* can do what they like, and *They* don't want factories to stop. I'll bet there were some places worked on Christmas Day. After all, the killing doesn't stop for Christmas, does it? Our own bombers were flying on Christmas Night. We heard them go.'

The killing, Lorna thought soberly. Air raids. Not one major city that wasn't taking terrible punishment from the Luftwaffe. Thousands of civilians killed. Thousands and thousands injured. The hospitals didn't expect time off at Christmas.

'I saw Ewan MacMillan in church on Christmas Day. I forgot to tell you.'

'And what did he have to say?'

Ness had not been to church, offering to help with morning milking and feeding the stock so Glebe Farm could at least have Christmas afternoon off.

'Say? He said "Happy Christmas", then asked me, since it was the season of goodwill to all, if I would volunteer to help occasionally at the manor.'

'You? Nursing? Why can't they get some Red Cross nurses?'

'Because it seems there's none available at the moment. And it wouldn't be nursing, Ness. They have three men there who are blind and can't read their letters or write to their families. They can't read newspapers, either. All they've got is the wireless – and each other. But Ewan said it's an all-male establishment and it might make a change to hear a woman's voice. That's why he was casting around for people to help; the orderlies are there to nurse, after all. Anyway, I said I'd try my best. A sort of thank you to God, I suppose, because I can see.'

'And would that be every day?'

'Don't suppose so. I won't be the only volunteer. He'll give me a ring, he said. Or he'd see me in the cookhouse one morning soon, on the round. I'd like to do it. A few letters and papers through letterboxes doesn't seem much of a contribution to the war effort.'

'You often talk to the doctor, don't you?'

'No. Only if he happens to be in the cookhouse when I deliver.'

'So it's pretty regular?' Ness persisted.

'I hadn't thought. I – I suppose it just happens that the sergeant makes a pot of tea at about the time I call.'

'And medical officers have their tea break in the cookhouse?'

'I don't know, I'm sure. What are you trying to say?' Lorna bent to place a log carefully on the fire, eyes downcast.

'Nuthin'. Only you two seem to bump into each other quite a lot.'

'Well, of course we do. Most mornings and sometimes in the village. He lives here, Ness. Can't I be pleasant to a man without anyone getting ideas? It's our duty to be nice to our soldiers and I shall find the time to read to the ones who can't see, and maybe write letters for them!'

'All right! I only said that –'

'*Said*! You think me and Ewan have a date every morning, do you, in the cookhouse?' Lorna demanded, pink-cheeked.

'Well, of course you do! You deliver the mail there every morning! And apart from the doctor, there's that nice sergeant who looks forward to seeing you! You make his day!' Ness grinned. 'And I was only kidding! My, but you don't half blush easily, Mrs Hatherwood!'

'Then you shouldn't tease. Things like that turn into rumours – especially in Ainsty! And we were talking about how lucky we are and –'

'Yes, and that Liverpool is getting bombed again but they're all right, at Ruth Street.' Ness forced herself to think of the safe snug shelter. 'And, hey! Talking about blessings!' she gasped as the phone began to ring. 'You get it!'

Lorna hurried to pick up the phone. 'Meltonby 223. For you, Ness. Think it's from Liverpool.' She closed the door behind her, hoping it wasn't bad news.

'They're OK,' Ness beamed, returning contentedly to her chair. 'Ringing from the bottom of the street. Only got three minutes, but Mum said they're all fine. They were on their way to the Sefton Arms for a couple of drinks and to see the New Year in – if Wailing Winnie doesn't go, that is. But it's thick fog, there, so fingers crossed they'll be all right tonight. Ar! Fancy them ringing, just as we were talkin' about them.' Her smile was wide and happy. 'And there's one blessing we've forgotten. What about our hens!'

'Oh my word, yes! I'm glad we got them, Ness.'

More than glad. They had had boiled eggs for breakfast, scrambled eggs on toast when the meat ration was used, poached eggs for high tea. A blessing indeed, now that eggs were to be rationed, together with jam and marmalade. And bananas not to be imported for the duration because they were not considered essential cargo and so were not worth transporting, not when ships' holds could be filled with wheat and sugar and meat. But imagine? No more bananas!

'Talking about hens, they're going to be threshing at Glebe in the New Year, so I'll try to get my hands on some gleanings – see if I can get some wheat and barley to eke the hen food out. There's bound to be a bit of spillage.'

Ness had never experienced the threshing of the corn harvest. She had helped gather it, pile it onto carts and stack it in the loft, but she had yet to do her first thresh. Rowley said it was a nasty, dusty job and there would probably be rats nesting amongst the sheaves of corn, so she had better make sure her trouser bottoms were tucked into her stocking tops.

'Glebe has been promised the threshing machine for the 6th, and we can only have it for two days, so we'll have to work like mad. Everybody who can will lend a hand. I'm quite looking forward to it.' Apart from the rats, that was.

The mantel clock chimed the half-hour. Thirty more minutes and another year would begin. Another year of war and of worrying again about spring tides and the invasion. Because as sure as made no matter, Hitler would try. He had rampaged through Europe so there was nowhere left for him to go but Britain. And the British were taking everything he could throw against them. Blitzkrieg, shelling, food ships sunk. It was getting so bad at sea that rumour had it, Ness said, that convoys were getting to Liverpool with half their ships sent to the bottom by packs of U-boats. But tonight they were counting blessings, so she said,

'Do you think the rations will run to a little pot of tea since it's New Year? And can we spare another log?'

'Yes to both,' Ness smiled, still happy about the phone call. 'But let's leave the tea till midnight, then we can toast the New Year. And what's to do with that phone? Twice in one night! Hurry up, Lorna. Bound to be for you, this time!'

'Darling! Oh, William, how lovely of you to ring. And a Happy New Year to you, too!'

Ness closed the door quietly, selecting the largest log. Lorna would be pleased, grateful her man had phoned – pathetically grateful. Ness did not like William, she brooded, eyes on the flames already licking the beech log. She hadn't even met him yet she knew he was selfish, pompous and full of himself. Dog ugly, too, and Lorna so beautiful she could have taken her pick from half the Riding. Which was part of Lorna's charm, she supposed, not knowing how attractive she was.

Take that doctor. Always there whenever Lorna was around. And now he was trying to persuade her to spend more time at the manor, reading to soldiers! And her so naive you just couldn't believe it!

'Ness! Aren't we just the lucky ones?' Lorna, cheeks flushed. 'Both of us getting calls and on busy New Year's Eve, too!'

'So how was he,' Ness felt bound to ask.

'Just fine! There was a party going on in the background. He seemed to be enjoying himself.'

'And he still loves you?'

'Of course he does. He actually said he did which isn't like William, especially in a room full of people.'

'Ar. Takes all sorts,' Ness acknowledged. Probably William had had one or two – got a bit reckless. 'So are you going to put the kettle on?' She glanced at the clock. 'Ten minutes to go.'

'Yes. You switch the wireless on, so we can hear Big Ben and know it's time.'

They wouldn't actually hear the most famous clock in the world, of course. Big Ben had ceased to strike, but a recording of its chimes was played over the wireless because to hear Big Ben was a comfort. Rather like Ness's Liver Birds, Lorna supposed. A sort of talisman; a promise that some things endured.

'By the way,' she called from the kitchen. 'What say we go to York, next week? *Rebecca*'s on at the Odeon.'

'Fine by me.' Ness switched on the wireless, waiting for it to warm into sound, adjusting the dial. A watch-night service was being broadcast from a church Somewhere in England.

'Made it!' Lorna laid the tea tray on the floor, covering the pot with a knitted cosy. You stirred tea, nowadays, then left it to brew – *mash*, as Yorkshire people said – for at least a minute. And when the amount of tea leaves you could spare was smaller than it ought to be, you stirred it some more, and gave it another minute.

The strains of the hymn faded, there was a small silence, then the first stroke of Big Ben; the first second of another year. 1940, with all its sorrow was gone. Now it was time to look forward and to pray, Lorna thought, as you had never prayed before, for a miracle. Just one wonderful miracle that would stop the invasion of this precious, bomb-happy island. Quickly she filled cups, smiling as she raised hers high.

'Happy New Year, Ness. And thank you for coming to Ladybower.'

'Happy New Year to you, too, and thanks for havin' me!'

'Do we want this?' The chimes had stopped, the news bulletin had begun. Lorna reached to turn off the wireless.

'Nah.' Ness sipped tea, pleased that Lorna had used her best rosebud china cups. 'Did you make your wish?'

'Of course. As soon as the chimes started. Did you?'

'Me, an' all!'

Ness had wished for the year to be over so she might forget. Not the calendar year, but *her* year; one of anniversaries.

'When I have seen a twelve-month through,' she had told herself so many times, 'I shall have turned the corner. It can't be as bad, after that. Not the second year around.'

So now she was beginning another year without Patrick – well, almost. In one more week, the remembering of hope gone; January 8th, when it really finally ended. So hang on till next Wednesday, Ness girl, and after that it won't hurt so much, nor the remembering. Because some things she was able, now, to recall without pain, whilst other things, she supposed, must always be there.

'More tea? Think it will run to it, if I squeeze the pot,' Lorna smiled, confident in her wish, glad the old year was gone.

'Please. And what time does the blackout finish in the morning, I wonder. Got to be up early.'

Ness shook open the paper, searching the pages which only numbered six, so it wasn't hard to find that curtains would remain drawn until almost nine in the morning. Still dark, she brooded, when kids set out for school. Awful, awful winter. Sun sets, the newspaper informed, at 4.59 p.m. Rises 8.38 a.m.

'The thing I shall remember most about this war,' she frowned, 'is the blackout. It isn't natural.'

'Nothing is natural about this war.' Lorna picked up the paper. 'But look at this, will you? Doesn't it make you proud? And even if this war goes on as long as the last one did, will there ever be a picture like that one?' She pointed to the headline: *St Paul's Stands Unharmed in the Midst of a Burning City*.

There, taking up almost half a page, was the dome of St Paul's Cathedral, rising from the darkness and smoke, etched starkly against a sky bright with flames.

'That's what it's all about, Ness. Hitler firebombs London. The second Great Fire of London they're calling it. A city blazing, yet that church is still standing. It's like an omen, isn't it? Everything around it an inferno, yet the cross on top of the dome stands out like a sign. Us against Them. Right against Wrong and oh dear, too stupid, aren't I?' Tears of love and pride filled her eyes. 'I do wish I'd been the one who took that picture. I wonder if he realizes how right and wonderful it is?'

'Reckon he does, queen,' Ness said chokily. 'That picture is us; it's Britain.'

'It is! Bomb-happy and stubborn. Aren't we the crazy ones? We're the backs-to-the-wall British who don't know when they're beaten.' Tears gone, she raised her teacup. 'So here's to our lot, 'cause we're going to win – one day, that is.'

'And God bless 1941,' Ness smiled, 'and all who sail in her! Is anyone coming to let the New Year in?'

'Don't suppose so. Nobody seems to bother here.'

'Well, they do in Liverpewl! Someone dark it has to be and he brings coal and bread and salt. And the ships in dock and in the river start up with their hooters and sirens. Doesn't half make a din. Mind, they won't be doing it now, till peace comes.'

'Peace. I often think not when it will be, but how it will be. People going crazy with happiness, like they did when the last war was over. Grandpa told me about it.'

'You thought a lot about your grandad, didn't you?'

'Mm. When he was ill – when we knew he wouldn't get better – we put the wedding forward; a quiet one in St Philippa's. He was very happy about it. He wanted me to marry William – trusted him completely.'

'Trusted?' Ness frowned.

'Oh, yes. You see, William was a Hatherwood, too. It was what first made Grandpa notice him. Seems that about four generations back, the great-great-greats were brothers. Made William and I ever so slightly related.'

'And how did youse two meet?'

'William came to the house, on business. He worked for Grandpa's solicitors – on the accounting side. Gave Grandpa some good advice about investing his money.'

'And it grew between you from there?'

'I – I suppose so. Grandpa wanted to see me settled before – well, he felt responsible for me, I suppose; wanted things sorted before he died. I think he actually chose William to take over from him. I knew he was manoeuvring us to the altar, bless him.'

'And you went along with it?' She'd gone and married William, Ness frowned, instead of having a good look around at what else was on offer.

'Why ever not? I liked him a lot and I knew the feeling was mutual.'

'Ar.' It would be mutual. William knew which side his bread was buttered; knew to the last ten bob how much Lorna would inherit. And the house. 'So you had your quiet wedding and your grandad died happy?'

'Yes. Peacefully, at the end. And I was happy, too. I wanted children, you see, and to bring them up at Ladybower the way it should have been for me. My mother never married my father.' She stared into the fire, poking the log to coax the last few flames from it.

'And?' Ness prompted.

'Well, I wanted my children to have a father who was around and most of all, I wanted them – *want*, when we have them – to be loved.'

'And your mother didn't love you?' Ness whispered. 'You were a poor little rich girl?'

'No. Just poor. When my mother ran off with her – with my father – there was no more contact with Ladybower, no handouts. And Mother did love me. I can dimly recall being hugged and kissed. The hugs and kisses came when she'd been drinking. When she was sober, she wasn't very nice, or so it seemed. And don't look so sorry about it. I'm not. Like I said, it's only vague memories. Gran and Grandpa took me. It was good, until Gran died suddenly. Boarding school after that, but I quite liked it,' she shrugged. 'No complaints. But here's me, going on and on. Sorry, Ness.'

'Be my guest, queen. After all, it's New Year. And thanks for tellin' me – trusting me, like . . .'

'And thank you for listening. Y'know, Ness, I'm glad you're here. I'd have been very lonely, with William away.

It's like having a sister.' She smiled tremulously, taking Ness in her arms, hugging her tightly. 'You won't leave, will you – even though William might sometimes get a bit stroppy about my lodger?'

''Course I won't, unless the powers-that-be say I've got to move on. I like it here. I'm stoppin'.'

Stopping, she thought when she lay snuggled in the fat feather mattress, hot bottle at her feet. And not only because she liked being at Ladybower; she liked Glebe Farm, too, and Bob and Kate. Mind, Rowley was a pain at times, but he couldn't help being what he was any more than Mick could help being a conchie. It took all sorts, didn't it?

A sister, she thought fondly. But that cut both ways. Ness Nightingale could use a sister, too, her being an only child. There were a lot of only children around. People hadn't gone in for big families in the bad years after the Great War; had learned a bit of sense.

She blinked herself awake and because these were the first hours of a new beginning she felt obliged to sort out her thoughts about Lorna, and what she had said about William. Funny, the way she had accepted it. Her grandad wanted the marriage and Lorna accepted it gladly, because for as long as she could remember, hadn't she said, there had been people to smooth her way, help her forget her early childhood.

Almost an arranged marriage. The Victorians had been good at it, but it shouldn't happen these days. A girl had a choice, now; even to choose unwisely. And Lorna had married unwisely, on that Ness would bet a month's pay; had taken the least line of resistance because she hadn't a clue about real love. Hell! Twice a week, regular! It wasn't natural, yet Lorna put up with it because innocent as she was, she had enough sense to realize that if she wanted children, that was the only way to get them! All very well, Ness sighed, all at once wide awake, but there would be a right old carry-on if something happened – like if Lorna really fell in love!

But she wouldn't. She was married to William so that, in Lorna's book, was love, and Lorna's sort didn't fall in love outside marriage. The priest's magic words took care of that! But what if something mind-boggling happened to make her doubt? What would happen to Lorna's safe world then?

Yet Ness was as sure as she could be that Lorna would be faithful, no matter what. The constant wife, true to her vows. Something hardly remembered from her past took care of that. Her mother had been a wild one; Lorna, though she might not even know why, wanted – *craved* – stability and respectability and she had found it in William. Nothing Ness Nightingale could do about it and anyway, who was she to judge; she whose mind-blowing love had ended a year ago, turning her world into a different place and her heart into a block of stone.

She sucked in a deep calming breath, closed her eyes tightly and stuck her face into the pillow. This was a new year, wasn't it; a clean, bright beginning, so be damned if she would weep!

EIGHT

Hanging on

1941

Larkspur Cottage, Ness had long ago decided, would suit her very nicely should she decide – when the war was over, that was – to take up residence in the country. And provided that Flora Petch should up sticks and leave it. It was a love of a house; very small but with a large, tree-filled garden. Upstairs were two bedrooms; downstairs, a small sitting room and a kitchen so big it had a working end and a sitting end and the most enormous cast-iron cooking range Ness had ever seen.

It was where she and Flora sat that February night in front of a crackling fire. Flora had been lucky. The November gales had uprooted an old tree and though sad at its loss, Nun Ainsty's district nurse had realized that before her lay not so much a stricken beech, but more logs than she had ever dreamed of when Jacob Tuthey got his saw to it. Logs to eke out the coal ration and fill her kitchen grate for the duration, or for at least three winters if you wanted to err on the side of caution.

'I'm packed and ready.' Ness stretched out her legs to warm her stockinged feet. 'You'll be glad to be rid of me.'

'I won't. I shall feel the quietness again, once you've gone. Mr Hatherwood going back tomorrow, is he?'

'Mm. It should only have been a week, but he had a pass

left over from Christmas and he tacked it onto his long leave. Seems he can do that.'

William, Ness thought testily, seemed able to do anything he set his mind to.

'Decent of you to move out,' Flora smiled.

'Decent of you to take me in. We'd have been in a right old mess, if you hadn't. William didn't want –' She stopped, hand over mouth.

'Didn't want what?' Flora broke the embarrassed silence.

'We-e-ll, he wasn't best pleased to find a land girl in his spare bedroom, but it was either me or evacuees – or so Mrs Ellery said.'

'But they haven't sent us any more evacuees.'

'No, and if Lorna had known that, I don't suppose she'd have panicked and taken me in. And I know I shouldn't be saying this, but she took me because William doesn't like children in the house. Seems he's not very fond of them.'

'Strange. I'm sure Lorna wants a family. She told me herself. Said I wasn't to retire until I'd delivered her children. Some hopes of retiring with a war on and anyway, I don't want to stop working yet. I never had babes of my own, so delivering other people's is very special – and watching them grow up, too.'

'Why did you never marry – or shouldn't I ask?'

'Ask away, Ness. It's no secret that my young man was killed in the last war. Never wanted anyone but Joe. My life is in Ainsty now. This cottage goes with the job, but I've set my eyes on the middle almshouse.'

'The one the artist lives in now? Funny feller, him. Seems to come and go.'

'He works for the government – something to do with a film unit – propaganda. No one knows, exactly, but it's his cottage I'm hoping to get, one day. But about Mr Hatherwood. Are you sure he's the reason for you moving in with me? I thought you were doing it so the two of them could be alone when he's on leave.'

'That's what me an' Lorna tell people. But when he found I was at Ladybower, he told Lorna she was to get rid of me pretty damn quick, but she wanted me to stay, and let him think I'd moved out. Mind, he knows now that I'm there for the duration and Lorna got a telling off for going behind his back, so it's best for me to move out when he's on leave. You won't repeat anything I've said, will you? I wouldn't want Lorna to think I'd been talking behind her back.'

'Not a word. I'm the district nurse, don't forget. Some of the things I see and hear you wouldn't believe, so I know I mustn't gossip. I'm sorry about Lorna getting into trouble for taking you in. Surely it's up to her who has her spare room. The house does belong to her, did you know?'

'Yes, but between you an' me, Flora, William is fond of his own way. He didn't like it when Lorna had her hair cut and she wouldn't dare let him see her with lipstick on. He acts like he's her father sometimes.'

'He's certainly a lot older than she is, and inclined to be staid, at times. And why the fuss about her hair I can't understand. It looks lovely, short.'

'Thanks. Was me that cut it.' Ness blushed with pleasure. 'Was a hairdresser, see. Any time you want your hair done, you've only got to ask.'

'I'll remember that. And since we're being thoroughly nosy tonight, what made you give up hairdressing?'

'Oh – I suppose I knew I'd have to register sooner or later, so I did it sooner. And I haven't regretted it. I like it here.'

'And is your young man overseas, Ness?'

'Haven't got one.'

'You haven't! An attractive girl like you?'

'No. Heart-whole and fancy free.'

'Sorry.' The nurse's cheeks pinked. 'I – I'm not being inquisitive or anything, but I'd have thought that young man at Glebe Farm was worth a second glance.'

'You can't mean Rowley,' Ness gasped.

'You know I don't. The other one – he seems a pleasant young man.'

'Mick? I get on well with him, but –'

'But he's a conscientious objector, is that it?'

'Nah. He's got his reasons and he's taken a lot of stick over it. I respect him for that.'

'I respect him, too. People look down on conchies and say they're worse than the Nazis, but I wish Joe had been one. He'd be alive today, if he had. But it was different in the last war. Conchies – if they dared to admit it – were put in prison without the right to appeal, and soldiers could be shot without a trial. At least this war isn't quite so savage.'

'It's bad enough. And they didn't call up women in the last war.'

'True. By the way, Ness, have you registered?'

'My age group hasn't come up, yet when it does it won't make any difference, farm work being classed as a reserved occupation. Lorna registered last week with the under twenty-fours. They told her part-time work isn't enough; that she'll have to find something more.'

'And is she worried?'

'Not her! William thinks that doing papers and letters is beneath her, but she loves it. The first time she's ever had a job. She'll have to work full time, though, her not having a family. She'd like to keep up the deliveries and find something for afternoons. You'd think that would satisfy the labour exchange? Trouble is, there isn't a lot of work around here – apart from her reading to soldiers at the manor, and that doesn't count. But she'll find sumthin'. Since that husband of hers joined up, she's learning to stand on her own two feet.'

'Good for her! Now – shall we listen to the wireless? It's Henry Hall at seven-fifteen. Or would you like to read?'

'I'd rather listen in.' Ness was not an avid reader, but dance music set her toes tapping. 'And shall I make us a cup of cocoa?'

'Would you? Thank goodness cocoa isn't rationed – yet. And thanks for the milk you've been bringing. I'm only allowed three pints a week. Kind of Kate to send it.'

'She didn't. I nicked it. Farm worker's perks, sort of. They've got churns and churns of it there. Won't miss the odd pint,' she shrugged. 'Kate wouldn't mind, if she found out, though Rowley might make a fuss. Nasty little piece, that Rowley.'

'And much too interested in the opposite sex – if village talk is anything to go by! But we're gossiping . . .'

'I know, but it's nice, innit, Flora?'

'Provided it doesn't go outside these four walls.'

The grey-haired, middle-aged nurse smiled as she laid more logs on the fire. She would miss Ness when she went back to Ladybower, but for all that, she was glad Lorna had company. She was fond of her, had watched her grow from childhood into a shy girl who blushed easily and spoke in whispers. Had been glad, she recalled, when Lorna had married, even though it was remarked upon at the time that the bridegroom seemed a little set in his ways. But it was none of Flora Petch's business, she thought, as she swept ash from the hearth.

'Hurry up!' she called to Ness at the other end of the kitchen. 'I'm switching on now.'

They sat in the drowsy warmth of the fire as dance music played softly; two women, each without a man of her own. Small wonder, Ness thought, they got on so well; Flora who had never wanted anyone but her Joe, had accepted a life without him. And what of Ness Nightingale? She didn't know. She really, really didn't.

'Cheers!' She lifted the white china mug, arranging a smile on her lips. 'And thanks again for havin' me!'

'I'm back!' Ness closed the outside door and swished the blackout curtain over it. 'Gawd! It's freezin' out there! Didn't throw me hat in first. Knew I'd be welcome.'

'You'd have been welcome last night,' Lorna flung, button-mouthed. 'William went back yesterday afternoon. Imagine – driving all that way in the blackout!'

'A day early? But why?'

'Haven't a clue, nor had he. The phone went yesterday morning – a woman, asking for William. She said, "Good morning, ma'am," to me – very servile, I thought – though she had a bossy voice.'

'And did they say why he had to go back early?' Ness hung her jacket on the door peg, then hurried to the fire.

'If they did, I wasn't told. The Army doesn't have to give excuses. Anyway, he packed his kit, had a spot of lunch, then left at half past two.'

'Was he fed up?'

'No. "Orders is orders", was all he said.'

'Something to do with his promotion, maybe?'

William's elevation to the rank of captain had been a long time coming.

'Hardly likely. I think he's given up on another pip, but he still grumbles that the job he does at Aldershot should carry higher rank with it. All I got to know was that the woman who phoned was an ATS sergeant and that she's some kind of secretary there. And let's face it, it was only a day off his leave. Nothing for me to get upset about when there are bombed-outs sleeping in the Underground, still, and no let-up on the air raids. And our own bombers flying ops most nights and not all of them coming back. Who am I to complain, Ness – or William, for that matter?'

'Well, there'll be no bombers goin' anywhere tonight – ours or theirs – unless they can see in thick fog! Glad you're not too upset about the leave.'

'Would be all the same if I was. And having leave in February can't be a lot of fun. William just seemed to sit by the fire all day, reading. Would have been better if he'd been able to get outside, into the garden. Or go for walks. And me getting up so early for work didn't help. He calls it my little job, though he's going to hit the roof when he finds out I've got to find another one.'

'You haven't told him you've been to register at the Labour?'

'No. I meant to, and that part-time work isn't enough when you haven't got young children. He doesn't like me delivering letters and papers. That's why I said nothing about registering or having to go to the labour exchange next week. He just won't accept that a married woman should go out to work. It's so old-fashioned, with a war on.'

'And are you sure you didn't have words, and that my name wasn't mentioned a time or two?'

'No Ness, it wasn't. Honestly! Your name never came up at all. And we didn't have words, though something was wrong, I knew it.'

'But why? Because the weather was lousy and he couldn't get out and his promotion hasn't come through and the alarm woke him every mornin' at half past five? Pity he hasn't something to really worry about like them poor sods gettin' torpedoed in the Atlantic!'

'Something *is* worrying him, Ness, but he isn't telling me.'

'And you didn't ask him?'

'How could I?'

'How could you? You're his wife and you've a right to know if anything's wrong. And what's more, he should tell you!'

'Well, he didn't, but I'm right, and I know it.'

'Then you aren't goin' to get to the bottom of it by worrying and imagining all sorts of things. Best thing you can do, girl, is to write to him; ask him outright what has made him so quiet. Let him know he's got you upset. Better still, ring him. Book a call now, then you've got a better chance of getting through. And when you do, tell him that – oh, you don't need me to tell you what to say! Just get it off your chest, clear the air, like.'

'If – if you really think I should . . . ?'

'Think? I'm sure you should so shift yerself, queen, and get that number booked, 'cause there'll be no living with you till you do!'

After supper they sat beside the kitchen fire, grateful for its warmth that drab February night, Lorna looking at the clock every few minutes. Ness determined that if she checked that clock with her watch just once more, she would hit the roof. And it was at the exact moment she opened her mouth to order Lorna to keep her eyes off the clock and didn't she know that a watched pot never boiled, that the phone rang.

'My call! Meltonby 223,' Ness heard her say breathlessly, before closing the door quietly. Then she crossed her fingers, closed her eyes tightly and wished with all her heart that William was around; that the precious three minutes would not be wasted in trying to find him.

'Would you believe it!' Three minutes obviously not wasted and Lorna, pink-cheeked and happy. 'That was William phoning *me*! And nothing is wrong, Ness – at least, nothing *I've* done!'

'Then thanks be for that.' Ness uncrossed her fingers. 'Am I to be told, then, or is it private?'

'Not really. It threw me a bit, William deciding to ring me, then I took a deep breath and asked him if anything was worrying him. And he said there was.'

'Ar . . . ?'

'Well, it's to do with the war, I'm almost sure. He couldn't tell me exactly – only hint at it. Perfectly understandable, I suppose. Careless talk over the phone . . .'

'So what do you *think* he was hinting at?'

'I can't be sure, Ness, but it's something that is happening down there, and he has to keep quiet about it. We-e-ll, that's what I was given to understand. And he said sorry his leave hadn't been a bundle of laughs, exactly, but he'd had things on his mind.'

'Things he couldn't tell anyone – not even his wife?'

'Well, how could he, on the phone? Telephones are listened-in to, monitored.'

'All right – but why didn't he say sumthin' when he was on leave, when you were in bed – pillow talk?'

'I don't know why. All I know is I was imagining all sorts of things; even got to thinking something was wrong between us.'

'And there wasn't – isn't?'

'Of course not. And I'm as sure as I can be that he knows something about the invasion and can't tell me.'

'Oh, *no*! I'd got around to thinking that fingers crossed it wasn't going to happen, that Hitler had decided to sink all our food ships and starve us out instead.'

'I don't think so. Of course Hitler will try to invade us when the weather is right. And William knows something. Either he's been told or he's found out by accident. It is possible – invoices for stores and where things are being sent . . .'

'Invoices? I thought your feller was in the Pay Corps and that he looked after soldiers' wages.'

'He is also an accountant, Ness, and he did say that the job he does should carry higher rank with it.'

'So you're goin' to start worrying yourself half to death about the invasion, again? Listen, queen – when it comes, *if* it comes – it won't be Nun Ainsty the tanks and parachutists make for. *If* it happens it'll be London and important places like ports and railway centres that'll get the worst of it. You worry about that dratted invasion as if it concerns you personally!'

'No, Ness. I just don't want Germans goose-stepping all over London and I don't want them in York, either. I don't want them here at all. Full stop! I happen to love my country!'

'And you think because I come from Liverpewl that I don't? Listen, girl, I love the bones of that place. All right

– so it's a port and it's got slums and it's been bombed to smithereens. It was never the prettiest of places at the best of times, but it's my city and I care about it like you care about Ainsty! I don't want them *Jairmans* in my neck of the woods, either!'

'Ness, I'm sorry.'

'Then don't be. We're all bothered about bein' invaded, but Hitler hasn't even tried yet, and who's to say that if he does we're goin' to throw up our hands and give in without a fight?'

'I said I was sorry. I won't talk about it any more.'

'And you're not to think about it, either! We're all in the same boat and we'll start worrying when there's sumthin' to worry about! A couple of hours ago you were worrying 'cause you thought your feller had gone all quiet on you, and now you know he hasn't we're back to the invasion again. Had you even once thought it mightn't be anything to do with that? What if William has come across sumthin' to do with Army accounts, somebody on the fiddle and he doesn't know what to do about it. Had you thought about that, eh?'

'Well – no.'

'Then give it your serious attention, queen.'

'Yes. And I'm sorry, Ness. I always seem to get things wrong.'

'So stop your worrying and go and cancel that call you put in – tell Mrs Benson you don't want it.'

'I will! Right now!'

Get things wrong, Ness brooded. Oh no! Not Lorna. It was William who was acting moody and William who was to blame for Lorna's worrying. Big things on his mind, had he, and letting the poor girl think he knew something about the invasion! A lieutenant being entrusted with such top-secret knowledge or even being in a position to know about it? Didn't make sense. If the government knew when Hitler was going to invade, they wouldn't make it known to a lieutenant in the Pay Corps!

All right. So maybe she was being nasty-minded? Maybe she didn't like William, anyway, and was happy to think the worst of him? Maybe William did have something that was bothering him, but no way was it about Hitler invading Britain in the spring and it was rotten of him to let Lorna think it was!

'Got it sorted with the exchange?'

'I did,' Lorna smiled, closing the door behind her. 'So what say we build up the fire and forget this awful night and the fog and –'

'And the war and the invasion? Just for tonight, shall we?'

'Yes, and remind myself that nothing should really matter except that William comes home safely.'

'Exactly!' Ness laid logs carefully on the fire.

'And just to cheer us both up, did you know there are snowdrops out in the garden, and snowdrops mean that winter is nearly over.'

'Ar. Pretty little things. Y'know, I can't wait for warm days again, though I wouldn't call fog awful. Bombers don't fly when there's fog – neither theirs nor ours – and fog means I don't have to worry about Ruth Street tonight.' Ness pushed off her slippers and tucked her feet beneath her, snuggling into the old, sagging chair. 'And might I say that it's good to be back. It was smashin' at Larkspur Cottage, but it's great to be – be –'

'Home?' Lorna whispered, all at once happy again.

Ness stood to count to fifteen which she always did to accustom her eyes to the blackout, then blinking rapidly – which also helped – she walked carefully to the gate.

Six steps, and she should be at the pillar box. You counted, too, so you knew approximately where you were until you could pick out dark shapes and lighter shapes and begin to walk with more confidence.

She gazed past the almshouses to the east, where a lightening in the sky told her that the darkness would soon be gone;

that soon, heavy curtains could be drawn and the blackout would be over for another day. Until five o'clock tonight, that was, which was really four o'clock if *They* hadn't messed about with the hour. Then tonight at five would come complete, compulsory darkness again, with never a sliver of light showing, nor car headlights. The blackout was unnatural and dangerous. Apart from people getting killed, Ness brooded, it was the worst thing about the war. People walked into lampposts and into walls and missed their footing at the kerb edge because of it. Drivers of cars and lorries, who could not see without proper lights, caused even more accidents. Yet the blackout was a necessary evil which, she was bound to admit, did more good than harm.

Yet for all their efforts, no one could black out the moon, Ness grinned cheerfully, and for almost one week every month – clouds and fog permitting, that was – the moon shone brightly and was welcomed by all, especially by bomber crews who could find their way to a target, it was said, with no bother at all. On the other hand, it had to be admitted that patrolling fighter pilots could see bombers more easily; could fly out of the moon and make a killing with ease. Mind, it was a two-way thing. Our fighters did it to *their* bombers every bit as easily.

She dug her hands into her pockets then stood stock-still as she heard the click of an opening gate.

'Flora? It's Ness . . .'

'Hi, there,' came the voice out of the darkness. 'Going to work? Me, too. I'm away to Meltonby to see Dr Summers – try to get a word with him before morning surgery. And Ness! Something's just hit me. Didn't you say Lorna was needing work?'

'Not so much needing as having to. Why?'

'Only that Doc Summers could do with a bit of help, and it wouldn't be far for Lorna to go – better than having to travel to York. Think she'd be interested?'

'I'm sure she would. If she can tell the bods at the labour

exchange she's found herself another job, they'll leave her alone, I shouldn't wonder. What would she have to do? I don't think she'd be very keen on blood.'

'Nothing like that. I think it would be more on the clerical side – like keeping accounts and sending out the doctor's bills once a month. And answering the phone.'

'Then I'll tell her. Thanks for the info and mind how you go, Flora. See you!'

Well now, didn't things have a habit of working out, given time? Mornings for the GPO, afternoons at the surgery in Meltonby, and Lorna gainfully employed to the satisfaction of His Majesty's Government and the war effort. All nice and neat and on her doorstep with hardly any travelling. Lorna would be relieved – provided she was suited to it, that was.

Come to think of it, Ness considered as she reached Glebe Farm, the only person who wouldn't be pleased was William, who wouldn't like it one bit; a thought that made Ness smile. Very wickedly.

'So you've arrived! Mother wants you, in the kitchen!'

'And good morning to you, too!' Ness flung back. 'What's eatin' Rowley,' she asked of a red-cheeked Kate.

'Nothing – oh, it's the milking machine broken down, and he's just been trying to get the mechanic who isn't answering.'

'Oh, my Lor'.' This was it, the day she had dreaded, the day Glebe Farm would realize that the land girl was only a Liverpool hairdresser who couldn't milk a cow. 'I – I'm afraid I –'

'Drat! I'd forgotten we never got around to teaching you. Never mind. It isn't the end of the world. I'll go out and give them a hand; you take over here. The kettles are on. Do toast and jam and a jug of tea, will you, and bring them to the shippon?'

'I'm sorry, Kate . . .'

'But it isn't your fault, lass. Nothing to it. I was brought up to hand-milking, never did like those machines, newfangled things. But Rowley was all for it and got Bob on his side. Mind, they save a lot of time – when they aren't breaking down, that is.'

'What must you think of me – a land girl who can't milk.'

'And I, Ness Nightingale, can't cut hair nor perm it, either! So see to the drinkings for me and when you bring them in, someone will show you how it's done. You'll pick it up in no time. No butter on the toast, and saccharin in the tea, don't forget!'

And with that, Kate was gone, doubtless looking forward to helping with the milking – the old-fashioned way, of course!

Ness tied on Kate's pinafore then cut bread into thick slices, thinking that farming wasn't all romps in the hay and collecting eggs or even bottle-feeding an orphan lamb. Farming was threshing which was always done in winter and was cold and dusty and noisy. It was dangerous, too, as she had quickly realized when gazing down from the top of the stack into the flailing thresher below. And farming in winter was hedging and ditching; hedges to be cut with a razor-sharp slasher, ditches to be unblocked so field drains could better empty into them. She and Mick had had a week of it, with hands numbed, eyes streaming from the cold north-easter that seemed never to stop blowing. And now the milking machine had broken down and Ness Nightingale couldn't hand-milk!

She jabbed long-handled forks into two slices of bread, holding them to the glowing coals, feeling the heat sear her face and not caring. At least, she thought, her year was over and she could no longer think, 'This time, last year . . .' because on January 8th, the day the threshing machine had clanked and bumped out of the stackyard, she had told herself that all her sad rememberings must go with it.

January 8th, when her last link with Patrick was broken,

and her mother telling her it was for the best. That was when she knew she must make a fresh start; get away from Liverpool and everything that reminded her of the way it had been, before Patrick. And as luck – or maybe it was fate – would have it, she had been within ten paces of the labour exchange; found herself asking in a strange voice if they had any work of national importance that a fully-fledged hairdresser and hairstylist could do and if possible, not in Liverpool, please?

'Have you considered the Women's Land Army?' the clerk asked, one eye closed in a wink, the other on the bright red nails of the woman who sat on the edge of her chair and bit her lip nervously. It had been said as a joke, but there the joke ended when the fully-fledged hairdresser replied,

'As good as anythin', I suppose. Does it count? Is it work of national importance?'

And the clerk assured her it most certainly was and if she really wanted to give it a try, had she realized the work would be hard and at times heavy, and almost certainly would take her away from home.

Away from Liverpool. That had clinched it.

'Tell me more,' Ness Nightingale had said, though on looking back she had to admit that no warning had been given about working under a blazing summer sun or freezing half to death, up to the ankles in icy ditchwater.

Mind, no one had told her, then, about Nun Ainsty and Lorna and Ladybower and a village so small she had known every living soul in it within a couple of weeks. No one had told her, either, about the utter joy of a May morning or listening, as dusk came, to birdsong in Dickon's Wood.

'Oops!' Quickly she turned the bread on the forks, knowing that even the horrors of hand-milking were as nothing, when she could enjoy being a land girl and living deep in the country and sometimes, now, could think of Patrick and not weep inside herself.

* * *

‘Drinkings!’ Ness called, sniffing the familiar shippon smell; a warm, cow-dungy, milky smell, mixing in with the scent of wheat straw that reminded her of harvest time and threshing time, and made her think that when – oh, please, *when* – she could milk a cow by hand, then maybe life as a land girl in Nun Ainsty was something she would be glad she had chanced upon.

She set down a plate of jammed toast, four large mugs and an enamelled jug of tea, and was about to slip away to the safety of the kitchen when a voice called,

‘Not so fast, Ness Nightingale! If you can’t milk a cow, now’s the time to learn!’

‘Leave it, lad. Not now. Some other time!’ came Bob’s voice from the far end of the stalls.

‘Oh, no. Now is as good a time as any.’ Rowley poured tea from the jug and took a slice of toast. ‘Get yourself a stool and a milking cap and give your hands a good scrub. There’s soap and water in the dairy, and be sharp about it!’

It was then, very briefly, that Ness wished she were back in the over-scented, over-hot salon in Liverpool, then she stuck out her chin, straightened her shoulders and thought that if someone like Rowley who was as thick as two short planks could milk a cow, then so could Ness Nightingale. She had comforted herself with the thought that her first year of memories was over, so why not start afresh by learning to hand-milk a cow, show the arrogant little sod who stood there chewing toast with his mouth open, that she wasn’t just a pretty face!

‘Won’t be a minute,’ she said softly, then walked head high to the dairy and the bucket of soapy water, the milking cap and stool, asking herself why shouldn’t today be the day on which she became a *real* land girl? Indeed, if she wanted to go the whole giddy hog, why shouldn’t this be the first day of the rest of her life!

‘Right!’ Rowley said when she returned, thick black hair tucked into a milking cap, hands warm from the soapy suds. 'You can start on this one – get yourself settled. Hold the bucket between your knees or the silly beast will kick it over.'

'OK. So how do I do it?' Ness gazed at the heifer, running her tongue round her lips, telling herself it would be all right.

'Do it? You take a teat in each hand and pull. That's all there is to it.' He was clearly enjoying himself. 'I thought everyone could milk a cow.'

'Sorry! We got our milk in bottles in Liverpool. I never found the need to learn,' Ness hissed. 'Now, will you please show me how?'

'Hey! Hang on!' Mick stood beside them, arms folded. 'Don't you think it would be better if you started Ness off on one of the older cows? That one there has not long calved down. She's never been hand-milked before – might be skittish.'

'And that's your considered opinion is it, conchie?' Rowley stuck out his jaw. 'You know all about it, then?'

'Enough to know it would be better for her to learn on a more placid beast. The one I'm milking now would be fine for you, Ness.' He smiled comfortingly, picking up her stool, leading her to where an elderly cow munched contentedly on hay, lazily flicking its tail. 'Now sit yourself down, make yourself comfortable and relax your hands. I've already milked out two quarters – you do the other two.'

'These teats?' Ness hardly dare touch them.

'That's right. Wrap your fingers round them – imitate the sucking of a calf.'

Ness squeezed gently and a squirt of milk hit her shoe.

'That's the idea. Now the other one. And direct it into the bucket this time.'

She did it again, tilting the udder with her right hand. There was a ping as the milk hit the bucket; and from her left hand came a similar sound.

'Fine! Slowly and gently, Ness. Rest your forehead on her side . . .'

Ness looked down at the froth of white milk. The old cow munched on, and the bucket began to fill as Ness relaxed her hands and arms. She was doing it! She was getting milk out!

'OK?' Mick smiled.

'Yes, thanks. How will I know when to stop?'

'When there's no more milk; when she stops letting it down. I'll leave you to it, then?'

'Thanks, Mick.' She could hardly bear to look up from the bucket, so elated did the sight of the milk make her. 'I – I've got the hang of it now.'

Almost mesmerized, she listened to the rhythmic hiss as the milk hit the bucket. She'd got it. She damn-well had! She let out a sigh that was a mixing of contentment and relief and a trembling hope that this really could be the first day of the rest of her life. And oh, just wait till she wrote home and told them she could milk a cow. Mam would fall off her chair laughing!

Rowley walked past with a full bucket of milk.

'I'm doing it! I've got the hang of it, Rowley!' she called from the depths of the cow's warm, earthy flank.

But Rowland Wintersgill walked on to the dairy with never a word.

Ness sang softly as she worked up to the elbows in soap suds, deciding that not even scrubbing clean the scrambled egg pan was a chore when you could milk a cow; could milk *three* cows. Well, two and a half to be strictly fair, since Mick had had a hand in the first.

'My word. Who's the happy one, then?' Lorna smiled as she dried plates. 'Mind, you've learned something I couldn't do. I'd be terrified to milk a cow.'

'Oh, there's nothing to it. Just relax your hands, you know – be gentle and –'

'Yes, I know. You've already told me – twice. And how understanding Mick was.'

'Sorry. But hand-milking was the one thing I dreaded – them findin' out, I mean, that I couldn't do it. It all came right, though. That number twenty-one will always be my favourite cow, after today. And that's sumthin' else, Lorna. I once thought cows had names, but at Glebe Farm they have numbers. But I'll never think of my first as a number, for all that. For me, that old cow will be Buttercup. And I wasn't going to tell you this, but I was so mad about it I nearly exploded!'

'Don't tell me, then, if it's private.'

'Oh, that's the last thing it was, Lorna! A right old carry-on there was in the yard, afterwards. Rowley chucking his weight about!'

'Giving orders again?'

'No. Giving down-the-banks to Mick. Said he'd pushed his nose in when he shouldn't have.'

Ness related the matter of the young, skittish cow and how Mick had intervened.

'So do you think Rowley wanted you to milk the young one because he knew it would be restless?'

'Not at the time, I didn't. It was just another cow. But then Mick told me to finish the one he had started, showed me how. Anyway, when we'd finished and got the milk through the cooler and into the churns, Rowley as good as told Mick not to interfere with his orders again; said he was only the hired hand and how come a conchie knew so much about milking cows. And Mick said he'd learned years ago, on his uncle's farm, so Rowley wanted to know why he hadn't gone to his uncle's farm to be a conchie.

'"Because my uncle died suddenly and my aunt sold up," Mick said, so I went up to them, 'cause Mick looked so mad and Rowley was goading him, calling him conchie all the time. I told them to grow up and stop acting like a pair of idiots.'

'And they stopped?'

'Yes, but it was only because Bob Wintersgill came out of the dairy, and Rowley was too crafty to be caught rowing, though he was the one who started it. He's a little creep.'

'And Mick?'

'Mick kept his cool, but only just. One of these days he's goin' to give Rowley a fourpenny one if he doesn't stop being so bluddy arrogant.'

'Then let's hope it doesn't come to blows, Ness, though I know how you feel. Rowley's just a year older than me, so I know him better than you might think. And I agree that he's a spoiled brat. He being an only child, Bob and Kate didn't realize till it was too late how much they'd indulged him. Well, that's what Nance Ellery told me. A few good spankings would have done him the world of good, she said. But forget Rowley Wintersgill. I'd far rather talk about working for Doc Summers. Think I'll ring him now. Surgery is usually over by seven.'

'Then off you go. I'll finish the dishes. And good luck, girl!'

Ness wiped the pan, then swirled the suds round the brown glazed sink, listening as they gurgled away. She hoped the job hadn't already been filled. Five afternoons a week would suit Lorna nicely. Mind, William wouldn't be best pleased to know his wife had two jobs, but few things seemed to please him. Only if his promotion came through and Lorna let her hair grow long and frizzy again, would he be anything near pleased. And for the land girl to vanish into the distant sunset, of course!

But to heck with the Williams and Rowleys of this world, she thought, pushing them from her mind, thinking instead of Mick Hardie and his kindness, wishing he were not a conchie and open to taunts and downright rudeness. But if he hadn't been a conscientious objector, he wouldn't have come to Glebe Farm and she was glad he had, because he was a decent man who had the courage to stand up for what he believed in.

'I spoke to Doc Summers,' Lorna slammed shut the kitchen door. 'He seemed pleased I was interested. Had given up on finding anyone, he said. I'm to go and have a chat to him about it tomorrow.'

'And you are pleased about it, too?'

'You bet I am! He said that working for the GPO and for him should satisfy the labour exchange. And before you ask, there won't be blood,' she grinned. 'Strictly clerical and being in the surgery afternoons when he's doing his calls so I can answer the phone. I've a feeling that the job is mine, if I want it. Doc Summers knows me well – won't want any references. Oh, my goodness, this has been quite a day, hasn't it?'

'Not half! Me milking cows, you finding yourself another job!'

'So why don't we drink to it? There's still some sherry in the dining room – it'll grow whiskers if we don't see it off soon. What say we raise a glass to success?'

'And another to all our fighting men and women everywhere?'

'And if there's any left after that and we're still sober, we'll drink to peace!'

'A very good idea, Mrs Hatherwood!' Ness liked Lorna even more when she threw caution aside and forgot the staid and sober William for a little time. If only, she thought cunningly, he could be sent overseas for a couple of years what a new, confident wife he might come back to! 'Well, get on with it,' she laughed, shaking such improbable thoughts from her head. 'Away with you and get the bottle, then we'll build up the fire and forget all about the war!'

Surely, for a little while, it might just be possible?

Ness stood aside to allow a van to drive through the gateway; distantly from the shippon came the *clunk clunk* of the repaired milking machine. She closed her eyes and made the most earnest wish that it would not break down again for the duration. But if ever it did, Ness Nightingale would be better able to cope!

'Morning, Kate. My, but that's a sweet sound for a cold morning.'

'Aye. The mechanic has just gone. I gave him half a dozen eggs; tickled pink, he was. Happen next time he'll remember the eggs, and come a bit quicker!'

'That's bribery and corruption, Mrs Wintersgill! Mind, if you could squeeze a mug of tea out of the pot, I'd be prepared not to report you to the Ministry of Food!'

'It's very weak . . .'

'It's hot. That's all that matters.' Ness wrapped her fingers gratefully around the thick mug. 'Well, just four days to go an' it'll be March. Thank heaven we've seen the last of the winter.'

'Don't be too sure. I've known it snow in April and you can't be certain you've seen the last of the frost till May – not around these parts, anyway.'

'Well, the daffodils are pushing through and before you know it, it'll be May and I'll be going on leave. Put in my request last week and had word from the hostel, to check it out with you.'

'May? Can't see it being a problem. The potatoes'll be planted by then, and the root crops. Would be as good a time as any. Going home, will you be?'

'Ar. Good old Liverpewl. It's taken a fair few air raids, but nothing as bad as London.'

'And you won't mind going there – risk being bombed?'

'Nah. They've got a good shelter at Ruth Street. Would need a direct hit, fingers crossed, to do them any harm. Leastways, that's what I'd like to believe.'

'We're lucky, aren't we, in Nun Ainsty?' Kate offered jammed toast. 'Mind, there's always the risk of the aerodromes getting bombed. Quite a lot of them around these parts, and if you remember what a terrible time the fighter stations in the south had last year – well, I just hope it doesn't happen up here.'

'Well, them Nazis are getting a bit of their own back now. I saw our new bomber yesterday. Lorna pointed it out to me. A Halifax it's called and much bigger than the old Whitleys. Talk has it that they've got two squadrons of them at Linton.'

'Oooh. Should we be talking like this?' Fearfully Kate dropped her voice to a whisper. 'Careless talk, I mean.'

'Well, I saw ever so many. Reckon if me and Lorna saw them, then so did lots of other people. Lorna said they can carry more bombs and fly a lot farther than the Whitleys.'

Very good at planes, Lorna was. Could tell you, when a Hurricane flew over, if it was a Mark-one or a Mark-two. Mind, it was all the rage now. Even small boys had deserted train spotting for plane spotting.

'Those poor lads were out bombing again last night. I'm grateful the war hasn't taken Rowley from us. I'd be worried half to death if I thought he might be flying in the blackout over Germany.'

'Well he isn't, and he won't be,' Ness comforted and all the time wishing Rowley could be sent on a raid or two – to Berlin or the Ruhr that were thick with searchlights and night fighters. Knock the wind out of his whistle, that would! 'And supping tea isn't going to get the war won. I'll be off to the shippon! Ta-ra, Kate!'

And she was off, with Kate watching her go, wishing Rowley could find a nice girl like Ness, wondering why she never talked about her boyfriend because surely she must have one – or two! But it was something you didn't ask, Kate sighed; wasn't wise to enquire where someone's boyfriend was – just in case . . .

And why, she thought irritably, had they let another war happen? Surely her generation had seen it coming? Seen it coming and swept it under the mat because it was beyond their thinking that only twenty years after the slaughter in the trenches another war could break out.

The first time, Sarajevo had been the excuse; this time it was Hitler marching his soldiers wherever the fancy took him! Why couldn't this country have minded its own business for once and let Europe get on with it, she thought, red-cheeked with indignation.

Then she took a steadying breath, closed her eyes and offered up thanks that her son was safe at Glebe Farm for the duration. A naughty lad at times, but he was her only child and she loved him. And oh, drat the war and drat Hitler and drat those submarines that were sinking our food ships in the Atlantic. And whilst she was about it, drat a lot of silly old men in Westminster who had called Mr Churchill a warmonger because he'd warned them about Hitler and how this country would be at war again, if they didn't watch out.

And now Mr Churchill was in charge of a country at war again, and people listened to every word he said; every challenge and insult he hurled at Hitler. A funny old world it was, and no mistake!

'Let me do that, Ness.' To Mick Hardie's way of thinking, milk churns were not for women to heave around.

'Thanks, but I've got the hang of it fine.' You learned to tilt them at an angle, then roll them. A terrible strain on the arm muscles, especially if they were full, but she had long ago come to the conclusion that there were two ways of doing things on a farm – the right way, or the hard way, and Ness Nightingale was a quick learner. 'Anyway, I've finished. Going inside, now, for drinkings and a warm by the fire. You coming, Mick?'

'Yes – but whilst we're alone, is it any use asking you for a date? You said you like dancing and –'

'No, Mick. Thanks, but no.' She felt her cheeks flush because her refusal came much too glibly. 'I – I don't go on dates, any more.'

'There's someone special, Ness? Is that it?'

'No. No one at all! But I – I –'

'But you don't go out with conscientious objectors?'

'Mick – no! I like you a lot, I really do. But I can't tell you why and – and –'

'And there's no reason why you should,' he finished, smiling gently. 'Sorry. I jumped the gun, didn't I? If I say I won't ask again, can we still be friends?'

'Of course we can! We get on well together and oh, dammit, it's all too involved! But I promise hand on heart that it's nuthin' to do with you being a – well, nuthin' to do with your beliefs, it truly hasn't. So shall we shake hands on it?'

'Gladly!' He took the hand she offered, holding it for a little while, smiling into her eyes.

'Fine,' she whispered croakily, because she had hurt him and he didn't deserve it. Mick Hardie was tall and good to look at and when he smiled, as he was doing now, it was enough to charm the birds from the trees and make your stomach go *boing!* into the bargain. And this wasn't the first time she had wondered what it would be like to kiss him or to dance with him, but since Patrick . . .

'Right!' He was taking her arm, jolting her out of her remembering, whilst she was telling herself that men like Michael Hardie didn't grow on trees and she was a fool to even think of refusing him. Yet a fool was born every minute, didn't they say, and Ness Nightingale was one of them.

All at once she wished she was at Ladybower, sitting opposite Lorna at the kitchen table. Lorna would understand, if she could tell her that was. But she couldn't tell Lorna any more than she could tell Mick. There were things you had to hold inside you, learn to live with, and her feelings for Patrick was one of those things. It was called taking it on the chin – growing up. Either way, it sometimes hurt, still; hurt a lot.

* * *

After years of walking past it with little thought and being used to its forlornness and neglect, Ainsty manor had all at once become very familiar to Lorna, part of her daily life. Mornings she delivered newspapers and letters to the back door; four afternoons a week she entered by the front door to read newspapers and letters to the three soldiers with bandaged eyes; wrote replies to those letters, too.

She pushed open the heavy, iron-studded door. 'Afternoon, Lance Corporal,' she smiled to a medical orderly. 'Just on my way to the snug.' She said it as a courtesy because he knew where she was going; to a small room at the end of the stone-flagged passage with *Snug. Private* on the door in faded gold script. Those words intrigued Lorna, made her wonder whose small private place it once had been and where he – or she – was now. Wondered, too, if that someone knew it now housed three iron beds, three wooden chairs and three lockers. And, most important, a table on which stood a wireless which was almost always switched on.

'Afternoon, Ma'am,' he said correctly, though there was a smile on his words because he liked the softly-spoken woman who didn't look a day over seventeen. 'I have a message from the MO – said he'd be obliged if you'd wait here for him – not go into the snug ward. Care to take a seat, Ma'am? He said he wouldn't be long.'

Lorna sat carefully on the rickety folding chair, gazing up the wide staircase to the tall window on the half landing, wondering why Ewan wanted to see her. Nothing serious, she hoped.

'Hullo, there. Hope you haven't been waiting long? And why the frown?'

'Frowning, Ewan? Oh, I – I was thinking that beautiful staircase looks so neglected.' She said the first thing that came into her mind. 'That old oak needs feeding – oiling and waxing . . .'

He looked at her, eyebrow raised. To him it was a set of

stairs leading from the ground floor to the attics and part of an old house he was doing his best to keep reasonably warm and clean and turn into a decent billet for wounded soldiers. And this afternoon he had no inclination to dwell upon the condition of the staircase.

'Look – can we talk, Lorna? There's no one in the surgery – I won't keep you long.'

'Sure.' She followed him to a room, on the door of which hung a notice: *MO, Please knock and wait*, and he reached up and turned it over to *Engaged.*

'We shouldn't be disturbed here.' He offered a cigarette packet, and she shook her head. 'Mind if I have one?'

'Please do.'

He looked tired, she thought, and his hair was in need of a trim. She watched him inhale deeply then said,

'When did you last have leave, Ewan?'

'Lord knows! I suppose they'd give me some if I kicked up a fuss, but I can't get away till we get another MO. And MOs are a bit thin on the ground these days.'

'So you are completely in charge here?' A lieutenant, as William was, who probably deserved promotion a whole lot more than her husband did.

'Afraid so. The bod who helped open up this place with me was drafted to North Africa months ago. But can we talk, Lorna? It's about Private Jones.'

'Alun?' She liked the young soldier who would be twenty-two in March. 'It's bad news?'

'Afraid so. You'll know that the three with eye injuries had a visit from a consultant a few days ago?'

'Y-yes?' Of course she knew. She knew more about the three soldiers with bandaged eyes than most. Didn't she write their letters, read out the replies? Didn't they all – Alun especially – trust her with their confidences? 'You've heard?'

'Last night, on the phone. There was written confirmation this morning. It isn't good, for Private Jones.'

'And the other two?'

'They'll be going to a special unit for surgery and from what was said last night, there's a fair chance they'll get some sight back. They've shoved off to the rest room. Jones is on his own and in need of a shoulder to cry on, I shouldn't wonder.'

'He knows? How did he take it?'

'How would you expect a lad of his age to take it?'

'Pretty badly. But what can I say that will help?'

Freckle-faced Alun Jones; tall and thin and seriously in love.

'I don't know what you'll say. I left him in a state of shock, but the anger will follow. Best if you were just to listen, at first. But you don't have to do it, Lorna. I thought, though, that you are nearer to him than I am and anyway, right now he needs to hear a woman's voice. Certainly not mine. He must hate my guts, after what I've just told him.'

'I'll go now.' Reluctantly she walked to the door. 'I'll do my best, Ewan. Listen, you said?'

'Yes. He's normal enough to want to curse the whole world right now. Leave the door open, though, if you'd like . . .'

'I'll be all right. And he's entitled to be angry. It must be terrible to be so young – and in love, too – and be told he won't ever see again.'

'He's got a girl?'

'Mm. I don't think I'm breaking any confidences if I tell you she's called Rebecca and it's pretty serious between them. In her last letter she said she was hoping to get time off to visit him. Hell! I hate this war!'

'Join the club, Lorna,' he said softly, opening the door for her. 'And thanks. I'll be somewhere around the place. Let me know how things go, will you?'

Lorna tapped on the ward door, then walked in. The young soldier was laid on his bed, an arm over his face. She wondered if he were sleeping – or even pretending sleep – so she said softly,

'It's Lorna. Can I come in?'

'Might as well.'

'Want to talk?'

'Talk! I'll say I want to talk!' He elbowed himself into a sitting position. 'But most of all I'd like to come face to face with the swine who did this to me – just him and me, Lorna!'

'Want to tell me about it?' She drew out a chair, grating the legs on the floor so he would know where she was sitting. 'Was it a bomb?'

'A shell. Our lot had made it to the beach – Dunkirk. I heard the thing coming, didn't know whether to freeze or to run. Then it fell so near I felt it hit the ground. Did you know that when something falls that close, you've got a better chance? So near, see, you escape the explosion – it passes over you. But the blast from it got my eyes. Not one shrapnel wound. Just my eyes. A pain, like a knife going into them . . .'

Unspeaking, she reached for his hand, holding it tightly, feeling the rage in him as he struggled to speak.

'Sorry, but I'm crying, see? Under these bloody bandages, Lorna, I'm crying like a girl. Not much of a man, eh? Not going to make much of a husband, either. Becky would be better off without me.'

'No Alun, she loves you!'

'But how's it going to be when she knows I'm blind – *really* knows?'

'She half knows it already. She knows I'm writing your letters – reading out hers to you.'

'All right! But we never once said I wasn't going to see again!'

'No, because we thought there was hope . . .'

'Well, now I know there isn't, so the sooner she knows the better. And I'm not going to give her the chance to marry me out of pity. I've made up my mind. I'm going to tell her it's over between us – finish it!'

'You can't! I – I won't write the letter!'

'Please yourself. I'll find someone who will.'

'Alun! You're bitter and I don't blame you. So would I be. Rebecca wants to come to see you. She's trying to get time off – she said so. At least give her the chance to make up her own mind. Please don't ask me to write that letter – not till you've calmed down a bit, thought it out.'

'I don't want her here! Oh, she might say she wants me, still, but I won't be able to see the pity in her eyes, will I, never be sure? It's for the best, Lorna.'

'Listen! I can't tell you what you should do. Before so very much longer you'll be leaving here I shouldn't wonder, and you and I won't ever see each other again. But for a long time, Alun, I have been your eyes; you and Becky have trusted me with your confidences and I know how much you love each other. Doesn't that give me some say in all this?'

'No, it doesn't. It's got to be my decision and the way I feel now is that I'd never be quite sure she hadn't married me out of pity – supposing she ever said she would, that is.'

'Pity! What has pity to do with it? You can't turn that girl's life upside down just because of your pride! Because that's all it is, Alun Jones, pig-headed pride!'

She was shaking now, because even as she was hurling the words at him, she knew she was wrong. But words, once spoken, cannot be taken back. They stay for ever in the memory, there to be recalled to taunt and to hurt. And he was right. She had no say at all in the matter. It was his life and Becky's and who was Lorna Hatherwood to offer an opinion?

'I'm sorry,' she whispered chokily when the silence between them had become too hard to bear. 'Forgive me, please? I'll write the letter, if you still want me to.'

'I don't want to, Lorna.' He sounded like a small, frightened boy. 'But it's got to be done. I've made up my mind, see, and there's no going back. So let's get on with it, eh?'

'Very well.' She took pen, ink and paper from the locker beside his bed. 'I won't interfere. I'll write exactly what you say I must. But before I do, there's something I've got to tell you. After Saturday I won't be coming any more. I've got an afternoon job with the doctor in Meltonby. Sad, isn't it, that if you ever think of me in times to come, I will be the one who wrote the letter you didn't want to send, and not Lorna who came to like you as a friend – and who was proud to be your eyes and Becky's voice.'

'*Duw*, Lorna, I've come to like you, too, and I'm grateful for what you've done. I've often wondered what you look like, though I'll never know now. Mind, the MO says you are beautiful; blonde hair and a lovely smile, so I've got my own picture. But let's get on with it. Ready? Dear Rebecca. I want to –'

'Not Becky *cariad*, like always?' she whispered. *Cariad*. Darling.

'No. Not any more. And you said you wouldn't interfere.'

'Very well.' Close to tears, she dipped the pen into the ink bottle.

'You're late!' Ness was peeling potatoes when Lorna opened the kitchen door.

'Yes. Been saying goodbye to two of the lads – they're leaving tomorrow. Wish I didn't have to go in any more. It was awful, today. Bad news for Private Jones.'

'Oh, *no*! So what's to become of him? Will he have to learn basket weavin' and things like that?'

'I don't know, Ness. All I do know is that he wanted me to write to his girl and break it off.'

'And you did?'

'No choice. And they were so in love. He'd talk about her. So beautiful, he said, and such tenderness in his voice whenever he said her name. Said he was sorry he didn't have a photo to show me, but photographs aren't a lot of use, he said, on a blind man's bedside locker. Oh, but this is a terrible war!'

'There now, queen. Don't take on so. Tears aren't goin' to help your soldier, are they?'

'No. Alun cried, though. Into his bandages, he said.'

'Ar, hey.' Ness offered a handkerchief. 'Now see here, you can't take on the sorrows of the world!'

'The world? What do I know of the real world – me, who's always had someone to look after her? Got it all on a plate, didn't I – this house and all Grandpa's money. And William. What about Alun who's never going to see again and Becky, who's a nurse in Swansea. Only she can't get time off to see him because of the bombing there. And now he's written, breaking it off!'

'You mean *you* wrote, Lorna, and now you're all upset.'

'If I hadn't, someone else would have done, and why am I going on like this? He'd made up his mind, he said, and I can't play God in their lives, can I?'

'No you can't so dry your eyes, queen, and blow your nose and listen to some good news instead. My leave is on. May first for one week!'

'But that's when William's next long leave is due.'

'I know. Ness Nightingale isn't just a pretty face! So off you go and feed the hens whilst it's still light and I'll see to the veggies. And cheer up, girl!'

Cheer up? Lorna measured wheat into a bowl. Couldn't play God? But the trouble was she just had, and what the outcome would be didn't bear thinking about. But she hadn't had a lot of choice and besides, it was done now.

She drew a calming breath, letting it go in little huffs, throwing grain into the hen run. Play God? But wasn't there a war on, and didn't people have to do it all the time?

'Four eggs, Ness.'

Lorna laid them carefully on the table, then smiled brilliantly as if her conscience was crystal clear. And it wasn't . . .

Things, Lorna was to think later when she had got over the shock of it, sometimes have a peculiar way of turning out – like bumping into your conscience at your front gate. Because that was what happened this morning. She had awakened, said 'White Rabbits' because it was the first day of a new month and new-month days had a wish on them. Childish, but there was a war on and anyone who wasted wishes didn't deserve to have them to come true. So she sat up in bed, crossed her fingers, whispered the magic words then said out loud, 'I wish for – for . . .'

All manner of wonderful things had come to mind like Hitler being dead and the war ending next week; or maybe a couple of ounces on the butter ration was worth a wish, and a spot more extra sugar? Then all at once deciding to leave it in Fate's hands she said,

'I wish for something good to happen today,' and even as the wish floated out and up and away, she hoped it wouldn't be something like catching sight of a celandine or a wild, white violet. Usually, to see those little flowers lifted her heart, told her that spring was really on the way, but with a white-rabbit wish surely she was entitled to expect something a little more out of the ordinary?

Yet this far, not even anything ordinary had happened. She had set out for Meltonby as the sky began to lighten into yellow and grey streaks, passing no one on the way there who might even remotely be the bearer of something good. And wasn't she being rather childish she demanded sternly as she looked carefully right and left at the top of Priory Lane. She was a grown woman now, a married woman, and believing in new-month wishes was like believing in fairies, or Father Christmas.

There had been nothing out of the ordinary, either, as she sorted Nun Ainsty's letters in the little room behind the post office. Nothing for Ladybower for herself or Ness and no letter for Private A Jones bearing the familiar Swansea postmark. But Rebecca was probably too tired even to think, because in her last letter she had written she was in the middle of a week of late shifts; particularly harassing when there were air raids to contend with, and patients to comfort and help to the safety of the hospital shelter – those who could be moved, that was.

She frowned at the woman in the mirror who arranged her hat at an angle. Funny, when you thought about it, how much she knew about Alun and Rebecca; remarkable that she, Lorna Hatherwood, should be allowed to see into the souls of two people – as if she really was God, she thought, pulling on her second-best gloves. And she continued to frown into the mirror, because now she was going to the manor to say her goodbyes; to the lance corporal who sat at a desk in the hall and answered the phone and ringing bells; goodbye to the room with *Snug. Private* on the door and to Alun, alone inside it. She hoped no more young men with bandaged eyes would occupy the two empty beds, though she would know nothing about it because this was the last of her visits. On Monday, at one o'clock, she would begin working for Doctor Summers; one till five-thirty, six afternoons a week with an hour extra on Mondays, because that was his extra-busy day.

She would still deliver letters and newspapers to the back door of the manor, of course; would still see the nice sergeant-cook and sometimes Ewan, sleepily drinking his first cup of tea. She was glad she would still see him, because he worked too hard, looked much too tired and needed an eye keeping on him! Ewan MacMillan, who three days ago had told a young man he would never see again. She set off down the path and was pulling shut the front gate when a voice called,

'Excuse me please, but can you tell me if this is Nun Ainsty? No signposts, see.'

'This is Nun Ainsty,' Lorna smiled.

'Then thank the good Lord for that! Couldn't have walked another step. Been travelling all night! Is it far to the Army hospital?'

'It isn't. As a matter of fact, I'm going there myself. Let me take your case – you must have carried it from the top of the lane?'

'I have. Funny, but it didn't seem all that heavy when I got off the bus!'

'Come far?' Lorna asked.

'From South Wales and two hours late that train was. Not that I'm complaining, mind.'

'You've come sick visiting?' There was something in the lilt of the voice that told Lorna she might well have come from Swansea. But this couldn't be Alun's girl, because Rebecca was tall and dark and very beautiful and this young woman, short and inclined to plumpness, had hair that could only be described as mousy, and in need of combing, too. And her lips were pale and cracked with a faint lipstick line around the edges. 'You couldn't, perhaps, have come from Swansea?'

'Right first time! There's clever!'

'No – easy, really. You speak exactly like one of my soldiers – Private Jones.'

'*Duw*! I don't believe it! Alun Jones, is it? Then you've got to be Lorna the Letter – well, that's how I always think of you. The lady who writes my young man's letters, are you?'

'Lorna Hatherwood.' She held out a hand. 'And you are Nurse Rebecca Pryce?'

'That's me. Small world, eh? There's good to meet you. Thank you for being so kind to my Alun.'

'Well, if this doesn't beat cock fighting – as they say in these parts,' Lorna laughed. 'And since we sort of already know each other would you like to come to my home, have a cup of tea and a rest first?'

'I could do with a bit of a wash. That train was so crowded and hot and dusty, too. But now I'm so near to Alun, I'd rather not, if you don't mind. Haven't seen him since they moved him up here. But there's one thing you could do for me, please? Could you tell me if anybody does bed and breakfast in Nun Ainsty? I came up all of a rush – before they changed their minds at the hospital and said I couldn't have leave, after all. I've not had time to find somewhere to stay.'

'Oh, dear – there's no one in the village does B and B . . .'

'Well, never mind. There'll be an Army Welfare Officer at the hospital; he's sure to be able to help.'

'I'm afraid there's no one like that at the manor,' Lorna said softly. 'That convalescent home is run on a shoestring and the medical officer seems to have the lot on his plate. But in the absence of a Welfare Officer, could I offer you a bed? You'd be welcome to stay at my place, Rebecca. No trouble at all.'

'You're sure? You'd take a stranger into your home without another thought? Oh, there's kind . . .'

'But you're not a stranger. I know you through your letters. Where else could you think of going?' Though where, Lorna thought, before the words had hardly left her lips, was she to sleep? But they would manage, somehow. There was a war on and they would have to! 'Y'know, it's funny when you think about it. A stranger walks into the village – and believe me, till the Army took the manor we didn't get many – and lo and behold it's Alun's girl!'

It was only then she remembered the wish for something good to happen today, and here was Alun's girl and fingers crossed that something good would come out of it. Oh, *please*, it would?

'So tell me about Alun?' Rebecca asked as they neared the manor. 'About his eyes, I mean. The last I heard was that a consultant was taking a look at him. Did you know – oh, of course you did! What I'm trying to say is has there been any word?'

'Look, Rebecca – I know this is a terrible way for you to be told. If I had the sense I was born with I ought to have said you should see the MO. But Alun knows. The MO told him on Tuesday – it was bad news.'

'I thought it might be,' came the quiet, controlled whisper. 'We've had a few cases like that – the bombing, it was. Wish I'd been there, though, when he was told. Wish he could have let me know, somehow. So how did he take it?'

'I believe he took it badly. The MO had just told him – asked me to sit with him, said it might help for him to hear a woman's voice. So Alun told me about it, got it out of his system. He was angry and afraid and then he said he was crying, behind his bandages. But he'll be able to tell you for himself, won't he, and you being a nurse – well, you'll be better able to deal with it than I was.'

'Was it bad for you, Lorna?'

'It was a whole lot worse for him – and today is his birthday . . .'

'Yes. St David's day – I haven't forgotten. There's a present for him in my case. I tried really hard to get time off for the first of March, you know. And Lorna – thank you for being there when he needed someone. It must be terrible not to see, but I love him so much that him being blind doesn't seem quite so bad when I tell myself he was within seconds – *inches* – of being killed. I still go cold, just to think of it. But we'll manage, Alun and me. And can I say thank you for being here for me, too, and ask one last favour? If you know your way around the place, will you take me to see the MO please, before I see Alun?'

And Lorna said she would and as they walked up the old, uneven steps to the manor door, she prayed with all her might and main for the first-day wish to come true; all-the-way true.

But that, she thought miserably, would take a miracle and even small miracles were thin on the ground, these days; especially for Lorna Hatherwood, who had done something completely unforgivable . . .

NINE

'Ewan – can you spare me just a couple of minutes?' Lorna asked anxiously, hand on the surgery door. 'I know you're busy and I won't keep you, but there's something I must tell you about Rebecca and Alun.'

'Then come in, do. I can spare you *at least* five minutes – and a cup of tea into the bargain. Nurse Pryce was badly in need of a hot drink – there's still some in the pot. And don't look so worried. She knows the worst, took it well.'

'And is she with him now?'

'She is. Best birthday present Private Jones could have.' He held up the teapot. 'Er . . . ?'

'No thanks, Ewan. And when I tell you, you'll never speak to me again, let alone offer me tea. I did something awful.'

'Awful, Lorna? *You*?'

'They're very much in love, those two. I know.' She looked down to the tightly clenched fingers on her lap. 'I wrote Alun's letters and read out Rebecca's replies – several times he wanted to hear them, actually. But last Tuesday, when you told him what the consultant had said then asked me to sit with him, he was very upset; insisted I write to Rebecca and end it between them. I tried to make him see sense, but he wouldn't listen. He was so bitter, Ewan.'

'So you wrote the letter?'

'Yes. Like I always do – word for word. It was a stinker

and what's worse, she hasn't got it yet. She told me she hadn't heard from him for quite a few days – thought it must be the bombing. They've had it bad, around Swansea.'

'Then let's hope the letter did get bombed.'

'Yes, but don't you see – she has no way of knowing he doesn't want to marry her. She'll have gone into that room thinking things are just the same between them – and they aren't!'

'Nurse Pryce will deal with it. She's a sensible sort.'

'But what if he really meant what he told me to write in that letter? She's going to be devastated.'

'What was the gist of it? Can you remember?'

'Gist? You can have it word for word, if you like.' She opened her handbag. 'It's here. I didn't post it, and I know it was wrong of me,' she whispered, unwilling to meet his eyes. 'Criminal, even. I above all should know you can't mess about with people's letters. But I just couldn't send it – not when I knew how much he loved her. I thought that if things were sort of delayed a bit he might calm down, change his mind. I was on my way here when Rebecca and I ran into each other.'

'Yes. She told me. And?'

'I was coming to see Alun, say goodbye, wish him well. Today is my last day, but you know that. Anyway, I was going to tell him what I'd done and ask him if he still wanted Becky to have the letter – I hoped he'd changed his mind. But I got cold feet – couldn't do it, and before you show me the door, just let me say that those two have a very special love and I didn't want it to be thrown away.' She pushed back her chair, reaching for her handbag. 'I'll go, now. I'm sorry, Ewan . . .'

'Lorna! Please stay? Shut the door and sit down?'

'Give me one good reason why I should?'

'Well, for one thing I'd like to know if you would think it unethical if I were to read the letter.'

'It's up to you. Maybe you should, then if you want to

give it back to Alun, you can. You'll have to tell him what happened, though – blame me.'

'Why should I? I could invent something like you had left it here for posting and it got misplaced.'

'Do as you think best. I don't think it will make a lot of difference. Becky will know now. But read it out loud, will you?'

'If you wish.' He laid the single sheet of paper on his desk. 'Sure you want me to?'

'Please. He usually called her *Becky cariad* – that's a Welsh love word. Darling. But that letter starts, Dear Rebecca. So formal and cold.'

'Right!' He took a steadying breath. 'Here goes . . .

Dear Rebecca

I want to let you know that I have had a lot of time, lately, to think about us and all we had hoped for from life. But when you are lying in the darkness, things seem to get clearer, if you see what I mean. What I am trying to say is that you and I have been together since we were kids at school, were brought up two doors from each other. We sort of drifted into this relationship and neither of us have had the chance to meet anyone else, which isn't right. I feel trapped, Rebecca, because of a promise I made to you when I was a kid of fourteen: it is why I am asking you to let me go. You and I aren't meant for each other, I realize it now. I am leaving this place because my eyes are going to be fine, with luck. The three of us here are going to a surgical unit for operations and it's fingers crossed we will all be able to see again.

So don't write to me any more. Just try to understand that we would have been making a terrible mistake if we had gone ahead with it. Think of me sometimes, and wish me luck. And try not to hate me too much. You'll be grateful to me, in the end. All the best, Alun . . .

'You're right, Lorna. It's a stinker.' He folded the sheet and returned it to the envelope. 'I don't know what's going on at the moment in the snug ward but one thing is certain – there's only one place for this.' He leaned over the desktop, taking careful aim to send the letter spinning into the fire. 'And that, I suppose, makes me an accomplice, or is it an accessory after the fact? Whatever it is,' he smiled, 'I'm in it up to the neck with you now.'

'Ewan – thank you, and thanks for understanding.' Already, the tenseness was leaving her. 'I've been worried about that letter for days.'

'What letter?' he grinned. 'By the way, Nurse Pryce told me she's staying the night at your place. Good of you, Lorna.'

'She is – if she still wants to. Just think – what if Alun insists he meant every word of it?'

'Somehow, I don't think that will happen. Nurse Pryce struck me as being a very determined young woman. If I were a betting man, my money would be on her.'

'Mine, too, but only because my conscience wants her to win. There's one thing, though, that puzzles me. From the way she writes it's obvious she thinks her Alun is the best thing that's happened since steam trains, and handsome with it, and bless him he isn't; you've got to admit it.'

'Agreed. And I'll bet Rebecca doesn't attract a lot of wolf-whistles, either.'

'Exactly. Yet Alun described her to me like she was Hedy Lamarr – long dark hair, exquisite nose and big brown come-to-bed eyes. And she's small and plump and mousy and motherly.'

'Oh dear.' Ewan bit his lip to control the laugh that threatened. 'But I suppose it's what you call the look of love.'

'Love is blind, you mean?'

'No, Lorna. I mean the look of love; what the other person sees. It's what love does – Dickon and Ursula, for instance.'

'Goodness! I'd forgotten them. But come to think of it,

word got around in a mind-I'm-not-admitting-anything kind of way, that what they *might* have seen in the wood wasn't disfigured at all.'

'The way Dickon saw her, Lorna,' he said matter of factly. 'The way Alun sees his Rebecca, and she him. Simple, really.'

'Oh, Ewan, you are such a dear person!' She stopped, cheeks flushing. 'I – I mean you're so understandingly *nice* . . .'

'Of course I am!' He walked to the door, holding it open for her, then stood as she walked away, thinking what a sickly little word nice was; stood until he heard the clicking of the front door sneck, then went to stand at the fireplace, hands behind his back. Nice? Oh, but that didn't describe his feelings for her! Lustful, more like, and she married to a man old enough to be her father if looks were to be believed! Yes, and whilst he was at it, damn this war for landing him in Nun Ainsty and the sooner he was out of the place and back on active service, the better! Then he let go a deep breath and glared at the face in the black-spotted mirror perched atop the mantelpiece.

Bloody idiot, Ewan MacMillan, that's what you are! Of all the women in this whole wide world, you've got to fall for a married one! A *respectably* married one at that, with only one thing on her mind at the moment – where she will sleep her overnight guest and if the rations will stretch to include supper and breakfast!

Nice, Lorna thought, as she walked past the pond. A thoroughly nice man with the most beautiful smile. In fact his smile was the first thing she had noticed about Ewan and she had then gone on to think how very attractive he was and wasn't it a good job she was a married woman and that married women got automatic absolution for thinking such things? A pity absolution didn't stop you wondering what he would be like to kiss!

She unlocked the door, stepping into the safe familiarity

of the front hall, closing her eyes, listening to the solemn tick of the grandfather clock. That clock had stood there ever since she could remember, safe and enduring, exactly like her marriage to William. Then she reminded herself that Alun's girl was coming to stay.

'Please let it be all right between them?' she whispered to the cherub on the face of the clock, then fastened on her pinafore and began to prepare supper, Ewan MacMillan and all other foolish thoughts banished from her mind.

'That was the best meal I've had for a long time.' Rebecca Pryce snuggled into the depths of the armchair. 'All the same, I feel guilty for eating your rations, Lorna.'

'But you didn't. We had rabbit pie and apples and custard. Rabbits aren't rationed, thanks be, nor are vegetables. And the pie crust was made from suet – also unrationed – which my butcher let me have from under the counter. As for the pudding – the apples are home-grown and the custard –'

'Was made from milk, nicked by me,' Ness grinned. 'We have six pints a week between us from the Meltonby milkie, so when we're getting a bit short I top us up, so to speak, from the farm. Thievin' so-and-so, aren't I?'

'You'll never go to heaven, that's for sure,' Rebecca laughed. They were sitting cosily in the front room. The last time it was used had been at new year, so it needed an airing was the excuse Lorna made for the lighting of a fire and the using of precious coal. And since there were only two chairs in the kitchen, anyway, and since Lorna's conscience was still troubling her over the letter, she told herself that you couldn't always be measuring out this or that or scrimping and saving things. Just once, it was lovely to sit in the lamplit room in old, chintz-covered chairs, with fireglow lighting the bumpy white walls into softest apricot. 'This is so peaceful, I think I could sit here for the duration. Does this little village know there's a war on?'

'It doesn't,' Ness supplied. 'I know, 'cause I come from Liverpewl.'

'Agreed. So you'll be able to go to bed – fingers crossed – and sleep right through,' Lorna smiled. 'By the way, I won't be able to see Alun again, but Pearl Tuthey says she'll take over from me to do the letter writing. She's a nice lady – got two sons in the Navy, so you needn't feel she's a stranger.'

'I won't, but talking about letters, it seems Alun's last one to me got lost in the post.'

'Oh? S-sorry . . .'

'Do you know what was in it, Lorna?'

'Yes, but I don't think he meant it,' Lorna whispered, cheeks flushing red.

'Of course he didn't – but do you want to hear how we got on?'

And Lorna said yes please, she did. Indeed, all she wanted to hear was that Alun had stopped being prickly and that everything really was all right again.

'If you don't mind telling us, Rebecca.'

'Of course I don't! Got to tell someone! Me and Alun are engaged. Official, it is. Now what do you think about that?'

'*Engaged*? I'm so glad.' Lorna really, really was. How much, no one would ever know. 'Congratulations to you both.'

'And from me, an' all,' Ness smiled. 'And we'd love to hear about it 'cause there's so much bad news these days, that sumthin' romantic and lovin' will make a nice change.'

'Well, things were a bit peculiar between us at first, I couldn't understand it. But shall I tell it from the start – from when I'd seen the MO and he'd told me what to expect? Oh, I was all churned up inside – not just because Alun wasn't going to see again, you'll understand, but because my heart was thumping twenty to the dozen because I wanted to see him and say happy birthday and kiss him. And then tell him that I knew about his eyes and that it was all right, that him and me would manage.

'So I knocked on the door and just stood there, all full up, just looking at him and he said, "Lorna . . . ?"

'"Happy birthday, *cariad*," I said, trying not to cry. "Told you I'd get time off, didn't I?" And then his face changed and he said, "Rebecca! What the hell are you doing here! Didn't you get my letter?" And I asked him what letter, and didn't he want to kiss his girl after all the months we'd been apart?'

She stared into the fire, struggling against tears, then took a deep breath and the smallest smile tilted the corners of her mouth.

'Oh, there was such love in me for him that I put my arms around him and kissed him, then I asked him what was wrong, because he just stood there, wooden, hands at his sides and never giving me so much as a hug.

'Anyway, to cut a long story short it seemed he'd sent me a letter, said you'd written it for him, but the words were his. Breaking it off, he said he was. He'd said he'd be leaving soon for an operation and that he would get his sight back, but it was all a big bluff, because he was afraid I wouldn't want him once I knew the truth.'

'Must have been awful for you, queen. So what happened, in the end?'

'Happened, Ness? I told him straight. "Now see you here, Private Jones," I said. "I've seen the medical officer and I know the truth. And what's more, I'm pulling rank because I'm a staff nurse now and I've got my own ward and I don't take orders from Army privates, see? So come you here and give me a kiss and don't talk so stupid. We were lovers before you left for the Army so that makes us engaged, to my way of thinking. And don't you try to get out of it, or I'll sue you for breach of promise!"'

'So it's all come right?' Lorna smiled shakily.

'*Duw*, of course it has. We're engaged now, so if ever that pesky letter does arrive, I won't even read it. And when he's got his bandages off and gets a bit more confidence moving around on his own, and maybe learns to read in Braille, the Army will discharge him. He'll have a pension – we'll manage. And things could have been much worse. He could have been killed . . .'

'So you'll be visiting again, tomorrow?'

'Yes. The MO says that since I'm a nurse I can take him to the pub for a pint. He's looking forward to that! And I've fallen lucky. Seems there's transport going to York station in the afternoon to pick up two patients and I can have a lift there – if I don't mind riding in an ambulance! So I told the MO it wasn't the first time I'd been in one and I doubted it would be the last. Oh, I'm so contented sitting here with everything come right for Alun and me but if you don't mind, I ought to go to bed now.'

'Of course we don't mind. I've put in a hot bottle for you. There's hot water in the tank – would you like a bath?'

'Wouldn't I just! Seems like a week since I had a decent wash. I still smell of that dusty old train.'

'Then I'll pop up with a drink when you're in bed.'

'Made with stolen milk, will it be?' Rebecca smiled wickedly.

'Stolen? Ness doesn't steal milk – she nicks it. There's a difference. Now off you go. You know where the bathroom is . . .'

'Ar, dunnit make you feel lovely,' Ness sighed when they were alone.

'Lovely – if you don't mind me sharing your bed, that is.'

'No problem – as long as you don't snore!'

And Lorna said she didn't and all at once felt very happy. And very relieved.

'This is nice, isn't it?' Lorna sat, pillow behind head, watching Ness wind her long black hair into flat curls, securing each one with two fine pins. 'It's fascinating the way you do that – your fingers seem to fly.'

'Well, it's me job, innit? And think yourself lucky you don't have to do this every night!'

Lorna smiled, loving her short, feathery curls that could be kept in order simply by running her fingers through them; loved the way everything had come right for Becky and Alun, loved sharing a bed with Ness.

'Y'know, tonight it's like we are sisters.'

'Mm. I've sometimes wished I had one, but if you haven't got one to laugh over you don't have one to cry over, either. I mean – well, sisters nick your clothes, don't they, and your make-up?'

'Wouldn't know. But I want William and I to have at least two children – when the war is over, that is.'

When the war was over. In a hundred years, maybe? And would she ever have the children she longed for? Had William weighed it all up in his mathematical mind and decided they couldn't afford them, or that he was too old to start a family, or would be by the time the Army sent him home to be a civilian again?

'What's the matter, girl?' Ness demanded through the dressing table mirror. 'Frownin' gives you wrinkles!'

'If you must know, I was wondering when we'll have children, and how many.'

'So thinking about kids makes your face go like you're sucking a lemon?'

'No. But I sometimes think William doesn't want a family – ever.'

'Then you'll have to stop your twice weeklies when the war is over, and really try hard.' Ness eased a bandeau over her pin-curled hair. 'There now, that'll keep them in place. And shift over. You're spreading into my half! Finished your drink? Want me to put the light out, or do you want to talk?'

'Both, please.' Lorna wriggled onto her back, pulling the bedclothes to her chin. 'If you don't mind, I'd like to talk about Becky and Alun.'

'Why? They've got it sorted, those two. Mind, I reckon he'll be worrying about that letter, and if it will turn up. Was it really nasty, Lorna?'

'It was. Cruel. It was his stupid pride – thought Becky wouldn't want him. I think he was finishing it before she did. Typical of men!'

'But she wouldn't be finished with! She's a smasher, that girl. No oil painting, mind, but she's got a lovely nature and she's dead in love with Alun. Her eyes go all dreamy when she talks about him.'

'I'd noticed that, too. Must be wonderful to be loved like that.'

'And you aren't, Mrs Hatherwood?'

'Ness! Don't twist things. What I meant was what those two have between them is pretty marvellous, all things considered.'

'So let's hope that if ever that letter arrives she doesn't read it – not that it would make any difference to her, I suppose.'

'No, because she won't get it, Ness. Not ever. I didn't post it, you see – couldn't bear to because I knew how much he really loved her. I suppose I was playing God – condoned by Ewan.'

'You did *what*! But how does Ewan come into it?'

'I told him. Said I'd been on my way to see Alun, own up to what I'd done and did he still want me to post the letter. But Becky turned up out of the blue so I couldn't – daren't – ask him. I went instead to Ewan and he agreed with me and threw the letter on the fire. And I'm glad he did; glad he understood – was on my side. He's such a lovely person, don't you think?'

'If I was on the look out for a feller, I suppose I'd agree with you. But I'm not, and neither are you, Lorna, so I reckon the poor bloke is wasting his talents in Nun Ainsty. Nuthin' here for him, is there?'

'You're presuming he's looking for a girl, then? What if he's married, Ness? He very well could be.'

'Nah. He's the straight sort, would have told you if he had been – talked about her. You've been in his surgery; is there a photo of a woman on his desk?'

'N-no.'

'There you are, then! A dead giveaway, photos on desks. Mind, he doesn't seem all that interested.'

'I don't see how he can be,' Lorna defended hotly. 'The way I see it is that he should still be a convalescent himself, not in charge of about thirty wounded. I don't suppose he's got the energy left to go dancing, nights, or even find a date to take out!'

'All right, girl! I was only teasing! Don't take it to heart so much or I'll think you fancy him on the quiet.'

'Ness, I'm a married woman! I don't fancy other men!'

'As if I could forget!'

As if, Ness thought, being married made any difference at all. If the spark was there, then that was it! *Boing*! That was one of the things war did. It parted wives and husbands, sweethearts and lovers, with no thought at all. Stood to reason things could happen, *did* happen. There would be a lot of broken marriages and engagements before it was over!

'Asleep?'

'No, Lorna. Just thinkin''. About people bein' apart through no fault of their own. Rotten, this war is.'

'I know. That's why I'm glad to be starting at the surgery on Monday. The busier I am, the more quickly the days will pass.'

'Until the first of May?'

'Yes. Until William comes on leave.'

She said it without emotion, Ness thought, as though stating a fact. For seven days and nights her husband would be home and they would make love. In bed. Regular as clockwork.

'So what made you tell Ewan,' she demanded, pushing Lorna's love life to the back of her mind where it rightly belonged. 'Why didn't you tell *me* about it?'

'Sorry, Ness. I should have, I suppose, but Ewan was the first person I thought of, and the nearest to hand. But I'm glad I did, because he did exactly what I'd wanted to do with it. It made us conspirators, I suppose, and –'

'And there's no one you'd rather conspire with than the MO?'

'No! I mean that he wouldn't tell on me, that he'd respect my confidence, not presume to judge. William wouldn't have –'

She stopped, suddenly, and in the darkness Ness heard the hiss of her indrawn breath.

'Your William wouldn't have done such a terrible thing, eh? William wouldn't dream of throwing a letter addressed to someone else on the fire?'

'N-no Ness, I don't think he would. Probably that's why I confided in Ewan. Ewan is more understanding – oh, hell! I don't mean that, and you know it! What I'm trying to say is –'

'What you're trying to say, queen, is that William's principles make him straight-laced, whereas Ewan is an ordinary mortal who was willing to help ease your conscience?'

'Well – yes. But William isn't straight-laced, Ness. He's a very nice man, really, and very dependable.'

'Of course he is. I never said he wasn't. He's a bit dull, though, you've got to admit it. Have you ever closed your eyes and pretended you were kissing another man? Ewan, for instance?'

'I have *not*! Don't try to put words into my mouth!'

'You mean to say you haven't, not even once, wondered what he'd be like to kiss? Cor! You're missin' sumthin', queen, because I tried it ages ago and decided his kiss would be warm and firm and he'd do it slow, like – tease a bit. An' I don't think he'd be a sloppy kisser, either. Can't stand wet kisses, meself!'

'Ness Nightingale! Will you shut up! If I didn't know you better, I'd think you'd been drinking! And – and I don't think he'd be a wet kisser, either,' she giggled. 'And yes, since you mention it, I think he'd take his time, too.'

'It's Englishmen who take their time, Lorna. Ewan MacMillan is a Scot! But what the heck! It'll all be the same in a hundred years, so close your eyes and go to sleep.' She yawned, wriggling herself into the feather mattress. 'G'night, queen. Sleep tight.'

Lorna did not sleep but lay unmoving, squinting into the darkness, thinking about kisses; Ewan's kisses and William's kisses and the way William's moustache scratched when he became passionate.

Then she relaxed and smiled, because Ness had been teasing, of course. Ness said outrageous things and didn't mean a word of them and what was more, she hoped Ness would always tease and say awful things because she was fun to have around. Life would be dull without her.

So Lorna thought about being William's wife – his *faithful* wife – and about all other lonely wives who were being faithful, too, yet who must sometimes wonder, as she did, what it would be like to kiss Clark Gable or Tyrone Power or Leslie Howard – or young medical officers – and not feel one bit guilty about it. Wondering was all right, she had long ago established, as long as you left it there.

She smiled again and thought about Alun and his Rebecca and could almost feel glad about the letter she hadn't posted and Ewan had thrown on the fire without a second thought.

Back to Ewan again! She closed her eyes tightly, whispered 'Our Father . . .' then commended William and all fighting men and women to Our Lord's keeping.

'And all the sweethearts and wives of fighting men,' she whispered softly, 'who are every bit as lonely as I am.'

Purposefully, she made herself think of ordinary things; about being able to give Rebecca a new-laid white egg for her breakfast and that tomorrow, which was always a meatless day, they would have cheese omelettes for supper and rice pudding – if Ness was able to come by another pint of milk.

Yet for all that, ordinary thoughts did not stop the tear that trickled down her cheek and fell wetly into her ear. It was annoying, really, because she did not know why she was weeping. She truly didn't.

Lorna waved as the tooting ambulance passed her in Priory Lane, smiling as the little Welsh nurse leaned out to blow a kiss. Then she watched it slow at the end of the lane and turn left onto the main road, heading for the railway station. It had been lovely having a guest for the night, even if she had slept in hers and William's bed! But she wouldn't tell William about it because what he didn't know he couldn't worry over and anyway, it would be far too complicated to explain why she had felt duty bound to ask Rebecca to stay.

Conscience eased, Lorna thought instead about her new job with Dr Summers, hoping she would be able to cope, knowing that if she did not, the labour exchange would immediately find another job for her, probably miles away. But Doc Summers was a nice man who had seen her through measles and chickenpox and countless attacks of croup. She would be all right. She was, she supposed, your average soldier's wife, doing the best she could for the war effort, not because the government said she must, but because she wanted to. She wanted the war over and done with; wanted an end to the killing and to men being blinded, and if delivering letters and newspapers, and working afternoons in the surgery of a country doctor and taking in a land girl would shorten the war by just one hour, then she was more than happy.

She stood at the crossroads as a convoy of Army lorries and trucks passed, waving back to the men who waved to her, giving them her brightest smile. It was something that not long ago she would never have dreamed of doing, but there was a war on now, which made it all right.

She looked right and left, hurried across the road, then took the lane that led to Meltonby, thinking that in no time at all, winter would be truly over and William would be coming home on leave.

Life, she told herself firmly, could be a whole lot worse!

'So how did it go?' Ness demanded when blackouts had been checked, supper eaten and pans and dishes washed and wiped and put away. 'Any blood?'

'Of course not! If there's blood, Mrs Summers gives a hand – she was a nurse, thank goodness. I'm more of a clerk – I work in a little side room. When I've got my bearings I'll answer phones, make appointments, arrange home visits and send out bills at the end of the month. But there are heaps of things to be gone through and sorted into piles for filing or throwing away. I'll get used to sorting the wheat from the chaff, Doc Summers says.'

'Bet he's glad to have you, Lorna.'

'I think he might be, once I've got used to things. Mrs Summers said thank God I had come, that now she could go out afternoons if she felt like it, and not be tied to the telephone all the time. That dratted instrument, she called it. But I'm so tired and I haven't done anything manual like you do, Ness. Just the strangeness of it, I suppose.' The novelty of being a working woman for the first time in her life and, if she dare admit it, actually enjoying it. 'How was your day, Ness?'

'Same as always, 'cept one of the young heifers started calving down and was having a bad time. Bob had to send for the vet in the end, but we got a lovely little heifer calf, so that's one that won't be going to the stock market on Thursday. I wouldn't like to be a cow, Lorna. A calf every year then milked twice a day till the poor things are past it. Not a lot of fun, when you think about it.'

'Suppose not.' Lorna already accepted that calves were taken from their mothers at birth. Ness, a town girl, did not and thought it cruel and vowed never to eat veal again. 'But that's the way life is.'

'Ar. Bein' in the country isn't all rosy-cheeked kids and romps in the hay. I'm beginning to find that out. And talking about hay – Glebe Farm's hay is almost used up, but the herd will soon be out in the fields again and eating grass. Less work for us.'

'You are starting to talk like a farmer, Ness, and not so long ago you were terrified even to think of milking a cow by hand. You've come on a lot.'

'Ar. It isn't so bad, bein' on a farm, especially now it's getting warmer and there's summer to look forward to. Only one fly in the ointment – Rowley.'

'And what has he been up to, then? Still as nasty as ever?'

'He is, and he'll never change. He's such a creep. When I walk past him, I know he's looking at my bottom, and yesterday he got an eyeful because my shirt had come unbuttoned. "Seen enough?" I asked him and he said he had, thanks very much, then walked away grinning. Only it wasn't a grin; more a leer. But enough about him. I saw Rebecca getting into the Army ambulance. I reckon those two will manage all right.'

'They will.' Briefly Lorna closed her eyes, hoping that maybe some time in the future there would be an operation that would help Alun to see again. 'I must remember Alun tonight, when I say my prayers. You never know, there might be the odd miracle going begging. I can ask Our Lord to at least put him in the queue.'

'You believe in all that stuff, don't you – prayin' and going to church?'

'Yes. I always have.'

'And you get prayers answered?'

'Sometimes, though you should ask for other people, not yourself – or so Gran said when I was little. I ask Our Lord to take care of William, though William can take very good care of himself. He always has, come to think of it. Very well organized, my husband is.'

'Ar,' Ness nodded. Little though she knew of William, that at least she knew to be true. And it wasn't down to his being well organized. In her considered opinion, Lieutenant Hatherwood put himself before all else. A selfish so-and-so to put it bluntly. But no use telling Lorna that. She would find out for herself one day. Sure as eggs was eggs, she would. 'Ar,' she said again, closing her eyes, setting her chair rocking. 'What do you think to them *Jairmans* – on the march again.'

'March? Where to this time? Who told you?' Lorna was all at once alert.

'Heard it on the one o'clock news in Glebe kitchen. And it's Bulgaria this time. Seems the prime minister there invited them in. To safeguard peace in the Balkans was the excuse. Oh, but that Hitler's got a cheek. What it really meant, Bob said, was that he wanted to get his soldiers nearer to Greece. Greece'll be the next, in Bob's opinion.'

'So is that good – for us, I mean? And I know it sounds selfish, but if Hitler has got his eyes on Greece, surely he won't be invading us?'

'Ha! Thought it was funny – you haven't mentioned the invasion for at least two weeks! But it might be as well to think on,' Ness frowned, 'that maybe the Bulgarian thing is a bluff; make us think he's lost interest in Britain and then him sneaking in through the back door, crafty, like he always is!'

'The *back* door, Ness? But surely they'd have to come from across the Channel?'

'Which is what everybody expects. But it would be just as easy for them to come from Holland and land on the east coast, hadn't you thought?'

'I – I don't know what to think, and that's the truth. It's awful being on edge all the time, waiting for it to happen.'

'So why don't you relax and think how much worse it is for the Bulgarians – and probably for them Greeks, an' all. At least whilst he's bothering them, Hitler is leaving us alone.'

'Oh, what the heck! Let's switch on and listen to Geraldo? It'll be the nine o'clock news after the dance music and we can hear if anything more has happened.' Lorna had been late home from the surgery and missed the six o'clock bulletin, thankful that Minnie had left the kitchen fire ready for lighting and the table set for supper. 'Maybe it won't be as bad as we think.'

'No. 'Cept that they've started bombing London again,' Ness murmured, feeling guilty that Londoners were still in the thick of the bombing, whilst Liverpool had had less raids than usual. 'There have been no visitors for two weeks,' her mother had written. *Visitors* meant German bombers. Very careful what she wrote in letters, Mam was.

'Poor old London,' Lorna sighed, feeling guilty because Nun Ainsty had never heard an air-raid siren, let alone bombs.

'Yes, an' it's the docks and the East End what's coppin' it, same as in Liverpool. The docks, and all the streets around them. Hitler ought to be hanged!'

'He will be, when the war is over. He'll have to answer for what he's done.'

'Yes, but right now he's casting his slitty eyes on Greece, so there'll be no hangin' just yet, queen!'

'Suppose not. Life's a bitch, isn't it?'

'It is – and then you die. Oh, let's listen to some dance music? Let's close our eyes and pretend the war is over and we're dancin' in lovely long frocks with two smashin' fellers.'

'Fine by me.' Lorna turned on the wireless. Two smashing fellows? But William didn't exactly fit the bill, did he? Rugged and dependable looking and fairly tall, but much as she cared for him, not what you could call smashing. And besides, William didn't dance. Disliked it, in fact. 'OK. Let's pretend . . .'

She closed her eyes as the toe-tingling throb of a rumba

beat filled the kitchen, and with a swish and a rustle of her cornflower-blue satin ball gown she began to dance, hips swaying.

And with whom, she wasn't telling. Oh my word, no!

TEN

Ness walked, hands in pockets, sniffing the air and the scent of green things growing. The willows at the back of the manor were already bursting into leaf and the elms that lined the drive were thick with blossom – if you could call the brown, tufty flowers that covered the bare twigs blossom, that was. She had learned a lot about the country; could name the bright yellow celandines and wild violets that grew beneath the hawthorn hedges. She recognized the chaffinch singing its heart out in Mrs Ellery's beech tree; knew, too, that a hen blackbird was brown, not black, and that they hatched two broods of fledglings each summer.

Tonight, daylight would last until almost eight o'clock; winter had gone, she thought gratefully. Now there was summer to look forward to and best of all, she would be going home at the end of next month.

It would be good to see them all again, even if Liverpool seemed a bit down at the heel from the bombing, with rubble piled high on bomb sites, and shattered shop windows covered with corrugated sheeting. Liverpool would always be home, though Nun Ainsty had come to rate a close second.

She smiled and waved to the landlady who was opening the doors of the White Hart. Ness knew everyone in the village, now, felt a part of it. There were worse places to be; far better here than in London and all the other bombed cities. And now Glasgow had come in for an almighty blitzkrieg.

Nowhere, except tucked-away villages like this one, seemed safe from Hitler's bombers. Being softened up, weren't we, so that when the tides were right Hitler could invade us as he should have done last year. And hadn't. But it would be soon, said the prophets of doom. Stood to reason, didn't it – after Greece it was bound to be us.

Then she clucked impatiently, straightening her shoulders and sticking out her chin. She had put in a good day's work for the war effort and now she was hungry. Meat and vegetables for supper tonight, and bottled gooseberries and custard. And wasn't Nun Ainsty Home Guard ready and waiting so what the heck was she worrying about?

'Hullo, luv,' she smiled to the driver of the red post office van who was emptying the pillar box beside Ladybower's front gate, then she made for the open door, calling, 'Hi! I'm home!' whilst hanging her jacket on the kitchen door peg. 'Any letters?'

'Not for you, Ness. The gas bill and one from William for me.'

'Ar.' William's weekly epistle. 'How is he?'

'Fine. And busy with the war and missing me and looking forward to his leave,' Lorna said matter-of-factly, stirring custard on the stove top.

'I haven't had a letter for almost a week.' Ness scrubbed her hands at the kitchen sink. 'Hope everything's OK at home.'

'There's been nothing on the news about Liverpool being bombed,' Lorna comforted.

'But they don't always tell you – well, not till days afterwards. Even news seems to be rationed by the government these days.'

'Yes! And talking about rationing, Ness – guess what? They're only rationing jam and marmalade now! From next week. Half a pound; half a jar for each person to last a month.'

'A pound between us? Won't go far,' Ness shrugged.

'Well, I've still got a bit of home-made jam on the pantry shelf, so I reckon we'll take our ration in marmalade. OK?'

'Fine by me.' Butterless toast and jam had been good at filling gaps, Ness thought, which jam rationing would put an end to. 'But let's look on the bright side, girl. Bread isn't rationed – yet.'

'Nor cocoa.'

'Nor vegetables.'

'Mm. Nor –' Lorna stopped. 'What else isn't rationed?'

'We-e-ll, suet isn't, nor sausages – when you can get them. And soap and soap powder . . .'

'*Soap*! They couldn't ration soap – could they? I mean, things would have come to a pretty pass if soap was rationed!'

And Ness agreed, and said of course they couldn't ration cleanliness, then offered to feed the hens. At least they had eggs in abundance; eggs you could eat without worrying if they had gone off, because shop eggs were at least three weeks old when they got to the grocer's, Ness calculated.

She gave the white and black hens a brilliant smile, then threw an extra handful of wheat to show how grateful she was. Four eggs today, five yesterday, which wasn't bad going for six hens. And soon, Kate said, she shouldn't wonder if they weren't providing *six* eggs a day because, for some reason, in April hens laid more eggs than in any other month. Even scraggy old past-it hens laid in April, the farmer's wife said.

'Four.' Ness inspected and wiped the eggs with an expertise born of much practice, then put them on the cold slab in the pantry.

'You must take some when you go on leave,' Lorna smiled. 'Are you counting the days yet?'

'Nah. Six weeks to go. I'll start crossing off days a week before. Are you counting, Lorna?'

'N-no. Like you, not just yet . . .'

* * *

It had all been very relaxed, Ness was to think later. She and Lorna sitting at the kitchen table, washing-up ignored, Ness recounting how she and Mick had done the milking and mucking-out between them because Bob and Rowley had been ploughing all day, now that the land wasn't so heavy and there was a good drying wind from the southeast. And Lorna said she had finished sorting and filing and could use the top of her desk now, and that the doctor's wife had gone off to York and stood in a queue and got a jar of cold cream at the end of it.

'So it's going to be all right at the surgery?' Ness smiled.

'I think so. But I'm going to have to organize myself. With two jobs I don't seem to have a lot of time for housework, and now the nights are lighter I've got to do some gardening.'

'Then we'll draw up a rota. We can do the cooking and washing between us like always, take care of what housework we can, then leave the rest to Minnie. Why not ask her if she could do a couple more hours? Bet she'd be glad of the extra.'

'Now why didn't I think of that?' Lorna sighed, jumping to her feet when the phone rang, eager to answer it, wondering why, these days, you always jumped and ran at the first strident ring.

'For you, Ness,' she called. 'Your mother, I think, in a call box. Hurry!'

'You were right. It was Mam,' Ness said when the three-minute call had seemed to be over in no time at all. 'More bombing. Two nights on the trot, it seems.'

'But there was nothing on the wireless or in the papers. Bad, was it?'

'Could have been worse. Mam phoned so I wouldn't worry when I heard. They're all right at Ruth Street. The bombing was over the water this time.'

'Where exactly?'

'Across the river, on the Cheshire side. Birkenhead

copped it, not Liverpool. A lot killed and the docks took a battering.'

'And your relatives there?'

'Perce and Tizzy? They're fine. Got themselves to Ruth Street. They weren't hit, but Perce said, "sod it, let's get out of it. Leave it. It's only an 'ouse!"'

'So they were all safe in your shelter? I feel guilty, sometimes, us not having air raids, but if you like I'll remember them tonight when I say my prayers.'

'Would you?' Not that Ness believed in praying, but it did no harm to be sure. 'Tell you what, Lorna. You see to your side of things and I'll send out a few ill-wishes, land Hitler with a bellyache, or sumthin'.'

'Then it's Hermann Goering you should concentrate on. It's he who sends the bombers over. But try not to worry too much, love? I'm sure they'll be all right.'

And Ness said just a little sniffily that she was sure they would be and that it was smashin' to have Lorna to listen to her woes.

'Sisters, eh?' Lorna gave Ness a hug. 'And you won't ever go to live in the hostel, will you?'

'I'm stoppin' – and listen! What's the din?'

They ran outside as a bomber flew low over the village, then another. And they watched as more took roaring to the sky.

'Those are the new Halifaxes,' Lorna whispered. 'Big, aren't they? I think it must be their first bombing raid. Let's hope they drop one on Fat Hermann for Perce and Tizzy, then all get safely back.'

So they stood as the huge planes circled and rose higher and higher and wished them Godspeed as they vanished, small as sparrows in the distant, darkening sky.

'Good on yer, lads,' Ness said chokily. 'Give 'em a bit back, eh?'

She wished Mam was on the phone at Ruth Street so she could ring her up and tell her about the bombers, then realized that that would never do, because those bomber crews were in enough danger without some fool civilian spouting careless talk into a telephone. Phones could be listened-in to, walls had ears and you had to be like Da', and keep mum. It was a queer old war, come to think of it!

'I don't feel so bad, now, about Perce and Tizzy, I mean. What say we take a walk round the garden before it gets dark, and listen to the quiet and tell ourselves how lucky we are?'

'Lucky,' Lorna said softly, soberly, linking Ness's arm. 'How *very* lucky . . .'

'So how are you feeling about things?' Doctor Reginald Summers asked. 'Time slips by, doesn't it – three weeks since you started here, Lorna.'

'You mean do I think I'll make a go of it? There's an awful lot to learn and it's a big responsibility, especially when I'm here alone.'

'Of course it is, but I know you can cope. And Jessie does so appreciate being able to take the odd afternoon off – from the dratted instrument,' he smiled wickedly.

'I'm glad about that. At least I'm some use. And I'll have to cope, won't I? If I don't, they'll make me work somewhere else – maybe even on munitions and I'd hate that. I think women who do that sort of job should be given a medal – even if the pay is high. William wouldn't want me to work in a factory, either.'

'So how is he, then?' Best change the subject. Lorna didn't seem too sure about working here – but then she had always been unsure about almost everything. Which was a pity, really. In his opinion, the doctor considered, she was a highly intelligent young woman, if only she would give herself a chance.

'William? Oh, he's fine. I get a very big letter once a week – a diary, almost, a bit each day. I don't think he likes being called up, though. Being a soldier just isn't William.'

'No. But like all the others, he'll have to put up with it.'

'Yes, of course! He hasn't complained,' she defended hastily. 'It's just that he isn't cut out for soldiering, even if he is in the Pay Corps. He's making the best of it, but I don't think he likes being away from home. When we were married, you know, I felt very relieved for him to take over – especially when Grandpa was so ill. When he went into the Army I was floundering a bit, for a time. But I'm managing – and there's Ness, of course.'

'Ah. The bonny lass from Liverpool.' He smiled and looked at Lorna over the top of his spectacles. 'She'll be good company for you – William must be pleased you've got her.'

'Oh, but he isn't!' She felt her cheeks flush because she hadn't meant to say such a thing. 'I – I mean, he doesn't like strangers in his house. He hated it when we had the evacuees. And I shouldn't be saying things like that, should I?'

'If you can't say things to an old man who's been your doctor – and friend, I hope – since you were a tot, then it's a poor lookout. And I've known you long enough to know when something is worrying you, so tell me – don't you like working here?'

'Oh, yes! I'm getting used to it and I know I'll improve. I don't want to leave – unless you want me to?'

'Of course I don't want you to, so what is bothering you? This is your GP asking . . .'

'Oh, everything and nothing. The war, I suppose, and not being able to do anything about it. And William being away from home and food rationing and –'

'But a great many husbands and sons are away at the war, Lorna, and rationing is fair. In the last war, food went unrationed till almost the end and poor people went very, very hungry. You wouldn't want that, now would you?'

'No.' She accepted the mild rebuke. 'And I'm not whingeing. I'm glad to do something for the war. If nothing else, it helps pass the days. And I know I'm lucky living in Nun Ainsty

– it's just that William seems – well, different.' The words came out in a rush. 'I can sense it from his letters.'

'Then a week together will do the pair of you good. He'll be home soon, didn't you say?'

'First of May.'

'Well, tomorrow will be the first of April – the day the accounts go out. Jessie will do them with you till you get the hang of it. You know most of the pensioners around here – they get a little off. And those who haven't paid get an 'Early settlement will be appreciated' note. And don't worry. You'll soon be able to manage on your own. I've known you a long time, Lorna, and you are brighter than you think! And if anything is troubling you, ever, you know you can tell old Doc Summers, now don't you?'

He squinted over his glasses again and smiled, and she smiled back because compliments were few and far between in her life and because she knew he meant what he said.

'Thanks. I'll be fine, truly. About time I started to grow up,' she shrugged.

'Lorna, you've been grown up for a long time – only you haven't realized it. Now off home with you. See you tomorrow – and thanks. I really mean it. You'll fit in here just fine, I know you will.'

He stood at the surgery window and watched her ride carefully down the drive. Such a nice young woman, if a little timid. He hoped she wasn't worrying over nothing or indeed that she had nothing to worry about. Sad for one so young and not long married, to have her husband go to war. Sad for a lot of women, he sighed, and when the damned war would end was anybody's guess. He was sick and tired of it already and any fool knew it wasn't even half over yet!

He closed the surgery door behind him and made for the kitchen and the smell of frying onions and sizzling sausages, and Jessie smiling. No evening surgery tonight and a good programme on the wireless. Feet up and a pipe of tobacco. Bliss!

Yet something *was* bothering young Lorna, and it wasn't only the war and her husband being away, either. He'd bet his last petrol coupon on it!

They were to have an air-raid siren at Nun Ainsty. An up-to-date one. The news came from Nance Ellery and she should know, since the existing one was kept in the garage at Beech Tree House, to be pulled out if necessary and operated manually. Very manually, because it took muscle to crank the cumbersome handle and keep it turning at speed for one minute. And all the effort produced only a strangulated groaning, which couldn't be heard at the bottom of the village unless the wind was in the right direction.

They had been lucky, mind. Apart from trial runs, the siren had only sounded once in anger and was quickly followed by the all clear, the danger being identified as an arrow of geese flying south and not a formation of enemy bombers.

The new siren, electrically operated, was to be installed on the flat roof of the sturdy stone garage at Beech Tree House, and would only require the flick of a switch to send out a wail that would be heard for miles around. And as before, the Air-Raid Warden at Meltonby would still ring Gilbert Ellery and warn him a raid was imminent; 'Air-raid warning Purple', the actual words were. Then would come a wait for 'Air-raid warning Red', at which the switch would be thrown whilst Nance counted off a minute on her wristwatch. And should there be no reply from Beech Tree House, the Meltonby warden would ring the Saddlery where a spare garage key was kept, and the honours would go to Jacob and Pearl.

It all sounded very bothersome and inefficient, yet this far the method had worked and would work still better with an electrified version capable, Lorna had been assured, of awaking the dead around St Philippa's!

'Why do you suppose,' she asked of Ness, 'we are suddenly in need of a louder siren?'

'Because the one we've got is neither use nor ornament.' Heaven help Ruth Street if it depended on such an outdated contraption.

'We can hear it all right,' Lorna defended, fearful that Nun Ainsty was being more thoroughly drawn into the war. 'You've heard it.'

'Yes, but only because I was standing not ten feet away.' Ness had been present for one of the trial runs, carried out at monthly intervals. 'It'd be heaven help Liverpool if they depended on things like that.'

'So you think we are going to get raided?' The bomber stations around were never far from Lorna's mind.

'No I don't. But if we are, then it'll be good to know we can hear the warnin'. I mean – imagine bein' in Glebe's far fields and a raid expected. You'd never know, would you? About time we got a real siren, and I know what I'm talkin' about.'

'Y-yes. Of course. Stupid of me. Sorry.'

'Oh, away with your bother,' Ness grinned. 'You're worryin' over nuthin'. And you've said it yourself, Nun Ainsty isn't worth bombin', even if they could find it.'

Nun Ainsty, Lorna had heard from someone who knew someone who was going out with a bomber boy from Linton, could not be seen from the air so hidden was it by trees.

'Mm. Over nothing.' She was glad to agree. 'And we're getting our act together, aren't we – after Dunkirk, I mean.'

New, heavy bombers at the aerodromes and the LDV had uniforms and rifles and ammunition, too. Left over from the Great War, Goff Leaman said, and the rifles in need of a good going-over, but better than nothing. The Home Guard, as it was now called, was ready for the invasion.

'Of course we are.' Still backs to the wall Ness was bound to admit. 'An' before so very much longer we'll be fightin' back!'

A victory, just one battle won to be glad about; something

worth printing in the newspapers and broadcasting by the BBC. Just for a change, some good news?

'Yes. And if you're sure you won't come to church with me, could you be a love and do the vegetables?'

And Ness said of course she could and for Lorna to get her Sunday hat on and be off, and to say one for her land girl whilst she was about it and one for Ruth Street – if she didn't mind, that was.

'A new siren – and not before time,' Ness muttered when she was alone in Ladybower's kitchen. 'And let's hope we never hear the dratted thing!'

'Ness, lass, are you missing anything?' said Kate Wintersgill at the other end of the phone. 'You've left your shoulder bag with your purse in it.'

'Goodness! I hadn't noticed. I'll be up for it straight away.'

'No need. Just thought I'd tell you in case you were worried. I'll lock it in the desk so it's safe.'

But Ness wanted the walk. The evening was brisk and the sky not yet dark, though blackout time was half past eight. April almost over and Ness had wished on her first swallow and seen primroses in the hedge bottoms and cowslips in creamy drifts in the far meadow. Winter was gone and with it the long dreary nights.

'Who was that?' Lorna looked up from the pad on her knee.

'Kate. I left my bag at the farm. Think I'll stroll up and get it – OK?'

'Sure.' Lorna was writing to William. 'Will you be all right?'

''Course I will. It isn't dark yet and besides, you said there should be a new moon tonight.'

'And you want to wish on it?'

'Might as well.' Dammit, she was getting as superstitious as the rest of Nun Ainsty, wanting to see it in the open and not through the window. Bad luck to see a new moon through glass! And, come to think of it, that moon would be almost full when she went on leave.

Leave. Seven days at Ruth Street and being with Mam and Da and Nan in that mucky, bawdy, dear old city again. Seven days of wearing civilian clothes and being able to queue for cosmetics. Then a trip over the water on the ferry to see Perce and Tizzy, or take the Overhead Railway to Sefton Park, perhaps, though its greenness wasn't quite so special since she had miles and miles of greenness and trees and flowers every day of her life now.

The kitchen clock chimed ten and Ness got to her feet, saying good night to Kate. She had not intended staying so long, but Bob and Rowley had gone to a Home Guard parade so it seemed right and proper for them to sit and chat a while.

'See you in the morning, then.' She had hitched her bag on her shoulder, waving to the farmer's wife who stood on the doorstep, then glanced to her left to the priory ruins standing black and jagged against a darkening sky. So quiet. As quiet as if nothing had changed from the long-ago time before the village was built and all that was here was the priory with its farm and chapel. It was to the nuns that lepers came to die and victims of cholera were carted from York to the burial ground around the little chapel. Quiet as the grave, in fact.

Ness hurried to the farm gate, then past the manor towards the White Hart. Its windows were darkened, but she could hear the sound of a piano playing, and laughter.

She thought about April 30th, and Kate who had said she should finish early and get herself to the station; thought, too, about Lorna who offered to run her to the bus stop in Meltonby so she could catch the six twenty-three to Liverpool, and with a bit of luck be in Lime Street by ten-thirty. In time, Ness calculated, for the last tram, and an extra day, almost, added to her leave.

'Hey – you!'

Ness turned to see Rowley in khaki battledress, rifle over his shoulder, cap askew.

'Rowley! Parade over, then?'

'Dunno. Didn't go. I mean, why the sod should I? Why should I be made to join the Home Guard? I'm on work of national importance, aren't I – shouldn't that be enough?'

'So you've been supping ale instead.' The fact was obvious as he stepped nearer. 'Well, goodnight, Rowley. Mind how you go.' He wasn't too steady on his feet. 'See you.'

She made to walk past him. Rowley sober was a pain; Rowley drunk was to be avoided at all costs.

'Hang on. I'll walk you home. Y'shouldn't be out on your own, you know. You might walk into the duck pond . . .'

'I won't. You take care, Rowley – don't bump into anything in the dark.'

But his hand was already on her arm, so she said,

'OK. But only as far as the gate, mind.' Best not upset him. It was only a cock's stride to Ladybower. She could be away and up the path in no time at all.

'I shall expect a g'night kiss, Ness.'

'Ha! Then blessed is he who expects nothing, 'cause your luck just ran out!'

'Did it, eh? Did it, Ness Nightingale? Well, I'm fed up with the way you ignore me! Is it because I'm not a conchie, then? Is Mick with the yellow streak more to your liking?'

He laid down his rifle and respirator, reaching for her, pulling her close, and she told him to behave himself and stamped on his foot with the heel of her shoe. But it made no difference through his thick army-issue boots.

'Let me go, will you!' His mouth was searching for hers. 'Stop it, Rowley!' If only he wasn't holding her so tightly; if only he would take a step back from her and give her room to swing her shoulderbag, catch him in the face, allow her to run. 'If you don't let me go, I'll scream!'

She struggled against the great strength of him and he

laughed because he knew it would do her no good.

'Don't be such a prude, Ness Nightingale. You know you want me to! Give in, eh?'

'*Yaaaaah*!' Ness opened her mouth wide and let out a scream, then another.

'What's going on! Who is it?' A voice in the darkness, feet running.

'Over here! Help me! Please help me!' Ness tore herself free as Goff Leaman reached them.

'Oh, Goff . . .' It was all she could say.

'Rowley! I might have known! Has he harmed you, Ness? Are you all right?'

'Y-yes. I – I'm fine.' She wasn't fine. She was shaking in every limb and her mouth had gone so dry she could hardly speak. 'I think he's been drinking.'

'Aye. I can smell it on him. But did he *touch* you?'

'No. N-not like that. But I'm glad you came when you did.'

'Touch her?' Rowley blustered. 'She should be so lucky! She doesn't interest me one bit! And if you've had your say, Goff Leaman, I'm going home.'

'Aye, lad. Best be off. I'll be talking to your dad in t'morning. Now, if you're sure, Ness . . . ?'

'I'll be all right. Really I will. But he's left his rifle and respirator, just threw them down. Will you take them?'

'Aye. I'll give 'em back tomorrow, give me a good excuse to let Bob know what went on. Want me to see you home, lass?'

'Please, Goff. And don't make too much of it, will you, or it'll be round the village in no time and heaven only knows how it'll end up. I've got to work with Rowley; I don't want more trouble. Please . . . ?'

'I'll have a quiet word with his dad – no one else. Y'know, one of these days, someone is going to give that young devil a right good hiding. Beats me how decent folk like Kate and Bob had to rear a wrong 'un like him. An only child, see?

Spoiled. And here we are.' He opened the gate. 'I'll wait till you're in. Good night, lass.'

''Night, Goff – and thanks.' She touched his cheek with her fingertips. 'I'm glad you came when you did. I don't think he knew what he was doing.'

'Oh, he knew all right, but get yourself inside. Us mustn't be seen hanging around your gate or folks'll be talking!'

She heard his chuckle as she ran to the kitchen door, closing her eyes with relief as she shut it behind her. Then she called, 'It's only me! Sorry I'm so late back,' and burst into tears.

Ness lay in bed, hushed and comforted by Lorna who had clucked over Rowley's behaviour, then bundled her upstairs with hot milk and honey – for the shock, she insisted.

'Rowley was a nasty little boy, y'know. He'd tear wings from butterflies and think it was funny. He once threw a kitten into the beck, then started blubbering when we threatened to tell on him. If it was up to me, I'd ring the police station this very minute!'

'No, Lorna. Like I told Goff, I've got to work with him. Don't want to make a bad job worse. And I've got the measure of him now. I'll tell him that if he comes within ten feet of me in future, I'll scream rape at the top of my voice!'

'You're getting upset again. Drink your milk.'

'Not upset, Lorna. Not any more. I'm really mad now and all I hope is that Bob will believe Goff, believe that Rowley forced himself on me.'

'He will. The village knows what Rowley's like.'

'He's a toerag!'

'Of the first water. Will I get you an aspirin to help you sleep?'

'Thanks, girl, but no. I'm over it now, but thanks for bein' there for me an' I'm sorry I broke down.'

'Glad to be there.'

'You won't say anything – especially to Mrs Ellery?'

'Not a word, if that's what you want. Now finish your milk, then snuggle down. And try to sleep? Try to forget him? He isn't worth a second thought.'

Yet Ness could not forget Rowley Wintersgill as she lay wide awake in bed. She had been very afraid, had seemed powerless against the strength of him. Fear had nearly paralysed her. She wondered how she had found the strength and courage to scream.

Yet it was over now, she insisted silently. Rowley Wintersgill was dangerous, a womanizer who would have to be watched in future. And he was arrogant, an' all; thought no woman could resist him! Preferred Mick to him, did she? Well, he was right, there! She preferred Mick Hardie a thousand times over, and if ever she allowed herself to love a man again, it might well be someone not unlike him!

She plumped her pillow, turned on her back and, hands behind head, began to count sheep. But they all looked like Rowley – not sheep, exactly, but rams.

She shut him from her mind and thought instead about next week and Mam and Ruth Street; about going home, to Liverpool. In just six more days . . .

ELEVEN

The train was less than an hour late arriving. Not bad going, Ness was bound to admit, taking in the sights and sounds of Lime Street station and the smell of coal smoke and hot, oily locomotives. And litter everywhere, because now there were too many jobs for too few men, and unswept rubbish came low in the order of things.

She made for the Pierhead. It was lighter out here, though twilight was already deepening into night. Ahead, the sky took on the fading light-glow from the river and over the water, on the Cheshire side, buildings stood starkly against the skyline.

With relief she heard the clank of the last tram and ran to the stop. Soon be there, now; home to Mam and Da and Nan and the little terraced house with its safe coal cellar.

'Scotty Road,' called the conductor.

'Ta.' Ness heaved her case aboard, dipping into her pocket for two pennies. 'Bottom of Ruth Street, luv.'

Ten more minutes, allowing for stops along the track, and she would be calling, 'It's me! Anybody in?' and finding Mam all flustered because she wasn't expected home until tomorrow; home to Liverpool, its river and docks as full of ships as she had ever seen them. More than enough work for the dockers, now, and for men long unemployed. It had taken a war to do it, mind, so wars couldn't be all bad. That same war had taken Ness Nightingale to live in an old house with a bathroom and water running hot and cold in the taps. Ladybower and Nun Ainsty, all trees and flowers and safeness.

'*Rewth* Street comin' up.' The conductor heaved the case from under the stairs. 'Hey up girl, what's in here, then?'

'Five legs of lamb, sixteen bags of sugar and a keg of best butter. What do you think is in it – me uniform and two pairs of boots for the mender?' Ness grinned. 'Ta-ra, luv.'

Ruth Street. She loved it, yet when she was at Ainsty she loved Ladybower every bit as much. She was lucky, all things considered, and content with her life if she didn't think too much about Patrick. And lately she had to admit that it didn't hurt quite so much to call him back to her remembering.

But she was on leave and for seven days there was no hosing-down and mucking-out; no collecting eggs and checking eggs and wiping eggs and laying them on trays ready for the man who came twice a week to collect them.

'Mam!'

Rose Nightingale stood on the doorstep of No. 3, gazing upwards.

'Ness, girl! Came out to check the blackout and there you are, a day early! You eloped, or sumthin'?'

'All above board. Oh, Mam, it's good to be back.'

'Good to have you, queen, and I swear you get bonnier every time I see you. Farm work must agree with you. Feeling better, are you?'

'Feeling fine, and give us a hug and a kiss, eh?' She closed her eyes and held her mother close. 'I've missed you,' she whispered chokily.

Today, William would be home. When he would arrive, Lorna had no idea, because he was driving his own car – how *did* he manage to get petrol for such a long run? – so it could be any time between noon and two o'clock.

She sighed, satisfied. The house was bright and welcoming; windows open to the May-Day sun and flowers in vases and the smell of beeswax polish made Ladybower a good place to come home to. Now all that remained was to have a six-inch bath, wash her hair, flick her fingers through it and sit on the bench outside to let it dry.

Doctor Summers had insisted she take the afternoons off whilst William was on leave.

'Jessie says she'll cope with the dratted instrument for a week. Only fair.'

With her morning job, Lorna had not been so lucky. Mrs Benson was unable to find a replacement, the shortage of labour being what it was. She was very sorry about it, but there *was* a war on.

'It doesn't matter, Mrs B. Truly.'

Of course it didn't. Nun Ainsty must have their papers and letters and what could be nicer than a May morning? Two hours, if she pedalled like mad, was all it would take. William wouldn't have time to miss her.

She took the scented soap from the bathroom cabinet. Toilet soap came unperfumed now, and if you were lucky enough to have a jealously hoarded tablet that smelled of lily of the valley, you used it only on special occasions.

Carefully, she ran a bath. Bath water must only be six inches deep. Water was a commodity of war, especially in bombed cities, and coal to heat water was in short supply. Some people had patriotically painted a six-inch-high line around the bath, but Lorna flinched from such vandalism and used instead an old toothbrush, kept behind the taps, as a measuring guide. One day, when the war was over of course, she would run a bath so deep that her feet would float upwards to meet the taps. And she would fling rose-scented salts into it – bath salts would be back in plenty in the shops again – and lather herself all over with rose-geranium soap. Meantime, for the duration, it must be a splash in water so shallow it hardly covered her bottom!

Everything was ready. Scones cooling on the kitchen table, a tray set with the best rosebud china, and in an hour's time she could begin to count away the minutes. William's letters had on occasion seemed a little distant, sometimes railing at service life in general and senior officers in particular, but a week at Ladybower would put everything to rights. There was a war on and who could blame any man, taken from his home and loved ones, if sometimes he wondered what exactly he was doing in the Army and how long it would be before his King and Country no longer needed him and sent him home. Home to Nun Ainsty, when there would be an end to rationing and the blackout and to killing and maiming. Peace. A long way off yet, but a word Lorna kept in her heart like a shining talisman because, one day, peace would come.

By three o'clock William had not arrived and Lorna wandered around the garden trying not to look at her watch. Two days ago, she and Ness had moved the hen ark to a position on the lawn from which it could not be seen from the sitting-room window. The hens still irritated William who saw no reason why his grass should be ruined. But she and Ness were fond of the plump white birds; grateful for unrationed eggs, though William would never see it that way. William could be very stubborn and was inclined to be dictatorial at times. William was –

She shook her head to empty it of mutinously uncharitable thoughts and allowed a glance at her watch. Three-thirty. He was overdue but she would not get upset. No end of reasons why he should be late. She would sit in the garden, eyes closed, face to the afternoon sun, and think instead about Ness and if her journey home had been a long one – and what she would be doing now. She would not worry about William who could look after himself no matter what. Not worry until four o'clock that was, when she might be forgiven for conceding that he really was late. But only then would she accept that something just might have gone wrong.

Ness. Lorna missed her already, needed her here now to

explain why William was late and when he would arrive. But Ness and William would never meet. Better that way.

Four-thirty. Time to get back to Ruth Street before the homeward rush of workers, when too many people would cram too few buses and trams and trains, because there was probably too few men to drive them and too little petrol, electricity or coal to fuel them.

Ness had had a satisfactory outing, calling first at Dale's salon to see if her friend the cosmetic buyer had anything tucked under the counter. She had not. Not even for Ness. She expected an allocation of cosmetics in about ten days' time, which she readily accepted was not a lot of use.

'Try the *Bon Marché*, Ness luv, and the chemist on Lime Street. You might get lucky there, and smashin' to see you. Pop in again, eh, before you go back?'

In the end, after rounds of chemists' shops and department stores, three hours of queueing produced a Sultry Scarlet lipstick, a pot of vanishing cream and a small tin of Nivea – unscented, of course. She also discovered that tomorrow morning at ten, a fish stall in the market would be selling their allocation on a first-come, first-served basis, one pound to each person. Ness made a mental note to be there early, wondering how housewives managed to look after children and homes and still find time to queue for anything unrationed or in short supply, fish being but one of them. It made her think, as she gazed from the tram window, of Nun Ainsty and rabbits in plenty and gardens full of vegetables, and Kate who never let anyone go short of milk. And of six white hens on Ladybower's lawn, which made her think of William. She wondered if he would comment on the absent land girl and hoped it would be a case of out-of-sight, out-of-mind. She was about to dwell upon what a miserable sod William could be and what madness had prompted Lorna to marry him when the conductor called '*Rewth* Street', and saved her the bother.

* * *

William arrived at five o'clock.

'Hullo, old girl.'

He placed his hands on Lorna's shoulders and kissed her cheek and she wrapped her arms around him and clung to him, relieved.

'Was something wrong?' she whispered, cheek against the brass button on his top pocket. 'I mean – well, what kept you?'

'Oh, anything and nothing.' He pushed her from him, taking off his cap, hanging his respirator on the door peg. 'The war in general and Aldershot in particular. Nothing for you to worry about.'

'Good. I *was* a little worried. You look very well, dear. I've made scones for afternoon tea. Do you want one or shall we wait till supper? Supper's cold, so it doesn't matter. I got a ham shank from the butcher and managed to get some salad, and I baked bread, especially for you . . .'

She stopped, taking a calming breath. She was babbling because she felt uncomfortable; actually felt uncomfortable in her husband's presence because she had not seen him for three months and the soldier who stood in her kitchen didn't seem to fit in at all. It was what happened, she thought wildly, when the Army took your husband and you were learning to manage on your own.

'I'll go upstairs and change. And yes, I could do with a cup of tea – er – and one of your scones.'

'Bring your uniform down with you, dear. I suppose it'll need sponging and pressing and –'

'No need.' He was halfway upstairs. 'I've got a batman to do that.'

She heard the closing of the bedroom door and said, '*Well*!'

William late, yet no outstretched arms, no, 'Hullo, darling,' no passionate kiss, nor explanation.

But the war was to blame. It wasn't natural for a man to be away from home for months on end then walk into his own kitchen as if he had never left it. William had been closeted with men. Like living, she shouldn't wonder, in a monastery.

She let go of her indrawn breath and smiled at the kettle to relax her button-round mouth. It would be all right when he came downstairs in the familiar civilian clothes she had laid out on the bed; all right when he'd had home-baked scones and tea from a civilized cup. Of course it would!

Ness sat in the back yard of No. 3. It was a tidy little yard, walls whitewashed, flagstones scrubbed every Monday with a stiff brush and leftover suds from the weekly wash. Mam's yard didn't smell of tom cats nor pee like some. There was a bench in Mam's yard and old buckets planted with nasturtiums and snapdragons. Nice to sit here, eyes closed, and wonder what was happening at Nun Ainsty.

The sky would be higher there, and wider, because rooftops didn't block it out, and in Lorna's back garden there would be a sort of sighing when the breeze stirred the trees in Dickon's Wood. Here she heard only the hum of Scotland Road; trams and buses and lorries that seemed never to stop. A city noise.

'Quiet, isn't it?' Rose Nightingale sat down beside her daughter.

'You reckon? An' there was me, thinking about the noise from Scotty Road, and how quiet it is at Ladybower.' She took her mother's hand. 'I wish there was some way you could get to see Nun Ainsty, Mam. You'd know, then, what quiet was.'

'No, Ness. Hush. It's *that* sort of quiet.'

She pulled her hand away and rose to her feet, head tilted, listening, eyes ranging the sky.

'What is it?' All at once, Ness felt uneasy.

'The quiet. Can't you feel it?'

'N-no, Mam.'

'Well I *can*. It's like a stillness you can almost smell – the quiet before the siren, I mean.'

'You think there's going to be a raid?' Ness sucked in her breath.

'I hope not, but I think there is. You get to recognize it – a sort of *waiting* . . .'

'Then hadn't we best go inside – if you're sure, I mean?'

'Not *sure*, Ness, but almost.'

They had hardly reached the back door when the first siren sounded distantly, then another, nearer, then the one just two streets away, at the ARP post.

Hell! Did they have to wail so, Ness thought, part in anger, part in fear. That awful howling was enough to send anyone into a panic. Her mouth had gone dry. To turn the key in the door behind her was an effort because her hands were shaking so.

'It's all right, Nan.' She laid an arm around her grandmother's shoulders. 'We'll go down to the cellar.'

'No, Ness. Not just yet.'

Rose was calmer now. Going through the air-raid routine helped ease the terror that always took her when the siren sounded. It helped to do familiar things; putting the fireguard in place, turning off the water and gas.

She took the small case in which she kept birth certificates, ration books, her bank book and precious photographs. Methodically, she checked the contents, placed her purse beside them, then snapped shut the lid.

'Gas masks, Sam? Don't forget them.'

They heard the first bomb then. Not so much an explosion; more a shuddering, shaking boom.

'Far enough away. The docks, most likely.' Sam Nightingale ran his tongue round his lips. 'Best we get downstairs. Come on, Nan. I'll give you a hand.'

'After you, Mam.' Ness stood with a finger on the light switch. 'I'll follow you down.'

She knew the drill. You didn't shut inside doors and it was best you left windows just a little way open. Because of the blast. A tightly-closed door or window took more of a battering than one with a bit of give in it. She pulled the door to behind her, clicked off the light, then felt her way down the stone steps with the toe of her shoe.

'Everybody all right, then?'

No one answered. Stupid to ask, really. Of course they were all right – until the next one fell. It was what they were listening for, and how much closer it might be; how soon they would need to huddle beneath the table.

Ness reached for her grandmother's hand and held it tightly. Such a frail, frightened old hand. Two wars, Nan had seen. It wasn't fair. She dismissed from her mind the fact that old people and children in Germany were being bombed by the RAF, and hated Hitler with all the strength inside her. Nan once told her that Hitler had stayed in Liverpool before the Great War with an aunt; some swore honest-to-God-true he'd actually been *born* in Liverpool. That being the case, more's the pity the midwife hadn't had a drop or two of gin inside her when she birthed him and dropped the kid on its head before she'd even slapped its bottom!

Another bomb fell and another and another. Ness closed her eyes and pulled the old woman closer.

''S all right, Nan. We're safe as houses, down here.'

Her tongue made little clicking noises against the roof of her mouth and she crossed her fingers as she said it and closed her eyes tightly and thought about Lorna and Ladybower and Glebe Farm, but it did not stop the shaking nor the anger inside her.

She wished she knew how to pray, but maybe hating was the next best thing . . .

Sunday, May 4th. Lorna smiled as she peeled potatoes. This morning they had made love. Everything was back to normal. William was more relaxed, probably because he had worn civilian clothes since his arrival on Thursday, and the Royal Army Pay Corps and everything khaki-coloured seemed to have been pushed to the back of his mind.

It was when they were drinking tea at the kitchen table that William shattered her mood of wellbeing.

'Seen the piece in the paper – about Liverpool, I mean?'

'What about Liverpool?' Her head jerked sharply upwards.

'Isn't that where your land girl lives?'

'You know she does! They haven't been bombed?'

'Seems like it. Pretty badly – three nights running. Thursday, Friday and last night.' He offered the paper. 'Read it for yourself.'

'But there was nothing on the wireless about it! Three nights, and they think not to tell us. Why do they sit on bad news for so long? Why do they treat us like children?'

'The government, Lorna, knows what it's about; it doesn't give out news willy-nilly. It's called censorship, my dear.'

'Whatever they call it, it doesn't help Ness, does it? Why hasn't she phoned to let me know they're all right at Ruth Street?'

'Because they might *not* be all right.'

'William! What a terrible thing to say!'

'We-e-ll – maybe she couldn't ring,' he shrugged. 'Maybe the phones are off. One hit could put the entire system out of action. Don't worry. I'm sure your land girl will be all right.'

'Ness! Her name is *Ness*,' Lorna hissed. 'There's tea in the pot if you want another cup. I'm going to see Nance.'

'Whatever for?'

'To ask her if she's heard anything on the news I might have missed – about Liverpool, of course!'

'But it won't be any different on the wireless. Don't you think you're worrying over much? Sorry I spoke now. Sorry I took the trouble to collect the paper.'

But he said it to an empty kitchen, because Lorna was running down the front path, heels flying, in search of news she didn't want to hear.

'*Women*!' Sighing, William made for the sitting room,

settled himself in his favourite chair beside the window, folded his arms over his stomach and closed his eyes. A little nap, perhaps, until she was back . . .

'It's the milkie, Mam,' Ness called from the door. 'Wants to know if you'd like extra. He's got some over.'

It made sense, she thought. Half the houses on his round were gone, or the people in them had taken off. It surprised her that, in spite of everything, the milkman was still trying to deliver.

'Please. Tell him to put it on the bill, will you – and thank him ever so much.'

'Two extra for number three.' The milkman wrote in his book. 'Ta-ra,' he grinned, as if he hadn't spent three nights in the shelter nor had to walk to the depot each morning, to pick up his float. 'See you tomorrow!'

Tomorrow. Would they see tomorrow? Would there be yet another night in the cellar? And would the milkie be calling, Ness thought despairingly. Would those bombers get the depot tonight, like they'd got the stations and the main telephone exchange and the sorting office? Because they hadn't seen sight nor sound of the postman since Friday morning. Maybe they'd got the postie, too?

'Why don't you two go to bed, get a bit of rest? I'll call you, if anything happens.'

Nan and Mam looked asleep on their feet. Three nights of bombing had seen to that. And as for Da – he'd walked to work every morning like nothing had happened. All the way to Lewis's despatch department, then walked back again at night, because it was quicker that way.

Mam looked worn out, and Nan seemed to have got smaller and slower, seemed dazed by it all. If there was one more night of it, Ness vowed tight-lipped, she would insist they try to get over the water to Perce and Tizzy's. Rumour had it that things weren't quite so bad on the Cheshire side. It might be worth a try, if the ferries were still sailing, that was. Street gossip had it that there had been no local trains into or out of Liverpool, so it was useless trying to get there by Underground.

Talks. Rumour. The Army called in because of looting, some said, and hospitals full and turning away injured. Mind, it might just be talk. She had no way of knowing and anyway, she was past caring.

All at once she longed for Ladybower and the peace of it and the quietness. And the safeness. But Nun Ainsty was a long way away, an impossible way away because right now, Ness thought despairingly, to be able to get to the Pierhead, even, would be nothing short of a miracle.

She closed her eyes tightly against tears. She *wouldn't* weep. Not in front of Mam and Nan but oh, what wouldn't she give to know that tonight the sirens would stay silent and the bombers wouldn't come. And maybe they wouldn't. After all, there was precious little left to drop their bombs on!

'Did you hear what I said, you two?' she said, as cheerfully as she was able. 'Bed! This minute, and no messin'.'

'It's serious, Nance thinks.'

Lorna burst into the room and William gave a little snort, blinked his eyes and straightened his back.

'Serious what?'

'Not what. *Where*. In Liverpool. Ewan MacMillan told Nance that one of his orderlies lives there and has gone home on compassionate leave. His wife is expecting and nearly due. He wants to get her somewhere safer.'

'Who is Ewan MacMillan?'

'You know who he is! He's the medical officer at the manor! I used to write letters for his blind soldiers. Things must be serious to warrant compassionate leave. The orderly is going to try to get his wife to her sister's place, in North Wales.'

'If he can get her there. If they've had it bad in Liverpool, maybe there is no transport. Well, it seems there are no phones . . .'

'Don't be sarcastic. Ness would have rung, if she could. They aren't on the phone at home. And I don't know how you can sit there so – so *complacent*, William. Doesn't it ever occur to you there's a war on?'

'It does, Lorna. I'm helping to fight it.' His reply was bland. 'And before you and I get heated up over something neither of us can do anything about, I think I'll take a walk round the village.'

She was about to say she was sorry, then changed her mind because she wasn't sorry. Then she almost said she would go with him, that a walk was just what they needed. But she didn't say that either because she knew that William was right; stupid of them to have a quarrel and spoil his leave because of words about Liverpool. Best accept what she could not change, even though she would still worry about Ness.

Sighing, she thought instead about this morning and their lovemaking. William had kissed the tip of her nose, her mouth, her nipples. For a little while it seemed as if the war had not happened, that he had never been away, yet two hours later they were on the verge of a quarrel because she was concerned about someone he did not even know, nor had any wish to meet.

For a little while she considered running after him, linking arms, telling him she was sorry, because wasn't it always she who apologized? It was easier that way, she had found.

So instead she rounded her mouth into a mutinous button, because just this once she would *not* say she was sorry. This time it was William's turn to give in – and he would. Before Tuesday night!

''Bye, William.' Lorna stood at the gate wiggling her fingers in a wave. 'Take care, darling. Try to ring – let me know you've got there.'

William stuck his arm out of the window in an answering goodbye, then turned left into Priory Lane, accelerating as if impatient to be away.

Lorna watched him go, wondering why this time she wasn't crying. Strange, because she always allowed a tear when he had gone. Maybe she was getting used to goodbyes.

'I'll get up when your alarm goes,' William had said. 'Might as well make an early start – take it easy.'

'But won't you be staying for lunch?'

'No point. Half the morning'll be gone before you're back, old girl.'

'But I always finish by nine. You know I do.'

He hadn't wanted to stay, she thought dully, hadn't wanted to eke out their last morning. It was as if he was punishing her for the jangling alarm at five-thirty every morning. But delivering letters was a part of her war work. She had no choice. Surely he understood?

A tear ran down her cheek; not because of William's leaving but for herself, and self-pity wouldn't do! She brushed it away and sniffed inelegantly, checking that the back door was shut. Six o'clock, and already late! She mounted her red GPO cycle and pedalled up the lane that led to Meltonby and Mrs B who would have the kettle on. And there would be the GPO driver from York and the friendly bus conductor who always waved. Nice people. Ordinary people like herself doing the best they could for the war effort. Nothing glamorous like being a fighter pilot or a commando; just decent folk trying to see that letters were delivered like always, and that the local bus ran on time.

And later, before she went to the surgery, she decided she would call at the manor, ask Ewan if his orderly was back and had brought any news with him. Because Liverpool had been bombed seven nights running, and today, Ness's leave ended. Today, she would be back – or would she?

'Oh, damn this war,' she hissed, not caring who might be

lurking behind the hedges either side of the lane. 'I'm sick of it! Bloody sick!'

The medical officer was leaning, arms folded, against a headless statue at the top of the stone steps leading to the front door, and he smiled and walked to meet her.

'Ewan. Can you spare me five minutes?'

'Surely. Was just taking a breather. Like to walk?'

The manor gardens were wild and overgrown, but paths still led to seats and an ornamental pond, green all over with slime.

'Water lilies grew there, once. I came here with Gran, sometimes, when the house was lived in.'

'Careful,' Ewan cautioned as they walked around the pond. 'The path is slippery here. Wouldn't want you to fall into that lot.' He offered a hand, guiding her over the wet moss, making for a wooden seat. 'Mind if I smoke?'

Lorna shook her head, watching him inhale deeply, then said,

'Your orderly – is he back from Liverpool yet?'

'Corporal Prentice? Back yesterday. Seems to have got things sorted.'

'Did he say how things were there? Ness went on leave and I haven't heard from her. She's due back today.'

'And you're worried?'

'Very worried. As far as we've been told, they've had seven nights of air raids; maybe they're still getting bombed. I wrote a couple of days ago – just in case – though how long it will take, if it gets there at all, I just don't know.'

'Prentice said it was pretty bad, but he managed to get his wife to her sister's place in North Wales. They hitched lifts most of the way, I believe.'

'Maybe because buses and trains aren't running there. They won't be, will they, if roads and streets are blocked, and stations bombed.'

'Makes sense, I suppose. But he got his wife out and

managed to get back here – things can't be all bad, Lorna.'

'But bad enough. I feel dreadful about it. Y'see, I'm pretty certain Ness took her leave because William was due home – didn't want to clash. William doesn't like Ness being at Ladybower.' She looked down at her hands, knowing she was being disloyal to her husband yet unable to stop the flow of guilt. 'Seems that between us, William and me landed her in the bombing. Our fault . . .'

'Why, for heaven's sake?'

'Because he told me Ness must go, but I didn't take any notice. I like having her. She's good company. I took her because Nance Ellery said we'd probably get evacuees again. I panicked, I suppose, because William didn't like the evacuees, either, and I thought a grown-up would be the lesser of two evils.'

'I see.' Ewan bit back the words he almost said; like asking if there was anything at all that William *did* like. 'Pity. Ness seems a nice young woman. I see her in the farmyard, you know – almost always smiling.'

'Well, I'll bet she isn't smiling right now. And I still think it's partly my fault she's there.'

'Partly William's fault, too. If blame there must be, don't take it all, Lorna. She'll turn up – bet you anything you like. Don't start worrying yet. There's any amount of things might have kept her.'

'You're right, but I think I'll call at Glebe after work. They might have heard something.'

'I doubt it. It would be you Ness would get in touch with. Promise you won't worry too much? And just think – when you get home she might be there.'

'Yes, she might. She's got her own key. She'll be there, smiling, saying, "Hullo, queen."' Lorna's voice trembled and she got to her feet. 'Got to go. Better not be late on my first day back. And thanks for listening. I appreciate it.'

'Any time. Confessions heard, comfort given. I'll walk you as far as the gates,' Ewan smiled. 'Ness will be all right.

She strikes me as being a young lady who can look after herself.'

He hoped so, he thought, as he watched Lorna ride away, because what Corporal Prentice had told him had been shocking in the extreme, and best not repeated. Lorna was miserable enough; her man gone back to his regiment, and Ness missing. It made him wonder if William was partly the cause of her worry and if so, why? William Hatherwood. A bit of a mystery, Ewan shrugged, sending his cigarette end spinning. He stood until she was out of sight, trying not to heed the small voice of his conscience that reminded him she was married and unavailable; to wipe from his mind that delightful little bottom, those so-blue eyes and the air of innocence about her, and get on with his war, if he knew what was good for him!

But what was good for us, he frowned, wasn't necessarily what we wanted, nor deserved. Life was funny that way.

On Saturday morning, Lorna opened William's letter. She had stuffed it into her pocket when sorting the mail on the long narrow table at the back of the post office, tutting that yet again there was nothing from Ness. And for all William's letter contained he might just as well not have sent it!

His journey back to Aldershot had been interrupted by a slow-moving convoy of Army lorries and trucks, otherwise he had arrived without incident. He thanked her for an enjoyable leave and said he would write more fully later as he was in haste to catch the 11 a.m. collection. The letter ended with, *Take care of yourself, Affectionately, William*, and not one word enquiring about Ness.

But he didn't care about Ness. He even blamed Ness for the hens on his lawn, yet ate one of their eggs every morning entirely without conscience!

'Where are you?' Lorna demanded of the geranium on the kitchen windowsill. 'Why haven't you got a message through to me? I'm worried, Ness.'

Kate was worried, too, and Bob, and Nance said there was nothing anyone could do but wait and hope and pray, none of which were options that appealed to Lorna who was in favour of something more drastic, like getting the next train to Liverpool, though whether there was a station for it to arrive at was open to debate.

'I am *sick* of this war!' She glared at the plant. Sick of trying her hardest for the war effort though in truth it was little enough; sick of a husband who, when he came on leave, was not very husbandly; sick of towns and cities being bombed and fed-up almost beyond endurance waiting for the invasion that must surely come any time now, or why were ports being bombed with such Teutonic thoroughness?

Then she whispered, 'Sorry', to the geranium because it was wrong and unpatriotic to complain when she was safe in Nun Ainsty and William in no danger. Not like soldiers in the North African desert nor merchant seamen who were sitting targets for U-boat packs that seemed to sink any ship they fancied, if what Ness had told her was true.

Ness. Where *was* she and oh, please let her be all right?

Sunday morning. Bright and sunny and no letters or papers to deliver and the surgery closed. Today was her own to do with as she wished; to potter in the garden, write to William. But she did not want to do any of those things nor go to Eucharist at St Philippa's because she was weary of praying to a god who took not one blind bit of notice of her pleadings. All she wanted was to think about Ness, will her back. She was missing her more than she thought possible, realizing that life at Ladybower was going to be very lonely if she had to endure a duration without the land girl who had come to mean so much to her. Lovely, happy, good-to-have-around Ness, and oh, where are you and how are you, and please try to phone?

But the phone did not ring and it was not until late that evening when Lorna was shutting up the hens that she heard a tractor stop outside and voices that sounded uncommonly like those of Bob Wintersgill and – no, it *couldn't* be!

'*Ness*!' She ran to the gate, arms wide open. 'You're all right! I've been worried sick!'

Ness was back, and Bob carrying her case up the path, smiling, saying he had picked her up at the top of Priory Lane.

'Hullo, queen. Good to be back. I missed you.'

'And *I* missed *you*! What on earth happened?'

'It's a long story and right now I'd kill for a cup of tea. And thanks, Bob, for the lift. See you tomorrow, eh?'

And Bob said it was fine by him and drove off with a roar and a belch of fumes to spread the good news.

'Was it terrible,' Lorna asked when they were seated at the kitchen table, almost as if Ness had never been away.

'Terrible. Couldn't get here any sooner. No trains. Got a bus, eventually, to Preston then a train to Leeds, then hitched a lift on an RAF lorry, goin' to Linton.'

Her voice trailed off and for the first time Lorna saw the paleness of her face, the dark rings beneath her eyes, a mouth set tight with fatigue.

'And your parents?'

'Fine, thanks be. And Tizzy and Perce. Them bombers came every night for a week, left the place in a right mess.'

'But they've stopped?'

'Two nights ago. Had to, I suppose. Nuthin' much left standing to bomb . . .'

'I am *so* sorry.' Lorna reached across the table, taking Ness's hands, holding them tightly. 'And *so* relieved to have you back.'

'I'm lucky to be back. But can we talk about it later and is there water for a bath? Don't seem to have had a decent wash for a week. No water, see, after the third night. No phones, either. Couldn't ring.' She closed her eyes tightly against tears. 'Sorry, Lorna, but I'm dead beat.'

'Of course you are and of course you can have a bath.

Take all the water you want and be blowed to the six inches lark. Want to use my best soap?'

'No, ta. All I need is a good long soak.'

'Then up you go and leave the bolt off the door so I can check you haven't fallen asleep.'

Lorna closed her eyes, said a fervent thank you for prayers answered, then picked up the phone to tell Mrs B and Nance that Ness was back. Yet for all her elation, she knew she would not mention it to William in her next letter. Some things it were best you didn't tell your husband.

Sneaky? She supposed it was, but the Lorna who gazed from the hall mirror had grown up a lot in the year since she waved her husband off at York station; had taken in a land girl, said goodbye to her long frizzy hair, ruined the back lawn, taken to using lipstick, and had two jobs.

'Not bad going, Mrs Hatherwood.' The woman in the mirror smiled smugly back, winking solemnly, and Lorna hugged herself tightly and did a little dance around the hall because all was well again at Ladybower.

Ness sat beside Mick on the grassy headland of the field, mug in hand. They had been thinning-out sugar beet seedlings, leaving a hoe's width between plants. Mick was at one end of a row, she at the other, meeting and passing with a smile, but saying little. Ness was still tired, still worried about Ruth Street and if the bombing would start again. Mick recognized her withdrawal and left her alone – until Kate arrived with drinkings and mugs, that was.

'Want to talk about it, Ness?' They settled themselves on the grass.

'Not especially, but I've got to tell someone – get it off my chest. Didn't say much to Lorna. Got myself straight off to bed last night and just flaked out. But it's wicked what they've done to Liverpool, Mick. I wanted to get out of it, yet I wanted to stay with Mam and Da. Nan was terrified, seemed to get older and smaller. We tried to sleep in the day.

Da's work has been bombed. He went in to help with the clearing up, but the place is badly knocked about; it'll take ages to get it sheeted over and back for business. Lewis's he works at – the despatch department. Nuthin' to despatch, at the moment. Nuthin' anywhere but piles of bomb rubble. They say there's still people to dig out. The Army came. Some said it was to stop the looting, but they're helping to get the streets opened up, and the phones going again.

'The stink is awful, Mick. Wet, burned wood, sewers blown wide open, people going round the mortuaries, looking for family – makeshift places in drill halls and schools and lines of dead, most of them white over with bomb dust. Or so people say.' Eyes narrowed she squinted into the sky at three bombers flying low overhead. 'Those are ours, aren't they?'

'Yes. Looks as if they're flying tonight . . .'

'Well, good on 'em. Give that lot a bit of their own back. D'you know, Mick, there are thousands homeless, in rest centres. Lost everything, most of them. At least number three is all right. One or two roof slates off and a couple of window panes broken, but we were lucky.'

'You'll be trying to get through to them tonight?'

'Nah. Phones all out of action and anyway, we haven't got one at home. They say the main sorting office in Liverpewl copped it as well, so it looks as if we'll be back to using carrier pigeons.' She tried to smile, but the tears in her throat were stopping her. 'I hate Hitler. What has me Nan ever done to him? And the woman next door – her husband's at sea and she's got two kids to bring up on her own. What did them kids ever do to them *Jairmans*, will you tell me?'

The tears were running down her cheeks now, her shoulders shook, and Mick hushed her and pulled her into his arms so that her cheek rested on his chest.

'It's all right, Ness. Let it come.'

He didn't think about her nearness. All he could think as he stroked her hair, was that he was a man who refused to fight.

Even though old people and children were being bombed, he was still a conscientious objector who refused to join the Armed Forces. Those people in Liverpool could not fight back; they must cower in shelters and pray they would make it through the night. Yet he, young and fit, refused to take up arms because of what he believed – *sincerely* believed.

Small wonder Ness refused him when he asked her for a date. What decent girl would want to be seen out with a conchie? And what about the man who lived next door in Liverpool who had left a wife and children and gone to sea and who would learn, through his ship's wireless office, that his home port was being blitzed. How would he feel? How would they all feel, those men who had gone to war?

He could not tell. All he knew was that he would not fight nor take part in killing, and being spat upon in the street was only the smallest part of it.

'All right now?' he whispered. 'Feel a bit better?' He took her chin, wiping dry her cheeks. 'Drink your tea, eh?'

'Ar. Better had,' she said sniffily, 'or anybody seein' us like this would think we were kissin' in the hedge bottom, and we aren't.'

'Of course not.' He got to his feet, offering his hand, pulling her up beside him, laughing. Yet, for all that, he thought of the many times he had wanted to do just that – kiss her breathlessly.

'Come on then, Mick Hardie,' she laughed with him. 'This and better may do, but this and worse isn't goin' to get this war won.'

Another bomber flew overhead, and he wondered what it would be like for the RAF crews who tonight would fly over Germany, knowing that many of them would not return.

But he was a conchie and conchies didn't fight. Nor get killed. It was why most people despised them.

TWELVE

Soon it would be Midsummer Day. Lorna sat, face to the Sunday morning sun, a smile lifting the corners of her mouth. She had read again William's once-weekly letter which had been unusually affectionate.

> *Take care of yourself,* he had ended. *I think of you often, and with love . . .*

Such affection came as a relief, especially as since he went back to Aldershot, William's letters had been businesslike and brief, with few loving thoughts in them.

She opened her eyes to gaze at the beech which overhung the garden. It was in full leaf now, as were all the trees in Dickon's Wood. And the air was warm again, the evenings long. No blackout until eleven and sun-up by six each morning.

'Asleep, Ness?'

'No. Just thinking.'

'Like . . . ?'

'Like Liverpool is back to normal again – well, as normal as it'll ever be.'

Mangled tram tracks repaired, buses running again, rubble cleared from the streets and piled high where shops and offices had stood. And telephones, too, more or less working. Da had phoned twice from the pub. Da wasn't soft. The pub was the best place from which to book a trunk call. Waiting for the exchange to get you through was more bearable with a pint of ale to help it along.

'And no more air raids?'

'Fingers crossed – no. But then, London's getting it all now. How they stand it, I don't know. Seven nights were more'n enough for me.' It would be a long time before she could think of the vicious bombing of her city and not hurt inside. 'Mam said in her letter that they are all going over the water for Sunday supper tonight. Uncle Perce came by a joint of beef, so they're sharing it.'

'Black market?' No one got joints of meat these days. 'Off the ration?'

'Mam didn't say. Well, she wouldn't. You never know if one of those snoopin' censors will open your letter.'

'Suppose not.' Censors were not popular. They read your private letters as their God-given right and cut things out of them they decided were a danger to the defence of the realm. 'Well, *we'll* be having corned beef for supper, and salad.'

If you could call a small lettuce, a very small piece of cucumber and two tomatoes a salad. But they wouldn't have had salad at all, had not the Meltonby greengrocer called at the surgery for his wife's indigestion mixture, with a bundle wrapped in newspaper.

'Salad. From under the counter, Mrs Hatherwood.'

She had thanked him sincerely, yet wishing it could have been the butcher's wife who suffered from indigestion. Imagine? Under-the-counter sausages!

'Isn't it lovely and warm?' Ness purred. 'This weather looks set for days. Wouldn't be surprised if Bob doesn't make a start on the hay tomorrow.'

She knew all about haymaking, this being her second summer at Glebe Farm.

'Mm. Bob usually cuts around after Barnaby-bright.'

'Wot?'

'Barnaby. St Barnabas' Day. Eleventh of June.'

'Then he's a bit adrift, isn't he?'

'Well, there or thereabouts and – oh! Phone!'

'You get it.' Ness closed her eyes, settling her head on her hands. She had had her call from home yesterday. This one would be for Lorna. William, perhaps?

'That was Nance!' Lorna was back in an instant. 'They've just interrupted the Home Service to say there'll be an important announcement on the six o'clock news. It's the invasion, Ness! I know it is!'

'Of course it isn't the invasion! If it had been, they'd have been ringing the church bells like mad.'

'St Philippa's hasn't got a bell.'

'*Not* the invasion,' Ness said with more conviction than she felt, because if Hitler was going to do it, now was the time. 'I mean – they'd have called the Home Guard out wouldn't they, and sounded the siren, and they haven't. And if it really is the invasion, they'd have said so there and then and not made us wait two hours till the six o'clock news. Stands to sense, dunnit?'

'Does it?' When did anything the government said or did make sense? 'Come to think of it, we've had one or two cheerful bits of news recently. Reasonable to suppose we can expect a slap in the teeth.'

'Granted – well, about the good news, I mean.' After all, Ness was bound to admit, there had been no more air raids on Liverpool since the May blitz, almost a hundred Hurricanes and Spitfires had got through to help defend poor little Malta that was getting bombed something rotten, and Rudolf Hess had deserted the Nazi party and landed up in Scotland. But Hess wasn't good news, exactly. Hess was mad as a hatter; had to be, or why else would he come to this bomb-happy island? 'And we sank the *Bismarck*, Lorna . . .'

'Yes, after they'd sunk our HMS *Hood*. But you really don't think it's the invasion?'

'Of course I don't. Maybe it's – it's an ounce on the butter ration.'

'Not important enough for a special announcement.'

'Now see here, queen, you asked me and I told you. I *don't* think the invasion has started. I can't tell you why, but I don't! And instead of worrying ourselves sick and spoiling our Sunday off, why don't we go for a walk, or sumthin' to take our minds off it.'

'When Gran was worried, she always baked a cake,' Lorna whispered. 'Wish I could.'

'Well you can't. Nobody's got rations to spare for cakes when there's a war on, so we'll cut the lawn instead – well, what's left of it.' Ness forced her lips into a grin. 'Or you can see to the grass and I'll make a start on the ironing – unless you want Minnie to do it tomorrow?'

Grass cutting, ironing, mucking-out the cowshed even, was better than waiting for the six o'clock news and Lorna's dratted invasion.

Reluctantly, Ness got to her feet, sad that the lovely day had been spoiled because surely after all the months of making up his mind, Hitler couldn't have decided that now was the time to invade the British?

But wasn't it always one step forward, two steps back? One piece of good news, then something really bad. It was the way the war seemed to be going – for our side, at least. At this rate it was going to be years and years before we got it over and done with!

Sending malevolent thoughts winging high, Ness made for the kitchen and the basket piled high with neatly folded clothes. She disliked ironing – would rather scrub a floor – but at this minute she disliked Hitler more, and wished she really could curse him. The war would be over next week, though, if she'd been any good at it.

But it did no harm to try, so she closed her eyes tightly and sent belly ache, toothache and a thumping headache in the direction of Berchtesgaden.

And oh please, *please* not the invasion . . . ?

*   *   *

The ironing was done, the grass cut and two corned beef salads sat on the slate slab in the pantry, because neither Ness nor Lorna was hungry. Ten long, aching minutes to go before the BBC announcer told them, in his funereal voice, what they least wanted to hear.

In the sitting room, windows wide open to the early evening, they sat, feet tucked beneath them, urging the mantel clock to tick faster, willing it not to.

'It *can't* be the invasion,' Ness muttered. 'I mean – the bombers would have taken off, wouldn't they, and there hasn't been a plane in the sky all day.'

'Then maybe that's significant.' Normally there seemed to always be bombers flying low overhead.

'And Mrs Ellery hasn't rung, has she? If there'd been anything to tell, surely she would have. Her husband's in the Home Guard, she'd have let us know if they'd all been put on standby?'

In Nun Ainsty, Ness had learned, news went round the houses with lightning speed.

'You'd think so – but who are you trying to convince, Ness? Yourself, or me?'

'That clock,' Ness avoided the question, 'hasn't moved for ages. I'll swear it hasn't! And I'm not trying to convince anybody! We'll be all right!'

Oh, please they would? No grey-uniformed soldiers goose stepping down London streets or Liverpool streets? No goose stepping *anywhere* in these islands?

'I'm going out.' Lorna jumped to her feet. 'Forgot to feed the hens. Give me a shout when the pips start?'

'I'll come with you.'

Ness did not want to face the clock and the wireless alone. Yet when they had thrown wheat and collected eggs and returned reluctantly to the house, six o'clock was still a minute away.

'I'm switching on now!' Button-mouthed, Lorna swung the dial and clicked on the switch. Then she closed her eyes to wait for the pips that would bleep out six o'clock, and when they had sounded there would be no turning back the clock. She ran her tongue round her lips, sucking in a calming breath, letting it go in little huffs.

'*This is the BBC Home Service. Here is the six o'clock news, and this is Alvar Lidell reading it.*

This morning, at first light, Nazi armed forces invaded the Soviet Union. Reports reaching Stockholm from Moscow indicate that on a front of 1800 miles from Finland to the Black Sea, 100 divisions crossed into Russia without a declaration of war. Waves of Luftwaffe bombers . . .'

'Russia!' Ness hissed. 'They've invaded *Russia*!'

'Ssssh! Listen!' Lorna's face was white, her eyes wide.

'. . . *have attacked airfields, gun positions and troop concentrations. Towns also attacked are Kiev, Sebastopol and Minsk.*

'*Moscow, Leningrad and Stalingrad are preparing to meet heavy air raids. Vice Commissar Molotov has already broadcast to the Russian people, stating that the responsibility for the attack falls upon the German Fascist leader.*

'*Mr Molotov called for self-sacrifice and self-discipline from all citizens of the Soviet Union and declared that the Red Army will wage war against the arrogant Hitler and beat back his forces . . .*'

'Oh, my Lord!' Lorna could remain silent no longer. 'Did you hear it? Has Hitler really attacked Russia?'

'Seems like it. And them two with a pact not to attack each other!'

'Not worth the paper it was printed on, Ness!'

'. . . *German forces have penetrated several miles within the Soviet borders and appear to have met with little resistance . . .*'

'I'm shaking all over.'

'Me, too. I feel sick.' Lorna switched off the wireless. 'Is nothing and nowhere sacred? That man is power mad; thinks he can do just what he likes!'

'Yes, and this far he's got away with it! I can't take it in! Could do with a brandy, or sumthin' – for the shock, I mean.'

'Well we haven't got any, nor sherry, so it'll have to be tea. We'll have a cup of tea, then try to talk about it sensibly.'

'There's nothing sensible about attacking a country you're supposed to be friends with.'

'Agreed. But we *did* hear it?' Lorna set the kettle to boil. 'Hitler *has* invaded Russia?'

'He has.' Ness pulled out a chair to sit, chin on hands, at the kitchen table. 'He's invaded Russia and we all thought it was going to be us!'

'And are you thinking what I'm thinking?'

'That we're very sorry for Russia, but we're glad Hitler changed his mind?'

'Something like that.' Lorna slid a carefully-levelled spoon of tea into the smallest pot. 'And there was me, thinking it was only a matter of time before we were invaded. I was sure we would be. It was always there, nagging at the back of my mind, yet now . . .'

'Now it seems we're off the hook – for the time being, at least. Seems them *Jairmans* have got bigger fish to fry. Will we be mates with the Russians now, do you think?'

'I don't know, but I suppose we're both fighting on the same side – their enemy is our enemy. Dammit! I feel like weeping, yet I know I should be glad, Ness.'

'Then get pouring, girl. I suppose we couldn't spare a spoon of sugar?'

'You suppose correctly.' Lorna plopped a saccharin tablet into each cup then stirred her own noisily. 'And do we listen to the nine o'clock news – make sure we got it right, or shall we go to the pub, find out what people think about it? I wish William wasn't so far away.'

William. This was the first time she had thought of him since Nance phoned this morning, and she should have thought about him, wished him with her to tell her there was nothing to worry about. But William was in the Army and she was learning to face her fears alone.

'Penny for them?' Ness's fingers snapped. 'You were miles away.'

'Oh, I was only thinking that William isn't here and that –' She shrugged, cheeks pinking. 'We-e-ll, I'm not doing too badly on my own, am I? And are you game for going to the pub, after supper – see if there's any more news?'

'Let's see how we feel when we've eaten.'

'Fine by me, Ness.' All at once, to think of chewing limp lettuce no longer dismayed Lorna. 'I'll cut the bread, you lay the table – OK?'

They did not go to the White Hart, deciding that Ladybower was the best place to be in case anyone phoned.

'William might try to get through.'

'And Mam. But I don't think they'll be lucky, Lorna. The phones will be buzzing with military calls since the news broke. There won't be any trunk lines for civilian calls.'

'So let's sit in the garden?'

Ladybower's garden was safe and familiar. The roses that climbed the walls were in bloom and the trees of Dickon's Wood ringed round it protectively. In the garden, you could shut out the war if you didn't look at the strips of criss-crossed brown paper on the windows; if the almost constant drone of planes overhead didn't remind you that some city in Germany would be bombed tonight.

'Do you suppose they'll let up on London now? If they're bombing Russia they can't bomb London, can they, Ness?'

'Suppose not. It's funny, innit – funny peculiar, I mean – that not so long ago, everywhere was dark and cold and miserable and we thought we'd never see summer again. Remember New Year's Eve, Lorna? We went mad, and lit a fire in the sitting room.'

'And made wishes when Big Ben chimed. What did you wish for, Ness?'

'Can't remember.'

'Well, I can. I wished for there not to be an invasion and there hasn't been – not England invaded, anyway. I was so sure it would happen. Everyone was sure. When the tides were right, they said, in early summer.'

'And now Russia has copped it instead. You've got to feel sorry for them, Lorna, even if they are Communists.'

'I do, especially for the children. They'll be terrified and bewildered, yet you and I are here feeling glad it isn't us. I should feel guilty, but I don't; just very, very thankful.'

Her voice trembled with tears and Ness reached for her hand.

'It's going to be all right. And there's one thing I do remember about New Year's Eve. We were talking about when the war would end. Didn't seem to be a lot of hope, us sticking it out on our own. Yet now there's another country fighting Hitler; some other country taking the brunt of it. Six months ago we were backs to the wall, yet now we just might start to fight back.'

'With the Russians, you mean? You think our soldiers will be sent there?'

'No. Our soldiers are needed here, but I think we'll help Russia in other ways and it wouldn't surprise me if Mr Roosevelt helps them, too. On the quiet, I mean, Lorna, like he helps us.'

'Reckon it'll be in all the papers in the morning.'

'And I suppose Mr Churchill will speak on the wireless. He usually does, when something happens – straight and to the point, no holds barred. I'm glad we've got Winston.'

'And I'll bet he's glad Hitler has attacked Russia, and not us. Sure you don't want to go to the pub, Ness?'

'Sure. Rather stay here.'

And sit quietly in Ladybower's garden, with the sun still warm and everything green and summer-fresh, like everywhere around was promising a new start after the long dark of winter; promising that for a time at least, this country would be just that bit safer than it had been this morning, before Nance Ellery rang.

No more backs-to-the-wall, dare she hope? Were we really going to start fighting back, somehow, somewhere? And after fighting back, would there come a day when we knew we were going to win?

'I wonder,' she said softly, gazing up into the green depths of the beech tree, 'what Dickon and Ursula would have made of all this . . .'

THIRTEEN

Fighting Back

Lorna glared at the two red ration books with a mixture of alarm and bewilderment. How *could* They ration clothes, she had thought, recalling the newspaper announcement – on a Sunday, would you believe, when all the shops were shut – which had sent the entire nation into shock. Yet here was the proof that They had; two books collected this morning at Meltonby Village Hall. One each for Ness and herself.

She had stood in the queue after finishing her deliveries, amazed she had been able to get Ness's coupons, too, though really it was because Nance, assisting the lady clerk from the Board of Trade, had made it possible.

'I'm not at all sure I can give you Agnes Nightingale's coupons,' the clerk frowned. 'By rights, she should collect them herself.'

'But how is she to get them? She's working, and can't get time off!'

'Yes indeed! War work!' Nance had intervened, declaring there was no reason at all why Lorna should not be given the coupons. 'I can vouch for Mrs Hatherwood!'

The clerk had taken one look at Nance Ellery's bristling bulk and decided against confrontation.

'We-e-ll – just this once I suppose it will be all right.'

Nance did have her uses, Lorna was bound to admit, opening her own book to look at what all the fuss had been about. Sixty-six coupons which must last a year. Ordinary, inch-square pieces of paper, grey-green on white, with Clothing Coupon printed on them and a crown above the letter T. Board of Trade, that stood for. Precious scraps of paper, said to be worth ten shillings each on the black market. Buy a thick winter coat, a pair of shoes, two pairs of silk stockings and you had seven left over for a blouse and two ounces of knitting wool. Six months' allowance gobbled up, which meant that to buy a warm coat was well-nigh impossible – if you needed knickers, a brassiere and a long nightdress, that was.

Clothes, now, were all at once precious and must be hoarded. No giving to jumble sales or to the Salvation Army for bombed-outs. Clothing, she had read in her weekly magazine, should not be discarded at a whim. No shame, now, in handing down or passing on. Or swopping! Or carefully unpicked and the best parts used for short trousers for a small boy, or a kilt for a little girl. Hand-knitted jumpers and cardigans could yield many ounces of coupon-free wool if unravelled and wound into balls. Yet who had the time to unpick trousers and jumpers Lorna sighed, when housework, war work and queueing for unrationed food took up so much time, apart from gardening and letter writing and –

Letter writing. It made her remember the envelope with the Swansea postmark, pushed into her jacket pocket that morning, to be read later. From Rebecca, she was almost sure. *Cariad*. She smiled to recall Private Jones's love name for the little nurse and hoped all was going well for them.

She pushed the coupon books behind the mantel clock, glared at them peevishly, then took out the letter.

'There was a letter this morning, from Rebecca.' Lorna dried the last plate then slotted it in the rack. 'Remember Rebecca?'

''Course I do. *And* a certain letter she never got! How is she?'

'Read it for yourself.' Lorna settled herself in the armchair, pushing off her shoes, wriggling herself comfortable.

'Want me to read it out to you?'

'If you like. I'll close my eyes and pretend it's Rebecca talking to me.'

Ness cleared her throat.

Dear Lorna,

You said to keep in touch, so this is to let you know that Alun and I are fine and looking forward to our wedding, once the Army finally releases him.

At the moment, he is still learning to cope with his blindness, how to do things for himself, like lighting a cigarette without burning his nose, and, more seriously, to learn to ask for help when he gets stuck. Still cussedly independent is my Alun, but gradually learning to live without his eyes . . .

'Ar, hey. Without his eyes, Lord-love-him. Livin' in the dark, havin' to learn to accept it, and him so young. It's shockin', Lorna.'

'But he'll still have his sense of smell and touch, and his memory. And he'll have Becky. But go on Ness, there's an interesting bit coming up.

You will be glad to know that the letter Alun sent me – the one asking me to set him free – has never arrived, but if it ever did, I would tear it up . . .

'And good for her, too. She'll never know what really happened to it, will she? You wouldn't ever tell?'

'Of course not.' Lorna smiled yearningly, remembering other letters between Alun and Rebecca; frank and uninhibited, telling of their need for each other.

I miss you so, cariad. *I want you in my arms, in my bed. I want to make love to you . . .*

She shook away such thoughts and recalled instead the bitterness with which Alun had dictated that end-it-all letter, the sadness it had caused her to put his words on paper. Yet Ewan had thrown it on the fire, taking the blame on himself, absolving her guilt. He would be glad to know, she thought, *deserved* to know, that things were working out well for Private Jones and Nurse Rebecca Pryce.

'I – I suppose Ewan might like to be told,' she said hesitantly. 'After all, he had a hand in it.'

'Good idea. Phone him, why don't you?' Ness said softly, searching the other's face for telltale blushes.

'If you think so . . . ?'

'Of course I do. Reckon he'd appreciate it.'

'Oh. Er – right, then.'

Lorna walked nonchalantly into the hall, lifting the phone, putting it down at once because she had glimpsed her face in the hall mirror, been shocked to see the pleasure in her eyes, the small, shy smile.

She stood, eyes closed, telling herself it was all right, that she had not rushed to get in touch with Ewan MacMillan on the flimsiest of excuses, had not blushed to think that soon she would speak to him. Of course she hadn't! It was just that Ewan was a nice man to talk to – especially if you were lonely and had not had a letter from your husband since Saturday.

'I've changed my mind, Ness.' She sat down heavily. 'I think a short note would be better.'

'Please yourself,' Ness muttered from the deeps of the book she had picked up. 'Ring, write – it's up to you.'

'Like I said, I'll write.' In control again, Lorna sat down at her desk, selecting a sheet of her best, pre-war notepaper.

Dear Ewan,

This is to let you know that today I heard from Nurse Pryce and that she and Alun are fine and planning their wedding.

They are such a lovely couple and I know you will be as pleased as I was to learn that things are working out well for them, and that they seem so happy.

Rebecca mentioned that THE letter had still not arrived, but if it did, she would tear it up. I could not agree with her more!

With all good wishes.

There now! What was wrong with that? Carefully she underlined the word she had written in capitals, then signed her name. A perfectly ordinary letter, which she would leave at the manor in the morning with the rest of the mail.

She folded the sheet of paper, slid it into an envelope, and wrote his name formally in the centre of it: Lieut. E MacMillan, RAMC. Then she moistened the flap with her tongue, taking care not to leave even a trace of lipstick, sealed it carefully, and laid it on the hall table. A letter to a friend, that was all. She glanced quickly into the mirror above the table. She was blushing again; blushing like a teenager! Oh, grow up, Lorna!

At exactly ten-thirty the next morning the phone rang, and Lorna knew it was Ewan. Taking a deep breath, she lifted the receiver.

'Meltonby 223 . . .'

'Lorna! I got your note. Good of you to write.'

'No problem. I thought you would like to know – especially about the – er – missing letter.'

'The one that must have been bombed in Swansea, you mean?' There was laughter in his voice. 'I missed you this morning. The sergeant told me you'd only just left. I ran after you, but never a sign. Wanted to tell you I'm away –'

'*Away*, Ewan? You've been drafted?'

'No! Away on leave! Do you realize I've been here ten months and not had so much as a day off?'

'Oh, *leave*.' Relief she could not prevent washed over her. 'To Scotland?'

'Aye. For ten days, though it'll waste two days of it getting there and back. My locum just arrived.'

'Your – er – family will be pleased to see you.' Small, superfluous talk.

'If they can remember what I look like. Tell you what – it's a bit early for the heather, but if I see any in flower I'll bring you some back. Will that suit?'

'It will, and thank you. I've never been to Scotland.'

'Not ever? Then come with me, and I'll show you.'

'Ha! Where will you be?' She didn't know where he lived.

'In the Highlands. By Ardnamurchan.'

'I'm no wiser, but I'll look it up. And you're to have a good leave – get plenty of rest. Must go now. Thanks for ringing. 'Bye, Ewan.'

''Bye,' she whispered again into the receiver, but the line was dead. Mrs Benson had already pulled out the plugs.

'*Well!*' she said to the empty hall. 'That's it, then,' she said to the face in the mirror.

Abruptly she made for the kitchen, realizing she would miss him. No! Not *miss* him! Why should she? She hardly ever saw him these days. Yet she would know that for ten days he would be miles and miles away, in Scotland. By Ardnamurchan. Even to think it made her strangely sad because although she wouldn't miss him exactly, she would miss the happy feeling that any day, any time, she might turn a corner and see him.

And that was no way for a married woman to feel! How could she even think such a thing; she, who had just about everything any woman could want. But the war was to blame. So many husbands and wives parted through no fault of their own, and all of them lonely.

And there lay the answer! She was a happily-married, *lonely* wife. One of many. Minnie, walking up the path, was lonely too, so why was hoping just sometimes to see Ewan so very awful? Thinking about a man didn't mean she was unfaithful. Well, *did* it?

'Morning, Mrs Hatherwood.' Minnie Holmes hung her jacket on the door peg.

'Hullo. I was about to make a pot of tea. Like a cup?'

'Please – if you don't mind paying me for tea-drinking, that is.'

'Of course I don't, and tell me,' Lorna turned away to fill the kettle because she knew she was blushing. 'Do you ever get lonely?'

'I'll say I do! I miss my man something awful. Thank heaven I've got the bairns.'

'I miss William, too. I – I don't suppose you – er – you could spare me an extra hour, tomorrow?' The words came in a rush. 'Just to do the downstairs inside windows?'

She hadn't intended saying that. She had almost asked if Minnie had fantasies, too – like kissing a film star or hoping to see a certain man when she turned a corner? Somehow, she had bitten back the words.

'Of course I can. Glad of the money. Any time. You've only got to ask.'

'Thanks.' Lorna really meant it. Thanks for making her realize that women were the same the world over and that Minnie, too, might have foolish thoughts, yet it didn't mean she didn't love her husband! 'Tea won't be long,' she smiled.

All at once she did not feel so guilty, and whilst pouring boiling water into the smallest teapot she sent loving thoughts in the direction of Aldershot.

Because William was lonely, too!

Ness kicked off her shoes at the back door then let herself into the empty kitchen.

Won't be home till seven, read the note propped against the geranium on the window-ledge. *Omelettes for supper. L.*

Monday evening. Not unusual for Lorna to be late home, which gave Ness time to get out of her working clothes and into a cool cotton frock. Haymaking was hot and dusty, she had come to learn, but the last load had been stacked and sheeted not an hour ago, she and Kate having made a wish on it – a last-load-of-hay wish being a particularly potent one. Kate had done the afternoon milking alone because a break in the weather threatened, and all hands were needed in the field in a race against time.

'Made it!' Ness had sighed, tired but elated. 'Will I take the cows back to the field or help you hose down?' she had asked of the farmer's wife.

Mick Hardie, standing in the shippon doorway, answered for her. 'Ness and I'll finish off here. Take the weight of your feet, Kate. You look fit to drop.'

'Bless you, lad – if you're sure, that is?'

'I'm sure. Away with you. Ness will help me.'

So Ness had unfastened the cows' neck chains and sent them lumbering across the yard in the direction of the pasture. Being a land girl had its bonuses, especially in summer and more especially since she was beginning to learn the ways of farming. The salon in which she once worked seemed a long way away now.

Mind, Rowley was still a nuisance, though his manners had improved since the night he'd been sent on his staggering way by Goff Leaman. But that was all in the past and since then she had learned from Flora Petch that the young man in question had been seen recently in Meltonby in the company of a young woman with peroxided hair and red nails. Ainsty talk also had it that the young woman had something of a reputation; in short, common as muck, and that Kate wouldn't be best pleased when she learned what was going on. But until she did, good luck to all red-nailed bottle-blondes, if that was what kept Rowley out of Ness Nightingale's hair!

She drank deeply from a glass of water, deciding not to

listen to the six o'clock news when she knew it would be all about bombing. Malta being bombed, London being bombed, Russia being bombed. German planes were even dropping bombs on Moscow now. There seemed to be no stopping the Luftwaffe and no stopping the German soldiers who were pushing deeper into Russia, aiming for Leningrad. Now the Russian people had their backs to the wall, too. It was not an enviable position to be in, especially if you lived in Smolensk which had gone up in flames. The entire city!

'Burn everything as you retreat,' Stalin had ordered. 'Leave nothing but scorched earth behind you!'

Yet in Nun Ainsty all was quiet and still. Here, nothing happened, not even a haunting, Ness thought, as she opened wide her bedroom window to look out on Dickon's Wood. And thinking about the nun made her think about Martha Hugwitty, who had let it be known she was prepared to tell a lady's fortune for the price of a shilling, laid in her left hand. For charity, of course, and the utmost secrecy and discretion guaranteed at all times!

It might be a laugh to part with a shilling, especially if Martha could be persuaded to talk about Ainsty's ghost. Maybe Lorna would agree to go, too, because come to think of it, Lorna could do with a laugh these days. Lorna had something on her mind which Martha's cunning might well draw out.

The open window made little difference to the heat in the room. Outside, nothing moved, not even the leaves on the trees. To the west, low yellow clouds threatened thunder and Ness hoped it would hold off until Lorna was home.

She stepped out of her clothes and walked naked to the bathroom, deciding to suggest a visit to Martha over supper. Just for fun, she would stress, and for a good cause. And because you didn't get many laughs for a shilling these days!

* * *

The air became hotter, the sky more dark. In the distance, thunder rumbled. Ness stood at the front gate, looking left into Priory Lane. The first drops of rain fell darkly on the dry earth as Lorna, pedalling furiously, hurtled up the path.

'Phew! I could see it coming. Went like the clappers. Saw some lightning over near York and it's heading our way. Are you afraid of thunder, Ness?'

'No.' Not if she was home and dry, that was, and could watch it from the window. 'Are you?'

'Not any more. I used to be until Grandpa explained about lightning taking the shortest path to earth. The manor, he said, was the tallest building and most likely to attract it.'

'And he didn't think to mention the trees next door?'

'He didn't. But talking about the manor, Ness, there was a postcard from Ewan.'

'For you?' Ness's head jerked up.

'No, silly! To the surgery. He and Doc Summers are quite good friends. A view of Ardnamurchan. I really must look it up and – ooooh!' Lorna gasped as a lightning flash lit up the room. 'Count, Ness!'

'What on earth for?'

'Because –' A peal of thunder drowned her words, and when it had lessened then rumbled away, Lorna said, 'Because if you count the seconds between flash and crash, that's how many miles away the eye of the storm is.'

'Then it's two seconds – two miles – away. Meltonby, I'd say.'

It was raining hard now. Water ran down the path and into the road and spilled from gutters too full to take the deluge. And when it was over, Ness thought, the sticky heat would be gone and sun-scorched grass would grow green again. The air would be fresh and cool, and would smell of the rose petals the storm had scattered everywhere.

'In any hurry for your supper, Ness? Omelettes don't take long.'

'No. Let's sit here, and watch it. And talking about eggs,

I've seen to the hens. Three eggs today. I suppose you realize they'll go into a moult this autumn? No eggs for weeks.'

'How long?'

'I reckon they'll start laying less about November, then they'll stop altogether, and lose their feathers. Real scraggy they'll look.' Ness was an authority on poultry. 'Mind, they'll feather up and start laying again about Christmas or New Year.'

New Year. Lorna closed her eyes and wondered where they would be, what they would be doing by the time 1942 came round, which led her to wonder how long the war would last and how much more lonely dare she allow herself to become.

She was glad when a crash of thunder overhead cleared her mind of such thoughts, especially as lonely thoughts might well lead to Ewan MacMillan – probably because of today's postcard. And that was foolish, since all the card had contained was *Best wishes from Scotland* and signed *E MacM*.

'When the thunder is over, shall we go out – get some lovely cool air,' Ness asked.

'Yes!' Lorna replied too promptly. 'Anything to get out of the house! As soon as we've had supper, if you want!'

For goodness' sake, Lorna Hatherwood, what is the matter with you! Nothing seems to suit, these days!

Or was her period due? Again. If only William would be careless, just once. But William never did anything without first having thought it out carefully, and a baby was not on the agenda. Not until the war was over, by which time she would be too old to conceive!

Oh, damn this war!

They decided after supper, not to go for a walk because it was still raining. Soft, gentle rain, for all that. You could almost hear the parched earth guzzling it down and the soft *Aaah*! from trees and hedges as it dripped off them. The country-woman in Ness decided it were best it continued all night, nice and steady, because now the hay was safely in, rain was desperately needed for growing crops.

'It's going to be a bit wet for a walk,' she ventured.

'I know, and I really wanted to go out,' Lorna fretted. 'I feel shut in.'

'But you've been out, on and off, all day.'

'OK. So I want to go out again! I don't want to look at four walls, that's all.'

'There'll be dance music on the wireless . . .'

'Out! We can wrap up. A drop of rain won't hurt us,' Lorna persisted.

'Fine by me. Or we could – well – nip over to Martha's?'

'Martha's? Why?'

''Cause she's telling fortunes, for a shilling. For charity. It'd be a giggle, Lorna.'

'We-e-ll . . .' Perhaps it would, at that. Martha was harmless enough. And it *was* for charity. 'I'm game then if you are, though I hope nobody sees us going in.'

'So what if they do? She hasn't got a notice on her door saying *Gypsy Hugwitty – Fortunes told for a bob*, has she?'

'But William might phone, and I'd be out.' Lorna was having second thoughts.

'You reckon?'

William hardly ever phoned. Very difficult getting a trunk line from so far away, Lorna always said. So many soldiers at Aldershot and half of them trying to ring home.

'You're right, Ness. He won't ring. So are we going for a shilling's worth, then?' She forced a smile. 'Like you said, it might be a laugh.'

'Come you in, ladies,' Martha Hugwitty beamed, 'and sit you both down and tell me what I can do for you?'

'Well, we've come to –' Ness hesitated. 'We'd heard you might –'

'Come to support my charity, eh? And very nice, too. Everything confidential. And you can ask one question – if you want to, that is.'

Her cheeks were round and red, her eyes small and black and beady; eyes to make Ness doubt the wisdom of laying her life open – but only for a moment. For fun, they had come. She would take everything Martha might say with a pinch of salt, even if she got close to something best forgotten . . .

'What's the matter, Ness Nightingale? Having doubts, are you? If you don't want to hear anything bad, either of you, just say so and I'll leave it out.'

'Doubts? Of course I'm not. And I don't want anything left out,' Ness said recklessly, dipping into the pocket of her cardigan. 'And here's me money. I'll go first!'

Martha held out her left hand, closed her fingers on the shilling, then placed it in a small glass pot on the mantelpiece.

'Let's get comfortable, then. Draw up a chair. Best we sit at the table, by the window. Can see better. Now, give me your right hand, lass. I never bother with the left. The left is what was intended for you the day you were born; the right is what you've made of life. And no talking. Don't like having my concentration broken. You can ask your question when I'm finished.'

Ness laid her hand palm up on the table top, looking at Lorna because she would rather not look into Martha's eyes, winking slowly.

Lorna did not return the wink but sat there, eyes wide, thinking, Ness shouldn't wonder, if perhaps they had made a mistake in coming and wouldn't it be awful if William ever found out she'd had her fortune told. And by Martha Hugwitty, of all people!

Martha reached for Ness's hand, holding it between her own, taking a long deep breath then letting it out slowly.

'You worry, lass, all the time, about nearest and dearest. Don't. They've got a good guardian angel.'

Mam and Da and Nan, Ness thought. Of course she worried about them! What was new?

'You put on a brave face. You try to hide inside yourself. Stop it. It'll get you nowhere.' Martha's head jerked up, her eyes opened and she laid Ness's hand on the table again. 'There now, that's the clairvoyance. That's what I feel. Now I'll have a look at what else you might expect.'

She took Ness's hand, pursing her lips, holding it closer to the window. Then she said,

'You'll have a long life, Ness Nightingale, and a happy one, an' all. You'll have good health and you'll have two bairns – both of a kind. You and them will never want. There's a break in your lifeline, of no importance now. Whatever it was, you weathered it. Like I said, a good life to come.'

'And that's all?' Hardly a shilling's-worth.

'That's all. Good health and bairns to rear. Isn't that enough for any woman? What more do you want?' Her eyes found Ness's eyes, holding them in a long, significant stare. Then she folded the upturned palm into a fist, covering it with her hand. 'Hold on tight to that luck, Ness. There's not many palms I've seen set as fair as yours.'

'Thanks.' Ness still felt cheated. 'Can I ask my question now?'

'You can.'

'Why haven't you told me the bad things? There's got to be something . . .'

'I told you your life is set fair. If there's bad in your life, it's over and done with. A break in your lifeline, I said. Behind you now. But ask your question, lass.'

'You say I'll never want and I'll have children, which means I'm goin' to marry. Will you just tell me – have I met him yet?'

'You've met him and that's all I'm prepared to say.'

'Thanks.' Ness let go of her breath, tilting her chin. 'You now, Lorna.'

'Y-yes.' Lorna opened her purse, taking out a shilling,

laying it as Ness had done, on Martha's outstretched palm. Then she laid another beside it. 'For your charity, Martha.'

'I thank you. Won't make no difference, though. I say what I see, no matter how much you give.'

'Yes. Of course . . .'

And oh, please don't, Martha? Because if your eyes look into mine, they'll see nothing but a muddle!

'Right, then.' Again the deep breath, the closed eyes and Lorna's right hand held between two old ones. 'Ssssh. Ah, yes. There are troubled waters ahead. You won't expect them, but you'll sail into them, head on. And you'll be strong, and weather the storm. You'll find happiness at the end of it, nothing's more certain.'

'Trouble?' Lorna whispered. 'But –'

'Whisht! I said no talking. And no buts, either. Trouble you will have, and happiness in plenty, an' all.' Martha's eyes opened and she breathed deeply again, as if she were glad the bad bit was over. 'Now, let's have a look at your palm, see what we can make of it.'

'I – I don't think I want to know.' Lorna snatched her hand away. 'And you didn't ask me if I wanted the bad bits, Martha. I'd have told you no, if you had.'

'Troubled seas I said, then a calm and peaceful landfall. A safe and loving haven. And till that comes, you'll learn to stand on your own two feet, Lorna Hatherwood! And there's nothing but good, in the end – once you've weathered that storm, that is. There's a long life and a healthy one for you, and a good man beside you.'

'But I've already got a good man!'

'Then that's as well, isn't it, because there are bairns for you. Three. Now what do you think to that?'

'Children? Three! Martha – if only you knew how much I'd give for just *one*!'

'Then have patience. Like I said, it'll come right.'

'Then can I ask my question? What sex will my children be, Martha, and when?'

'Two of a kind, an' then one. Two lads and a lass, or t'other way round. And you'll conceive them carelessly and happily, but not till the fighting is done. Peacetime bairns, they'll be.'

'Peacetime,' Lorna whispered huskily. 'Well – thanks, Martha.'

'My pleasure, lass. Pity about that old tea rationing. We could have had a go with the tea leaves, an' all.'

'Think we've heard enough.' Ness pushed back her chair. 'Best be off. Things to do, like.'

'I'll see you to the gate. And don't forget, any time you have a problem – well, a trouble shared is a trouble halved, as they say,' Martha nodded. 'Always glad to be of service, and not one word about my lady clients ever passes my lips, be sure of it.'

'Hang on! I've left my purse,' Lorna gasped. 'Won't be a minute.'

'Did you have to say that to her?' Ness said when she and Martha were alone. 'Trouble to come. She'll worry herself sick now!'

'Stop your fretting. Trouble there is and trouble she'll get over. It's you, Ness, needs to bear in mind that your own trouble is over, if you'll let it be. Look to the future. Don't let what is past shape what is to come. And don't look at me so gormless. You know what I'm talking about. And sssssh! She's coming!'

'Sorry! Couldn't find it. It had fallen under the table. Well – I suppose we'd better be off then, and thanks, Martha,' Lorna smiled.

'Any time. You've only got to call. Take care, both of you.'

She smiled as Lorna turned at the gate and held up a hand. Then she closed her door and reached for the glass pot on the mantelpiece, tipping the coins into her hand. Her left hand.

Eight shillings so far, and another lady expected later tonight. Her charity was doing well. She replaced the pot, then set her chair rocking, thinking about the land girl so determined to cling to the past that she was making a rod for her own back. Pity, for all that, about the trouble ahead for Lorna. Bad trouble, though it would make a woman of her. Sheltered, she had been. Suffocated with kindness. And her so meek and eager to please, when underneath it all there was fire and passion, aye, and curiosity an' all, struggling to get out, did the lass but know it.

She replaced the pot, smiling fondly at her accumulation of shillings. Soon she would be able to pay the coalman what she owed him, make sure that when winter came she had a fire in her grate. After all, didn't heaven help them as helped themselves? And didn't charity begin at home and wasn't Martha Hugwitty, spinster of this parish, her own favourite charity?

She closed her eyes to wait for the knock on the door that would come as soon as it was dark, with another shilling to add to her pot! Not a bad night's work, all in all!

'Well! That was short and sweet, if you like!' Ness closed the door firmly behind her as if to put an end to Martha and her nonsense. 'Not bothered, are you, about what she said? Trouble, indeed! You're to take no notice, girl! That one is an old fraud!'

'No, Ness! I don't think she is, and I certainly don't want her to be! Oh, no one in her right mind wants to be told there's a sticky time ahead, but as far as I'm concerned, I want, *need*, to believe her! Forewarned is forearmed, don't they say, so I'll be prepared for it, won't I?'

'But there's a war on, girl, and trouble could mean all sorts of awful things!'

'I know. But it would all come right, Martha said, so I'll have to put up with it when it happens, like other women have to! After all, what's so special about Lorna Hatherwood? And won't it all be worth it? Children, she said. *Three*, and happily got. All I have to do is wait for the war to be over!'

'So you believe what she said? You believe an old biddy like her, just because you want children?'

'I would believe the moon was made of green cheese, if I thought that one day I would have even one child! I'm upset, but I'll cope – *if* it happens. Surely you want to believe what she said? There were children for you, too, and luck and love and happiness in your hand, Ness!'

'Yes, and the band played "Believe It If You Like"!'

'Ness Nightingale, what *is* the matter with you? You've already met the man you are going to marry – the one you are going to have two children with – and you shrug it off as if it doesn't matter!'

'Yes I do, because life isn't like that and because I coughed up a shillin' for a lot of old malarkey! Who does that Martha think she's kidding? Sorry I told you about it now.'

'Well I'm not. But tell me, who is he? Your man, I mean. Rowley? Mick? Ewan? Aren't you just a little bit curious?'

'Lorna! I have met hundreds and hundreds of men! Heaven help us – it might be the conductor of the Lime Street tram or the street sweeper that does Ruth Street or the milkie or the postie! I couldn't care less because I don't believe it – all right? Now then, are we going to listen to dance music or Tommy Handley? Or are we going to make a cup of cocoa and go to bed and read?'

'Well, I've had rather a busy day and I wouldn't say no to an early night, if that's all right with you, Ness?'

'Of course it is and don't take any notice of me, girl. You believe Martha if you want to, and good luck to you an' your three kids. And bags I be godmother to the first!'

'Granted, soon as asked. But what did Martha mean when she said you put on a brave face and that there was a break in your lifeline, Ness, but it's all behind you now? Were you ever seriously ill?'

'No, I wasn't. Fit as a butcher's dog, that's me! Always

was. So stop your bothering and I'll put the kettle on. The storm has cleared the air. It'll be lovely and cool in bed tonight. Come to think of it, I fancy an early night myself.'

An early night! Some good it had done and her still awake! Ness thumped and turned her pillow, wondering if Lorna was awake. Probably was. Too excited, most likely, to sleep; too busy choosing names for those three kids she was going to have. When peace came. If ever it did! And drat that Martha! Poking and prying with her beady eyes. Mind, it was good that Mam and Da and Nan were going to be all right, because she *did* worry about them and the bombing, and it was good to know they had a guardian angel – if you believed in angels. But for the rest of it – how *dare* she hint about putting on a brave face, telling her to forget what had been? What did Martha Hugwitty know about it? No right at all to bring it up, Ness fretted, especially now she was learning to live with what happened almost two years ago.

Ever been seriously ill, Lorna had asked. My, but Ness Nightingale was getting good at lying. Break in her lifeline the old woman said it had been. Did that include broken hearts, an' all? And being told that her trouble was over if only she'd let it be. Of course it was over and she *was* trying to look to the future. But how could you forget when tonight it had come back to remind her; when black eyes had looked into her past and dug it all up?

Two children, indeed! That had hurt, because she wasn't ever going to love again, and you had to have a man to get kids and she was done with being in love. She was getting over Patrick, she really was, and she must forget tonight and the veiled hints and knowing nods. Martha had been fishing and hard luck, because Ness Nightingale wasn't telling!

'Oh, flamin' Norah!' she hissed, throwing back the bedclothes, drawing aside the curtains, staring into the blackness that was Dickon's Wood. She blinked until her eyes became accustomed to the denseness of the night and could make out the vague shapes of trees and bushes.

Nothing moved. There was no moon. This was the time that country people called the dark of the moon, when witches did their witching and things went bump in the night, if you were daft enough to believe it.

She took a deep, soothing breath and wondered about Ursula and Dickon. They had known about lost love. Ursula, people said, only appeared to star-crossed lovers, to those who had loved and lost.

'So why don't you appear to me?' Ness whispered softly into the night. 'Why haven't I seen you, Ursula Ainsty? Don't you know about what happened to Glebe Farm's land girl?'

She waited, breath indrawn, thinking how stupid she was being. Talking to herself now. Talking to ghosts and there weren't such things as ghosts, no matter if some people in Nun Ainsty half believed there were!

Angrily, she swished closed the curtains and got into bed, wishing they had never gone to Martha Hugwitty's almshouse, because people who could tell you what was past and what was to be were frauds who took shillings off stupid people who wanted to hear something good. Like Lorna did. Gawd! If Lorna had parted with a ten-bob note instead of an extra shilling, that old biddy would have seen at least six kids in her hand!

Bunkum! Mumbo jumbo! Codswallop! She didn't believe any of it and she *wasn't* weeping. She damn well wasn't!

FOURTEEN

'What *is* that?' Lorna gazed with disbelief at so large a piece of meat.

'Venison. Ewan brought it back with him,' Jessie Summers beamed. 'He said I was to ask no questions, but there's more than enough for Reggie and me so I told him he was to come and help eat it. Why don't you come, too, Lorna?'

'Thanks. I'd love to.'

'Then that's settled. Let's make an occasion of it. The recipe needs wine vinegar, which I have got, and two glasses of red wine.'

'Never mind. No one has wine these days – except people who have bottles of it put down in their cellars. None in the shops now, but everything French stopped after Dunkirk, didn't it? Perfume, too,' Lorna sighed.

'You're wrong there – about the wine, I mean. Reggie has a few bottles hoarded for special occasions. I'll see if I can wheedle one out of him; use a drop in the cooking and we'll drink the rest. Like I said, we'll have a bit of a party.'

'Then I'll look forward to it.' Lorna draped her cardigan over the back of her chair, ran her fingers through her hair, then sat down at her desk. 'Anything new?'

'A couple of settled accounts, but you can see to those, can't you? He looked very well.'

'Er – who?'

'Ewan. Said he'd had a lazy leave and felt the better for it.

Got to go. Helping out at the baby clinic. I'll let you know what night it'll be. Oh, and Reggie's out on a call. Accident at Low Meadow Farm.'

And with that the doctor's wife was off, leaving a strange silence behind her and Lorna with no option but to think about Ewan MacMillan.

She had known, of course, that by now he would be back from leave, though she had not seen him. Not that she had looked exactly, dropping this morning's mail and papers with a quick hullo and goodbye to the sergeant in the cookhouse before he even had time to ask if she wanted a cup of tea.

Things were straight in her mind now. She had accepted that it was quite in order to be lonely, since half the women in the country were lonely, too. And she had forgiven herself for thinking Ewan was attractive, because thinking was all right. Thoughts couldn't get anyone into trouble – if kept in check, that was.

Mind, she had accepted Jessie Summer's invitation eagerly without so much as an 'Are you sure?' or 'I couldn't eat your rations.' Had accepted because the doctor's wife had been gifted a large piece of meat and wanted to share it and not because Ewan would be there, too. It really wasn't.

She gave her attention, then, to Low Meadow Farm, looking up the number in the directory, scribbling it on her jotter in case it should be needed. Farm accidents were nothing new. A farm could be a dangerous place; farm implements could wound, threshing machines had been known to kill, severe cuts with scythes and billhooks were commonplace.

Then she tidied and dusted her desk, opened the windows wide and reached for the accounts book, pleased she seemed to be settling in at last and was learning to cope with being left alone in charge sometimes. She was learning complicated medical terms and not only how to pronounce them, but how to spell them, too. Timid and compliant Lorna Hatherwood might be at Ladybower, but here at the surgery in Meltonby,

Dr Summers' receptionist was calm and confident and a different person altogether. Lorna rather admired the new person she became for four and a half hours a day, six days a week, and wondered what it would be like when the war was over and she returned to being Mrs William Hatherwood.

Then she laughed out loud, because she would love being a peacetime wife and the mother of three. Quickly and carelessly their children would be conceived Martha had said, and whether or not she really believed in the hocus-pocus of fortune-telling, the shilling-promise of three babies of her own would be something to cling to when trouble came and her spirits were low. Two boys and a girl. When the war was over, that was. Lovely, lovely thought.

Ness clanged shut the farm gate behind her, sighing with pleasure. Another day gone. Another day nearer the end of the war. And she had to admit it, from where she was standing, it wasn't a bad old war. Above her, a clear sunny sky; at her feet, green grass with wild flowers, dog roses and honeysuckle in the hedges and butterflies everywhere. Now it seemed that the Luftwaffe had decided to leave Liverpool alone, so life was good again. So good, in fact, that at times she felt guilty for feeling such contentment when there was a war on.

'Ar, what the 'eck!' She waved to Flora Petch who was leaning dangerously out of an upstairs window, polishing it vigorously, then stuck her hands in the pockets of her overalls and made for Ladybower. Lorna would not be home yet, which would give her time, Ness thought, to open windows and lay the table for supper.

An aircraft flew low overhead and she watched it disappear beyond the far trees. Off bombing tonight, were they? Then good luck, lads. Come back safely, eh?

She was closing the back door behind her when the phone rang. Should she answer it? It might be William. But then again, it might be Lorna, saying she would be a little late and could Ness peel potatoes and carrots, please?

Hesitantly she said, 'Meltonby 223.'

'Ness! Ewan MacMillan here. Is Lorna about?'

'She isn't home from the surgery yet. Shall I ask her to ring you back?'

'Don't bother. Just thought I'd call round, later on. Will half past seven be all right – just for five minutes?'

'I'm as sure as I can be that it will. Did you have a good leave, Ewan?'

'Just fine. Slept a lot, walked a lot. Tell you about it later. 'Bye, Ness. See you.'

So Mrs Hatherwood had a date tonight with the gorgeous Scot, Ness grinned wickedly. No sooner was he back from leave than he was ringing her up. Interesting!

'But didn't he say what it was about?' Lorna demanded impatiently of Ness.

'No, 'cause I didn't ask. Seven-thirty for five minutes, he said, so whatever it is won't take long. No reason why he shouldn't call, is there? I'm here, as chaperone.'

'Chaperone, Ness? This is 1941!'

'Then shall I shove off?' Again the teasing grin.

'No you shall *not*!' Lorna was surprised how calm she felt. 'It's a friendly visit, to the two of us. Nothing to get het up about.'

Ewan, Lorna had already decided, might be bringing her a cut of venison, too. Where was the harm in that?

Yet she had to admit it would be nice to see him again, if only for five minutes. Very nice indeed.

Ness opened the door to Ewan's knock, and if she had thought him handsome before he went away, she was obliged to admit he looked downright devastating tonight. She took in the tanned face, eyes no longer tired, the tousled fair hair.

'Come in.' She gazed enquiringly at the large envelope marked OHMS tucked beneath his arm. 'And yer hair's a mess. I'd better cut it, whilst you're here.'

'Sorry.' He pulled his fingers through the thick mass. 'The barber at home is six miles away. Didn't feel like wasting the time.'

'Go through. Lorna's in the kitchen. I'll nip upstairs for me scissors and a towel.' Her fingers itched to bring order to Ewan's hair, just as they had itched when first she laid eyes on Lorna's tangled curls.

'Ewan!' Lorna smiled, offering her hand. 'How nice to see you. And how well you look!'

'Aye. I had a thoroughly lazy time. I have a present for you – hope you'll like it.' He offered the large envelope. 'Remember I said if the heather was out, I'd bring you some? Sadly it wasn't, so this is the next best thing. Take a look at it.'

All at once dry-mouthed, Lorna took out a painting. She had been so calm, yet now the warm glow of pleasure she always felt in his company was back, and she gazed long and hard at the picture so she might thank him for it in a voice that was normal.

'It's beautiful,' she whispered. 'You did it?'

'Mm. Like it?'

'I love it. Is it of Ardnamurchan?'

'No, it's the wee bay at Ardurie, where I live. Ardurie is by Ardnamurchan – a sort of straggle of houses and crofts. You can hardly call it a village. It doesn't warrant even a dot on the map.'

'It's in watercolour, isn't it?' Flush-cheeked, Lorna held it at a distance, taking in dim grey hills, a glint of water and, in the foreground, a tangle of foxgloves and ferns.

'Watercolour is quick to work in. Oils take a lot longer. Do you really like it?'

'I really do. Thank you so much, Ewan. I don't know what to say.'

'Then don't say anything. I painted it for you and I'm glad you are pleased with it. I signed it, by the way. Discreetly, of course.'

'I can see it – but only just.' Lorna pointed to a tiny E MacM. tucked beside a cobble and a leaf of fern. 'But you have no need to be discreet. I shall tell William I bought it at a charity sale for – er – for the Red Cross.'

'So he wouldn't want one of my watercolours in his house?'

His eyes found hers and held them, and because she could feel her cheeks flushing hotly, she said,

'Not at all, Ewan! What I meant was that he might think it extravagant if I had bought something so obviously professional, except, of course, for a good cause.'

'But why tell him you bought it?' There was a stubborn tilt to his chin, a dare-you look in his eyes. 'Why not say I gave it to you – a thank you for all you did to help at the manor?'

'Because I – I . . .' Lorna let go her breath, relieved to hear Ness clattering down the stairs.

'Lost the dratted scissors. Couldn't find them anywhere!'

'And where were they?' Lorna asked shakily.

'In the bathroom cabinet, and hey! Will you look at that! It's smashing!'

'Ewan painted it. For me.' Lorna was in control of her emotions again.

'Well, all I can say is that I told you so! Didn't I say it, Ewan, that day we met you in the woods? You startled me 'cause I thought you was – *were* – someone else.'

'I remember, Ness. You were looking for fallen branches; I was sketching trees.'

'Then you'll remember I said you could do that sort of thing for a living? And if you ever gave up doctoring, you could! That is one heck of a picture. Where will you put it, Lorna? Over the fireplace?'

'N-no. The fireplace wall gets too much sun, and there's

the risk of smoke. Over my desk would be better, I think – when I've had it framed.' Above the desk at which she sat to write William's letters. 'In fact, I'm pretty sure I have a frame it would fit, in the storeroom. And Ness is right. You *do* need a trim, Ewan.'

'If Ness will let me pay the rate for the job, I'd be grateful.'

'Away with you! What's a haircut between friends? Any time at all for a wounded soldier.'

'Then what if I give you one of the pencil sketches I was doing when we met? I've still got them, somewhere.'

'Honest? I'd love one. And you've just got yourself free haircuts for the duration – well, for as long as you stay at the manor. Just ring 223 and ask for Ness.'

They laughed, easy together. But then, Lorna thought, Ness was like that; always comfortable in the company of men. No lash-fluttering or simpering or flirting. What you saw with Ness Nightingale, was what you got. But for all that, it made Lorna wonder yet again why there was no man in the land girl's life. Peculiar, to her way of thinking. Very peculiar.

The second Saturday in July was one to be remembered; a bad day, Ness was to think later. One not to be repeated. It had started with a dreary news bulletin; Hitler's soldiers laying siege to Leningrad, the Luftwaffe bombing London still; the RAF bombing Cologne and Essen and Berlin. You had to expect things like that, Ness brooded, but not Kate being taken to hospital and not, most definitely not, what was to follow.

Ness had heard the startled cry, the thud of Kate hitting the concrete floor of the cow shed, and hurried to help.

'Dratted cow muck! Wouldn't you think I'd know by now not to slip on it! Give me a hand up, Ness, and *oh*! My arm . . .'

'You've hurt it? I don't wonder. You went down with a right old bang. Let's get you inside, clean you up. You're covered in the stuff!'

There had been no doubt at all that Kate had broken her left arm.

'I'll be as gentle as I can,' Ness soothed. 'Let's get these clothes off you, then I'll give you a sponge down. Think I'd better ring for Doc Summers.'

'No, lass. It'll be all right. Just bruised . . .'

But Ness was already asking the exchange for the doctor's number.

'He won't be long. Just finished morning surgery. And he says you're not to eat or drink anything, just in case. And it isn't just bruised if you ask me, so sit there quiet, and I'll get Bob.'

Ness cupped a cold face cloth to her aching jaw, recalling the morning. Kate, white-faced, arm in a sling, being taken to hospital, and what happened afterwards still took a bit of believing; still made her sick inside if she thought too long about it.

Rowley, selfish as ever, had watched his father's car disappear then demanded to know who was to make the midday meal.

'I suppose it'll be me, but you'll have to make do with cheese sarnies and what's left of the apple pie,' Ness had shrugged. 'I'm a farm worker, not a cook.'

'You're here, Ness Nightingale, to do what you're told and till my father gets back you take your orders from me! So get on with it. I'm starving.'

'Then starve!' Ness, shaking with anger, pushed past him, but he took her arm, flinging her round to face him. 'And take your hands off me, Rowley Wintersgill! I'm not your Meltonby tart!'

'No! You're a Liverpool tart and you've been asking for it since the day you got here!'

'You reckon? Sorry, but I don't fancy you at all, so get out of my way. I've got work to do outside so you can make your own sarnies!'

Ness had not expected the blow to her face. It sent her reeling to the floor and before she could get to her feet he was kneeling beside her, pulling at the straps of her overalls, her shirt.

'Stop it! Leave me alone!'

'Asking for it, I said!' His eyes were wide and wild as he brought his mouth down on hers.

'*Aaaagh*!' Ness bit his lip savagely, rolling away from him, grabbing the table leg, crying, 'Mick! Help me! Someone help me!'

'So you want to play rough, do you?' He was straddling her, tugging at her clothes again. Ness planted her feet squarely on the floor, arching her back, trying to free herself. But it was useless, and shaking with terror she wondered if she could reach out to the hearth, and the iron poker that lay there.

She struggled, but he held her, his mouth a taunting leer. He was enjoying it, Ness thought desperately. He really meant it! She called,

'No! *No*! Leave me be!'

'Give in, Ness Nightingale. You've made your point – lay back and enjoy it!'

He was mad, she thought, choking back a sob. And bad and arrogant.

'Stop it!' She pulled her nails down his face. 'Get off me! Don't, Rowley? Please don't . . . ?' She closed her eyes, turning her head from side to side as his mouth sought hers again.

It was then she heard running feet, saw the shape that for an instant blocked the light from the doorway.

'That's enough!'

Mick Hardie grasped Rowley's hair and the back of his shirt. Ness felt him thrown from her.

'What the hell are you up to! Has he harmed you, Ness?'

'No! But if you hadn't come he'd –' She drew in her breath as Mick took the full force of Rowley's fist.

'Get out of here, conchie, or I'll give you the hiding of your life!' He drew back his fist to hit out again, but Mick ducked, throwing himself at his assailant, knocking him to the floor.

'Stop it! Stop it, both of you!' Ness scrambled to her feet. 'Don't Mick! He isn't worth it!'

But Mick Hardie had the advantage. Savagely he slammed a fist into the arrogant face. Then again.

'Don't, Mick!' She pulled at his arm, throwing herself between the struggling men. 'Stop it, or you'll kill him!'

'I'd like to,' he panted, 'but you're right. He isn't worth it.'

Grabbing Rowley in an arm lock, he pushed him to the open door, flinging him on the cobbles outside.

'Try that again, Wintersgill, and I'll *really* hurt you! Now, get out of my sight!' He turned, rubbing his right hand. 'Are you all right, Ness? You're sure?'

Mutely, Ness nodded.

'So tell me what happened.'

'I – I told him to make his own sandwiches. He ordered me to make him something to eat, and I told him where to go. It was why he hit me, knocked me down. That was the start of it.' Her voice shook, tears filled her eyes.

'Sssh, now. It's all right. He won't hurt you again.'

'Did you have to hit him so hard? He'll make trouble for you now. He's a nasty little piece.' She pulled a hand across her eyes.

'Afraid I just saw red, Ness. I thought he was trying to rape you.'

'He was. Lord knows what would have happened if he'd managed to get my overalls down. He kissed me, and I bit him. And I scratched his face.' She sat down heavily on the fireside chair.

'Good for you.'

'No, Mick. There'll be trouble. He isn't the sort to take it lying down. He's vindictive. I don't suppose anyone has ever belted him, till now.'

'Well, now he knows what it's like to be on the receiving end! He'll be in trouble when his father finds out. As if Bob isn't going to have enough on his plate with Kate out of action. Will Lorna be at home?'

'No. She'll have left for the surgery.'

'Then best you stay here a while. Come to think of it, Bob should see the state you are in. Could you do with a cup of tea?'

'No thanks. I'll get a glass of water. And put your hand under the tap, Mick. Your knuckles are bleeding.'

'Don't know my own strength. Like I said, something just snapped. But don't worry about me. Your face is swollen. Did he hit you hard?'

'Yes. I'll be in a right mess in the morning. What are we to do, Mick? Whichever way you look at it, we're in trouble.'

'No, Ness. Bob will believe you and me. I can take care of myself, but it's you I'm worried about. I think you should see them at the hostel, tell the warden what happened. At least it might make her think twice about sending another land girl to Glebe Farm.'

'Another? You talk as if I'll be leaving, Mick.'

'And won't you be? You can't stay here, after this. There are plenty of farms around here begging for a land girl.'

'But how can I ask to leave? Kate is going to be home from hospital soon. How is she going to manage with an arm in plaster? How is it going to be for her if I walk out?'

'Both Kate and Bob should have thought about that when they were spoiling Rowley rotten. It's too late now.'

'But I've got to stay, Mick. Rowley's learned his lesson. Maybe Bob will believe what we say.'

'Well, we're about to find out. He's back!'

'So what's been going on around here, then?' Bob Wintersgill gazed around the kitchen. 'Looks like somebody's had a fight. And where is Rowley?'

'I threw him out. I found him messing around with Ness and I had to hit him. But how is Kate?'

'She'll do. Got her arm in plaster now. She's staying in there for the night. I'm to collect her in the morning. But it seems it's not only Kate who's been in the wars. What happened to your face, Ness?'

'Rowley tried – well, he wanted to – I . . .' Tears filled her eyes again.

'He damn well tried to rape her, that's all. Here, in the kitchen. I pulled him off her and he lashed out at me, so –'

'So you hit him back?'

'I did. Wouldn't you have? Look at the mess Ness's face is in.'

'Aye. I've seen it and the state she's in, too. Button yourself up lass, and get off home. I'm sorry if you're upset. You're sure nothing happened?'

'Nothing happened, but it might have done if Mick hadn't got here. And I think I would like to go home now, get out of these things, wash myself . . .'

'Oh no you don't, Ness Nightingale!' Rowley stood, arms folded, in the doorway. 'She goes nowhere till you've heard my side of it. I don't know what they've cooked up between them, but all I asked was for her to make me some sandwiches, and she refused. Got very cocky with it.'

'Is that right, lass?' Bob raised an eyebrow.

'Yes, it is. He told me he was giving the orders around here till you got back, so I walked out. At least, I tried to. He just grabbed my arm and hit me. He hurt me. I fell over. And then – then he tried to –'

'You lifted your hand to a woman, son? You punched Ness?'

'Only a tap – and she'd asked for it!'

'A tap? Have you looked at her face, her eye?' The farmer's face was white with fury. 'Spoiled you may be, but I thought we'd instilled some sort of decency into you! Have you ever seen me strike your mother?'

'No, but mother isn't a tart!'

'And neither is Ness!' Mick flung. 'I heard her calling out to him to stop. And he threw the first punch. What do you think I was going to do – stand there and let him?'

'All right. Go to the first-aid box and get some ointment and a bandage on that hand, lad. Then get back to the field. I'll deal with things here. And you, Rowley, get your head under the pump, take the swelling out of your face, cool you down a bit.'

'And that's all you've got to say, Father? It's going to take more than cold water to fix my face. What are people going to think when they see it? What will I tell them?'

'You'll tell them, if you've got one iota left of the brain you were born with, that a cow kicked you. A young heifer with a sore udder – all right?'

'But that's a lie, and you know it! I'm going to look a right fool, aren't I, getting myself kicked by a cow!'

'You'll look more than a fool if the police get wind of this lot. Can't you get it into your head that when a lass says no, she means no. Didn't you even stop to think that what you tried to do is a matter for the law, if Ness cares to make a complaint against you?'

'So you'd go against your own son?' Rowley's bruised face grew redder. 'You'd take the word of a Liverpool tart and a conchie?'

'When it comes to you and your womanizing ways, yes I would! So you'll do nothing to upset your mother when she comes home, is that understood? You'll get yourself cleaned up and you'll keep your mouth shut!'

He turned to Ness, eyes sad.

'Are you going home then, lass? And I'll understand if you

want to send for the constable. What Rowley did was wrong, and you'd be within your rights.'

'No, Bob. I think he's got the message. I won't be reporting anything. But if he tries it on again . . .'

'He won't. Be sure of that. Mind, it's a nasty eye you've got.'

'I know. I walked into a lamppost in the blackout.'

'What blackout? It's high summer.'

'Don't worry. I'll think of something. I don't want Kate worried any more than she need be. But I hope you'll believe I didn't encourage him.'

'I believe you, though Kate will have to know.'

'Why should she, if we stick to the cow story? Best we do . . .'

So she had walked back to Ladybower, and then held cold face cloths to her bruises and swallowed an aspirin. And waited tearfully for Lorna to come home.

'Good grief! Your face!' Lorna gasped. 'I knew about Kate, but no one said anything about you being hurt. What happened?'

'Do I have to tell you?'

'You most certainly do! Did you fall or something?'

'Not exactly. And I suppose you're entitled to know, but I don't want it blabbed round the village.'

'Ness, I do *not* blab. Just tell me?'

'OK. I didn't fall. I was pushed, sort of. Rowley wanted me to make sandwiches and –'

'Rowley! I might have known! But sorry. Won't interrupt again.'

'To cut a long story short, I told him to make his own sarnies. It was the way he ordered me to do it that got me mad. We had words and he hit me and I fell over and before I could pick meself up he was on top of me, trying to get me clothes off, telling me I'd been asking for it. I yelled and Mick came.

‘Anyway, one thing led to another and the two of them had a set-to. Mick won. Then Bob came back from the hospital and played hell with Rowley.’

‘Mick won? But he’s a pacifist. Surely he wouldn’t do a thing like that?’

‘He did, though. Rowley’s face will be a mess in the morning and oh, I don’t know where it’s all going to end.’

Tears came again in big jerking sobs, and Lorna sat on the arm of Ness’s chair and hugged her and told her it would be all right.

‘You won’t be going to the farm tomorrow, anyway. Sunday is your day off,’ she comforted. ‘I’ll get some witch hazel and dab your bruises with it and maybe by Monday they won’t look so bad. And by then, Rowley will have been given the hard word. He’ll behave himself in future.’

‘I hope he will, Lorna. But if I hadn’t been wearing overalls, it might have been a different matter. He couldn’t get my trouser legs down, I was kicking so much. But he meant to. I bit him and scratched him and I’m glad Mick hit him. Mick said I should ask for another farm, but I want to give it another chance. Kate will need help around the house now. I won’t be taking my day off tomorrow. I’ll go in,’ she shrugged.

‘And what is Kate going to say when she sees your face, and Rowley’s?’

‘And Mick’s too, don’t forget. There’ll be three of us bruised and battered. Kate isn’t going to buy the story we cooked up that a heifer kicked Rowley. She’ll want to get to the bottom of it. I’m sorry for Kate.’

‘And I’ll be sorry when it gets around the village, Ness. Ainsty is only a little place. Everybody gets to know everybody’s business, sooner or later. The three of you can’t go into hiding till your faces are back to normal. Just wait till Nance Ellery sniffs it out. She’ll have a field day!’

‘I didn’t egg him on, Lorna. Honest.’

‘I know you didn’t, and I’ll get that stuff for your bruises now. Then I'll whip us up an omelette and we'll sit in the back garden when we've eaten it. The sun is still warm. Sunshine will help heal your face. And as for Rowley Wintersgill – oh, I knew his ways would get him into trouble one day!'

Mind, you could expect such a thing from him Lorna thought. He'd been a nasty little boy and he'd grown up into a nasty, lewd man. That someone would give him a hiding had been on the cards for a long time, Lorna brooded as she went in search of witch hazel and gauze.

What surprised her, though, was Mick Hardie lashing out. Quiet, she had always thought him, and brave in his own way for standing up for his beliefs. She hadn't thought he would let himself be drawn into a brawl. Yet wouldn't any man have defended a woman in Ness's situation – one about to be raped. My God! *Raped*?

'Are you going to report it,' she asked as she dabbed soothing liquid on Ness's face. 'I mean – an attack like that is serious. I don't like to say it, but what Rowley Wintersgill had in mind was –'

'Rape,' Ness supplied, dully. 'Bob said I'd be within my rights to call the constable, but I'm not going to. It'll be something to hold over Rowley – keep him in his place. And as far as I'm concerned it's over and done with now, bar one or two black eyes that are going to have to be explained away. And thanks for being so decent, Lorna. I was glad when you walked in tonight. I feel a bit better about it now.'

'And you aren't going to ask for a transfer?'

'Best I give it another try, because even with Rowley to put up with I still like being at Nun Ainsty. I don't want to risk having to leave here, Lorna. Let's hope that village gossip doesn't spread into Meltonby, and the charge hand at the hostel doesn't get to hear about it. I might not have a choice if she does.'

'Then fingers crossed, and keep that pad over your eye whilst I get supper.'

'Bless you, Lorna. You're good to me.'

'And you are good to me, and good *for* me, too. I'd be miserable if you ever left.'

And Ness said that fingers crossed she was stopping, in spite of that little sod Rowley. Too right she was!

They sat in the garden after supper, faces to the sun. Ness felt calmer now, though her face still throbbed and no matter how she tried, she could not get Rowley Wintersgill – or Mick – out of her mind.

'What are you thinking about, Ness?'

'I – oh – I was wondering if you'd had your Saturday epistle from William.'

'I did, and he's well. And it's almost certain he'll be due long leave, sometime in August.'

'August! Don't think I could ask for time off in August, Lorna. They'll be busy with the harvest, and then there'll be potatoes to lift and sugar beet. I don't think I can ask for leave till November. Let's hope there'll be a vacant bed for a week at the hostel, though I don't think there will be in August.'

'But surely you could go to Flora's?'

'Mm. Wouldn't mind that. But plenty of time. It's nearly a month before your William's due. Are you looking forward to it?'

'Of course I am. And I forgot to tell you. I've been asked to the surgery for dinner, though Jessie isn't sure when. Ewan brought her a big piece of venison back, so she said we were both to help eat it. It'll be good, knowing I'm not taking someone else's meat ration.'

'And lookin' forward to being walked home by Ewan?'

'Walking home with Ewan might be rather nice, but I've already decided to drive there. I'm not too badly off for petrol, and Meltonby and back won't use much.'

'So you'll be offering him a lift?'

'Ness Nightingale! You seem determined to get him and me together!' Lorna's cheeks pinked.

'There's no harm in giving a wounded soldier a lift!'

'None. But his wounds are OK now, he told me so. And there's the phone!'

She was on her feet and away, only to return to say, 'It wasn't William. It's Bob, for you.'

'Heck! I wonder what he wants.'

'Pick up the phone, and you'll find out!'

'Will you tell me, Mrs Hatherwood, how Bob and Kate managed to have a son like Rowley?' Ness asked on her return. 'Bob is really concerned about me. Said I wasn't to go in tomorrow and that he was going to ask Martha to help with the housework. I mustn't even think of working on my day off. He was very firm about it.'

'Martha will be glad to oblige. Did Bob say anything else?'

'Only that he's thought about things and decided Kate will have to be told. And he's right. She's nobody's fool. Sad for her, for all that, and her feeling groggy with her arm. But maybe by Monday my face won't look so bad.'

'And maybe you'll have developed a real shiner! But what about Rowley – you say Mick hit him twice?'

'At least. Mick looked real angry and when he threw him into the yard. Rowley landed pretty heavily, an' all. Bet he aches all over.'

'Which is only what he deserves! So shall we go in and listen to the nine o'clock news, or shall we stay here?'

'Let's sit here till it starts getting dark.' Ness loved the garden as twilight came; loved the goodnight whispering of the trees and the blackbird that almost always sang from the tallest oak; loved everything about Ladybower's garden, truth known. 'I'll nip inside – bring us both a cardie.'

And *why* had this morning's bother happened, she fretted. Right up until today, Nun Ainsty had been absolutely wonderful. But then there had been a serpent in the Garden of Eden, or so Auntie Agnes had told her. Seemed nowhere was perfect.

Ness shivered and shrugged on her cardigan, wondering why she wasn't thinking about Mick Hardie instead; about how he had just made sure that from now on Rowley would give him an even worse time, find even more dirty jobs for him to do.

But it wouldn't worry him. Mick Hardie made two of Rowley Wintersgill. Mick was a decent sort. Pity she hadn't said yes that time he asked her for a date, but it was too late now.

Ness hesitated at the open door, telling herself it would be all right, yet all the time sad because this was the very first time she had entered Kate's kitchen with apprehension.

'Lass?' Kate rose to her feet, her face anxious. 'Let me have a look at you. I'm that ashamed I don't know what to say.'

'Then don't say anything. It's over and done with.'

'You've got a nasty eye, for all that.' Hesitantly she touched Ness's face.

'It's heaps better. The swelling has gone now, and the bruising will have faded by the end of the week. It's you I'm worried about. How are you feeling?'

'A bit better today. Not so painful. Doc Summers came yesterday tea time to have a look at me. He says the hospital will put a lighter plaster on it soon, and it'll be a lot more comfortable. But do you want to tell me what happened, Ness?'

'How much do you know?'

'I know,' Kate sighed, 'that Rowley went for you and –' She stopped, eyes filling with tears.

'Hush, now. Don't get yourself upset.' Ness took the agitated hand, holding it tightly. 'What happened wasn't very nice and I'm sorry it developed into a fight. But best not dwell on it? I haven't seen Mick or Rowley yet. How are things between them?'

'Glowering and growling the pair of them, like a pair of snarling dogs, and Bob with a face like thunder. And how we're going to keep it from the village, I don't know. A heifer kicked out, indeed! Got the three of you, did it? People aren't daft, you know.'

'Kate love, it isn't the first time two men have had a fight, and it won't be the last. It'll be a five-minute wonder.'

'Happen so. But village gossip being what it is, they're going to want to know what started it in the first place. Our Rowley's got a bit of a reputation, don't forget.'

'Maybe he has, but the village isn't entitled to know what really happened. They'll have to be content with what we choose to tell them – that it was a fight over me.' The idea came suddenly. 'It's none of their business anyway.'

'No, but that's the way it is in villages, Ness. I don't know what's to become of that lad of ours.'

'Stop your worrying, Kate. Rowley isn't stupid. I reckon he's learned his lesson. There's no need to dwell on what might have happened. I'll admit I was terrified, but Mick sorted things. It's him we have to thank.' She lifted the knitted tea cosy, feeling the pot. 'This tea is good and hot, still. What say I give it a drop of boiling water? Like a cup, would you?'

'Please. And you can put us both a spoon of sugar in it – for medicinal reasons! You'll not be leaving us? I'd miss you cruel, if you did.'

'I'm stoppin'.' Ness set the black iron kettle on the fire. 'So what do you want me to do today?'

'The men are doing the milking – best you find yourself something else to do.'

'I'll see to the poultry then, and there'll be yesterday's eggs to be wiped and checked. Now don't worry. Things are never as bad as they seem. It'll sort itself out, given time.'

'Aye, but Martha's coming to give me a hand. She'll put two and two together, and that'll be it.'

'So you tell her – in strictest confidence, of course – that

Rowley and Mick had an argument over me. The village will be more inclined to accept that than the frisky heifer story.'

'But what about *your* eye, Ness?'

'My own fault. I tried to separate them, and took a punch myself. Now, we've said all we're going to say on the matter. When the men come in for drinkings you can tell them what we've decided – after I've made myself scarce, that is.' She took Kate's face in her hands, kissing her cheek. 'We women have got to stick together. And the worst didn't happen, so let's be thankful for that. What really happened won't ever go beyond these four walls. All right?'

'You're a good lass, Ness Nightingale. Just the sort I'd have picked for our Rowley, if things had been different!'

'Sorry, Kate.' Smiling, Ness lifted her cup in salute. 'Thanks, but no thanks!'

Ness opened wide the cow pasture gate, urging the herd through it for afternoon milking. This far, things had not been too bad. Bob had gone to market with calves and Mick and Rowley still maintained a guarded silence, each avoiding the other whenever possible. Both had bruised faces. Mick's hand still seemed painful and Ness could clearly see the effects of her teeth on Rowley's lip.

This morning, Martha Hugwitty had arrived at ten on the dot, determined to be the first in the village to inspect Kate's plaster, hear at first hand every last detail of it. That there was even more to tell only added to her pleasure. She returned from the far field where she had taken drinkings and would be put off no longer.

'Is someone going to tell me what is going on around here,' she demanded testily. 'There's Ness acting coy about her eye and now Rowley and Mick look like they've been in a fight. What happened, Kate? You can tell me . . .'

'Then before Ness comes in and in the strictest confidence, Martha, there was a bit of a set-to.'

'I can see that! What I'd like to know – confidentially, of

course – is what it was about and why Ness seems to have been in on it, an' all.'

'Well, Martha, it seems both Rowley and Mick are interested in Ness; both would like to take her out. And to cut a long story short, they had words over it which led to blows. And poor Ness, who tried to come between them, got in the way of a fist! My Bob has read the riot act and it's all over now, we hope. But that's the truth of it.'

'Ah,' Martha nodded. 'Makes sense. Ness Nightingale is a bonny lass, though quiet. Has she got a young man overseas or something?'

'I couldn't tell you, Martha. She has never confided in me and I wouldn't dream of asking, even though I'd have thought a good-looking lass like her would have a following of men around these parts by now.'

'Could she, do you think,' Martha glanced towards the open door, lowering her voice, 'be a war widow, and doesn't want to let on?'

'It's possible, but she doesn't wear a ring. Mind, a person has to be careful in times like these, not to ask anything that might upset. And you'll say nowt in the village about what I told you?'

'Not a word.' Martha tapped her nose with a forefinger. 'And how long, do you think, before you get back to normal?'

'Could be up to four weeks, according to how the bone mends, but I hope it'll be healed before we start the harvest.'

'Mustn't rush things,' Martha advised sagely while all the time thinking that up to four weeks of regular employment would suit her nicely. 'I'll be glad to oblige for as long as you want me, be sure of that.'

And not only four weeks' wages, but all the goodies that went with it. A drop extra of milk, happen, an egg or two, or a rabbit? And a sit-down dinner every day at twelve-thirty sharp! Life was looking up for Martha

Hugwitty, spinster and fortune-teller of this parish. Oh my word, yes!

Mick Hardie was waiting at the gate as Ness left the farm, just as she was congratulating herself for keeping more or less out of the way of both him and Rowley. She had sat down for the midday meal with them both, so that was one hurdle behind her. But she wasn't ready, yet, to talk about it.

'Shall I walk you home, Ness?'

'Thanks, Mick, but I'd rather you didn't. And thank you for what you did. Things could have been a lot worse if you hadn't been nearby. I'm grateful to you, but can we let it rest, please?'

'If that's the way you want it. I just needed to know you were all right. No one spoke a word, hardly, over dinner.'

'There wasn't a lot to say. And by now, Martha will have broadcast the official version.'

'Which is?'

'Kate will be telling everyone that you and Rowley came to blows over me, and that I tried to stop you and came off the worse for it. Leastways, that was what we agreed. Best not say anything about – well, what really happened.'

'If that's the way you want it. You're staying on, Bob tells me.'

'I am. Rowley apart, I like working here and lodging with Lorna. I'll be all right, Mick. And thanks again for what you did. I appreciate it. And sorry about your face.'

'I was going to say, "Think nothing of it, Ness. Any time at all!" but I think if it happened again, I'd swing for the little swine!'

'It won't happen again. Bob and Kate will see to that. And I'll be careful him and me aren't alone anywhere.' She reached on tiptoe and kissed his cheek; a soft brushing of her lips. 'Good night, Mick. Take care. You know what I mean.'

'I'll take care,' he smiled.

Such a lovely smile, Ness thought as she walked quickly,

head down, to Ladybower. But Mick Hardie was a lovely man, when you thought about it. Really lovely, but not for her. Not for Ness Nightingale who would never quite forget the pain that loving a man could bring. Never completely forget . . .

Next day, at a little before noon, Nance Ellery came full sail up Ladybower's path.

'So, Lorna – is it true that Rowley Wintersgill and the farmhand nearly killed each other? A fist fight, I believe?'

'Nance! Who told you such a story?'

'I had it on good authority. Martha told Mary Ackroyd, and Mary told Gilbert when he went for a drink there last night. Martha was at Glebe Farm all day, so she should know!'

'Martha was there for a few hours to help Kate out. And no one nearly killed anyone. Rowley and Mike had words. Both of them interested, it seems, in Ness.'

'Ah! And words came to blows?'

'I believe a few punches were thrown.'

'And the land girl tried to separate them and got a bruised face for her pains! Believe me, Lorna, there's nothing new under the sun! Women and religion. What most men fight over. And what about the farm hand, then? I thought he was against violence?'

'He was – *is* – I suppose. But Rowley started it all. What did you expect Mick to do? Stand there and turn the other cheek?'

'Lorna! You sound as if you're siding with the conchie.'

'I'm not siding with anyone, but Rowley can be a little too arrogant! Maybe he provoked Mick.'

Provoked, Lorna fretted inside her. If only she could tell the half of it!

'Well, sufficient to say that Master Rowley has met his match at last. A few more slappings like that might be the making of him!'

'It wasn't a slapping, exactly, any more than it was anyone being nearly killed, Nance. A bit of healthy horseplay over a young woman, that's all. I'm surprised at you, believing Martha's romancing,' Lorna said snappily. 'And would you mind if I got on with things. I haven't had my lunch yet, and I've got to be at the surgery by one. And please, as a person whose opinion is respected in this village, do put people straight, Nance, when you hear such lurid stories? Boys will be boys, don't they say?'

'Horseplay, you reckon?' Nance rose to her feet. 'I suppose you could be right – especially if there's a girl in it. Fond of her, are you?'

'Of course I am. Ness wouldn't be living here if I wasn't. She's nice to have around.'

'Then don't forget it was I who sent her to you. Remember, Lorna, not long after William left? And how is he, by the way?'

'Due on leave next month.' Lorna gazed long and steadily at the wall clock.

'Then I'll leave you, my dear, to get on with your little job for the war effort. Every little helps, I suppose.'

And with that she straightened her hat, gathered up her large handbag, and left. And Lorna smiled, allowing her the last word, thinking that not so very long ago Nance Ellery's bossiness had made her stammer and shake. It was rather nice to be able to hold her own against the she-dragon of Nun Ainsty, though sad it had taken a war to convince her she was capable of standing on her own two feet.

Her own two feet. If the war went on much longer, she could get to like it, and that would never do!

'There's a wonderful smell coming from your kitchen,' Lorna said to Jessie Summers.

'Mm. It's the marinade. I shall do the venison very slowly in the bottom of the oven. Tomorrow night, it'll be. Seven-ish. That suit you, Lorna?'

'You bet. I'm going the whole hog and driving over, so I can wear a pretty dress.'

'Then I can do better than that. I phoned Ewan not long ago and arranged for him to pick you up.'

'But Jessie – an army truck? Is that wise?'

'What's wrong with it? I figured the Army has more petrol than you. Anyway, it's fixed. He'll be calling at ten to seven – all right?'

It would have to be all right, Lorna brooded. Fingers crossed that no one saw him calling for her, or there'd be even more gossip about Ladybower. Mind, Jessie seemed to think it was all right that a woman whose husband was away could be picked up – no! – *called for* by a young doctor in a truck with a red cross painted on the side, so what the heck! And if she waited at the front-room window until she saw him drive down the village, she could be out of the door and into the truck before he'd hardly had time to stop. Before Martha Hugwitty, opposite, had time even to get to her window!

'What's wrong, Lorna?'

'Nothing really. I was just hoping that when Ewan calls, Martha won't be peeping through her lace curtains.'

'And what if she is? There's a war on. Women can't go into purdah, especially since the government seems hellbent on making them register for war work, calling up young women into the Armed Forces who have never been away from home before. Goodness, girls stand at the side of the road and hitch lifts these days without a second thought, so think nothing of it! And that's the phone!'

She smiled complacently as Lorna hurried to answer it, then went on with her marinating and peeling and chopping in readiness for tomorrow night's dinner. She was quite looking forward to it, and it would take Lorna out of herself. Far too introverted, that one. Worried about accepting a lift from a man, indeed! Whatever next!

* * *

Lorna was at the gate when Ewan MacMillan arrived with a grey army blanket draped carefully over the front seat of the truck. He jumped down to help her.

'A bit high, that step. Up you go, lassie. And can I say you look extremely smart?'

Blue suited her, he thought, taking in the slim-fitting evening dress that only just tipped her knees, the silk stole over her arm.

'Thank you! I must say that dressing up is quite a luxury these days. Nice to make the effort. And might I return the compliment?'

In what was obviously his best uniform and without the habitual white coat and furrowed forehead, there was no denying he was attractive. And since she might as well be hanged for a sheep, she turned to smile brilliantly into his eyes. After all, if Martha Hugwitty was talking about Lorna Hatherwood's carryings-on, at least she would have to leave Ness's black eye alone!

Ness snuggled into the armchair, a cushion at her head, a chocolate bar at her side. It was weeks and weeks since she'd had such a luxury. She had found it on her bed with a note.

To keep you company tonight whilst I am out gadding. Don't wait up. L.

In very short supply now, chocolate no longer came packaged in silver paper and a gaudy wrapper. Now, by government order, chocolate – when you were lucky enough to get even a very small bar – came in a simple paper packet and was a blend of milk and plain chocolate and not for ages had there been bars filled with cream, or strawberry, or soft toffee. Everything was so basic now, Ness sighed, looking longingly at the chocolate, wondering if she should try to make it last all night or gobble it down. She had reluctantly decided on the former when the phone rang, making such a sudden clamour that she jumped startled to her feet.

'Meltonby 223.' She smiled as she said it, because it might be Mam.

'Is my wife there, and would you hurry please!'

William, and Lorna out with a feller!

'Sorry, but she's at the surgery – at Dr Summers's. The number is Meltonby 108, if you'd like to ring her there . . . ?'

'No thanks! I'll write!' The call ended abruptly with a slamming down of the phone.

Ar, wouldn't you know it. Once in a blue moon William rang and Lorna wasn't waiting at the end of the phone when he did!

She looked at the hall clock, ticking loudly, with detached unconcern. A quarter past seven. She must remember the time. If William did decide to try to get through again – and with a bit of luck the trunk lines would all be busy – she hoped he wouldn't say anything to upset Lorna, because she had gone out tonight looking absolutely smashing; looking as if she were really looking forward to a meal in Ewan MacMillan's company.

Ness sat down heavily, annoyed that she was shaking, amazed that a man she had never met and had spoken barely a dozen words to, had the ability to upset her. So arrogant, and with never a hullo or a please or thank you! She reached for the comfort of the chocolate bar, wondering yet again what Lorna saw in the pompous man with the ridiculous moustache.

Your feller phoned, girl. She sent her thoughts speeding to the surgery in Meltonby. *But don't give it another thought. Have a smashing time, eh?*

Ness, in pyjamas and dressing gown, her carefully pincurled hair wrapped in a turban, was waiting when Lorna got home. Little stop-out! Nearly midnight, and her coming in, flopping in a chair, smiling like the cat that'd been at the cream.

'Ness! It's been great, tonight. It's ages since I've been out!'

'So why don't you do it more often, queen?'

'Because it'll be ages before Ewan goes on leave again. Hunks of venison don't grow on trees. Jessie is a marvellous cook. The smell hit us as we walked in and Ewan said it reminded him of his mother's kitchen. We didn't have a pudding, we were so full up. I was greedy. Had second helpings.'

Ness smiled fondly. Lorna looked so pleased with herself, had had such a good time, that it wouldn't be right to tell her about William.

'Made a pig of yourself, Mrs Hatherwood, and a war on! And gettin' back late, an' all. Hope nobody saw you creepin' in.'

'Not at this hour, surely? Even Martha's got to sleep,' Lorna giggled. 'When Ewan saw me up the path and shone his torch so I could get the key in, I didn't care who saw me. Not even when he kissed me goodnight!'

'You *what*? Have you been drinkin', girl?'

'Yes. Two glasses of red wine.'

'Very relaxin', red wine must be.'

'No. Just makes you feel nice. And I'm not drunk, Ness; not even a bit tiddly. Relaxed, though, and happy all over. And you can wipe that holier-than-thou look off your face, because he only kissed my forehead. Took my face in his hands and said, "Night, Lorna. I've enjoyed tonight." Then he kissed me – very brotherly – and that was it!'

'So what did you all talk about?' Ness settled herself, feet tucked under her, knowing that Lorna was in no mood for bed because there were things to be told.

'Well, war talk was banished. Forbidden, Jessie said. As a matter of fact, you came into the conversation, Ness. They know at the surgery about what went on last Saturday – well, they do now.'

'Lorna! You didn't tell!'

'Of course I didn't. It was Ewan.'

'Ewan MacMillan? What business is it of his? And who told him?'

'Mick Hardie did. The two of them were talking over the fence – you know, where the farm and manor meet, at the back. Ewan asked Mick if he'd like him to take a look at his eye and Mick said, "No thanks", and to wait until he saw the other bloke, or words to that effect. Mick told Ewan he'd given Rowley a hiding because he'd been pestering you, *pestering* he said, then asked Ewan if he could spare him a few minutes for a talk. And before you ask, I don't know what they talked about. Ewan didn't say.'

'So it's halfway round Meltonby by now? And before you know it, the warden and the charge hand at the hostel will know, too!'

'Ness! It won't be, I promise you,' Lorna soothed. 'The dinner-table talk was between two doctors, a doctor's wife and me, the receptionist. Nothing will go outside that room, I promise you. Doctors don't blab. They *can't*. Only amongst themselves. And it was Mick who took it on himself to tell Ewan, don't forget. You've nothing to worry about. Ewan was most sympathetic, and Jessie was really pleased someone had squared up to Rowley at last. And there's something else,' she said, offhandedly, 'but you won't want to hear it.'

'Tell!' Ness hissed. 'Might as well have the lot!'

'Ah, but this isn't about you, and this bit of gossip *is* doing the rounds of Meltonby. He who shall be nameless nearly got himself another good hiding. You know about the blonde in Meltonby?'

'The one Rowley has been seeing? The common one?'

'Yes. Well, he nearly got caught in the act, or so local gossip has it.'

'Local gossip being . . . ?'

'Jessie's cleaning lady. It seems Rowley was visiting his blonde and her husband arrived unexpectedly on leave.

Almost caught the two of them. Someone had to make a quick exit over the back fence. He was seen!'

'With his trousers in his hand?' Ness managed a grin.

'Jessie's informant didn't say, but Doc Summers said it was a pity the husband didn't get to Rowley before Mick did. Seems he's a physical training instructor in the Army; very strong, and mean. He'd have made a better job of it than Mick, the Doc said. Probably torn Rowley's head off!'

'Rowley Wintersgill's goings-on make me sick,' Ness said flatly. 'But you're sure nothing is going to get back to the hostel about what happened to me?'

'Absolutely sure. Ewan made a point of sending his good wishes to you and that he hoped you weren't too upset, and Doc Summers said that if you wanted to nip in any time before surgery starts, you're at liberty to do so. Just for a chat, if anything is bothering you, he said. So you mustn't worry. You had the sympathy of everyone there tonight.'

'We-e-ll, I suppose it'll be all right, if you say so. And I'm for bed. We have to be up early, or had you forgotten? What say I make us a drink – the milk will run to it. Ovaltine, eh? Why don't you nip upstairs and get into bed. I'll check the doors and windows and bring the drinks up.'

And Lorna said that that would be wonderful, and went upstairs with a dreamy expression on her face which made Ness think it was surprising what two glasses of red wine could do!

Then she smiled wickedly, because in the morning, when the ruby red glow had worn off a little, she would mention William's phone call and bring Mrs Hatherwood down to earth with a bump. But not, she decided as she measured milk into a pan, until tomorrow. Wouldn't be fair to tell her tonight. Not whilst she was still in the throes of that first kiss – not to mention the wine! On her forehead, indeed! What was Ewan thinking about? That was where a man kissed his granny!

*   *   *

Lorna was about to leave for Meltonby post office when Ness walked into the kitchen.

'There's one in the pot, if you squeeze it, Ness. Got to be off. See you!'

'Hold on a tick! Didn't tell you last night, but your feller phoned.'

'William phoned, and you forgot to tell me! How *could* you forget, Ness?'

'Very easily, as a matter of fact. You were in such a good mood last night that I decided not to spoil it.'

'What an awful thing to do! Just because I'd had a nice time was no excuse for you to –'

'OK!' Ness held up her hands. 'Wrong of me, I suppose, but you'd only have fretted and said you shouldn't have been out and what must poor William be thinking.'

'But he isn't able to get through often and when he does, I'm not here! And sorry. It wasn't your fault, Ness. Mine, I suppose, for not being in. What did he say?'

'Nothing much. I told him you were at the surgery, *not* that you were out to dinner, and gave him the number so he could ring you there. But he said he would write, so it can't have been all that important, now can it?'

'N-no. My punishment, for all that, for being out gadding.'

'And for necking on the doorstep with another feller,' Ness smiled wickedly. 'Oh, for goodness' sake, get yourself off to work! There's a war on, and people need their post. There'll be a letter – an extra one – for you in the morning. Better'n a quick phone call, a letter is!'

And with that Ness opened the kitchen door and with a sideways jerk of her head, indicated it was time for Lorna to be off.

'What a fuss over nothing,' she said out loud, setting the kettle to boil. Now Lorna would feel guilty all day that she had enjoyed a night out and, if you wanted to rub it in, been kissed good night into the bargain! A scarlet woman she was turning into! Shame on you, queen! And shame on William, too, because he wouldn't write. There wouldn't be a letter until Saturday, when the regular epistle arrived. It made Ness wonder if he had an aversion to addressing envelopes. Or maybe he thought that to post a letter every day was a waste of stamps!

Carefully she poured just enough boiling water into the tiny teapot and stirred it vigorously. Give it a minute to brew, then Ness Nightingale would enjoy one of the pleasures of life; her first cup of tea of the day.

Utter, utter bliss.

FIFTEEN

Ness crossed her fingers and closed her eyes to wish the white-rabbit wish that came with the first day of every month. She was, there was no doubt about it, becoming as countrified as the rest of Nun Ainsty, and even if white-rabbit wishes were a load of superstition, it did no harm to try. Country people did peculiar things all the time and thought it perfectly normal, like tipping your forelock and saying, 'Good day, Sir,' each time you saw a magpie.

'Devil's birds. Nasty things,' Martha Hugwitty had explained. 'Give 'em a bit of respect, though, and they'll fly past you with their bad luck.'

As yet, Ness had not saluted the sleek, black and white birds. Handsome creatures they were, with a long sharp beak and a harsh cry. But devil's birds? She smiled, shook her head and said, 'White rabbits', firmly and clearly. 'I wish that Liverpool won't be bombed for the whole of this month. I wish Mam and Da and Nan and Tizzy and Perce to be safe.' And a good job it was that Lorna had left for work or she would think her lodger was going ga-ga and talking to herself!

Lorna. Still down in the mouth about William's leave. August he had said yet, without explanation or regret, the Army cancelled it and told him it would probably be in September now. Lorna had burst into tears on reading his letter and said she was sick, sick, *sick* of the war and sick of Hitler and sick of the Army and oh, of *everything!*

'Well, hard luck, Mrs Hatherwood,' Ness had been forced to issue a reprimand. 'For the duration of this war the powers that be can do what they like, when they like and you are no exception! So your William's leave has been put back? There's plenty who'll never go on leave again, don't forget, and every one of them would give a lot to be safe at Aldershot, leave or no leave!'

'I know. I'm sorry. Childish of me,' Lorna sniffed. 'But I was so looking forward to it. And will you tell me, please, how am I ever going to start a baby if William keeps getting his leave postponed?'

'So that's it! You're still on about a baby when you know it isn't goin' to be until the war is over. Didn't Martha tell you so?'

'And you believe her, Ness?'

'Dunno. But it's a bit of a laugh, I suppose. Them fortune tellers always tell young women what they want to know, don't they? The married ones they tell they'll have children and for the single ones there's a tall, dark, handsome man just around the corner.'

'But Martha saw two children in your hand, Ness, and you haven't even got a man – or have you?'

'You know I haven't.'

'Martha said you'd already met him. Why didn't you ask her who?'

'I – er – well, there's a war on, and if being married in wartime made me as miserable as it sometimes makes you, then I'll postpone my Prince Charming and two kids, if you don't mind.'

'Sorry. I've been acting like a spoiled brat, haven't I? I know I'm not the only woman with a husband in the Army, and William will be home in September – with a bit of luck. I'd like to know the reason, for all that. You don't think there's something going on – like he's going to be sent overseas?'

'Of course he isn't. If he was going abroad they'd give him embarkation leave. Even the Army isn't so rotten as to send a married man overseas without leave.'

'Then do you suppose he's being sent on a course? They're always doing it, aren't they – sending men on courses, I mean.'

'That's it! That's what it'll be!' Eagerly Ness agreed. 'And had you thought that William won't be telling you about it because he might be going on a course at York, or Catterick Camp, nice and near to home!'

'You think so?' Lorna's tears were forgotten.

'We-e-ll, it's as good a reason as any for holding back leave, when you think about it.'

An assurance that made Ness feel distinctly mean, because she had only gone along with the course idea to please Lorna and now the poor girl was clinging to it like it was the God's-honest truth! Just as if, she had thought scornfully, there were courses in pen pushing. Not even the Army could think up something as barmy as that!

Yet that had been all of a week ago, and still William was in barracks at Aldershot and still he had no idea when his next long leave would be. It was, Ness supposed, like Nan always said: 'All be water under the bridge a hundred years from now, so why worry about it?'

And so it would be, and Ness Nightingale had better shift herself and be off to Glebe Farm to dig for victory. And who, she frowned, was lucky enough to enjoy being on war work when war work wasn't supposed to be enjoyable? But life as a land girl in Nun Ainsty was just about as good as it got – Rowley Wintersgill excepted, that was!

Ness was crossing the stackyard when she heard a low whistle and turned to see Mick Hardie.

'Have you a minute?'

'Sure, Mick. If you're going to the kitchen for drinkings, I'll walk with you.'

'Fine. And Ness – I've tried to keep my distance since the upset – don't want to provoke Rowley any more than need be – but I want to talk to you. Come out with me tonight – just for an hour? A walk, or maybe a drink at the White Hart?'

'OK.' She said it reluctantly. 'An hour?'

'Won't take any longer. Just something I need to tell you. Meet you by the pillar box at half seven?'

And Ness said half seven would be fine and hurried ahead of him to the kitchen, where Martha Hugwitty was tying on her apron.

'Morning each. I'll pour. No use you trying to lift that big pot with one hand, Kate. And how are things today, then,' she asked solicitously.

'Doing much better with a lighter plaster on. They said if all goes well I might get the dratted thing taken off in time for harvest. And here come the men. I'll swear they can smell tea a mile off!'

Ness took her mug and excused herself as she often did now, and made for the pump trough. She needed to think about tonight; about why she had agreed to meet Mick and why he had made the meeting sound urgent. Mind, not so long ago she had almost decided that if he asked her again for a date, she would say yes. She owed him that. Yet tonight he needed an hour of her time. Why one hour?

She squinted into the sky. Hardly a cloud. If the good weather lasted, they could start cutting the wheat in ten-acre field, Bob said. And the weather would hold good if the swallows were anything to go by, because today they flew so high in the sky she could hardly see them. A sure sign.

There was something new to learn about country ways every day of the week, when you thought about it. By the time the war was over, she would be as good as Goff Leaman when it came to weather forecasting; she would have turned into a real country bumpkin.

She rinsed her mug under the pump, then took it to Martha, who was up to the elbows in suds, to wash.

'Will I see to the hen huts, Kate? It's Saturday tomorrow, don't forget.'

Every other Friday, Ness cleaned out the hen arks, putting fresh straw in the nest boxes, clearing the floor of droppings which she left in a tidy pile at the far gate from where, every other Saturday, Goff Leaman collected them in his wheelbarrow. Best thing for tomatoes, Goff had said. Brought them on a treat and cost nowt into the bargain.

Ness smiled to think that not so very long ago, she would have considered hen muck as being nasty and smelly and of no value at all. But then, if you lived in Nun Ainsty, there was nothing new under the sun except, perhaps, that she had promised to meet Mick Hardie at half past seven. For an hour.

It gave her something to think about as she scraped and swept and barrowed, yet when the arks were sweet and clean again and fresh chaff thrown on the floors, she was still none the wiser.

That evening, they ate what Lorna called an almost-unrationed supper. Cauliflower with cheese sauce, bread baked by Martha in Kate's iron oven, followed by stewed apples – the first of the season's windfalls – and custard, the milk for which Glebe Farm had unknowingly provided.

'A scrape of margarine on the bread and the last of the cheese ration,' Lorna beamed. 'Y'know, I'm getting quite good at making do, though I says it as shouldn't.'

Lorna was brighter now, Ness thought; seemed almost to have accepted that in four days' time William should have been on leave, and would not be.

'Ten out of ten, Mrs Hatherwood. And there'll be the letter tomorrow, don't forget.'

William's once-a-week letter; a page written every day and posted to arrive on Saturday. Lorna picked it out when sorting Nun Ainsty's mail and pushed it in her pocket to be read later, at leisure. You would have thought he could have spread it out to two or three letters, Ness brooded, but she supposed it was in William's nature to be sparing with anything that cost money, him being an accountant. He even wrote on Army notepaper and used an OHMS envelope, which didn't need stamping. Mean, that's what. It was something else she didn't like about him.

'Mm. Maybe tomorrow he'll know when his leave will be. I still haven't forgiven the Army for stopping it.'

'They haven't stopped it, Lorna, just put it back. And we'd better get on with the washing-up, 'cause I've got a date.'

She said it matter-of-factly and out of the blue, yet it so shocked Lorna that she gasped,

'You've got a *what*?'

'A date. With Mick. At half past seven by the pillar box.'

'Well, you sly old thing! And you never said a word!'

'He's only just asked. And don't make a big thing of it if you don't mind. He'd like an hour of my time, he said.'

'An hour? But you don't make dates and specify how long!'

'It isn't a date, exactly. Just something he wants me to know, he said.'

'And he didn't give you a hint?'

'Nope. I reckoned that after what he did when Rowley got stroppy, I owed him that. He asked me out once before, see, and I said no. And I've got to admit I'm a bit curious.'

'But curiosity apart, you like Mick, don't you? It isn't just curiosity and gratitude?'

'Of course I like him and it doesn't bother me one bit that he's a conchie. Anyway, now you know.'

'So what will you wear?' Lorna filled the biggest kettle and set it to boil. 'The blue frock with the swirly skirt suits you.'

'Oh, for Pete's sake, it isn't *that* kind of a date. A walk, he said, or a drink at the pub. No need to look so pleased about it.'

'But I *am* pleased. It's the first date you've ever had – well, since you came here.'

Ness began to collect dishes, refusing to be drawn further because Lorna had put her finger right on it. It *was* her first date since a November night when her world fell apart. She drew in her breath sharply.

'So it is,' she said softly. 'And can we get a move on, please? Don't want him hanging about outside, waiting, or Martha's sure to see him and it'll be back at Glebe Farm in the morning!'

'They'll know about it at Glebe whether Martha sees you or not. This is Nun Ainsty, lovey. Nothing goes unnoticed here!'

And at half past seven that evening, Lorna was proved right. Martha Hugwitty's lace curtains twitched noticeably just as Mick smiled and said,

'Hi. Thanks for coming, Ness.'

'Did you think I wouldn't?'

He looked good in flannel trousers and a white shirt, buttoned low, sleeves rolled to his elbows, setting off his brown skin. And tall and slim, too. She wouldn't be surprised if he danced like a dream.

'If you hadn't come, I'd have knocked on your door.'

'Oh? Must be important, Mick.'

'Only to me, but I want you to know.'

'Then let's go? Priory Lane would be fine.'

Priory Lane, half a mile long, led to the main road. There was little traffic on it. Better than walking through the village to the pub; better than going to the White Hart where half of the drinkers would make it their business to hear what they said, the other half probably being lip-readers!

'So what's your news, Mick?'

They stopped at the first field gate and leaned on it companionably, looking over pastures and fields yellow with ripe wheat. And trees throwing long evening shadows.

'I'm leaving.' He said it softly, staring ahead.

'*Leaving*, Mick! Why? Where to?'

'To the Army, eventually.'

'The *Army*! But you're a – a –' She stopped, eyes on her hands.

'A conscientious objector? Not any longer.'

'So you went through all you did, had to go before a tribunal, took a load of flack for what you believed in, and now you're going to pack it in! Am I to be told why?'

She was shocked and all at once afraid. Afraid for Mick.

'I've told them at Glebe.' He laid a forearm on the gate top then turned to face her. 'Now I want you to know, but I'd rather you didn't talk about it to anyone else.'

'Not even Lorna?' Her heart was thudding and she didn't know why.

'Maybe Lorna, but no one else. So where do I begin, Ness?'

'At the beginning, I suppose.' Her voice was croaky. Probably because she felt so choked. 'Right from the time you decided you wanted to be a soldier.'

'I don't *want* to be – not exactly – but lately I've had to admit that maybe it's best I should go.'

'In heaven's name, why?' Cheeks blazing, she raised her eyes to his and saw that his face was calm, his smile gentle. 'You said you couldn't – *wouldn't* – take a life. What happened to change you, Mick?'

'Oh. Me, I suppose – and my temper. I saw red, wanted to beat Rowley half to death . . .'

'Oh, no. All this isn't because of me and Rowley?' she whispered. 'It wasn't him made you –'

'Made me want to kill him? He had you on the floor. He was hitting you. What was I supposed to do, then? Stand there and let him?'

'No, Mick. Of course you couldn't. But did you have to get so mad at him? Did you have to punch him then heave him into the yard? Rowley Wintersgill isn't worth it. OK – someone had to teach him a lesson, but did it have to be you?'

'He was going to harm you. I didn't have much choice. As a matter of fact, I think I enjoyed belting him – at the time. I wanted to wipe the arrogance off his face, and that was just for starters.'

'So he's arrogant and he annoys me, too. But what you did was out of character. You hit him so hard your hand was bleeding. You must really dislike him.'

'I hate him. And that's something else I never knew I had in me.' He shrugged, staring ahead. 'I think I actually hate him.'

'Because of me?' Her voice was little more than a whisper. 'But Mick, I had my dungarees on! I'd have been all right. I'm sure I'd have got away from him.'

'After he'd knocked you black and blue, maybe. And from where I stood, I only knew he was all over you and you were screaming for help.'

'Oh, Mick Hardie.' She laid a hand on his. 'I didn't say thank you, did I? Not properly. Didn't seem to get the chance with the pair of us avoiding Rowley and avoiding each other whenever we could. But I was – *am* – grateful for what you did. That kitchen floor is hard. I was praying he wouldn't bang my head on it and knock me senseless. Heaven only knows what might have happened then.'

She held her hands to her face, closing her eyes tightly, pulling in gulps of air, refusing to weep because if she did, Rowley would have won.

'Hey! It's all right. It didn't happen and your face is fine now.'

He moved closer then placed an arm around her shoulders, drawing her to him. And because she was a little off-guard trying not to cry, and because she felt safe being near him, she relaxed and laid her head on his chest, fighting sobs.

'Ssssh.' He pushed her a little way from him, taking a handkerchief, mopping the tears that filled her eyes. 'And I'm sorry. I should have known you aren't over it yet.'

'But I *am* over it. He won't try it again; not now his father knows. But it makes me mad because he's the reason you are going into the Army, when if there was any justice in this world, it ought to be him! And it's my fault.'

'But Ness, I knew what I was doing. All you did was make me realize I'm capable of acting like any other man when the need arises. In fact, I was so blazing mad I could have killed him. Seems my principles aren't worth as much as I thought.'

'So how long have you felt like this, Mick? When did it all start?'

'A couple of days after, I suppose. I saw Ewan MacMillan over the back wall and he asked me what was wrong with my hand and face, and did I want him to take a look at them. Anyway, one thing led to another. Seems he'd heard about me losing my rag and belting Rowley, so I asked him if I could have a word with him – wanted his advice, I said.'

'About joining the Army? But couldn't you have thought about it, instead of jumping in feet first?'

'I'd thought enough. I told Ewan I wanted to jack in being an objector and what did he think about it? And he told me that if I was set on the Army, best join the Medical Corps. They aren't a combatant unit, he said. A lot of men who thought the way I did had joined the Medics. The exact opposite, he said, to taking life – or words to that effect,' he shrugged.

'So you are determined? Because of Rowley Wintersgill you're going to join up?'

'I *have* joined up, Ness. The Medical Corps have accepted me.'

'*No!* When are you going?' Her mouth had gone dry and she was shaking.

'Do you mind when?'

'Of course I mind since it's all down to me you've volunteered.' She flung round to face him, cheeks flushed. 'You're working like a dog for the war effort. You're doing your bit here, without harming anybody!'

'I'll be doing my bit as a medical orderly, without harming anybody. Like I said, I won't have to do any shooting. And it'll make a change from being a conchie.'

He said it without bitterness yet his words filled Ness with guilt.

'Hell! I wish Kate hadn't broken her arm,' she said. 'Wish she hadn't been taken to hospital. None of this would have happened but for that kitchen floor!'

'Will you miss me, Ness Nightingale?'

'Don't ask such damn stupid questions! Of course I'll miss you. I like you a lot. It never bothered me that you were a conchie, you know that!'

'I like you a lot, too, so maybe it's as well I'm shoving off since you aren't interested.'

'So who says I'm not interested?'

'Sorry, but I'd got the impression you weren't. I asked you out once, and you said no. A very firm no, as I remember. I took it there was a man in your life – overseas in the Forces or something. Am I right, Ness?'

'No! We-e-ll, yes. There was Patrick.' It hurt to say his name.

'Ah. I might have known a girl like you would be spoken for. But you said *was*. Have I blundered in? If I have, I'm sorry. If you don't want to talk about it . . . ?'

'I don't, but he was called Patrick Martin. It happened more than a year ago. It's why I joined the Land Army. A fresh start. And I'm trying to get over it, Mick. I truly am.'

'I've upset you. Forgive me? Leave it, shall we?'

'Yes, please. I'd rather not talk about him, if you don't mind. Reckon I've had enough bother for one day – you going into the Army, I mean, because of me. And you didn't say when you are going.'

'Not just yet. Bob saw them at the labour exchange about my call-up, asked them to defer it till he'd found someone to replace me. Told them there was harvest coming up, then potatoes to be lifted and swedes and sugar beet. Looks like it could be the end of November, if Bob gets his way.'

'Then I hope he does. And I'd like to go home, Mick. Sorry if tonight hasn't been a bundle of laughs.'

'Necessary, for all that. Seems we both had things to get off our chest.'

They said little as they walked back to the village because there was nothing, really, to say. Yet when they said good night beside Dickon's Wood, Ness reached on tiptoe to kiss his cheek, not caring who might see them.

'See you in the morning, Mick. And I'm sorry about tonight; sorry about everything.'

She turned abruptly, making for Ladybower, thankful to see Lorna on her hands and knees weeding, her bottom only just visible between two rose bushes. It gave Ness time to order her thoughts, straighten her shoulders, then call, 'Hi!', as she walked reluctantly to face Lorna's eager curiosity.

A little before six the next morning when she heard the door bang behind Lorna, Ness jumped quickly out of bed, ignoring the fifteen minutes due to her before the alarm clock rang. Quickly she washed and dressed, then made for Glebe Farm. She wanted – *needed* – to talk to Mick. It would not wait. There were things he should know and if she hurried she knew exactly where he would be at a little after six in the morning; where they could get a few minutes together without being seen.

She made for the pasture, then stopped, pulling in deep breaths, trying to compose herself, calm the uneasy thudding of her heart.

Mick almost always brought the cows from the pasture for milking. Cows stayed in the open overnight in the summer months and she knew he would still be in the field, rounding up stragglers, urging them towards the gate. She saw him in the far corner and held up her arm, reluctant to call out, and when he saw her and returned her wave she ran towards him, avoiding the animals that walked clumsily past her, bags swollen with milk.

'You're early, Ness.'

'I know. I wanted to see you.' His smile was worth missing breakfast for. 'I want to say I'm sorry and ask you if we can talk tonight. Another hour, maybe?'

'Fine by me. Whatever you want.'

'Then is half past seven at the ruins all right? Can you meet me there?'

'Sure. But has something happened? You look as if you haven't slept all night.' He took in the pallor of her face, the smudges beneath her eyes.

'I didn't. I was going over things again and again. Oh, I told Lorna about you joining up, but that was all. I didn't tell her about Patrick, but I want you to know, Mick.'

She slapped the flank of a cow that had stopped to pull on the grass, then fell into step beside him, eyes on her boots.

'And it must wait until tonight, Ness?'

'Afraid so, if you can make it.'

'OK. Half seven at the ruins, then. You don't mind if anyone sees us? It's very near to Glebe.'

'I realize that, but it's so peaceful there – seems as good a place as any.'

'You sound upset.'

'Look, Mick – can we leave it?' They were beside the field gate from where they could see Bob and Rowley crossing the yard to the cow shed. 'I'll go to the kitchen, give Kate a hand with early drinkings. It worries me when she tries to lift heavy kettles. 'Bye, Mick. See you.'

She ran towards the open kitchen door, cheeks burning. Then she stopped, forced a smile to her lips and called,

'Hi, Kate. Want me to put the kettle on?'

That night, the minute she set foot in Ladybower's kitchen, Ness knew there was news for the telling.

'Guess what?' Lorna smiled. 'A phone call from William just as I was leaving for the surgery.'

'And? Good news?'

'The best! Seven days' leave, probably the third week in August. It was all he had time to say. I think he was using the office phone for a crafty call, and had to keep it short. All news in the letter, he said, so now I've got to wait till Saturday.'

'But it's definite?'

'Seems so. I haven't got a date yet, but he wouldn't have gone to the bother of ringing unless it was official. Aren't you pleased for me, Ness?'

'You know I am. I'll warn the warden at the hostel as soon as you can give me a date, but I don't hold out much hope of a bed there. Don't reckon any of the girls would dare to ask for leave at harvest time.'

'Nearly ready.' Lorna checked the potatoes. 'I know it's a nuisance, and I hope you won't mind too much.'

Of course Ness didn't mind moving out. Ladybower, with William on leave, was the last place she wanted to be. Although Ness had not met William, not actually been introduced, she had seen him, distantly, with Lorna in the village and she knew exactly what he looked like. And you couldn't miss the large, silver-framed photograph of him in uniform. It seemed to dominate the sitting room and Ness swore his eyes followed her whenever she walked past it.

'You know I don't mind. We agreed, didn't we, that for the sake of peace and quiet I would move out when William was home. The least I can do. After all, he could have refused to have me here.'

'No he couldn't.' Lorna said it quietly, cheeks flushing. 'I'm the one who says who shall live here. It's *my* house, didn't I tell you? I feel guilty about it, sometimes, but there's nothing I can do about it and besides, I think I like it that way. But no more of who owns what! William's leave is on again and I'm sure you'll be able to stay with Flora. You enjoyed being with her last time, you said.'

'I'll have a word with her tonight. She likes a bit of company, I think. Anyway, what's for supper? Something smells good.'

'Stew. Very little meat, lots of gravy – and peas and cabbage. And courtesy of a crafty land girl I know, sago pudding. Oh, don't you sometimes wish for a big sinful steak, or is that unpatriotic?'

'Not a bit. I think of steak an' all, and fried onions. And cream cakes and buttered toast. Most people do, if they're honest.'

'Mm. And tinned peaches in thick syrup, and rich fruit cake.'

'Well, never mind. As soon as Glebe starts on the harvest, Goff Leaman will be there with his gun, shootin' all the rabbits in the cornfield.' Rabbits. Unrationed, and like gold dust. 'But I'll just nip upstairs and clean up – if I've got time, that is?'

'On the table in ten minutes.'

Lorna Hatherwood was happy once more. Her man would be home soon, and it didn't take a genius to guess, Ness thought, that already she was thinking of babies again.

Ness sat in the cloister, face to the evening sun, looking around at the ruins of the priory, trying to imagine how it had been in its glory days, wondering about the sick who came there to be nursed. Once upon a time, Lorna had said, no religious house could turn anyone away, neither travellers in need of a bed for the night, nor a leper, nor anyone begging for food.

What had happened to those nuns, Ness frowned, when their possessions had been taken by a king at war with the pope. Where had they gone, who had taken them in when the roof had been torn from the building; who, after that, cared for the ill and the hungry? It was a funny old world, when you thought about it; always bother and fighting, mostly over religion. Pity the priory hadn't been gutted a bit earlier. Ursula would have been glad to see the back of the place, and the faithful Dickon only too willing to take care of her. Ursula would have –

'Hi! Am I late, or are you early?'

Mick. She had not seen him coming, so wrapped up in her daydreaming was she.

'I'm early,' Ness smiled. 'I was going to see Flora Petch to beg a bed from her, but she must be out on a call. Lorna's husband is coming home on leave and I usually make myself scarce when that happens.'

'And what were you thinking about? Obviously something rather nice. Your eyes were closed and you were smiling.' He sat down beside her.

'I was thinking about this place, actually, and wishing they could have chucked the nuns out a bit earlier than they did – for Ursula, you see. She wouldn't have minded bein' thrown on the street. She didn't want to be there in the first place!'

'And you believe the ghost story? I thought you were too level-headed for that, Ness Nightingale.'

He was smiling at her, his eyes teasing, and it prompted her to demand,

'All right, then, so tell me why it's nonsense?'

'Well – it's my opinion that after the monasteries and nunneries were looted and closed, it was all right for anyone to take what they wanted from them. The king took the land, and anyone else could help themselves to the stone, which they obviously did. Every house in this village is built with stone from the priory, had you noticed? A nice little tucked-away community, probably most of them related in one way or another. So what was to stop them, when they didn't want any more houses in their village, to try their hardest to keep people away?'

'You mean they invented a ghostly nun to frighten people off. A bit much, wouldn't you say?'

'Not at all. Quite crafty, really. But it's only a theory. If you want to believe in the nun, then feel free.'

'Of course I don't believe in the nun. I don't believe in ghosts, full stop! Think I'm simple or sumthin'? Mind, they do say there's no smoke without fire, so you make up your own mind, I reckon. But I – well, I didn't ask you here to talk about what happened four hundred years ago, Mick. I asked you because I want you to know the whole story.'

'About . . . ?'

'About Patrick. And will you keep it to yourself? It isn't something I talk about, you see. And before you say it isn't any of your business – well, I think it is, because last night I left you thinking that there had been a man in my life and that I'm still upset about it.'

'You did. It was the only reason I could think of why an attractive girl like you doesn't seem interested in men. It fitted, somehow.'

'Yes, and you're half right. Only Patrick wasn't killed. He wasn't even in the Armed Forces. He was, if you want it straight between the eyes, a married man. And before you ask, no, he didn't chuck me. It was me walked out on the affair. Because that's all it was. A cheap, stupid affair!'

'Ness, love – don't get upset. I don't have to know. Let's leave it, shall we?'

He ached to take her in his arms and tell her it was all right, but most of all he felt a sudden dislike for the man; just as he had felt when he snapped, and thrashed Rowley Wintersgill. So he took a deep breath, stuffed his fists in his trouser pockets and stared at the ground.

'And what if I don't want to leave it? What if I want you to know, because I think you're too good for the likes of me! He was married, Mick, and I never suspected. No! That's wrong. Looking back, there were all sorts of vague things, but I chose to ignore them.

'I was besotted. I'd never met anyone like him before – not anyone interested in me. He spoke lovely like he'd been to a posh school. None of your Scouse accent. He had a big car, an' all, and he didn't buy his suits from the Fifty Shilling Tailors, that's for sure. Want me to go on?'

'Not if it upsets you.'

'Not any more. Sickens me, more like. But it's best you know what you landed yourself in the Army for. Looking back, y'see, it all added up. He never met my folks, never picked me up at work. And when I asked about his family, I realize I only got half answers. I only *think* he lived in the Sefton Park area and he never gave me his phone number. I could have insisted, I suppose, but I didn't want to rock the boat. I was just willing to be there when he could manage it. He was away a lot on business. Government business he said it was.'

'So why did you end it, Ness. How did you find out?'

'Me,' she said bluntly, harshly. 'Me getting pregnant.'

'Hell, I'm sorry. I shouldn't have asked.'

'No, but you did, so I'm telling you. I fell for a baby, didn't I? On a dirty weekend in Blackpool. And when I told him I'd missed, it all came out that he was married and his wife wouldn't even consider a divorce, her being a devout Catholic. Two children he had, and another on the way. Imagine! Him messing about with me, then going home to his pregnant wife! I felt used and cheap and dirty. I'm what you would call a tart, Mick.'

'Don't say things like that. You aren't the first girl to be taken in and you won't be the last.' He said it so softly, so gently, that she lifted her eyes to his.

'You aren't shocked? Then you should be. First Patrick, then Rowley. What is it about me that attracts the wrong types? Do I give out the impression I'm easy?'

'I wouldn't think so. You slapped me down pretty quickly when I asked you for a date. Thought all men were the same, did you?'

'No, Mick. Not you. Anyway, now I've told you maybe you can understand why I was off men. I acted like a fool over Patrick, but I didn't know he was married and I didn't give Rowley the come-on, honest I didn't.'

'So you got pregnant?' He asked it so suddenly that for a moment she had to think hard to find the words.

'Y-yes I did and I didn't know what to do, where to turn. I couldn't tell anyone, not even Mam.'

'And Patrick didn't help you?'

'I didn't ask him; didn't want to talk to him or see him ever again. Trouble was, I couldn't stop thinking about him and what a fool I'd been – and about the baby, too. I started being sick in the mornings. I got expert at getting to the lavvy in the yard without anyone knowing. It was all just – well – awful.'

'And where is the baby now? With your mother?'

'No, Mick. I miscarried it. In the January. I had terrible pains at work and they called an ambulance. I didn't do anything to get rid of it. It just happened. The ward sister was kind, didn't treat me like I was no better than I ought to be. She said it was probably due to my job. Hairdressers are run off their feet around Christmas and the New Year; probably all the standing, she said, and the worry of it. They didn't tell me if it had been a boy or a girl, and I didn't ask. Best I shouldn't know.'

Her eyes filled with tears and she wiped them angrily away with the back of her hand.

'Ness. I don't like to see you like this. Is there anything I can say that will help?'

'Nothing at all. It happened and the best thing I can do is to learn from it. I won't get caught out again in a hurry, I can tell you!'

'Well at least I can see why you didn't want to go out with me.' He got to his feet, holding out his hands to her. 'Want to walk?'

'Please. If you really want to. Can we look at the ruins? Can you explain how it once was – you bein' an architect, I mean.'

'Not exactly an architect. I'd only got my degree when I had to register for service, and the conscientious objector thing came up. I've a lot to learn yet.'

He took her hand in his own and was glad she did not snatch it away.

'Mick – just one thing. No one knows about the baby but Mam. She couldn't believe it when I told her, in the hospital. We decided not to tell Da and that we'd say that the pains were due to a grumbling appendix, whatever that is! It seemed as good an excuse as any, and Nan and Da seemed to accept it. Lorna doesn't know either. I wouldn't dream of telling her.'

'But why not? She's a lovely lady. I don't think she would judge you.'

'I'm sure she wouldn't, but she's desperate to have a child of her own. She had a sad time when she was little and all she seems to want now is a family she can really call her own. Trouble is, I think William isn't all that keen. So you see, if she knew I'd been with child, and a child I didn't want into the bargain, then it would upset her. She might feel badly done to.'

'I can see what you mean and, Ness, can I say how sorry I am, and ask you to believe that not all men are like Patrick? Don't let what happened spoil it for you when you meet a decent man.'

'So you don't think I'm common – and stupid, into the bargain?'

'Of course I don't. You were unlucky and a bit too trusting, if you really want to know what I think.' He drew her arm into his, smiling down at her. 'So shall we start at the far end over by the oak trees, where the fishponds used to be? You can still see the outline of them. And tell me when you want to be back home – an hour, didn't you say?'

'Better not be much longer. I told Lorna I was going to see Flora; didn't tell her I was meeting you. Her eyes would have lit up, if I had. Well – twice, in two nights! I know she thinks I'm a bit peculiar not going out on dates. Mind, she hasn't asked why, but I know she's bursting to.'

'So why don't you make her day and tell her you're coming out with me tomorrow night – if the harvest allows, that is?'

'Mick! After what I've told you, you still want to know me?'

'Of course I do. And before you read the riot act, I promise to behave myself at all times – not even a good night kiss, unless you allow it.'

'Then fingers crossed,' she whispered, 'for half past seven, tomorrow night?'

'Here at the ruins, and for a little longer, perhaps?'

'Fine by me.' She managed a small, uncertain smile. 'And Mick – thanks a lot.'

'Any time at all,' he grinned teasingly. 'And I think we'd better be making tracks – I'll walk you as far as the village, see if Miss Petch is back. And Ness . . . ?'

He cupped her face in his hands and kissed her forehead. A gentle, whispering kiss that seemed to seal their new-found friendship because that, Ness was sure, was all that would ever come of it. And besides, in November, he would be gone.

'Well, that's enough gardening for one night.' Lorna tipped a bucket of leaves and weeds onto the compost heap. 'I think William will be pleased with the garden when he comes home, don't you?'

'He should be. It looks pretty good to me. Shall I lock the hens up?'

'Please. But not before you've told me about you and Mick Hardie. And before you answer, let me tell you that you were seen!'

'What? Me an' him. Who was it?' she demanded, flush-faced. 'Who split on me?'

'Me, if you must know. I was posting a letter to William

and saw you both outside Larkspur Cottage. This is a very small village, don't forget. You can't get away with anything here.'

'Get away? I bumped into him.' We-e-ll, almost true. 'Flora wasn't in when I called, so I went for a walk in the ruins, then called again to see if she was in. No law against talking to a feller you work with, is there?'

'Ness! Nobody said there was. Just tell me why you've gone so red?'

'Because he – well, he asked me to meet him tomorrow night if we aren't all of us busy with the corn harvest, that is. Nothing definite, I mean.' Best come clean about tomorrow, Ness decided, since she had already lied about tonight.

'Then I hope you said yes, and I hope it pours down all day tomorrow so Bob can't start cutting!'

'Don't let him hear you saying that! But that's all there was in it, so don't go reading things into it.'

'But you like him? Come on, Ness, admit it.'

'Of course I like him, but there's no big romance so you can wipe that smug smile off your face, and remember he's going away in November, so it'll be goodbye then. And in case you're interested, Flora said yes. Glad to have me, so that's something else taken care of. Now – are you coming inside to wash your hands, and shall I make us a drink of cocoa?'

'Not cocoa. Let's have tea to celebrate – er – you and Mick getting together, I mean.'

'We haven't *got together*! We're just going out. Perhaps. So don't go telling it with every letter you deliver in the morning!'

'Won't need to, old love. I'm pretty certain I'm not the only one who saw you. The sergeant-cook at the manor doesn't miss much, and his kitchen – er, cookhouse – looks right over the priory. And if I might say so without having my head snapped off, I've often wondered what the matter was with the pair of you! Began to think you had a secret lover, Ness!'

'Well, I haven't, so get your hands cleaned whilst I see to the hens and put the kettle on. And if you don't mind, shurrup about me and Mick Hardie!'

Shut up about Mick, Ness thought as she lay in bed, determined to sleep and not toss around half the night worrying. But yet again, sleep seemed not to come easily because she was going over everything in her mind; every word, every look that passed between them, every smile. And a kiss. Very brotherly, but a kiss for all that. Michael Hardie, now that she was prepared to admit it, was so good-looking it wasn't fair. Thick dark hair, blue eyes and a smile that would charm the birds from the trees! He was well educated, and, in spite of everything, seemed to want to be with her.

Or was it that he thought as Patrick Martin had done, that she was easy? Did Mick, now he knew she had been biddable and beddable, fancy his luck with some more of the same?

She turned her pillow and punched it angrily. Why had she told him about Patrick and the baby? Could it have been to remind herself that even though she had always thought Mick attractive, it would be a long time before she got over the shame of her affair with a married man; a long time before she could let herself trust again? Had telling it been intended to warn Mick off; let him know she was no better than she ought to be; a young woman who no decent man would want to take home to meet his folks? But meeting his family wasn't going to happen! By the time winter had set in Mick would be gone, and that would be the end of it. 'The *end*, Ness Nightingale,' she hissed, throwing back the bedclothes, making for the window and drawing back the curtains.

Below her, the garden was dimly lit by a half-waned moon that softened shapes and darkened shadows. And beyond it was Dickon's Wood where a long-ago horseman waited.

What nonsense! She shook her head crossly. There were no such things as ghosts! She drew deeply on the night air, holding each breath, letting it out slowly. Deep, gentle breathing usually calmed her, but it was going to take more than that to quieten her mind and clear her head of thoughts. Chin on hands, she closed her eyes and whispered,

> Heaven has no rage,
> like love to hatred turned,
> Nor Hell a fury,
> like a woman scorned.

Lines recited in school and, for some strange reason, still remembered from a boring English lesson. Written by a man who, had he known it, put them on paper all those years ago for Ness Nightingale. And for every other woman who was to allow herself be deceived by a man.

Hatred and fury. That was what she had felt for Patrick the instant he told her he was married, so it could not have been love between them. Not real love. Not the love Dickon felt for Ursula with her poor, disfigured face; Dickon who had waited in the trees near the priory every saint's day. A humble horseman who probably could not read or write but who loved with all his simple heart.

Mick was a latter-day Dickon, Ness brooded. Mick was good and kind and had defended her when she cried for help. It would be easy to love him; good to lift her mouth, eyes closed, for his kiss.

But Mick was not for the likes of Ness Nightingale who had been stupid and too trusting and hadn't wanted to recognize the truth when it stared her in the face. Not until it was too late, that was; when love had turned to hate.

'Good night youse two if you're there,' she said softly, then closed the window, pulling down the blackout blind, swishing the curtains together with such force that they rattled on their wires.

She wished she believed in heaven like Lorna did, and that one day she would go there and see Auntie Agnes and

Granda', and those two from the wood happy together, with Ursula beautiful the way Dickon had thought of her in life, with nothing to make people turn away from her and cross themselves against evil, because a witch had been responsible for her lip.

Ness pulled the bedclothes up to her chin and thought instead about Ruth Street and about Perce and Tizzy on the other side of the Mersey, hoping they were safe as she was, tucked up in bed with no wailing siren to spoil their sleep. Then she thought again about Mick, wondered if he too were awake, still, and thinking about Glebe Farm's land girl. And then, for shame, she wondered if he slept in the nude and was sure as she could be that he did.

'You're right, Ness Nightingale,' she whispered into the pillow as tears choked in her throat. 'You really aren't one iota better than you need be, thinking about a man in the nude!'

But oh, Mick, why are you so attractive and so safe to be with? And why are you too good for the likes of me?

SIXTEEN

It seemed, Ness thought, as if their date tonight was on. The harvest proper would begin tomorrow. Today, she and Mick had done the milking whilst Bob and Rowley opened up ten-acre field swinging razor-sharp scythes in the hot August sun. Not a job for the faint-hearted, or weak.

'We're to go for drinkings, Mick – Kate's orders,' Ness said when the herd was safely back in the pasture and the shippon cleaned. 'Then you'll be relieving Rowley, don't forget.'

'How could I? I'm to take over Rowley's cutting so he can drive Kate to hospital.' Mick washed hands and arms at the pump trough. 'Clever, that. Seems Bob isn't willing to leave you and Rowley unchaperoned nor, for that matter, to leave Rowley and me in ten-acre with scythes in our hands!'

'Good thinking,' Ness laughed, walking ahead of him across the yard.

'Ready for a sup of tea,' Kate beamed, relieved the day of deliverance had come. 'And won't I be glad to get this pesky thing off my arm! It hinders the housework and I'm fed up having a bath with one arm hanging over the side! But get your drinkings, Mick, then tell our Rowley to hurry up and get himself shaved and out of his working clothes. The sooner I get to hospital the sooner I'll be back with two good arms.'

And with two good arms Kate had returned triumphant,

though a little put out to find that with the plaster gone, the arm looked pale and thin.

'They said at the hospital that I'm to treat it gently and remember that the muscles will be weak for a while. But there's nothing wrong with it that an afternoon's stooking in the sun won't cure.'

Whereupon Bob reminded his wife that heaving stooks of wheat was not the way to treat a bad arm, and she was to keep herself away from ten-acre for at least a week!

'Amen to that!' Martha scolded. 'You take heed of what your man says, Kate lass. I'm more than willing to give you a couple of extra hours tonight; keep an eye on you, see to the supper.'

Sincerely meant, even if Martha was more concerned in keeping her job at Glebe Farm until the harvest was in. Longer, if she had anything to do with it, having become used to farm dinners and the odd egg and pint of milk. Indeed, she had not eaten so well since rationing started.

It was accepted that a woman without a man must look out for herself and Martha had become very good at it over the years. Times when she was not obliging someone in Nun Ainsty – as now – there was always fortune-telling to fall back on. Fortune-telling seemed to have become popular with the onset of war; it was not so readily looked down upon now that women had men in the Armed Forces to worry about.

Bob had agreed with Martha, then returned to ten-acre and the scything, content that for the first time in many weeks, all seemed set fair at Glebe Farm.

Dear Lorna. She had left milk in the pan and cocoa measured into a mug and taken herself off to bed, Ness smiled, when all the time she must have been aching to know how the date had gone.

Ness lit the gas under the pan then leaned against the draining board, arms folded, thinking about Mick and the ruins and how late she had got home to Ladybower. Mind, Lorna would be disappointed to learn they had talked and talked like best friends who have been a long time apart. It was easy now for Ness, knowing there was no longer secrets between them.

'D'you know, Mick, that I've no idea where you come from, you not havin' an accent like me.'

'No accent? Then wait till I've been home a few days,' he laughed, 'and you'd know I was a Janner. Devon born and reared, though it seems ages since I lived there.'

Mick had been to Durham University and had twin sisters, Madeline and Lydia; one training to be a nurse, the other a lance corporal in the ATS.

Ness watched the milk begin to rise boiling, then added the cocoa, whipping it to a froth. She had told Mick about No. 3, Ruth Street and the Mersey ferries. And about the amazing Overhead Railway that ran the length of the docks, north and south, and must surely have been a boon to spies who could ride on it and see every merchantman and warship in the river.

As a little girl she had often ridden its length with Auntie Agnes, she told Mick, marvelling at the Cunarders and the sleek white cruise liners, wondering who could be rich enough to sail on them. Now, to see so many ships no longer pleased her because she knew that soon they would sail down river and out to sea and that many would not come home.

And Mick had said that his mother had returned to part-time teaching when war started and that his father worked long hours in an Exeter bank because so many of the younger men were gone to join the armed forces.

'What is your house like, Mick?'

'Deep Hay? Higgledy-piggledy. First built in 1350 and bits added on ever since. No two windows the same size and doors never intended for men six feet tall. And there's an apple orchard, and quite a few plum trees.'

Ness had closed her eyes and imagined the house called Deep Hay, whilst Mick told her about a man, centuries ago, who'd had charge of the fences and boundaries thereabouts and had lived in the 1350 part of it before the rest was added – a one-up, one-down at that stage, Mick said. It was probably why he'd always been interested in houses and his reason for becoming an architect.

'A hayward that man was called, Ness, because hay wasn't just something fed to cows in winter; a hay was also a fence or hedge – and I'm boring you!'

'No, you aren't! It's just that before I came here, I'd never known anyone with a garden big enough to have an orchard in it. In Ruth Street our front door opens onto the street, and we have a yard at the back. That house of yours must be really something.'

'Suppose it must. I was born there, you see, and if I make it through this war it'll be mine, one day. I'm glad about that. Wouldn't want a stranger to live there.'

'So you're quite at home in the country, Mick? Not like me, who once thought that Sefton Park was the nearest I'd ever get to sumthin' like this.'

She waved an arm that took in fields as far as she could see and woods and an evening sky so beautiful it didn't seem fair people should live in the terraces of houses that ran from Scotland Road in long straight rows, each one the same. No apple orchards. Only a cobbled jigger that ran between the backs of the houses and more often than not smelling of tom cats.

'Why the sigh?' he had asked, and she had said it was because one day she would have to go back to Liverpool when it was all over.

'Not that I don't love the bones of the place,' she hastened, 'but I won't ever forget Nun Ainsty and the quiet and all the flowers.'

Nor Glebe Farm and cows and hosing down and Kate's kitchen. And six white and black hens and Dickon's Wood that sheltered Ladybower from winter winds and the sun in summer.

'Bob is letting me go a week early, so I can have time at home before I join up,' Mick had said. 'November seems a long way away, but it isn't, really.'

Nor was it. Ness sipped the hot drink and calculated it was about eleven weeks and that when he went, she would miss him.

'So is there a girl in your life, Mick?' she said softly, as they walked home.

She had not meant to ask but it came easily for all that, because she really wanted to know.

'Apart from the terrible two at home, no one at the moment. What made you ask?'

'Oh – curiosity, I suppose.' She felt her cheeks redden. 'What I mean is why isn't a man like you spoken for?'

'Like me?' His eyes held hers and she could not look away because all at once she realized how very blue they were. 'And why should I be spoken for?'

'Because – well, you're good-looking . . .' She'd had to make a conscious effort to look away, stare at her feet. 'And you are kind and know how to treat a girl and I'll bet,' she hastened because now she had started she might as well be hanged for a sheep! '. . . I'll bet you're a smashing dancer, an' all.'

'Don't know about smashing, but I like dancing. Don't you, Ness?'

'Ooh, yes. Bet I've gone through more dancing partners than you've had hot dinners, Mick Hardie. But no steady bloke. Patrick was the first I took seriously and look where it got me!'

'Then why don't we go to a dance in York, once the harvest is over? We could get the bus there and hitch a lift back.' He sidestepped Patrick so firmly that Ness felt bound to insist,

'But have you *never* had a steady girl, Mick?'

'I've had lots of girlfriends, but only in passing. A student can hardly afford to eat, let alone take girls out. What Bob pays me every week is the first serious money I've ever earned, which means I can now afford the luxury of a real date. So what do you think?'

'All right.' She still refused to look at him. 'When we get some time off, I'd like that. But there'll be no time off for the next three weeks. There's the barley to be seen to, when ten-acre is finished with. And when that happens, make sure you cover up, Mick. Last year my arms were scratched all over and sore for days. Barley has nasty little needles on it. You can't strip off when you're hot.'

Which was a pity, she thought, rinsing and drying her mug. Mick had taken off his shirt when the hay was being cut and turned. She remembered thinking how tanned his chest and back were, how broad his shoulders.

And she was getting obsessed with the man, she thought impatiently. Wondering if he slept in the nude; remembering haytime.

'Oh, get yourself off to bed, you silly woman!' she whispered, reminding herself yet again that someone like Mick did not get serious with someone whose accent was undeniably Scouse and had been cheap enough to spend a dirty weekend with a man. Because that was what it had been, though at the time she hadn't been able to think straight, or see through the stardust.

She snapped out the kitchen light and walked quietly upstairs. And why, she would like to know, had she told Mick about that weekend and the baby that had been the result of it? Wouldn't it have been wiser to have said nothing?

No! You told the truth and shamed the devil. That was what Auntie Agnes always said, and be blowed to the consequences. Even if, Ness thought yearningly, opening up her heart to Mick had put paid to anything but friendship between them.

She got into bed without pin-curling her hair. Why bother

when tomorrow it would be tucked into a bright green snood in the cornfield. Why bother to look attractive when no man with a ha'p'orth of sense in his head would want her – except what Patrick had wanted her for!

She lay still, thinking about what she had done less than an hour ago.

'Good night,' Mick had said at Ladybower's gate.

''Night, Mick.' Then, fool that she was, she had taken his face in her hands and reached up to kiss him. On his mouth. She wondered now at her stupidity, yet hadn't he said, she reasoned, that he would not expect so much as a good night kiss.

. . . And before you read the riot act, I promise to behave myself at all times. She could remember every word of it. *Not even a good night kiss, unless you allow it.*

So she had kissed him to let him know, she supposed, that kisses were all right between them. And now it would be up to Mick. Their next kiss would be his, if he wanted it; if he wanted to take her out again, that was.

'See you,' he had whispered, touching her cheek with his fingertips. 'Thanks for tonight – and I did mean it about us going dancing.'

Those last few words had seemed to make it come right. She had kissed him – a thing no girl should do on a first date – and still he wanted to see her again.

She sighed deeply, trying not to admit how attractive she found him, and that no matter how much she told herself she must never trust a man again, Mick Hardie had only to smile and she could, if she let herself, be utterly charmed by him.

'You're a fool,' she whispered into the darkness. 'Will you never learn?'

'Just pack the essentials,' Lorna said the day before her husband was due home on leave. 'No need to clear everything out of your room. After all, William knows you are here, so why bother?'

'You're sure?'

'Quite, quite sure.' The firmness of her reply surprised Lorna who, not so long ago, would have leaned over backwards to avoid Ness's name being mentioned. 'And if you find you need anything, just give me a ring.'

'I've got all I need, ta.' Ness had no wish to ring Meltonby 223 to find it answered by William. 'Martha is still doing Kate's weekly wash and she said she would do my shirts and overalls with Glebe's, so Flora won't be too put out.'

'Yes, but what if you need a cotton frock, and some shoes? I thought you and Mick were going dancing.'

'We are, harvest permitting. Don't forget that when you've worked till the light goes, there's not a lot of energy left for dancing!'

'But didn't Bob say he was taking a day off from the wheat?'

'He did. Sunday. He never allows Sunday work unless it's urgent. Mick and I will do morning milking and Bob and Rowley will do afternoon milking. Other than that, it's a rest day.'

'You like Mick Hardie, don't you? I don't know why the pair of you were so long getting together,' Lorna scolded. 'You told me you didn't mind him being a conchie, so why did you say no, the first time he asked you for a date?'

'Hey! You take care of your love life and I'll take care of mine!'

'In short, mind your own business, Lorna!'

'Yes. Oh, heck – *no*! Look – if I tell you something will you treat it in the strictest confidence?' Dammit, Lorna deserved to know. It couldn't be kept from her for ever!

'Of course. I don't blab, especially when asked not to! So tell me?'

'We-e-ll, I didn't go out with Mick because there was someone else, you see.'

'*Was*? Ness! I'm sorry. He wasn't . . . ?'

'No. He wasn't killed. Wasn't even in the Armed Forces.

To cut a long story short, I found out he was married. What's more, he had two children and another expected. It kind of put me off men for a long time.'

'Lordy! It would.' Lorna's eyes opened wide. 'I'm sorry, truly I am. I shouldn't have asked, but I always thought it peculiar you didn't seem interested in men. You being so attractive and such good fun, I should have known there was a reason for it. Are you over him yet?'

'I am. It's why I joined the Land Army. New start, and all that. You'll not tell anyone?'

'Not even William. Cross my heart and hope to die! How awful for you, Ness, and for his poor wife, too. Thank heaven William isn't like that. A bit bossy at times, but faithful.'

'He was called Patrick, by the way.' Ness snapped open her case. 'And it really is over and done with.' She said it very firmly to make sure Lorna would never, ever, mention his name again. 'Be an old love and pass that pile of shirts, will you?'

Over and done with? Oh, no. Never quite forgotten, especially the baby. But that was one thing she couldn't tell Lorna; couldn't say, 'Oh, and by the way, I got pregnant, too, and miscarried it.' You couldn't say something so hurtful to someone who desperately wanted a child and was being denied one, it was almost certain, by a selfish husband.

'But you'll see Mick again?'

'Of course. Ten-acre will be ready for stacking by Tuesday and when that's been seen to, Rowley and Bob will start opening up the barley. We'll both have a break on Wednesday – apart from milking. Maybe that's when we'll be able to get away to York.'

'So hadn't you better pack a frock and shoes, just to be on the safe side? And would you like to borrow my perfume? I still have some left.'

'Yes to the frock and shoes, no to the perfume. Thanks a lot, but perfume is like gold dust these days. You hang on to it. Anyway, won't you need it yourself, William being home?'

'No. You take it, Ness. William doesn't appreciate perfume. Doesn't do anything for his ardour. Says it makes him sneeze,' Lorna laughed.

And Ness laughed with her, secretly suspecting that nothing on earth would arouse William Hatherwood to passion. What a pompous creature he was. Whatever had got into Lorna's head when she married him?

But then, she thought, all at once serious, everyone was allowed one mistake, surely? Ness Nightingale above all should know that!

'Well, that's about it. Only my sponge bag to put in.' Ness pushed the case under the bed. 'I'll leave it at Flora's in the morning, on the way to Glebe. By the way, what time do you expect William?'

'Arrives in York early evening. He's coming by train this time, and wants me to meet him.'

'Run out of petrol coupons, has he?'

'Don't think so. Something needs doing to the car, he said, so the Army mechanic is fixing it for him – on the quiet, of course.'

'Of course.' And on the cheap, too, Ness shouldn't wonder. William wouldn't spend money taking his car to a garage when he could get it done on the quiet.

'I shall ask him for a petrol coupon, you know. York and back, twice, will make a hole in my rations.'

'Good for you, Lorna. Beats me why he wants his own car down there.'

'The trains irritate him. Always late, he says, and crowded and dirty, too.'

'Well, 'ard luck! Your William gets a first-class ticket on the train. At least he gets a seat. Not like the poor sods who have to pack in like sardines in third class!'

'I know, Ness, but William is a bit set in his ways. I'm sorry . . .'

'Now see here, girl, I thought you'd learned to stop saying

you were sorry. You don't have to apologize for him, you know. I thought you were learning to stand up to him.'

'I am. I've got time off from the surgery, but there's no way I can get out of the mail and papers and I shall tell William there's a war on, if he complains. He objects to the alarm disturbing him at half past five, you see, but at least he can have the pleasure of going back to sleep.'

'Hm.' Ness knew exactly what she meant. Her weary bones ached for bed. 'I'm whacked, but can we have a walk around the garden before I turn in? I won't see it for a week.'

She loved the garden even more when the night flowers smelled so sweetly and the blackbird sang on the tallest tree in the wood as twilight came. Nights came earlier in August. Soon it would be autumn, and then November. But she wouldn't think about Mick leaving. Tonight she and Lorna would walk amiably around the garden, breathing deeply on the cool air, taking in the scent of honeysuckle that climbed up through the hedge and spilled over in a shower of blossom. Beside the path grew night-scented stocks; very small, ordinary little flowers until the sun set and their sweet, soothing perfume demanded you notice them.

'Y'know sumthin', Lorna? Even when I'm real old, I shall still remember Ladybower's garden and the flowers and the trees around it.'

'Real old! Steady on, love. We've hardly had time to be young yet, thanks to this war! But I know what you mean. When all this is over and you and me both have children of our own and nothing to worry about any longer, I think I shall always look back on the war and remember the good things. And that we won it, eventually.'

'You reckon? We're going to win?'

'No doubt about it, though don't ask me when! But we are fighting back now, not waiting to be invaded, though I still feel guilty when I think about what the Russians are going through instead of us.'

'Ar.' Ness closed her eyes and breathed deeply, and the scents and the quiet and the absolute safeness of Ladybower washed over her and relaxed her work-weary limbs. It was almost, she thought, like praying without words.

She sent a silent good night to Ruth Street and to Perce and Tizzy and to Mick who would be in bed already in the room above the kitchen. Probably sleeping naked.

'It's me for bed!' She jumped to her feet, closing down such thoughts. 'If I stay here much longer, I'll fall asleep standing up!' She kissed Lorna's cheek. ''Night, queen.'

''Night, Ness. Sleep tight. Think I'll sit here a little longer.'

And think about tomorrow, no doubt, when her man would be home, or have little dreams, Ness wouldn't be at all surprised, about the war being over and the three children Martha had promised.

Dear, lovely Lorna, who deserved better than William.

William's train was late, the station porter told Lorna. Something to do with a goods train brought to a stop by a flock of sheep straying onto the line. Sabotage, to his way of thinking, he said gloomily. Those animals had been let out on purpose to upset the timing of all the down trains and a sneakier way of causing an upset than if they'd put explosives on the line and blown it up! Spies all over the place!

So there was nothing for it but to find a place to sit and read the magazine she had bought on the station; a very thin magazine compared to pre-war. But there was a paper shortage so luxuries suffered accordingly. Mind, the government would never dare forbid the publication of women's magazines. Women drew the line at the shortage of cosmetics and clothing and the complete absence of perfume. To deny them their cookery recipes, beauty hints and fashion pages would be too cruel. Even though there was precious little to cook with or smooth on faces, those pages were an affectionate reminder of the way it had been. As for fashion, with clothing and shoes rationed, those pages consisted more of make do and mend, and how to make two clothing coupons do the work of four, rather than what was new in Paris for the season.

Paris. That magical city occupied by the Nazis, and what made it so awful to think about was that but for the invasion of Russia, London might now be occupied, too!

She flicked over the pages. There were short stories in most magazines; almost always about women at war; women with heads held high, managing alone, assuring their man they were just fine and counting off the days to his next leave. Like most women who had a son, husband or sweetheart gone to war. Like Lorna Hatherwood who waited for her soldier and who must wait still longer because of a flock of stupid sheep. Or a saboteur!

She smiled to recall the pained face of the porter who probably started work at six that morning and would be expected to work a long shift for the sake of King and Country and patriotism. She wouldn't be surprised if his feet were hurting like mad and he was out of cigarettes, poor man. Poor Lorna, too, with an hour still to wait. Poor William, who would be clucking impatiently and seething silently about the state of the railways and the idiots who ran them!

Tea! It would take care of fifteen minutes. She made her way to the refreshment room where she could buy an almost tealess, almost milkless cup of liquid for thruppence and into which she would drop one of her own saccharin tablets, sugar having disappeared from buffets and refreshment rooms since food rationing.

She walked across the bridge, trying not to look down at couples who probably waited for the train William would get off, wishing it would never arrive so they could stand there, hands clasped, and never part.

She smiled at the lady behind the counter, old too like the porter and who, but for the war, would be at home drinking tea from her own pot and listening to the wireless.

Lorna thanked her, offered three pennies then stirred her tea, returning the tethered spoon to the counter. Fifty-five minutes still to go. She sighed, found an empty corner table, then, chin on hands, began her favourite daydream which was always about the day peace came and everyone threw their blackout curtains on a bonfire on the Green at Nun Ainsty. And went completely mad with joy!

'Lorna! What on earth are you doing here?' She looked up, startled. 'I've been looking for you all over the station!'

'William! Oh my goodness!' She reached up to kiss him. 'They told me the Edinburgh train was at least an hour late. Sheep on the line and all the down traffic delayed.'

'Then they told you wrong. The train to Edinburgh – my train – on the *up* line was only a little late, as you can see. Most likely it was the train *from* Edinburgh they were talking about!'

'Sorry,' she whispered, making for the door and away from the curious stares of people killing time and eager to listen to any conversation that might relieve the monotony. People who obviously knew the difference between Edinburgh-up and Edinburgh-down! 'I really am sorry you had to hang about.' She smiled, but it did nothing to remove the pique from his face, so she took his respirator and the smallest of his cases, set her lips at stubborn and reminded herself that the sorry-days were over and that Lorna Hatherwood no longer apologized for matters beyond her control. She set off briskly and it was not until they had crossed the footbridge that she said, very calmly, 'How is it, William, that whenever you and I meet at this station, there seems to be words between us? I was given to understand that your train was an hour late, but the man who told me so was old and looked very tired and probably misunderstood what I said. Now! Can we please go to the car and not stand here glaring at each other?'

‘B-but . . .’ William’s face flushed red, his eyes opened wide. ‘I only said that –’

‘Look dear, let’s leave it shall we? I was given wrong information, obviously, but there *is* a war on and people *do* make mistakes!’

Chin jutting, she made for the car park and it was not until they had left the city behind them that William said,

‘Now see here, Lorna, you’re getting yourself upset . . .’

‘I am not upset, but I don’t like being shouted at in public.’

‘Sorry. Was just a bit tetchy, that’s all.’

‘Thank you, dear. Apology accepted.’ She pushed down the window, sticking out an arm, signalling right into Priory Lane. ‘And we’re nearly home, so can we both forget sheep on the line and enjoy your leave. And you never said – why was it put back?’

‘Oh, anything and nothing. You know what the Army is like.’ William accepted the olive branch. ‘They do what they want and don’t see the need to explain. Actually, I think it was because of the move.’

‘Move?’ She turned her head sharply. ‘Where to?’

‘Not *that* kind of a move. Not a posting. We were all set to move offices, that’s all.’

‘And moving office warranted putting your leave back?’

‘Like I said – the top brass does what it wants.’

‘So where have you moved to?’ She slowed the car.

‘Well, that’s just it. We’re still in the same place. I’ll be glad when we get into bigger offices – more chance of my promotion coming up.’

‘Aaaah . . .’ Lorna pressed the accelerator, not wanting to talk about the elusive third pip that would proclaim William’s rank as captain. The promotion had been a long time coming. Best not talk about it. ‘Lovely weather, isn’t it. Glebe Farm is busy with the harvest. And here we are – home.’ It always pleased her to see Ladybower’s roof and chimney stacks half hidden by trees. She smiled indulgently,

William's outburst forgotten. 'Home. Lovely word, isn't it? And let's have a good week? Let's forget the war and oh, *everything*!'

'I think we can manage that, Lorna, if the war allows.'

'If the war allows.' She smiled into his eyes as he opened the car door and helped her out. 'And somehow I think it will.'

For seven days, Laura thought tremulously, they could pretend the war had never happened. If they didn't turn on the news bulletins, that was, nor open a newspaper and if William didn't insist on wearing his uniform to Sunday church. Still smiling, she opened the front door, half expecting a, 'Hullo, queen,' from Ness.

'Welcome home, soldier,' she said softly.

Ness took off her boots at the back door of Larkspur Cottage then called,

'Flora? It's only me . . . !'

'Hullo, there.' District Nurse Petch was still in her navy blue uniform. 'Had to stay with a patient till the ambulance arrived. Put me back a bit. Supper won't be long, though I'm afraid it's going to be pot luck.'

'Then how about these?' Carefully Ness took a large brown egg from each pocket. 'Boiled egg would be fine by me. And here's a drop of milk.'

'Bless you. Half a pint a day doesn't go far. Are you sure it's all right, Ness?' She regarded the large lemonade bottle fondly.

'Reckon so. I'm in charge of the eggs and nobody saw me take the milk. And if they had, it would only be Rowley who'd kick up a fuss.' Glebe Farm produced more than a hundred gallons a day. Two pints was neither here nor there.

'How's the harvest going? We're in for a storm, Goff Leaman said.'

'Bob won't like that. We've got the wheat cut and stacked

and tomorrow he was hoping to make a start on the barley – weather permitting. Mind, we need rain for the potatoes, but not just yet . . .'

'Well, it looks as if we're going to get it.' Flora looked uneasily at the sky from the kitchen window. 'Nasty clouds up there.'

'Then let's hope there's no thunder.' Thunder often brought heavy rain; the kind that did no good at all to ripe, standing barley. 'Anyway – is it to be eggs?'

'Fine by me. You lay the table, Ness, and I'll cut the bread. And I must say it's nice having you – especially if there's going to be a storm. They terrify me.'

At eight they heard the first, faraway rumble of thunder.

'Mind if I close the curtains?' Flora whispered. 'And I think I'll unplug the wireless – just in case.'

Just before war started, the district nurse had bought a new, ultramodern Bakelite set which ran on electricity, and it would be awful to have the aerial struck by lightning and the set ruined, especially since wirelesses had joined the can't-get-one-for-love-nor-money list. 'And I'm sorry for being a big baby. So glad you're here.'

'Think nuthin' of it.' Ness joined her on the sofa at the sitting end of the huge kitchen, thinking it was nice to be wanted which immediately brought William to mind. She hoped he had arrived safely and that he wouldn't object too much to being awakened at the crack of dawn; hoped too, that Lorna had a good week. She flinched as thunder cracked overhead and rain lashed against the window. 'Ouch! That was right on top of us. This is going to mess up the barley. There'll be no cutting tomorrow. It'll take at least a day to dry out.'

It was only then that Ness realized that nothing was wholly bad, not even a storm in the middle of harvest, because now a date had become a distinct possibility. If Mick remembered, that was.

She closed her eyes, crossed her fingers and wished fervently that he would.

'Not a very good start to my leave.' William glared moodily through the window pane. 'That rain is really battering the roses.'

'Mm. It'll be knocking hell out of Glebe's barley, too. Ness said they were hoping to start cutting it tomorrow,' Lorna said. 'Heaven only knows the state it'll be in if this rain doesn't stop soon. Half of it laid flat, I shouldn't wonder.'

The roses! Lorna thought peevishly. Ladybower was lucky to have roses. Other, more patriotic people, had long ago dug out their bushes and now grew vegetables for the war effort.

Ness! William brooded. He might have known it wouldn't be long before her name was mentioned. The land girl had made an impression on Lorna. Must have, since the woman was still here, though what his wife saw in her was a mystery. Peculiar, that. Never before had Lorna questioned his wishes, let alone defied him outright! But it was the fault of the war and a propaganda campaign directed at women to make them feel more important in the scheme of things; inveigle them from their homes where they rightly belonged, to work for the war effort.

'Think I'll have forty winks.' He eased off his slippers. 'Train journeys are dashed tiring. Don't need any help in the kitchen, do you?'

'No thanks.'

Of course I don't! I do two part-time jobs, worry about you, William, worry about finding enough to eat, worry about the war, but it's all right! I've only been up since half past five! You have your forty winks, dear. I'll do the washing-up, she fumed silently.

Men! She glared at the geranium on the kitchen window-ledge, then sighing, rolled up her sleeves.

* * *

'You're early, Ness. I didn't expect you back just yet.' Flora Petch laid down the book she was reading. 'Had a good time? Enjoy the dancing?'

'Had a super time, but no dancing. When we got there, there was a notice on the door. DANCE CANCELLED. NO BAND. So we just strolled around York and talked and talked. Mick knows so much about houses. He said that from where we were standing outside the Minster, he could see so many different styles of architecture; mediaeval, early and late Tudor, Georgian. Mick's so educated. And here's me, thick as two short planks. Left school at fourteen and I know nuthin'.'

'I'm for bed, but I'll make us a drink first. And don't say you know nothing, Ness. You're marvellous with hair.'

'Ar. Not too bad. But I'll never understand why someone like Mick wants to go out with someone like me.' Ness really meant it.

'Then look in the mirror, lass. You're very attractive and nice with it, too. Don't undervalue yourself. Mind if it's cocoa?'

Ness said she didn't mind at all. Truth known, she was forced to admit, if Flora had offered a glass of rainwater from the tub outside, she wouldn't have noticed, so high-as-a-kite was she. All she wanted was to go to bed, snuggle under the eiderdown and think of tonight; of everything they had seen and said and laughed over. Yes, and in spite of what Flora had just said, wonder yet again how a man like Mick should want to take out someone like Ness Nightingale when he could have taken his pick from half the land girls in Meltonby hostel who thought he was gorgeous!

'Penny for them. You were miles away, Ness.'

'Oh – was just thinking the barley should be dry enough to cut with a day of good weather to dry it out.'

Today had been warm and sunny after the storm; had been a beautiful August day that made you glad to be alive. And tonight had been pretty marvellous, too.

'You look sleepy. Take your cocoa upstairs and drink it in bed. You'll have to be up good and early. There's wheat flakes in the cupboard and bread in the bin; you can see to your own breakfast.'

Flora did not rise until eight, by which time Ness would be in the shippon, helping to milk the herd.

'Then I'll say night-night.'

'Good night, Ness. Sleep tight.'

Flora watched her cross the kitchen and open the staircase door in the corner of the room, listened to the ten steps she would take to the landing, waited for the clicking of the sneck on the spare bedroom door.

Sleep tight, indeed! Ness's cheeks were flushed, her eyes over-bright and without a doubt she would lie there thinking about Mick Hardie and that good night kiss. Mind, she hadn't been snooping, Flora brooded; had just happened to be at the front-room window checking the blackout and in time to see a kiss that would make any girl pink-cheeked.

She smiled, and sipped her drink. And good luck to them. They made a lovely pair. Young, straight and beautiful, with the shadow of war always there to remind them that time was short. Time had been short in the Great War. If only she had known how little of it she and her young man had left, Flora sighed.

And oh, damn all wars!

With deliberate concentration, Ness wound her hair into pin curls, trying not to think too much about the evening she had spent with Mick. But it was useless, because she wanted to think about it; bring back every word and smile, every laugh.

No dance, of course, so they had strolled along the quaint streets; some so narrow you couldn't have got a hay waggon down them. And they had marvelled at the age of the city; that it had stood enduring even though the Scots had had designs on it and Vikings and Romans had actually occupied it.

'I wonder how many wars this old place has seen,' Ness had asked.

'Lord knows. But no looking back? One day at a time, eh, and let's enjoy tonight, even though there isn't a dance?'

'I *am* enjoying myself, and there'll be loads of chances to get to a dance and –'

She had stopped, breath indrawn, because there wouldn't be loads of chances to go dancing or do anything else, for that matter. Mick was leaving in November and after that it would be anybody's guess.

'Goodbye, Ness,' he would say. 'It's been great knowing you.' And he would hold out his hand, kiss her cheek maybe, and that would be that. No promising to write to her; no asking her to keep in touch. November, that cold, miserable, dark month would be the end of it, because only when the war was over and he could provide for a wife, would Mick marry. And it would be a girl who wasn't second-hand nor shop-soiled as Ness Nightingale was. Mick would marry a girl who lived around his Devon village, and he would marry her or at least give her a ring before he asked any favours.

That was what she thought before they had caught the last bus to Meltonby and got off it at the top of Priory Lane; before they walked the half-mile to Nun Ainsty, fingers entwined, arms linked. And not even as she held out her hand and wished him good night at Flora's gate had she so much as hoped for that kiss. One on the cheek would have been fine, she would have been glad of it. But after he said,

'Thanks for tonight, Ness. We'll do it again, once the harvest is over?'

And she had said she would like to very much and that she would see him tomorrow, good and early, in the shippon; had said it matter-of-factly, whispered a soft good night and turned to go because she hadn't, she truly hadn't, expected what was to come.

'So don't I get a kiss?'

Gently he took her elbow and turned her to face him, so

she had said that of course he did and reached to touch his cheek with her lips.

'I said a kiss, Ness Nightingale!'

And with that she was in his arms and because it felt the right and proper place to be, she had closed her eyes and offered her mouth to him for that kiss; for that toe-curling, breathtaking, dizzy-making kiss.

'Oh, lordy,' she whispered to the face in the mirror. 'Oh, my word!'

Because it had been one unbelievable kiss. Gentle but firm, and him making it last until she had to gasp for breath and let out an 'Aaaagh . . .' then stand there, shoulders heaving.

And he had laughed softly and said, 'That's better', and would have kissed her again, she was sure of it, had she not broken from his arms and fled, bewildered, up the path of Larkspur Cottage to fumble the unfamiliar key into the back door lock.

She pulled her tongue round her lips, sitting chin on hands, looking at her wide-eyed mirror image, wondering where it would all end.

Yet she knew where it would end. At Glebe Farm it would be, on a cold late-autumn morning. And Kate and Bob would be there and maybe Rowley, too, so they would only be able to shake hands and she to offer her cheek for a last goodbye, because in spite of that unbelievable kiss, it would all end when Mick left for the Medical Corps.

And she would be so miserable, so inconsolable that not even Lorna would be able to do or say anything that would help. And what did Lorna, whose life was so well-ordered, know about heartache; who had known no awful downs nor marvellous highs?

Ness turned from the mirror and forced herself to think about how it had been for Lorna and William; how it had been last night, which was a Tuesday night, and how on earth William was able to produce passion on the dot and as regular as clockwork.

Passion? Not on your life was it! Making love should be a let's-do-it-now thing, no matter what the day or where two lovers were and oh, for heaven's sake, she was thinking about Mick again!

She turned to the mirror once more.

'Grow up, girl! Mick Hardie is not for you and don't forget it, if you know what's good for you! Don't *ever* forget it!'

SEVENTEEN

Things were beter now, Lorna thought as she straightened her hat in the hall mirror, because she had been a little uneasy about William's behaviour. It was nothing she could put a finger on, nothing to really worry about. Just a nagging at the back of her mind that the husband who had come home to her wasn't the William who had gone to war. Which was to be understood, she supposed. William was a soldier for as long as the war lasted, she had to accept that, so of course it took a little time to settle into being a civilian again, albeit for only seven days.

Yet he had snapped at her in the station buffet, then later on, even though he had put on civilian clothes and eaten supper with obvious enjoyment, he still seemed to have left half of himself at Aldershot.

After which, he had prowled about the house, angry that the heavy rain was damaging the roses, annoyed that his leave had started with a thunderstorm.

Then, to add to her worries, he had gone early to bed and was sleeping deeply when she joined him at ten o'clock, which wasn't at all usual for a Tuesday night. She stood in the dimness, gazing at him, getting used again to his head on the pillow, wondering if she should bounce into bed and awaken him, or creep between the sheets and lie very still on the edge of the bed.

She looked at his mouth which even in sleep was tightly set, and decided on the latter, to lay unmoving, finding excuses for what had happened.

William disliked trains and was obviously tired; the quiet of Ladybower was a contrast to Army life and the company of men, and by far the best explanation for the uneasiness between them was that in all the bother of getting here, he had forgotten it was Tuesday night. Thus comforted, she reluctantly awaited sleep, which had been a long time coming.

As the days passed, though, things had been more comfortable between them. William had not objected to the early alarm, had helped with the washing-up and on Friday spent the day in York, visiting the office and taking the senior partner to lunch. After all, he reasoned, it was politic to make sure he was not forgotten and that his desk would be waiting for him when his demobilization came. He had left the house at ten and been away all day which at the time had annoyed her slightly, since he had used her car to get there.

'You know I can't stand public transport, old love – OK?'

It had had to be OK, she supposed, and waved him off with a smile, because even though it might have been nice to be asked along, she realized how sensible the visit was. You might even call it diplomatic. William was very astute that way.

'Lorna! I can't find my tiepin!' His voice jerked her back to here and now. 'Where have you put it?'

'Coming!' She took off her Sunday hat and ran upstairs, knowing exactly where it was; knowing too that things were back to normal between them – bed-wise, that was. This morning they had loved, then she had carried morning tea upstairs to drink in bed like always, even though she knew that later William would wear his uniform to church so she would not be able to forget that just two days from now she would be driving him to the station and waving him goodbye.

'Here it is, you old softie. Right in front of your nose with your cufflinks!' She met his gaze in the dressing-table mirror and smiled into his eyes, then began to brush his jacket. 'And though I wish you'd never had to wear it, I must say, darling, that you look very smart in khaki.'

At which he had shrugged and dropped his eyes from hers to fiddle with his shirt cuffs and say, gruffly,

'You think so?'

'Yes, indeed. But do hurry, William? We mustn't be late for church. I'll pop down and see to the casserole. You've got two minutes!'

She hurried into the hall, put on her hat, jabbed it with a hatpin, glancing as she did so at her top lip. And it was all right. This morning's loving had left no angry red mark there. She turned to smile at her husband as he walked down the stairs.

'Oh, yes,' she said softly. 'Very smart, dear. Very smart indeed.'

Ness heard the noise of the tractor and hurried to the kitchen door, raising her hand to her mouth in a drinking motion, holding up five fingers. Mick grinned and waved. Behind him, the trailer of empty milk churns clattered and clanked. At the speed at which he worked, Ness calculated, it would take him about five minutes to unload the trailer and roll the churns to the dairy. She pushed the iron kettle further into the coals, then tipped a spoonful of tea leaves into the smallest pot. Then she laid milk jug and saccharin tablets on the table beside the big brown mugs and sat down, in the unaccustomed quiet of the kitchen, to wait.

It was ten minutes since Kate, in her Sunday coat and hat, and Bob and Rowley, in Home Guard uniform, had left for the chapel on the Green where at eleven a special service of prayer was to be held. Today, too, there would be a church parade, with Nun Ainsty's Home Guard, six in all, and those from the manor able to walk, filling four of the pews.

Eucharist would be said – it was never sung, there being no choir nor ever had been – then prayers would be offered for all servicemen and women and for civilians and the bombing they endured almost nightly. Prayers, too, for the King and Queen and the royal family and for the government and all in high office. And for men posted missing in action, that they may soon return safely; a most hushed and earnest asking.

There were so many prayers, in fact, that the vicar dispensed with his usual sermon to the relief of the congregation because the Meltonby vicar, who also ministered to St Philippa's, was inclined to go on a bit.

So Kate had asked Ness if she and Mick would mind staying behind and finishing off in the milking parlour and seeing to the poultry, to which Ness had replied, just a little too eagerly, that she didn't mind one bit and was sure that Mick wouldn't either.

'It's going to be another warm one.' Ness smiled as he came into the kitchen. 'Another few more days like this and the barley will be dry enough to stack.'

'Good. Then maybe we'll be able to fix another date?'

'I'd like that. Think we'll find a dancehall that's open next time?'

'Surely.' He stirred his tea, then looked up suddenly to find she was gazing at him intently. 'Why the frown?'

'I was thinking there won't be a lot more time to go dancing.'

She had not been thinking that at all, but the words came unbidden to her tongue.

'And will you miss me when I go?'

'You know I will.' She stared fixedly at the table top.

'I'll miss you, too, Ness. I'll miss you a lot.'

'Then we'll have to keep in touch, won't we?' She forced her eyes to his. 'The odd letter, perhaps?'

'And is that to be it? The odd letter?'

'Every week, then?'

'Not enough, Ness Nightingale. When I get my call-up

date, Bob says I'm to have a few extra days at home. Will you come with me?'

'To Devon?' she whispered, shocked. 'But if I went to your place, your folks might get the wrong idea, think we were serious about each other.'

'And can you honestly say we aren't? The other night, when we kissed, didn't it mean anything to you? It did to me.'

'Yes, but you can't take a girl to meet your parents on the strength of one kiss now, can you?'

Her cheeks burned, her mouth had gone dry. His directness unnerved her.

'Why not, when I *am* serious about us? And as for the one kiss you talk about – would it help if we made it two?' He drew her to her feet and wrapped her in his arms. 'Or three, perhaps?'

'No, Mick!' She stood back from him. 'Not here. Not in this kitchen?'

What had happened on this very spot, almost, warned her that this was not the place. Not where Rowley Wintersgill had –

'OK, then.' He kissed the tip of her nose as he released her. 'But I meant what I said about coming with me to Deep Hay.'

'I'm sure you did, but there'll be things to talk over first, Mick, and there's work to be done. Later we'll talk, so drink your tea, then I've got to see to the hens.'

She crossed to the opposite side of the table as if to place its safe sturdiness between them and because she remembered the morning Kate went to hospital and knew that if anything wonderful was to happen to them, it must not be here.

'And if you've got nothing more urgent to do, Mick Hardie, you can carry the hen water for me – save me making two trips and slopping it all over my shoes.'

'Very well. Maybe right now is neither the time nor the

place, but I want you to come home with me, so you'd best get used to the idea. Understood?'

And she whispered shakily that of course she understood and that it might be very nice to see Devon, only next time he mentioned it, would he please not spring it on her so suddenly, and scare the living daylights out of her?

And they laughed, the tension between them gone, and filled buckets at the pump to carry to the hen troughs, and she determined not to think about when he left, let alone meeting his family. On this Sunday morning she was glad just to be with him, happy to anticipate kisses to come; passionate kisses that made her pull in her breath just to think of them, because Mick had put his cards on the table, said he was serious about her. And he would be easy to love, if only she dare.

Yet the hurt of Patrick had gone deep and deep wounds took a long time to heal.

When the service was over and the customary chat with the vicar at the church door had ended in handshakes and smiles, the men made for the White Hart and Mary Ackroyd's best bitter.

William was first away with Gilbert Ellery, and Nance, who was about to call a reminder that Sunday lunch was at one sharp, decided instead to smile at the medical officer from the manor and ask if he had enjoyed the service and wasn't it nice to see the little chapel filled almost to capacity? And Ewan MacMillan had agreed with her and asked to be excused for a minute, then hurried to where the corporal formed ten men in hospital blue uniforms into lines of two, to be marched back to the manor.

'Corporal.'

'Sir!' They were in public now, the easiness of the army hospital not allowed.

'If the men would like a quick drink, tell them to feel free, but I want them back by one o'clock sharp. And sober!'

And the corporal stamped his feet, saluted, then told the soldiers to fall in sharpish if they wanted a couple of pints, and marched them to the White Hart before the MO changed his mind. A decent sort, Lieutenant MacMillan. They would be sorry to see him go.

'Sorry about that.' Ewan returned to the ladies.

'The men weren't,' Nance laughed. 'And how have you been keeping, Lieutenant? We hardly see you in the village now.'

'Still here, as you see, though busy.' He turned to smile at Lorna. 'We miss your visits, Mrs Hatherwood. Is all going well at the surgery?'

Polite talk for Nance's benefit, since Ewan visited Dr Summers at least once a week.

'I'm getting the hang of it; I'm not so afraid, now, of the medical words – and how to spell them. I'll be back at work on Wednesday so if you ever call on the doctor, I might see you.' A diplomatic answer because Nance Ellery liked to have her finger on Nun Ainsty's pulse and what she didn't know couldn't cause palpitations. 'And if you don't mind, I'll have to go. Got to make the batter for the Yorkshire puddings.' A feeble excuse, because the batter was already made and standing in the cool of the pantry. 'And – er – the casserole, too. Imagine having beef stew for Sunday dinner. Hitler has a lot to answer for!'

'Then count your blessings, Lorna, that you have fresh eggs and milk, it seems, to make Yorkshires with! A great many of us haven't!'

At which Lorna, suitably chastened, blushed pink and said, 'Goodbye Nance, Lieutenant . . .' and was rewarded with the slowest of winks from Ewan which he was careful not to let Nance see. Which was just as well. Nance Ellery could get the wrong idea entirely, had she been witness to the lovely smile that went with it!

Lorna hurried home, strangely happy, wondering if William

ever winked at ladies, dismissing the thought with a laugh. William winking? Never!

She was still smiling as she took off her hat and gloves and jacket, and the woman in the hall mirror ran her fingers through her hair, and smiled back.

Then she straightened her shoulders, tied on her Sunday pinafore and thought about this morning, in bed. And all at once, for some reason that mystified her greatly, the smile was gone.

William said the stew they ate for Sunday dinner was very tasty indeed and that he had enjoyed it.

'That's because I put the last of the Bovril in it,' Lorna sighed, because heaven only knew when she would get more. She was on the grocer's list, of course, and would be furtively given a small jar from under the counter when her turn came. She was on the salad cream list and the list for Horlicks and Oxo cubes and Ovaltine and tomato sauce, all of which were unrationed but in such short supply that they were extremely hard to get. Indeed, William had had to make do with baked custard for pudding when she had hoped to make jam roly poly, his absolute favourite and which, sadly, needed under the counter suet she had not been able to get.

'Did you enjoy the pudding, too? We have a baked custard every week because of the hens and the extra milk Ness – er – brings.'

Then she made great play of rolling up her napkin and easing it into the silver ring, because she realized that she had mentioned Ness's name and should not have done. She had also mentioned the hens, which William blamed Ness for, and was relieved when he scraped back his chair and said he felt like having forty winks in the sitting room.

'Nice to be able to have a little snooze when you feel like it, Lorna. One of the nice things about being home.'

'A good idea. But I insist you take off your uniform first,

and get into something more comfortable – and your slippers. I'll wake you at half three with a cup of tea.'

The washing-up would not take long, Lorna was forced to admit. The pans were already done and the earthenware casserole dish, which would need a lot of scraping and scrubbing, could be left in the suds to soak. And when she had dried and put away and wiped down she would go into the garden with the Sunday paper, kick off her shoes and thank heaven that this far, albeit after a shaky start, William's leave had gone well and seemed to have done him good.

She crossed her fingers and thought about his next one three months hence in November, when it would be cold and dreary and require blackout curtains to be drawn at half past four in the afternoon. It would be November when Mick left Glebe Farm and by which time, too, Ewan could be gone.

'I'm passed fit, now,' he had said on one of his visits to the Meltonby surgery. 'Fingers crossed that I get a bit more time at the manor. I'm getting to like the place!'

Ewan, gone. She would miss him, Lorna brooded. He was so nice, and tall and handsome, dare she admit it. The evening they had eaten venison in Jessie Summers' kitchen, and drank wine and laughed a lot, had been four hours of bliss with the war not even mentioned.

The night before, Ewan gave her the watercolour that hung above her desk. William had not remarked on it, let alone asked who painted it and what had prompted him to give it to her. And however soon Ewan went and however far, she would always have the picture of distant hills and shimmering water and foxgloves to remember him by.

She pushed him out of her mind. William was coming downstairs and she could hear the slap of carpet slippers as he made for his favourite chair at the sitting-room window. She wished, not for the first time, that he would shave off his moustache. Not only would it make him look less middle-aged, but because she had never kissed a man who didn't have one and often wondered what it would be like.

Come to think of it, she had only ever kissed William – passionately, that was, so she would never know. And more the pity, she thought, as she glared at the casserole dish and the baked-on gravy. She dunked it in the sink without another thought and listened to the gurgle as it filled with suds.

She peeped through the open door of the sitting room as she went upstairs to put on a cool cotton frock and take off her stockings and roll-on. William was already asleep, his arms crossed over his stomach. He wasn't snoring, but his mouth was open and it made him look like a contented walrus.

Immediately she raised her eyes heavenwards and said sorry to God for thinking such a thing, and of course He would understand that she hadn't meant it at all; that really she had been fed up with the casserole dish, and taken it out on William.

Absolved, she opened the bedroom window wide and gazed out onto Dickon's Wood and beyond it to her left to Glebe Farm, wondering if Ness was in the barley field shifting stooks even though it was Sunday.

She had missed Ness a lot and wondered how she would feel if one day Ness was to tell her that the Land Army was moving her to Somerset, or Suffolk. Or Scotland.

She dismissed so awful a thought from her mind and concentrated on the careful removal of her silk stockings, all two coupons-worth of them, then wriggled out of her roll-on with a sigh of relief.

From the garden, Lorna heard the ringing of the telephone and hoped Ness was not on the other end of it. William would not be best pleased to be awakened, especially by Ness, but by the time she had reached the back door the ringing had stopped and she stood, waiting for William to testily call her with the badly-done-to look on his face of a man who was being denied peace and quiet in his own front room.

But he didn't call out. Indeed, his voice was perfectly normal as he spoke into the phone, so she walked quietly back to the garden, knowing he would soon be out to tell her who had called. And she was right.

'Who was that, dear?'

'The Army, dammit.'

'*Your* Army, William?' She drew in her breath sharply. 'Aldershot?'

'Yes. And on a Sunday of all days. I've got to go back,' he said tersely, face flushed.

'But *when*?'

'By tomorrow, midnight at the outside. Before, if possible.'

'Not overseas, William?' Her lips were stiff. 'Who rang?'

'The Adjutant's office, and it isn't overseas. It's to do with the office move. They're starting tomorrow, they said.'

'And can't they do it without you? Surely they won't panic over one extra day?'

'Seems they're panicking already. I'm responsible for my section and that's all there is to it. I'll have to be there.'

'But you're going to have to travel overnight and that won't be a lot of fun.'

'I'm not in the Army to have fun,' he said crossly, and she took heed of it.

'Then why don't I ring enquiries, ask about a train and getting you a sleeper?'

'No! Hang on a minute. Just a thought, but there might be a way round it. Primmy might be able to help.'

'*Primmy*? Who is he?'

'*She* is the ATS sergeant in charge of the clerks and typists and the switchboard.'

'And she can hold the fort till you get back tomorrow night?'

'No, dear. She's on leave, too,' William explained patiently.

'If they've called her back as well, she'll be leaving in the morning, early, I shouldn't wonder. Got her own car, y'see?'

'But how does that help you? I think I must be missing something because it doesn't make a lot of sense to me. I'll make a cup of tea.' When in doubt, make tea, and damn the rationing! 'I was going to make one soon anyway, and then you can tell me why your Sergeant Primmy can help.'

'That isn't her name.' William followed Lorna to the kitchen. 'Actually she's Primrose Smythe-Parker. I've heard it said that the girls under her call her Primmy P.' He settled himself at the kitchen table.

'But how can your sergeant help?' Lorna was fast losing patience.

'She lives the other side of York, I'm almost sure. It would solve all our problems if she could be persuaded to make a detour and pick me up.'

'And will she?' To Lorna's way of thinking, it wasn't a good idea at all. 'The poor girl would feel obliged to help and it might not be convenient, you know.'

'Maybe not, but it's worth a try. Anything's better than travelling overnight or even catching the early train in the morning. It would make you very late with your round, Lorna.'

'Then for once, the papers and letters would have to be late!'

'Good for you, old dear. But I'm going to chance it. Primmy will be in the phone book.' He made for the hall and the telephone directory. 'Now will she be under S or P?'

'I'd try P first. And I really don't think it's fair of you to ring her at home. She might be out, anyway. Shouldn't you be getting on to railway enquiries instead?'

'You were right. Under Parker.' William picked up the receiver. 'Hullo, Mrs Benson. Can you get me Kinderston 177? Won't count as a trunk call, will it? Rather urgent, I'm afraid. Oh, bless you . . .' He turned to smile at Lorna.

'Lucky, that. Mrs B has got a line to York. She's putting me through,' he mouthed.

'The kettle's boiling,' Lorna said flatly, closing the kitchen door behind her because she didn't want to hear William coerce the poor young woman into picking him up, especially when she could hardly refuse, he being an officer. He was pulling rank, and she didn't think it was right.

And why was she worrying about the way William was getting back to Aldershot? Shouldn't he be hopping mad at losing two days of his leave? And was it right that the people down at Aldershot should send for her husband – and the ATS sergeant, too – at the drop of a hat, merely because of an office move? People seemed to have been conditioned to blindly accept anything at all these days. William was wanted in barracks as soon as possible, and there was nothing to be done about it. No use getting herself into a state!

She poured hot water into the rosebud teapot, swirling it round to warm, glaring at the geranium on the window-ledge, thinking that the poor plant took an awful lot of flack these days and thank goodness it couldn't answer back and tell her what a spoiled brat she was being!

'There you are!' a beaming William announced. 'Nothing ventured, nothing gained! Primmy P has been called back, too, and she'll give me a lift – provided I'm ready by six, tomorrow morning.'

'But the poor girl is going to have to be up at the crack of dawn to get here that early!'

'Won't be a problem, she said. She'll have to come through York, but there won't be much traffic about at that hour of the morning. Decent of her, I'd say.'

'*Very* decent, so the least I can do is make sandwiches for on the way. I'll do egg and salad cream. And I'll have to see if I can sweetheart a couple of tomatoes out of Goff to go with them.'

'But can you manage the rations, dear? I don't want to put you out.'

'Bread isn't rationed and I can surely spare a scrape of margarine. And there are plenty of eggs in the pantry,' she offered pointedly. 'Like I said, it's the very least I can do, especially since finding something to eat on the way back won't be easy. And I've got to be grateful, I suppose, that I'm not taking you to the station tonight. At least you've got the rest of the day at home.'

'And I'm grateful, too. What say we go for a walk tonight? Through the ruins and on to the riverbank? Then we can call at the pub on the way back – see if Mary can find us a gin under the counter, since it'll be my last night.'

'I'd like that,' Lorna smiled, even though she was still put out about the sergeant and wondered, for the first time, what the young woman was like. Small, she decided, and pretty and modest like the flower after which she was named.

'Then shall you put the cosy on the pot, Lorna, and shall I carry the tray into the garden so I can have a last glimpse? It won't be looking as pretty next time I'm home on leave.'

And Lorna said it was a good idea, whilst all the time wondering how he could be so calm about everything when the William of old would have been furious. But then, she thought as she held open the kitchen door for him, it seemed that Army life had at least taught him he couldn't have everything his own way.

'I've just thought,' she said as she poured milk into the rosebud china cups, 'that now you are moving to bigger offices, there'll be a better chance of promotion.'

And William said yes, promotion might very well be on the way at last, then lifted his cup and said, 'Cheers, my dear. And thanks for being so good about what's happened.'

She was about to ask him if she had any choice, but bit back the words and smiled and said, 'Cheers!' and set about wondering what they would have for supper tonight, deciding it would have to be omelettes again. Lorna wondered how women who were not able to keep their own hens managed on one egg per person per week. One distinctly not-so-fresh egg, if what she heard was to be true, and thank heaven for those six little creatures who scratched away contentedly at William's once immaculate lawn, bless their fluffy little bottoms!

Only when they had walked past the almshouses and Larkspur Cottage and Nance Ellery's house; when they had passed St Philippa's and the gate that led to Glebe Farm and turned left into the priory ruins, did William tuck Lorna's arm into his.

'Lovely evening.'

'Mm.' Lorna looked to her right where the outbuildings at the back of the manor yard met Glebe Farm's land. 'All seems quiet at the farm. Wonder if they've got the barley safely stacked.'

'You'll know in the morning, dear, when you deliver the post. Right now, let's talk about us.'

'*What* about us?' Lorna frowned.

'Well, that I've had a good leave and enjoyed the peace and quiet – even if you had to do your war work.'

'Every woman my age has to work, if she hasn't got children. I've managed to get home by half past nine every morning, William, and Doc Summers was very good giving me time off.'

'Yes, I suppose so. But I never thought I'd see the day my wife went out to work.'

'Most men would agree with you, but the war has changed all that. Now it's all right for a married woman to have a job – indeed, she's expected to.'

'I know, dear.' He sensed the edge to her voice and took heed of it. 'And if I appear a little – well, short at times, it's only because Army life is so different. Not a lot of privacy for a fellow.'

'No. It must be awful.'

There wasn't a lot of privacy, either, for the Russian people who had to set light to their homes on Stalin's orders before they retreated, or for the bombed-outs in London, but she didn't say so. Because this was William's last night at home and she mustn't upset him.

'And you do know, Lorna,' he squeezed her hand tightly, 'that you are very dear to me. I care deeply for you.'

'Well of course you do, softie!' she laughed. 'I'm your wife, aren't I?'

It was best she made little of William's rare romantic outburst, because he was naturally upset at being recalled, and if she was to tell him, tearfully, that it was awful to have to go back two days early, she would only make matters worse. William could not abide tears, so it was best they talked of trivialities with tomorrow's early departure not mentioned.

She almost said he must remind her to set the alarm clock half an hour early so he could have a bath and eat his breakfast in peace before the sergeant arrived, but bit back her words and said instead,

'Look, William.' She pointed, squinting into the sky. 'See how high the swallows are flying. There'll be another good day tomorrow. If Glebe hasn't got all the barley in, then they'll manage it with another day of sun.'

For want of words she had said it and at once wished she had not, because his reply was unexpected and hurtful.

'Yes, and tomorrow your land girl will be able to creep back into the spare room, won't she?'

Dismay overtook Lorna but she closed her eyes and took a deep breath. Then very deliberately she pulled her arm from his and said much, much too softly,

'She will indeed. And aren't you glad I won't be alone in that big house when you've gone?' And since, in spite of her efforts, they were talking about tomorrow, she added, 'And can you remind me, when we get home, to hard-boil the eggs for your sandwiches?'

Then Lorna wondered how soon she could safely suggest that they should return to Ladybower.

* * *

They did not call at the White Hart on the way back because William thought it very unlikely that Mary would have anything under the bar counter and anyway, he no longer felt like facing the joviality there. And Lorna agreed with him, because all at once she felt edgy and morose and knew the feelings were more due to her coming monthly period than to William's departure. And it would arrive as it always had, because you couldn't hope to conceive on just the once – this morning – which was the only time they had made love. And since working at the surgery, she had learned that the best time to get pregnant was in the middle of the cycle and that it was then, if you wanted a child, you should try hardest.

But William didn't want a child yet, so why was she bothering about dates and periods, telling herself it would be all right, once the war was over. There would be children for her one day, hadn't Martha said?

She cleared her head of such fantasies. There was a war on and you learned to live it from day to day. You accepted existing from one leave to the next; accepted the rationing of food and clothing and that civilians were as much in the front line, sometimes, as fighting men and women. And when you went to bed each night, you knew that another day had been lived through and that peace, when it came, was at least one day nearer.

'I'll be ready for my bed tonight,' William said as they walked up the path and Lorna wondered what exactly he could mean. 'Mind if I turn in early, old love?'

I, not *we*, so Lorna said it was fine by her as she had a few things to do anyway, and would he like a drink bringing up?

'Er – no. Thanks all the same. Is my uniform all right?'

'Nothing has happened to it since you wore it this morning.' She forced a smile. 'I cleaned your buttons and badges yesterday and everything is laid out ready for you on the spare bedroom bed. Now, off you go.'

'G'night, then.' He kissed her cheek, then took her face in his hands and kissed her forehead, too. 'It's been a good leave . . .'

'Yes, it has.' She watched him go, listened as he climbed the stairs, then heard the closing of the bedroom door.

A good leave? She supposed so. Nothing mind-boggling, but what the heck? It was a lot worse for William who, this time tomorrow, would be back at Aldershot in the middle of all the upheaval whilst she, Lorna, was safe in her very dear Ladybower. And tomorrow, Ness might be back; if she could see her when she delivered to the farm and explain what had happened and that if it was all right with Flora, her bed would be ready as soon as she wanted. Then she said,

'Oh, *damn* this war!' and, tight-lipped, set three eggs to boil on the gas stove.

EIGHTEEN

Lorna awoke at five, cancelled the alarm and decided to let William sleep on for a few more minutes, ticking off in her mind as she washed and dressed if anything was still to be done.

Sandwiches? Made last night and wrapped in a damp tea towel on the cold slab. William's kit? Uniform sponged and pressed, buttons and shoes polished and all laid out in the spare bedroom. Only a phone call to make to the post office to let Mrs B know she would be half an hour late this morning, and how very sorry she was.

She pulled a comb through her hair, flicking it with her fingers. It made her think yet again about Ness who would be back tonight to say all the right things to a friend whose husband's leave had been cut short by two days.

She shook self pity out of her mind. William was only at Aldershot. He wasn't being fired on, nor baking in the North African desert, nor even taking-off almost every other night to bomb Germany, so when six o'clock came she would smile him on his way and be thankful they were only hours apart and not half a world away from each other.

On the other hand, of course, she could have closed up Ladybower and found lodgings near him as some wives did. She had actually discussed it with William but he argued against it.

'Leave Ladybower empty? But haven't you thought, Lorna,

what could happen to it if you did? The government would commandeer it without a by-your-leave. When they take a rundown place like the manor, this house wouldn't stand a chance!'

William was thinking, she had known, of bombed-out families being housed in it or it being used as a billet by the Army or the Air Force. Nothing was sacred these days, he argued. If the powers that be thought they wanted it, then an Englishman's home was no longer his castle. They just threw the Defence of the Realm Act at you, and out you got! Ladybower, William had stressed, was far more important than being together in doubtful lodgings and paying through the nose for it. Besides, there was no guarantee he would have been given permission to sleep out of quarters. Matter closed. They had talked no more about it.

Lorna filled the extra-large cup William always liked to drink his morning tea from, thinking that he needn't have made such a fuss about the place being left unoccupied, because Ladybower was more important to her than almost anything she could bring to mind. Come to think of it, she had not for one moment even considered leaving it – not *really* considered.

'Wake up, darling.' Gently she shook his arm. 'Twenty past five.' She opened the curtains. 'Careful. Don't knock the tea over. Shall I run your bath?'

And William grunted sleepily, twice, which she took to mean that he would not knock over the tea and that yes, he would like a bath.

'Breakfast in fifteen minutes!' Best he should not keep the sergeant waiting. 'And I'll bring up your shaving water.' Tap water was never hot enough for shaving he always said, so right from the start of their marriage she had made sure that his shaving mug was filled with near-boiling water. Just one of William's little peculiarities. You got used to them all, in time.

* * *

At a little before six, as Lorna was opening the front gates, a black car drew up outside.

'Is this Ladybower?' the driver asked and Lorna said it was, and held out her hand.

'Good of you to come so far out of your way, Sergeant. Are you sure you weren't too put out?'

And Sergeant Primrose Smythe-Parker offered a hand through the open window and said it was no bother at all.

It was not until she got out of the car, tugged at her jacket to straighten it and stood full height, that Lorna realized that here was no modest, shrinking flower. The lady was tall, straight-backed and fresh-complexioned – ruddy, if you wanted to be unkind – and her feet, in flat-heeled brown shoes could only be described as on the large side.

'Would you – er – like a cup of tea? There's some in the pot.'

To which the sergeant replied thank you, no, though if the bathroom was available she would like the use of it. Which made Lorna very thankful that instinct had warned her to put out the best embroidered hand towels, though she wouldn't be at all surprised if William had failed to rinse the basin after shaving, and left a tide mark of short ginger hairs halfway up it!

'Top of the stairs,' she instructed. 'On the right,' then hurried to tell William to get a move on; that the sergeant was upstairs and didn't look the sort who liked to be kept waiting.

'She's got a very big car, William.'

'Yes. A Wolseley. Got it for her twenty-first, I believe.' He seemed not to be impressed.

'Is your shaving gear still in the bathroom?'

'No. It's packed. All ready for the off. And don't look so agitated, Lorna. The poor girl is probably feeling far more embarrassed than you.'

He patted his moustache with his napkin, then pushed back his chair, which set Lorna's teeth on edge, because she couldn't abide grating chairs. Just like at school, when the English mistress seemed always to catch her fingernails on the blackboard.

'I doubt it, dear.' Sergeant Smythe-Parker had not been in the least put out; she had the air of one who gave orders and expected them to be carried out on the dot. 'Why isn't she an officer? She's got the bearing for it.'

'Heavens, why ask me? Haven't a clue, Lorna. And I suppose we'd better make a start.'

The sergeant was coming downstairs; she hesitated a moment, then coughed before entering the kitchen.

'Everything all right?' William picked up the cap and respirator Lorna had laid on the chair beside him.

'Fine, Sir. And it's six. We'd best be off. I'll just turn the car round, if you'll excuse me, Mrs Hatherwood.'

'Of course. And thank you so much.' Lorna held out a hand. 'So nice to have met you.' Then, when she heard the car engine she wrapped her arms around William's neck, kissing his mouth, gently stroking his cheeks with her fingertips. 'Safe journey, darling. Try to let me know you've got there all right?'

'I'll try, but I doubt I'll be lucky. You know what it's like in the mess – everyone wanting calls. And we'll be OK. The sergeant is a very capable driver. Take care of yourself now.' He kissed her cheek. 'And don't wave me off?'

'I won't, William.' She knew how much he disliked being waved off. Welcomed, yes. Waved goodbye to – no. Some kind of superstition they had in the Army, she supposed.

She heard the banging of the car door, then ran upstairs to watch him go, making sure she could not be seen from the window.

And that was that, she sighed, as the car disappeared at speed up the lane, until November, so no moping, Lorna. You're half an hour late for work already, so shift yourself!

Quickly she checked the house, slammed the door behind

her, then wheeled the red GPO cycle from the garage, pedalling furiously up the lane. And anyway, she reasoned, William would enjoy being driven in comfort; far better than enduring hours of stop and start on the train. Funny, she thought as she waited at the crossroads, how things seemed to always work out for him. She wouldn't be surprised if even as a little boy, his toast never landed on the floor butter-side down! And oh, who was a fool, then! Who hadn't given her husband the sandwiches she so carefully made? What would Sergeant Primmy P think of her?

So? she shrugged. Nothing she could do about it now. She crossed the road quickly. And they wouldn't be wasted. She and Ness could eat them for supper. There was a silver lining to every cloud! Ness would be home tonight.

Ness did not move back to Ladybower that evening. She was, she had told Lorna later, going dancing with Mick. The barley was stacked in the gantry, awaiting threshing when winter came. Rowley was going to Meltonby to a Young Farmers' meeting – or so he said, Ness winked – and Kate and Bob planned a restful evening listening to the wireless in the front parlour.

'I see,' Lorna said, disappointed. 'Well, I hope you have a lovely time. It'll be tomorrow, then . . . ?'

'Straight after work. There isn't much to move. You'll be expecting me for supper? We can have a good natter, then – catch up with all the gossip, eh?'

Gossip, Lorna thought as she knocked on the kitchen door at the manor and laid letters and papers on the table.

'Post!' she called, then hurried out before the sergeant-cook returned from the storeroom and asked her to stay for a cup of tea. She didn't want tea and she certainly didn't want to see Ewan because she was still put out over William's too-soon departure and didn't want to think how much better her husband would look if he were clean-shaven like the medical officer.

So now, as she ate her way through the egg and salad-cream sandwiches with stubborn determination, she wondered how to fill her time for the rest of the evening, then remembered, almost with relief, that her bed had still to be made. So why not strip off the sheets, turn the mattress and clean the room? And after that she could clean Ness's bedroom, lay out towels for her, then she could – What could she do? What more to stop her feeling so utterly miserable about the loneliness of the house and the way her feet seemed to echo on the kitchen floor.

'Dammit!' She set down a half-eaten sandwich. She wanted no more. The hens could have what remained!

She went into the garden, heels slamming, throwing the bread into the run, watching as the hens pecked and squawked and scratched until there was not a crumb left. And oh! What a way to spend a summer evening; how attractive the drudge of making beds and dusting dressing-table tops when everyone else seemed to be doing something far more enjoyable with someone they wanted to be with. Ness and Mick, Rowley and his latest fancy, Bob and Kate. Couples, all of them, and not like Lorna Hatherwood whose husband had left more than twelve hours ago and who wouldn't, she was sure, ring to let her know he was safely there.

Tears filled her eyes and she hurried into the house and up the stairs. Tears were still wetting her cheeks when all was finished and the bedrooms were to her satisfaction. She glared into the mirror at the swollen eyes, the runny nose, the droop of her mouth.

'Lorna Hatherwood, you look awful! You do! You really do!' She took a deep breath, dabbed her eyes, then blew her nose noisily. 'So – finished, have you?'

Of course she had finished. There had been nothing to weep about in the first place; nothing but self-pity, as if she were the only woman in the country whose husband had had his leave cut short!

She splashed her face with cold water then gently dabbed

it dry, sighing because her nose was still red, her eyes still puffy, so there seemed nothing for it but a walk to the top of the lane and back; to slam down her heels and knock the anger, or whatever it was, out of her. And hope, she thought as she closed the gate behind her, that she didn't meet anyone on the way. Just her luck to run into Nance Ellery who would ask why she had been weeping and demand a detailed explanation of something Lorna could not have explained, then go on to lecture her on how lucky she was, did she but stop to think about it. And if that happened, Lorna vowed, she would fly off the handle, tell Nance Ellery she would cry if she wanted to, that it was no business of hers and that she was much too bossy. And it was about time someone told her so!

But wasn't all this because her period was due? She was always weepy for a few days before and surely her wayward female hormones could be indulged once in a while? She wasn't weeping because she was lonely for William or because Ness would not be coming back until tomorrow. Nor that the leave she had been looking forward to, turned out to be very ordinary indeed. She was weeping, she supposed, because she felt like it. Surely that was reason enough? All normal and natural, if you were a woman.

But what was not normal or natural was this dreadful, heart-hurting feeling of aloneness and her need to be loved and teased and kissed, and be damned to female hormones!

The tears began again and she did not bother to wipe them away, nor did she care if Nance Ellery saw her; didn't care if the entire village saw her!

She closed her eyes and sniffed and snuffled and wished that tonight could be the night she had been collected in an Army truck with a blanket over the seat, and driven to Doc Summers's house to eat venison in Jessie's kitchen and drink red wine and feel thoroughly relaxed and happy. And just a little tipsy.

And if wishes were horses, then beggars would ride,

wouldn't they, so stop your whingeing and pull yourself together!

Ness's 'It's only me!' took Lorna hurrying to the back door. 'Sorry I'm late, queen, but I had a bit of a chat with Flora when I picked up my things. I've brought a drop of milk and some windfalls.' She pushed the bounty into Lorna's eager hands then padded into the kitchen. 'Ar, but it's good to be back. Flora's a love, but here's where I like it best.'

'It's good to have you back.' Lorna's voice was distinctly wobbly. 'The house has seemed so empty since William left.'

'Got there all right, did he?'

'He never said. You know what trunk calls are like.'

'So? No news is good news, girl, and whatever's for supper smells good!'

'Woolton pie, that's all, and bread and butter pudding without the butter,' Lorna shrugged. 'But Goff gave me a rabbit, so we'll eat well tomorrow. And Ness – don't ever leave Nun Ainsty, will you?'

'Not if I've got anything to do with it. And I'll just nip upstairs for a wash. Won't be a tick!'

Happy again, Lorna took the suet-crusted, meatless pie from the oven and checked the pudding on the bottom shelf and the potatoes baking on the top shelf. An economy meal tonight, but the rabbit would take care of two suppers, and windfall apples from Glebe's orchard and custard made with doubtfully acquired milk would keep body and soul together until the meat ration was due. Life could be a whole lot worse, she was forced to admit, and smiled at the geranium on the window-ledge.

'So what happened – about William's leave, I mean?' Ness tucked her feet beneath her, wriggling into the soft sagginess of the armchair.

'There was a phone call from Aldershot. Be back by tomorrow, they told him.'

'Funny, innit, that you can't get a long-distance phone call for love nor money, but when the Army wants one, they get it right away.'

'Too right,' Lorna shrugged. 'But to cut a long story short, there was an ATS sergeant from William's office on leave, too. He gave her a ring and found she'd been called back as well. So he asked her to give him a lift. I was so embarrassed, but she called for him yesterday morning at six. Not at all what I'd expected. Her name is Primrose, William said, so I expected someone fragile, sort of, though she was anything but. And you should have seen her car!'

'Goff mentioned he'd seen one.' Ness was glad the matter of the mysterious car had been cleared up.

'A Wolseley. William said she's supposed to have got it for her twenty-first birthday! She seemed very upper class. Cut-glass accent, y'know. Big feet, though,' she added.

'A sergeant? But I thought the posh ones always got to be officers.'

'I thought that, too. Smythe-Parker she's called. I believe the ATS girls she's in charge of call her Primmy P.'

'Now fair play, Lorna. I don't suppose her folks could have known she was goin' to grow up like she did or they'd have called her Brünnhilde, or sumthin'.'

They began to giggle and Ness said it wasn't fair to mock the poor woman just because she had an unsuitable name, whilst secretly thinking that anybody who would oblige by carrying William off two days early had to have something good about her.

'Aren't we being bitchy?' Lorna's giggles began again. 'She can't help being well-built.'

'Suppose not. You weren't jealous, were you, when you saw your William drive off with her?'

'Not in the least. Anyway, the poor woman couldn't very well refuse, him being a superior officer. And William wouldn't do anything like that if he thought I'd be jealous and Brünnhilde knows he's a married man. But tell me, how did your date go? Did you manage to find a dance?'

'We did – and a smashing band. The floor wasn't too crowded, but it got a bit hot when they had to shut the windows and close the blackouts. Mick's a smashing dancer.'

Better than smashing. It had been fantastic, dancing closely – especially for the last waltz. They had danced that one cheek on cheek and Mick had asked if he might take her home, because the man you gave the last dance to should, by rights, have the privilege. And she had told him to stop teasing, and of course he was taking her home! There'd be trouble, she said, if he didn't! And oh, that good night kiss. Kisses. Her lips tingled even yet to think of them.

'Ness Nightingale! Will you take that silly look off your face? Either that, or tell me what you were thinking about!'

'About Mick, if you must know,' she said softly. 'He really is something. Good looking, good dancer . . .'

'Good kisser?'

'*Very* good.'

'Well, come on then. Tell! You've fallen for him, haven't you? You're blushing!'

'Fallen? We-e-ll, I could if I let myself, I suppose.'

'So what's stopping you? Not Patrick the skunk? But he's history, surely?'

'Yes, but once bitten . . .'

'Ness! I'd bet you anything you like that Mick Hardie is a perfect gentleman. And I think he's smitten, too.'

'Maybe he is, Lorna. In fact, he said next time he goes home he wants me to go with him to meet his folks, but I –'

'There you are, then! What more do you want? You're practically engaged when they ask you that. You'll go, of course?'

'I'd like to, but what would his mam and dad make of me – if they could understand my accent, that is? I come from a Liverpool street, we don't have a big house with an apple orchard and all that.'

'Mick's told you he lives in a big house? You surprise me.'

'No!' Ness jumped to her feet to stand by the window, arms folded. 'And it's goin' to rain – not that we don't need it. Just look at them black clouds.'

'Don't change the subject, Ness. We were talking about you and Mick!'

'All right! He didn't tell me it was a big house; it was just the impression I got. Seems it's all higgledy-piggledy 'cause it's been added on to since the year dot. It's called Deep Hay. Ours is called number three, and it hasn't got a garden.'

'Well, if that doesn't beat cock fighting! I never took you for a snob, Ness Nightingale, and an inverted snob at that. Does it matter where either of you come from, what your background is, as long as you suit each other?'

'Oh, you can talk, Lorna. You with this house and money in the bank and you and William both with cars. I'd say your background was very posh!'

'Yes, but it *wasn't*. My background was a mother who drank and a man who didn't have the decency to marry her! There isn't even a father's name on my birth certificate, did you know? Lord knows what would have happened if Gran and Grandpa hadn't been here for me! So forget Ruth Street and forget higgledy-piggledy houses in Devon. All that matters is that you love the guy, and you do, don't you?'

'Yes, I think I do love him. When he kisses me I just fall apart. Tell you sumthin', Lorna – I trust Mick, but I don't trust myself. And if you'd ever been kissed by him you'd know what I mean!'

'Mm. But maybe I *do* know. I haven't kissed Ewan, but I've often wondered what it would be like. Good job I'm a married woman.'

'So when you kissed him – in your wonderings, I mean – did it make you fall apart, too?'

'Of course it didn't,' Lorna said huffily, then her face broke into a grin. 'It was a bit toe-curling, though!'

And they laughed together like the best of friends they had become, and because Ness was home again.

'It's getting dark, all of a sudden. Shall I switch on the lamp, Lorna?'

'Better not. We'll have to draw the blackout if we do. Let's just sit in the gloaming and think about all the good things; do a blessings-count, sort of.'

'Like it's going to rain, and we need it?'

'Mm. And that we've got a rabbit, so it's big eats tomorrow,' Lorna offered.

'And that kissing Mick and Ewan is just out of this world?'

'Mick and *William*, if you don't mind!'

So they sat, contented, and Ness thought about Deep Hay and that maybe, if Mick asked her again, she just might tell him that yes, she would like to go there with him. If he was sure, that was.

And Lorna thought about William and knew he would be safely back in barracks; no doubt about it with the efficient Primmy at the wheel. And there would be a letter on Saturday morning, telling her all about it. Then she set her lips into a *moue*, and wished fervently that her husband would go stark raving mad, and shave off his moustache!

Lorna stood at the sorting table in the room behind Meltonby Post Office, arranging the letters in order. First came Ladybower, then the White Hart followed by the Saddlery and Throstle Cottage. After which, with a rubber band to keep them together, a thick bundle for the soldiers at the manor. Only then would come the call she was so looking forward to, because this morning there was a letter for Ness, addressed to Ladybower and which, because of the unfamiliar handwriting and an Exeter postmark, Lorna decided must be delivered at once, and in person. It made her fingers itch, and so eager was she to give it to Ness that she did the round almost at a run.

'Morning, Kate!' She laid morning paper and letters on the kitchen table. 'Most of them from His Majesty! More forms to annoy Bob. Got one for Ness. I'll just pop across the yard and give it to her.'

She made for the sound of the slow clunk-clunk of the milking machine and saw Ness at once, making for the cooler with two pails of milk.

'Hi there.' She sent her most brilliant smile in Bob's direction. 'Can I nip into the dairy? Got one for Ness.'

And Bob said of course she could, only be sure to walk carefully. They didn't want any more broken arms, if she didn't mind!

'So what brings you here?' Ness frowned. 'And what on earth is making you look so pleased with yourself at this hour of the morning?'

'Got a letter, for you. Thought you'd better have it right away.'

'But couldn't it have waited?'

'No, because it isn't from Ruth Street. Take a look at the postmark.'

And with that Lorna was off to finish her deliveries, still not able to stop smiling, hoping it was what she thought it might be, waving to Mick who was trundling milk churns at the far end of the yard.

'Hi!' she called. 'Just given Ness a letter!'

'Good!' He stuck up a thumb, then disappeared into the dairy with a smile that seemed to suggest he knew who had written that letter, and what it contained.

Ness had no time to kick off her shoes, nor comment on the rabbit-stew smell that met her at the kitchen door. Instead she thrust a familiar envelope at Lorna.

'Here! Read that, will you. Mick's doing, that's what! Talk about a fast worker!'

'You're sure?' Lorna hesitated.

''Course I'm sure! Just read it, queen!'

The envelope was pale blue with matching notepaper; the handwriting was firm and feminine.

Dear Miss Nightingale,
Michael has often mentioned you in his letters, so now that he expects to be home in early November, I am wondering if you would like to come with him? His father and I would be so pleased to meet you and make you welcome. Write soon, and tell me you will come?
With warmest good wishes,
Viola Hardie

'Well now. Isn't that nice, Ness? You'll go, of course?'

'Seems there's no way out of it now, without sounding ungrateful.'

'What do you mean? To my way of thinking it's a perfectly friendly note and I think you should write back at once, accepting. But tell me – what did Mick say about it? I got the impression he knew the letter was on its way.'

'He did. Said he'd asked his mother to be sure to write to me. I dithered when he asked me to go home with him, so he said it seemed the only way was for his mother to invite me. I'm stuck between a rock and a hard place now.'

'Of course you aren't! All you have to do is to send back an equally nice letter saying you'd love to go.'

'But that's the trouble, Lorna! I'm no use at letter writing – well, not to people like Mrs Hardie.'

'Then if you'd like, I'll help you. Surely between us we can put something together. And I'll give you some of my best notepaper, so there's no more to be said. Get yourself out of those dungarees, and when we've eaten we'll get down to it. I'll put it in the York bag in the morning so it'll be on its way to Devon before the pillar box outside has even been emptied.' She scanned the address at the top of the letter. 'To Deep Hay, Borton-under-Whytchwood, Devon. What a lovely place it sounds.'

'Y-yes,' Ness said dubiously. 'Looks as if Mick has really pulled a fast one. I told him so, but he only laughed. I've been on my high horse with him ever since. And his Mam calls him Michael. Makes him sound strange.'

'And you, too, Agnes. I Michael take thee Agnes to be my lawful wedded wife. You'll both wonder who you are getting married to!'

'Now, stop it!' All at once, Ness was laughing. 'Just be careful what you're saying. Didn't you know that's how rumours start?'

She was still smiling as she took off her dungarees and shirt and thick socks, because she knew she wanted to meet Mick's parents; wanted, on some far-flung day, to say the wonderful words, too. I Agnes take thee Michael. Wanted it more than anything she could ever dream of, or hope for.

She walked naked to the bathroom and washed herself all over in cold water, because there was nothing like cold water for wiping the smug smirk from anyone's face! Slowly, she patted herself dry, gazing at herself in the mirror, all at once wide-eyed and serious.

Now look here, girl, she urged silently. Just watch it, see? Don't get carried away. Remember what happened before. Think about it before you write that letter. Think good and hard, and don't let Lorna push you into anything! All right?

Mick held his arms wide and Ness went into them gladly, offering her lips.

'Am I forgiven, Ness, for jumping the gun and asking Mother to write? Are you cross? Is that why you've been avoiding me all day?'

'Cross – no. Was a bit of a shock, for all that.'

'But you'll think about it? I really want my folks to meet you.'

'Why, Mick?' She laid her cheek on his chest because she didn't want him to see her face.

'Because – hell, girl, do you want me to spell it out?'

'Yes. I think I'd like you to.' She took a step away from him, raising her eyes to his, her heart thudding.

'All right. I suppose I've been wanting to say it for a long time – since I first saw you – and I thought there must be someone else. But all that is behind us. Forgotten. So you can ditch that letter, throw it on the fire and forget it was ever written. I'd like to know where I stand, that's all. It's up to you now. It's make your mind up time.'

'The letter. I see.' All at once she felt very calm. 'As a matter of fact I've already answered it. It's on the hall table for Lorna to post at Meltonby. I told your mother I'd love to come with you . . .'

'Darling!' He hugged her tightly, but they did not kiss; just stood together close, as if neither quite believed what was happening. Then Mick said softly, 'I love you and I want you to marry me. But we won't talk about that just yet, or you'll run like a startled hen. But I *will* ask you, Ness, before so very much longer.'

'Then maybe when you do I just might say yes, because I love you, too. I've tried not to, but it isn't any use.' She took his face in her hands, kissing him gently. 'Looks as if you're stuck with me, Mick Hardie.'

And as they kissed again, urgently and with passion, she closed her eyes, clinging to him because all at once she felt happy, and desperately in love. And very giddy.

I Agnes take thee Michael . . .

Silly little tears pricked her eyes and smiling she brushed them away, taking in the look of him, his tallness and slimness and the absolute beauty of his face; snapped it as if she were taking a picture to keep in her mind for ever. And all at once she wondered why she had wasted so much precious time, knowing that after November she might not see him again for a long, long time.

At that moment in the silent ruins, with the sun low in the sky and sending age-old shadows over the grass, she loved him so much she felt as if she could fly; that if he did not keep hold of her tightly she would shoot off crazily and be lost for ever.

So, because all at once she could not cope with the magic around her and because she was Ness and Liverpool-blunt, she looked at him sternly and said,

'And what did you mean, exactly – a startled hen!'

NINETEEN

It was all right. William's Saturday letter had arrived. Less of it than usual but that was to be expected.

Lorna pushed it into her jacket pocket and carried on sorting, doing it automatically, thinking that when the round was over she must get to the butcher's early or she would miss the cheap cuts of meat; meat being allocated by price and not by weight. Between them, she and Ness were allowed two shillings and fourpence-worth of meat, which meant one pound of stewing beef or four lamb chops, and lamb chops were an extravagance when you considered the bone!

Draining her mug, she called goodbye to Mrs Benson and the driver of the red GPO van, then waved to the conductor and driver of the early bus as she passed, glad to be back in the familiar, safe routine again, with mornings for deliveries and housework and afternoons at the surgery. And she must remember to ask Minnie if she could spare an extra hour to give the inside windows a clean and polish. Minnie, whose soldier husband had not been sent abroad yet, fingers crossed, and recently promoted to lance corporal with a shilling a day rise in pay.

'I told him,' Minnie had said, 'to keep that seven bob for himself and not make it over to me. At least now he can afford a pint and a smoke.'

Dear Minnie, who had two children, Lorna thought as she crossed the main road and into Priory Lane, though Minnie had said to take comfort; that if you had none to laugh over you had none to cry over either. Because cry over them she had, money being so short when her man had been called into the Army that she hadn't known, some days, which way to turn. Until she had come to Ladybower, she had added, and that Mrs Hatherwood was not to hesitate to ask for the hour or two extra if she felt so minded.

Lorna smiled, partly to see her home ahead of her and partly because although the war had taken William from her, it had given her Ness, new friends, and two jobs, both of which, in all modesty, she did very well. And that same war, dare she admit it, had given her a confidence she had never believed existed in the old days of depending on Grandpa and latterly on William. It made her wonder what would happen when the war was over and she became a dependent again.

But the war was a long way from being over. Soon it would start its third year, and the Allies no further forward, if you dare think about it. Hitler's armies sweeping all before them in Russia to get to Moscow before winter set in, and Leningrad, standing defiant and preparing for siege. A long, cold and hungry siege.

Mind, on the count-your-blessings side, the twins from the Saddlery had managed, for the first time since joining the Navy, to get leave at the same time, and Mr Churchill had told Parliament that fewer of our merchant ships were being lost at sea, which everyone was delighted to accept as fact, because Winston always told the truth; always had done, even when things were going so badly for us.

She leaned her cycle against the pillar box, pushing her morning paper through her own letterbox, calculating that if she did the round at a run, almost, she could be back in Meltonby in good time to be near the top of the queue when the butcher opened his shop early, as he always did on Saturdays. She might get stewing beef, which could be stretched to two meals, half a pound of off-the-ration sausages, perhaps, and a lump of under-the-counter suet, if she were lucky enough and early enough. Fingers crossed, of course, so no allowing herself to be coaxed into a tea break at the manor by the genial sergeant-cook! She pedalled past the wood at speed and on to the White Hart, thinking about sausages and suet and about doing her bit to help win the war, which was going to last a lot longer than the Great War had. Which made her think that if something miraculous didn't happen before so very much longer, she would be past the age of childbearing before peace came, dammit!

When Lorna arrived at the surgery all was quiet, which was to be expected since she had come to realize that the majority of Reginald Summers's patients were content to put up with weekend ailments until Monday mornings.

'He's out on calls,' Jessie Summers supplied as Lorna hung up her jacket. 'Nothing much doing. Come and see what I've got!' She opened the pantry door with a flourish. 'There now! Dinner on Tuesday, off the ration. Want to come?'

A brace of grouse hung from a hook beside the gauze-covered open window, tied together at the neck with strong string from which hung a stamped label. Delivered that morning, Lorna shouldn't wonder, by the driver of the red GPO van.

'Jessie!' The birds were very stiff, eyes tightly shut. 'I didn't know you could send them by post. And aren't they a bit early?'

'No, dear. Grouse came in on the twelfth. It's pheasants that are later. But isn't someone good?'

'Are they a present?'

'Mm. One of Reggie's pals from his medical school days comes up trumps every year, so what say you come on Tuesday night, and help us to eat them?'

'But I *couldn't*!' You didn't eat other people's food, even though game birds and rabbits and hares were not rationed.

'Yes you could! Why don't you let Ewan pick you up at a quarter to seven, so we can have a drink beforehand?'

'Ewan?' So he had already been asked. It made her want to refuse; some small white lie would do, surely? 'That would be fine,' she said instead, 'if he wouldn't mind calling for me.'

'Of course he won't. As a matter of fact I've already phoned him and he said that transport would be no problem.' Or words to that effect, if she were strictly truthful.

'What do you mean, would I mind, Jessie?' he'd said and there was no doubting the pleasure in his voice. 'Be glad to, you should know that.'

Should know *what*? she had thought at the time. That Ewan was smitten with Lorna? Probably was, though thank the good Lord he wasn't the type to mess about with an unworldly young woman whose husband was away at the war.

'Then in that case – fine. Thanks. I'd love to come,' Lorna whispered, knowing she was blushing.

'That's settled, then. Ewan said he would bring a bottle of sherry though I wasn't to ask where he got it.'

The surgery phone rang then and the older woman noted the relief with which Lorna ran to answer it. And thank that same good Lord, she frowned, that Lorna was not the sort to mess about behind her husband's back, or it would be anybody's guess what could happen between those two – given the inclination, the opportunity and a fair amount of luck, of course. But by the heck, this was a funny old war, and no mistake!

'What's news,' Ness demanded, padding into the kitchen.

'Letter from William. All's well.'

He had written a short but satisfactory letter. The drive to Aldershot had gone well, apart from being slowed down by a crawling convoy of Army lorries and transports. The office move was not mentioned, nor were the missing egg sandwiches, for which she was grateful. His car, satisfactorily repaired, was running like a dream.

Then he had thanked her for a splendid leave, said he was sorry about the recall, but that all seemed back to normal now, and he would see her again in November, King and Country permitting.

Take care of yourself, Lorna dear. I think of you and Ladybower often.
With love,
William

Not the most passionate of letters, but William was not the most passionate of men, even when they made love. But you couldn't have it all ways. William was protective and caring and dependable, which must surely be better than passion which often burned itself out, Nance Ellery said, and what would be left, then?

'Hey!' A hand passed in front of Lorna's eyes. 'You were miles away!'

'Sorry. Only thinking about William's letter and how dependable he is and how lucky I am.'

'As in what, queen?'

'We-e-ll – having a good marriage and Ladybower and living in a safe little backwater when half the population is being bombed night after night and . . .' She stopped, searching her mind.

'And what else, Mrs Hatherwood?'

'Ness! You can be very cynical. Surely that's more than enough? And if you have nothing better to do than stand around looking calf-eyed, could you please slice the carrots?'

'Hey! I'm not calf-eyed,' Ness whispered, all at once serious, 'though as a matter of fact what you see is one lucky land girl who is meeting her feller tonight, and can't help feelin' dead chuffed about it. Called being happy, I suppose.'

'Happy? Y'know something, Ness? You were attractive when you first came here, but now you positively glow. It must be obvious to all and sundry you are head over heels in love. For heaven's sake watch it, or you'll shoot off like a rocket, never to be seen again. Where are you going, by the way?'

'There's a hop in Meltonby,' Ness crunched on a piece of carrot. 'Not the best of floors and I've no idea what the band will be like.'

But did it matter? Dancing anywhere with Mick was wonderful. The nearness of him excited her and the closeness of her lips to his ear, to his mouth, made it even more tantalizing; made her ache for afterwards, when they could find a hidden place, and kiss. It sometimes made her afraid that one night she would no longer be able to fight the emotion between them in time to draw back from the brink. She had let it happen once. Only a fool would let it happen again. But she loved Mick so much that –

'Now who's miles away?' Lorna teased.

'Sorry, queen. I was thinking about Mick.'

'Which made you frown? What has Mick done to make you look so fierce?'

'Nothing. It's me. Usually one of us draws back when things get a bit – well, you know. But what's going to happen if just once neither of us bothers to count to ten?'

'You know what will happen, Ness. Just try to be careful, that's all.'

'Careful! When sometimes there's nothing in this world you want more than to – well, want to . . .'

'Then for goodness' sake, tell Mick how things are for you, because it's obvious he feels the same. Men can take – er – *precautions*, and don't ask me since when have I been an expert on birth control. I'm not, but William obviously does something or why haven't I got pregnant?'

'Precautions. Yes.' Ness stared at the chopping board, not knowing how to deal with Lorna's forthrightness. Who'd have ever thought she would know about such things? But then she worked for a doctor, didn't she?

'Maybe you're right. Maybe I should talk to Mick.'

'Too darn right you should, Ness Nightingale! And for heaven's sake, will you get those carrots on to boil! By the way, I'm going out on Tuesday night to Jessie's and Ewan is calling for me. You and Mick can have the front room, if you like.'

'You *what*!' Bless us and save us, what had got into Lorna! 'Have you considered for one moment what people would think if they saw Mick coming here?'

'Think? What do you think they'll think when they see me get into an army truck with Ewan? This village always *thinks*, Ness, so just for once let's give it something concrete to chew over, because I'm sick of what Nun Ainsty thinks!' And to add weight to her outburst, she slammed the lid down hard on the potato pan. 'Sick and tired!'

On Tuesday, Lorna awoke to grey skies and an unfamiliar chill in the air to remind her that soon August would be gone and with it, the end of summer. In Dickon's Wood, leaves on the trees had already taken on a darker, leathery look and in Priory Lane the brambles, once tightly green, were swelling and starting to ripen. Once, going brambling had been worth the effort in spite of scratched arms and purple-stained fingers. Once, you made bramble and apple pies and bramble jelly, yet how could you do such things now on four ounces of sugar a week? Four heaped tablespoons, then that was it!

A familiar sound made her look up to watch the downward flight of a bomber. One of the big ones coming back to the aerodrome, its undercarriage down, its engines making a different sound; tired, kind of, as if that great black-underbellied thing had feelings, and was glad to be safely home.

The sight of it wiped all thoughts of the sugar shortage from her mind because this morning, many of those bombers would not come back. This morning six – or perhaps three, or ten – of our aircraft failed to return from raids over enemy territory, the newsreader would give out in faultless English, devoid of any emotion. Six – or three, or ten – multiplied by seven crew to each bomber, and you had the number of telegrams speeding the awful news to all those families. She was glad she didn't have to deliver those small yellow envelopes.

She began to pedal as quickly as she could, so she would be gasping for breath when she got to the post office; a kind of penance, perhaps, for worrying about the shortage of sugar when so many young men were never coming home again.

Tears threatened and she sniffed them impatiently away, all at once feeling guilty because not one of those telegrams would be delivered to Ladybower. Her husband had a safe job behind a desk in Aldershot, didn't he? He'd made sure of it. But if she were honest, mostly she felt guilty about tonight. Not because she was going out to dinner with friends, but because she was looking forward to it; really looking forward to it. And she shouldn't be.

Ness sat, chin on hand, gazing at Mick's face because she loved it so much; loved Mick so much she was unwilling to take her eyes off him.

They sat at a corner table in the White Hart – where else was there around here to keep dry this miserably wet evening – except Lorna's front parlour, that was.

'Penny for them?' Mick smiled.

'You won't like me when I tell you. What would you say,' she faltered, dropping her gaze, 'if I told you that Lorna said we could have the use of her sitting room tonight. She's out, by the way.'

'I'd say it was very kind of her, and what are we waiting for?'

'But it isn't as simple as that, Mick. I wasn't going to tell you about it. I'm sorry, now, that I did.'

'Why, Ness?' All at once his face was grave. 'Is something wrong?'

'As a matter of fact there is. Look – finish your drink and we'll try to find somewhere dry – and *not* Ladybower.'

'But why ever not? Sounds just the job for a wet night in Ainsty.'

'Because I don't think we should. The way I feel, Mick, heaven only knows what might happen. And we can't talk here. Let's go to the ruins? I know where there's a dry bit in the cloisters. It's better than sitting here with people listening to every word.'

'Ness! There's hardly a soul in the place tonight!'

Only a few soldiers in hospital blue uniforms who didn't appear to be remotely interested in the corner table.

'OK. But we've got to talk and we can't do it in here. Not what I want to say, that is . . .'

'Then the ruins it is,' he smiled, 'if that's what you want.'

'I don't want, exactly. Where I'd like to be this very minute, is sitting on Lorna's sofa with you, but you an' me on our own like that would be asking for trouble, and you know it.'

'Darling girl, I know no such thing. But it's pretty obvious you've got something on your mind.' He got to his feet, holding out a hand. 'Come on, then. Let's make a dash for it.'

When they were standing beneath an overhang of stone from which a time-smoothed gargoyle dripped rainwater, Mick took Ness in his arms, holding her close, kissing her gently.

'So tell me, Ness?'

'It's me. I'm the trouble, and if you knew the way I feel you'd agree with me – about not going to Lorna's, I mean.'

'And what if I feel the same? What if it's every bit as bad for me?'

'Then it's just asking for disaster, isn't it? It's not that I don't trust you, Mick. I do. Even after what happened, I do. But I don't trust myself. And,' she hesitated, resting her head on his chest. 'And I'm scared stiff, if you want the truth, that if it – if it happened between us, you'd dump me.'

'Dump you like *he* did? Do a Patrick on you?'

'It could happen, Mick.'

'Well, it won't. For one thing I'm not married and you know it, but I've got to admit there's nothing I want more at this moment than to make love to you on Lorna's sofa!'

'There you are, then!' She laid her hands on his chest, straining from him. 'That's why we've got to stop out here, in the wet.'

'I'm inclined to agree with you. There's nothing better for damping the ardour than standing under a monotonous cold drip.' He took her face in his hands. 'So I reckon the only way out for us is for you and me to get married. Soon.'

'*Married*? Are you askin'?' she gasped.

'Of course I am. I've hinted at it often enough, but you've always managed to evade the issue. So, Agnes Nightingale darling, for the very last time, will you marry me? Please?'

'You mean it, don't you?' Her voice was a whisper of emotion. 'But when? And where? I don't believe any of this. I really don't.'

'Then you better had, because it's the last time of asking. Now – as to where. Liverpool, shall it be, or Borton-under-Whytchwood? Or St Philippa's? And how? We could get a special licence – easy enough, these days.'

'You *do* mean it,' Ness whispered, pulling her tongue around suddenly-dry lips. 'You really do! And will you tell me how you and me can get married when I haven't met your folks and you haven't met mine? What if my Nan doesn't like you because you're a conchie, and –'

'But I'm not, am I? By Christmas I'll be in khaki.'

'And what if your Mam thinks I talk common. What if she doesn't like my Liverpewl accent?'

'She'll hardly object to any accent, lovely girl, when she's as broad a Janner as you're likely to meet. Mind, she sometimes uses her telephone voice, but she can't keep it up for long.

So don't spoil it, Ness? Don't go all uptight now that we're almost there? And if I seem to be panicking you down the aisle then say so, and we'll talk it over calmly and sensibly. Only say you'll marry me, then we can start making plans. I do love you. I always have. I always will.'

'And I love you, Mick, and yes please, I'll marry you.' She reached on tiptoe to kiss him gently, all at once shy.

'Then from now on,' he smiled, 'consider yourself engaged. I think you should have a ring.'

'Oh, Mick Hardie, don't you know you can't buy engagement rings these days? Only second-hand, and they're hard to come by and dead expensive. Don't you know there's a waiting list for rings – even wedding rings?'

'I didn't know. But then,' he grinned, 'I'm not up to date on such things, never having proposed before. But surely we can find something, somewhere? I'd like you to have a ring, Ness.'

'And I don't want one. I couldn't wear it around the farm. It'd be lost in no time at all. I'd have to wear it on a chain around my neck, and where's the sense in that? Thanks, darling. No to an engagement ring, but yes please to a wedding ring. Maybe I'd beter put my name down – get on a few waiting lists. And even if I'm lucky, it'll only be nine-carat gold. Against the law to sell anything else now.'

'Then blow the lists. Mum was left her grandmother's jewellery. Old fashioned Victorian brooches, mostly, but I know there's a wedding ring amongst it. Maybe she would give it, or even loan it till we can get a decent one for you. Would that be all right, Ness?'

'It would be very all right, sweetheart.' She took his face in her hands, offering her lips, whispering, 'And if you'd like, maybe we could go back to Lorna's. If she's as late as last time, it'll be midnight before she's in.'

'Bless you, darling, but no. When you and me do share a bed, it'll be on our wedding night. So let's tell our folks we want to be married as soon as we can manage it, then start making plans?'

So they stood there in the rain and kissed, and kissed again. And the gargoyle dripped and dripped, and they didn't even notice it.

'Good night, dear.' Lorna kissed Jessie's cheek. 'And good night, Doc. I've had a lovely time.'

She really had. The evening had started with a scolding from Ness because she was in a dither about what to wear.

'The cocktail dress I wore last time was far too revealing,' she frowned. 'Something simple but nice would be more in keeping.'

'For goodness' sake, queen! You're carrying on like it's your first date!'

She had settled, eventually, for a floral cotton shirtwaister, her pearl beads and a touch of lipstick and mascara.

'And you're wearin' perfume, an' all!' Ness had accused.

'No I'm not! It's my best soap you can smell.' The precious lily-scented soap that was almost used up. 'And I'm not going on a date. I'm going to Jessie's for a meal.'

'Is that so? Well, the dashin' doctor is callin' for you in five minutes and you don't want him waitin' outside, do you, so everybody in the village is sure to see him.'

It was why Lorna was waiting at the gate when the Army truck pulled up and had opened the door and scrambled inside before Ewan had even stopped the engine.

And now she was going home in it, only this time Ewan helped her in, waiting until she had gathered up her skirts before he slammed shut the door.

'Reg and Jessie are great people, the salt of the earth.'

'Mm. I feel so at home with them. They're good to work for. I was told that when I first came to live with Gran and Grandpa, I was spotted all over with chickenpox. Doc Summers looked after me then. I seem to have known him all my life. I wish I could cook like Jessie,' she added hastily, because she didn't want Ewan to ask about when she was little. All she wanted to do was enjoy what was left of tonight, because even driving carefully because of the blackout, they would be back at Ladybower in only ten minutes.

'Jessie cooks like my mother. Some women do it naturally. It's a gift, I believe. I shall miss those two, when I go.'

'Go, Ewan?' She was far too relaxed to grasp the sudden seriousness in his voice. 'Go where? You'll be at the manor for the duration!'

'No, Lorna.' Carefully he crossed the main road, making for the white-painted stones either side of Priory Lane. 'Afraid I won't. As soon as my relief arrives, I'll be on my way.'

'You mean you're leaving Ainsty? But how long have you known? And will you pull in, please? We've got to talk.'

'Sadly it's past the talking stage.' He drove onto the wide grass verge and stopped the engine. 'It's fact. My relief could arrive any day and when I've settled him in, that'll be it.'

'But where are you going? Abroad, will it be?'

Her heart thudded with dismay because she did not want him to leave. Just to think of some other medical officer drinking early-morning tea in the manor kitchen was almost beyond belief.

'On a week's leave, and then to some place near London for a final medical and all that sort of thing. Then they'll post me to a regiment and it's almost certain I'll be going overseas.'

Overseas, Lorna thought dully. Miles and miles away. Half a world away, maybe.

'The Middle East, Ewan?'

'Could be. Or perhaps the Far East – Hong Kong, Singapore. Lord knows.'

'And He has a habit of never telling.' Lorna sighed. 'Oh, damn this war. You get yourself wounded at Dunkirk and now, when you're fit again, they're sending you into action.'

'That's the way war is. And it was very easy to get wounded at Dunkirk. I'll be more careful, in future, don't worry.'

'I'm not worrying, Ewan. Not exactly.' Liar, Lorna Hatherwood. This has hit you for six! 'It's just that it's going to be strange you not being around. And yes, I suppose I'm just a bit worried. I've got to know the manor people pretty well, don't forget. I felt pretty cut up when Private Jones – Alun – left, even though he had his Rebecca. He'd become a friend, you see, not just a blind soldier I read to and wrote letters for. I'm going to feel the same about you going. Sad . . .'

All at once the wine glow had gone. Now she felt flatly sober and not only sad he was leaving, but dismayed, too.

'It's the way life is, Lorna. I won't forget you, or Nun Ainsty.'

'I won't forget you, either. I won't be able to. The watercolour – remember it?'

'I do. You said you'd hang it over your desk.'

'And I did. I'll remember you every time I see it – every day, in fact.' She wrote to William at that desk every day, didn't she; of course she would remember Ewan. 'Do you remember when we met in the woods?'

'Of course I do. You were in the wood with Ness, scavenging fallen branches after the gale. I was leaning against a tree, sketching. I think I startled Ness.'

'You did. She was hoping to see the ghost.'

'And now I shall never see Ursula. Reckon I'll give her a wave in passing when I go – just in case.'

'She won't be there, Ewan. Only star-crossed lovers see her – are *supposed* to see her.'

'Is that so?' he laughed, reaching to start the engine. 'I suppose you know it's past midnight?'

'No, I didn't, but it seems it's time for Cinderella to go home.'

And not only time to go home, Lorna brooded. She *wanted* to go home; go home to Ladybower, and weep!

* * *

'Ness! What on earth are you doing still up at this hour?'

Lorna had closed the door carefully behind her, prepared to tiptoe upstairs, when she noticed the kitchen light.

'Waiting for you, of course. And what time of night do you think this is, Mrs Hatherwood!'

'Past twelve, I know.' Lorna sat in the opposite rocking chair and eased off her shoes, only then noticing Ness's face which, in spite of the turban that hid her pin-curled hair, was unusually radiant. 'Something's happened, hasn't it?'

'Mm. Want me to make a cup of cocoa, 'cause there's a lot to tell.' She filled the kettle without waiting for a reply. 'And we didn't take advantage of your offer of the front room, thanks all the same. Mick wanted to, but I said no way!'

'Why on earth not?'

'Thought it best we went to the ruins instead. By the way, Mick asked me to marry him.'

Ness stood, spoon poised, waiting for her bombshell to burst.

'Marry you! And about time, too! You said yes, of course?'

'I did,' Ness smiled broadly, 'so congratulations are in order.'

'And I do congratulate you.' Lorna jumped to her feet, arms wide. 'I'm really, really pleased for you both.' She hugged Ness to her. 'When is it to be?'

'As soon as we can manage it. We've got to tell the folks first. Do you realize, Lorna, that Mam and Da and Nan don't know a thing about Mick, except that he works at Glebe. I've been a bit cautious about mentioning him in letters.'

'Then I suggest you book a phone call to Ruth Street tomorrow. Ring the pub, why don't you, and ask the landlord to ask your mother to phone you here, after work. That way, it should take care of the initial shock. Explain that you're writing a letter telling her all about it, because you'll not be able to say a lot in three minutes.'

'You can say that again. When Mam's picked herself up off the floor of the phone box, there won't be a lot of time left. I still can't take it in, y'know.' She shook her head in delighted disbelief. 'Me, I mean, marrying someone like Mick. Mind, I'll be meeting his family when I go there with him, but what about my folks, and where would he sleep at Ruth Street? We haven't got a spare room; suppose he'd have my bed and I'd bunk up with Nan.'

'Ness! The kettle's boiling! And is it important who sleeps where? What matters most is that you and Mick get married.'

'Ar. You're right. It happened so suddenly, see, so we didn't get to talk about it much. We were both a bit light-headed, I suppose. But my fiancé – imagine? And just think – none of this would have happened if I hadn't come to Glebe Farm. I keep thinking I'm dreaming and that I'll wake up in Liverpool, still hairdressing at Dale's!'

'I'll pinch you, if you like,' Lorna smiled. 'In fact I'll pinch you hard if you don't get on with that drink! But seriously, love, I'm thrilled for you both. Won't you make a lovely couple. You'll have such lovely children.'

'Hey! Let's get hitched first! And you don't half go on about kids, Lorna . . .'

She concentrated hard, then, on the hot drink, because she suddenly remembered the dismay she had felt, knowing she was pregnant with Patrick's child; the aching relief, almost, when it had slipped from her in a hospital ward.

'I know I do, but it looks as if I'm going to have to wait. But here's to you and Mick.' She held her mug high. 'And d'you know what? I think I'm going to cry, and isn't that too stupid of me,' she sniffed. 'I seem to weep at the drop of a hat these days.'

'You wouldn't be you if you didn't. But let's take our drinks upstairs? You look worn out, queen, and you've got to be up before me in the morning. Just wanted you to know, that's all.'

'Well, you've told me and I'm glad. Now, off you go. I'll lock up and put the lights out. 'Night, Ness. I was going to say sleep tight, but I think that would be too much to expect.'

Gently she kissed Ness good night; sadly she watched her walk upstairs, knowing that she couldn't tell her about Ewan; couldn't dim such happiness with her own dismay. Because she *was* sad, Lorna was bound to admit, and she would miss him more than she thought possible; more than she should.

But it was the fault of the war, she brooded, placing the guard over a fire already dead, sliding home the bolts on the back door, turning the key. The war tore husbands and wives apart and didn't care one jot about the misery it caused, and the awful aching loneliness. And why shouldn't she miss Ewan? He had become a good friend, so why shouldn't it be all right for her to be upset at his leaving?

'Because you are married,' she mouthed to the pale-faced woman in the hall mirror. 'Because you have no right to feel anything for any other man. Not anything at all!'

She snapped off the hall light, walking carefully upstairs in the darkness and along the landing, wondering if perhaps she should tell Ness about it. But then the sliver of light that shone beneath the spare bedroom door went out, and Lorna knew that such news must wait until tomorrow.

All at once she felt very lonely, and more miserable than she cared – *dared* – to admit.

'Talk about a bush telegraph! The whole village knows. I've been stopped three times! I suppose you passed on the news with every letter?' Ness collapsed dramatically into the kitchen rocker. 'And when I told Kate, she said I should be married here in Ainsty, so all the village could get together for a bit of a do. Oh, Lorna, I'm so happy that I'm starting to worry now in case something happens to spoil it.'

'But why should it? You've had your fair share of trouble, Ness, so you're due a bit of luck for a change. Are you meeting Mick tonight?'

'Can a duck swim? And what smells so good, 'cause I'm starving!'

'You know what it is. Today's Wednesday and on Wednesdays it's always Woolton pie for supper. And baked apples and custard. And Ness, I hate to be a wet blanket, but I've got to tell you. Ewan is leaving.'

'Leavin' Nun Ainsty?'

'Yes. As soon as his relief arrives. Could be within a week. He told me last night.'

'Then why didn't you say something before now? Why did you keep it back? Come to think of it, I thought last night you looked a bit down in the dumps, but reckoned you were tired.'

'Didn't want to spoil your good news, I suppose. He told me when we were on the way home. He'll probably go abroad, he says.'

'And you're going to miss him, aren't you, queen?'

'I am. And I know I shouldn't, but there it is. I feel awful about it.'

'Awful about what, Lorna? About him going or about you being cut up about it?'

'Both, I suppose. He said he'd be in touch with me once he knows when he's going, but you never know. Things happen so quickly these days. I'm telling myself that last night was the last time I shall see him, just in case.'

'Listen, Lorna – I know I shouldn't ask this and you'd be well in order if you bit my head off, but did anything happen last night?'

'Like what?' Lorna's chin shot up, her mouth made an indignant round.

'Like maybe he kissed you, and things got out of hand . . .'

'Nothing got out of hand but we did kiss, or more to the point, I kissed *him*. At the front gate, actually. I put my arms round his neck and said good night then kissed him on the mouth. I wanted to, so I don't care. All I mind about is that I think I shocked him.'

'Now why, will you tell me, would he be shocked? Ewan is a doctor, not a pretty-faced crooner. He knows how many beans make five, I shouldn't wonder. One kiss, and you get all het up about it? Unless –' She got to her feet, placing her hands on Lorna's shoulders, turning her round so they stood eye to eye. 'And look at me when I'm talkin' to you. Did you get passionate last night?'

'Of course we didn't! We were at the gate. What could have happened in full view of the entire village?'

'With the entire village – excepting you an' me – in bed and asleep?'

'Oh, you know what I mean. I kissed *him*! A goodbye kiss, not a no-holds-barred necking session! I know I should have kissed his cheek, but I didn't. And do you want to know why? I think that deep down I wanted it to develop into something. I really wanted it to. I don't know what got into me and I know I should feel ashamed, but I don't, so what do you think about that, Ness?'

Her face had paled, her fingers gripped so hard on the chair back that her knuckles showed white.

'So tell me, Lorna – did he take the hint, and kiss you back?'

'No, he didn't. That was what made it so humiliating. I acted like a tart.'

'Oh, Mrs Hatherwood, don't you just take the plate of biscuits! You kiss a soldier goodbye – a very nice feller, incidentally, who I wouldn't mind gettin' into a clinch with myself! It would be no trouble at all to give him a goodbye kiss. We've had quite a few chats, Ewan and me, over the farm wall. I'm goin' to miss him, too.

'But you haven't seen the last of him, Lorna. He said he'd let you know when he was leaving, so he will. And when he does, I hope you make the most of it and do what you know you want to do – give him something to remember you by!'

'Ness Nightingale, you amaze me! Surely you don't mean that we should – that we should –'

She stopped, cheeks blazing, trying to forget that she had wondered not just what kissing Ewan would be like, but more, much more than that! It was as if Ness had read right inside her mind.

'What I mean is that kissin' a feller – really kissin' him – doesn't amount to adultery, surely even you know that. Oh, Lorna, you're so – so *innocent*, you really are! But what you're in need of right now is supper, then a good night's sleep, 'cause I shouldn't wonder if you didn't sleep a wink last night.'

'I didn't. I felt so miserable and guilty, too.'

'Guilty? One kiss isn't worth missing your sleep over. Tell you what, though, if it's guilt you want, why not be hanged for a sheep and go the whole – *almost* the whole – hog. Now that just might be worth a sleepless night, queen!'

And in spite of herself, Lorna laughed and admitted that an early night might not be a bad idea – after she had written to William, of course – then asked Ness if she had remembered to book the call to Liverpool.

'I did. Mrs Benson said she'd give me the first trunk line she could get hold of after seven.'

'Fine. Now, get your hands washed! Supper's ready!'

All at once she knew why she was so very fond of Ness. Not because she was the next best thing to a sister; not because she was fun to be with, either, but because she had an uncanny knack of saying the right thing at exactly the right time. A friend who was totally unshockable!

TWENTY

The day had been sunny and some of its warmth lingered in the stones of the priory ruins. Behind them the sun was setting brightly red, and to the east a pale white moon began to rise over the tree tops.

'A full moon,' Ness said softly. 'The harvest moon.'

'Suppose you could call it a bombers' moon, too. There'll be no blackout tonight.'

'It doesn't seem as if they're flying.' Ness settled her head on Mick's shoulder. 'Hope not. It'll be like daylight up there; fine for the Gerry fighters, though.'

'Y'know, darling, when I'm here I sometimes wonder what those nuns would have made of this war. Tanks, dirty great bombs, planes. They'd have thought the end of the world had come. An innocent age, I suppose. Uncomplicated.'

'You what? If that was innocence then give me today, war and all! Theirs was an *awful* world, Mick. Lepers came here to die, but we can cure them now. And what about fathers sending their daughters into convents, just because they had a hare lip? You can have an operation for that, an' all. And they didn't have penicillin, either.'

'The wonder drug? We've only just discovered that ourselves, Ness.'

'Granted. But it wasn't a very good world for women, though. They did as their father told them, then did as their husband told them. Good old Mrs Pankhurst!'

‘They didn’t call women up into factories and the Armed Forces in Ursula’s day. They didn’t have a Land Army – didn’t need one, I suppose. Peasants came cheap when this priory was built.’

‘Well, it’s water under the bridge now.’ She lifted his hand to her lips, kissing it gently. ‘And if the bombers don’t go tonight, we can pretend there isn’t a war on and that if we sit here real quiet, we’ll hear them nuns singing prayers.’

‘Vespers, Ness. And if we hear singing nuns, you won’t see my behind for dust! Want to walk?’

‘No, ta.’

‘Nip over to the Hart for a drink?’

‘Later, maybe. Just want to sit here for a bit, in the quiet.’

She nestled closer, twining her fingers in his, feeling a contentment she had never thought possible. They were living life on the edge of destruction yet here, tonight, the tranquillity of a past world seeped into them as though they were a part of it. All because, Ness thought, things had come right for them. Soon, they would be married and life would be good – for a little while at least.

Yet dark November would come and with it an awful, aching loneliness, because Mick would be gone. Dreary days and cold nights and not a light to be seen from dusk to dawn. Sixteen hours of blackout come November, and Mick a soldier.

‘Did you know Ewan MacMillan expects to be moved on soon?’ Mick broke into her broodings. ‘I’ll miss our talks at the fence.’

‘Lorna’s going to miss him too, though she won’t admit it. He told her about it on Tuesday night. She got in late – they’d been at the doctor’s for a meal.’

‘Do they see each other often?’

‘No. Only when properly chaperoned, so to speak. He called to take her to Meltonby and she was all of a dither, trying to make up her mind what to wear. I wish she wasn’t married to that William. I can’t stand him.’

'But you've never actually met him, Ness.'

'And I hope I never do. I just know I don't like the man. There's a photograph of him in a silver frame in the sittin' room. Every time I see it, I want to poke tongues at it! He's toffee-nosed; he gave Lorna down-the-banks for taking me in, told her she was to get rid of me, but she didn't. It's why I go to Flora's when he's on leave – keeps the peace. Poor Lorna. She doesn't know what she's missing.'

'OK. We've established you're not particularly fond of William.' His eyes teased her. 'So let's talk about us? Have you told your parents yet?'

'Thought you'd never ask! Of course I've told them. Was on the phone to Mam tonight, and there's a long letter on the hall table for Lorna to post in Meltonby in the morning. I couldn't say much. You don't get long, you know.'

'And what did your mother say?'

'She said, "Good heavens to Murgatroyd, our Ness. Have you been drinking?" when I told her. Then she said that I'd kept you a bit quiet, so I said it was because I wanted to be sure – after – well, after what happened, you see. It took a while for it to sink in and that I was serious.'

'But was she pleased for us, Ness?'

'I think she was, darling. Just a bit shocked at first. Asked me if I was sure and I told her I was so sure she could put it in the *Echo*, if she wanted. They do that a lot now, you know – announce engagements and suchlike in the *Liverpool Echo*. I told her what to put when I wrote tonight. Had to, since she didn't know the first thing about you. Like she said, I'd kept you pretty quiet.'

'So what is our official announcement to say?'

'I wrote it in capitals, so she'd get it right. MICHAEL HARDIE (RAMC) TO AGNES NIGHTINGALE (WLA). CONGRATULATIONS FROM BOTH FAMILIES.'

'You're jumping the gun a bit. I'm not in the Royal Army Medical Corps yet.'

'No, but you will be. And I said congratulations because

that's what they always seem to put. Let's hope your Mam and Dad do the same.'

'I'm hoping that when it happens at my end, it'll be in the Marriages column. I want it to be as soon as we can make it, sweetheart.'

'Me, too.' She turned in his arms and lifted her lips to his, and as they kissed she wished that Lorna could be as happy. Half as happy would do.

Poor Lorna, all alone in that big house. It wasn't fair.

Lorna sat at her desk, chin on hand, wondering what more she could write to William. There was news, of course, but not all of it could she put in a letter to her husband.

That Ewan was leaving the manor? Best not to. That Ness and Mick were engaged and crazily happy? No to that, too. Ness was never mentioned except in exceptional circumstances, and getting engaged to a conscientious objector would only make the telling worse. William hated conchies. Cowards, who would have been taken out and shot in the last war, or at the very least sent to prison for the duration.

She sighed, reading what she had written.

Wed. August 27th, '41
7.30 p.m.

Dearest William,

Today has been warm and sunny, exceptionally so since we are almost into September.

Last night I went to Meltonby to have dinner with Reg and Jessie Summers. They had a brace of grouse as a present and invited me to share their good luck. So kind of them.

All right to tell William that. Sneaky not mentioning that Ewan had been there, too.

This far, I have not used any of my clothing coupons,

but I will soon be in need of winter shoes and had thought to go to York to get a pair – between jobs, that is. They will eat up five coupons and I will be left with sixty-one to last until next June. I have decided to wear trousers when the cold weather comes, for the morning round. That way, I can wear socks in place of stockings which are the biggest blight of all. They ladder so easily and are certainly not worth two clothing coupons! And I am not being selfish or complaining, my dear, because I would gladly go shoeless, even, if you could be at home with me.

Which was a pretty stupid thing to write, since William wouldn't be seen dead walking through the village with a shoeless wife at his side! Indeed, he had asked if she had gone gypsy when once she walked barefoot across the lawn in fun, because it was midsummer morning.

I met Nance on the way home from the surgery and she asked if you had enjoyed your leave and what a shame it was that you lost two days of it. She sent her best regards.

And oh, what else could she say? What else could she write without causing William to be jealous or angry? Because William was easily upset, could turn tetchy for no reason at all these days. The war was to blame, of course, because it was not natural for man and wife to be parted and to sleep apart.

The brambles in Priory Lane are starting to ripen. Remember our brambling afternoons when we came home with scratches and nettle stings and purple fingers? Such fun, had we but realized it.

Bob Wintersgill has finished with the corn harvest

and he let me glean the barley field to help feed the hens.

And why she had written that she didn't know, because mention of their hens would remind him of Ness who was taboo; as indeed was Lorna Hatherwood, scratching for barley, gleaning a field like a peasant in a Victorian watercolour.

'Oh, *hell*!'

She ripped the page from the pad, screwing it into a ball, throwing it into the empty fire grate because it was a letter you would write to your godmother or an elderly aunt. It was not the sort of thing you wrote to husbands; to a soldier who was miles from home and hearth. Yes, and his bed, too!

My darling William,

I miss you tonight. I miss you every night. Soon, I shall go early to bed and wish you were with me: wish I could be in your arms and kiss you and love you and make love with you . . .

That was what she should have written; what she would never write to William because he would be embarrassed that his wife ached to be loved, even though it wasn't a Tuesday or a Sunday. And far worse, that she had put it in a letter that might be opened by the Censor's office, and read!

Not that any of it mattered because she did not want William to make love to her tonight. William wasn't ever very passionate. Rough, sometimes, but never passionate. And his moustache scratched, especially when the grunting started. And when the grunting and pushing was over, he would turn from her and say, 'Aaaaah', instead of holding her close and kissing her gently and whispering that he loved her.

Her eyes began to fill with tears and she brushed them away and blew her nose loudly. She didn't know what the matter was these days; why she was irritable and impatient and more tired than a woman of her age should be. Was it because of the shortage of food and clothing and scented soap and face cream and just about every small luxury everyone had taken for granted not so very long ago?

Or was it because, just sometimes, she needed to love and be loved? She did not know, yet there was one thing certainly not responsible for her moods and lethargy. She was not pregnant!

She glanced at the picture on the wall above her desk; Ewan's watercolour of distant, shining water and misty hills and foxgloves. It was the most beautiful thing she owned.

She got to her feet and began to pace the floor, arms folded as if to hold in her anger, knowing that if she had any sense at all she would take down that picture and put it out of sight and never look at it again. Never, ever, let it remind her of Ewan who was leaving Nun Ainsty maybe even tomorrow, and who she would never see again.

Tears came to her eyes once more and because it was useless trying to stop them, she threw herself face down on the sofa, pushed her face into a cushion, and wept.

'So what's to do, queen?' Ness scolded. 'You were supposed to have an early night, not sit here in the dark!'

The moon shone through the window, half lighting the room, and Ness had been surprised to find Lorna, hands round knees, on the front-room sofa.

'Oh – well, I didn't feel like it, in the end. Wrote to William, then –'

'Then sat here on your own with not even the wireless on! What is it? Has William phoned or something?'

'William hardly ever phones, you know that. I suppose I was too tired to shift myself and get into bed.'

'Well, you're going to get your nightie and dressing gown on this minute and I'll make you a butty and a hot drink. You hardly touched your supper. How do you think you're goin' to get to sleep on an empty stomach? And watch it with the lights. You haven't even seen to the blackouts!'

'OK. I'll do upstairs. Will you do downstairs, Ness?'

What was wrong, Ness thought as she swished curtains and pulled down blinds. Could Lorna really be upset about Ewan's posting? Surely not the dutiful wife who was faithful to her marriage vows and wouldn't dream of looking at another man?

But was that entirely true? Frowning, Ness set the kettle to boil and took mugs from the dresser. Could it, perhaps, be that Lorna had become fond of Ewan MacMillan – through no fault of her own, of course. Maybe, because he was kind and considerate not to mention handsome and because she was lonely, could Lorna have enjoyed his company – well, just a little?

Wrong! It was more than just a little or why had Lorna made such a song and dance about kissing him good night; been full of guilt about it? If it had meant nothing, it shouldn't have been worth a mention.

But surely they had established that a kiss between friends was fine, and Lorna had agreed, yet now she was back to square one and looking as if she had been having a good old cry, from the state of her face, that was. Lorna couldn't weep prettily; she went the whole hog and ended up with puffy eyes and a red nose.

Ness turned to see her standing in the kitchen doorway and looking so downtrodden that she was all at once worried.

'Now see here, girl, sumthin's up, it's pretty obvious, so why don't we sit ourselves down and have a good old natter about it? I'll make you a jam butty and then you can tell me what's really bothering you, eh?'

At which Lorna pulled out a chair and sat at the table, chin on hands, and said she didn't know why she felt so rotten.

'The curse due, is it?' Ness asked, slicing bread, taking care not to force Lorna to meet her eyes.

'No. You know I've just had it.'

'So you're not – mightn't be –'

'Overdue? Not a chance.'

'Mind, I wasn't meanin' you're miserable cause you might be late or anything. Far from it. What I thought was that sometimes, early on that is, it does make you a bit out of sorts. Before the mornin' sickness starts, of course . . .'

'You'd know, would you?'

'N-no, Lorna. But I know women who have felt that way – they said.'

Careful, Ness Nightingale!

'Well, you can count that one out. I'll admit I feel a bit under the weather, but I think if I was late, I wouldn't feel miserable. Far from it.'

'So what is it, do you think?'

'Wish I knew. I've been weeping – I suppose you noticed?'

'I did. You'll have to splash your face with cold water or you'll look a mess in the morning. Haven't you even the remotest idea what it is you were weeping about?'

Eyes still down, Ness sliced the sandwiches into dainty triangles then arranged them on a china plate.

'Nothing in particular. Just the war, I suppose. And I know I should be ashamed of myself because there are thousands of women worse off than me. Some have lost their husbands and their homes – or sleep in the Underground because they've got nowhere to go at night. And I'm sure there can't be anywhere much safer than Ainsty. If it wasn't for the aerodrome close by, you could kid yourself that the war was happening to some other country. When you think about it, the war has hardly touched me – apart from William going, that is.'

'So it isn't the war, really?'

'I suppose not. It's just – oh, everything and nothing. Nothing I can put a finger on.'

'Then maybe it's me to blame, Lorna. Maybe me being so cockeyed happy makes it worse for you, being alone. I'm sorry if it's me, queen.'

'No, Ness. It isn't. In fact, if you weren't here I think I'd have gone quietly mad by now; done something stupid like shutting up Ladybower and running away to sea, or something equally crazy. I'm glad you're here, truly I am, and I'm glad you and Mick are so happy.'

'Then eat up those sarnies and get yourself into bed. You're just about shattered.'

'Think I must be. And I know I shouldn't talk about it, but there are women coming to the surgery who are so fed up with the war it's getting them down. Doc Summers has been prescribing bottles of iron tonic. Maybe I need one, too.'

'Maybe you do, at that! Have a word, tomorrow afternoon. Free consultation, like. And don't look at them sarnies as if they've grown fungus. Get them eaten, and when you wake up in the morning, you'll wonder what on earth you were worrying about!'

Worrying, Ness pondered, when Lorna had gone to bed. Oh, but she knew what was the cause of it just as Lorna knew it, too. But admitting it, talking about it, was altogether another thing. It was the way things were, she supposed, for lonely, childless women; women who wouldn't dream of going off the rails even though the war was getting them down. Yet in Lorna's case the war wasn't entirely to blame; not if you were hand-on-heart honest. Lorna's problem was something best brushed under the hearthrug and forgotten, truth known. And in time Lorna would do just that, Ness thought sadly, which would be a pity. A very great pity.

Lorna completed the post and paper deliveries in record time, determined to think about nothing but the task in hand; keeping her thoughts in check. Tuesday's fall from grace was nothing short of disgraceful. You'd have thought she was the only woman in the North Riding with a husband at war, so miserable had she been.

Thankfully, she had slept soundly last night and awakened to another beautiful day; slightly misty, a little chilly, but a glad-to-be-alive morning, for all that. Until she got to the manor, that was, and said a cheery-enough good morning to the sergeant-cook, who said he was sorry but he hadn't made the tea yet and to which Lorna replied that that was all right; maybe tomorrow morning, eh? Then all the while wondering why she was pedalling down Glebe Farm lane as if the air-raid siren on top of Nance Ellery's garage had just gone off at full blast.

She spied Rowley beside the pump trough and thrust the mail and newspaper into his hands, calling a goodbye, making for the gate at which she had propped her cycle. Just Beech Tree House to do now, and Larkspur Cottage, and the almshouses. They would all be in bed, still. Even Martha's curtains would not twitch. And she was being very foolish, Lorna knew, but this morning she didn't want to talk to anyone, not even to Ness.

She heard a motor behind her and pulled in to let it pass, knowing it would be the truck from the manor, hoping it would stop, praying it wouldn't. But it slowed, then passed her and through the open window a hand waved and she knew the driver to be the corporal, not Ewan. Not Ewan on his way to York station.

She looked at her watch and wondered where the truck was off to so early in the morning, then tutted impatiently. She was getting as nosy as Martha, and that would never do!

'Good morning.' Ness felt hands from behind cover her eyes. 'Guess who this is and you've won a coconut.'

'I'd rather have a kiss.' She turned to whisper her lips across Mick's cheek. 'Love you. See you later.'

She forced herself to walk away from him and into the kitchen.

'Morning, Kate. Any tea left in the pot?'

'You can take mugs to the menfolk, if you want. I've just made a mash. And no need to ask how you are this fine morning.'

'As well as can be expected, in the circumstances.' Ness set a large wooden tray with mugs and spoons and milk and saccharin tablets, eyes bright with mischief. 'Ar, it doesn't half knock you for six – courtin', I mean. Shall I stay or have my drinkings with the men?'

'Have it here, lass, and tell me the news from the village.'

'Was still there ten minutes ago when I walked through it,' Ness grinned. 'But if it's tittle-tattle you want, reckon Martha'll have to bring you up-to-date when she gets here. My head's in the clouds these days.'

'Then it seems courting is in the air at Glebe Farm. It wouldn't surprise me if our Rowley isn't settling himself down at last. He seems serious about the lass from t'other side of Meltonby. Asked if he could bring her to tea on Sunday. He's never brought a girl home before, so what do you think to that?'

'It looks, Kate, as if he's halfway down the aisle already. What is she like?'

'Bonny, and inclined to plumpness, if what I remember of her is correct. She was in school with Rowley; I haven't set eyes on her since. Olivia, she's called. But I'm not counting my chickens, Ness, though I'd like nothing more than to see the lad settled serious. Mind, if she's anything like her mother, she won't stand any nonsense from him!'

'So fingers crossed, Kate. And have you had any news, yet, from the labour exchange? Not that I want Mick to go, but there'll come the day when –'

'Aye, when he has to. And I'll miss him, too. Lord knows what we'll get in his place, but he'll be a hard one to follow. Bob was making enquiries about another land girl, but half the farms around seem to be asking for them, so we'll have to look elsewhere. Trouble is, farming is for the young and strong, and most men who'd suit are in uniform now. Still, there's a while to go till November.'

'Nine weeks, at least.' Ness stirred her tea. 'And then heaven only knows where he'll end up.'

'But surely they'll have to train him first; not just as a soldier but there'll be medical things to learn, I shouldn't wonder. Wouldn't it be grand if he ended up at that big military hospital in York? It doesn't follow that he'll be sent abroad right away. And whilst we're about it, Ness, don't you get any ideas about leaving us, an' all. I'd miss you, if you did.'

'Leave? Not if I can help it. I'm stoppin', Kate, if it's anything to do with me. So let's be getting the tea to the workers, eh? See you at ten.'

Nice to be wanted, she thought, as she walked carefully, mugs clinking, across the yard. Hadn't Lorna said pretty much the same? And wasn't life in this gorgeous little village absolutely smashing? And wasn't Ness Nightingale the lucky one being sent to Meltonby hostel to find there was no bed for her? And wasn't Lorna a real sweetie? Pity about William, but you couldn't have it all ways.

'Tea up, gentlemen,' she called. 'Come and get it!'

Lorna laid a list of appointments on Reginald Summers's desk. Only four, so far, for late surgery. With luck she would be home on time tonight. And hadn't she better be making a start with the monthly accounts so they were as ready as they could be for posting on the first of next month. She heard the inside bell tinkle and opened the hatch, smiling.

'Ewan!' She had expected a patient. 'The – er – he's out on calls and Jessie's out, too. I'll tell them you called, ask them to ring you back, shall I?' She drew in a deep, steadying breath.

'It isn't them I've come to see. It's you. My relief arrived early this morning. I'll be away to Ardnamurchan on Saturday. Can I call tonight, or tomorrow perhaps? Can you spare me an hour?'

'Of course I can. But would you mind if – well, if I came to see you, at the manor? What I mean is that Ness will be out, and –'

She stopped, embarrassed, because why shouldn't he call at Ladybower, even though she was there alone? Why was she making a big thing about it?

'Sorry, Ewan. I'm putting it very badly, but you know the way things are around Ainsty.'

'I do. I come from a little village, too. Ness goes out and not long after, I'm knocking on your door. Should have thought. Stupid of me, but I'd like to say goodbye to you and thank you for – well, for all the things you did for the blind soldiers and for being so very nice to talk to. I've enjoyed your company.'

'Well, then – half seven tomorrow night suit you?'

'It would be fine. The new MO hasn't taken my office over yet. Won't keep you, Lorna. See you tomorrow.' He smiled into her eyes and she was surprised to find she was smiling back and saying, ''Bye. See you,' as if she was in control again and that saying goodbye to a friend was nothing at all.

Getting to be quite an actress, wasn't she?

'I'll be off, then.' Ness stuck her head round the sitting-room door. 'Got my key. Don't wait up.'

''Bye, Ness. Have a nice time.'

Lorna turned to watch her run up the path, slamming the gate behind her, impatient to be off, then turned back to her desk.

Thursday August 28th, '41
7.20 p.m.

Dearest William,

I am so sorry I didn't write last night; sorrier still

that it was the first time ever I missed. Sadly, I felt under the weather; had a headache so went early to bed. I think I must have been tired after the night before; dining out isn't exactly my thing these days. Still, I feel fine tonight. Everything OK. Nothing to bother about. Back to my usual self.

And of course you won't know that I went to dinner on Tuesday evening at Reg and Jessie's. They had a brace of grouse given and very kindly invited me to eat with them.

I think I will go to the shops on Saturday, splash out five clothing coupons on a pair of stout winter shoes. They will be the first coupons I have spent since I got them in June, and allowing five for the shoes, it will only leave sixty-one to last until next June.

She decided not to mention the shoeless bit she had written last night. Silly, even to think of it. If she walked out shoeless, William would disown her. She remembered about the brambles.

The brambles in Priory Lane are starting to ripen. Remember our brambling afternoons and the fun we had? And all the jars of bramble jelly I used to make when sugar was not rationed?

She remembered about gleaning Glebe's barley field with Ness, and decided that, too, was better left out.

There is not a lot of news. Life goes on, most times, as it always did. Sometimes I can sit in the garden and think that the war is a long way from Ainsty.

She sighed, keeping her eyes on the desktop and not allowing even a glance at the wall above. Because if she did, if she looked at that picture and thought about Ewan, she would not be able to write the final few lines of the letter. Not without blushing for shame.

I miss you so much, William. Nights can be very lonely without you. I ache for the war to be over so we can live our lives together again and sleep together every night.

Take care of your dear self. This letter comes with love and longing.

Always,

Lorna.

Carefully, she addressed an envelope; meticulously she stuck on a stamp then got to her feet, stretching. She laid the letter on the hall table beside the one Ness had written to Ruth Street. Another one. Two letters home in two days and almost certainly all about Mick. Ness, who was desperately in love. Mick, who loved her equally desperately. She shrugged, wondering how she could fill the rest of the evening. A walk, perhaps, in the fresh air? Along the riverbank, or to the top of Priory Lane? Thanks, but no.

She recalled that once, when she was in a dithery mood like now, she had often baked cakes and pies and sometimes, to knock the moodiness out of herself, she had baked bread, too, pummelling the dough with clenched fists.

But that seemed a long time ago now, and there were no rations to spare for cakes or pastries. Even to bake bread didn't bear thinking about because flour was so awful. National flour, the Ministry of Food called it, and it was all brown and bitty. It made her long for the beautiful white flour of old that ran softly through her fingers and she knew there would be no more of it for the duration.

Which left the garden, she supposed, sighing just to think of the weeds she had ignored for far too long. Surely weeding and energetic hoeing and running the mower over the parts of the lawn the hens were not using would take care of her restlessness?

Or was it anger she felt? Could it even be envy of Ness, and her happiness? One thing it was not, Lorna decided, was because Ewan was leaving. She wasn't in a state because she was going to the manor tomorrow night; she had been to the manor lots of times. Nor was it that soon she was never to see him again.

Yet maybe she was entitled to be a little sad at the leaving of someone she had come to like and admire. What was wrong in that?

But it wasn't sadness, because if she were truthful she would admit that what she felt was an emotion far stronger. What churned inside her now was frustration and a hatred of a war that had brought her to this and made her want to stamp her feet and bang doors, and weep.

So it was either tears, or gardening. Nothing like getting soil on her hands and down her fingernails, and shoving a mower and tugging out weeds, to knock the mood out of her.

She chose the garden. She had wept too much recently, and in wartime tears were a luxury allowed only to those who had something to weep about. And when you looked at it that way, Lorna Hatherwood was so lucky she should be laughing her head off right now.

So why wasn't she?

Ness and Lorna left Ladybower together and walked through the village as far as the chapel.

'See you, then.' Ness turned left toward the ruins.

'Got your key? I'll be in long before you.' Lorna turned right towards the manor. 'Shall I tell Ewan all the best from you, Ness?'

'No ta. Already done. I saw him this afternoon at the fence and he told me he was going tomorrow, early. I shall miss him. Bet you will, too.'

'Of course I will. Everyone will. Well – see you . . .'

She wished she felt as Ness did; wished she was going to meet her lover, run into his arms eager for his kiss. She and William had had few dates. Either William came to Ladybower – at first, on business – or she had met him at Grandpa's solicitor's office where he worked on the accounting side of the practice. Then William phoned her occasionally, and sometimes suggested they go for a meal, and for a long time she thought he was doing it only because Grandpa wanted it, expected him to keep an eye on her. On her wellbeing, of course. And to be fair, a lot of the money she later inherited was due to William's good advice about when to buy shares and when to sell them. William liked money whether real or on paper and never spent tuppence when a penny-ha'penny would suffice. Steady, that's what. William was the type of person best thought about when you were on your way to see a man who was leaving in the morning. To do that cleared your head of all foolish thoughts, because to think of her husband counting money like Ebenezer Scrooge was very sobering. Indeed, William at his most stern was a formidable man and she wondered what he would do if he knew she was going to meet a man. Because even if she called it popping in to say goodbye to Ewan and wish him all the very best, when push came to shove she was meeting another man. It was usually called a date.

The front right-hand gate of the manor still creaked when she pushed it open. The front left-hand gate still hung low on its hinges and had not been opened for years. Now it was clogged with earth and tall weeds; the drive was weed-grown, too. Poor old house that no one had wanted until war came, and would be unwanted again when the war was over. Built solid of pilfered stone, it would probably last another three hundred years, if the roof held up.

Lorna wondered if ghosts from the past ever haunted Nun Ainsty Manor. After all, it was built from priory stones, hallowed stones, which could act as a magnet to restless spirits; to the ghosts of lepers and cholera dead who probably had been buried unblessed hereabouts, too.

She was glad that when she looked up it was to see Ewan standing beside the broken statue at the top of the steps. His face wore a quizzical look.

'What is so interesting about the drive? You had such concentration on your face, Lorna.'

'It wasn't the drive, exactly. I was thinking about ghosts and spirits and what will happen to the manor when the war is over and the Army doesn't want it any more.'

'It will go back to being the sad and sorry place it was when first I came here. Your ghosts and spirits can have it to live in, then.'

He was laughing, so she laughed with him, and when she held out her hand, he kept it in his, leading her into his office.

This far, Lorna thought as she took off her jacket, it had gone splendidly; everything nice and normal and uncomplicated as indeed it should be.

'It felt chilly, out there.' Ewan set a match to the fire. 'Might as well be cheerful, on my last night.'

Lorna looked around her. Shelves were empty of books and medical paraphernalia; two half-packed boxes stood at the back of the room.

'You're taking all this with you on the train – as well as your kit?'

'Afraid so. Didn't realize I'd collected so much clobber. And there's my painting stuff, too. Stupid of me to bring it here. Might have known this billet wouldn't last for ever. But the corporal will give me a lift onto the train with it and I'll worry about getting it off when I have to. Wonder where all the porters and their trolleys disappeared to?'

'Away to war,' Lorna smiled, still at ease, still accepting that in an hour they would shake hands and say goodbye like the civilized people they were. Like ships that pass . . .

'Tea?' Ewan settled himself in the chair opposite.

'No thanks. But the first time I had tea in this room, we were conspiring to law-breaking – remember?'

'Like burning a letter, interfering with the Royal Mail? You'd got yourself pretty upset, Lorna. Do you always take other people's troubles so much to heart?'

'Oh, but what happened was *my* trouble. Alun – a blind man – trusted me with a letter, and look what I did. Do you wonder I got upset?'

'You being what you are, I suppose it's to be expected. And anyway, it all turned out for the best. Private Jones might well have lost his little nurse for all time, and that would never have done. Do you ever hear from them?'

'Just the once, to say they were looking forward to their wedding as soon as Alun was discharged from the Army. I'll probably get another when they finally make it down the aisle. It's sad to meet people and get to like them, then have the war move them on. And there's nothing anyone can do about it.'

'Like you and me, Lorna? We've got to know each other yet tomorrow I'll be moving on. Will you be sad about us?'

'I – I – yes of course I will. It's going to be strange, having another MO here. Where is he, by the way? Am I to meet him?'

'Not tonight. He's taken the truck and gone to York. Probably be late back.'

'Never mind. I'll see him around I suppose, and say hullo. What is he like?'

She was making small talk, but Ewan had asked her if she would miss him and she had answered that she would, which had been a mistake. So small talk it had to be.

'Like? Forty-ish. Walks with a slight limp. Not enough to get him his discharge, though. His leg was badly injured in the Plymouth bombing. An easy billet like this one is just what he needs right now.'

'And you, Ewan – abroad, will it be?'

'Almost certainly. Against the law of averages to get

another UK posting. And about postings – well, comings and goings, actually – I was talking to little Miss Hugwitty this morning, mentioned that I was leaving. She was hanging out washing at the farm and came to the fence for a chat.'

'Good old Martha. Never misses an opportunity to ferret out what's going on.'

'I'd gathered that, but she said something rather strange. First she told me not to worry; that my aura was good and that I'd be around at the next armistice, or words to that effect. And then she said she wondered who the third man would be. "You see, things always happen in threes," she said. "Deaths, births. And now there are two men leaving this village, so who's to be the third?" Got any ideas, Lorna?'

'N-no.' Her mind went from house to house, starting with her own. 'Only maybe the man from the middle almshouse – the commercial artist. But he's hardly ever here. Away in London, most of the time, doing something for the Ministry of Information, talk has it. Even Martha hasn't got to the bottom of what he does. Did she say anything else?'

'About the third man? Nothing, except that it's going to happen fairly soon. "Afore the year is out," she said, and to mark her words!'

'A lot of the things she predicts do come true. She believes in Ursula, though admits she's never seen her. All the same, she'll probably be right. First yourself, then Mick. Maybe the third one will be another soldier from the manor – simple as that. Martha likes her bit of drama, though even I could have worked that one out,' Lorna laughed. 'So what else is news?'

'Fresh from the War Office. I heard this morning. I've got another pip up. As from September the first I'll be a captain. What do you think of that?'

To which Lorna said she was delighted, she truly was, even though it made her wonder where William's third pip had gone.

'A mixed blessing, I suppose. A little more pay; a lot more responsibility. How are things at the farm? Is Bob having any luck with Mick's replacement?'

'No, and he's getting a bit worried,' Lorna frowned. 'Ness said it was beginning to look as if he was going to ask Goff Leaman to work at least part-time at Glebe, and Martha, too. Martha's been there since Kate broke her arm. Kate said she would gladly do farm work if Martha would take on the cooking and some of the housework. Ness and Kate could manage the herd and the hens between them and oh, Ewan, had you thought! It could be Ness leaving Ainsty! The powers-that-be could move her to any farm they want and there's nothing she could do about it!'

'Not Ness. Miss Hugwitty was adamant it would be three men, so stop worrying, Lorna, and don't listen too much to what she says. Now, who else is there to talk about?' He bent to lay logs on the fire. 'Or shall we talk about you and me? Will you write to me sometimes?'

Write? Could she? Should she? Yet who would be any the wiser? Letters could be intercepted at the post office, slipped into her pocket. William need never know.

'Well, perhaps the odd one . . .' A letter, sometimes, to a soldier serving abroad, a friendly letter. Where was the harm in it?

And that agreed, they settled themselves either side of the fire and chatted like the friends they were; talked about everything and anything and in the comfortable silences between, they listened to the soothing spit and crackle of burning logs as if the war were miles away, in some other country.

'Did you know it's past ten?' It was Ewan who shattered the idyll.

'Heavens! I hadn't realized!'

Whatever had she been thinking about to stay so long when Ewan must surely be busy and have more packing to do.

'Ssssh.' He laid a finger on her lips and smiled as if he too had only just realized their hour was long gone.

'It's getting dark. I'll see you home.' He pulled down the blind and closed the curtains.

'No! There's no need. I'll be fine. There's a moon tonight. Thanks all the same . . .'

So this was it. This was where she smiled and offered her hand and wished him well. And where she told him it had been nice knowing him. Might even add she would miss him. But she would not kiss him as she had done, had foolishly done, when last they said good night.

'I said I would walk you home.' He held out her jacket and she slipped her arms into it obediently.

'Won't be long,' he called to the corporal. 'Just seeing Mrs Hatherwood home.'

Only then did she realize she would not see him again; only then did she allow the feeling she had pretended not to exist to surface, and be faced. She said huskily,

'I'm going to miss you, and I shouldn't.'

'Why ever not?'

'Because I'm married.'

'I've always been aware of the fact, Lorna.'

He closed the front door behind them, then took her elbow, guiding her down the steps.

'Then that's fine, isn't it?' She moved a little way from him. 'And the moon is very bright. I'm sure I'll be OK now.'

'I'll see you to Ladybower,' he said stubbornly. 'And if you're so worried about being seen with me, why don't we go through the wood?'

'The *wood*?' She turned to face him. 'That wouldn't be very wise, Ewan. It might be quite dark in there and besides, how would it look if someone saw us climbing the fence back onto the Green?'

'You're determined we're going to be seen, aren't you, and that the village will be scandalized. But what makes you think Ainsty is one bit interested in you and me?'

'I don't think, I *know*. Nun Ainsty doesn't approve of women sneaking into woods with soldiers and anyway, we should act our age. We aren't teenagers, Ewan!'

'Then let's pretend we are. Let's pretend that the wood really is haunted and that I've dared you to walk through it!'

'Oh, for heaven's sake, I'm not afraid of ghosts. Not even when I *was* a teenager did Ursula bother me! And we can't stand here all night debating the point, so if you are determined to walk me home, then let's go. Through the village!'

She was trying not to laugh because she really couldn't be cross with him for not realizing what a gossipy little place Nun Ainsty could be, given half a chance.

'Hold on! Can't you take a dare, Lorna Hatherwood?'

'Of course I can! All right. Just to show you I'm not scared of Ursula, then the wood it is! But we go in the back way and leave it through the gap – the gap that leads into my garden!'

'I didn't know there was a back way.'

'You wouldn't, but there is. You take the path left from here, as if you're going into the gardens, then you turn right, halfway up it. It leads to the Saddlery, which was once the manor's stables and grooms' quarters. Then you go on to where the path is overgrown – behind the pub is as far as it goes now.'

'And that way you're making sure that no one sees us! Is it where you took your sweetheart, Lorna, when you were a teenager?'

'No, it isn't.' Come to think of it, she'd never had a sweetheart. The Saddlery twins had been too young and Rowley too awful and there'd been no one else. William had been her first young man – and her last. 'Are you getting cold feet now?'

'Absolutely not. Never let it be said a MacMillan was afraid of a poor, lovesick nun!'

'Right, then.' She reached for his hand. 'I'll go first. And it isn't a nun you need worry about. Just watch out for brambles and nettles and don't say I didn't warn you.'

All at once she felt more sure of herself; in charge. And in charge of her emotions, too, because wasn't she the stupid one, making a drama out of a walk in Dickon's Wood?

'Who does the wood belong to? Is it yours, Lorna?'

'Afraid not.' They were talking in whispers. 'It belongs to the manor, I'm almost sure. That's why it's got so neglected. There was once a path through it, but it's overgrown now. That's why there's a little gap in my boundary hedge. The path led directly to our garden, and a stile, which has also gone. Ladybower was once the dower house of the manor – where the dowager lived when her son took over. My great-grandfather bought the house from the people at the manor, but there's nothing in the deeds to say he bought the wood.'

They had stopped at a clearing beside an old beech tree. She had asked him to walk carefully, because its thick roots ran along the surface and could be dangerous to someone who did not know they were there.

'Did you know this beech was supposed to have been planted by the manor in honour of England defeating the Armada, but it couldn't have been.'

'Then could it be here that Dickon waited every saint's day for Ursula to run away with him?'

'Sorry, no. The manor hadn't even been built in Ursula's time. The Priory was still intact but roofless at the time of the Armada. There were only the almshouses hereabouts, and the little lepers' chapel. People hadn't got around to stealing the stones to build with. But legend is repeated so often, it gets to be fact.'

'Like Ursula and Dickon?'

'Exactly, though I do believe a rich York merchant once paid his daughter's marriage dowry to the priory to be rid of her. I'm surprised the Prioress took in someone supposed to be tainted by witchcraft. I've always thought they would have given her the most menial things to do, because of it. No wonder she tried to run away.'

'Lorna, do you realize we are standing in a haunted wood under a practically full moon and talking about a ghost as if she were your best friend?'

'Yes, I do. But Ursula isn't a best friend; never was, though when I was little I felt sorry for her. She's been a part of my growing up, even though I don't believe in her.'

'And that's a contradiction in terms, if you like!'

He laughed so loudly that Lorna was bound to hush him; whisper that someone might hear and then who knew what stories of ghostly laughter would fly round the village?

'Careful, Ewan.' She held out her hand again because they were coming to the brambly part.

The moonlight filtered through the trees and they could make out the silvered trunks around them, but there were parts where moss grew thickly and which would be wet with dew and slippery to walk on.

'You'll go back to the manor by the road, won't you?' She was still whispering. 'I wouldn't want you to fall into the bushes or anything.'

'Or meet up with Ursula?'

'Idiot!' She gave his hand a squeeze. 'Just follow me and mind what you're doing. We're almost there now.'

She pointed through the trees to where Ladybower's chimneys stood dark against the brightness of the sky.

'So soon it's goodbye, Lorna?'

'Yes. And here's the gap. You can hardly make it out, but I know it's there because there's a climbing rose beside it, and I can smell it.'

'Moonlight and roses. A right and proper setting for fond farewells.'

'Stop it! No fond farewells. Just so long, take care, and all that. And we're here now, so this is it, Ewan.'

She turned to face him, thinking how good he was to

look at, and how, when she remembered him it would be at this place, in the half light, with the scent of roses around them.

'Well – so long. Take care of yourself.' She held out a hand, then withdrew it hastily. 'It's been nice knowing you.'

'Can't you do better than that old cliché, Lorna?' He was speaking softly, tenderly almost. 'Can't you, just this once, forget you are a respectably married woman and say goodbye decently? One kiss? Pity to waste the moonlight and roses.'

'Don't tease, Ewan?' This was the time to go. All she need do was walk away, push through the hedge where the stile had been and into the safety of her own garden. 'Anyway, give me one good reason why you deserve a goodbye kiss?'

'Because the last one you gave me I didn't appreciate at the time.'

'So I shocked you?' Last Tuesday night! A mistake, that. 'Did you think I was forward – common?'

'Not at all. All I could think of, afterwards, was what a clot I'd been not to have kissed you back. Very thoroughly. I'd wanted to, heaven knows. I still want to.'

'Then what is a kiss between friends?' She took his face gently in her hands, softly she kissed his lips. 'Goodbye, Ewan MacMillan . . .'

That was when she should have made for the gap, conscience intact, but that was the moment she found she was no longer in charge of her head or her feet and stood there, bewildered.

'And goodbye to you, Lorna Hatherwood. Don't forget me entirely?'

He reached for her then, and she went easily into his arms, resting her cheek on his chest. His nearness did not seem wrong. They were friends who must part and she wanted, needed, him to kiss her. She raised her head, parting her lips, closing her eyes.

He held her closer, tilting her chin with a forefinger, touching her mouth gently with his own, and because she wanted the moment to last, she clasped her arms around his neck and kissed him back.

How long they stood enchanted, she did not know. All she was sure of was that this time between them would be locked away in the depths of her remembering and left, forgotten. It must be.

'I have to go,' she said softly, though she made no move to free herself from his arms. 'One last goodbye, please?'

It was her way of asking him to meet her halfway; make it easier for them both.

''Bye. Take care of yourself, Lorna.'

His mouth found hers again and she clung to him for one last, breathless moment. Then she pushed from him and ran to the gap beside the climbing rose, across the grass and down the paved path to Ladybower, and sanity.

The kitchen door was unlocked and Ness sat at the kitchen table, reading the paper. She looked up quizzically.

'So what's to do with you, queen? Been running?'

'N-no. Actually, we walked back through the wood. Creepy, in the moonlight . . .' She ran her tongue round lips gone suddenly dry. 'Did it for a dare, actually. Stupid of me, wasn't it?'

'So have the pair of you been kissin'. Your lipstick's all gone.'

'Has it? Well, I always lick it off, you know I do.'

'I asked if you'd been kissin'. him. Have you?'

'No, I haven't! You're getting as bad as Martha!'

Did it show, then? Were her eyes too bright, her cheeks too flushed? And was the throbbing in her lips plain for Ness to see?

'Kettle's still hot. Want a drink, girl?'

'Please.' She didn't, but it would give her time to pull herself together, get Ewan out of her mind.

'You're upset he's gone, aren't you, Lorna?'

'N-not upset. Sad, maybe. He was a nice man.'

'*Was*? You're talking like he doesn't exist any more. Just

because he's gone doesn't mean he's forgotten. You won't forget him, will you?' Ness persisted.

'Oh, don't probe so. OK, I'm a bit upset. Wouldn't you be if someone you knew was going abroad, into the fighting?'

'I will be, when Mick goes. No shame in that when there's a war on, is there?'

'Shame doesn't come into it, Ness. You are going to marry Mick. You're in love. Ewan and I were just friends and I'm sad he's gone if that's what you want me to say. And can you hurry up with that drink? I'll take it into the sitting room with me. I missed writing to William today.'

'So what's a day? Go to bed, girl. You look shattered.'

'Yes, but not till I've written to William. I write every day, you know I do.'

'Now see here, Lorna, you're in no fit state to be writing letters. Get yourself off to sleep. It'll all seem a lot better in the morning.'

'No. Only a few lines. I'll pop it in the York bag in the morning. There won't be any delay then.'

She was determined to write to William. It was the very least she could do. Not in need of absolution, exactly, but to help calm the panic inside her, bring her down to earth. And she would sit at her desk, tell her husband she loved him and not once glance up at the picture of shining water and foxgloves.

Friday 29th August, '41

Dear William,

Nothing much has happened today. The weather is being kind to us; today was gloriously sunny. Tonight, I did a little weeding and pruning in the garden.

Lie number one, Lorna.

Bob has still not been able to find a replacement for the farmhand who is leaving. There is talk of Martha staying on at the farm and Goff Leaman working there part-time on a regular basis.

Dammit! Why couldn't she write that Mick Hardie was going into the Medical Corps soon, and the reason for Bob being a man short at Glebe? Why couldn't she say that Mick and Ness were engaged and getting married as soon as they could make it? Because Mick was – had been – a conscientious objector and because Ness was a land girl with a Liverpool accent who had no right at all to be at Ladybower!

We have been having quite a slack time at the surgery, but Reg says not to worry. The season of coughs and sneezes will soon be upon us.

I still have not been to town to buy winter shoes: perhaps I will squander half a petrol coupon and go next Saturday.

You are not to worry about me.

And that was a good one, if you please, because William ought to be worrying like mad about her because tonight she had stood just a few yards from their home and –

I am very well, but missing you. I haven't started, yet, to count off the days to your next leave because it seems so far away. Perhaps, when October comes . . .

Take care of yourself, William. I think of you all the time.

With love,
Lorna

She had not said she loved him, but that would have to do. She had tried to make amends and from this very minute, what had happened tonight was over. In the past. Forgotten.

She addressed an envelope, stuck on a stamp, then sat chin on hands, knowing that if she let herself she would look up at the shining water and weep, though why she did not know. She had nothing to weep about. Nothing at all.

She laid the letter on the hall table, switched off the lights and went to her bedroom. She did not clean her teeth nor wash her face but lay there, looking through the uncurtained window at tree tops silver in the moonlight, wondering what Ewan was doing and if he regretted what happened tonight.

She wished she could tell Ness about it. Ness would listen, then offer the answer she wanted most to hear. Ness always did. It was why she would never tell her, because this was something that could not be shared and halved. This was a problem that for the first time in her life, it seemed, Lorna Hatherwood would have to work out for herself. If problem there was. Maybe Ewan had forgotten those kisses long before he got back to the manor.

And now, so must she.

Midnight. Another day. The day he would leave Nun Ainsty manor, and Lorna.

So why was he sitting here glowering into a dead fire instead of finishing his packing? Why was he still trying to make it all add up? Or better still, why didn't he just forget what happened in the wood, wipe it from his mind and never think of it again?

Yet he would think of Lorna often; remember the softness of her in his arms and the kisses that aroused him more than he'd intended they should. He had wanted to kiss her, come to think of it, since the first time he saw her. There was such an innocence about her that he had not been able to believe she was a married woman. A few more minutes of her nearness tonight and the sweetness of her mouth, and what might have happened was any fool's guess. Had she not been Lorna he would probably have taken advantage of her trust. Had she been some other woman, things might well have been different. But now it was over. He would not see her again, yet he would remember her always and think what might have been, had the Fates allowed.

Though she was not the entire cause of his bewilderment; not Lorna, but some other woman. He had decided to walk back through the wood, had passed the beech tree and was making for the muted sounds coming from the White Hart. His hands were deep in his pockets and his head was down when he heard footsteps. It was why he stopped, because a sudden wildness inside him made him think it was Lorna, following him.

So he turned, his heart thudding, telling himself she wanted him as much as he wanted her and that a man could only take so much. Lorna had come back to him, and he was only human, dammit.

That was when a breeze blew into his face and he smelled not roses but a strange mustiness, mingled with lavender; the way old, unwanted clothes smelled when they had lain in a chest for years.

And then she had passed him, and he saw the long, shapeless coat and the thick dark hair pulled back from her face into a plait. And eyes, not Lorna's eyes, that were black and luminous in the moonlight; lips that were sensuous and red, tilting at the corners into a small smile.

She stopped, lowered her head in a little bow and was gone, and it was then he knew he had imagined her; had hoped it would be Lorna and that his mind was playing tricks. He had been sad at their parting, so had seen – *thought* he had seen – the nun, offering her comfort as she was said to do to star-crossed lovers.

So was he star-crossed? Had Ursula come to his thoughts? Had he imagined her and not actually seen her?

Yet it was not Ursula Ainsty he had conjured up. Ursula was a nun required to walk with downcast eyes. Ursula had a cleft palate and what people called a harelip. She would have worn a habit and not a homespun coat. Nor would she have the most perfect mouth he had ever seen – apart from Lorna's, that was.

So who had the woman been, if a woman he had seen? And whose footsteps had he heard – *thought* he heard – behind him? Not Lorna's. Not Ursula's. So which physician should heal himself, drink the last of his whisky and get into bed?

Because tomorrow had already come. Lorna and yesterday were gone. Soon he would take a train north; by this time tomorrow he would be in his own bed in his parents' home in a hamlet beside Ardnamurchan. And one week from now his leave would end and he'd be on the way to God only knew where.

So away with your ghosts, Ewan MacMillan! Away with thoughts of Lorna and with the woman – the beautiful woman – in Dickon's Wood. Oh, away with that one because if he had been drinking he would have dismissed her long ago, and easily, as fantasy.

He walked to the littered desk, opened the bottom drawer and took out a bottle and glass. A good stiff drink would put him to sleep in no time at all. Dreamless sleep, if he were lucky. He raised his glass to his reflection in the cracked mirror over the fireplace.

'So here's to ghosties, Ewan, real or imagined. And here's to Lorna Hatherwood. Goodbye, darling girl. Take care . . .'

TWENTY-ONE

Lorna wrote, *Sat. September 13th '41* in the top, right-hand corner of the page.

Dear William,

This is the most beautiful afternoon. We seem to be having a little Indian summer. I am sitting in the garden without a cardigan, watching a thrush feeding on Rowan berries.

With a 'Tsk!' of annoyance she laid down her pen. 'Why should I sit here writing, when all I want to do is think how beautiful the garden still looks. The trees don't seem to be shedding their leaves yet. I wonder if it's an omen.'

'Like what?' Ness lay barefoot on the grass, eyes closed, face to the sun.

'Like summer doesn't want to go.'

'Or maybe because it's goin' to be such a rotten winter that this weather is meant as compensation in advance, sort of.'

'Then we'd best enjoy it.' Lorna closed her eyes, inhaling deeply. 'Can you smell the meadowsweet? It's thick in the lane.'

She loved the clusters of cream-coloured flowers that grew either side of Priory Lane, remembering that Gran once told her the flower had been sacred to the Druids and that it had been used to flavour mead. She said as much to Ness.

'O, ah?' Ness would rather think about tonight, and Mick, and that they were lucky that Bob had decided to postpone the cutting of the four acres of oats still standing. Bob was not a lover of oats as a crop, but the subsidy given by the Ministry of Food for growing it was not to be scoffed at. Harvesting cereals Ness could take in her stride now. It was thoughts of October, when roots – crops that grew beneath the soil – would be harvested that made Ness sigh with tiredness. Turnips, swedes for cattle fodder, potatoes and, most important to Ness's mind, sugar beet. Because sugar had to be brought here by sea and merchant ships were being sunk bringing it, which she, a Liverpudlian, knew only too well. To grow sugar beet was patriotic. To harvest it was a dirty, cold and muddy job.

And by the time the roots were in, and empty fields ploughed and left to lay fallow over winter, it would be November and Mick would be gone. An awful month, November, in more ways than one now. Ness decided not to think about it.

'Writin' to Himself, are you?'

'No Ness. I've made a start, but I'm not in the mood this afternoon. I want to make the most of the sun. Won't be many more days like this.'

She laid the writing pad beneath the wooden seat, then screwed on the top of her fountain pen. Yesterday, Jessie had told her to take Saturday afternoon off; in lieu, she said, of the overtime she would have to work when winter ailments filled the surgery waiting room.

'Kate took delivery of a hundred pullets this morning,' Ness supplied. 'The old hens will be goin' into the moult before so very much longer. Some of them are getting past laying. Kate will be putting them in the pot.'

'Oh, dear. How old is *old*, would you say?'

'Well, I reckon those six over there will be good for another year, then they won't lay so many eggs. We'll have to keep it in mind.'

'Ness! I couldn't do it!' Not eat the little hens that were a part of the family, almost, and had given them dozens of off-the-ration eggs. 'Besides, if we decided they were past it, who would – well . . .'

'Wring their necks? I suppose Goff would do it, and pluck them, too, for a couple of bob.'

'Ness! I will *not* eat those hens! I couldn't!'

'Then you can't be all that hungry. I'll bet them Russians in Leningrad wouldn't think twice about it. Short of food already and winter comes early there. Can't be a bundle of laughs, bein' under siege.'

'I suppose not. And did you see it in the paper that the Germans are being told – *told*, mind you – that it's an offence, now, to peel potatoes. Potatoes have got to be cooked in their skins, would you believe? Surely they can't be all that short of food?'

'Well, that's Hitler to blame, if they are. Shouldn't have started the war, should he? At least us Brits can still peel potatoes. Mind, we boil peelings, and feed them to the hens.' Now they were back to the hens again! 'I reckon we could keep those six of ours a bit longer. A couple more years, perhaps?'

Which made Lorna smile brilliantly and say that next Saturday morning she was going to York and did Ness want to tag along for the ride? And to which Ness smiled dreamily and said,

'No. Thanks all the same. Don't want to be tempted. I'm saving my coupons for something nice to wear for my wedding.'

'Got anything in mind?'

'Something I can get my wear out of.' Wedding dresses, which seemed not to be in the shops any more, were too much of an extravagance only to be worn once. 'Mind, women in the Forces are getting married in their uniforms, which is nice, I think.'

'Women in the Forces have no choice, unless they can

borrow a white dress and veil. They don't get clothing coupons.'

'Hmm. I suppose it being November I could get married in my walking-out clobber. Do you think a vicar would allow a bride to walk down the aisle in trousers?'

'Are you getting married so soon, then? I thought you'd resigned yourself to waiting until Mick got leave after his training was finished. Next March, you thought it would be.'

'Listen, girl, I'm getting so desperate I'd wed the man tomorrow, wearing a potato sack, if that was what it took! All I want is for us to be married. Any time. Anywhere.'

'Couldn't agree more. Live for the day.'

'So tell me – how did you feel, Lorna, when your feller went off to the Army, then?'

'Oh – you know? It wasn't as bad for me, I suppose. He'd joined the Reserve a year before war broke out – I'd seen him in uniform quite a bit. Got used to it. I remember seeing him off at the station when he got his calling up papers. Somehow, I knew he'd be all right. William always considers things very carefully, you know. I daren't have dissolved into floods of tears on the station platform. He'd have been most embarrassed. And I hadn't time to feel lonely. You came, not long after.'

'Ar, so I did.' Ness would never cease to remind herself how lucky she was. More than ever lucky, since Mick. 'And I'll try not to whinge when my turn comes. I'll only be in the same boat as a lot of other women – you included. I'll manage.'

On September 27th, which was a Saturday, Lorna delivered a buff envelope to Glebe Farm. It had *On His Majesty's Service* printed large across the top and she knew at once what was in it because it was addressed to Mick.

At ten that morning, when everyone had gathered in Glebe kitchen for drinkings, Kate took the envelope from the mantelpiece and gave it to him, unspeaking.

'Mick! Surely not yet,' Ness whispered, to which Rowley said he wouldn't be surprised if it was calling-up papers, and what was That Lot thinking about, sending for him when there were still the roots to be harvested?

Mick read the single sheet of paper then said,

'Monday, November 24th. Travel warrant and further instructions follow by post later. That's it, then. Sorry, Ness love, but we knew this would happen.'

'Yes, but they didn't have to tell you yet!'

'Never mind. At least now we know. You said I could have a week off beforehand, Bob. Is that still all right?'

'You're taking all this much too calmly, Mick Hardie.' Ness's voice trembled with tears. 'It's only –' She walked over to the calendar hanging beside the fireplace. 'Only eight weeks, then that's it! The Army!'

'Then we'd better count on six,' Bob said quietly. 'I reckon Mick should have a couple of weeks with his folks.'

'*Two* weeks! Can we spare him? We'll be right in the middle of –'

'Yes, I know, Rowley. Up to the armpits in sugar beet. But I reckon Mick should go a couple of weeks before. He's been a good worker and he'll be missed. Wondered what we were getting when we knew you were coming, lad, but now I'm right sorry you're going.'

'Sorry! And what are we to do, then, till a replacement comes?' Rowley was red-faced now, and scowling.

'*If* one ever comes. Reckon we'll have to be content with Martha and Goff. They'll do their best, they said. And think on, son – you're sitting out the war here at Glebe, so I reckon you're the last one to complain.'

'But farming is just as important as soldiering, Dad! I'm in a reserved occupation – nothing to be ashamed about in that!'

'No. But Mick was in a reserved occupation, an' all.' Kate sent her son a shut-up glare. 'He didn't have to leave here. Give him credit for that and stop being so worried you'll have to work a bit harder. We all will. There's a war on, remember, and Mick is away to join it soon. And I'm right sorry he's leaving.'

'Then let's work things out.' Bob joined Ness at the calendar. 'And let's hear no more about it from anybody. You'll be leaving us on the tenth, Mick, and you Ness will have your leave on the seventeenth. Sorry I can't give you the extra time, too, but I can't be two hands down, not for two weeks. Is that all right with you?'

'As right as it'll ever be, Bob. And do you mind if I leave my tea, Kate? Could do with a breath of fresh air . . .'

Ness ran from the kitchen, eyes bright with tears and Kate glared at Mick and said,

'Well, off you go, lad! The lass is in need of a shoulder to cry on. Give her a bit of a hug, eh? And as for you, our Rowley, you just watch what you say, 'cause it's my belief you were at the bottom of all this!'

'*Me*? I don't know what you mean!'

'Oh, but you do. It wasn't long after Mick was obliged to give you a sorting out that he was talking about going into the Army. If you'd behaved yourself and kept your feelings in check, this might never have happened. So be prepared to take on more'n your fair share of his work!'

At which Rowley slammed his mug on the table and walked out because no one, not even his father, was a match for his mother when she had a mood on her. No one ever gainsaid Kate Wintersgill and got away with it lightly! Give him credit at least, for being a quick learner!

Mick found Ness in the dairy, lips set stubbornly against tears.

'Sorry, sweetheart.' He folded her in his arms and laid his cheek on her hair. 'Didn't expect it to be so final, so soon. But we've known all along it would be about the end of November.'

'Suppose so. But seeing it in black and white brought it home a bit. And you'll like it, having a week extra at home.'

'I will. There'll be plenty to think about, a lot to do. And then you'll be there and we'll have the most marvellous week, I promise you.'

'You don't sound too put out, Mick Hardie,' she sniffed.

'Oh, I am, darling, but like I said, there'll be things to do at home and people to see. I'll worry about the Army when I've got to. After all, it was my choice. I was doing a decent job here at Glebe, if you count it in terms of the war effort. But the time came to move on, so as long as they don't order me to fire a gun, then I'll put all my efforts into being a medic. The only thing that's going to bug me is that you'll be here and I'll be God knows where, and for how long. It'll hurt a lot, Ness, saying goodbye.'

'Yes, but when the time comes, we mustn't say goodbye. It's bad luck, don't forget.' She whispered a kiss on his cheek. 'And we'll have to work out some kind of code so that if you are sent overseas –'

'*When* I'm sent overseas, I'll find a way of letting you know where I am without the Censor cutting lumps out of my letters. And as from now, we have six weeks before I leave here, so tell me you love me?'

'You know I do. I adore you, Mick Hardie.' She closed her eyes and lifted her lips to his. 'And I'm all right now; over the shock. So kiss me, please?'

'So how did things go this morning?' Lorna hung her jacket on the kitchen door peg. 'Was the letter anything to do with Mick's call-up?'

'It was. Knocked the stuffing out of me, for a bit. Mind, we'd both been expecting it, but to see it in black and white, all impersonal and final – I felt like yelling my head off.'

'But you didn't.'

'No. Bob was very decent about it; said Mick could finish at Glebe two weeks beforehand – November twenty-fourth the letter said.'

'You'll be seeing him tonight?'

'He's calling for me here at half past seven – if that's all right, Lorna? There's a hop in Meltonby. Rowley said they've hired a decent band, for a change. He's going, too – taking his girlfriend. I heard him tell Kate he'll be wearing his Home Guard uniform. Suppose he thinks he'll pass as a soldier, cheeky little devil. How's William, by the way?'

'Fine, as far as I know. There wasn't a letter this morning.'

'What! No Saturday epistle!'

'No. But it often happens that mailbags are delayed – bombing along the way, or something. I know for a fact the mails from London aren't at all reliable.'

'You don't seem much bothered.'

'I'm not. There'll be a good reason for it. If anything awful had happened, William – or someone – would have phoned.'

'Ar,' Ness nodded, at a loss for words because once, the non-arrival of the Saturday letter would have upset Lorna. But maybe Lorna was getting used to William being away and letters sometimes arriving late. It happened all the time. 'It'll turn up on Monday,' she comforted.

'I'm sure it will. And tonight or tomorrow there just might be a phone call, explaining. And for all the news he puts in letters, I think I'd much rather have a phone call. So when you go to meet Mick's folks, will you take a nice dress with you? I know the weather will be cold, but you're sure to go dancing.'

'Good idea. Mind, I'll have to go down there in my uniform 'cause I'll be travelling on a railway warrant. But once I'm there, I won't be wearing it again till – well, till my leave is over.'

'Good idea. You'll want warm civvy clothes, though. Will you write home for some, or better still and to save the bother, why don't you take some of mine? You'd be very welcome, and what fits me fits you.'

'Could I, Lorna? I'd take good care of them. You're sure?'

'I've just said so, haven't I? The plaid pleated skirt and red twinset would suit you fine. And why don't you take my grey costume? You'll have to look smart when Mick takes you around the relations, don't forget. Mind, you look great in your walking-out uniform, but Mick will still be wearing civvies. He's not in the Army yet. Oops! Sorry! Stupid thing to say, wasn't it?'

'No, queen. Don't go round as if you're walking on eggshells. Mick is going into the Army soon, and nothing is going to change it. And thanks for the offer of the clothes, Lorna.'

'You're welcome. There's one dress I'd particularly like you to take. It's short, mind, but you've got good legs. A cocktail dress. I last wore it when Ewan and I went to Reg and Jessie's – the time Ewan brought venison back with him from leave, and –'

Her voice trailed away, because it was not the first time today she had thought about Ewan MacMillan. There had been this morning, too, at the manor. This morning the sergeant in the kitchen had a pot of tea already made and two cups beside it.

'Now don't tell me you haven't got time to have a cuppa, Mrs Hatherwood. You always seem to be in a hurry these mornings. Frightened of the new MO, are you?'

And she had been obliged to stay, though she wasn't one bit afraid of meeting the new medical officer; just that when she did, it wouldn't be Ewan. And that had made her sad.

'And *what*?' Ness said, uncannily invading her thoughts. 'Tell me what you was thinkin' about, just now? Big eats with off-the-ration venison, or was it Ewan?'

'Neither, as a matter of fact.' She was getting good at evading Ness's bluntness. 'I was thinking, if you must know, about the cook at the manor. I sometimes stop for a cup of tea with him, that's all. And don't ask me why I was thinking about him, because I don't know.'

'You were thinkin' about him because you'd been talking

about going out with Ewan and you straight away thought about him not being at the manor any more. Association of ideas, it is. I'm not just a pretty face, you know! Have you heard from him, by the way?'

'No, I haven't.' Drat Ness. She was getting as bad as Martha! 'And I don't expect to.'

Of course Ewan wouldn't write. He'd said he would, but after what happened in the wood, any man with an iota of sense would cut and run. After all, those kisses had not been the goodbye-between-friends type.

'Why not, queen?'

'Because we were friends, that's all. Ships that pass in the night I suppose you'd call us. Now, do you want to get changed whilst I make supper? If Mick is calling at half seven, you'll have to get a move on.'

She had never danced with Ewan, Lorna brooded as she peeled potatoes. Ness was lucky, going out with a man she adored, dancing close, cheek on cheek and not caring who saw them. Tonight, Ness would come home very late, eyes bright, cheeks flushed.

And what would Lorna Hatherwood do? She would wash up after supper, then sit at the kitchen table and write to William. And she would make sure the door was wide open so she would be able to hear the telephone when William rang. If he rang. Which he wouldn't.

And oh, wasn't her life just one big bundle of laughs, and wasn't she sick, sick, *sick* of this bloody war!

On Monday, which was also Michaelmas Day and important for all kinds of reasons if you lived in the country, Lorna unfastened the string on the Nun Ainsty bundle and spread the letters on the sorting table.

As if drawn to it, she picked out the buff envelope with William's writing on it. She had known all along it would be there and instead of slipping it in her pocket she slit it open, just to make sure that all was well. And it was.

She read it quickly then lingered her eyes on the postscript at the end of the page.

P.S. Was holding this back, awaiting a date. Leave just confirmed. Seven days from Tuesday 18 Nov.

So it was all right. Nothing to worry about. She stuffed the letter in her jacket pocket and began sorting.

The oats had been cut, dried and carted into the gantry to await threshing. Now it was October and potato harvest had begun. The mild autumnal weather was holding, the soil was dry.

Ness remembered last year's potato lifting and sodden earth sticking to her gumboots so it had seemed she had lead weights in them. And cold, soil-caked hands and Rowley being a pig, doing as little of the stooping, bending and heaving as needs be, never missing a chance to belittle Mick.

Things were different this year. Rowley had learned the hard way to watch his manners and she, Ness, had fallen deeply in love. Yet in four weeks, Mick would leave Glebe Farm, so they must be together every minute they could and try not to count the days that seemed now to fleet past.

Lorna was not counting, either. Time for marking off the days when November came, she had said last night.

'Goodness only knows what we will do, Ness. November isn't the best of months anyway, and they'll be busy at the surgery. I shall feel awful asking for time off. And I know that by rights, Mrs Benson should give me a week off, too. A married woman is entitled to time off when her husband is on leave. But goodness only knows who she would get to do the Ainsty round. Reckon I just won't ask . . .'

Besides, Lorna had pointed out, William would not mind her doing mornings. William only disliked the alarm waking him so early in the morning. And if she did the delivery at a gallop, she could be back home in time to cook his breakfast.

That had been last night, Ness shrugged, with Lorna in one of her uncertain moods, and this was another day; one day nearer November 24th, and twelve sacks of potatoes – about as many as the small truck would hold – stood ready for loading.

'Listen, you two,' she said, as if she were used to giving orders, 'how about loading the sacks, then I'll take them to the yard.'

'Hey! Stop being so bossy, Ness Nightingale,' Rowley scowled.

'Well, you can please yourself, but if you want me to bring drinkings back with me, young master, you'd best get heaving!'

'All right, then. And ask Mum for some dripping toast, whilst you're about it.' It was Rowley's way of giving in gracefully. 'And maybe Dad will give a hand here when the milking is finished.'

'And maybe he'll still be busy, so don't bank on it!'

As Rowley heaved the last potato sack on the truck, Ness stood on tiptoe and, unseen, kissed Mick gently, smiling into his eyes.

'And what was that for?' he smiled.

'Oh, just because I wanted to.'

And because, truth known, it was for the day he could no longer be with her; gathering rosebuds, she supposed.

She started the engine, driving carefully towards the field gate. That was something else she had learned. Now, she could drive a tractor. Soon, Bob said, she must apply for a driving licence so she could take it on the road, and since driving tests had been suspended for the duration, it would present no problem.

The only problem Ness could see, was how to drive between the gateposts without mishap, because if she got it wrong, she would have to reverse and try again, and going backwards with a load behind her was not Ness Nightingale's strong point. Especially with Rowley watching.

She exited the field magnificently and made for the farmyard, triumph singing through her. She was so happy, here at Glebe. If only she need not count off days, life in this hidden-away little world would be marvellous. But you couldn't have it all ways, so count your blessings, Ness girl!

She slowed, eyes steady ahead for the farmyard gateposts, and manoeuvred through them with aplomb.

'Hi!' she called to Kate who stood in the kitchen doorway. 'Where does Bob want this lot, then? And the workers in the top field could do with tea and dripping toast, please!'

Oh, yes. She could be deliriously happy; would be, if she could turn back the clock to last year's potato harvest; mud, Rowley and all. And if she had known, then, what she knew now.

Lorna frowned at the calendar hanging on the side of the kitchen dresser, trying to work out the hieroglyphics on it. Today's date, the ninth, was circled in red and beside it, written small, was M sup 7. And below it a cross in black and the figure ten, which all meant that tonight Mick was coming to supper at seven, and that in ten days' time William would be home on leave.

'Would you like to bring Mick for a meal?' she had asked of Ness. 'I know it's his last night and that maybe you might rather go to the pub or for a walk somewhere or –'

'Or come to supper? Ladybower wins hands down,' Ness had accepted eagerly. 'It would be lovely. It's so cold outside.'

Nights began early in November. Gone were the bright mornings with the sun already shining even as she set out for Meltonby. Gone, too, the birdsong and hedgerows thick with flowers, and swallows flying high. Now it was early darkness and skimpy fires and bitterly cold bedrooms and tomorrow, Lorna frowned, she would stow Mick's luggage in her car and take him to Meltonby and the early bus to York that waited outside the post office. Ness had said it was best she should not go with them; she wanted their parting kiss to be at the front gate, so she could stand there when he was gone, listening as the car drove into the darkness.

'I shall tell myself,' she had said, 'that in a week I'll be with him again.'

And she had said there would be no tears, because tomorrow, November 10th was not the end of the world. Monday, November 24th *was*.

Ness opened the kitchen door, closing it quickly behind her, blinking her eyes in the sudden glare of light. She found Lorna consulting the calendar.

'Hi, Ness. I'm just working things out. According to all this scribble, it's ten days to William's leave and in the morning I'm giving Mick a lift to the bus – Bob having deposited him and his baggage at Ladybower's gate. And the following week,' she added quickly, on seeing the sadness in Ness's eyes, 'I will be doing the same for you; getting you to the bus that drops you off outside the station. Then it'll be all systems go to Exeter, and seven days with Mick.'

'You're a smashing lady, Mrs Hatherwood,' Ness smiled. 'And you don't have to go to so much trouble. Will the rations run to one extra for supper?'

'You bet. Take a quick peep.' Lorna opened the oven door. 'I'm doing what the Ministry of Food leaflet said we should all do and not lighting the oven for just one item. You will see, therefore, large potatoes jacketing on the top shelf, a rabbit stew in the middle, and doing nice and gently on the bottom shelf, a baked custard.

'So tonight, at the risk of being locked up for wasting electricity, I switched on the immersion so you can have a lovely soak and get all the soil from under your fingernails. And don't bother about only six inches. Be a devil and have as much bathwater as you like!'

'Bless you.' Ness smiled shakily. After a cold, earthy day in the sugar beet field, a deep, hot bath would be forbidden heaven. 'And thanks for taking Mick to the bus tomorrow. You'll be using your petrol ration and don't think we don't appreciate it.'

Come to think of it, next time she was home, she would have a word with Uncle Perce. Perce was good at getting things. Maybe he could come by the odd petrol coupon.

'The least I can do, Ness, and anyway, that little car goes a mile on a squirt of petrol, though don't tell William, will you? I usually manage to wheedle a coupon out of him when he's home. I think he's grateful that I don't ask how he manages to get enough petrol to drive that big car around Aldershot, and to drive it all the way up here as well! But get off upstairs and make yourself beautiful. I'm going out after supper, by the way. Nance wants a word about helping the WVS with collection boxes. Sorry there isn't coal to spare for a fire in the sitting room.'

'Goin' out? Who are you kidding? But it's smashing of you, queen. And we wouldn't expect a fire in the parlour, though next time there's a gale we'll go into the wood, eh, and gather branches for logs – like we were doing the day we bumped into Ewan – remember?'

'Er – no. Did we?'

'You know we did. He was drawing trees.'

Sketching bare branches – of course Lorna remembered. How could she not remember, and more so now, since the night she had run from him to the safety of her own garden. Hardly a day passed but that she remembered Ewan MacMillan. And her husband coming on leave in little more than a week! What a mess her mind was in, and how hard it was going to be to get Ewan out of it!

'Of course. Drawing trees. Quite an artist, Ewan was.' He was in the past now. And one day, when she could find the courage, she would take down the painting above her desk and never look at it again. 'So are you going to run that bath, Ness Nightingale, or aren't you!'

* * *

'So glad you've managed to come, Lorna. We don't seem to have had a chat for ages. Both of us busy winning the war, eh?'

Nance Ellery stood at her front door. Unlike most Yorkshire people who always used the back door, Nance received only at the front.

'Suppose that's it. But being busy helps the days along.'

'So it does. Have you time to stay a while? I always enjoy a little chat when Gilbert is out – he's Home Guarding tonight. Well now,' she wriggled herself comfortable in the plush-covered easy chair in her sitting room. She did not use her coal ration, as most did, for the kitchen fire. Instead, she cooked on the gas stove and when the kitchen became unbearably cold in winter she used a paraffin stove to heat it – which smelled awful, Lorna always thought, and gave out black fumes. 'Thanks for taking a collecting box. You'll do Ainsty and Meltonby?'

'Ainsty. William is coming home next week, so I won't be able to do Meltonby,' Lorna said firmly, thinking that once, no matter what, she would have found time to do exactly as she was told, so intimidating had she found Nance.

'Ah, well. It all helps, no matter how little. And I ran into your cleaning lady in the post office yesterday. She told me her husband will be on leave, too.'

'Yes. Exactly the same dates as William and Ness.'

'Well! Isn't that convenient? Not having anyone under your feet when you want to be alone together, I mean.'

'Together. Of course. And Minnie's husband is a corporal now.'

'Splendid. Have you met the new medical officer at the manor, by the way?'

'No, though I suppose I will eventually in my official capacity as post lady and newspaper boy.'

'Hm. Funny, that, when you knew Lieutenant MacMillan rather well, I believe.'

'So I did, Nance. Don't forget I used to go to the manor

to read to the blind soldiers. Oh, and yes! I went out with him a couple of times.'

'You did *what*? I didn't know about it. Did you stop to think about the danger of going on dates, and you a married woman, Lorna!'

'You didn't know about it because I didn't tell you, until now. Martha knew, though. She saw him pick me up at Ladybower in the Army truck,' Lorna said, eyes wide with mischief.

'B-but you don't seem very concerned about it. I mean – William home next week and sure to find out. It wasn't very wise of you, was it?'

'William knows. I told him.' Lorna was enjoying the pained expression on the older woman's face, even though she had to admit that though William knew she had been to dinner twice at the surgery, she had not mentioned Ewan being there, too. Yet now, crazily, she was telling the village crier about it and feeling not one iota worried. 'Oh, dear. I forgot to tell you. On both occasions we were invited to supper by Jessie Summers. Ewan very thoughtfully gave me a lift there. Twice. All above board. We were well chaperoned!'

'My dear! I'm not meaning – I wasn't hinting that anything improper might have happened. I know you too well for that!'

'Of course you do, Nance. And Lieutenant MacMillan is a captain now.'

'You hear from him, then?'

'Of course I don't. He told me about the promotion before he left.'

'Ah. You've heard about Rowley Wintersgill?' Defeated, Nance changed direction abruptly. 'You'll have heard about him and Olivia Smithson?'

'That they're going out together and that Olivia has been to Sunday tea at Glebe Farm? Ness told me.'

'Ah, yes. But had you heard there could be an announcement? Seems Rowley is very keen!'

'Engaged? But I thought Rowley just loved 'em and left 'em.'

'Oh my word no, Lorna. Not this time around. The Smithson girl can't be called a beauty by any manner of means, but she's got things going for her – if talk is to be believed.'

'*What* things? That she's eager for a husband? Heavens!' Lorna giggled. 'She must be if she even considers Rowley!'

'Not exactly. I don't think the lad is having it all his own way, for all that. He's getting frustrated. Miss Olivia is keeping her hand on her ha'penny till he comes up with a ring. I heard that on very good authority. Mind, the girl isn't as attractive as Rowley's last fling – the soldier's wife in Meltonby, I'm talking about.'

'You know about that one, too?' My, but there wasn't much escaped Nance Ellery!

'I know he was nearly caught with his pants down,' Nance smirked. 'And I'll take bets on Olivia. Dumpy and a tad gormless she might be, but she has one big attraction – being an only child and her father's money. He's got the biggest acreage around these parts. Mark my words, Lorna, she's got Rowley hooked, but not a word to your land girl. Wouldn't want it to get back to Kate. And what about the land girl, eh? Her and the conchie engaged, I believe.'

'Nance! Mick isn't an objector now, as you well know!' Lorna looked at the mantel clock and decided that at nine forty-five on the dot, she would pick up the collection tin and leave. 'And yes, they are engaged, though Ness doesn't wear a ring; not much point when it could so easily get lost. And they're hoping to get married, soon; maybe in spring. He's leaving Glebe in the morning, did you know? Joins the Medical Corps at the end of the month.' She stopped only to draw breath, then rushed on. 'Mick's parents live in Devon. Ness is going to meet his family next week. Did you know that when the war is over, Mick will be an architect?' Useless snippets, eagerly gobbled up by Nance. 'And did you know he has twin sisters? One a nurse and the other in the ATS?'

'I didn't.' Nance's eyes glowed. 'Mind, I've known all along that Rowley had designs on Ness Nightingale and he and Mick Hardie came to blows over her!'

'That's right. And Ness got in their way and got a black eye for her pains. Common knowledge, Nance.'

But oh, Lorna yearned inside her, wouldn't it be marvellous if she could tell the truth of it and to see her ignite and go off like an eager, gossip-laden rocket? But for Ness's sake – Kate and Bob's, too – the truth was best forgotten.

'Mm. Nice to think that the con— that Mick Hardie got the fair lady. A handsome young man if ever I saw one. The MO at the manor was a good-looker, too, wouldn't you agree, my dear?'

'Yes, I would.' What the heck, Lorna! Tell the truth and shame the devil! 'Very handsome. Ewan is a gifted artist, too. He gave me a watercolour, a thank you for helping at the manor. You must remind me to show it to you, when you next call.'

And he kisses like – but she couldn't say that to Nance, because what happened in Dickon's Wood was not a useless snippet to be passed around Ainsty. It was something that should never have happened, yet something she would never regret.

'Call? Now I just might find time to do that – when William has gone back to his regiment. You'll be in need of cheering up, then, won't you? Yes! I'll most certainly call – do my duty as a friend and neighbour. And Lorna' – she shifted uneasily in her chair – 'there's something I've always meant to say to you, but never got around to it. You see, I've known you almost all your life; known you since your – since your grandparents brought you here to live with them. So that almost makes me an aunt – or a godmother, don't you think?'

'We-e-ll, yes. And since I have no living relations that I

know of, I wouldn't mind the odd aunt. But what do you want to say to me, Nance?'

'Well, just that having no children of my own, I've watched you grow up with affection, and knowing that William isn't always at hand, now, for you to lean on, I want you to feel – if ever the need arose, of course – that you can always count on me if you need an older person to confide in. And yes, I'll admit to being a bit of a gossip – damn all else to do in this village – but I do know when to keep it shut.' She placed a forefinger across her lips.

'Yes. Of course, Nance. Most kind of you.' Good grief! Surely Nance couldn't know – couldn't even suspect – about Dickon's Wood and the kisses? The goodbye kisses. 'If ever I needed to confide, then I'm sure you would be the first person I would turn to. And it's kind of you to offer, but what made you say it, will you tell me? You're not turning into another Martha? *Feelings*, sort of?'

'Heaven forbid! And goodness only knows why I said it. I suppose it's just that sometimes you look so girlish and vulnerable. And William away at the war and you having to cope on your own.'

'But I'm not alone. I've got Ness. And I'm only the same as half the women in this country. Minnie, for instance. She had to learn to get on with it – and two children into the bargain.'

'Yes. But you and Minnie Holmes are quite different. Minnie's father was killed in the last war. She was reared on a widow's pension; not like you, Lorna. And that's Gilbert shutting the front gate. He's back early! Amazing how those Home Guard parades seem to finish just before the White Hart closes!'

'It's past ten, Nance. I'd better be going.' Lorna shrugged into her coat, knotted her headscarf under her chin, then picked up the collecting tin. 'I've enjoyed our chat.'

'Good. And I'll be sure to call on you when William's leave is over.' Affectionately, amazingly, she kissed Lorna's cheek.

'Just stay long enough to say hullo and goodnight to the man of the house, will you – then take care how you go in the dark. Watch out for the duck pond. Oh, how I do dislike the blackout! So dangerous . . .'

Ness was sitting, chin on hand, at the table when Lorna opened the kitchen door.

'Hullo, love. Cheer up, eh?'

'Mick's just gone. A wonder you didn't bump into him. And I'm all right, Lorna. No need for the mother hen look. I'll be seeing him again in a week. "Think Exeter station," he said. "I'll be waiting for you." I'll tell you something – he wasn't much put out when I kissed him at the gate.'

'Men never are, Ness. Against their upbringing to show emotion.'

' "Don't get up in the morning to wave me off," he said, but I will Lorna, so give me a shake when your alarm goes?'

'If you're sure?'

'That I want one more quick kiss? Sure I'm sure. Then I'll wish like mad for next week to fly. And when it has, I'll be on my way to Devon and your William will be home. It's all go at Ladybower, innit?'

And Lorna agreed that it was and said why didn't they have a mug of Ovaltine since Ness had so sneakily appropriated a two-pint can of milk?

And they laughed, because you had to laugh these days, if only over two mugs of under-the-counter milk. If you didn't, then the only alternative was tears.

Ness, all at once cold, hugged her dressing-gown round her and made for the kitchen. She had waited with Lorna for the sound of Glebe tractor, then ran to Mick's arms, kissing him in the darkness, whispering, 'I love you. See you. Take care,' whilst Bob made sure that the cases were safely stowed on the rack of Lorna's little car. Then he had taken Mick's hand and wished him luck and said he was right sorry he'd decided to go and not to forget Glebe Farm, and the folk there.

And Ness had stood, listening to the sound of the tractor and trailer clanking off and to the protesting purr of the overloaded little car as it made for the red bus that would be waiting outside Meltonby post office.

She walked quickly up the path, banging the kitchen door behind her, blinking in the sudden brightness. Mick was gone but a minute and she felt lonely already. No Mick now, at morning milking nor in Kate's kitchen for ten o'clock drinkings. Nor would he be there for midday dinner nor beside her in the cold of the potato field. Nor ever again tossing and turning hay or making sheaves of wheat into stooks.

In two weeks' time, the man she loved so deeply would join a war he did not believe in. Because of what happened in Kate's kitchen, Mick had turned his back on his beliefs and enlisted in the Army, though to help save lives rather than take them. Darling, wonderful Mick. How much she had longed these last few days for him to take her; belonging would have made parting just that little easier. But they had decided, in a moment of unnatural reason, to wait until they were married. If they could, of course. Yet now it seemed they would have no choice. Not for a week, that was – then who knew what might happen?

'I love you, Mick Hardie,' she said out loud to the cold, uncaring kitchen. 'I always will.'

Then she shook away the tears that had threatened since Lorna parped a goodbye on her horn as the car drew away. In a week she and Mick would be together again and even when that week was over, there would be letters to write and, fingers-crossed, phone calls to hang around waiting for – just in case. And then, when Mick had done his training, there would be another leave in spring. Would it be then they would marry?

She made for the stairs, taking them two at a time, washed,

then quickly dressed. So what the heck? She wasn't due at Glebe for another hour, but her need to be near someone, feel the warmth of Kate's kitchen and maybe a mug of tea and a slice of dripping toast became almost overpowering, because it stood to reason, didn't it, that the sooner she got herself off to work, the sooner the day would pass and the sooner she would be on that train.

'See you in Exeter, Mick,' she whispered as she closed the door behind her, then stood for the obligatory fifteen seconds to blink her eyes to get them adjusted to the unyielding darkness. 'See you soon, my darling.'

TWENTY-TWO

Ness watched the unfamiliar landscape slip by. All was drab with winter, yet it might as well be high summer in Glebe Farm's hayfield, so warm-hearted and happy was she. Soon, more than an hour late because trains were always late these days, they would stop at Exeter station and Mick would be there. Happiness wriggled through her. Just a week ago she had felt alone and depressed, determined to work until she dropped if that was what it took to make the time pass quickly. She had been toasting bread at the fire in Glebe Farm kitchen when Lorna opened the door, laying newspaper and letters on the table.

'Anything important in it?' She winked at Kate who had taken the hint and sorted through the envelopes.

'Well, goodness me! Him not an hour gone and here's a letter for Miss A Nightingale!'

'I told you last night I hadn't seen him, but I did, Ness. He was going to post a letter but gave it to me instead. Asked if the nice postlady could deliver it for him first thing in the morning,' Lorna laughed.

'There now,' Kate beamed. 'I reckon the nice postlady deserves tea and dripping toast by way of a thank you. Ness, lass, will you toast a slice more bread – if you can manage to come down to earth, that is.'

Then all at once it was a lovely morning on which to be alive and have friends like Lorna and Kate and a man who loved her and wanted her every bit as much as she loved and wanted him.

'I'll read it later.' She stuffed the envelope into the back pocket of her dungarees. And she would hold out against reading it, because just to feel it there, crackling as she moved, would be like unfastening every knot in the string around her birthday present parcel, just to prolong the excitement.

It was eleven o'clock when she had wiped clean the last of a bucket of eggs and set them with more care than usual into papier mâché trays, when she gave in, and opened it.

Sweetheart,

When you read this letter you'll be goodness only knows where. The kitchen, the dairy or maybe in the far potato field. Wherever and whenever, it is to tell you how much I will miss you until the 17th.

Did I tell you I love you? I love you, love you, love you. I always will,

Mick

And at a little past eleven on that cold November morning, Ness had clasped her hands together and closed her eyes tightly and whispered,

'Please God, *please* let Mick come safely back from the war. I love him so much. Take care of him?'

And that was something, if you like! Ness Nightingale, who could take God or leave Him, praying as if her life depended on it. Or Mick's life . . . ?

People were beginning to move, to take cases from racks and shrug into coats, and servicemen to collect kitbags from the pile at the end of the corridor.

They were approaching Exeter. All at once excited she pushed her way to the door to scan the platform as the train slowed and squealed juddering to a stop.

'Darling!' She saw him way down the platform, head and shoulders above most. He was wearing a thick jacket and had a scarf wound round his neck. 'Mick! Here!'

And then she was in his arms, eyes closed, loving the familiar nearness of him. And it was as if they had never spent a week apart because their kiss wiped out all the long days between.

'Mick, I've missed you.'

'And I've missed you, my darling. And I've got a surprise for you, but you can't see it just yet.'

'Something nice?'

'I think so. Very nice.' He picked up her case, then fingers entwined, they left the platform. 'We'll get a bus to Borton just down the road. On the hour and half past the hour. Not long to wait. Mum's looking forward to meeting you. Sorry Maddy and Lydia won't be there. Maddy is taking her finals and the Army doesn't give compassionate leave for meeting fiancées.'

'Well, you haven't even been to Ruth Street yet. It's the war to blame. And can't you give just a little hint about my surprise?'

'Not just yet.' He kissed the tip of her nose. 'And here's the bus stop. They're pretty well on time, our local buses.'

They joined the queue, at the back, then Ness whispered,

'I'm so excited to be here, but do you think your folks will like me, Mick? I'm a bit nervous about meeting your Mam.'

'After what I've told them about you they love you already. And Ness, let's make this leave very special, shall we?'

'Every bit as special as we can.' She moved nearer so her lips were close to his ear. 'I want you. I'm tired of waiting.'

'Me, too. We'll have to see what we can do about it.' He stepped a little way from her then, smiling into her face. 'It's been a long week, Ness. Nun Ainsty has seemed so far away.'

'It is. More than eight hours on the train away, but everything's fine now.'

She thought briefly about the faraway village, and about Lorna who would be thinking about tomorrow, when William would arrive on leave.

Then she smiled contentedly, because she and Mick were together again. Darling Mick – who had a surprise for her.

Ladybower shone. It smelled of beeswax polish and chrysanthemums picked from the garden. Today, Ness had left for Devon. Tomorrow, around noon, Lorna thought, William would arrive and meantime there was nothing to do but wait. She wished she could have done an old-fashioned bake – cakes, pies and scones – but baking days were out, for the duration. It was unpatriotic even to think longingly of them.

She was debating whether to make a very small pot of tea or drink a glass of water, which was more patriotic and better for her health, anyway, when the knocker sounded through the kitchen. Four times, and firmly brought down on the back door.

She hurried to answer it, remembering that Goff Leaman had promised her a rabbit, if he could lay hands on one.

'Goff?' She squinted into the darkness, because lights must be switched off before opening an outside door. 'Is it –'

'It's Primrose Smythe-Parker. Can I come in?'

'Sergeant – er – yes, of course. Come in . . .' Quickly Lorna closed the door then switched on the light. 'Er – you'll be on leave, too?' It was all she could think of to say. 'I mean, last time William was home you –'

'That's right. I gave him a lift back to barracks. We were both recalled a day early.'

'Yes. We-e-ll, how can I help you, Sergeant?'

'I rather wanted to talk to your husband, Mrs Hatherwood. He's on leave, isn't he?'

'Not until tomorrow. Surely he told you?'

'No. I didn't know. I'm not at Aldershot now. I must have got it wrong.'

'I'm afraid you have. I'm expecting him any time after midday tomorrow. Where are you stationed now?'

She was making polite conversation now, but politeness cost nothing, Lorna supposed. And anyway, Sergeant Smythe-Parker made her feel uneasy – and in her own kitchen, too!

'I'm not. Stationed anywhere, I mean. I left the Army a week ago. Discharged. Medical grounds.'

'Then I'm sorry. Nothing too serious, I hope.' This was becoming embarrassing. 'I mean – well, you don't look too bad.'

'I'm fine. One gets on with things. I'll go now. I'm sure you are busy.'

'Well, yes. Have been. Just finished. Was wondering if I could spare a spoonful of tea. Would you like a cup? You must have driven quite a way, in the dark. At least stay and –'

'Thank you, no. And I live only a few miles from here. No problem. Will you ask your husband to give me a ring as soon as he can? He knows my number.'

'Yes. Of course.'

She was bossy and arrogant, Lorna thought, as she opened the back door. Sergeant Primmy Parker could well develop into another Nance Ellery, given time. And why did she want William to ring her?

'Thank you, Mrs Hatherwood. Good night.'

'Well!' Lorna shook her head in bewilderment. Walking in like she were still a sergeant, giving orders! She lowered herself into the wooden rocking chair, concerned that maybe being discharged from the Army on medical grounds was serious, and made you a bit edgy? Perhaps she should feel sorry for her? She closed her eyes, wishing that Ness were here – which was pretty stupid because by now Ness would be with Mick in Devon and wouldn't take kindly to being wished back to Nun Ainsty.

Primrose, Lorna frowned. A strange name for someone so tall, so angular. Even wearing a pleated skirt and a powder-blue jumper, she was no modest flower. But it was a pity she was ill. Perhaps William would know what was wrong. After all, they had worked together.

Lorna got to her feet, said, 'Blow it!' and set the kettle to boil. One small spoonful of tea! Surely just this once she could spare it? And didn't she deserve it after so strange an encounter?

But it would all be explained away tomorrow, after William had made the phone call. Maybe then she would realize there was nothing to be puzzled about.

She said, 'Blow it!' again, deciding to have sugar in her tea instead of a saccharin tablet. 'Live dangerously, Lorna!'

The kettle began to whistle and she cleared her mind of all doubts and irritations and thought instead of William who would be home in a few hours' time and the cup of tea she would enjoy in a few minutes' time, and out of the best rosebud china, too!

Strange, for all that, the sergeant arriving at her door. Stranger still that she, Lorna, was foolish enough to give it a second thought.

She wished again that Ness were here to share the tea – and to sort out, as only Ness could – the matter of Primrose Smythe-Parker. And the phone call William had to make to her home.

William arrived at ten minutes past twelve, which was surprising Lorna thought, running down the path, arms wide to meet him.

'Darling!' She gathered him close, kissing his cheek.

'Hullo, Lorna.' He handed her his respirator. 'I'd kill for a cup of tea.'

'Can do.' She hurried to the kitchen, cheeks flushed. The

same old William. Undemonstrative as ever. After three months apart, a kiss on the cheek when she longed for him to hug her breathless. But that was his way, she had long ago accepted it.

'Need a hand?' She held open the door as he manoeuvred his case through.

'No thanks. Just a hot drink. It was freezing cold all the way up.'

'Then come into the kitchen. It's warm there. And William, can you ring Miss Smythe-Parker?'

'She's been on the phone?' His head jerked up.

'No. She was here, last night.'

'*Here*? You're sure, Lorna?'

'Of course I am.' Already she regretted passing on the message. 'She told me she's left the Army.'

'So she has. Well, best I ring her and get it over with.'

'Yes. Do that.' She could hear the tightness in her voice. 'She says you know her number. Don't be too long?'

But William had already closed the kitchen door behind him.

'So what was that all about?' she demanded when he returned. 'And don't look so hurt. Surely I'm entitled to know?'

'Of course you are.' He stood at the fireplace, fingers spread to the coals. 'Primmy apologized for calling on you last night. She realizes she shouldn't have.'

'No, she shouldn't. A phone call would have been better. So what did she want?'

'She's still at sixes and sevens since her discharge. She's been in the ATS since the outbreak of war; being a civilian again is taking a bit of getting used to.'

'I'm sure it is, William. And she'll be worried, I shouldn't wonder, about her – er – condition. She told me about that last night, too.'

'*Told* you?'

'That she'd been discharged on medical grounds. She

didn't go into details, though. Do you know what is the matter with her? Did she tell you?'

Lorna asked it sharply, because her husband had hardly set foot in the house and already there was an atmosphere.

'As a matter of fact, she did. But I'd like to get myself settled in and thawed out first, if you don't mind. My feet are like blocks of ice. Are my slippers about?'

'In the hearth, where they usually are. But I'd like to know why Primrose called here last night and why she wanted you to get in touch with her. And why, whilst we are on the subject, did you scurry like a startled rabbit to phone her?'

'All right, then. She was discharged because she's pregnant. The Army bods like to get a woman back into civvy street within three months.'

'Which means she's three months gone?'

'Yes.' He was still looking into the fire, his back to her.

'And does she know who the father is?' Bitchy, that, but it got results.

'What do you mean – does she know?' He turned to face her. 'Do you think she's been at it with the entire regiment?'

Only then did Lorna realize something was very wrong. Normally, she couldn't care less how the sergeant got pregnant, but all at once the small voice of reason warned her to tread carefully.

'You know I didn't mean it that way. Don't be so uppity. What she does with her life has nothing to do with you and I, especially as she is no longer in the Army, no longer a colleague. Let's keep it in proportion? You've hardly stepped inside the door and we are arguing. Why does it always seem to come to words between us? So upstairs with you, and take that uniform off. I've put your civvies on the bed. And William, let's forget about the Army for seven days – please?'

'Yes, I think we should, for now. Let a fellow get his breath, eh – and a cup of tea.'

'Nearly ready. But I can't help, now that you've told me, thinking about the mess the poor girl has got herself into. I hope her parents don't give her a bad time over it. Will the father marry her? I've got to admit I was a bit fussed about her calling last night. She was quite abrupt, I've got to say it, but she was probably worried, poor thing.'

'All right! Since it seems you can't let the matter drop, Lorna, her parents are one hundred per cent behind her. The baby will be welcomed, especially if it's a boy. Primmy's brother was killed in France, early on in the war, you see. And she won't have to worry financially. Her people are very well-heeled. The child won't want for a thing.'

'Good. All children should be wanted. I hope things go well for them both.' She truly did, even though it made her sad to think that anyone but herself could get pregnant. 'So go upstairs and put Lieutenant Hatherwood away, and come downstairs the man I married, if you wouldn't mind.'

'I'll do that. Early start, see? Tired. I suppose there wouldn't be a spot of lunch about?'

'Of course there is. Sandwiches and home-made broth. And for supper there's beef and vegetable pie. And William,' she said softly, 'welcome home to Ladybower – and to me.'

It was when they had eaten supper that the phone rang again.

'Answer it will you, William?'

Instinct told Lorna it was Primrose, and when he had put the phone down she would ask him, very firmly, exactly what she had said to him and why she thought she could phone whenever she felt like it. After all, she would point out reasonably, the sergeant was nothing at all to do with them. Or was she? Did William know more about it than he was prepared to admit? Did he know who the father was? A married fellow officer, perhaps? Men were notoriously clannish when the chips were down. They closed ranks, didn't they, like an old-boys' club.

‘That was Primrose.’ She went into the attack the minute William came into the room. ‘So tell me – what is it this time?’

‘She was worried, so she rang me.’ He sat in the chair opposite and picked up the newspaper.

‘Please put that paper down, William, and tell me why, if the woman is worried, she doesn’t try ringing the father of the child. It’s him she should – *Oh, my God*!’

It came to her with the force of a physical blow. Three months pregnant and exactly three months ago the sergeant and William had been recalled from leave a day early. Primrose had given him a lift back to barracks, had arrived at Ladybower in her big Wolseley car *three months ago*!

Slowly he folded the newspaper and laid it on the floor beside his chair. Only then did he raise his head and meet her eyes.

‘William, please answer me truthfully. Perhaps I am wrong to ask it, but will you tell me where you and she spent the night, three months ago, when the two of you were recalled from leave?’ Her lips were so stiff with fear she could hardly speak. ‘Did you spend it together? Was that early recall a put-up job? Did you agree it between you?’

Please say no, she pleaded inside her. Only tell me I’ve got it terribly wrong and I will apologize humbly and gladly.

‘Y-yes, we did.’ He sounded almost relieved. ‘We were desperate to spend a whole night together.’

‘So how long, when that woman came to my house three months ago in her flash car, had it been going on between you?’

‘Since New Year’s Eve. There was a party in the mess. We’d both had a bit too much to drink.’

‘Yes, I remember.’ She and Ness had toasted the New Year, and made a wish. ‘You phoned and I could hear a party going on in the background. It all adds up.’

Talk of anything at all, she thought desperately, except the one question she did not want to ask – and had to, even though she already knew the answer. She clasped her hands tightly together, but it did nothing to stop their shaking. She ran her tongue around her lips, yet the question remained unasked.

'Please say something?' she said instead, gazing into the fireglow because she could not look at him; didn't dare read in his eyes what she knew to be true.

'What is there to say, Lorna? You and Primmy have forced everything into the open. She by coming here; you by demanding to know every last word of it.'

'So it's her fault and mine? Not yours?' She was no longer tongue-tied. Released from shock, the words came in a torrent. 'And all I need now is to hear you say that the baby is yours; that the child she's carrying was got in some hotel room when you both crept away, a day early. Don't take me for a fool, William.'

The disbelief that held her was gone now, and in its place was white-hot anger.

'All right. It's my child,' he shrugged.

'So does it please you, William, to tell me about that child when I have longed for one of my own? Do you know what this is doing to me? I suppose you're going to tell me next that you love her.'

'I do, Lorna.' His face was pale; suddenly he looked old. 'I should be ashamed to say it, but I'm not. Oh, I know she's no pin-up girl, but she's a real woman; *all* woman.'

'And I'm not? God! I don't believe I'm hearing all this! And would you have come clean about it if she hadn't arrived at the house asking for you, thinking you were already home? But she knew *exactly* when you'd be home. She came here to start the ball rolling, didn't she? So she's pregnant, so what do you intend doing about it? Are you going to acknowledge the child, maintain it, see to its education? Did you realize, you and she, what you were doing when you started this affair?'

'Yes, Lorna, I think we must have.'

'Then why in heaven's name did you let it go on?'

'I don't know. I suppose we, neither of us, wanted to stop it.'

'You love her *that* much? And she loves you so much she was willing to get pregnant to get you? Tell me – what is there about her – apart from being all woman?'

'Then since you ask, she's good to make love to. She wants me.'

'And I don't? I'm not a real woman, then?'

Her hands grasped the chair arms, her body shook and it felt as if someone had slammed a vicious fist into her stomach.

'Compared to her you're cold, Lorna. An ice maiden.'

'But I've never refused you! I've always been there for you!'

'I'll grant you that, but you always just lay there, never tried to love me in return. Every time, I could almost read your thoughts. Will it be a baby, this time? You wanted a child – children – not a lover!'

'Oh, but you know how to hurt! Splendid of you, William, to tell me just how good your woman is between the sheets, what a hot bit of stuff! And now she's carrying your child and I'm never going to have one! Because I could never share a bed with you after this. Do you realize what you have done to me, William Hatherwood, how much I despise you?'

Her entire body hurt. There was a pain inside her belly exactly where a child would have been, and it was as if he had ripped from her all hopes of ever conceiving. And big, awkward Primrose, with her damn great feet and eager loins, had won!

The pain was getting worse. She got to her feet, walking two unsteady steps to his side. Then she lifted her hand and brought it against his cheek with all the venom in her.

'Aaaagh!' The force of it stunned her. Her hand hurt. She hoped his face hurt, too.

'Lorna! What the hell!' He grasped her shoulders, shaking her. 'What has got into you? Have you gone mad?'

'No. I just came to my senses.' She said it slowly, quietly. 'This is the end of the road for us, isn't it? Do you want to marry her?'

'Yes, and she wants to marry me. Like I said, we love each other.'

'Then go to her and your love child, William. The sight of you sickens me. Get out of my house, *now*! You can come back for your things later. Just get out of here!'

'All right. If I must. But will you be all right? And we'll have to talk, you know . . .'

'So all at once you're concerned for me! Isn't it a bit late for that? And what is there to talk about? I'll divorce you, if that'll make it any easier.'

Divorce in Nun Ainsty! How sordid, and she with no choice.

'No, my dear.' His voice was eager now, and placating. 'There's an easy way. I'll give you grounds. You know how it's done? There are women you can hire for the night –'

'Yes. I believe they're called prostitutes, tarts!'

'No! They stay with you in your room all night – nothing happens – and the next morning the chambermaid brings in tea and sees you together. So simple, Lorna.'

'And then the private detective in his greasy mac just happens to be there on cue, to scribble the mucky details in his notebook!'

'That's it, Lorna. It's the way most divorces are managed these days. It's the gentlemanly way to do it, so neither lady is directly involved. I admit to adultery with an unnamed woman.'

'You've got it all thought out, haven't you? You didn't just come up with it. It's been buzzing inside your head for a long time. You want Primrose and she's having your child, so what is there in it for me, then?'

'I'd pay you alimony, Lorna . . .'

'Thanks, but I don't want your money. I've got enough of my own as well you knew when you married me, promised Grandpa you'd look after me, that I'd be safe with you. He died happy seeing us married, I'll grant you that, William. But now you've found someone else who's a hot little trick with expectations greater than mine, eh? What is it about you and women? And you looking like a middle-aged walrus with that stupid moustache.'

'Lorna! You're not yourself! I'm sorry to have brought this on you, and clumsily, too. But try to calm down? Let's you and me talk it over like the sensible people we are?'

'All right! You've got your divorce, William. I'll see you are rid of me as soon as possible. We might, if we don't start slinging accusations about and bargaining about money, get it over and done with in time for you to marry your Primmy before the child is born.'

She was calm now, and exacting revenge for all the Tuesday nights and Sunday mornings; for the scratchy moustache and most heartbreakingly of all, for denying her the child she wanted so desperately.

'Bless you, Lorna. I knew you'd do the right thing in the end.'

'What choice do I have? We wouldn't want the child to be born out of wedlock, would we; don't want it to be a bastard, especially if it's a boy! But I want you to go now. Let's hope we can talk like two grown-ups tomorrow, then you can pack your things and that's the last I shall want to see of you. Be sure to tell your pregnant Primmy that Lorna has seen sense; that she can have you with my blessing. Good night, William.'

She walked calmly to the front door, holding it open; did it as if her marriage hadn't just ended and that nothing had changed between them. Then she turned the key in the lock, walking in disbelief to the once-familiar sitting room, switching off the lamp so she might sit in the firelight, find comfort in it. She might even convince herself that tonight had never happened; that it was only a bad dream and that tomorrow William would be home around midday on leave; convince herself, too, that Primrose Smythe-Parker had never been to Ladybower and did not carry William's child.

In her numbness, Lorna did not weep. She could only wonder that this morning she was looking forward to William's leave, yet only a few hours later he had admitted to adultery, and to fathering a child. And he had walked out of Ladybower, left her as if she were worthless; to be discarded when something better chanced along – someone whose family was well-heeled; a woman who was eager to please and everything a man could want in bed. Plain women, she had heard, were often like that. It was their only way to get a man.

She wished she could weep, let go of her anger, slam doors, throw William's photograph across the room. But it was too late now for either and besides, what good would tears do? Maybe when Ness came back she could unburden her torment? Ness would understand, would hold her tightly as she sobbed the misery out of herself.

Until then, she must live her life one day at a time, starting with tomorrow, when William would return to pack his things, then drive off, out of her life. Until then, she would try to forget she had lost control, acted like a hoyden, slammed her hand into his face and all the time feeling so sick with disgust she could have, should have, drawn her fingernails down his cheeks and left her mark there for his woman to see.

She bent to lay another log on the fire, then drew her feet beneath her and hugged a cushion tightly to her chest. Tomorrow was another day, but she must think about it – *now*.

Lorna had done the morning round, lit the kitchen fire and, by the time William arrived, the iron kettle was puffing complacently on the hob. He was wearing the clothes he had left in, with a borrowed jacket thrown over them.

'So you went to her?' A stupid thing to say, because where else would he go?

'I went to her parents' home. How are you, Lorna?'

'How do you think I am? Yesterday I had a husband. This morning . . .'

'I'm sorry.'

'And you expect me to believe that? The time to have been sorry was at that drunken party, when it all started. It's three months too late now, so I hope we can talk like reasonable people, even though just to look at you makes me want to puke. Last night I wished I had scratched your face, but this morning I awoke and did the post round as usual. I still feel a little peculiar, but I'll get used to being discarded – a much better word than divorced, don't you think? So sit down, please.' She indicated the chair opposite. She would feel better with the sturdy table top between them. 'The kettle is on the boil. Would you like tea?'

'Thank you, no. And, Lorna, I really want you to know how sad I am about all this.'

'Yes. You just said. But we've gone a little beyond the recrimination and regrets stage. We have to talk about – well, *things*.'

'Very well. But first can I say that Primrose feels badly about it, too. She wanted me to tell you that.'

'And you can tell Primrose to go to hell. Now – there are tea chests in the outhouse. You can take two of them. And your cases are in the middle bedroom, with all the other things we moved down from the attics. That, and your car space should be enough for your things. And don't forget to take your books? Apart from that, the furniture here is mine, as is the house. Funny, isn't it – Grandpa stating in his will that Ladybower should remain in my name? Not such an old softie, was he?'

'I respected your grandfather, Lorna.'

'Yes. Being an accountant you would, because you knew down to the last brass farthing how much he was worth, how much I would inherit. I suppose that when you and she have a son together, Primrose will inherit her parents' estate. You have a penchant for picking up heiresses.'

'Now see here, Lorna! This isn't a bit like you. It's like you're taking advantage of the situation.'

'Do you know, I believe I am! The boot is on the other foot now. I haven't shed one tear, did you know that? I thought it strange, but there are no tears in me. Maybe you aren't worth weeping over, William. And as for taking advantage, didn't you do the same? Weren't you taking advantage of me – of my trust – when you first got Primrose's knickers down?'

'Stop it, will you!' He jumped to his feet, pushing back the chair so the legs scraped on the floor tiles and set her teeth on edge. 'You're talking common – dirty!'

'And Lorna doesn't do that! Lorna is – *was* – a sweet trusting girl, grateful to you for marrying her – is that it? Someone you could order about and get away with it, eh?'

'I'm not standing for this.' He reached for his jacket, making for the door. 'I won't sit here listening to your vicious tongue!'

'Then go, William. If you don't want to talk to me, talk to solicitors, mine and yours. Solicitors can be wondrous slow. You just might have to wait longer than you can afford to be rid of me, haven't you thought? So please sit down again and listen to what I have to say. After all, it's you and Primrose want this divorce, not me. I can, if I want, drag the whole business on for the duration, so don't push your luck! In short, William, you started it and don't ever forget that!'

'Then can I say that you are not the young girl I married; that you have changed into someone I don't recognize. I never thought to hear you talk as you are talking now.' He pulled the chair up to the table again, resting his forearms on the table top, twining his fingers into a fist. Lorna was gratified to see his knuckles showed white.

'Say exactly what you want, William. I don't care any

more. All I want to talk about is this divorce and how to get it over as quickly as possible. But if you want a fuss, want it all your own way . . .'

'There'll be no fuss. I just want as little scandal as possible.'

'Thank you, William. I'm glad we can see the way ahead, at last.' She dropped her gaze to the table top. 'So this is what I suggest we do. I will divorce you. It will be far the quickest way out – and speed is essential, we both know that.'

'Yes, and I'm grateful. The adultery-with-an-unknown-woman way is the best, the gentlemanly way of doing it, you've got to agree. I'll get it all going when I get back to Aldershot. There's a hotel there I hear can be relied on to co-operate. No problem that I can see. And I'm sorry it has ended like this. I never wanted to hurt you, Lorna. This is embarrassing for me, too, please believe me?'

'I'll never believe another thing you say, William.' She stared fixedly down at her hands, breathing slowly and evenly. 'And as for being embarrassed – well, hold your horses. There's more of it to come! I will divorce you – gladly – and name Primrose as co-respondent. There is no way I'm going to let her come out of this whiter than white. She went to great lengths to get you, so she can pay the going rate!'

'But you *can't* do this, Lorna!' He spread his hands in a gesture of bewilderment. 'It's going to make Primrose seem no better than she need be! Think of the scandal it's going to cause, naming her. She'll be treated as a – a –'

'Scarlet woman? Marriage breaker? Trollop?' Lorna frowned. 'Yes, I suppose she will, now you mention it. Anyway, take it or leave it. No compromise, William. Either Primrose is named or I'll forget the whole thing and you'll have to wait years and years to divorce me for desertion. I don't know where refusal of conjugal rights comes into it, but you can use that as well, if you want to.'

'Dammit! You've got me over a barrel!' He brought the flats of his hands down on the table top. 'You're enjoying this, aren't you – all wide-eyed and injured innocence! But you're as crafty as they come, Lorna. You're mad. You're like your mother. That's what they say about breeding, isn't it – that it will out!'

He was angry now and red-faced with frustration, she supposed, because timid Lorna was giving as good as she got! It must be a great shock to him. The thought pleased her.

'I wondered,' she said calmly, 'when that would be brought into it. Now it has come to hitting below the belt, it seems, and all because you can't have your own way, William. You want Primrose and you want the divorce your own way, too. The gentlemanly way, didn't you call it? But I don't think there's anything gentlemanly in sleeping with a woman when you've already got a wife. So sorry. I'm divorcing you for adultery and I shall name your Primrose as co-respondent, and there's nothing more to talk about.

'Now, will you take what is yours, which isn't a lot as I recall, and get out of my house? And don't make me more angry than I am, William, because being my mother's daughter I just might scratch your face – might even throw plates! So back your car up to the kitchen door, please, and get it loaded as quietly and quickly as possible and then, if we're lucky, Martha mightn't even see you go!'

It was not until he had driven away, straight-backed with indignation, biting his bottom lip as he did when angry, that Lorna let go of her breath and gave way to the panic held in check for so long. Now she was afraid, bewildered and alone with no one to turn to. She did not know how she would cope with not only the break-up of her marriage, but of being a divorcée. Divorce was a terrible thing; something people didn't like talking about. To be in the company of a husband who had committed adultery or a wife who hadn't been able to hold on to her man made people uneasy. Even the innocent party – herself – would be held partly to blame if only for not soldiering on, making the best of a bad job, sticking with a dead marriage. She supposed there were a lot of people who would be better apart, yet who could not face the stigma of divorce. Nice people, decent people just didn't accept it. Divorce was for people like King Edward and Mrs Simpson and look at the trouble that had caused! She began to shake. What in heaven's name had she done and where was she to go from here?

'I'll divorce you, and name Primrose.'

Brave words when hurled in anger, but how would it be; how would it all end? Was she upset because she had lost her husband or was it because she had allowed another woman to take him from her? Could it be that she didn't, deep down, want William, but was determined another woman shouldn't have him? Was her pride injured or was she upset that another woman carried the child she had so desperately longed for? Had William been right? Had she, in those together times, thought only of becoming pregnant?

She looked at the mantel clock. By rights, now, she should be at the surgery had things been normal. But after tomorrow, when she went to York to see Grandpa's solicitors, nothing would be normal again. And think what would happen when Nun Ainsty found out. How many would be on her side? Nance would be against; Flora sympathetic. Martha would be on a rosy cloud because never before had there been a divorce in the village. Kate would be neutral, she supposed, and Pearl Tuthey at the Saddlery, too. Neither would express an opinion because neither took pleasure from another's misfortunes.

And Ness? How would she take it? Ness disliked William even though they had never met. They never would now. Ness would say, 'Ar hey, queen! Tell them all to mind their own business. Who cares what the village thinks!'

But there were still four more days to live through before Ness came home to Ladybower. Four days of self-pity and anger and accepting that the chances now of her ever having a child were almost nil. Four days before she could pour out her heart, then let go the tears she was holding back; that pride would not let her shed. When Ness came home it would be all right, but what was to be done *now*? How was she to muddle through until then? Who was to give her comfort?

Without thinking or knowing why, she went to stand at her desk, looking up. Then she drew a trembling breath and gazed at the picture of misty hills and distant shining water and foxgloves.

'What am I to do, Ewan?' she whispered. 'And why aren't you here when I so need a friend?'

She sent her mind back to the time they first met in Dickon's Wood. He had been sketching there and helped she and Ness drag fallen boughs into Ladybower's garden. Through the gap in the hedge she had pushed through, guilt-ridden, the night they said goodbye.

Dickon's Wood! She would go there again; stand by the tree Ewan had leaned on, pad in hand. And she would send her thoughts to him, wherever he was. And those thoughts would be about the last time they met and the kisses she could not forget; kisses she had been unable to tell even Ness about, so passionate had they been.

She reached for her jacket. The light was beginning to fade but she would still be able to find the tree. Closing the door behind her she ran across the garden to the gap, pushing through it impatiently. Then she closed her eyes and gave herself up to remembering. Two people saying goodbye. A kiss of friendship between them, then each would go their separate way; he to another country, she to her life as Lorna Hatherwood.

Yet it did not work out that way. They had held each other closely, lips clinging in a desperation that had shaken her to the depths of her imaginings. They had not spoken a word, but kissed and kissed again, neither wanting to break the magic, both knowing they must.

It had been she, eventually, who tore herself free, who

pushed, bewildered, through the hedge to the safe familiarity of Ladybower's garden; away from the woman who had kissed like a wanton, and back into Lorna Hatherwood's body and mind.

That secret must never be told, so ashamed and bewildered had she been. What happened that night could never be shared, not even with Ness.

She shrugged away all regrets. It had happened. No one could change those moments that even yet made her want to close her eyes and lift her mouth to his.

She began to walk to the far boundary and Ewan's tree. The old pathway was easier to see now that summer's grasses had withered, and she trod carefully because soon she would come to the clawing brambles which shed their leaves in winter, but not their thorns. Then she saw the tree; saw it distinctly because only in the depths of the wood had it been almost too dark to see. Here, on the outskirts, the November afternoon still lingered, and ahead of her she could make out the bare, graceful branches of the beech tree.

With a small sigh she leaned against the trunk as he had done, and closing her eyes she sent her thoughts high and wide and far, to where he was, wherever he was.

It's Lorna, Ewan. Remember me? Remember the woman who kissed you like there was no tomorrow, here in Dickon's Wood? Do you remember Nun Ainsty, sometimes think of it, still?

I think about you. Today especially I thought about you because Ness isn't here so there's only you to tell that I'm lonely and angry. And afraid, too, Ewan, that I shall grow into a dried-up old woman who will never know the joy of a child in her arms . . .

She breathed in, holding it, then let it go in little puffs, opening her eyes on hearing slippered footsteps, standing still and unafraid.

The footsteps stopped and in the distant gloom was a woman in a drab, shapeless coat. An army blanket made into a coat to save clothing coupons, was it? She made a picture in her mind of a beautiful young woman with a small smile that tilted the corners of her full, sensuous mouth and hair, thick and black, woven into a plait.

Startled, Lorna looked around her, but the woman had gone. She had dreamed up the shabby coat; dreamed the beauty of the face, the deep compassionate eyes. There was no one here; never had been. In the half light, nothing moved. There were no footsteps. All that was left of her imaginings was the scent of lavender and there was no lavender in Dickon's Wood; nor did it flower in winter.

Still bemused she whispered, 'Ursula?' but the only sound was the cawing of rooks, flying home to roost.

Home! All at once afraid, she turned in her tracks, walking as quickly as she dare until she passed the bramble patch, not looking back, grateful to see Ladybower's chimney stacks ahead, solid against the fading light.

Gratefully she pushed open the kitchen door, fumbling to pull down the blackout blind before swishing the curtains across the window. Then she switched on the light, looking around her at things familiar. She walked through each room, darkening windows, switching on lights, relieved that at least everything was normal.

Almost normal. In the sitting room was an empty bookcase and a silver photograph frame with William's picture removed. He had taken it, but left the frame. And in the bedroom they had shared, all things to remind her of him were gone. Instead there was an empty wardrobe and a tallboy with empty drawers. Everything was emptiness now in her life. In two days, it had changed as cruelly as if someone had knocked on her door, handing her a telegram; a message folded into the small yellow envelope of dread. And it was as if it told her William had been killed in action and gone from her life for ever. Because it was as final as could be. She would never see him again. He belonged so completely to another woman that she might just as well think him to be dead. She trailed into the bathroom, still checking, but even his toothbrush had been taken from the tumbler that held it, and the tube of toothpaste. There was nothing there but a photograph at the bedside of William in a new suit and sober tie; she in a pale-blue frock and matching hat, carrying a posy of white rosebuds. No bridal white, no veil. The wedding had been hurried because Grandpa had wanted it and because, Doc Summers had warned, to delay it might mean that soon her grandfather would be incapable of walking her down the aisle.

She reached for it, took out the photograph and laid the frame at the back of the top drawer of the tallboy. Then she walked downstairs and, tearing the photograph into two, threw it on the kitchen fire. She was glad to see it burn. William looking posed and stiff, she with a pillbox hat perched on top of a pile of frizzy hair. She had changed now. Why keep a photograph of two people best forgotten?

She stood in the emptiness of the kitchen, willing the phone to ring suddenly to shatter the silence, but it did not. The emptiness pressed in on her and she hurried into the hall, picking up the phone.

'Hi!' she said when a familiar voice answered. 'It's me, Mrs B. Did my phone just ring?'

'N-no, Lorna. Why do you ask?'

'Because I thought I heard it. I – I was outside, shutting up the hens . . .'

'No call from here. Are you all right, Lorna? You looked a little pale this morning.'

'Did I? Tired, maybe. William and I sat up late, talking. Everything's fine. See you in the morning . . .'

She stared at the instrument, black and cold, her only link with the real world until tomorrow, when she went to the post office. She wished Ness would ring, but it would be out of the question. Calls from Devon were long-distance and you didn't have trunk calls on other people's phones.

Ness, please hurry back? You'll never believe one word of it, when I tell you. I don't think I believe it myself . . .

She sat in the rocking chair beside the kitchen fire, to think of Ness who was in Devon and of William who had left her, but she thought of neither, because the scent of lavender was all around her still. So she thought instead of the woman she had seen – *thought* she had seen – in the wood, and the shabby coat and the absolute beauty of her face.

But you could be forgiven for imagining things, for being just a little deranged, when your marriage was over and there was no one to talk to, glean comfort from. How many hours until Ness came back? More than a hundred, and they would tick away so very slowly.

She closed her eyes, and wished she could weep.

TWENTY-THREE

Ness would soon be back. One more night, then she would burst into Ladybower's kitchen, her wide smile lifting the gloom.

It had been an awful week. Mornings were bearable – just. Lorna had obeyed the peevish clamour of the alarm clock, had washed and dressed and set out on the red GPO cycle. She had not once eaten breakfast nor even made tea. No need, when Mrs Benson would have the big brown pot ready beside the fire, and bless the faceless person at the Ministry of Food who had sanctioned Mrs B's request for a tea ration for the Meltonby post office workers. Only four ounces a week, which had to be eked out for the Meltonby postman, the Nun Ainsty postlady, Mrs B, the switchboard night operator, and the driver of the red GPO van who delivered parcels and letters to outlying farms and cottages. And because they were decent, and brought the morning papers, the driver and conductor of the early bus were included too. Seven mugs of tea, six days a week. The tea allowance had to be stretched to the very limit and Mrs B had got it to a fine art. Mrs B also provided milk and saccharin tablets and no one, yet, had dared ask how she came by the milk.

The post office at Meltonby had been Lorna's only contact with the real world, and she was grateful for it because there she did not have to watch every word she said. It was altogether another matter in Nun Ainsty where people might be inclined to ask how William was and if he was enjoying his leave. Deliveries in Ainsty were made on the run, almost. Even Kate was not given the chance to ask her to stop for a bite of toast, and she was thinking, no doubt, that the postlady was in a hurry to be home to her husband.

Lorna wondered, as she cycled down Priory Lane, eyes squinting into the early-morning darkness, how soon it would be before someone in the village remarked that they had not seen the two of them together at church or in the White Hart, or even walking out. This far, even Martha had made no comment, which meant, Lorna supposed, that she had not seen William load his car and leave. Sometimes the blackout was a blessing.

Mornings Lorna coped with; afternoons dragged because she could not go to the surgery and bring herself to say that because William had left her, she was available for work as usual. The day she was due back would be soon enough to face Jessie Summers who was nobody's fool. But this far, the secret was hers, still – except for old Mr Wainwright, the solicitor in York who was struggling to keep the practice going because young Mr Wainwright had been called up into the Royal Air Force. A divorce was the last thing the overworked solicitor needed.

'You surprise me, Lorna! I would never have connected William with – er – er, *that* sort of thing.' The bombshell of William's infidelity was serious indeed. He had been a trusted member of Wainwright and Wainwright's staff, dealing with clients' accounting problems, giving sound monetary advice. 'You'll realize, my dear, that it will be impossible for him to work here when the war is over. Divorce – people won't like it . . .'

She returned to Ladybower never more in need of tea to soothe her and a bath to wash away the experience of laying her soul bare. She opened the tea caddy to find it almost empty. The tea ration, she was bound to admit, had taken a bashing these last few days and no more due for days. Tea she must reluctantly do without; a bath and a change of clothes was a must, and what was more, she fully intended to use more than the patriotic six inches of water! That day, she had taken the first step towards divorce. A decent bath was nothing less than she deserved, and wasn't her life in a mess, and please hurry back, Ness? Don't miss that train? You can't know how much I need you.

Ness arrived a little after midnight. Lorna heard her key in the lock and ran to the door.

'You're back! I'd given you up! Did you manage all right, from York?'

'Struck lucky. It was well past eleven when the train got in and I knew I'd have to try hitching a lift; there was an RAF transport outside the station and it was going to the aerodrome, would you believe? So I hopped up into the back with about twenty airmen and when I banged on the side for the driver to stop, I told him that this was as far as it went and that I only had half a mile down the lane to go.

'And didn't he tell me to sit tight, and brought me here. "All part of the service," he said. Wasn't it smashin' of him? And hey – what's to do with you? You look fit to drop, queen.'

'I feel a bit rough. Didn't know it showed.'

'Rough? You look like you're in the middle of a severe attack of mornin' sickness. What's the matter? In for a dose of flu?'

'No to both.' It was all she could manage to say. Ness's joke tipped the scales and the tears, so long held back, came in great gasping sobs.

'I've been trying not to weep. Been bottling it up,' she choked. 'But the morning sickness did it. Oh, Ness, it isn't me that's pregnant! It's William's lady friend, would you believe!' The sobs began again.

'His *what*? Now see here, Lorna, just let me get out of this jacket and stick my cases out of the way, then I'm goin' to put the kettle on. Tea is what we both need, and then you can tell me all about it. You've got it right, haven't you – William's got a fancy woman?'

'He has. And there's no tea till I get the new rations, so we'll have to make do with cocoa. Sorry, but I've been going a bit heavy on the cuppas, these last few days. And I'm sorry about the hysterics, but I haven't known who to talk to. And yes, William has got another woman. Seems it started last New Year. Primrose Smythe-Parker, and she's three months pregnant.'

'Pregnant? Flamin' Norah! I turn my back for a week and look at the trouble I come home to. I never liked your feller, but I never thought he'd go off the rails, honest-to-God I didn't. He'll have to marry her, won't he?'

'Yes, and he wants to. Says he wants a divorce as soon as possible. Mustn't have the baby born out of wedlock, must we? And you know how much I've always wanted a child, Ness, then he goes and does this to me.'

'So what say we get into our dressing gowns and slippers, then get that fire going again and talk it all over, eh?'

'But you must be tired, Ness. Let's go to bed? We both have to be up early. I'd like a hot drink, though, and did I tell you I'm so glad you're back?'

'You did, queen. Twice. And I think we'd better liven up that fire, 'cause I've got news for you. Anyway, I'm past sleep. I'd only go to bed and think about Mick. Might as well stay down here and catch up on things, eh?'

So they sat either side of the kitchen fire, and Lorna was glad, now that the tears had stopped, to tell all, right from Primrose calling at Ladybower to William with his worldly goods crammed into his car and on top of his car, to the visit to Grandpa's solicitor who had been most embarrassed by her determination to divorce William and name Primrose as co-respondent.

'Bitchy of me, I know, but those were my terms. Mr

Wainwright told me he knew of the Smythe-Parkers. Very rich, he thought. Made a small fortune during the last war, making shell cases, and they're doing it again this time around.'

'Seems your William has landed on his feet, again.'

'He's not my William; not any longer. And the more I think about it, the surer I am that I'm more worried about the scandal of divorce than I am about losing him. Lord knows what I'll do when it gets out.'

'Nobody knows, then?'

'Not a soul. Even Martha hasn't ferreted it out, yet. But I shall have to tell Mrs B and Doc Summers before so very much longer. And Kate, too, I suppose. It's what Nance Ellery will make of it that bothers me. And why I'm worrying, I don't know. Dammit, I'm the injured party, aren't I? It isn't me wanting the blasted divorce.'

'No, girl. But it seems like you're goin' to get one. And things might not be as bad as you thought. I'll be on your side, you know that. If I hear anybody slaggin' you off, Lorna, they'll get down-the-banks from me! And as for that William! Well, he's a right little sod and it's my belief you're better off without him.'

'Bless you, love. I don't feel so adrift, now you're back. And can we talk about it tomorrow? I've told you the worst, got it off my chest, and I'm being selfish. You must have had a lovely time and here's me, moaning since the minute you got in. Tell me, Ness – how was Devon?'

'Thought you'd never ask! And lovely time doesn't come into it. It was absolute heaven, just like in the films.' She smiled dreamily, then held up her left hand, wiggling her fingers in front of Lorna's nose. 'And you never noticed!'

'Ness! That isn't a wedding ring?'

'It is, girl!'

'You and Mick – *married*?'

'We are. On the nineteenth, at the Registry Office by special licence! Mick said he had a surprise for me, but I never imagined anything like that. But it's nearly one in the morning. Maybe we should get off to bed, and take your divorce and my wedding with us. Like you said, we can talk about it tomorrow night.'

'You'll not say anything about William and me, Ness? Not just yet?'

'Not a word. I've got good news for the telling. Your bad news is best swept under the rug for a few days. And I'm sorry to come back with stars in my eyes and you so miserable, Lorna.'

'Not miserable, exactly. Now that I'm getting a bit more used to it I think that even worse than William walking out is the baby. Her being pregnant hurts a lot.'

'Yes. An' we're off to bed this minute! Let's not get on to babies tonight, eh? And anyway, what are you worrying about? Martha told you there'd be three for you and two for me, didn't she?'

'Without a husband?'

'That Primrose got one without a husband, didn't she? Anything's possible, queen. I'm just startin' to find it out! So check the doors whilst I bank the fire down, then it's upstairs!'

And Lorna smiled for the first time in many days and said,

'I'm glad you're back, Ness.'

'I know. You keep saying. Now up them stairs, lady – no messing!'

'I made up your bed. And Ness, you'll have to cuddle the pillow tonight.'

'I know. It'll be awful!'

But tomorrow was another day, Ness thought, as she followed Lorna upstairs. Tomorrow there was sure to be a letter from Mick – there might even be a phone call. And if she couldn't be with Mick, then this gossipy little village was the next best place to be.

''Night,' she smiled, opening the bedroom door.

‘’Night, Ness. God bless. I can’t believe you’re married, y’know. We’ll talk some more tomorrow.’

‘You bet we will. You’re goin’ to have a word for word account of Ness Nightingale’s – oops! – Hardie’s weddin’ and all the Is dotted and the Ts crossed. You haven’t heard the half of it yet.’

‘I shall enjoy every word.’ Some of the tension was leaving her. Ness was back, and married. One really good thing had happened – surely from now on things could only get better? Oh, please – couldn’t they?

They sat in deep, saggy chairs in the lamp glow, recklessly deciding to throw coal rationing to the wind and light a fire in the sitting room. Just for once.

Outside, stark bare trees stood like monuments to a summer long gone and a fog had come down, thick and black, in a swirling, silencing blanket. So, because Ness was missing Mick and because Lorna had troubles of her own, it went without saying that the comfort of the sitting room for just one night was well in order.

‘Once the fire is red, we can keep it going with logs,’ Ness had said. Already this winter, gales had torn down dead branches which they had eagerly dragged into the back garden and sawn up with Christmas in mind – with just a basketful to be used tonight. Because this was the first day of a new life for each of them, and it was going to take a lot of getting used to.

‘I missed Mick something awful when I got to Glebe this morning.’ Ness looked up from the letter she was writing. ‘I half expected him to be there; thought that any minute I’d hear him whistle from the dairy and smile at me, and wave.’

‘But there was a letter for you . . .’

Lorna had recognized the writing on the envelope with an Exeter postmark and delivered it to Glebe Farm.

‘What do you make of that, then?’ she asked of Kate. ‘Mrs Ness Hardie, no less.’

'Married? Our Ness got wed, then?' Kate had pounced on the letter, eyes wide.

'She did, and that's all I'm saying.' Lorna was halfway to the door. 'Anyway, I don't know a lot. Ness was late back last night, but she'll tell you all about it.'

And with that she was away, hurrying to Larkspur cottage with an important-looking envelope for Miss Flora Petch SCM, and the last letter of the round. Only newspapers to the almshouses now, then she could congratulate herself on getting another delivery over and the divorce still under cover.

'There now; that's a few lines to Ruth Street, too. Can you post it in the morning for me, Lorna? Mick's letter will have to wait till I've got an address for it. I wonder what he's doing now.'

'Probably being given the run-around – the new recruit's routine. And he'll be wishing he was back with you. Letters are important to a man away from home – leastways, I used to think so.' She ran her fingers through her hair, then smiled. 'But we aren't talking about *that*, are we?'

They had agreed not to speak of the divorce unless absolutely necessary. Sadly, it had become necessary, because Mr Wainwright, on being unable to get Lorna on the Ladybower phone, had obligingly – and in all innocence – been plugged through to the Meltonby surgery by a helpful Mrs Benson. So now Reg and Jessie Summers knew. Red-faced, Lorna had admitted she had been phoned by her solicitor and promised it would not happen again.

'I know the phone mustn't be used for private calls, but it was important, Jessie.' Then a reckless rush of courage had prompted her to say. 'William has left me, you see. I'm divorcing him. For adultery.'

'*Divorcing* William?' To Jessie Summers's credit she recovered her wits in an amazingly short time. 'Well, you aren't going to be the first in these parts.' The doctor's wife, on consideration, had not been unduly shocked, though a little surprised. 'Mark my words, Lorna, there'll be a lot more marriages breaking up before this war is over. I know what I'm talking about. No names, no pack drill, though. But let me know if there's anything we can do – and I'm so sorry. Is Reggie to know?'

And Lorna had said that perhaps it might be as well to tell him, which for the time being had been the end of it and not as traumatic as Lorna had thought.

'How long do you think it will be,' Ness frowned, 'before Mick has an address to send me?'

'I imagine he'll be given one straight away. There'll be a letter tomorrow, or the next day. Trust me, Mrs Hardie, I'm a postlady. I'll rush it to you, special delivery! So if you're finished writing your letters, tell me about the wedding? But before you start, Mr Wainwright phoned me at the surgery this afternoon. He says he's heard from William's solicitors and William and Primrose are accepting that she's to be cited as co-respondent. I think they are desperate not to hold things up.'

'Your bloke will be back in Aldershot by now. I wonder if she's gone with him?'

'He's not my bloke and I couldn't care less if she's with him or not. And we said no more divorce talk – just wanted to let you know the latest, that's all. Tell me about the wedding, Ness? Don't leave anything out?'

'I'll leave out anything I think is private between husband and wife,' she added, smiling smugly. 'But the rest – oh, I think about it all the time. I can close my eyes and hear his voice. Mind, I'll admit I thought he was a bit matter-of-fact when he left Glebe Farm, but I know now that he was planning all the time to get a special licence. Didn't say anything about it, though, in case he couldn't manage it.

'We were at the bus stop in Exeter and I whispered to him – we were in a queue at the time – that I was sick of waiting. Well, one of us had to give way, and I reckoned there'd been enough counting to ten already.

'Anyway, he said he agreed with me and had given it a lot of thought and that he had a surprise for me but he wouldn't tell me what. I thought maybe he'd got me a ring, even though I'd told him not to, but when he showed me it knocked me for six. A special licence, Lorna, and a wedding, he said, the day after tomorrow, and did I mind very much that it wasn't going to be a grand affair?'

'And you didn't. Where was it, Ness?'

'At the Registry Office. Mick's parents were all for it, but turned down being our two witnesses. They said if my parents couldn't be there, it was only fair that neither of them should be. So we roped in a couple of witnesses from outside. We spent the night at a lovely hotel in Tiverton, then went back to Deep Hay for the rest of the leave. His parents are great. They said that in March, when Mick should get leave again, why don't we have a church blessing at Borton with both families there? There'd be room for Mam and Da and Nan – Tizzy and Perce, an' all. And if they're given notice, Mick's twin sisters should be able to wangle a weekend off, too.'

'That's a marvellous idea, Ness, and I hope I shall be invited, too. Wouldn't want to intrude but I'm sure there'll be a bed and breakfast nearby that I can stay at. That will be something good to look forward to. It'll be beautiful in Devon then. It's much warmer than here. There'll be spring flowers and the blossom in the apple orchard might be out. By the way, what did you wear?'

'Your costume, Ness. I was glad you said I should take it. We went to a florist nearby and Mick bought me a red rose – they actually had some, in the shop. Said it was because I was a Lancashire lass. I kept it in water overnight, and Mick's Mam wrapped it in tissue paper and pressed it for me in the big old family Bible they've got. She wrote our names in it, and the wedding date. There are loads of Hardies there – births, marriages and deaths – going back years and years.'

'Mick's mother sounds lovely.'

'She is, Lorna. And his dad, too. They didn't mind a bit about my accent. In fact, when Mick introduced me his mother said, "I see what you mean, Michael. She's every bit as lovely as you said." And that house, Lorna. It's all ups and downs like they've built bits on regardless, over the years. Six bedrooms and two attics. Really beautiful, even in winter. A smashing place for kids to grow up in. Me and Mick will live there, one day. You wouldn't believe it, but there are two kitchens. Mrs Hardie said that would make it all right. Two women sharing a house would get on just fine as long as they each had their own kitchen. I'm so lucky, I can't believe it.' Her eyes filled with tears and she dashed them away, forcing a smile. 'I'm stupid, aren't I, but I can't get used to being this happy. I love Mick so much and it isn't right, not when you're so miserable. Sorry, queen.'

'Then don't be. There's something I didn't tell you – about me and Ewan. I think you should know, then maybe you won't feel quite so sorry for me.' Lorna dropped her gaze to her hands. 'It was the night before he left the manor.'

'Oh?' Ness sat bolt upright, tears forgotten. 'You went up there to see him, didn't you?'

'And he walked me home, through the wood.'

'Yes, you said. A daft thing to have done if you ask me, and you a married woman. There could have been talk.'

'I know. But whilst you're pitying me for being landed with a divorce, will you think about me and Ewan and the fact that we – well, it was a passionate goodbye. I decided not to tell you.'

'Lorna! Not you and him? You didn't . . . ?'

'We weren't lovers, but it could have happened. I wish now that it had.'

'Then don't go wishing anything of the sort. I got tangled up with Patrick, don't forget. I know all about the adultery bit. Oh, I know he'd no intention of leaving his wife, but even if he'd wanted to he couldn't have got a divorce. He was the guilty party, see? Divorce can be very messy.'

'You reckon, Ness? Mine seems to be going through all right.'

'Yes, but don't you see – if you'd just once gone off the rails with Ewan, you'd not have been able to get a divorce so easily? You'd have had to declare your own infidelity and that would have gone in William's favour.'

'You could be right. William wanted to use the adultery with an unnamed woman thing. Said it was the gentlemanly way to do it. But I was determined to bring Primrose into it. After all, she'd taken my husband. I reckoned she shouldn't get away scot-free.'

'I see. You nearly ended up sinning with Ewan and you're pointing the finger at William's bit of stuff? Luckily, you're in the clear so never mind about those two – tell me about Ewan MacMillan?'

'There's nothing to tell, sadly. We got a bit – got a *lot* passionate. It would have been easy, just the once, for it to happen. But he's gone and no one has heard from him, not even Jessie and Reg. You'd have thought he'd have been in touch with them. I reckon it's because I made a fool of myself in the wood. Probably thinks he had a lucky escape – me being married, I mean.'

'But you aren't married – or you soon won't be. When it's all done and dusted, will you write and tell him, Lorna?'

'No address to write to. And anyway, he mightn't be interested.'

'Pity. Though I must say you seem a lot better about – well – *things* than you did last night.'

'It's helped being able to talk to you. And I was dreading it coming into the open, yet when I told Jessie she was only mildly surprised, after the initial shock. Didn't seem to think of me as being – well – not quite nice to know. But I suppose there are people I always knew I could rely on, and people I knew would be hostile, even though it's none of my fault. Nance Ellery, for one.'

'Well, it's bugger-all to do with her! Nuthin' to do with

nobody, come to think about it, but you and Himself. As far as I'm concerned, Primrose is welcome to him.'

'Suppose she is. It's having to give up all hope of a family that really bugs me.'

'You won't be having babies with William, so best get it out of your mind. But you're due for three, didn't Martha tell you? Carelessly got, she said. So maybe it's a pity you weren't a bit more careless when you said goodbye to Ewan MacMillan.'

'And knowing my luck nothing would have come of it. Do you suppose it's maybe because I'm not able to have children? Barren? I hadn't thought of that.'

'Oh for Pete's sake, girl, why shouldn't you have kids? Primrose just struck lucky, that's all. Shouldn't wonder if she didn't set her cap at William. You said she wasn't much to look at, didn't you?'

'She isn't. Tall and gangly and nothing to write home about. And big feet.'

'Ar. That'll be why. They say plain women with big feet are good at it, don't they? I suppose it's Mother Nature compensating them for bein' dog ugly.'

'Poor thing. You could almost feel sorry for her, but when push comes to shove, she's the one who's laughing. She's well-pregnant, Ness.'

'And so will you be, girl, when you meet the right feller. And do you know what we should do, tomorrow night? We should go to the White Hart, you and me, and I should flash my weddin' ring around and you should tell them that you're divorcin' William because he's been messin' about. You've got nuthin' to apologize for, Lorna. What say we do it?'

'Well, it's some ring to flash. Nothing utility or nine-carat about it. Where on earth did you get it, Ness?'

'Mick's Mam gave it to me. Belonged to her grandmother. And it fitted, too, so she said it looked as if I was meant to have it. But what do you think about tomorrow night – let the whole village know?'

'Married women don't go to pubs unescorted, even when there's a war on – you'd better get used to that, Ness. And as for letting the whole village know, if I tell either Martha or Nance, or both, then the job is as good as done. But I'm not ready for it to be village gossip just yet, if you don't mind. Let's stick with your good news? Leave the divorce for a little while? It still hurts, you know; I still feel I've been used – let down. William made a fool of me and I can't forgive him for that just yet. Why must divorce be so complicated and have such stigma attached to it? Why can't couples separate the same way as they get married? We go into marriage of our own free will – well, most people do – so why can't we say sorry, it hasn't worked, and end it in a civilized way?'

'A civilized divorce? There'll never be such a thing, Lorna. Getting out of a marriage you've promised is till death do you part has *got* to be a complicated matter. There's no way I'd let Mick go without a fight – not that he'd go off the rails, mind.'

'I didn't think William would either, but I'll not fight Primrose for him. She's welcome. And when you come to think of it, there's nowt so queer as folk. I'll be glad when this year is gone. It hasn't been a good one for me. As far as I'm concerned, the sooner it's on its way, the better.'

'Ar. Remember last New Year, Lorna? You and Himself were still a couple and I hadn't as much as kissed Mick! You an' me sat here and made wishes when Big Ben began to strike. Y'know what? I wished Patrick out of my life, absolutely, every last rotten memory of him, so that's a New Year wish come true, if you like. Not only did I stop bein' mad about Patrick bein' such a smarmy swine, but I got a bonus, an' all.'

Yet still Lorna didn't know about the baby, Ness brooded. She had not been able to tell her, and about the way she lost it almost two years ago. But you didn't tell things like that to a woman who was desperate for a child. Only Mam and Mick knew, and that was the way it would stay. 'So what did you wish for last New Year, Lorna? Any good, was it?'

'No, it wasn't. Primrose got what I wished for, as a matter of fact.'

'Then I'm sorry, queen. But Martha saw children for both of us, so let's hang onto that, and this coming New Year it'll be your turn to get what you want.'

'Won't be long now. About six weeks and then it'll be 1942. How many more will we welcome in before this war is over, Ness?'

'Dunno. But surely it's our turn to win some battles? Surely soon we'll have a bit of luck?'

'Long overdue, I'd say. We're getting good at hanging on, aren't we? If only there could be just one victory for us. Something marvellous to shout about.'

'It'll happen, queen. We'll win, in the end, only don't ask me when!'

And they smiled, and decided they could spare just two more logs for the fire, after which they would go to bed, Ness to think of Mick and she, Lorna, discarded woman of this parish – what would she think of? About William and Primrose, and their child, or would she fall blessedly asleep the minute she closed her eyes? Nice, if she could, but she doubted it.

'Win? Of course we will. And since I got the ration this morning, how about cocoa and toast? Let's be devils, live dangerously!'

And Ness said it was fine by her, and placed *three* logs on the fire.

It was as she was toasting bread that Lorna remembered the third man and that Martha had said things always happened in threes.

'Is the cocoa done?' Lorna decided against even a scrape of margarine on the toast. ''Cause I've got something to tell you. Talking about Ewan must have jogged my memory.'

'About you and him?'

'Not exactly. About something Martha said to him as a matter of fact. One of her predictions, actually. Take the mugs through whilst I jam the toast.'

'So?' Ness said when they were settled and the logs were spitting and crackling and dancing flames. 'What about Martha Hugwitty?'

'She was hanging out washing at Glebe – you know, at the drying green near the manor back yard? And she had a chat with Ewan. Said his aura was good and he would come through the war all right. And then she said that she wondered who would be the third man. Things always happened in threes, she said, be it births or deaths or whatever.

'"Two men are leaving Nun Ainsty – yourself and Mick," she said. "So who's going to be the third?" Because mark her words, there would be one and before so very much longer.'

'So the two men, Mick and Ewan she knew about, but the third . . .'

'Has turned out to be William!'

'Heck! So it has! And nobody would ever think he'd take himself off to pastures new, so maybe there really is something in Martha's predictions?'

'Oh, Ness, do you think she really is clairvoyant? Could there be something in what she said, that night she told our fortunes?'

'Dunno, girl, but it might be a good idea to go and see her again – see what else she can turn up. You might get to know who's going to be father to those children. Ewan, do you think it could be?'

'No, Ness. I don't want to know about the future yet. I'm too busy dealing with the present. And as for Ewan – I won't ever see him again. It's a feeling I have. Ewan is in the past. I could have loved him, but him and me – no, it isn't to be.'

'But don't you see, Lorna? Now that William's out of your life, it'll give Martha more scope, sort of.'

'More scope to dig up another man for me, you mean? After all, she'd feel obliged to, wouldn't she, since she'd wished up three children. And didn't she say I had trouble ahead – troubled waters that I would sail into, head on? Not so daft our Martha, is she?'

So they laughed, because that was all they could do about it really, and licked fingers sticky with jam and lifted their mugs high to toast whatever was to befall them.

'Cheers, Mrs Hardie,' Lorna smiled.

'Ar. Mud in yer eye, girl.'

And Lorna thought that now Ness was home things might start to come right again.

And Ness thought about Mick and wondered what he was doing this very minute, and sent her love to him in great warm gusts. Thought, too, that if she couldn't be in Mick's arms this very minute, then Ladybower's front parlour was the next best place to be.

TWENTY-FOUR

'Post, Kate – and the usual for Ness.' Lorna laid letters and the morning paper on the well-scrubbed table top in Glebe Farm's kitchen.

'Not a day without a letter – 'cept Sundays and two on a Monday to make up for it. They've made a lovely couple, those two – when they finally got around to it, that is. And how is your man, Lorna? Still at Aldershot?'

'I – I think so.' Now was the time to tell Kate. Two weeks gone by and into December, and still no one knew. It had been a small miracle, really.

'You *think* so? Is he on his way somewhere else, then? And it's a raw morning. Surely there's time for a bite of toast? Teapot's on the hob . . .'

'If you're sure?' Lorna glanced round the empty kitchen. 'Martha not here?'

'Not yet. Now that Mick's gone – now that she's working here on a regular basis – she comes in at eight. Stays till four. Same hours as Goff. Didn't Ness tell you?'

'She probably did. I've had a lot on my mind lately.' To tell Kate was only fair to Ness; would save her having to watch every word she said when Lorna's name was mentioned. She sat at the table, staring down at her gloves, knitted from odd bits of wool. No two fingers the same colour. 'Look, Kate – this is in confidence, not that I think you'll blab it round the village. Only Ness knows, this far – and the solicitor in York.'

'Solicitor?' Kate's head jerked up from the bread she was toasting at the fire.

'Sounds ominous, doesn't it? And it is. William has left me and I've agreed to a divorce.' It hurt more than she had thought to say it out loud.

'A *what*? Divorce, did you say?' She said it as if Lorna had gone out of her mind. 'Well! I don't know what to say! And what was the cause of it – or can't you tell me?'

She turned her attention to the toast, arranging the bread on the fork, unable to meet Lorna's gaze.

'Oh, I can tell you. You might as well have the lot! William was seeing a woman in Aldershot and to cut a sordid story short, she's having his child. I don't have any option, Kate. The baby is due early summer by my reckoning. They'd like to marry before it's born.'

'Well!' Kate said again, reaching down with the knife to the bottom of the dripping jar to where the meaty sediment lay. 'Can't ever remember a divorce in Ainsty! Don't know what to say, lass, except that I'm sorry – for you, I mean – though I never thought your William had one bad bone in his body, him so – so –'

'Respectable?'

'Yes. I suppose that's the word I'm looking for. But how about yourself? Is Ness looking after you, then?'

'I'd be lost without her, Kate. And now that I'm over the initial shock, it isn't so bad. Not being wanted, discarded, that hurts. But he isn't contesting the divorce. It'll go through fairly quickly. Uncontested they do, Mr Wainwright said.'

'Then you just eat up this dripping toast, my girl; get some goodness inside you! And I can't say I'm not shocked, because I am. But I'll say nothing. Ness never let slip a word, you know.'

'She'll be relieved now, not having to watch it. And I shall tell Flora because I trust her, too. Won't be long before it gets out, I suppose, but by then I'll be better able to cope with it. Once it gets to be village gossip, I don't suppose

I'll mind much what people say.' She bit into the toast and was surprised how good it tasted. 'Mind, Martha's going to have a field day once she finds out. And Nance will go all holier-than-thou on me, she being a pillar of the church.'

'Then we'll keep it quiet for as long as we can, eh? And thank you for trusting me, Lorna. I'm fair shaken up. Reckon it must have taken a lot of courage to tell me, and none of it your fault, either. Oh – *men*!'

It wasn't until after Lorna had gone that Kate finally came to terms with what she had just learned. Nasty business, divorce, especially when there was adultery attached and a baby on the way, an' all. And him back with his unit and Lorna, poor lass, having to take all the backwash.

But William Hatherwood going off the rails? Didn't seem possible, him so staid and more like Lorna's father than her man. Kate had often wondered why there had been no bairns at Ladybower – they'd been married long enough – and had come to the conclusion that him being middle-aged and set in his ways it was going to take a little longer to get around to it. You couldn't exactly call him an eager young tup.

Yet he hadn't been backward with the woman in Aldershot, had he? Made you wonder what the world was coming to. The war to blame, she supposed. But poor Lorna. It just wasn't fair.

'It just isn't fair on Lorna.' She heard Ness's footsteps on the cobbles outside. 'A right dirty old man that William of hers has turned out to be. Who'd have thought she'd ever have to divorce him, though.' She turned to see Martha transformed into wonder on the step. 'Oh, my Lord, what have I done? And me thinking you was Ness! Why didn't you cough or something? And what are you doing here so early, Martha Hugwitty?' she demanded testily. 'You aren't due for a good half hour yet!'

'And that's all the thanks I'm offered for getting myself here early. "Kate can do with a hand with the breakfasts,"

I said to myself. "Got to pull together with Mick gone off to the war." And I get nasty looks and accusations for my pains! Sorry, I'm sure!'

'No you're not, Martha Hugwitty. You just heard something you shouldn't have and more fool me for thinking you were Ness!'

'Well I'm not, so are you going to tell me?'

'Indeed I am *not*! You've heard too much already! And how I'm going to face Lorna I don't know, and her trusting me with a confidence!'

'So William Hatherwood has been messing about and Lorna's divorcing him? That's all I heard. And that he's a dirty old man!'

Martha's eyes were bright. Here was scandal, gossip at its very best. But she must tread carefully; didn't want to get on the wrong side of Kate Wintersgill who was mild as a summer's day most times, but could be very firm and forthright when crossed.

''Twas me said he was a dirty old man, not Lorna. But all else is the truth, though you got it out of me by stealth, creeping about the place, listening.'

'Not a word shall pass my lips, Kate, you have my word – leastways, not till it's common knowledge, and then –'

'Then you'll be in like a shot with your two-penn'orth, saying you'd known all the time, I suppose! Well, you'd better say nothing, 'cause if it gets around Ainsty I'll know who's responsible for spreading nasty rumours!'

'Rumour? Sounded like fact the way you said it. But Lorna's secret is safe with me.' Martha unwound her muffler and hung her coat on the door peg. 'Forgotten, I said. Now, would there be a cup of tea on this cold morning?'

'Not unless you put that pot to warm on the side hob and pour some boiling water into it. Then you can take a mug to Rowley and Bob in the shippon. Tell them it's warmed up and watered down and if they don't like it, they can lump it!'

And with that Kate took herself upstairs to make the beds. She would plump pillows and turn mattresses and get rid of the anger inside her. Because she was very angry and mostly with herself, fool she had been! But she would tell Ness, who was due in any minute, what had happened and would she tell Lorna how very grieved Kate Wintersgill was about the way it had happened. And that Martha had had the hard word from Kate's own lips and wouldn't dare to say one word in the village – or else!

She billowed a sheet onto the bed and felt a little better. Ness would help; she was fond of Lorna. Ness, Kate shouldn't wonder, wouldn't give Martha the time of day; and tell her to keep her mouth shut if she knew what was good for her. And Martha *did* know what was good for her; knew to keep on the right side of Glebe Farm who lately had provided her with a regular job with midday dinner and a few off-the-ration eggs. And milk every night to take home with her. Even Martha wouldn't be so daft as to blab!

Comforted, Kate patted the rose silk eiderdown she and Bob had slept beneath these last twenty-eight years and hoped that maybe – with a little conniving and a lot of luck, nothing of what Lorna had said this morning would get past these four walls.

Kate Wintersgill was the original eternal optimist. At half past twelve, when Lorna was setting out for the surgery, Nance Ellery called,

'Lorna! *Wait*! I must speak to you!'

So Lorna stood to watch her puffing past the duck pond, face red, hat askew.

'I'm on my way to work, Nance. Is it important?'

'*Important*! Divorcing your husband and I have to hear about it second-hand! Me, your friend and confidant! Didn't I say to you – and not so very long ago at that – that if ever you needed to talk, ask advice, you only had to come to me. Yet it's Martha Hugwitty tells me!'

'Told you?' Lorna's mouth had gone dry. '*Martha* told you? And who told *her*?'

'She got it from Glebe Farm.'

'But *how*?' She had only a few hours ago told Kate. Surely Kate above all people hadn't –

'Martha went to work early this morning. Seems she overheard a conversation. Or something like that! Anyway, I am hurt, Lorna. Why you couldn't have confided in me, I will never know!'

'I didn't tell you, Nance, because I thought you'd be angry with me – that you didn't approve of divorce.' It was as near to the truth as she dare say.

'Nor do I! Marriage is for ever. Whom God hath joined. So William went off the rails?'

'Yes, Nance. And I'm sorry, but I'm only just coming to terms with it myself! I feel guilty, you see, even though it wasn't my fault.'

'No need to sound so apologetic, young woman! As far as I'm concerned, that marriage of yours was a total mismatch right from the start! Never agreed with it, myself. "She's taking the first man who's asked her," I said to Gilbert. "Why on earth does she want a man who's old enough to be her father – well – who *looks* old enough!" So who did he go off the rails with? Anyone I know?'

'She's called Primrose Smythe-Parker. She was stationed at Aldershot, too. She – she's pregnant, Nance.'

There now, Lorna, tell the truth and shame the devil!

'Ha! I ought to say you surprise me, but I can't. Never liked William Hatherwood. I said to Gilbert at the time, "He's doing all right for himself, and Lorna worth a pound or two! Knows what he's doing!" Anyway, I warned Martha Hugwitty. Told her to be careful what she said and not go spreading nasty gossip. Said she'd have me to contend with, if she did!'

'But how did you get to know? Martha was at the farm, surely?'

'So she was. But Gilbert knocked over the milk jug and the day's ration with it. I'd gone to Glebe to beg a drop more – just this once, I said. Kate and Ness weren't there, but Martha let me have the milk – and the news!'

'So you're on my side? You don't blame me?'

'Of course I'm on your side, Lorna. And what is more, if there is tittle-tattle in Ainsty, they'll have me to deal with! Now, what are the true facts of the matter, so I can put the gossipmongers right?'

'The bare facts, Nance, but true. William came on leave and told me he wanted a divorce because someone he was going out with was three months pregnant. He admitted the child was his. He wants it all over with as soon as possible so the baby can be born in wedlock.'

'Right! That's all I need to know. I'll put the village straight if they start embroidering it! And you *are* the innocent party, don't forget. Now off with you to work. I'm sorry things have turned out so badly for you. You did the right thing, though.'

And with that she was off, straightening her official WVS hat as she went, tucking in wisps of hair, her back quivering with indignation – or was it triumph – at being the recipient of the official version?

Old fraud, Lorna thought fondly, knowing that if Nance was on her side, who then would dare be against her!

She let go a sigh of relief and set off for the surgery. The worst, gossip-wise, was over. She had been tried by Nun Ainsty's Grand Panjandrum and adjudged the innocent party. So what had she to worry about? Only the end of a marriage; only an awful aloneness as if nothing could ever be the same again. And the feeling of failure, of course. She had failed as a wife and a lover. An Ice Maiden, wasn't she?

Yet she had known passion, briefly, in a moonlit wood when a goodbye kiss had aroused something inside her she had not known to exist. Her kisses were abandoned and urgent and for a few unbelievably wonderful moments, she wanted Ewan desperately, with every wilful pulse in her body urging her on. She had run from him and now he was a part of her loneliness, too.

'Stop it, Lorna,' the voice of reason inside her commanded. 'You are not a war widow; merely a casualty of war. And you have Ladybower and Ness and gossipy little Nun Ainsty which has never heard an air-raid siren, let alone been bombed.'

And soon it would be Christmas, then New Year and new hopes and beginnings, and, in no time at all, February and snowdrops and nights getting lighter. So roll on spring and Ness's blessing in a Devon church and oh, so many good things to look forward to. No more looking back. She must learn to think dispassionately not only about William but about Ewan MacMillan, too. She must never, ever, allow herself to think of Ewan again.

'You are young, Lorna, and alive,' she insisted as she waited at the crossroads. 'And if you need a bonus, you have no one to answer to now but yourself.'

She looked right and left, not just for oncoming traffic but in case someone had been lurking in the hedgeback and heard her talking to herself; the mad divorcée!

'Oh, for Pete's sake, get yourself to work,' she muttered, not caring. And why should she care when there was nothing she could do to change any of it?

Lorna had been to church at St Philippa's. Evensong was held once a month there, in winter. All other evensongs were held at Meltonby church, at three in the afternoon because of the high windows and the impossibility of blacking them out. St Philippa's on the other hand was tiny, with small windows that were easy to fit blackout curtains to. Consequently, evensong was at half past six, at the time it should be.

Lorna had left it until the very last minute to go in; had pushed aside the door curtain at six twenty-nine exactly, knowing that all who were going would be there. The entire village, plus one or two from Meltonby, were seated as she walked slowly down the aisle to the very front pew, head defiantly high. This was her coming out as a single woman; was where she must confront Nun Ainsty, and where better a place? Was she picking up her life, three weeks after, or was she testing her grit and granite to its utmost? She wished she knew. Maybe, really, she needed the reassurance of the people of Nun Ainsty before she finally wrote The End to her marriage.

She rose from her knees when the priest entered. Once, there had not even been pews in St Philippa's because those for whom it was built had been expected to stand, or to kneel. Pews had been added by the squire who built the manor house. He had taken stones from the roofless priory, then put pews in St Philippa's, it was thought, to salve his conscience for stealing holy stones. That was how legend had it, but no one knew for certain if it were true. Like Ursula and Dickon.

The priest intoned the Trinity, then announced the number of the first hymn. Nance, already seated at the little reedy organ with Gilbert beside her to operate the bellows, gave the standing-up chord, then launched into 'Fight the Good Fight'. Nance always launched into things. Both feet first usually, yet now, gratefully, Nance Ellery was her ally and it would be a tribute to that lady's standing in the village, if, when the service was over, people treated her as they had always done when she was William's wife. And amazingly, they did, and Lorna left the little chapel feeling both forgiven and uplifted.

'I'll walk with you, Lorna, as far as the pillar box. Got my flashlight,' Martha offered when the congregation was outside and blinking in the darkness. 'Glad you felt able to come to church tonight.'

'Oh, yes, Martha. Christian charity is a great comfort. I have so many good friends in Ainsty, you know.'

'I notice Ness Nightingale wasn't there.'

'No. Ness – er – *Hardie* is of a different persuasion. When I left her, she was writing to her husband. He's in Northumberland, doing his initial Army training; the drilling and square bashing bit, you know, but he expects very soon to be sent to do his medical orderly training.'

Lorna dared her, mentally, to say one – just *one* word about William's fall from grace, but not one word did Martha utter.

'I'm in a bit of a hurry,' she confided. 'Want to get home and switch the wireless on. Was having a word with Flora Petch. She asked me what I made of the announcement after the six o'clock news and I had to confess I hadn't listened. Well, nowt but bad news, these days. Best ignore it, when you can.'

'But what did Flora say was on the wireless, Martha?'

'Oh, the usual news, then it seems the announcer said that there would be an extended news bulletin at nine, and they don't do that unless there's something awful happened.' Like the fall of France, Martha recalled, and the evacuation at Dunkirk. And the invasion of Russia, an' all. 'Reckon Hitler's invaded somewhere else, if you ask me.'

'Martha! Hitler is having a bad enough time of it in Russia.' Even though Leningrad was under siege and Moscow surrounded, nothing much was happening on the Eastern Front at the moment. The winter had seen to that. German soldiers had no Arctic clothing and tanks could not be moved because their tracks were frozen. 'I'm sure another invasion is the last thing on Hitler's mind.'

'Then what do you suppose it is? They can't cut the rations any more. We're starving already!'

'We are *not* starving, Martha. We have fair shares and enough to get by on. The people in Leningrad would give their right arm for rations like ours. And electricity and gas, and a warm fire to sit beside.'

'Hm.' It was all Martha Hugwitty could say because she wasn't used to such an assertive Lorna. Maybe being deserted had made her a bit bossy. Tragedy affected different people in different ways. 'Well, here's the pillar box.' She pointed her blacked-out torch at it to make out a dull red glimmer. 'Bid you good night, Lorna.'

'And you, Martha. Mind how you go.' Then she hurried indoors to tell Ness about the nine o'clock news.

The announcer who read the nine o'clock news spoke the King's English in the clipped, unemotional tones that announcers were obliged to use. Their funereal voices, Ness always said. But even Ness, who was still high on a cloud of happiness, was unprepared for what was to come.

It has been released by the Ministry of Information that this morning, Japanese planes attacked the American Pacific Fleet at Pearl Harbor. It is understood that grave damage was inflicted and that there are many casualties.

It is also understood that the United States of America has declared war on Japan and that Mr Churchill will speak to both Houses of Parliament at three p.m. tomorrow, it was officially announced from Downing Street. Mr Churchill is expected to give MPs a full review of the situation arising from Japan's aggression.

The Ministry of Information has advised that more news may be released shortly and, if this is so, it will be announced on the BBC's regular ten forty-five or midnight bulletins . . .

'You *what*!' Ness demanded, wide-eyed. 'What are them stupid Japs thinkin' about? You can't start bombing somebody else's ships without declaring war on them first! They're acting like bluddy Hitler! Anyway, I don't know how they managed to find them warships. They're all short-sighted; they all wear glasses!'

'Well, it seems they've upset the applecart all right. You don't want any more of this, do you?' Lorna, white faced, turned off the set.

'Nah. We'll read about it in the papers in the mornin'. No use looking for trouble.'

'But will there be any of it in the newspapers? The government censors everything they print. Maybe they'll slap a D-notice on it – or whatever it's called.'

'It'll be in the papers in the mornin',' Ness said positively. 'And till then, there's nuthin' you and me can do about it.'

'You aren't taking it very seriously, Ness. You just don't go messing with the Americans. Look what happened in the Great War when the Kaiser's lot sunk the *Lusitania*.'

'That was different. It was women and innocent children that got killed.'

Ness, now that she had thought about it, was of a mind to wait until morning – see what the papers made of it. She was not prepared to get herself into a state over what those slitty-eyed little fellers did thousands of miles away.

'Ness. Just *think* won't you? Or are you shoving your head in the sand because you don't want to know? It happened. The BBC don't get things wrong.'

'Then are we stoppin' up for the ten forty-five bulletin?'

'N-no. What we've just heard is bad enough. I don't want to hear any more. Like you say, it'll wait until morning. There'll be dance music on the Forces programme soon. We'll listen to that . . .'

And Ness agreed. It would be far nicer to listen to dance music and close her eyes and pretend she was dancing with Mick. Far better than worrying about something she could do nothing about. Tomorrow would be time enough for that.

Mrs Benson pounced on the newspapers the bus conductor carried into the room at the back of the post office, cutting the string instead of unpicking the knot in her eagerness to read that the Japanese pilots had only sunk a fishing boat and that somewhere along the line, someone had got it wrong.

'It's true, then!'

'Seems like it.' Lorna picked up a *Daily Mail*, all four pages of it. Indeed, so serious was the news that it took up the entire front page.

'Y'know, Mrs B, it means that America and us will have to declare war on *them*. That's going to mean that the entire world is at war, because sure as anything, the Commonwealth will follow suit. God! How stupid men can be! Why was it allowed to happen!'

'Don't ask me, Lorna! More's the pity there weren't a few more women in power – in Germany, as well as this country. Women wouldn't allow wars. Got a bit more sense than men; don't like rearing sons to be killed.'

'I – I don't think women in government would be a good thing, Mrs B. Women are too tender-hearted. I mean – it isn't all that long ago that women got the vote. Will we be having tea this morning?' It seemed politic to change the subject.

'Of course we're having tea! Meltonby Post Office doing without its morning tea, indeed! The world's on the edge of disaster it seems to me. Let's keep a bit of sanity here, at least.'

'But won't people want their newspapers good and early this morning?'

'Tea'll be ready in five minutes. That gives you time to sort your letters and papers, Lorna, which will be delivered at the usual time and not a minute before!'

And time, for Nun Ainsty letters and newspapers, was six forty-five; there or thereabouts. Come to think about it, Mrs B was right, Lorna conceded. People who lived around these parts were lucky, could sometimes think the war hadn't happened.

Mind, they would soon realize it had, especially Friday mornings when food rations for the week were doled out and when the new huge planes, some flown by boys not yet of age, took off almost every other night. Except foggy nights or when ice on the runway made takeoff impossible.

Lorna began to sort. Silly of her, really, to think that even for a moment could she forget the war. Or William and Primrose. Or Ewan, who had vanished from her life.

She placed the letters in delivery order, slipping one addressed to herself in her pocket. It was from Mr Wainwright, she could tell by the typing on the envelope, because the keys were in need of a clean. The letters b, d and o, for instance, came out as solid blobs which didn't look very efficient, if you wanted to be nit-picky. The keys of her own machine at the surgery were cleaned with a toothbrush every Monday morning. She typed quite well now. It was amazing how many things the war had insisted she should learn.

'Tea!' called Mrs Benson. 'Come and get it and go easy on the milk!'

That had been the start of the day and Lorna was quite sure it could get no worse; that having accepted it was only a matter of hours before Mr Churchill announced that Great Britain, too, was at war with Japan, surely nothing so awful could happen again for a long time – much less today.

Yet when she read Mr Wainwright's letter asking her to ring him on a matter most urgent, she realized that that day was to turn out to be even more awful.

Ringing York wasn't too bad. Telephone delays were worst on trunk calls which could take hours coming through – if at all. But, because bad news was known to travel fast, she was able to call his office with little delay.

'Ah, Lorna my dear. Good of you to ring. And I'll be brief. The solicitors for Hatherwood and Smythe-Parker have already been told and they accepted the news with bad grace, I'm afraid.'

'*Bad* news?' Lorna whispered.

'Bad news for them. I'm afraid, you see, that we are going to have to wait until late February for a hearing. And whilst I am hopeful that undefended your petition would go through without too many problems, even if you are granted a decree nisi by early March, for instance, there is still six months to wait for your decree absolute. Do you understand me, my dear?'

'I think I do. It looks as if – well – the baby is going to be a few months old when – when –'

'The child, as far as I can see, will not be born to married parents.'

Later, she told Ness about it.

'It's the baby I'm sorry for, being born illegitimate.'

'I don't understand all the delay. William wants a divorce; you're willing to give him one – why the wait?'

'Because after the divorce is granted, there's got to be a period of six months before it's completely final; before the decree absolute kicks in. And during that time, would you believe, Ness, I'm going to have to keep my nose clean – not do anything wrong, like taking a lover or anything.'

'But why shouldn't you? You're the innocent party and her and William aren't going to defend it – what's to do with the six-months thing?'

'I'm not altogether sure. All I know is there's this King's proctor. If I do anything I shouldn't and he gets to know about it, then I'm in trouble and I suppose the divorce proceedings will have to start all over again.'

'Sounds a shifty little sod to me. Think you might have got it wrong, Lorna?'

'No. Mr Wainwright explained it all, this morning. And the King's proctor isn't a little man in a bowler hat who hides behind bushes, spying on me. He's a legal person, sort of, and it's him – or his office – who could come down on me. There's no such thing, I'm beginning to learn, as a cut and dried divorce.'

'I think,' Ness said after due consideration, 'that divorce isn't very nice. Apart from the sinning you've got to do to get one, it's innocent people who've got to mind their Ps and Qs an' all. You, for instance.'

'And that baby, too, poor little thing. Everything seems to get worse, doesn't it? And to think that not so long ago I was worrying about blobby Bs and Ds.'

'Worrying about *what*?'

'Oh, nothing. Just something to do with typewriter keys. Not important at all, when you come to think of it.'

'I suppose it isn't. By the way – and this isn't definite – I might be going to Ruth Street at Christmas. Mind, it's entirely up to Rowley and if he says he can cope with the extra work. Leastways, that's what Kate said. "If our Rowley is willing, then I don't see why you shouldn't go to see your folks." '

'And is he willing?'

'Put it this way – he hasn't said no. And I know you'd be alone on Christmas Eve and for all Christmas Day, but I'd be back on the Friday, as early as I can. It's just that Kate thought that since I spent my leave at Devon, they might be glad to see me at number three – hear all the wedding gossip. And about the blessing later on. There's that to be talked about, an' all.'

'You'd go on the twenty-fourth – early? I can always take you to Meltonby for the first bus. You'd be in York station a little after seven. You could be in Liverpool by about one o'clock, if you're lucky.'

'If I can get on the train, don't you mean? Everybody'll be wanting to be home for Christmas.'

'Worth it, Ness, for all that.'

'So you don't mind me going; don't mind having Christmas Day on your own?'

'Why should I? If you hadn't come to Ladybower, I'd be on my own anyway. I'll have to get used to that, won't I? William not coming on leave any more, I mean.'

'Reckon you will, queen. But if you're sure you don't mind . . .'

'Of course not. Things slow up a bit on farms over Christmas; they do only the essential work. Better you have time off then, before threshing starts. And it means you'll be here for New Year's Eve. I'd like us to be together then – make our wishes when Big Ben chimes, and all that jazz.'

'Then I'll tell Kate I'd like to go. And I know Rowley'll

say yes. I think Christmas is going to be a big day at Glebe. I rather think him and Olivia are getting engaged – but not a word to anyone.'

'Rowley engaged? I never thought the girl existed who could corner him! Kate will be relieved. That was a nasty run-in you had with him, Ness.'

'Yes. Looking back, it was great the way Mick heaved him through the door face down onto the yard. But it's all forgotten now. And you're sure about Christmas?'

'Sure. Your folks haven't seen you for ages, and anyway, I'd rather we were together at New Year. One thing's certain, Ness. 1942 has got to be better – well, for me, anyway!'

Ness walked up the platform at Lime Street Station. The bus station was conveniently near, and she would get on the first red bus that was going along Scotland Road.

Excitement quickened her step. This was her town, this knocked-about, bomb-blasted port with its boarded-up windows and rubble-piled bomb sites. It was everything Nun Ainsty was not; dirty, down at the heel, bustling with signs of war. The docks, though she could not see them, would be full of warships and merchant ships, and down river, where the Mersey met the sea, many more would wait at anchor for a river pilot to guide them into a berth.

Liverpool was prosperous now. The war had made it so. Employment for all and every race and creed and religion crowding its streets. Loads of servicemen and women, too, mostly Royal Navy. They said there was a secret headquarters somewhere near the Pierhead; an underground place safe from bombs that looked after all the Atlantic convoys and, lately, the convoys trying to reach Murmansk with tanks and guns and ammunition for Russia.

'Thanks, queen.' The woman at the barrier punched her ticket and it was good to hear Scouse-as-it-was-spoke all around her. A change from the flat accents of Ainsty people.

A number fifty-nine bus stood ready to leave and Ness

found a window seat. A lot less crowded than the train. The compartment, intended for six, had had ten crammed into it plus kitbags and cases shoved onto the luggage racks and piled on the floor. The corridor outside had been no better, with people prepared to stand all the way, if that was what it took to get to Liverpool.

Now she rested her elbow on the sill and sat, chin on hand, to see familiar streets and squares of houses, then start as a tram crashed past them. She loved the green trams. Always had. They were so noisy, so aggressive as they clanked and hurtled along. When she was little, a ride on a tram was something special, especially if it was with Uncle Perce who seemed to know all the drivers and always got a seat at the front.

Dear old Liverpool. She was going to forsake it when the war was over, to live in a village not very much bigger than Nun Ainsty in a house called Deep Hay where no two windows were the same size, and there were wide, low doors and open stone fireplaces. When the war was over, of course. She crossed her fingers and watched the ends of terraces of houses as they passed. Soon, she would get off at the second stop along Scotland Road and there would be Ruth Street, only a cock's stride away. Number three. Home.

It only occurred to Ness as she opened the front door that it could well have been locked; that Mam and Nan might have been queueing at the shops, but she tiptoed down the red and black tiled passage to the open kitchen door.

'Mam! Happy Christmas!'

'Ness! Oh, lovely girl, let's have a look at you.' Rose Nightingale hugged her daughter then pushed her to arm's length, regarding her gravely.

'No, Mam. I'm not expecting! We didn't have to get married! And I'm on a flying visit. Got to leave early Friday but, oh, it's smashin' to see you! Where's Nan?'

'Gone down to the baker's for the bun loaf.' In Liverpool

you always had bun loaf at Christmas. It ranked equally with the cake and the plum pudding. 'Not that it'll be up to much, rationin' bein' what it is. Was lucky to get one, when you think of it. I'm taking it to Tizzy's. Said I'd provide the pudding and the bun loaf; Perce is providing the goose, and don't ask where he got it!'

Perce could get things, but you didn't ask which lorry it had fallen off the back of, or outside which pub he had acquired it.

'We're going over the water for Christmas dinner! It'll be like old times again!'

'Almost. And Ness, girl, I'm glad you're wed and happy. You *are* happy? And what about that ring! Where on earth did you get it? It's twenty-four-carat, if I'm not mistaken.'

'Mick's Mam gave it to me. She inherited it. Victorian, she said it was.'

'Ar. Them Victorians were a funny lot, but they made things to last. Now get out of that coat, then you can dry the dishes whilst I put the kettle on. Your Nan will be back soon, then you can tell us all about your Mick and – oh – *everything*.'

Ness smiled and the awful journey was forgotten and the equally awful journey back in a crowded, smoke-filled compartment, which was not to be thought about because she was one of the lucky ones, with her family for Christmas Day. It made her think about Lorna being alone – alone for ever now.

'And there's more to tell, Mam. Lorna's divorcing her husband!'

Rose Nightingale's eyes went saucer-wide and her cheeks flushed red, because ten minutes ago she had been washing dishes in the sink, yet now Ness had arrived with never one word to say she was coming, bringing gossip about the wedding and a divorce of all things, to oh and ah over. And Christmas with Perce and Tizzy. It was just too much. For two pins she would break down and cry her head off with happiness. But because Liverpudlians are made of sterner stuff, she smiled and said,

'Ar, Ness, you can't begin to imagine how lovely it is to have you home.'

The armchairs in the sitting room at Ladybower were old and should have, would have been replaced had the war not happened and everything that made life pleasant declared unnecessary – and unobtainable. Ness was glad the chairs were old and saggy, because they were lovely to curl up in, to burrow into like nests. And with firelight on the white, uneven walls and lamplight throwing shadows into corners, you had to feel lucky this New Year's Eve. Because weren't there women with husbands away at war and whose homes had been bombed, being forced to live in government centres during the day and in the Underground at night? If she let herself, she could feel guilty, Ness thought, especially when she had Mick, who had phoned her from Northumberland only a few minutes ago. Got lucky, he'd said.

'Funny, when you think, that a year has just flown past since we last sat here, hoping for a phone call,' Lorna sighed.

'Only it was you, hoping William might ring.'

'Yes, and when he did, remember, I could hear a party going on. Pity he ever went to it. That was where it all started between him and – and *her*.' Lorna's knitting needles clicked faster.

'It makes a change, though, you not everlastingly scribbling, Lorna. You must have saved a small fortune on writing pads and stamps since it happened. At least now you can sit down and knit sometimes. You're not too upset, are you; not putting a brave face on it?'

'No, Ness. It was a shock I'll admit, but now it's just a question of getting through a messy divorce – that's all it seems to amount to.'

'Messy! It's pretty straightforward, if you ask me. No

property to haggle over and no kids to want custody of. And all right, I'm hitting below the belt, but didn't someone once say that if you have none to laugh over you have none to cry over, either? It's a good job, as things have turned out, that you and him never had a family. Children should have a mother and a father in the same house.'

'OK, Ness. You've made your point. And I do know what it's like not to have two parents. Life was pretty rough for me until Grandpa brought me to Ladybower.'

'Sorry, queen. Shouldn't have said what I did. And there *will* be kids for you, Martha said so. Tell you what – why don't we have another go? Let's nip over there one night, see if anything's changed.'

'Everything has changed for me, Ness. And knowing what she knows now, Martha would tell us exactly what we wanted to hear; that Mick would come safely home from the war and for me – well, there would be a tall dark man, dimly in the future. And three children, of course.'

'Don't forget the carelessly got bit! And she'd be wrong about you. He isn't dark, is he?'

'I don't know what you mean, Ness!'

'Yes, you do. And if I were you, I'd wish like mad when it's midnight, for Ewan – who is *fair* – to appear out of the dim future and be sharp about it.'

'Ness! I'm sorry I told you about Ewan now. He's gone. Not a word from him to anybody. He hasn't even written to Reg Summers. Don't pin your hopes on him, Ness. I'm not. And I'm going to take that picture he gave me off the wall!'

'Whatever you say, girl. It's your picture and your wall!'

'I do say!' She folded her knitting and stuffed it into a carrier bag, wondering how she would feel if the Land Army sent Ness somewhere else, and she didn't phone or write; disappeared completely as Ewan had done. Because, all things considered, she had no one in the world now, but Ness. No mother, and if her father were alive he was in no hurry to find her! No husband, no grandparents. And if Ness, who had become almost a sister, vanished from her life, she would be alone in the world.

Imagine having to wonder who to leave Ladybower to, and the grandfather clock in the hall? And her rings and Grandpa's gold pocket watch. Was anyone in this village as alone as Lorna Hatherwood?

She glanced at Ness, who sat, eyes closed, a smile lifting the corners of her mouth, doubtless thinking of Mick and what they had said tonight. Ness had always been notice-me attractive; now she was beautiful. Love had made her so. It glowed vibrant and golden around her.

Lorna Hatherwood's love – if you could call it that – had been timid and pinkish. It had faded quickly because it had had no substance. Ewan was gone, and she accepted she would never see him again, but at least now she knew how a kiss should be, how it could excite, send need screaming through her. But that episode in her life must be forgotten – the kisses, the moonlit wood and the scent of roses growing beside the gap in the hedge.

'Penny for them, queen! You were miles away.'

'So were you. Thinking about Mick, I shouldn't wonder. You had a very smug look on your face, Mrs Hardie.'

'Mm. A few minutes – that's all there was but . . .'

'But you made the most of it – full of I-love-yous, I shouldn't wonder.'

'Oh, we talked about other things – in-between. Like he's getting moved on Wednesday to start his medical training. Somewhere south, to a place in Suffolk. A lot further away.'

'Never mind. The time will soon pass. It'll be the end of March before you know it.'

'Time doesn't soon pass, Lorna – not when you're apart. But I'll have to put up with it. There's a whole lot more like me. By the way, I told him I'd been to Ruth Street and that they were all dead chuffed to be goin' to Devon. He was pleased about that. Then he said he was going to the NAAFI to see the New Year in with a couple of pints. Said he'd think about me when Big Ben came on the wireless. I do love him. It hurts, wanting him. I'm glad I've got you to help me through it.'

'Funny, that. I was thinking much the same thing; hoping you'd never get sent away from Nun Ainsty. So, because we haven't got anything better, or more alcoholic, shall we have a cup of tea?'

'Later. Nearer to midnight? We'll use the best cups and saucers, and make our wishes then. But don't you think we should talk about last year – count blessings? Mind, you haven't many to count, Lorna, but I have Mick, and I know things will turn out right for you, too.'

'Well – if you're talking about the war, things are going better than at last New Year. We've got America on our side now, don't forget.'

'Happen we have, but America's goin' to be fighting them Japs. They won't want to be bothered about what's happening this side of the Atlantic. And somebody's got to square up to Japan. The cheek of them, taking Hong Kong. And waiting till Christmas Day to do it!'

'I suppose they've got their eyes on India now. When is it going to end, Ness!'

'Dunno. But it was flamin' Hitler started it, so maybe you should ask him.'

'Or Martha?' Lorna forced a smile.

'Listen, queen, if Martha Hugwitty knew when it's all going to end, she could make a fortune, putting bets on with the bookies! Anyway, I know what I shall wish for – what about you, Lorna?'

'Afraid there isn't one constructive wish in my head, right now, so I don't think I'll bother, when midnight comes.'

All the same, it might be good to know, not when it would all end, but *how*. Because if you thought about it, there were an awful lot of battles to be fought. Perhaps, though, something absolutely marvellous would happen; something like us winning just *one* battle? More in the way of a miracle, perhaps.

And miracles, Lorna knew, were pretty thin on the ground these days.

TWENTY-FIVE

How It All Ended

New Year's Eve, 1946. A time to look back, a time to look forward. Many times she had sat in this room and dreamed and wished and hoped. She and Ness together it had been until now, yet tonight would be different. For the first time since war started, Lorna was alone to dream and wish and to hope. Yet before she could even begin to look forward, she must arrange things in order in her mind, help decide what she must do with her life and hope that some peevish trick of Fate would not remind her that few things ever went to plan. For Lorna Hatherwood, that was.

Tonight she had done everything as it had always been done; had lit the fire with only a few pieces of coal – the war over these sixteen months, and coal still rationed – then piled it with logs gleaned in the wood after the October gale; she and Ness sawing logs for the last time. Both had known and accepted it, because soon Ness was to leave Glebe Farm.

And when the fire was burning brightly and the room warmer, Lorna had laid the tea tray with a starched cloth and the rosebud china, ready for the chimes-of-Big-Ben ritual, when they had solemnly raised their cups in a toast to the year to come.

Tonight she would not indulge in self-pity. Tonight she would think back. Every New Year's Eve to come she would do it, so it became a rite of remembering lovely things, and trying hard to forget things best forgotten. And above all else, a time to accept with humility what she could not change. There were many women who would spend this night in loneliness, remembering; women whose husbands or sweethearts had not come back from the war, and of whom Lorna Hatherwood was one, for couldn't she too be called a war widow?

Yet thinking too much about her aloneness must be forbidden, too, so she tucked her feet beneath her, wriggling herself comfortable in the armchair, to dip into her memories.

She chose a favourite one. April 4th, 1942. Mick had been given ten days' embarkation leave and a starry-eyed Ness counting off days, then hours.

'Mick's Mam wants a proper wedding,' Ness had said. 'Not just a blessing. She wants the whole lot and for Mick and me to say the vows as if it was the first time.'

Mind, the vicar at Borton-under-Whytchwood hadn't been at all sure he could do it, and referred the matter to his bishop. It had turned out all right. The bishop said yes – with the reservation that it would not be possible to have the ceremony entered in the parish register, which no one was the least bit bothered about as long as the *words* were said.

So beautiful, that Devon village and the age-old house called Deep Hay. Daffodils massed yellow in the apple orchard, the trees a cloud of pink blossom and hedgerows freshly green as if all the beauty was a backcloth, especially ordered for that special day.

So lovely a family. So many Hardies and Nightingales and all of them packed into six bedrooms and two attics. Mick's twin sisters; Ness's Mam, Da and Nan from Ruth Street and Perce and Tizzy from over the water. And she, Lorna, had insisted on being there and stayed at a bed and breakfast in the village, arranged for her by Mick's mother; with a lady whose husband was an anti-aircraft gunner stationed on Malta and who had yet to see his youngest son.

Mick's twin sisters were each given a forty-eight hour leave pass and had worn their prettiest dresses and picked bunches of daffodils to carry as bouquets down the aisle, behind Ness on her father's arm.

Ness had been so happy it made her even more beautiful. She too wore a simple cotton dress and carried a sheaf of cherry blossom, picked that morning from the garden and tied with a long white ribbon.

Both mothers had wept a little as Mick slipped the old gold ring on Ness's finger for the second time.

'With this ring I thee wed . . .'

They had smiled into each other's eyes and Lorna had pleaded silently, *Please God, let Mick come safely home* . . .

Afterwards they drank cider made by Mick's great uncle and no one had cared that there was no wedding cake, nor a wedding feast.

'Hey, queen – me twice married, eh?' Ness had whispered.

'Twice, Mrs Hardie. Reckon you must both mean it. Be happy, Ness.'

She thought fleetingly of her own marriage, when three weeks ago she had stood in court with Mr Wainwright beside her, to be granted a decree nisi. Six months more, then it had all been finally over.

'Happy? You bet we will.' Ness said, hugging her. 'And I'm glad you made it. Wouldn't have been the same without my sister.'

Such a happy day, meeting Ness's family and Mick's family, shutting out the war until Madeline had returned to her hospital ward and Lydia to the Army transport unit and the lorry she drove. And when she, Lorna, had said goodbye to Mam and Da and Nan and to Perce and Tizzy, too, Mick's mother said,

'You must come again, Lorna, and stay longer. We would love to have you. Such a long way to come for just two days.' They waited for the bus that went to Exeter and the train that would take Lorna to York. 'This is Ness's home, too, now.'

So Lorna had gone back to her war work and to count off the days until Ness returned; a Ness in need of comfort it would be, because she would not know where Mick would be posted, nor when they would see each other again. Not for years and years, maybe. But such a lovely, lovely wedding to think back on. A golden day, to keep special for ever.

Ness returned to Ladybower on the tenth, tired from the long, stop-start journey, desolate that she and Mick had parted.

'Reckon he'll be back in barracks by now. He saw me on the train, y'know. Him in his uniform, me in mine. Standing there, the pair of us, saying nothing. Just holding hands. It was him pushed me on the York train. "All right, Mrs Hardie, this is it – unless you want it to go without you, that is."

'And I said I didn't care if we stood on that platform for the duration and he kissed me and said, "Take care, my wife. I love you." And I told him I loved him, too, though it was all a bit of a blur after that. I stood at the window till I couldn't see him any more. Platform Two. Exeter station. I can't get that train out of my mind, taking me from him. And don't say anything kind, Lorna, or I'll burst out crying and never stop. Sympathy, right now, I can do without.'

There had been only one letter for Ness; it arrived two days later and bore no address; just the stark words, 'Somewhere in England'.

'Suppose by this time he'll be on the way to wherever he's going; some port, maybe, to pick up a troopship.'

'You're sure he's going abroad, Ness?'

'He said so. All I can do now is wait, think about how much I love him, and will him to be safe. We've got a code worked out so he can tell me where he is without the Censor cutting it out with his razor blade. At least I'll know . . .'

It had been on April 28th that the letter came. Lorna was sorting her post on the long table and pounced on it.

'At last! Mrs B. There's a letter for Ness!' She turned it over to read the sender's name.

157663 Pte Hardie M. D. Coy RAMC MELF c/o GPO London.

'MELF means Middle East Land Forces, doesn't it?' Not for nothing had Lorna been a postlady all those months.

'I think so. All the letters for overseas go to GPO London first, that I do know. Well, get your tea drunk, lass, and get that letter delivered. Ness has been waiting for it for a long time, don't forget!'

'Nearly three weeks. I can't wait to see her face.'

And Ness's face, when Lorna arrived out of breath from pedalling so hard, was marvellous to see. She was waiting at Ladybower's gate, dressed ready for work.

'I knew about it. Mrs Benson phoned. Said you'd just left with something for me – and isn't everybody kind?'

'Kind? Let me tell you I haven't made it so fast down Priory Lane before. Open it, Ness? Where is he?'

'Just a quickie to give me his address, he says,' Ness smiled, her voice husky. 'And he loves me, loves me, loves me, loves me – four times he loves me which means, for four of them, that he's in North Africa. Now I can post all those letters I've written.'

'It's a long way away, Ness, but at least he made it there safely. And if you shift yourself and get those letters addressed, I'll pick them up on my way back and post them in Meltonby. There's a collection there at noon.'

'He'll wonder what hit him! There are ten.'

'Good. Keep him out of mischief, reading them. So get a move on, Mrs Hardie. I'll be back in about twenty minutes!'

Lorna had pedalled off, feeling happy because Ness was happy. Happy, too, because the long dark winter was truly over and things could only get better from now on.

But days – especially good ones – tick away, and neither had been prepared for what was to happen, in just a few more hours.

They had been sitting in the garden, Lorna recalled, talking about a day that had been warm and sunny; about Mick, who was safe for the time being, because there had been no reports, lately, of fighting in North Africa.

'I had a letter, too, this morning,' Lorna offered, reluctant to break the mood of contentment. 'From Mr Wainwright. He's heard from the other solicitors. They told him that William is willing to pay the entire cost of the divorce – could be as much as eight hundred pounds, I believe.'

'*That* much? It would buy a nice little house! Only fair, for all that. It was him started it, don't forget. Do you ever think about him, queen?'

'As little as needs be. I'm not properly free yet. Until it's absolute, either of us could call it off.'

'Hey! You wouldn't do that!' Ness was glad to be shot of William, and didn't want him back in Lorna's life.

'No. And nor would he. It's just one of the technicalities Mr Wainwright was duty-bound to tell me – just in case.'

'Good! This has been a lovely day, so don't go spoiling it!'

Ness closed her eyes and lifted her face to the evening sun, thinking about what Mick had really written in the letter – apart from the four I-love-yous. It made her feel loved and cherished – and just a little smug.

'Look at the moon.' Lorna pointed to the tree tops in the wood and the full, white moon that was slowly rising above them. 'A bombers' moon tonight.'

'Oh, shurrup. I told you, didn't I, not to go spoilin' this smashin' day . . .'

Someone was shaking her. Someone was calling 'Lorna! Wake up! Listen!'

'Wha-a-at?' Still half-asleep, Lorna groped for the light switch.

'No! Don't put it on! *Listen . . .*'

There had been no mistaking it. An air-raid alert. The siren on Nance Ellery's garage roof wailed like a soul in hell. They had heard it before. On a trial run, and always at eleven in the morning. No one had minded – until now, because this must be the real thing.

'It can't be! Not at Nun Ainsty.'

Lorna pushed her feet into her slippers then slid her arms into the dressing gown Ness held.

'Come on, Lorna. Downstairs!'

The siren had run its ninety seconds warning. Now, after a last gasping groan it stopped, leaving a silence so dense it was frightening.

'It can't be us, Ness . . .'

'No. It could be Leeds or one of the aerodromes. But bombs fall anywhere. A couple of miles off target is as near as a direct hit.'

This brought it all back to Ness; the night after night bombing when she had been home last May. And them all going into the shelter that had once been a coal cellar.

'You'd think there'd be a cellar in a house this size.'

'Well, there isn't. Only the manor and Glebe Farm have cellars. Shall we go to Glebe, Ness?'

'To Glebe? Are you mad? We stay put, that's what. We stay here till something happens.'

'Happens?' Lorna's hands shook, her mouth had gone dry. She filled a glass at the tap and drank deeply. 'Happens – like what?'

'Like when something drops. We'll know how far away it is, then.'

'They won't hit the village? Nun Ainsty isn't all that important, surely?'

'Then keep your fingers crossed. And *if* they drop anything, we either go under the stairs or under this table. Mind, it might be a false alarm . . .'

It was then they heard the first bomb and hurried beneath the kitchen table to sit, arms clasped round knees, heads lowered.

'How far away was it, Ness?'

'Dunno. Could have been anywhere. Reckon about three or four miles, though.' Ness Hardie was an authority on air raids. 'Too near for Leeds. York, maybe. Or one of the aerodromes. Plenty of them around . . .'

'Oh, Ness – tonight, remember? I said it would be a bombers' moon. Well, nothing has taken off from Dishforth. It's the Luftwaffe's moon tonight, Ness!'

More bombs fell then, dully distant, and Lorna closed her eyes tightly.

'Do you think we could take a quick look outside,' Ness whispered. 'They didn't seem too near . . .'

'If you're sure? I'll turn out the light first.'

They stood on the back doorstep, the red glow that lit the sky to the west plain to see.

'I thought so,' Ness said, tight-lipped. 'They've dropped incendiaries first, then there'll be another wave of bombers soon, bombing on the fires. They did that in Liverpool, the rotten sods! Come on, girl, let's get inside. It won't be long before –'

A shattering roar sent them back to the shelter of the kitchen table.

'I said, didn't I? Knew they'd bomb on them fires. What time is it?'

'Five past three, and Ness, from the direction of the fires it looked like York.'

'But what is there at York that's worth an air raid?'

'Lots of Army, I suppose. And they say that all the aerodromes around here are controlled from some secret HQ in York. But I don't think there are any war factories.'

More bombs fell. Still a distance away, but always a reminder that if only one pilot got it wrong by only a few seconds, other places could suffer. Meltonby and Nun Ainsty weren't all that far away – not as a bomb dropped.

'I suppose there are anti-aircraft guns at York. I wonder if they'll send up our fighters, Lorna? Where's the nearest fighter station?'

'Church Fenton, I think. Ness, I'm afraid.'

'Me, too.' Hands met and clasped under the sheltering table. 'It was like this in the May blitz, back home – only they came back night after night, the pigs!'

'I hate this war.'

'Join the club, queen.'

The all clear sounded at five in the morning; the sweetest sound, high and unwavering. Danger over.

'So that's it, then. Shall I put the kettle on, Ness? Hardly worth going back to bed now.'

'Do that. I'll take a look outside. It's almost light.'

Ness walked to the gate. Nun Ainsty had not changed. Only the sick-making stink of destruction that came to her on the breeze.

'Hullo, Ness.'

Nance Ellery in her WVS uniform, doing the rounds of the village, checking.

'Lorna's put the kettle on. Want a cup?'

'No, thanks all the same. Nasty business. Gilbert said it was York. Damned vandals. After the Minster, I shouldn't wonder.'

'But what harm did an old church ever do to them *Jairmans*?'

'How would I know? I only know they couldn't have picked a better night for it. A full moon. Clear as day below them. Ah, well, I'll go and see if they're all right at the almshouses.'

Straight-backed, she was off, quivering with indignation at the bombing of a city once the capital of the north. A place of great importance then, secure behind its walls. No match for bombs, though. She knocked on Martha Hugwitty's front door and Ness went back to the kitchen.

'That was Mrs Ellery, checking up. Her Gilbert said it was York copped it. She's bonny and mad about it.'

'Who wouldn't be?'

'She said they were after the Minster.'

'Then let's hope they didn't get it. That Minster has survived for hundreds of years – even Henry the Eighth had the decency to leave it alone. And then some pesky Nazi thinks he can drop bombs on it!'

'That's war for you, queen.' Ness was shocked that the war had crept nearer to Nun Ainsty. 'Nothing sacred. They'll have to hang Hitler, y'know, when this lot is over. Hanging would be too good for him, come to think of it.'

'Then maybe Mr Churchill will tell them they can draw and quarter him as well.'

'What's that?' Ness had never come across drawing and quartering, but it sounded interesting. 'Does it hurt?'

'It would hurt a lot, love.' Her hands, she was glad to see, were steadier. 'In fact, I'd like to be there to watch it. But drink your tea. I'll have the bathroom first, if you don't mind.'

Lorna wondered how it would be in the post office at Meltonby and if it had been the night telephone operator there who passed on the alert call to Nance Ellery's house.

'There'll have been a lot of people killed and injured, Ness.'

'There usually is, with an air raid.'

Ness recalled Liverpool and makeshift mortuaries and people going from one to the other, desperately looking for missing family. And she remembered twisted tram rails and sewers blasted open, and stinking. And unexploded bombs, and –

'There won't be another war, will there, Ness? After all this, surely they can't let another happen?'

'No, queen. I reckon that this one, when we get to the end of it, should be the last.'

Her eyes filled with tears and Lorna knew it was because she was missing Mick, needed his arms around her, telling her not to worry, that he would come back safely.

'Hey! It's all right!' Lorna folded her dearest friend in her arms. 'We're both in one piece, thanks be. Chin up, old love.'

'I'm all right,' Ness had sniffed. 'Just wanted Mick, that's all. And I can't have him, can I, so what the 'ell am I whingeing about?' She raised her mug in salute, then drank deeply, smiling suddenly to become the Ness of old again. 'Oh, damn and blast Hitler and his dratted Luftwaffe.'

And Lorna agreed entirely, then made for the bathroom.

Lorna had arrived at Meltonby Post Office to find it almost deserted; no early-morning bus nor red GPO van outside. Mrs Benson sat at the little switchboard.

'Hullo, lass. Come you in. I've just been talking to York exchange. I've sent Ted home. He was worried sick.'

'He lives in York?' Lorna had not known where the night operator lived, only that he always caught the first bus out of Meltonby.

'Aye. Though how he'll get there, I don't know. Thumb a lift, maybe. My, but it's a right carry-on.'

'Did they tell you anything?'

'Only what they thought might have happened. They were on the switchboards all night – right through the raid. Deserve a medal. Anyroad, there's no bus with the papers and no van with mail. Isn't much point you stopping, Lorna. Nothing to deliver.'

'So – so what do they *think* might have happened?'

'The supervisor said that as far as she knew, the Minster was all right, but there's been terrible damage.'

'Poor old York. Why did it have to be bombed, Mrs B?'

'Didn't you know, then? Reprisal, that's what. Baedeker raids on historic towns, and all because we bombed Lübeck and Rostock. Nasty and peevish, if you ask me. And you'd better put the kettle on, lass. This switchboard's going mad this morning. People ringing up, worried, I suppose it is. Wish we could find out what's really happened.' She jabbed in a plug and said, 'Number, please?' and Lorna went to the tiny kitchen, to set the kettle to boil.

It was whilst she was gazing through the window that she saw the early morning bus outside.

'Thank God,' she whispered, grateful that something at least seemed normal, running to the door.

'Morning, love. No papers,' the conductor said.

'Papers come in on the train from Manchester, see,' the driver said, climbing down from his cab.

'And has the railway station been hit?' Lorna asked, frowning.

'Can't say. We picked the bus up at the depot. Only got rumour to go on. Nobody seems to know anything.'

'Are your families all right?' Lorna remembered how afraid she had been.

'Aye. Shaken up, but weren't we all? Mrs Benson wouldn't have the kettle on, would she? Our water is off at home. That lot must've got a water main, somewhere or other. I'd not say no to a mug of tea.'

'Mrs Benson is on the switchboard, but I've made tea.' She filled three mugs and a china cup. Mrs B always liked her first drink of the day from a civilized cup. 'I'll take this to the switchboard. Maybe there'll be more news.'

But the postmistress motioned to Lorna to set the cup and saucer beside her, so busy was she.

'Bus arrived. No papers,' Lorna mouthed, because Mrs B had her headset on.

'Then you'd best go home, Lorna. Let them know in Ainsty, will you, and if anyone complains, tell them from me they're lucky they didn't get bombed, an' all! Off you go, lass. See you tomorrow.'

Lorna told Nance Ellery there would be no letters nor newspapers that morning. Nance would put it around – and take no grumbling from anyone. Then she called at the manor kitchen and told the sergeant-cook that she was sorry, no letters for the patients today, nor papers.

'Then you'll have time to stop for a cup?'

Lorna recalled the plump sergeant with affection. Light of my life, he had called her. She wondered where he was now.

'Please. No sugar, though. Got any news?'

'As a matter of fact, I have. The MO rang York – offered his services. Went there straight away. There was an express jam-packed with people in the station when it took a direct hit. Heavy casualties, the MO was told. Nowhere's safe, these days. Sure you won't have a spoon of sugar? Good for shock.'

And Lorna said she wouldn't, thanks all the same, and pulled out a chair resting her elbows on the table top.

'Mrs Benson at Meltonby post office said the raid was a reprisal, but isn't all war a reprisal, sort of?'

'You could say that, I suppose. I'm grateful for being here, safe. Came here after Dunkirk. It wasn't a lot of laughs on those beaches. Think they've forgotten me. Pity they ever sent Lieutenant MacMillan away.'

'Isn't the new MO very nice, then?' A warm feeling had taken Lorna, just to be talking about Ewan.

'He's fine. Knows his job, all right. But he never comes here to the cookhouse for tea. You and him were close, weren't you?'

'We were friends. And we had mutual friends in Meltonby who sometimes asked us over for a meal. That's all,' Lorna said firmly. She'd had to be firm because at the time she had been on her six months' probation, so to speak, when anything the least bit compromising could have been pounced on by the faceless King's proctor.

'Aaaah,' the sergeant had said, knowing when enough was enough.

Lorna stretched her right leg which had begun to tingle with pins and needles, then looked at the mantel clock.

Half past eight. More than three hours to go until Big Ben chimed midnight. She gazed at the uncurtained window. Nice not to have to worry about showing even the tiniest chink of light. Almost everything was still rationed, even though peace had come, but the immediate benefit of the ending of World War Two, as it was now called, was the instant abolition of the blackout. People had danced in streets so lit up it didn't seem possible. Lights everywhere, and no mean-minded ARP warden yelling, 'Get that light out!'

The light from her sitting-room window streamed down the front path and out onto the Green. Nice to know that no one would ever fall again in the darkness nor run into the pillar box outside her gate, and smash their spectacles or cut a knee. At half past eight on New Year's Eve 1946, at least there had been another blessing to add to the end of killing and maiming and blinding. Which made her think of Private Alun Jones and the Christmas card he and Rebecca had sent. *Baby on the way*, Becky had written. Alun would never see his child, but he would hear it laugh, and cry, and listen to its baby talk. The child that might never have been, Lorna thought, had she not withheld a letter; had Ewan not thrown it on the fire. But she didn't think of Ewan now, if she could help it. Ships that pass, they'd had to be.

She started as the phone rang briskly, hurrying to pick it up.

'Meltonby 223.'

'Hullo, queen! Just phoning in case it gets busy later on and I can't get through. Happy New Year! What are you doing?'

'Happy New Year, Ness – and what do you think I'm doing? The tea tray is set with one cup and your chair is empty. I miss you. Any news of Mick?'

'*News*? He's *here*! Came yesterday. A civilian! He's made it, Lorna! Just walked in. We were all flabbergasted. But you're to come to Deep Hay when the weather gets better. No excuse, now your war work has finished. Promise?'

'I promise, Ness. And say welcome home to Mick for me.'

'You're sure you're all right, Lorna?'

'Fine. I'm getting used to things. Haven't started talking to myself yet.'

The warning pips sounded. Telephone calls were still unofficially rationed.

'Happy New Year, Lorna. Take care.'

'And to you and Mick. Be happy, Ness . . .'

She replaced the receiver then gazed at the dejected face in the mirror before her, tears filling her eyes.

'Weeping on New Year's Eve! Stop it, woman!'

Anyway, was she weeping for herself and her loneliness or was it because Ness was so happy in Devon with Mick safely home? Was she envious?

Maybe just a little, but never jealous. Not of Ness who had come into her life so many years ago when they were expecting to hear the ringing of church bells, warning of invasion from across the Channel. Backs-to-the-wall days, those. Six years together the two of them, yet now –

She pulled her hand impatiently across her eyes, blew her nose noisily, defiantly, then returned to her armchair, deliberately leaving the hall light burning, because you couldn't be fined nor sent to prison now for wasting electricity.

She threw a log on the fire, watching it ignite and blaze, then thought about what she had said to Ness about the empty chair opposite. William's chair it had been, but every time she looked at it, it became Ness's chair; always would be.

Lorna rarely thought of William, and if she did it was without bitterness. Their divorce had become absolute three months after Primrose had her child, a little girl. They had married quietly a month later – or so Mr Wainwright had said.

Now, there was only the aimlessness of her life to get used to and tonight she was determined to come to terms with it. Tonight was not only for remembering but for looking forward, too. Tonight, she would sort out her future, make resolutions, make such a good job of it that no one would be able, ever again, to look at her with pity in their eyes.

Nine o'clock. She sighed, took up her knitting, and began to think when things – things to do with the war, that was – had started to come right. November, 1942, she supposed. Even the reader of the special midnight news bulletin had thrown away his funereal voice to announce that the North African coast had been cleared of enemy forces in one mighty battle. A battle *we* had won! Prisoners taken by the thousand, more ammunition and lorries and tanks than we knew what to do with, captured or destroyed.

'Imagine! We've won something! The Allies have scored a bull's-eye,' Lorna laughed.

'And not before time.' Ness was every bit as jubilant. 'But there's just one thing we've got to remember . . .'

'Yes. Mick is there.' Lorna reached for her friend's hand. 'But he'll be all right. We both know he will. There'll be a letter soon.'

The letter arrived. It bore a date one week after the battle was over and Lorna had hurried to deliver it to Glebe Farm.

'He's all right,' Ness smiled. 'Says he's only just found time to write, now that things have calmed down a bit in their neck of the woods.'

No mentioning the battle, nor place names. Not allowed. People at home had got used to reading between the lines, anyway.

'And just listen to this, queen! "I saw Ewan MacMillan, though he didn't see me. Impossible even to get near enough to speak to him, both of us being up to the eyes in it. But it was Ewan, no mistake about it." Well, we know what that means, don't we? Your feller's in North Africa, too, Lorna. Small world, innit?'

'He isn't my feller, but what a pity they couldn't have met.'

'Ar. Mick could have told him about your divorce.

Interestin', that would have been,' Ness had observed with her usual directness.

A long time ago that had been and, over the years, Lorna tried not to think of Ewan, who had not cared enough to write – not even to Jessie and Reg. Nor even to drop a line when the war was over, because surely he would be home again, a civilian, by now. Yet even knowing he had forgotten her had not stopped Lorna thinking of him sometimes and wondering where he was, and how he was. She was doing it again, tonight, and it just wouldn't do!

She glanced towards her desk and the picture of shining water and distant hills she had not been able to bring herself to take down, wondering if she should be glad or sorry that Mick had not been able to tell Ewan about the divorce.

Yet that amazing victory in the North African desert at El Alamein had been the first of the battles won. Indeed, the Allies seemed not to have lost one since, with the Russian armies fighting back at last. Even Stalingrad and starving Leningrad had been freed from siege.

Then on and on to the peace Mr Churchill had promised – vowed – would come. The landings in Normandy that were soon to be known as D-day and the Nazi defeat and surrender, a year later.

Such rejoicings! Lights everywhere. Bonfires blazing, parties in the streets. In Nun Ainsty there had been amazing celebrations. Even Nance Ellery had lifted her skirt above her knees and danced round the Green!

So absolutely wonderful. Europe at peace at last. It had been some days before it was realized that the war was not entirely over, with the Far East yet to be freed from the Japanese invaders. And because America had been with us on D-day, it seemed the right thing for the Allies to do to pitch in with the Pacific War.

How much longer, Ness had asked? When would Mick be home? How many more years to wait?

'I'm stopping at Glebe, if they still want me, Lorna,' she

had said. 'Might as well – if it's all right with you.'

Yet the long wait for peace came in just months, with the dropping of two atomic bombs on the mainland of Japan. No one had ever heard of atomic bombs. Of blockbusters that caused terrible damage, yes. Of two bombs that could wipe out two entire cities, no.

Those bombs had been vicious, Lorna frowned, yet they had shortened the war, saved thousands of Allied lives.

She looked at the mantel clock. Half an hour to go to midnight and she had done nothing about her future, made no brave new decisions. The past she had taken care of, the remembering done, but what of the future?

She shrugged, still undecided, because she had not yet found the courage to admit that in all probability it was to be a lonely one and she would live on her own in Ladybower, accepting it as Martha had done; Flora, too. Would it be so very awful, never to have a child of her own?

Yes, it would! But a child of love, it must be, not the product of duty done on Tuesday nights and Sunday mornings. A child – children – carelessly got, Martha had promised – so what went wrong? Had it all been a joke, like Ursula Ainsty? There were no such things as ghosts. Nothing could resurrect the past, not even star-crossed lovers. And no one could foretell the future, either.

Surely the clock had stopped? Still ten minutes to go until midnight, when she would toast 1947 with the rosebud teacup held high, then take herself off to bed; forget all the yesterdays – and as for tomorrow? But tomorrow never came, did it?

The knocker on the front door came down three times and she wondered who had come to wish her a Happy New Year. Martha, perhaps, or Bob Wintersgill on Kate's instructions?

'Go and fetch Lorna – ask her to see in the New Year with us. She'll be lonely, this being the first one without Ness.'

She opened the door. There was a car outside which did not belong to anyone in Nun Ainsty.

'Yes?'

'Hullo, Lorna.'

She stood, shocked. Something was happening to her insides; something that ran cold and tingling down to her toes and all the way to the ends of her fingers. She drew in her breath, not believing it.

'Ewan?'

TWENTY-SIX

She spoke his name softly, and with disbelief. The sight of him, more good to look at than she had ever dared remember, set small agitated pulses fluttering in her throat.

'It's very cold out here. Am I to be asked in, Lorna?'

'Of course. Sorry. A shock, you see.' She stood aside, then closed the door. 'I can't believe this. It's been so long . . .'

'I'm sorry. There were – *reasons*. But will it do for now if I say I'm here to wish you a Happy New Year?'

'Thank you. Please – sit down.' She indicated the chair opposite. Then taking a deep, steadying breath, making a tremendous effort to speak normally and naturally as if her world hadn't just turned upside down, she whispered,

'You said you would write, Ewan. Sometimes, you said. As a friend.'

'I couldn't. I thought about you a lot, but there wasn't any hope for you and me, Lorna – not then. Then out of the blue, Jessie tells me you are divorced.'

'Jessie Summers? You're staying there? But you didn't write to them, either.'

'No.'

He sat relaxed. As if, she thought, this was any old visit; someone she once knew who was passing through and called on an impulse because it was New Year's Eve. And he had no right to look so attractive. She had no right to think it.

'Best not, I decided. They might have given me news of you if I'd kept in touch and that wouldn't have done, Lorna.'

'I see. The night in the wood, was it? The night we said goodbye? Thought I'd been a bit too eager? Best get the hell out of it – was that how it was, Ewan?' It hurt to ask it, but she had to know.

'No. Not like that at all, but when Jessie told me how things were, I had to see you right away. And before you ask, I'm here on business. Reg Summers is looking for a partner. The new National Health Service – it's going to happen though some doctors don't want it. Only a matter of time – in about a year . . .'

'But I always thought you'd join your father when the war was over.'

Small talk. He was here, in this room, yet she was sitting numb and shocked, saying all the wrong things.

'I might have done – it would have made things easier for him. But he's sold his practice. It's a small one, but hard work. Some of his patients live at the back of beyond. The house at Ardurie is part of the deal; they've bought a smaller place, near Edinburgh. Get a bit of culture, mother said. Then I found that Reg Summers wanted in on the Health Service; wanted a partner, too.'

He had tried to forget how completely he wanted her. He'd said goodbye to her then walked away because he had no choice. Nor had he ever stopped wanting her, even with other women in his arms. Yet they were acting as if none of this mattered.

'So you might be coming back, Ewan?'

She could not believe any of it. She had thought of him, wished herself back to the night of their goodbye, lived those kisses so many times. And now he was here and she was making a mess of it, when all she wanted to tell him was how glad she was to see him and how very much she wanted to be kissed again.

'Nothing is certain yet. But your clock says it's midnight. Happy New Year, Lorna.' He said it gravely, his eyes on hers.

'And to you, too. Happy New Year, Ewan.'

She held out a hand, but he did not take it. Instead, he unwound his muffler and unbuttoned his jacket.

'We've got to talk. Now, Lorna . . .'

'About you going into partnership with Doc Summers, you mean?'

'That, and other things. I hadn't any intention of going this far. Just thought I'd give them a ring, for old times' sake. That was when Reggie told me he was on the lookout for a partner – someone like me, preferably – and I told him I'd almost decided against general practice. It wouldn't have done – not in Meltonby.

'Then I heard Jessie's voice in the background. "Tell him Lorna Hatherwood is divorced," she called, and Reggie said had I heard what she'd said and did it make any difference to his offer?'

'And?' she whispered.

'And of course it made a difference! I said I'd be there right away – and here I am.'

All at once she was calm. All at once she realized there was all the time in the world for them.

'So here we both are, Ewan. Four years on,' she prompted, almost breathless with relief.

'And over those years, have you changed, Lorna? Had you forgotten me?'

'No, though I tried very hard not to think about you. And the times I almost took that picture down – the one over the desk, I mean – was nobody's business.'

'I've brought you another. It's in the car. But I won't let you see it, just yet. We've got to talk first, haven't we?'

'Yes. You said. But can we take it easy? There's been a lot of water under a lot of bridges and I still can't take it in

– you being here, I mean. Can we take things calmly, then we can –'

'Can take up where we left off? In the wood, when we said goodbye?'

'Yes. Oh, I don't know! Later, perhaps. We've got years to catch up on and my head is still spinning. You first . . .' she whispered.

'Well, I went overseas, like I thought I would.'

'Mm. North Africa. Mick Hardie saw you, but couldn't manage to get a word with you. He and Ness are married. Ness stayed on at Glebe; only left a month ago. Mick is back home – yesterday – and a civilian again. When were you demobbed, Ewan?' Dear, sweet heaven – did it matter?

'A year ago. Been stooging about, helping Father out, making up my mind what to do; doing a spot of painting . . .'

'And you never once thought about picking up the phone? I'll bet you've forgotten my number, even.'

'Meltonby 223,' he said softly. 'And the times I almost rang, just to hear you at the other end of it. Then I'd tell myself it would most likely be your husband who'd answer, so best forget it. Jessie told me you don't work at the surgery now.'

'There were women coming out of the Armed Forces when war ended who needed the job more than I did. The divorce didn't leave me destitute. I didn't ask for alimony; didn't want it. I don't work at the post office, either. By the way, the Army left the manor a year ago. It's empty again, up for sale.'

'So do you want to talk about the divorce, Lorna? Was it bad? Does it still hurt?'

'When it happened – yes I was hurt, and very shocked. But I finally realized it was only because Primrose – the other woman – was pregnant. I wanted a child, you see, and I felt cheated. And by the way, William said she was better than me, between the sheets. Seems I was an ice maiden.'

She laughed, glad she could talk about it and feel no emotion other than relief.

'It wasn't an ice maiden who kissed me goodbye that night in the wood.'

She had felt so soft, so very lovable in his arms. He'd been relieved she had been the one to cut and run. Relieved at the time, that was.

'And did you know that Rowley Wintersgill is married?' she rushed on, not yet ready to face up to the passionate goodbye. 'He has a son and another baby expected. Kate is delighted.'

'So nothing much has changed here?'

'No. All in all we had a quiet war – except when York was bombed. But talking about the village – you remember how bossy Nance Ellery was? Well, she came up trumps over the divorce. I hadn't expected her to be on my side, but the whole village was, including Martha.'

'And is Martha still seeing ghosts, telling fortunes?'

'She doesn't see ghosts. She's always been a bit sceptical about Ursula. Says she knows people who have sworn they've seen her, but her lips are sealed! And do you remember she said that two men were leaving the village – you and Mick and that mark her words! – there would be a third. And there was! William!'

'Lorna! I have been here almost half an hour and we are still putting the past to rights! Isn't it time we started to act like two people who haven't seen each other for four years – and take into account that I didn't know you were free, until now?'

'Fine by me.' She could hold back no longer. Nor did she want to. She needed to touch him, tweak his tie straight, take his face between her hands and kiss him, gently, teasingly.

'I think you'd better see the picture I've brought.'

'What is it, Ewan? Pyramids and camels?'

'No. It's a woman, and it's about time you saw her. I'll fetch it. Won't be a tick.'

He was quickly back, carrying something quite large, wrapped round in brown paper, tied with string. Avoiding her eyes, he tore away the wrapping, then held up the likeness of a beautiful girl. She was set mistily against a background of trees touched by moonlight. 'Do you know who she is – who I *think* she is?'

For a moment Lorna could not speak, so shocked was she to see the homespun coat, the sensuous mouth, the plait of dark hair. Then she let go of her breath and whispered,

'Ursula! You've seen her, too?'

'I don't know. Only star-crossed lovers are supposed to see her,' he challenged.

'Yes. So they say. I went into the wood; I missed you, Ewan, I wanted you to be there. So I went to stand beside the tree – where you were sketching – remember? And to this day, I don't know if I imagined her or saw her, but she was exactly as you have painted her. I tried to tell myself it was all in my mind – that it wasn't Ursula; that she should have been wearing a nun's habit. It was such a shabby coat she wore.'

'I agree about the coat. Shapeless. When it happened to me, she left a sweet smell behind her and I realized it was a scent of lavender. You and I had just said goodbye and I heard footsteps; I thought – hoped – it was you, coming back to me. But it was –'

'Ursula,' they said in unison.

'But why did she look like that, Ewan? So shabbily dressed, yet so absolutely beautiful? She's supposed to have been a nun who had a harelip, yet her mouth is perfect.'

She stared, bewildered, at the painting.

'I think it is the look of love. That was perhaps how Dickon must have seen her. Maybe that is how he made her feel; how she felt when she died – in his arms, wasn't it?'

'I hope so. And she probably wasn't a nun at all, Ewan. Maybe the greedy prioress grabbed her dowry, then gave her all the menial jobs to do – scrubbing, washing bedding in the hospice. I don't think that, tainted by witchcraft, she would have been allowed in the chapel, or near any of the shrines.

'Maybe they made her work in the garden. I think that's probably what she did. And I smelled lavender, too, when she had gone. There would be lavender bushes in the priory herb garden, perhaps?'

'Almost certainly. Most people went unwashed in Ursula's time. Sweet-smelling herbs were often used to disguise it. Maybe she carried sprigs of it in her pockets. Hell! We're talking about her as if she's real!'

'I think she once was and you and I saw – *sensed* – her presence, because she must have known we both needed her. But we mustn't say a word about it, Ewan. People would think we'd gone mad. And where do I hang the picture, will you tell me? Not where anyone would see her. I wouldn't want them to ask who she is.'

'In your bedroom?'

'Good idea. Mind, Minnie still cleans for me, so she's bound to see it. I'll tell her it's a gypsy girl. And it's reasonable to suppose that most people around here – if they believe in Ursula at all – would expect a woman in a nun's habit and certainly not someone so beautiful.'

'Lorna! What has got into the pair of us? Here's me, a doctor, and you an intelligent woman of this century, and we've both kidded ourselves into believing in a woman who, if she existed at all, lived more than four hundred years ago! The whole thing is ridiculous. We're both behaving like mediaeval peasants. I think we should forget Ursula. She really doesn't – *didn't* exist!'

'So why did you paint her, Ewan? And why did I recognize her as someone I saw in the wood? And there's the lavender . . .'

'Then what do we do?'

'We accept her, keep her as our secret.'

'Convince me, Lorna? Give me one good reason why we should?'

'Because she's been around for centuries – why try to exorcise her? Anyway, she seems happy comforting star-crossed lovers, so leave her be.'

'So you and I were both star-crossed when we saw her?'

'*I* was, Ewan, though at the time I didn't realize it. I was a married woman and I'd just kissed a man goodbye in a way married women shouldn't kiss. All things being equal, I was star-crossed. How did you qualify?'

'I had it bad for a married woman,' he said, his voice low.

'Well, then. That's Ursula settled. And since she seems to like it in Dickon's Wood, I vote we leave her there to get on with it.'

'And accept that we're both crazy?'

'Crazy? Like I said, it was you who painted her, don't forget!'

She was laughing now, and looking completely relaxed and beautiful and every bit as desirable as the Lorna he had first met. No, dammit! *More* desirable, because he had wanted her for four years and that made it a whole lot worse – or was it better? And as he looked at her, loving every bit of her, her face became all at once serious and she wrinkled her nose as if, all at once, something troubled her.

'Why are you looking at me like that, Lorna? Is something the matter?'

'I suppose it is. I've just realized that I've never danced with you.'

'*Danced*, for heaven's sake!' He got to his feet, holding out his arms, laughing. 'Easily remedied.'

'But there's no dance music on the wireless.' She was prevaricating, right until the end! 'And if you touch me, Ewan, hold me, will I be like Ursula, and vanish? Are we dreaming all this? Is it really you and me . . . ?'

'Lorna! The dreaming is over! I've done plenty of it, mind, since the night we said goodbye. I've kissed you so often, and held you and –'

'Yes?' She laid an arm around his shoulder, took his hand in hers. They were so close now. She moved nearer to lay her cheek on his. 'So now you are holding me again,' she whispered, 'and we can either pretend we are waltzing up there on a pink cloud or we can stay here, feet on the ground and you can kiss me. Kiss me hullo, this time.' She closed her eyes and parted her lips.

'Hullo, you,' he said softly. 'We've wasted too much time. There's a lot of catching up to do.'

He kissed her then, and she opened her eyes just long enough to murmur,

'Your fault. You should have written, like you said you would.'

'The only cure, when you're in love with a married woman you know you can't have, is to try to forget her.'

'I'm not married now.' She closed her eyes again, searching with her mouth for his.

'No,' he said, when they had kissed again. 'And I think we should do something about it very soon. I don't want to wait, Lorna.'

'Then why bother? We said goodbye once – I don't want to lose you again.'

'And you won't, sweetheart. Marry me?'

Now she really was on a pretty pink cloud, so she said, 'Yes, please. When?' before she fell off it, back into lonely reality.

'As soon as we can make it?'

'Mm. But do we have to wait? Stay with me tonight, Ewan. Don't go? And did I tell you I love you?'

'Not in so many words . . .'

'Then I love you, love you.'

'Mrs Hatherwood.' He took her face in his hands, so their eyes met. 'Are we being completely mad?'

'I hope so, Captain MacMillan.' She held out a hand. 'Oh, I *do* hope so.'

* * *

She stirred, then opened her eyes. The room was dark; only starglow palely lit the uncurtained window. It was all right. He was still beside her, sleeping softly.

The room was cold but the bed was warm with their loving, their nearness. She turned her head so she could hear the sound of his breathing, then gently moved closer, so their bodies touched. She wanted to whisper kisses on his cheek and waken him, but best not. Better to lie here and live again the kisses, a little hesitant, a little disbelieving, at first. And then the touching, the gentling and, when she could bear it no longer, the wonder of their coupling.

They had loved twice. The first soon gone in a blaze of passion; the second loving so completely wonderful that she knew that before this night, she had never been properly loved. And she knew that he knew it, too, and was glad.

From across the room, where they had propped her against the wall, Lorna knew that the woman in the painting knew about their loving and had blessed it with a smile.

She raised her head a little, carefully so as not to awaken him, glancing towards the fireplace wall. She could not see Ursula in the half dark, though she knew she was there for them. And that she always would be.

TWENTY-SEVEN

It was all so wonderful, so completely unbelievable, that even now she had to look at the wedding ring Ewan had put there that morning in February they were married. And then, for good measure, to gaze enchanted at the baby; her baby. Touch her, feel her softness and realness.

'Comfortable, sweetheart?'

'Mm. Just thought I'd take a peep at her, make sure she's all right.' Lorna looked into the Moses basket beside the bed.

'She is perfectly all right, woman!'

'She's making those little snuffling noises again.'

'Four-day-old babies often do. She has just been fed, is warm and tucked in and enjoying a snuffle before she goes to sleep,' he said firmly. Then he laughed out loud. 'Lorna – can you believe all this? You and I married –'

'Seven months ago,' she offered, impishly.

'Married, and a child.'

'Who is completely beautiful and adorable and I can't believe she's here.'

'Well, she *is*, and a perfect specimen.'

'Ewan! Stop talking like a doctor and act besotted, like you know you want to. Aaah. She's stopped snuffling.'

'I said she would. So shall we talk?' He sat on the bed beside her, laying an arm around her shoulders. 'There's news.'

'It's settled, then?' She laced her fingers in his.

'Settled. Contract ready for signing tomorrow. There's just one more thing – if you're up to talking about it, but I'll tell you first about the middle almshouse. It should be all finished in time for when the new Health Service starts next summer.'

'I never thought there'd be a surgery in Ainsty.'

'Well, there will be. Open alternate mornings and afternoons, Monday to Friday. And a clinic there that Flora will run.'

'Poor Flora. She thought she'd retire into that middle almshouse one day, and now you and Reggie have grabbed it. Is it going to be big enough?'

'For Ainsty – yes, of course. The little front parlour will be the waiting room and the big kitchen at the back the surgery. And upstairs will be toilets and storage and medical records. Quite a bit of work to do, of course, but it should be ready on time.'

'You're like a child with a new toy. You're going to be very busy, once it gets under way.'

'The new Health Service? It'll be a nine days' wonder at first – people getting doctoring free – free everything. It'll settle down, though. Some doctors are against it, but it's a good thing, Lorna,' he said earnestly. 'So many have had to physic themselves because they had no choice.'

'Well, Jessie Summers will be glad. No more sending out accounts on the first of the month.'

'By the way, Flora is all for it. She's decided not to retire just yet and, when she does, she'll stay put in Larkspur Cottage. Hardly anything will change in Nun Ainsty.'

'But that's just it, Ewan – it's changing already. The manor and the outbuildings to be made into flats and houses for one thing; eight dwellings, they're calling them. Nance says goodness knows who we're going to get. But if there are young couples there is sure to be children and the village needs children. It's always been a bit of a sleepy hollow. I won't mind a bit.'

In her present state of contentment, Lorna MacMillan would not care if someone decided to build a picture palace on the Green.

'Penny for them, darling,' he asked when she fell silent.

'Oh, just thinking about all the new things that are happening. Good job the man who's developing the manor was able to trace who owned it – and the almshouses, too.'

'And a good job the owner wanted to sell. Seems he never wanted to live there. Had only visited it a couple of times since he inherited. I think he was glad to have a white elephant taken off his hands. Anyway – we've sorted almost everything, including the little one's name, so there's just one thing to straighten out. The manor owns Dickon's Wood . . .'

'Well, we know that – always did. Oh, Lordy, Ewan, they haven't sold that, too?'

'They've had an offer of two thousand pounds for it.'

'*Two thousand pounds*! But whoever wants a wood that badly?'

'A timber merchant, Preston way.'

'*Timber*! He's going to cut it down!'

'Seems like it. Sorry.'

'*You're* sorry! What about Dickon and Ursula? What are they going to do when someone takes their wood?'

'Ssssh. Don't get upset. If I'd known, I wouldn't have told you – not just yet, anyway.'

'Then I'm glad you did, because tomorrow, when you go to sign the contract, you can tell the solicitor that selling Dickon's Wood isn't on – at least, not to a vandal who only wants it for the timber!'

'But Lorna . . .'

'No buts, Ewan. I imagine the absentee owner won't say no to a couple of hundred pounds more?'

'Buy it, you mean? *You* buy it? Can you afford it, Lorna? Sorry, but I can't help you. My cash is spoken for, for the time being. Have you really got that much in the bank?'

'Actually – yes. Grandpa left me Ladybower and – and ten thousand pounds besides. It was meant to make sure I'd be all right, financially, and he didn't change his will when I married William. He must have known.'

'Aye, he must. Mind, I knew the house was yours – but all that money, Lorna . . .'

'Most of it isn't money. It's invested, and I was living on the interest since the divorce. But I've got you to keep me now, so would you mind if I bought Dickon's Wood? We can't let it be destroyed, Ewan. And I'm sorry I didn't tell you about the money. I did tell you I had some, but I should have said how much. Things happened so quickly, that I didn't get around to mentioning it.'

'Then I'm glad you didn't. At least you can't say I married you for your money!'

'You married me, darling, to make an honest woman of me – but we won't go into that now. But you *will* do all you can to get the wood?'

'Promise. I'll tell the solicitor there are trees there hundreds of years old that shouldn't be cut down and could cause a lot of trouble for anyone who might try. If that doesn't work, then I'll have to start talking money. And I'll get it for you as cheaply as I can.'

'Good. Then what about Martha? I told you she had written, didn't I? She wants to see the baby.' Lorna reached for a letter from the bedside table. 'Read it.'

Dear Lorna,

This letter is to tell you how pleased I am to hear about your little girl and glad you are safely through it.

Congratulations to you both. I hope I will be able to call soon and see the babe.

Take care of yourself, and that dear little child.

With best wishes to all.

Yours sincerely,

Martha Hugwitty (Miss)

‘Good of her,’ Ewan smiled. ‘Do you want her to call?’

‘Oh, yes please! Tomorrow afternoon, when I’ll know we’ve got Dickon’s Wood, then I can tell her the news about the surgery as well. It’ll make her day!’

‘Nance will be quite put out.’

‘Nance is in Whitby seeing her sister, so hard luck. I’ll ask Minnie to pop across in the morning and ask Martha to call.’

‘You’re a devious woman, Mrs MacMillan. Tell Martha, and the news’ll be round like a flash fire!’

‘Yes, I know. You *do* think we’ll get the wood?’

‘Fingers crossed, we’re in with a chance. Ursula will be on our side, don’t forget. And you’ve had enough for one night. I’ll bring you a drink up, then tuck you in.’

‘And kiss me good night?’

‘That, too. Now settle down and rest. No arguing. Doctor’s orders!’

‘No arguing, darling.’

She laid a cheek on his chest and thought that no woman had the right to be this happy.

‘I love you,’ she whispered, into his woolly pullover.

Lorna heard the front door knocker and laid down the magazine she was reading, hoping Martha had come because it was very boring in bed, being compelled to take it easy for a week, when all she wanted was to push the pram round and round the village Green. Proudly and smugly.

She wriggled herself comfortable, rearranging her pillows, recognizing the voice of the caller. And then the phone in the hall downstairs began to ring and she listened, trying to hear what Minnie was saying.

‘That was the doctor on the phone.’ Minnie’s head, round the door. ‘And he says to tell you that for better or for worse, you’ve got yourself a wood.’ She wrinkled her nose. ‘Did I hear him right, Mrs MacMillan? A *wood*?’

'You did. I'll tell you about it, later. Is that Martha, come to see the baby?'

'To see *mother* and baby, she said.'

Martha stood in the bedroom doorway wearing a wide smile, her going-to-church hat, a silk scarf tied in a bow at her neck, and her best jacket.

'Oh, come in, Martha, do!'

'Hope I'm not intruding?'

'Of course not! Here's me, stuck in bed for three more days, and bored to tears – well, not bored, exactly; not with the baby. Look at her, Martha. Isn't she beautiful, or is it just me being smug?'

Martha gazed at the sleeping child with long fair eyelashes like her mother's and a round, pink mouth, milk-stained.

'She's beautiful. A lovely little girl. And you have every right to be pleased, Lorna. You've waited a long time for a bairn, haven't you?'

'Yes. But before – before Ewan, I mean – well, it wasn't meant to be.'

'No. This one's been worth waiting for – and the doctor was worth waiting for, an' all, if you want my opinion. But let's forget what's past, eh? I suppose you need all the news – what's going on in Ainsty, I mean.'

'Martha! It's only been five days! Whatever can have happened in five days?' Lorna laughed.

'Well – there's goings-on at the middle almshouse, for a start. I can't get to the bottom of it.'

'And you want to know why Ewan is interested in it?'

'We-e-ll – yes. Wouldn't have thought he'd have any use for an old cottage, but he's been there a time or two.'

'He has, Martha.'

'And it isn't only me that's noticed.'

'No? Then you can tell them it's going to be a surgery. Ewan is with the solicitor, completing the deal.'

'A surgery? What'll us do with a surgery in Nun Ainsty?'

'Do? Well, for one thing it'll save you the trip to Meltonby.'

'I'll grant you that. But you got used to the walk, even when your bronchials were bad. Better'n paying for a visit from Doctor Summers.'

'Yes, but when free medicine starts next year, no one will pay for visits.'

'Aaaah. And will glasses come into it, an' all?'

'Spectacles? Yes, of course.'

'That's right grand, then, 'cause I've been thinking these past few years that maybe I could do with some reading glasses.'

'Then hang on for a few more months, and you'll get them for nothing.'

'So this surgery next door to me, then – will the doctor be in need of a caretaker?'

'Not a caretaker. It'll only be open half the time. But it'll need a cleaner, without a doubt.'

'Well, then?' Being a cleaner at a medical establishment would be more seemly than scrubbing at Glebe Farm. 'Happen the doctor would consider me? I'm known for being particular, as Kate Wintersgill will verify, if asked.'

'Then I'll certainly mention it to Ewan.'

'Much obliged, I'm sure. Mind, there'll be a lot needs doing to it. Been very neglected, over the years.'

'It's all in hand. Before the doctors even considered it as a surgery they made enquiries about things. There are a lot of wartime building regulations still in force, and bricks and mortar in short supply still. But the Board of Trade will sanction the materials. There'll be a builder coming to have a look at it, give an estimate, so you'll know what he's about, Martha.'

'I'll keep an eye open, never fear.' It sounded very exciting, especially since it would happen on her own doorstep, almost. Watching the surgery, in particular, would make a change from watching the village, in general. 'But here's us going on about Ainsty, when all the time it's the little one we should be concerning ourselves about. She's a beautiful bairn, Lorna. You've done well.'

'Would you like to hold her? Pick her up – support her head – and give her a cuddle.'

And that, Lorna thought mischievously, was another one up for Martha on Nance Ellery!

'My, but she's a fair weight.'

'Seven pounds, six ounces. That's good for a girl, Flora said.'

'It is indeed, especially since she wasn't expected till November.'

'November? Who said anything about November, Martha?'

'Nance Ellery did. When you and the doctor let it be known you was expecting, Nance went all over coy and said you'd started the bairn on your honeymoon, and a honeymoon baby –'

'To a couple married late February . . . ?'

'Should arrive in November, or so Nance would have it. And to think she doesn't even know the little one is here yet. Serve her right for being away!'

'Martha! You can be very naughty at times,' Lorna said as seriously as she was able. 'So what do you suppose she'll think when she comes to visit?'

'Which she will, before she's unpacked her cases! Well, since you ask, lass, she'll think like I did – that the bairn is a good weight for a baby born two months early.'

'So you thought – *think* – Martha, that . . . ?' Lorna ran her tongue round her lips.

'That this lovely little honeymoon baby has timed it just about right – considering she was got on New Year's Eve.'

'Oh!' Lorna was clearly surprised. 'We-e-ll! Now Martha, look at me, will you? Look me in the eyes and tell me you aren't clairvoyant?'

'I'm not. But I'm able to see things – *sense* things. Come to think of it, there's something else we're going to have to talk about, and that is things happening in threes. You'll grant me that it does, on past experience?'

'Oh, yes. But why threes? And why now?'

'Because there have been two bairns in this village, lately. Rowley Wintersgill's second a month ago, and now your little one. So who do we know between us who's going to make up the magic number? 'Cause there's somebody as knows they're expecting and we haven't been told about it! Got to be. My reliable instinct tells me so.'

'Martha! We were talking about honeymoon babies!'

'So we were, lass. But then it suddenly struck me about something else, that's all.'

'So if I told you that Ness Nightingale – Hardie – is expecting at Christmas, would that do?'

'Ah, now, isn't that lovely! And they'll have a bonny bairn, an' all, them both being so comely. You'll give Ness and Mick my very best wishes when you next write, and tell her I'm glad she didn't let me down.'

'With the *three*, I suppose you mean?'

'Not exactly to do with that. Remember you two once came to me and I told your future?'

'I do, Martha. I remember it very well! And that there was trouble ahead for me.'

'Aye. Trouble you'd come through, which you have! And I told Ness she would have two bairns. Two of a kind.'

'Yes, and you also told me I would have three children, yet when things happened – the divorce, I mean – I wanted to believe you, but I couldn't.'

'Three bairns I saw in your hand, Lorna MacMillan, and three you'll have. And what else did I say?'

'I – I don't remember. Three children carelessly got, you said. Oh, my goodness! I think I know what you mean!'

'Of course you do. Carelessly got on New Year's Eve this little love child was.'

'But how did you *know*? Clairvoyant, like I said?'

'Nay, lass.' Martha let go a chuckle. 'Observant, more like.

There was a car outside Ladybower – the doctor's – and it was there all night. I saw it when I opened my front door to have a look at the New Year. And it was still there next morning! Clairvoyance? Oh my word, no. It's called putting two and two together!'

'Oh dear.' Lorna straightened her bed sheet, eyes down. 'We didn't deny anything, exactly. Just thought we wouldn't mention it, that's all. Does anyone else – er – suspect?'

'Not that I've heard of and no one will hear it from me. After all, a body has to have the odd secret. If I blabbed it around the village they'd know as much as you and me, and that wouldn't do, now would it?'

'Indeed it would not, Martha,' she replied gravely. 'Is she getting too heavy for your arms? Shall I put her back in her cot?'

'Nay, leave her be? Let me hold her a little longer?'

'All right, then. And in return for our secret, shall I tell you one? As a matter of fact, it won't be a secret for long, but at least you'll be the first to know. I've bought Dickon's Wood, Martha.'

'You've *what*? And what do you want with an overgrown old wood?' Martha was clearly taken aback.

'It was either that, or a timber merchant would fell it. I couldn't let that happen.'

'But it's a right shambles, all nettles and brambles and choked with self-seeded trees. And the path has been overgrown these many years. What are you going to do with it?'

'We-e-ll, you're right. It's going to need work done on it – opening it up, getting a bit of light into it. I'll have to find someone who knows what they're about, especially with all the rubbish that's grown up.'

'Then if you ask me, it sounds just the job for Goff Leaman, and his billhook.'

'I was rather hoping he'd be interested in taking it in hand. Bit by bit, of course.'

'Hmm. Be a nice hobby. You'd pay him, of course?'

'Of course. And in time, I can plant a few shrubs – rhododendrons, azaleas. Maybe a few lavender bushes?'

'First two – yes. They grow fine in woodland. But not lavender; wouldn't grow under trees. It'll thrive in poorish soil, but it needs sun. Snowdrops would be nice, if you're keen on planting though. Make a bonny carpet in February. But I'd forget lavender in Dickon's Wood, lass.'

'Of course. Just a thought. And there's Ewan's car . . .'

'Then I'll be off. And not a word shall pass my lips about – well . . .'

'New Year's Eve? Our secret, Martha. Thank you for coming.' Smiling, she held out her arms for the baby. 'And I didn't tell you. We're calling her Ursula.'

'Calling her *what*? After a nun that's nobbut a ghost?'

'I think it's a lovely name. Ewan said I could name girls, but that he would choose if we had a son. A good Scottish name that would sit well with MacMillan, he said. And since it seems that this morning I bought a wood . . .'

'Nay! Not *Ursula's* Wood. Not when it's always belonged to Dickon?'

'You're right, Martha. It will always be Dickon's Wood.'

Always. No matter who owned it, it would always belong to a long-ago horseman who loved a girl with all his simple heart, and who would love her for ever.

'That was Martha. What on earth has got into her?' Ewan said, standing mystified in the doorway. 'She was out of the front door with hardly a word.'

'That's because she has news for the telling. I've missed you. Kiss me, then tell me you love me.'

'You know I love you.' He took the baby and laid her back in her basket. 'News about what?'

'Oh, this and that. She's worked it out about New Year's Eve, but her lips are sealed. I told her about the new surgery – that's OK, isn't it?'

'Sure. And what else came under discussion?' He sat on the bed, taking her hand in his.

'That the baby's name is Ursula. It caused not a little consternation, especially as I'd just told her about the wood. And it was all right, darling? You didn't have to offer a lot more for it?'

'Not a penny more, actually. The solicitor phoned the timber merchant in Preston there and then; told him there was likely to be local opposition if he tried to cut it down. And the man said if that was the case, he was withdrawing his offer; didn't want any fuss or bother, especially over a few trees. Wasn't much of a wood, anyway; not all that special, he said.'

'*Not all that special*? The man's a Philistine! But aren't I the lucky one. Think of it, Ewan – I have you and Ursula, and now I, *we*, have Dickon's Wood. What more could I want?'

'That kiss you asked me for, perhaps? Will you have it now, or later?'

'Now, please.' She clasped her arms around his neck and closed her eyes. 'And later, when you can find the time.'

And when they had kissed, she looked over his shoulder to the wall opposite, and the picture that hung there; the likeness of a woman they had carried upstairs with them on New Year's Eve and who had been witness to their first loving.

'Y'know, Ewan, there might be some in the village who'll wonder about the baby's name, but it had to be Ursula, didn't it?'

She looked again at the gilt-framed portrait; a beautiful young woman whose soft smile and deep, secret-filled eyes gave memory to the long ago, when she, too, was loved.

It's all right, Ursula. You and Dickon don't need to worry. No one is going to cut down your wood . . .

Then she stirred in her husband's arms, and asked to be kissed again.

The Willow Pool

Elizabeth Elgin

A city ravaged by war, a girl on the brink of passion, a secret past to be uncovered ...

Against the background of bomb-ravaged Liverpool, Meg Blundell mourns the death of her beloved mother. She is nineteen, father unknown, her past veiled in mystery by her Ma. Why, she wonders, does the rent man never call at No. 1 Tippet's Yard? He does everywhere else. Why did Ma avoid talk of her father, but speak only of the idyllic house called Candlefold – a haven and a heaven to her?

With Ma gone, Meg must go back to her roots and, in the long sweet summer of 1941, find and lose love.

Thronged with unforgettable characters, both above and below stairs, with young women on the verge of passion and the men who must leave them, *The Willow Pool* enchants and enthrals.

Praise for Elizabeth Elgin:

'Once again Elizabeth Elgin has used her personal knowledge to fill it with the vivid kind of detail to keep her readers happy.' *Yorkshire Evening Post*

'A poignant, powerful saga that will stay in your memory long after you've read it.' *Woman and Home*

ISBN 0 00 651430 8